John Willis with Ben Hodges
THEATRE WORLD®

Volume 58
2001–2002

APPLAUSE
THEATRE & CINEMA BOOKS

Theatre World
Volume 58

Art direction: Mark Lerner
Book design: Kristina Rolander

ISBN (hardcover): 1-55783-625-6
ISBN (paperback): 1-55783-626-4
ISSN 1088-4564

APPLAUSE THEATRE & CINEMA BOOKS
151 West 46th Street, 8th Floor
New York, NY 10036
PHONE: (212) 575-9265
FAX: (646) 562-5852
EMAIL: info@applausepub.com
INTERNET: www.applausepub.com

Applause books are available through your local bookstore, or
you may order at www.applausepub.com or call Music Dispatch
at 800-637-2852

Sales & Distribution

NORTH AMERICA:
  Hal Leonard Corp.
  7777 West Bluemound Road
  P. O. Box 13819
  Milwaukee, WI 53213
  PHONE: (414) 774-3630
  FAX: (414) 774-3259
  EMAIL: halinfo@halleonard.com
  INTERNET: www.halleonard.com

EUROPE:
  Roundhouse Publishing Ltd.
  Millstone, Limers Lane
  Northam, North Devon EX 39 2RG
  PHONE: (0) 1237-474-474
  FAX: (0) 1237-474-774
  EMAIL: roundhouse.group@ukgateway.net

To Gerald Schoenfeld
Chairman of The Shubert Organization

For over fifty years of dedication to superlative theatrical productions,
untiring efforts to revitalize the New York theatre district and
Times Square, and faithful preservation of our theatres in
New York and throughout America.

CONTENTS

ACKNOWLEDGEMENTS

EDITOR John Willis

ASSOCIATE EDITOR Ben Hodges

ASSISTANT EDITORS Lucy Nathanson
Rachel Werbel

ASSISTANTS Brittany Brown
Brad Hampton
Barry Monush
John Sala
Huck Song
Matthew Wolf

STAFF PHOTOGRAPHERS Aubrey Reuben
Michael Riordan
Laura Viade
Michael Viade
Jack Williams
Van Williams

APPLAUSE BOOKS STAFF Mark Lerner
Michael Messina
Kay Radtke
Kristina Rolander
Kallie Shimek

BROADWAY HIGHLIGHTS

MOSTLY SONDHEIM
Barbara Cook (Mike Martin)

**BEA ARTHUR ON BROADWAY:
JUST BETWEEN FRIENDS**
Bea Arthur (Joan Marcus)

THE CRUCIBLE
Liam Neeson, Brian Murray,
Laura Linney, Jack Willis (Joan Marcus)

ELAINE STRITCH AT LIBERTY
Elaine Stritch (Michal Daniel)

THE ELEPHANT MAN
Billy Crudup, Rupert Graves, Kate Burton (Joan Marcus)

FORTUNE'S FOOL
Enid Graham, Alan Bates (Carol Rosegg)

THE GOAT, OR WHO IS SYLVIA?
Mercedes Ruehl, Bill Pullman, Jeffrey Carlson
(Carol Rosegg)

HEDDA GABLER
Kate Burton, David Lansbury
(T. Charles Erickson)

INTO THE WOODS
Melissa Dye, Vanessa Williams (Joan Marcus)

METAMORPHOSES
Doug Hara, Erik Lochtefeld (Joan Marcus)

MAMMA MIA!
Karen Mason, Louise Pitre, Judy Kaye (Joan Marcus)

MORNING'S AT SEVEN
Christopher Lloyd, Frances Sternhagen
(Joan Marcus)

NOISES OFF
Patti Lupone (Joan Marcus)

OKLAHOMA!
The Company (Michael LePoer Trench)

PRIVATE LIVES
Alan Rickman, Lindsay Duncan (Joan Marcus)

SEXAHOLIX...A LOVE STORY
John Leguizamo (Joan Marcus)

SWEET SMELL OF SUCCESS
John Lithgow (Paul Kolnik)

THOROUGHLY MODERN MILLIE
Sutton Foster (Joan Marcus)

THOU SHALT NOT
The Company (Paul Kolnik)

TOPDOG/UNDERDOG
Mos Def, Jeffrey Wright
(Michal Daniel)

URINETOWN
The Company (Joan Marcus)

BROADWAY

Productions that opened June 1, 2001 – May 31, 2002

A THOUSAND CLOWNS

By Herb Gardner; Director, John Rando; Sets, Allen Moyer; Lighting, Brian MacDevitt; Costumes, Martin Pakledinaz; Sound, Peter Fitzgerald; Casting, Liz Woodman; Production Stage Manager, Jane Grey; Presented by Jeffrey Richards, Raymond J. Greenwald, Norma Langworthy, James Fuld Jr., Irving Welzer, Kardana, Swinsky Productions, in association with Theatre Previews at Duke; Press, Jeffrey Richards Associates. Opened at the Longacre Theatre July 11, 2001*

CAST

Murray Burns . . . . Tom Selleck
Nick Burns . . . . Nicolas King
Albert Amundson . . . . Bradford Cover
Sandra Markowitz . . . . Barbara Garrick
Arnold Burns . . . . Robert LuPone
Leo Herman . . . . Mark Blum
UNDERSTUDIES: Ms. Garrick (Lauren Bone); Messers. Cover, LuPone, Blum (Eric Seigel); Mr. Selleck (Russ Anderson); Mr. King (Harley Adams)

A play in three acts. Time: April 1962. Place: Murray's apartment and Arnold's office in Manhattan. A writer for a children's television program struggles to maintain his free-spirited lifestyle while rearing his precocious nephew. The original Broadway production opened at the Eugene O'Neill Theatre, April 5, 1962.

*Closed September 23, 2001, after 84 performances

Photo by Carol Rosegg

Nicolas King, Tom Selleck

MAJOR BARBARA

By George Bernard Shaw; Director, Daniel Sullivan; Set, John Lee Beatty; Lighting, Brian MacDevitt; Costumes, Jane Greenwood; Original Music, Dan Moses Schrier; Associate Artistic Director, Scott Ellis; Stage Manager, Roy Harris; A Roundabout Theatre Company Production; Press, Bonueau/Bryan-Brown, Adrian Bryan-Brown. Opened at the American Airlines Theatre July 12, 2001*

CAST

Lady Britomart Undershaft . . . . Dana Ivey
Stephen Undershaft . . . . Zak Orth
Morrison . . . . Denis Holmes
Barbara Undershaft . . . . Cherry Jones
Sarah Undershaft . . . . Henny Russell
Charles Lomax . . . . Rick Holmes
Adolphus Cusins . . . . Denis O'Hare
Andrew Undershaft . . . . David Warner
Rummy Mitchens . . . . Jenny Sterlin
Snobby Price . . . . James Gale
Jenny Hill . . . . Kelly Hutchinson
Peter Shirley . . . . Richard Russell Ramos
Bill Walker . . . . David Lansbury
Mrs. Baines . . . . Beth Dixon
Bilton . . . . Brennan Brown
Factory Workers . . . . Eli Gonda, Jeremy Furhman,
Jeremy Lewitt, Brian Shoaf

Time: 1906. Place: England. Presented in two acts. A revival of George Bernard Shaw's play about the relative nature of mortality and notions of the common good. First produced at the Playhouse in New York, December 9, 1915.

*Closed September 16, 2001, after 74 performances

Photos by Joan Marcus

David Warner, Cherry Jones

Cherry Jones

Dana Ivey

IF YOU EVER LEAVE ME...
I'M GOING WITH YOU!

By Renée Taylor and Joe Bologna; Directed by Ms. Taylor and Mr. Bologna; Sets, Kenneth Foy; Lighting, Ken Billington; Sound, Jon Gottlieb; Stage Manager, Frederick H. Orner; Press, Pete Sanders Group-Pete Sanders, Erin Dunn; Produced by Martin Melzer, Stephen Melzer, Leonard Soloway, and Steven Levy; Associate Producers, Larry Scott, Bob Bender, Donald R. DeCiccio, Sandra L. DeCiccio. Opened at the Cort Theatre August 6, 2001*

Performed by Ms. Taylor and Mr. Bologna.

Presented without intermission. A ninety-minute comedy covering the pleasures and pitfalls of a show business marriage.

*Closed September 23, 2001, after 53 performances.

Photos by Joan Marcus

Renée Taylor, Joseph Bologna

Joseph Bologna, Renée Taylor

URINETOWN

Book and Lyrics by Greg Kotis; Director, John Rando; Music and Lyrics, Mark Hollman; Sets, Scott Pask; Lighting, Brian MacDevitt; Choreography, John Carrafa; Costumes, Jonathan Bixby; Sound, Jeff Curtis and Lew Mead; Fight Direction, Rick Sordelet; Orchestrations, Bruce Coughlin; Musical Direction, Edwin Strauss; Music Coordination, John Miller; Casting, Jay Binder, Cindi Rush, Laura Stanczyk; Production Stage Manager, Julia P. Jones; Stage Manager, Matthew Lacey; Press, Boneau/Bryan-Brown, Adrian Bryan-Brown, Jim Byk, Jackie Green, Martin Sainvil; Produced by the Araca Group and Dodger Theatricals, in association with TheaterDreams, Inc. and Lauren Mitchell. Opened at the Henry Miller Theatre, September 20, 2001*

CAST

Officer Lockstock . . . . Jeff McCarthy
Little Sally . . . . Spencer Kayden
Penelope Pennywise . . . . Nancy Opel
Bobby Strong . . . . Hunter Foster
Hope Cladwell . . . . Jennifer Laura Thompson
Mr. McQueen . . . . David Beach
Senator Fipp . . . . John Deyle
Old Man Strong; Hot Blades Harry . . . . Ken Jennings
Tiny Tom; Dr. Billeaux . . . . Rick Crom
Soupy Sue; Cladwell's Secretary . . . . Rachel Coloff
Little Becky Two-Shoes; Mrs. Millenium . . . . Jennifer Cody
Robbie the Stockfish; Business Man #1 . . . . Victor Hawks
Billy Boy Bill; Business Man #2 . . . . Lawrence Street
Old Woman; Josephine Strong . . . . Kay Walbye
Officer Barrell . . . . Daniel Marcus
Cladwell B. Cladwell . . . . John Cullum
UNDERSTUDIES: Mr. McCarthy (Don Richard, Peter Reardon); Ms. Kayden (Jennifer Cody, Erin Hill); Mr. Foster (Peter Reardon, Victor W. Hawkes); Ms. Thopmson (Erin Hill, Rachel Coloff); Mr. Cullum (Don Richard, Daniel Marcus); Ms. Opel (Kay Walbye, Rachel Coloff); Mr. Beach (Rick Crom, Lawrence Street); Mr. Marcus (Victor W. Hawkes, Don Richard); Mr. Deyle (Rick Crom, Don Richard); Ms. Walbye (Erin Hill, Rachel Coloff); Messrs. Crom, Hawkes (Lawrence Street, Peter Reardon); Mses. Coloff, Cody (Erin Hill); Mr. Street (Peter Reardon)

MUSICAL NUMBERS: Urinetown, It's a Privilege to Pee, It's a Privilege to Pee (reprise), Mr. Cladwell, Cop Song, Follow Your Heart, Look at the Sky, Don't Be the Bunny, Act 1 Finale, What Is Urinetown?, Snuff That Girl, Run Freedom Run, Follow Your Heart (reprise), Why Did I Listen to That Man?, Tell Her I Love Her, We're Not Sorry, We're Not Sorry (reprise), I See a River

ORCHESTRA: Ed Goldschneider, conductor, piano; Paul Garment, clarinet, bass clarinet, alto sax, soprano sax; Ben Herrington, tenor trombone, euphonium; Tim McLafferty, drums, percussion; Dick Sarpola, bass

A musical presented in two acts. A town with a water shortage finds itself paying dearly for one of the most basic human needs in this eco-satire and spoof of Broadway musicals; winner of three Tony Awards (for Book, Score and Director). Originally presented as part of the 1999 New York International Fringe Festival before a 2001 Off-Broadway engagement.

*Still playing May 31, 2002.

Photo by Joan Marcus

The Company

HEDDA GABLER

Adapted by Jon Robin Baitz from the play by Henrik Ibsen; based on a literal translation by Anne-Charlotte Hanes Harvey; Director, Nicholas Martin; Sets, Alexander Dodge; Lighting, Kevin Adams; Costumes, Michael Krass; Sound, Jerry M. Yager; Casting, Amy Christopher; Original Music, Peter Golub; Production Stage Manager, Kelley Kirkpatrick; Produced by Randall L. Werghitt, Harriet Newman Leve, Gallin Productions, USA Ostar Theatricals and Bob Boyett, in association with Bay Street Theatre, Huntington Theatre Company and the Williamstown Theatre Festival; Press, Boneau/Bryan-Brown, Adrian Bryan-Brown, Jackie Green, Ellen Levene, Aaron Meier. Opened at the Ambassador Theatre October 4, 2001*

CAST

Berta . . . . Maria Cellario
Miss Julia Tesman . . . . Angela Thornton
George Tesman . . . . Michael Emerson
Hedda Tessman . . . . Kate Burton
Mrs. Elvsted . . . . Jennifer Van Dyck
Judge Brack . . . . Harris Yulin
Servant . . . . Claire Lautier
Eilert Lovborg . . . . David Lansbury
UNDERSTUDIES: Ms. Burton (Tina Benko); Messrs. Emerson and Lansbury and Ms. Lautier (Patrick Boll); Ms. Thornton (Maria Cellario); Mr. Yulin (Martin La Platney); Mses. Van Dyck and Cellario (Claire Lautier)

A play in two acts. Time: Late 1800s. Place: The Tesman home, Christiania, Norway. Ibsen's tale of an unhappy housewife who seeks vicarious thrills as she attempts to influence the destiny of others. First New York English language production at the Fifth Avenue Theatre, March 30, 1898. Elizabeth Robins played the title role.

*Closed January 13, 2002, after 117 performances.

Photo by T. Charles Erickson

Kate Burton, David Lansbury

DANCE OF DEATH

Adapted by Richard Greenberg from the play by August Strindberg; Director, Sean Mathias; Sets and Costumes, Santo Loquasto; Lighting, Natasha Katz; Sound and Original Music, Dan Moses Schreier; Production Stage Manager, Arthur Gaffin; Casting, Ilene Starger; Produced by the Schubert Organization, Roger Berlind, USA Ostar Theatricals and Chase Miskin; Press, Barlow-Hartman Public Relations, John Barlow, Michael Hartman, Bill Coyle. Opened at the Broadhurst Theatre October 11, 2001*

CAST

Edgar, an army captain . . . . Ian McKellen
Alice, his wife . . . . Helen Mirren
Kurt, her cousin . . . . David Strathairn
Maja . . . . Anne Pitoniak
Jenny . . . . Keira Naughton
Sentry . . . . Eric Martin Brown
UNDERSTUDIES: Mr. McKellen (Edmond Genest); Ms. Mirren (Suzanna Hay); Mses. Naughton, Pitoniak (Alicia Roper); Messrs. Strathairn, Brown (James Riordan)

A play in two acts. Time: Autumn 1900. Place: The Captain and Alice's home, a fortress on an island off the coast of Sweden.

*Closed January 13, 2001, after 108 performances.

Photo by Joan Marcus

Helen Mirren, David Strathairn

MAMMA MIA!

Book by Catherine Johnson; Music and Lyrics, Benny Andersson and Björn Ulvaeus, some songs with Stig Anderson; Director, Phyllida Lloyd; Sets and Costumes, Mark Thompson; Lighting, Howard Harrison; Sound, Andrew Bruce and Bobby Aitken; Choreography, Anthony Van Laast; Musical Supervision, Martin Koch; Musical Direction, David Holcenberg; Musical Coordination, Michael Keller; Associate Director, Robert McQueen; Associate Choreographer, Nichola Treherne; Produced by Judy Craymer, Richard East and Björn Ulvaeus for LittleStar, in association with Universal Casting, Tara Rubin; Press, Boneau/Bryan-Brown, Adrian Bryan-Brown, Steven Padla, Jackie Green, Karalee Dawn. Opened at the Winter Garden Theatre October 18, 2001*

CAST

Sophie Sheridan	Tina Maddigan
Ali	Sara Inbar
Lisa	Tonya Doran
Tanya	Karen Mason
Rosie	Judy Kaye
Donna Sheridan	Louise Pitre
Sky	Joe Machota
Pepper	Mark Price
Eddie	Michael Benjamin Washington
Harry Bright	Dean Nolen
Bill Austin	Ken Marks
Sam Carmicheal	David W. Keeley
Father Alexandrios	Bill Carmichael

UNDERSTUDIES: Ms. Madigan (Meghann Dreyfuss, Somer Lee Graham); Ms. Inbar (Kim-e J. Balmilero, Kristin McDonald); Ms. Doran (Meredith Atkins, Yuka Takahara); Ms. Pitre (Marsha Waterbury); Ms. Mason (Leslie Alexander, Marsha Waterbury); Ms. Kaye (Robin Baxter, Marsha Waterbury); Mr. Machota (Adam Monley, Peter Matthew Smith); Mr. Price (Stephen Alexander, Jon-Erik Goldberg); Mr. Washington (Chris Prinzo, Peter Matthew Smith); Mr. Nolen (Tony Carlin, Bill Carmichael); Messrs. Marks, Keeley (Brent Black, Tony Carlin)

MUSICAL NUMBERS: Chiquitita, Dancing Queen, Does Your Mother Know?, Gimme! Gimmie! Gimmie!, Honey, Honey, I Do, I Do, I Do, I Do, I Have a Dream, Knowing Me Knowing You, Lay All Your Love on Me, Mamma Mia, Money Money Money, One of Us, Our Last Summer, Slipping Through My Fingers, S.O.S., Super Trouper, Take a Chance on Me, Thank You For the Music, The Name of the Game, The Winner Takes All, Under Attack, Voulez-Vous

ORCHESTRA: David Holcenberg, conductor, keyboard; Rob Preuss, associate music director, keyboard 3; Steve Marzullo, keyboard 2; Myles Chase, keyboard 4; Doug Quinn, guitar 1; Jeff Campbell, guitar 2; Paul Adamy, bass; Gary Tillman, drums; David Nyberg, percussion

A musical in two acts. Time: A wedding weekend. Place: A tiny Greek island. Songs of the 1970s group ABBA strung together in a story of baby-boomer wistfulness and a girl's search for her unknown father.

*Still playing May 31, 2002

Photos by Joan Marcus

Louise Pitre

Karen Mason, Louise Pitre, Judy Kaye

Tina Maddigan, Joe Machota

Ken Marks, David W. Keeley, Dean Nolen

The Company

The Company

THOU SHALT NOT

By Susan Stroman, David Thompson and Harry Connick, Jr.; based on *Thérèsè Raquin* by Émile Zola; Director and Choreographer, Ms. Stroman; Artistic Director, André Bishop; Sets, Thomas Lynch; Lighting, Peter Kaczorowski; Costumes, William Ivey Long; Sound, Scott Lehrer; Orchestrations and Arrangements, Harry Connick, Jr.; Music Direction, Phil Reno; Music Coordination, John Miller; Associate Director and Choreographer, Tara Young; Casting, Tara Rubin; Production Stage Manager, Peter Wolf; Assistant Stage Managers, Lisa Buxbaum, Mark Dobrow; Executive Producer, Bernard Gersten; Press, Philip Rinaldi, Barbara Carroll. Opened at the Plymouth Theatre October 25, 2001*

CAST

Flim Flam . . . . J.C. Montgomery
Papa Jack, Busker, Sanctify Sam . . . . Ted L. Levy
Monsignor, Antoine . . . . Patrick Wetzel
Sass . . . . Rachelle Rak
Sugar Hips . . . . Davis Kirby
Laurent LeClair . . . . Craig Bierko
Therese Raquin . . . . Kate Levering
Madame Raquin . . . . Debra Monk
Camille Raquin . . . . Norbert Leo Butz
Officer Michaud . . . . Leo Burmester
Oliver . . . . Brad Bradley
Suzanne . . . . JoAnn M. Hunter
UNDERSTUDIES: Ms. Levering (Dylis Croman, Kelli Severson); Mr. Bierko (Timothy J. Alex); Mr. Butz (Timothy J. Alex, Brad Bradley); Ms. Monk (Pam Bradley, Ellen Harvey); Mr. Burmester (J.C. Montgomery, David New); Mr. Bradley (James Hadley, Patrick Wetzel); Mr. Levy as Papa Jack (Timothy J. Alex, Kent Zimmerman); Ms. Hunter (Dylis Croman, Emily Hsu); Mr. Levy as Sanctify Sam (J.C. Montgomery)

MUSICAL NUMBERS: It's Good to Be Home, I Need to Be in Love, My Little World, While You're Young, I Need to Be in Love, The Other Hours, All Things, Sovereign Lover, I've Got My Eye on You, Light the Way, Take Her to the Mardi Gras, Tug Boat, My Little World, Won't You Sanctify, Time Passing, Take Advantage, Oh! Ain't That Sweet

ORCHESTRA: Phil Reno, conductor; Gregory J. Dlugos, associate conductor; Jonathan Levine, Jerry Weldon, David Schumacher, Sal Spicola, reeds; Joe Magnarelli, Derrick Gardner, John Reid, trumpet; John Allred, Joe Barati, trombone; Philip Fortenberry, Gregory J. Dlugos, keyboards; Benjamin Franklin Brown, bass; Brian Grice, drums; Walter "Willy" Usiatynski, percussion; Martin Agee, concertmaster; Cenovia Cummins, violin; Maxine Roach, viola; Roger Shell, cello

A musical in two acts. Time: 1946–47. Place: New Orleans, in and around the ninth ward. Steamy, jazz-inflected retelling of Émile Zola's tale of lust, betrayal, murder and madness.

*Closed January 6, 2002, after 85 performances.

Photos by Paul Kolnik

The Company

Craig Bierko, Kate Levering

BY JEEVES

Book and Lyrics, Alan Ayckbourn; Music, Andrew Lloyd Webber; based on the Jeeves books by P.G. Wodehouse; Director, Mr. Ayckbourn; Sets, Roger Glossop; Lighting, Mick Hughes; Costumes, Louise Belson; Sound, Richard Ryan; Choreography, Sheila Carter; Music Supervision and Direction, Michael O'Flaherty; Music Coordination, John Miller; Music Arrangements, David Cullen and Mr. Lloyd Webber; Production Stage Manager, Daniel S. Rosokoff; Produced by Goodspeed Musicals, Michael P. Price, Producer; Press, Barlow-Hartman Public Relations, John Barlow, Michael Hartman, Jeremy Shaffer. Opened at the Helen Hayes Theatre October 28, 2001*

CAST

Bertie Wooster . . . . John Scherer
Jeeves . . . . Martin Jarvis
Honoria Glossop . . . . Donna Lynn Champlin
Bingo Little . . . . Don Stephenson
Gussie Fink-Nottle . . . . James Kall
Sir Watkyn Bassett . . . . Sam Tsoutsouvas
Madeline Bassett . . . . Becky Watson
Stiffy Byng . . . . Emily Loesser
Harold "Stinker" Pinker . . . . Ian Knauer
Cyrus Budge III (Junior) . . . . Steve Wilson
Other Personages . . . . Tom Ford, Molly Renfroe, Court Whisman
UNDERSTUDIES: Messrs. Scherer, Stephenson, Kall (Tom Ford, Jamison Stern); Mses. Loesser, Watson, Champlin (Cristin Mortenson, Molly Renfroe); Messrs. Jarvis, Wilson, Tsoutsouvas, Knauer (David Edwards, Court Whisman)

MUSICAL NUMBERS: A False Start, Never Fear, Travel Hopefully, That Was Nearly Us, Love's Maze, The Hallo Song, By Jeeves, When Love Arrives, What Have You Got to Say Jeeves, Half a Moment, It's a Pig, Banjo Boy, The Wizard Rainbow Finale

ORCHESTRA: Michael O'Flaherty, conductor, piano; F. Wade Russo, associate conductor, keyboard; Eddie Salkin, reeds; Jack Cavari, guitar; Brian Cassier, bass; Brad Flickinger, drums, percussion

Time: This very evening. Place: A church hall, later to represent a London flat. A musical version in two acts of the Jeeves stories by Mr. Wodehouse that show the English upper classes to be helpless, harmless ninnies who must be rescued by their loyal sensible servants.

*Closed December 30, 2001, after 73 performances.

Martin Jarvis

NOISES OFF

By Michael Frayn; Director, Jeremy Sams; Sets and Costumes, Robert Jones; Lighting, Tim Mitchell; Sound, Fergus O'Hare; Production Stage Manager, David O'Brien; Casting, Jim Carnahan; Produced by Ambassador Theatre Group and Act Productions, Waxman Williams Entertainment, Dede Harris/Morton Swinsky, USA Ostar Theatricals and Nederlander Presentations, Inc.; Associate Producers, Pre-Eminence, Incidental Colman Tod, Jane Curtis/Ann Johnson; Press, Barlow-Hartman Public Relations, Michael Hartman, John Barlow, Wayne Wolfe; Opened at the Brooks Atkinson Theatre, November 1, 2001*

CAST

Dotty Otley . . . . Patti Lupone
Lloyd Dallas . . . . Peter Gallagher
Garry Lejeune . . . . Thomas McCarthy
Brooke Ashton . . . . Katie Finneran
Poppy Norton-Taylor . . . . Robin Weigert
Belinda Blair . . . . Faith Prince
Frederick Fellowes . . . . Edward Hibben
Tim Allgood . . . . T.R. Knight
Selsdon Mowbray . . . . Richard Easton
UNDERSTUDIES: Ms. Lupone (Barbara Sims); Mr. Gallagher (Doug Sender); Messrs. McCarthy, Knight (Michael Bakkenson); Mses. Finneran, Weigert (Virginia Louise Smith); Ms. Prince (Barbara Sims); Mr. Hibbert (Ross Bickell, Doug Sender); Mr. Easton (Ross Bickell)

A two-act play. Time: Three months of a theatrical tour. Place: Three regional theatres in England. A farcical take on the challenges—love, lust, inept actors, ego clashes—facing a touring theatre company in England; original Broadway production opened at the Brooks Atkinson Theatre December 11, 1983.

*Still playing May 31, 2002

Photo by Joan Marcus

Patti Lupone

THE WOMEN

By Claire Booth Luce; Director, Scott Elliott; Sets, Derek McClane; Lighting, Brian MacDevitt; Costumes, Isaac Mizrahi; Sound and Musical Arrangements, Douglas Cuomo; Casting, Jim Carnahan; Production Stage Manager, Peter Hanson; Stage Manager, Valerie Peterson; Presented by the Roundabout Theatre Company (Artistic Director, Todd Haimes; Managing Director, Ellen Richard; Executive Director of External Affairs, Julia Levy); Press, Boneau/Bryan-Brown, Adrian Bryan-Brown, Matt Polk, Jackie Green, Karlalee Dawn, Cindy Valk. Opened at the American Airlines Theatre November 8, 2001*

CAST

Jane . . . . Heather Matarazzo
Sylvia (Mrs. Howard Fowler) . . . . Kristen Johnston
Nancy Blake . . . . Lisa Emery
Peggy (Mrs. John Day) . . . . Amy Ryan
Edith (Mrs. Phelps Potter) . . . . Jennifer Coolidge
Mary (Mrs. Stephen Haines) . . . . Cynthia Nixon
Mrs. Wagstaff . . . . Barbara Marineau
Olga . . . . Jennifer Butt
1st Hairdresser . . . . Gayton Scott
2nd Hairdresser . . . . Roxanna Hope
Pedicurist . . . . Cheryl Stern
Mud Mask . . . . Julie Halston
Euphie . . . . Adina Poeter
Miss Fordyce . . . . Jane Cronin
Little Mary . . . . Hallie Kate Eisenberg
Mrs. Morehead . . . . Mary Louise Wilson
1st Salesgirl . . . . Ann Talman
2nd Salesgirl . . . . Barbara Marineau
Miss Shapiro . . . . Cheryl Stern
1st Saleswoman . . . . Julie Halston
2nd Saleswoman . . . . Susan Bruce
Miss Myrtle (a model) . . . . Adina Potter
Crystal Allen . . . . Jennifer Tilly
1st Model (negligee) . . . . Jen Davis
2nd Model (corset) . . . . Kelly Mares
A Fitter . . . . Jennifer Butt
Princess Tamara . . . . Roxanna Hope
Exercise Instructions . . . . Gayton Scott
Maggie . . . . Mary Bond Davis
Miss Watts . . . . Susan Bruce
Miss Trimmerback . . . . Ann Talman
A Nurse . . . . Adina Porter
Lucy . . . . Julie Halston
Countess De Lage . . . . Rue McClanahan
Miriam Aarons . . . . Lynn Collins
Helene . . . . Roxanna Hope
1st Girl . . . . Jennifer Butt
2nd Girl . . . . Gayton Scott
1st Woman . . . . Julie Halston
2nd Woman . . . . Susan Bruce
Sadie . . . . Cheryl Stern
Cigarette Girl . . . . Adina Porter
Dowager . . . . Barbara Marineau
Debutante . . . . Roxanna Hope
Girl in Distress . . . . Ann Talman

The Company

UNDERSTUDIES: Mses. Matarazzo, Stern, Scott (Jen Davis); Ms. Johnston (Julie Halston); Mses. Emery, Coolidge (Jennifer Butt); Mses. Ryan, Hope (Kelly Mares); Ms. Nixon (Ann Talman); Mses. Marineau, Davis, Talman (Jane Cronin); Mses. Bruce, Butt, Porter (Cheryl Stern); Ms. Cronin (Brandy Mitchell); Ms. Eisenberg (Madeline Rogan); Mses. Wilson, McClanahan (Barbara Marineau); Ms. Tilly (Roxanna Hope); Mses. Collins, Halston (Gayton Scott)

A play in two acts. Time: 1930s. Place: New York City and Nevada. Acid-tinged (and -tongued) chronicle of life amid a group of women who take pleasure in the betrayals and humiliations of their "sisters"; the original Broadway production opened at the Ethel Barrymore Theatre on December 26, 1936.

*Closed January 13, 2002 after 77 performances.

Photo by Joan Marcus

45 SECONDS FROM BROADWAY

By Neil Simon; Director, Jerry Zaks; Sets, John Lee Beatty; Lighting, Paul Gallo; Costumes, William Ivey Long; Sound, Peter Fitzgerald; Casting, Jay Binder Casting; Stage Manager, J. Philip Bassett; Produced by Emanuel Azenberg, Ira Pittelman, James Nederlander, Scott Nederlander and Kevin McCollum; Press, Bill Evans and Associates, Jim Randolph, Terry M. Lilly. Opened at the Richard Rodgers Theatre November 11, 2001*

CAST

Mickey Fox . . . . Lewis J. Stadlen
Andrew Duncan . . . . Dennis Creaghan
Bernie . . . . Louis Zorich
Soloman Mantutu . . . . Kevin Carroll
Megan Woods . . . . Julie Lund
Arleen . . . . Alix Korey
Cindy . . . . Judith Blazer
Rayleen . . . . Marian Seldes
Charles W. Browning III . . . . Bill Moor
Zelda . . . . Rebecca Schull
Bessie James . . . . Lydia Gravátt
Harry Fox . . . . David Margulies
UNDERSTUDIES: Mr. Stadlen (Adam Grupper); Mses. Seldes, Schull (Maggie Burke); Messers. Zorich, Margulies (Herbert Rubens); Ms. Gravátt (Tonye Patano); Mses. Blazer, Korey (Maria Redanty); Mr. Carroll (Teagle F. Bougere); Messers. Creaghan, Moor (James A. Stephens); Ms. Lund (Rhea Seehorn)

A play in two acts. Time: The four seasons. Place: A coffee shop in New York. Comic celebration of the famous Broadway theatre district coffee shop, located in the Edison Hotel, known as the "Polish Tea Room."

*Closed January 13, 2002 after 73 performances

Photos by Carol Rosegg

Alix Korey, Judy Blazer

Lewis J. Stadlen, Louis Zorich, Alix Korey

David Margulies, Rebecca Schull, Lewis J. Stadlen

QED

By Peter Parnell; inspired by the writings of Richard Feynman and Ralph Leighton's *Tuva or Bust*; Director, Gordon Davidson; Artistic Director, André Bishop; Sets, Ralph Funicello; Lighting, D. Martyn Bookwalter; Costumes, Marianna Elliot; Sound, Jon Gottlieb; Casting, Daniel Swee; Creative Consultant, Ralph Leighton; Stage Manager, Robin Veith; A Lincoln Center Theatre production; Executive Producer Bernard Gersten; Press, Philip Rinaldi, Barbara Carroll. Opened at the Vivian Beaumont Theatre November 18, 2001*

CAST

Richard Feynman . . . . Alan Alda
Miriam Field . . . . Kellie Overbey
UNDERSTUDY: Ms. Overbey (Piper Brooks)

A play in two acts. Time: June 1986. Place: California Institute of Technology, Pasadena. Physicist Richard Feynman's musings on the nature of life, death and science in a play that is nearly a one-man performance. Using an intermittent schedule, *QED* was performed when *Contact* was dark. The production also took a hiatus during winter holidays. *QED* was commissioned by and had its world premiere at the Mark Taper Forum.

*Still playing May 31, 2002

Photos by Craig Schwartz

Alan Alda

Alan Alda

Alan Alda

SEXAHOLIX...A LOVE STORY

By John Leguizamo; Director, Peter Askin; Lighting, Kevin Adams; Costume Consultant, Santiago; Production Stage Manager, Pat Sosnow; Produced by Tate Entertainment Group, Inc.; Press, Bill Evans and Associates, Bill Evans, Jim Randolph, Terry M. Lilly. Opened at the Royale Theatre December 2, 2001*

Performed by Mr. Leguizamo.

A performance in two acts. Comedic observations on race, culture, inter-marriage, family and sex.

*Closed February 10, 2002, after 67 performances.

Photos by Joan Marcus

John Leguizamo

John Leguizamo

John Leguizamo

MOSTLY SONDHEIM

Songs by Stephen Sondheim; Artistic Director, André Bishop; Musicians: Wally Harper (piano), Jon Burr (bass); A Lincoln Center Theatre Production; Executive Producer, Bernard Gersten. Opened at the Vivian Beaumont Theatre January 14, 2001*

Performed by Barbara Cook

Presented without intermission. Concert performance of songs by Stephen Sondheim and others.

*Closed February 11, 2002, after 9 performances.

Photos by Mike Martin

Barbara Cook

Barbara Cook

AN ALMOST HOLY PICTURE

By Heather McDonald; Director, Michael Mayer; Associate Director, Todd Lundquist; Sets, Mark Wendland; Lighting, Kevin Adams; Costumes, Michael Kass; Sound, Scott Meyers and Robert Kaplowitz; Original Music, Mitch Greenhill; Production Stage Manager, Kimberly Russell; A Roundabout Theatre Production (Artistic Director, Todd Haimes; Managing Director, Ellen Richard; Executive Director of External Affairs, Julia Levy); Press, Boneau/Bryan-Brown, Adrian Bryan-Brown, Matt Polk, Amy Dinnerman. Opened at the American Airlines Theatre February 7, 2002*

CAST

Samuel Gentle . . . . Kevin Bacon
Samuel Gentle (alternate) . . . . John Dossett

A one-man performance presented in two acts. Time: The present. Place: The grounds of a cathedral and other places. A story of trial and faith.

*Closed April 7, 2002, after 68 performances.

Photo by Joan Marcus

Kevin Bacon

BEA ARTHUR ON BROADWAY: JUST BETWEEN FRIENDS

By Bea Arthur and Billy Goldenberg, in collaboration with Charles Randolph Wright; Sets, Ray Klausen; Lighting and Sound, Matt Berman; Producers, Daryl Roth, M. Beverly Bartner, and USA Ostar Theatricals; Production Consultants, Mark Waldrop and Richard Maltby Jr.; Press, Barlow-Hartman Public Relations, John Barlow, Michael Hartman, Jeremy Shaffer. Opened at the Booth Theatre February 17, 2002*

Performed by Bea Arthur, with Billy Goldenberg on piano.

An autobiographical perspective on the life and career of Bea Arthur. Presented without intermission.

*Closed April 14, 2002, after 65 performances.

Photo by Joan Marcus

Bea Arthur

ELAINE STRITCH AT LIBERTY

By Elaine Stritch and John Lahr; Director, George C. Wolfe; Sets, Riccardo Hernandez; Lighting, Jules Fisher and Peggy Eisenhauer; Costumes, Paul Tazewell; Sound, Acme Sound Partners; Orchestrations, Jonathan Tunick; Music Direction, Rob Bowman; Music Coordination, Seymour Red Press; Producers, John Schreiber, Creative Battery, Margo Lion, Robert Cole, in association with Dede Harris/Morton Swinsky, Cheryl Weisenfeld and the Joseph Papp Public Theatre and the New York Shakespeare Festival; Associate Producers, Jay Furman, Roy Furman, Mark Krantz, Charles Flateman; Production Stage Manager, James D. Latus; Press, Carol R. Fineman. Opened at the Neil Simon Theatre February 21, 2002*

Performed by Elaine Stritch.

ORCHESTRA: Rob Bowman, conductor, piano; Les Scott, Richard Heckman, John Campo, woodwinds; Stu Satalof, Kamau Adilifu, trumpet; John Gale, trombone; Louis Bruno, bass; Willard Miller, drums, percussion

MUSICAL NUMBERS: All in Fun, Broadway Baby, But Not For Me, If Love Were All, Can You Use Any Money Today, Civilization, Hurray for Hollywood, I'm Still Here, I've Been to a Marvelous Party, I Want a Long Time Daddy, The Little Things You Do Together, Something Good, The Ladies Who Lunch, The Party's Over, There Never Was a Baby Like My Baby, There's No Business Like Show Business, Why Do the Wrong People Travel, Zip

Performed in two acts. Autobiographical perspective on the life and passions of Elaine Stritch. Originally presented Off-Broadway by the Joseph Papp Public Theatre/New York Shakespeare Festival; received a Tony Award for Special Theatrical Event; received a special citation from the New York Drama Critics Circle.

*Closed May 26, 2002, after 69 performances.

Photos by Michal Daniel

Elaine Stritch

Elaine Stritch

METAMORPHOSES

By Mary Zimmerman, based on a translation by David R. Slavitt of Ovid's *Metamorphoses*; Director, Ms. Zimmerman; Sets, David Ostling; Lighting, T.J. Geckens; Costumes, Mara Blumenfeld; Sound, Andre Pluess and Ben Sussman; Composer, Willy Schwarz; Production Stage Manager, Debra A. Aquavella; Stage Manager, Anjali Bidani; Produced by Roy Gabay, Robyn Goodman, Allan S. Gordon, Elan V. McAllister, Dede Harris/Morton Swinsky, Ruth Hendel, Sharon Karmazin, Randall I. Wreghitt/Jane Bergere, in association with Second Stage Theatre (Carole Rothman, Artistic Director; Carol Fishman, Managing Director); Press, Richard Kornberg and Associates, Richard Kornberg, Tom D'Ambrosio, Don Summa. Opened at the Circle in the Square March 4, 2002*

Raymond Fox, Doug Hara

CAST

Myrrha and others	Anjali Bhimani
Midas and others	Raymond Fox
Hermes and others	Kyle Hall
Phaeton and others	Doug Hara
Aphrodite and others	Felicity Jones
Erysichthon and others	Chris Kipiniak
Alcyon and others	Louise Lamson
Orpheus and others	Erik Lochtefeld
Eurydice and others	Mariann Mayberry
Therapist and others	Lisa Tejero

UNDERSTUDIES: Mses. Lamson, Jones, Tejero (Tara Falk); Messrs. Hall, Hara (Mario Campanaro); Messrs. Kipiniak, Fox, Lochtefeld (Gregory Derelian); Mses. Bhimani, Mayberry (Julienne Hanzelka Kim)

Presented without intermission. Contemporary adaptation of Ovid's *Metamorphoses*, with inspiration from Rainer Maria Rilke's *Orpheus, Eurydice, Hermes* (translated by Stephen Mitchell), Joseph Campbell, Carl Jung, Sigmund Freud and James Hillman; originally produced by by Lookingglass Theatre Company, Chicago. Current production transferred after a run at the Second Stage Theatre (opened October 9, 2001).

*Still playing May 31, 2002

Photos by Joan Marcus

Doug Hara, Louise Lamson

Doug Hara, Erik Lochtefeld

ONE MO' TIME

Book by Vernal Bagneris; music and lyrics by various artists; Sets, Campbell Baird; Lighting, John McKernon; Choreography, Eddie D. Robinson; Costumes, Toni-Leslie James; Sound, Kurt B. Kellenberger; Musical Supervision, Mr. Kellin; Musical Arrangements, Lars Edegran and Mr. Kellin; Vocal Arrangements, Mr. Edegran and Topsy Chapman; Casting, Amy Christopher; Production Stage Manager, Grayson Meritt; Produced by the Williamstown Theatre Festival, Michael Ritchie, Producer; in association with Bob Boyett; Press, The Pete Sanders Group, Pete Sanders, Glenna Freedman, Rick Miramontez. Opened at the Longacre Theatre March 6, 2002*

CAST

Papa Du . . . . Vernel Bagneris
Ma Reed . . . . B.J. Crosby
Thelma . . . . Rosalind Brown
Theatre Owner . . . . Wally Dunn
Bertha . . . . Roz Ryan
UNDERSTUDIES: Mr. Bagneris (Eugene Fleming); Mses. Crosby, Ryan (Aisha de Haas); Ms. Brown (Enga Davis); Mr. Dunn (John Ahlin)

ORCHESTRA: Mark Brand, trumpet; Conal Fowkes, piano; Orange Kellin, clarinet; Walter Payton, tuba; Kenneth Sara, drums, percussion

MUSICAL NUMBERS: Darktown Strutters Ball, Honky Tonk Town, Kiss Me Sweet, Don't Turn Your Back on Me, Jenny's Ball, Cake-Walkin' Babies, I've Got What It Takes, See See Rider, He's in the Jailhouse Now, He's Funny That Way, Tiger Rag, Kitchen Man, Wait Till You See My Baby Do the Charleston, Muscrat Ramble, Black Bottom, Louise Louise, Get on Out of Here, Weary Blues, New Orleans Hop-Scop Blues, Hindustan, What It Takes to Bring You Back, Everybody Loves My Baby, Right Key but the Wrong Keyhole, After You've Gone, My Man Blues, Papa De Da Da, Muddy Water, A Hot Time in the Old Town Tonight

Performed in two acts. Time: 1926. Place: The Lyric Theatre, New Orleans. A musical that juxtaposes backstage life and onstage performances by African American performers in the Theatre Owners Booking Association circuit.

*Closed March 24, 2002, after 21 performances

Photos by Carol Rosegg

Roz Ryan, B.J. Crosby, Rosalind Brown

Rosalind Brown, Vernel Bagneris, Roz Ryan, B.J. Crosby

THE CRUCIBLE

By Arthur Miller; Director, Richard Eyre; Sets and Costumes, Tim Hatley; Lighting, Paul Gallo; Sound, Scott Myers; Casting, Daniel Swee; Original Music, David Van Tieghem; Production Stage Manager, Susie Gordon; Produced by David Richenthal, Jennifer Manocherian/Harriet Newman Leve/Bob Boyett, Max Cooper, Allan S. Gordon, Roy Furman, Us Productions, Elan V. McAllister, Adam Epstein, Margo Lion, in association with Dede Harris/Morton Swinsky, Clear Channel Entertainment, Old Ivy Productions, Jujamcyn Theatres, Jeffrey Ash, Dori Bernstein/Roni Selig, Margaret McFeeley Golden/Michael Skipper, Gene Korf, Robert Cole and by special arrangement with the Roundabout Theatre; Associate Producers, Toby Simkin, Erick Falkenstein; Press, Richard Kornberg and Associates, Richard Kornberg, Don Summa. Opened at the Virginia Theatre March 7, 2002*

Liam Neeson, Brian Murray, Laura Linney, Jack Willis

CAST

Reverend Harris . . . . Christopher Evan Welch
Betty Parris . . . . Betsy Hogg
Tituba . . . . Patrice Johnson
Abigail Williams . . . . Angela Bettis
Susanna Walcott . . . . Kristen Bell
Mrs. Ann Putnam . . . . Jeanne Paulsen
Thomas Putnam . . . . Paul O'Brien
Mercy Lewis . . . . Severin Anne Mason
Mary Warren . . . . Jennifer Carpenter
John Proctor . . . . Liam Neeson
Rebecca Nurse . . . . Helen Sternborg
Giles Corey . . . . Tom Aldredge
Reverend John Hale . . . . John Benjamin Hickey
Elizabeth Proctor . . . . Laura Linney
Francis Nurse . . . . Frank Raiter
Ezekial Cheever . . . . Henry Stram
Marshal Herrick . . . . Jack Willis
Hopkins . . . . Stephen Lee Anderson
Judge Hathorne . . . . J.R. Horne
Voice of Martha Corey . . . . Lise Bruneau
Deputy Governor Danforth . . . . Brian Murray
Girl in Courtroom . . . . Laura Brekenridge
Sarah Good . . . . Dale Soules
UNDERSTUDIES: Mr. Neeson (Paul O'Brien); Mses. Linney, Paulsen, Soules (Lise Bruneau); Mr. Murray (J.R. Horne); Messrs. Hickey, Welch, Stram, Anderson (Michael Winther); Messrs. O'Brien, Welch, Willis (Stephen Lee Anderson); Ms. Bettis (Jenneifer Carpenter); Messrs. Horne, Aldredge, Raiter, Stram (MacIntyre Dixon); Mses. Mason, Bell, Hogg (Laura Breckenridge); Ms. Carpenter (Kristen Bell); Mses. Johnson, Bruneau (Marsha Stephanie Blake); Ms. Sternborg (Dale Soules)

A play in two acts. Time: 1692. Place: Locations around Salem, Massachusetts. A revival of Arthur Miller's 1953 meditation on the nature of group hysteria, community norms and their enforcement.

*Still playing May 31, 2002

Photos by Joan Marcus

Angela Bettis, Liam Neeson

THE GOAT, OR WHO IS SYLVIA?

By Edward Albee; Director, David Esbjornson; Sets, John Arnone; Lighting, Kenneth Posner; Costumes, Elizabeth Hope Clancy; Sound, Mark Bennett; Casting, Bernard Telsey Casting; Production Stage Manager, Erica Schwartz; Produced by Elizabeth Ireland McCann, Daryl Roth, Carole Shorenstein Hays, Terry Allen Kramer, Scott Rudin, Bob Boyett, Scott Nederlander, Jeffrey Sine/ZPI; Press, Shirley Herz Associates, Sam Rudy. Opened at the Golden Theatre March 10, 2002*

CAST

Stevie . . . . Mercedes Ruehl
Martin . . . . Bill Pullman
Ross . . . . Stephen Rowe
Billy . . . . Jeffrey Carlson
UNDERSTUDIES: Mr. Pullman (Richard Thompson); Ms. Ruehl (Felicity LaFortune); Mr. Rowe (Stephen Schnetzer); Mr. Carlson (Todd Swenson)

A drama presented without intermission. A man's life and family are thrown into chaos when his love for a four-legged creature comes to light. Honored as Best Play by the New York Drama Critics Circle and the Tony Awards.

*Still playing May 31, 2002

Photos by Carol Rosegg

Mercedes Ruehl, Bill Pullman, Jeffrey Carlson

Mercedes Ruehl, Bill Pullman

SWEET SMELL OF SUCCESS

Book by John Guare; Based on the novella by Ernest Lehman, and the United Artists motion picture with screenplay by Clifford Odets and Ernest Lehman; Director, Nicholas Hytner; Sets and Costumes, Bob Crowley; Lighting, Natasha Katz; Sound, Tony Meola; Choreography, Christopher Wheeldon; Orchestrations, William David Brohn; Musical Direction, Jeffrey Huard; Music Coordination, Michael Keller; Associate Choreographer, Jodi Moccia; Casting, Mark Simon; Produced by Clear Channel Entertainment, David Brown, Ernest Lehman, Marty Bell, Martin Richards, Roy Furman, Joan Cullman, Bob Boyett, East of Doheny, Bob and Harvey Weinstein; Executive Producers, Beth Williams and East Egg Entertainment; Associate Producers, Producers Circle, Allen Spivak and Larry Magid; Press, Barlow-Hartman Public Relations, Michael Hartman, John Barlow, Wayne Wolfe. Opened at the Martin Beck Theatre March 14, 2002*

CAST

J.J. Hunsecker	John Lithgow
Sidney Falco	Brian D'Arcy James
Susan	Kelli O'Hara
Dallas	Jack Noseworthy
Rita	Stacy Logan
Madge	Joanna Glushak
Abigail Barcley	Elena L. Shaddow
Billy Van Cleve	Michael Peternostro
Pregnant Woman	Jamie Chandler Torns
Pepper White's Escort	Eric Sciotto
Charlotte Von Habsburg	Michelle Kittrell
Otis Elwell	Eric Michael Gillett
Lester	Steven Ochoa
Kello	David Brummel
Club Zanzibar Singer	Bernard Dotson
Cathedral Soloist	Kate Coffman-Lloyd
Senator	Allen Fitzpatrick
Senator's Girlfriend	Jill Nicklaus
J.J.'s Vaudeville Partner	Jennie Ford
Press Agent	Timothy J. Alex

UNDERSTUDIES: Mr. Lithgow (Allen Fitzpatrick); Mr. James (Frank Vlastnik); Ms. O'Hara (Elena L. Shaddow); Mr. Noseworthy (Eric Sciotto); Ms. Logan (Jill Nicklaus)

MUSICAL NUMBERS: The Column, I Could Get You in J.J., I Cannot Hear the City, Welcome to the Night, Laughin' All the Way to the Bank, At the Fountain, Psalm 151, Don't Know Where You Leave Off, What If, For Susan, One Track Mind, I Cannot Hear the City (reprise), End of Act 1, Break It Up, Rita's Tune, Dirt, I Could Get You in J.J. (reprise), I Cannot Hear the City (reprise), Don't Look Now, At the Fountain (reprise)

ORCHESTRA: Jeffrey Huard, conductor; Ron Melrose, piano, associate conductor; Joel Fram, keyboard 2, assistant conductor; Steve Bartosik, drums; Ted Nash, Dennis Anderson, Charles Pillow, Ken Dybisz, Ron Janelli, reeds; Bob Millikan, Larry Lunetta, trumpet; Michael Davis, Randy Andos, trombone; Douglas Purviance, bass trombone; Roger Wendt, french horn; Clay Ruede, cello; John Beal, bass; Bill Hayes, percussion

A musical in two acts. Time: 1952. Place: New York City. Adaptation of the noirish 1957 Burt Lancaster–Tony Curtis movie about the corruptive power of the media.

*Still playing May 31, 2002

Photo by Paul Kolnik

John Lithgow

OKLAHOMA!

Book by Oscar Hammerstein; Lyrics by Richard Rodgers; based on the play *Green Grow the Lilacs* by Lynn Riggs; Director, Trevor Nunn; Sets and Costumes, Anthony Ward; Lighting, David Hersey; Choreography, Susan Stroman; Fight Direction, Malcom Ranson; Original Orchestrations, Robert Russell Bennett; Musical Supervision, David Caddick; Music Direction, Kevin Stites; Dance Music Arrangements, David Krane; Music Coordination, John Miller; Associate Choreographer, Warren Carlyle; Casting, Tara Rubin Casting, Johnson-Liff Associates; Production Stage Manager, Mahlon Kruse; Producer, Cameron Mackintosh; Press, The Publicity Office, Marc Thibodeau, Bob Fennell, Michael S. Borowski, Candi Adams. Opened at the Gershwin Theatre March 21, 2002*

CAST

Aunt Eller	Andrea Martin
Curly	Patrick Wilson
Laurey	Josefina Gabrielle
Ike Skidmore	Ron Carroll
Will Parker	Justin Bohon
Jud Fry	Shuler Hensley
Ado Annie Carnes	Jessica Boevers
Ali Hakim	Aasif Mandvi
Gertie Cummings	Mia Price
Andrew Carnes	Michael McCarty
Cord Elam	Michael X. Martin
Corky	Matt Allen
Jess	Clyde Alves
Susie	Bradley Benjamin
Slim	Kevin Bernard
Aggie	Amy Bodner
Joe	Stephen R. Buntrock
Sam	Nicolas Dromard
Chalmers	Merwin Foard
Ellen	Rosena M. Hill
Jake	Chris Holly
Mike	Michael Thomas Holmes
Kate	Elizabeth Loyacano
Armina	Audrie Neenan
Rosie	Rachelle Rak
Tom	Jermaine R. Rembert
Vivian	Laura Shoop
Emily	Sarah Spradlin-Bonomo
Sylvie	Kathy Voytko
Lucy	Catherine Wreford
Lil'Titch	Juliana Rose Mauriello
Travis	Stephen Scott Scarpulla
Desiree	Lauren Ullrich
Maverick	William Ullrich

UNDERSTUDIES: Mr. Wilson (Stephen R. Buntrock, Greg Stone); Ms Gabrielle (Amy Bodner, Laura Shoop); Ms. Martin (Audrie Neenan); Mr. Hensley (Merwin Foard, Michael X. Martin); Ms. Boevers (Kathy Voytko, Catherine Wreford); Mr. Bohon (Matt Allen, Nicolas Dromard); Mr. Mandvi (Michael Thomas Holmes, Tony Yazbeck); Messrs. McCarty, Carroll (Harvey Evans)

MUSICAL NUMBERS: Overture, Oh, What a Beautiful Mornin', The Surry with the Fringe on Top, Kansas City, I Cain't Say No, Many a New Day, It's a Scandal! It's an Outrage!, People Will Say We're in Love, Pore Jud Is Daid, Lonely Room, Out of My Dreams Ballet, The Farmer and the Cowman, All er Nuthin', People Will Say We're in Love (reprise), Oklahoma, Finale Ultimo

A musical in two acts. Time: Near the turn of the twentieth century. Place: The Oklahoma Territory. Revival of the Rodgers and Hammerstein classic about Americans carving a life on the frontier.

*Still playing May 31, 2002

Photos by Michael LePoer Trench

Patrick Wilson

Josefina Gabrielle, Patrick Wilson

Josefina Gabrielle, The Company

Andrea Martin, The Company

Andrea Martin, Josefina Gabrielle

Patrick Wilson, Josefina Gabrielle

THE SMELL OF THE KILL

By Michele Lowe; Director, Christopher Ashley; Sets, David Gallo;
Lighting, Kenneth Posner; Sound, Dan Moses; Fight Direction, Rick
Sordelet; Casting, Johnson-Liff Associates; Production Stage Manager,
David Hyslop; Produced by Elizabeth Ireland McCann, Nellie Nugent,
Milton and Tamar Maltz, and USA Ostar Theatricals; Press, Boneau/
Bryan-Brown, Adrian Bryan-Brown, Jackie Green, Martin Sainvil.
Opened at the Helen Hayes Theatre March 26, 2002*

CAST

Debra . . . . Claudia Shear
Milly . . . . Jessica Stone
Nicky . . . . Lisa Emery
Danny, Marty . . . . Patrick Garner
Jay . . . . Mark Lotito
UNDERSTUDIES: Mses. Shear, Stone, Emery (Julie Boyd, Liz Larsen);
Messrs. Garner, Lotito (James Mountcastle)

A play presented without intermission. Comedy about three upper-middle-
class women who take revenge on their clueless, haplessly retro husbands.
Originally produced at the Cleveland Playhouse.

*Closed April 28, 2002, after 40 performances.

Photo by Joan Marcus

Jessica Stone, Claudia Shear, Lisa Emery

FORTUNE'S FOOL

Adaptation of Ivan Turgenev's play by Mike Poulton; Director, Arthur Penn; Sets, John Arnone; Lighting, Brian Nason; Sound, Brian Ronan; Costumes, Jane Greenwood; Original Music, Kramer; Casting, Howard/ Schecter/Meltzer; Production Stage Manager, Jane Grey; Produced by Julian Schlossberg, Roy Furman, Ben Sprecher, Ted Tulchin, Aaron Levy, Peter May, Bob Boyett, James Fantaci; Associate Producers, Rita Gam, Jill Furman; Press, The Publicity Office, Bob Fennell, Marc Thibodeau, Candi Adams, Michael S. Borowski. Opened at the Music Box Theatre April 2, 2002*

CAST

Vassily Semyonitch Kuzovkin . . . . Alan Bates
Ivan Kuzmitch Ivanov . . . . George Morfogen
Olga Petrovna . . . . Enid Graham
Pavel Nikolaitch Yeletsky (Paul) . . . . Benedick Bates
Felgont Alexandrovitch Tropatchov . . . . Frank Langella
Karpatchov (Little Fish) . . . . Timothy Doyle
Praskovya Ivanova . . . . Lola Pashalinski
Nartzis Konstantinitch Trembinsky . . . . Edwin C. Owens
Pyotr . . . . Jeremy Hollingworth
Servants . . . . Beth Bartley, Ann Ducati, Patrick Hallahan, John Newton
UNDERSTUDIES: Mr. A. Bates (Edwin C. Owens, Jeff Talbott); Mr. Langella (Edwin C. Owens, Timothy Doyle); Mr. B. Bates (Jeremy Hollingworth, Patrick Hallahan); Messrs. Doyle, Hollingworth (Patrick Hallahan); Ms. Graham (Beth Bartley); Messrs. Morfogen, Owens (John Newton); Ms. Pashalinski (Ann Ducati); Servants (Jeff Talbott)

A drama in two acts. Time: Mid-nineteenth-century Russia. Place: A country house. Adaptation of an Ivan Turgenev play, alternately translated as *A Poor Gentleman* and *One of the Family* ... A member of the aristocracy suffers the slights of the contemptuous — and contemptible — bourgeoisie.

*Still playing May 31, 2002

Photos by Carol Rosegg

Enid Graham, Alan Bates

Timothy Doyle, Frank Langella, Alan Bates

THE GRADUATE

Adapted by Terry Johnson from the novel by Charles Webb and the screenplay by Calder Willingham and Buck Henry; Director, Terry Johnson; Sets and Costumes, Rob Howell; Lighting, Hugh Vanstone; Sound, Christopher Cronin; Songs, Paul Simon; Performed by Simon and Garfunkel; Other Music and Songs, Barrington Pheloung and other artists; Casting, Howard/Schecter/Meltzer; Stage Manager, Karen Moore; Produced by John Reid and Sacha Brooks, by special arrangement with StudioCanal; Press, Barlow-Hartman Public Relations, John Barlow, Michael Hartman, Bill Coyle. Opened at the Plymouth Theatre April 4, 2002*

Alicia Silverstone, Jason Biggs

CAST

Benjamin Braddock . . . . Jason Biggs
Mr. Braddock . . . . Murphy Guyer
Mr. Robinson . . . . Victor Slezak
Mrs. Braddock . . . . Kate Skinner
Mrs. Robinson . . . . Kathleen Turner
Elaine Robinson . . . . Alicia Silverstone
The Hotel Clerk,
The Bar Patron, The Psychiatrist . . . . Robert Emmet Lunney
The Bartender, The Priest, The Motel Manager . . . . John Hillner
The Assistant Desk Clerk . . . . Kelly Overton
The Bellhop, The Man in Bar . . . . Judson Pearce Morgan
The Stripper . . . . Susan Cella
UNDERSTUDIES: Mses. Turner, Skinner (Susan Cella, Jurian Hughes); Mr. Biggs (Judson Pearce Morgan); Ms. Silverstone (Kelly Overton); Mr. Guyer (John Hillner, Larry Cahn); Ms. Cella (Jurian Hughes, Kelly Overton); Men (Larry Cahn); Women (Jurian Hughes)

A play presented in two acts. Time: 1960s. Place: California. Coming of age story set in the angst-ridden, youth-worshipping era of the 1960s.

*Still playing May 31, 2002

Photos by Joan Marcus

Kathleen Turner

Jason Biggs

TOPDOG / UNDERDOG

By Suzan-Lori Parks; Director, George C. Wolfe; Sets, Riccardo Hernandez; Lighting, Scott Zielinski; Costumes, Emilio Sosa; Sound, Dan Moses Schreier; Casting, Jordan Thaler/Heidi Griffiths; Production Stage Manager, Rick Steiger; Produced by Carole Shorenstein-Hays, Waxman Williams Entertainment, Bob Boyett, Freddy De Mann, Susan Dietz/Ina Meibach, Scott Nederlander, Ira Pittelman, in association with *Hits* magazine, Kelpie Arts, Rick Steiner/Frederic H. Mayerson, Press, Boneau/Bryan-Brown, Chris Boneau, Amy Jacobs, Jim Mannino, Julianna Hannett. Opened at the Ambassador Theatre April 7, 2002*; Originally opened at the Joseph Papp/New York Shakespeare Festival July 26, 2001; Awarded the 2002 Pulitzer Prize for Drama.

CAST

Lincoln . . . . Jeffrey Wright
Booth . . . . Mos Def
UNDERSTUDIES: Mr. Wright (Kevin Jackson) Mr. Def (Jeremiah Birkett)

A play presented in two acts. Time: Now. Place: Here. A pair of African American brothers struggle for survival and primacy in their marginal existence.

*Still playing May 31, 2002

Photos by Michal Daniel

Mos Def, Jeffrey Wright

Mos Def

THE ELEPHANT MAN

By Bernard Pomerance; Director, Sean Mathias; Sets and Costumes, Santo Loquasto; Lighting, James F. Ingalls; Sound, David Shapiro for ADI Group; Original Music, Philip Glass; Projection, Michael Clark; Casting, Ilene Stager; Production Stage Manager, Arthur Gaffin; Produced by David Aukin for Act Productions, Waxman Williams Entertainment, Manhattan Theatre Club, Bob Boyett, Steve Martin and Joan Stein, in association with Boston Court Theatre/Eileen T. Kaye, Daniel Cohen, June Curtis, Hot Springs Ventures, Inc.; Press, Boneau/Bryan-Brown, Susanne Tighe, Adriana Douzos. Opened at the Royale Theatre April 14, 2002*

CAST

Frederick Treves	Rupert Graves
Carr Gomm, Belgian policeman	Edmond Genest
Ross; Bishop Walsham How	Jack Gilpin
John Merrick	Billy Crudup
London Policeman	Nick Toren
Pinhead, Manager,	
London Policeman, Will, Lord John	James Riordan
Pinhead, Mrs. Kendal	Kate Burton
Pinhead, Mrs. Sandwich, Duchess, Princess Alexandra	Jenna Stern
Pinhead	Lynn Wright
Belgian Policeman,	
Conductor, Conductor, Snork, Countess	Christopher Duva

All other parts played by the ensemble

UNDERSTUDIES: Messrs. Crudup, Duva, Riordan (Nick Toren); Mr. Graves (Steve Ray Dallimore); Ms. Burton (Jenna Stern); Messrs. Genest, Gilpin, Riordan, Toren (Joe Vincent); Ms. Stern (Lynn Wright)

A play presented without intermission. Time: 1884 through 1890. Place: London and Belgium. The emotional journey of a man who suffers from a congenital disfigurement that gradually snuffs out his life. Originally produced in London in 1977, by the Foco Novo.

*Still playing May 31, 2002

Photo by Joan Marcus

Billy Crudup, Rupert Graves, Kate Burton

THOROUGHLY MODERN MILLIE

Book by Richard Morris and Dick Scanlan; Based on the story and screenplay by Richard Morris (Universal Pictures production); Director, Michael Mayer; Sets, David Gallo; Lighting, Donald Holder; Costumes, Martin Pakledinaz; Sound, Jon Weston; New Music, Jeanine Tesori; New Lyrics, Dick Scanlan; Choreography, Rob Ashford; Orchestrations, Doug Besterman and Ralph Burns; Music Coordination, John Miller; Casting, Jim Carnahan; Produced by Michael Leavitt, Fox Theatricals, Hal Luftig, Stewart F. Lane, James L. Nederlander, Independent Presenters Network, Libby Adler Mages/Mari Glick, Dori Berinstein/Jennifer Manocherian, Dramatic Forces, John York Noble and Whoopi Goldberg; Associate Producers, Mike Isaacson, Krisitin Caskey, Clear Channel Entertainment; Press, Barlow-Hartman Public Relations, John Barlow, Michael Hartman, Jeremy Shaffer. Opened at the Marquis Theatre April 18, 2002*

Sheryl Lee Ralph

CAST

Millie Dillmount	Sutton Foster
Ruth	Megan Sikora
Gloria	JoAnn M. Hunter
Rita	Jessica Grové
Alice	Alisa Klein
Ethel Peas	Joyce Chittick
Cora	Catherine Brunell
Lucille	Kate Baldwin
Mrs. Meers	Harriet Harris
Miss Dorothy Brown	Angela Christian
Ching Ho	Ken Leung
Bun Foo	Francis Jue
Miss Flannery	Anne L. Nathan
Mr. Trevor Graydon	Marc Kudisch
Speed Tappists	Casey Nicholaw, Noah Racey
The Pearl Lady	Roxane Barlow
Jimmy Smith	Gavin Creel
The Letch	Noah Racey
Officer	Casey Nicholaw
Muzzy Van Hossmere	Sheryl Lee Ralph
Kenneth	Brandon Wardell
Mathilde	Catherine Brunell
George Gershwin	Noah Racey
Dorothy Parker	Julie Connors
Rodney	Aaron Ramey
Dishwashers	Aldrin Gonzalez, Aaron Ramey, Brandon Wardell
Muzzy's Boys	Gregg Goodbrod, Darren Lee, Dan LoBuono, John MacInnis, Noah Racey, T. Oliver Reid
Daphne	Kate Baldwin
Dexter	Casey Nicholaw
New Modern	Jessica Grové

ENSEMBLE: Kate Baldwin, Roxane Barlow, Catherine Brunell, Joyce Chittick, Julie Connors, David Eggers, Gregg Goodbrod, Aldrin Gonzalez, Jessica Grové, Amy Heggins, JoAnn M. Hunter, Alisa Klein, Darren Lee, Dan LoBuono, John MacInnis, Casey Nicholaw, Noah Racey, Aaron Ramey, T. Oliver Reid, Megan Sikora, Brandon Wardell

UNDERSTUDIES: Ms. Foster (Catherine Brunell, Susan Haefner); Mr. Creel (Aaron Ramey, Brandon Wardell); Ms. Christian (Kate Baldwin, Jessica Grové); Mr. Kudisch (Gregg Goodbrod, Aaron Ramey); Mr. Leung (Francis Jue, Darren Lee); Mr. Jue (JoAnn M. Hunter, Darren Lee) Ms. Nathan (Julie Connors, Susan Haefner)

ORCHESTRA: Michael Rafter, conductor, music director; Lawrence Goldberg, associate conductor and piano; Charles Descarfino, assistant conductor, percussion; Lawrence Feldman, Walt Weiskopf, Dan Willis, Allen Won, woodwinds; Craig Johnson, Brian O'Flaherty, Glenn Drewes, trumpet; Larry Farrell, Jeff Nelson, trombone; Brad Gemeinhardt, french horn; Belinda Whitney, Eric DeGioia, Laura Oatts, Karl Kawahara, Mary Whitaker, violin; Stephanie Cummins, Anik Oulianine, cello; Emily Mitchell, harp; Ray Kilday, bass; Jack Cavari, guitar; Warren Odze, drums

MUSICAL NUMBERS: Not For the Life of Me, Thoroughly Modern Millie, How the Other Half Lives, The Speed Test, They Don't Know, The Nuttycracker Suite, What Do I Need With Love?, Only in New York, Jimmy, Forget About the Boy, I'm Falling in Love With Someone, I Turned the Corner, Muqin, Long As I'm Here With You, Gimme Gimme

A musical in two acts. Time: 1920s. Place: New York City. Based on a 1967 movie about a kid from Kansas who struggles to survive amid adversity in the big city. Winner of six Tony Awards, 2002: Best Actress, Featured Actress, Choreography, Musical, Orchestrations, Costumes.

*Still playing May 31, 2002

Photos by Joan Marcus

The Company

MORNING'S AT SEVEN

By Paul Osborn; Director, Daniel Sullivan; Sets, John Lee Beatty; Lighting, Brian MacDevitt; Costumes, Jane Greenwood; Sound, Scott Myers; Casting, Daniel Swee; A Lincoln Center Theatre production, André Bishop, Artistic Director; Bernard Gersten, Executive Producer; Press, Philip Rinaldi, Barbara Carroll. Opened at the Lyceum Theatre April 21, 2002*

CAST

Theodore Swanson . . . . William Biff McGuire
Cora Swanson . . . . Estelle Parsons
Aaronetta Gibbs . . . . Elizabeth Franz
Ida Bolton . . . . Frances Sternhagen
Carl Bolton . . . . Christopher Lloyd
Homer Bolton . . . . Stephen Tobolowsky
Myrtle Brown . . . . Julie Hagerty
Esther Crampton . . . . Piper Laurie
David Crampton . . . . Buck Henry
UNDERSTUDIES: Mses. Sternhagen, Franz (Barbara Caruso); Messrs. Henry, McGuire, Lloyd (Jack Davidson); Mses. Laurie, Parsons (Rita Gardner); Ms. Hagerty (Linda Marie Larson); Messrs. Tobolowsky, Lloyd (David Manis)

A play in two acts. Time: 1938. Place: Two backyards in a small midwestern town. Revival of a gentle comedy of midwestern manners and mores, with parts for nine mature actors. 1980 revival earned Tony Awards for Best Revival and Director.

*Still playing May 31, 2002

Photos by Joan Marcus

Piper Laurie, Estelle Parsons

William Biff McGuire, Estelle Parsons

Frances Sternhagen, Stephen Tobolowsky

Christopher Lloyd, Frances Sternhagen

THE MYSTERY OF CHARLES DICKENS

By Peter Ackroyd; Director, Patrick Garland; Sets and Costumes, Christopher Woods; Lighting, Nick Richlings; Production Stage Manager, Frank Hartenstein; Produced by Ambassador Theatre Group, Act Productions, and Pre-Eminence Ltd.; Press, Boneau/Bryan-Brown, Adrian Bryan-Brown, Susanne Tighe, Karalee Dawn. Opened at the Belasco Theatre April 25, 2002*

Performed by Simon Callow.

A discourse presented in two acts. The life and times of Charles Dickens in his own words and the words of his characters.

*Closed May 12, 2002, after 20 performances.

Photos by Joan Marcus

Simon Callow

Simon Callow

PRIVATE LIVES

By Noël Coward; Director, Howard Davies; Sets, Tim Hatley; Lighting, Peter Mumford; Costumes, Jenny Beaven; Sound, John A. Leonard; Music, Paddy Cunneen; Fight Coordinator, Terry King; Production Stage Manager, Bonnie Panson; Produced by Emanuel Azenberg, Ira Pittelman, Scott Nederlander, Frederick Zollo, Nicholas Paleologos, Dana Broccoli/ Jeffrey Sine, James Nederlander, Kevin McCollum, Jeffrey Seller, and Duncan C. Weldon & Paul Elliot for Triumph Entertainment Partners, Ltd.; Press, Bill Evans and Associates, Bill Evans, Jim Randolph. Opened at the Richard Rodgers Theatre April 28, 2002*

Alan Rickman, Lindsay Duncaan

Lindsay Duncan, Alan Rickman

CAST

Sibyl . . . . Emma Fielding
Elyot . . . . Alan Rickman
Victor . . . . Adam Godley
Amanda . . . . Lindsay Duncan
Louise . . . . Alex Belcourt

A play in two acts. Time: 1930s. Place: A hotel terrace in France and Amanda's flat in Paris. When an acerbic divorced couple discover the flames of love for each other still burn hotly—even as they honeymoon with new mates—verbal and sexual fireworks ensue. 2002 Tony Awards for Best Revival of a Play, Leading Actress and Scenic Design. The first production opened at the Times Square Theatre on January 1, 1931, and starred Noël Coward, Gertrude Lawrence, Laurence Olivier and Jill Esmond.

*Still playing May 31, 2002

Photos by Joan Marcus

Alan Rickman

Lindsay Duncan, Alan Rickman

INTO THE WOODS

Music and lyrics by Stephen Sondheim; Book by James Lapine; Director, Mr. Lapine; Sets, Douglas Schmidt; Lighting, Brian MacDevitt; Costumes, Susan Hilferty; Sound, Dan Moses Schreier; Choreography, John Carrafa; Projections, Elaine J. McCarthy; Special Effects, Gregory Meeh; Illusion, Jim Steinmeyer; Fight Direction, Rick Sordelet; Orchestrations, Jonathan Tunick; Music Direction, Paul Gemignani; Casting, Jim Carnahan; Produced by Dodger Theatricals, Stage Holding/Joop van den Ende and TheatreDreams, Inc.; Press, Boneau/Bryan-Brown, Adrian Bryan-Brown, Amy Jacobs, Susanne Tighe, Juliana Hannett. Opened at the Broadhurst Theatre April 30, 2002*

CAST

Narrator	John McMartin
Cinderella	Laura Benanti
Jack	Adam Wylie
Milky-White	Chad Kimball
Baker	Stephen DeRosa
Baker's Wife	Kerry O'Malley
Cinderella's Stepmother	Pamela Myers
Florinda	Tracy Nicole Chapman
Jack's mother	Mary Louise Burke
Little Red Ridinghood	Molly Ephraim
Witch	Vanessa Williams
Cinderella's father	Dennis Kelly
Mysterious Man	John McMartin
Wolves	Gregg Edelman, Christopher Sieber
Rapunzel	Melissa Dye
Rapunzel's Prince	Christopher Sieber
Granny	Pamela Myers
Cinderella's Prince	Gregg Edelman
Steward	Trent Armand Kendall
Horse	Jennifer Malenke

UNDERSTUDIES: Mr. McMartin (Stephen Berger, Dennis Kelly); Mses. Benanti, Ephraim (Melissa Dye, Kate Reinders); Messrs. Sieber, Wylie (Adam Brazier, Chad Kimball); Mr. Kimball (Jennifer Malenke, Kate Reinders); Messrs. Kelly, DeRosa (Stephen Berger, Trent Armand Kendall); Ms. O'Malley (Linda Mugleston, Amanda Naughton); Ms. Meyers (Linda Mugleston); Ms. Chapman (Jennifer Malenke); Ms. Burke (Linda Mugleston, Pamela Myers); Ms. Williams (Tracy Nicole Chapman, Linda Mugleston); Ms. Dye (Jennifer Malenke, Kate Reinders); Mr. Edelman (Adam Brazier, Christopher Sieber); Mr. Kendall (Stephen Berger, Adam Brazier); Ms. Malenke (Adam Brazier)

MUSICAL NUMBERS: Into the Woods, Hello Little Girl, I Guess This Is Goodbye, Maybe They Are Magic, Our Little World, I Know Things Now, A Very Nice Prince, Giants in the Sky, Agony, It Takes Two, Stay With Me, On the Steps of the Palace, Ever After, So Happy, Lament, Any Moment, Moments in the Woods, Your Fault, Last Midnight, No More, No One Is Alone, Children Will Listen

ORCHESTRA: Paul Gemignani, conductor; Annbritt duChateau, associate conductor, keyboard 1; Mark Mitchell, assistant conductor, keyboard 2; Marilyn Reynolds, concertmaster, violin 1; Mineko Yajima, violin 2; Richard Brice, viola 1; Shelley Holland-Moritz, viola 2; Deborah Assael, cello; John Beal, bass; Les Scott, flute; Amy Zoloto, clarinet; John Campo, bassoon; Ron Sell, french horn 1; Nancy Billman, french horn 2; Dominic Derasse, trumpet; Paul Pizutti, percussion

A musical in two acts. Time: Once upon a time…. Place: A far-off kingdom. Classic fairy tales brought to musical life, before crossing into the dark side of "happily ever after…" 2002 Tony Award for Best Musical Revival; Original Broadway production opened at the Martin Beck Theatre on November 5, 1987, and ran for 765 performances.

*Still playing May 31, 2002

Photo by Joan Marcus

Vanessa Williams

THE MAN WHO HAD ALL THE LUCK

By Arthur Miller; Director, Scott Ellis; Sets, Allen Moyer; Lighting, Kenneth Posner; Costumes, Michael Krass; Sound, Eileen Tague; Fight Direction, Rick Sordelet; Original Music, Tom Kochan; Casting, Amy Christopher; Production Stage Manager, Andrea J. Testani; Stage Manager, Brendan Smith; Produced by The Roundabout Theatre Company; Todd Haimes, Artistic Director, Ellen Richard, Managing Director; Julia C. Levy, Executive Director of External Affairs. Opened at the American Airlines Theatre May 1, 2002*

CAST

David Beeves . . . . Chris O'Donnell
J.B. Feller . . . . Richard Riehle
Shory . . . . Dan Moran
Hester Falk . . . . Samantha Mathis
Dan Dibble . . . . Mason Adams
Andrew Falk . . . . Edward James Hyland
Aunt Belle . . . . Mary Catherine Wright
Pat Beeves . . . . James Reborn
Amos Beeves . . . . Ryan Shively
Gustav Elberson . . . . Sam Robards
Augie Belfast . . . . David Wohl
UNDERSTUDIES: Mr. O'Donnell (Ryan Shively); Mr. Reborn (Edward James Hyland); Mr. Shively (Will Bozarth); Messrs. Adams, Hyland, Riehle (Philip LeStrange); Messrs. Wohl, Moran, Robards (Blake Robbins); Mses. Mathis, Wright (Catherine Wadkins)

A play in three acts. Time: Several years during the 1930s. Place: Midwest. A man who feels he has had more than his share of blessings and good fortune struggles to understand why. Originally produced in New York at the Forrest Theatre in November 1944.

*Still playing May 31, 2002

Photo by Joan Marcus

Chris O'Donnell, James Reborn, Samantha Mathis

BROADWAY

Productions from past seasons that played through this season

AIDA

Music, Elton John; Lyrics, Tim Rice; Book, Linda Woolverton and Robert Falls and David Henry Hwang; Suggested by the opera; Director, Robert Falls; Choreography, Wayne Cilento; Set/Costumes, Bob Crowley; Lighting, Natasha Katz; Sound, Steve C. Kennedy; Music Producer and Musical Direction, Paul Bogaev; Music Arrangements, Guy Babylon, Paul Bogaev; Orchestrations, Steve Margoshes, Guy Babylon, Paul Bogaev; Casting, Bernard Telsey; Production Stage Manager, Clifford Schwartz; Cast Recording, Buena Vista; Presented by Hyperion Theatricals (Peter Schneider and Thomas Schumacher); Press, Chris Boneau–Adrian Bryan-Brown/Jackie Green, Steven Padla. Previewed from Friday, February 25, 2000; Opened in the Palace Theatre on Thursday, March 23, 2000*

The Company

CAST

Amneris . . . . Sherie René Scott †1
Radames . . . . Adam Pascal
Aida . . . . Heather Headley †2
Mereb . . . . Damian Perkins †3
Zoser . . . . John Hickok
Pharaoh . . . . Daniel Oreskes
Nehebka . . . . Schele Williams
Amonasro . . . . Tyrees Allen
ENSEMBLE: Robert M. Armitage, Troy Allan Burgess, Franne Calma, Bob Gaynor, Kisha Howard, Tim Hunter, Youn Kim, Kyra Little, Kenya Unique Massey, Corinne McFadden, Phineas Newborn III, Jody Ripplinger, Raymond Rodriguez, Eric Sciotto, Samuel N. Thiam, Jerald Vincent, Schele Williams, Natalia Zisa

UNDERSTUDIES: Franne Calma, Kelli Fournier (Amneris), Bob Gaynor, Raymond Rodriguez, Eric Sciotto (Radames), Schele Williams (Aida), Tim Hunter, Phineas Newborn III (Mereb), Troy Allan Burgess (Zoser), Robert M. Armitage (Pharaoh), Kyra Little, Endalyn Taylor-Shellman (Nehebka), Samuel N. Thiam, Jerald Vincent (Amonasro)

STANDBYS: Thursday Farrar (Aida), Neal Benari (Zoser/Pharaoh)

SWINGS: Chris Payne Dupré, Kelli Fournier, Timothy Edward Smith, Endalyn Taylor-Shellman

MUSICAL NUMBERS: Every Story Is a Love Story, Fortune Favors the Brave, The Past Is Another Land, Another Pyramid, How I Know You, My Strongest Suit, Enchantment Passing Through, The Dance of the Robe, Not Me, Elaborate Lives, The Gods Love Nubia, A Step Too Far, Easy as Life, Like Father Like Son, Radames' Letter, Written in the Stars, I Know the Truth

A musical in two acts. The action takes place in Egypt. Winner of 2000 Tony Awards for Original Score, Actress in a Musical (Heather Headley), Scenic Design, and Lighting Design.

*Still playing May 31, 2002.

†Succeeded by: 1. Taylor Dane, Idina Menzel, Felicia Finley 2. Maya Days, Simone 3. Delisco

Photos by Joan Marcus

Adam Pascal, Heather Headley

BEAUTY AND THE BEAST

Music, Alan Menken; Lyrics, Howard Ashman, Tim Rice; Book, Linda Woolverton; Director, Robert Jess Roth; Orchestrations, Danny Troob; Musical Supervision/Vocal Arrangements, David Friedman; Musical Director/Incidental Arrangements, Michael Kosarin; Choreography, Matt West; Set, Stan Meyer; Costumes, Ann Hould-Ward; Lighting, Natasha Katz; Sound, T. Richard Fitzgerald; Hairstylist, David H. Lawrence; Illusions, Jim Steinmeyer, John Gaughan; Prosthetics, John Dods; Fights, Rick Sordelet; Cast Recording, Walt Disney Records; General Manager, Dodger Productions; Production Supervisor, Jeremiah J. Harris; Company Manager, Kim Sellon; Stage Managers, James Harker, John M. Atherlay, Pat Sosnow, Kim Vernace; Presented by Walt Disney Productions; Press, Chris Boneau/Adrian Bryan-Brown, Amy Jacobs, Steven Padla. Previewed from Wednesday, March 9, 1994; Opened in the Palace Theatre on Monday, April 18, 1994*

CAST

Enchantress	Wendy Oliver
Young Prince	Tom Pardoe
Beast	Steve Blanchard
Belle	Andrea McArdle †1
Lefou	Gerard McIsaac †2
Gaston	Patrick Ryan Sullivan †3
Three Silly Girls	Lauren Goler-Kosarin, Pam Klinger, Linda Talcott Lee
Maurice	J.B. Adams
Cogsworth	Jeff Brooks
Lumiere	David deVries †4
Babette	Louisa Kendrick †5
Mrs. Potts	Barbara Marineau †6
Chip	Jonathan Andrew Bleicher, Joseph DiConcetto
Madame de la Grande Bouche	Judith Moore
Monsieur D'Arque	Gordon Stanley
Townspeople/Enchanted Objects	Anna Maria Andricain, Steven Ted Beckler, Kevin Berdini, Andrea Burns, Christophe Caballero, Sally Mae Dunn, Barbara Folts, Teri Furr, Gregory Garrison, Elmore James, Alisa Klein, Lauren Goler-Kosarin, Ellen Hoffman, Pam Klinger, Ken McMullen, Anna McNeely, Beth McVey, Bill Nabel, Wendy Oliver, Tom Pardoe, Raymond Sage, Joseph Savant, Sarah Solie Shannon, Matthew Shepard, Steven Sofia, Gordon Stanley, Linda Talcott Lee, David A. Wood, Wysandria Woolsey
Prologue Narrator	David Ogden Stiers

MUSICAL NUMBERS: Overture, Prologue (Enchantress), Belle, No Matter What, Me, Home, Gaston, How Long Must This Go On?, Be Our Guest, If I Can't Love Her, Entr'acte/Wolf Chase, Something There, Human Again, Maison des Lunes, Beauty and the Beast, Mob Song, The Battle, Transformation, Finale

A musical in two acts. An expanded, live action version of the 1992 animated film musical with additional songs. Winner of 1994 Tony for Best Costume Design. Since the opening, the role of "Belle" has been played by Susan Egan, Sarah Uriarte, Christianne Tisdale, Kerry Butler, Deborah Gibson, Kim Huber, Toni Braxton, Andrea McArdle, and Sarah Litzsinger. The role of "The Beast" has been played by Terrence Mann, Jeff McCarthy, Chuck Wagner, James Barbour, and Steve Blanchard.

*Still playing May 31, 2002. The production moved to the Lunt-Fontanne Theatre on November 12, 1999.

†Succeeded by: 1. Sarah Litzsinger 2. Brad Aspel 3. Christopher Seilber, Chris Hoch 4. Rob Lorey 5. Pam Klinger 6. Beth Fowler

Photo by Eduardo Patino

Andrea McArdle, Steve Blanchard

CABARET

Music, John Kander; Lyrics, Fred Ebb; Book, Joe Masteroff; Based on the play *I Am a Camera* by John Van Druten and stories by Christopher Isherwood; Director, Sam Mendes; Co-Director/Choreography, Rob Marshall; New Orchestrations, Michael Gibson; Musical Director, Patrick Vaccariello; Set/Club Design, Robert Brill; Costumes, William Ivey Long; Lighting, Peggy Eisenhauer, Mike Baldassari; Sound, Brian Ronan; Dance Arrangements, David Krane, David Baker; Company Manager, Denys Baker; Stage Manager, Peter Hanson; Cast Recording, RCA; Presented by Roundabout Theatre Company (Todd Haimes, Artistic Director; Ellen Richard, General Manager; Gene Feist, Founding Director); Press, Chris Boneau–Adrian Bryan-Brown/Erin Dunn, Jackie Green, Andrew Palladino, Amy Nieporent. Previewed from Friday, February 13, 1998; Opened in the Kit Kat Club (the Henry Miller Theatre) on Thursday, March 19, 1998*

CAST

Emcee	Matt McGrath †1

KIT KAT GIRLS:

Rosie	Christina Pawl
Lulu	Victoria Lecta Cave
Frenchie	Nicole Van Giesen
Texas	Leenya Rideout
Fritzie	Victoria Clark
Helga	Kristin Olness

KIT KAT BOYS:

Bobby	Michael O'Donnell
Victor	Brian Duguay
Hans	Richard Costa
Herman	Fred Rose
Sally Bowles	Joley Fisher †2
Clifford Bradshaw	Michael Hayden †3
Ernst Ludwig	Martin Moran †4
Customs Official/Max	Fred Rose
Fraulein Schneider	Carole Shelley †5
Fraulein Kost	Candy Buckley
Rudy	Richard Costa
Herr Schultz	Dick Latessa †6
Gorilla	Christina Pawl
Boy Soprano (recording)	Alex Bowen

UNDERSTUDIES: Linda Romoff, Victoria Lecta Cave (Sally), Brian Duguay, Michael O'Donnell (Cliff), Fred Rose, Manoel Felciano (Ernst), Vance Avery, Michael Arnold (Emcee), Maureen Moore (Schneider), Scott Robertson (Schultz), Leenya Rideout, Victoria Lecta Cave (Kost)

SWINGS: Linda Romoff, Penny Ayn Maas, Vance Avery, Manoel Felciano, Michael Arnold

A newly revised production of the 1966 musical in two acts. The action takes in Berlin, Germany, 1929–30. Winner of 1998 Tony Awards for Actor in a Musical (Alan Cumming), Actress in a Musical (Natasha Richardson), Featured Actor in a Musical (Ron Rifkin), and Best Revival of a Musical. For original Broadway production with Joel Grey, Jill Haworth, and Lotte Lenya, see *Theatre World* Vol. 23.

*Still playing May 31, 2002. The production moved to Studio 54 on November 12, 1998.

†Succeeded by: 1. Raúl Esparza, John Stamos 2. Lea Thompson, Katie Finneran, Gina Gershon, Kate Shindle, Brooke Shields, Molly Ringwald, Jane Leeves 3. Matthew Greer 4. Peter Benson 5. Polly Bergen 6. Larry Keith, Hal Linden

Photos by Joan Marcus

The Company

Matt McGrath

CHICAGO

Music, John Kander; Lyrics, Fred Ebb; Book, Mr. Ebb, Bob Fosse; Script Adaptation, David Thompson; Based on the play by Maurine Dallas Watkins; Original Production Directed and Choreographed by Bob Fosse; Director, Walter Bobbie; Choreography, Ann Reinking in the style of Bob Fosse; Music Director, Rob Fisher; Orchestrations, Ralph Burns; Set, John Lee Beatty; Costumes, William Ivey Long; Lighting, Ken Billington; Sound, Scott Lehrer; Dance Arrangements, Peter Howard; Cast Recording, RCA; General Manager, Darwell Associates and Maria Di Dia; Company Manager, Scott A. Moore; Stage Managers, Clifford Schwartz, Terrence J. Witter; Presented by Barry & Fran Weissler in association with Kardana Productions; Press, Pete Sanders/Helen Davis, Clint Bond Jr., Glenna Freedman, Bridget Klapinski. Previewed from Wednesday, October 23, 1996; Opened in the Richard Rodgers Theatre on Thursday, November 14, 1996*

CAST

Velma Kelly . . . . Sharon Lawrence †1
Roxie Hart . . . . Belle Calaway †2
Fred Casely . . . . Gregory Mitchell
Sergeant Fogarty . . . . Michael Kubala
Amos Hart . . . . P.J. Benjamin †3
Liz . . . . Michelle M. Robinson
Annie . . . . Mamie Duncan-Gibbs
June . . . . Donna Marie Asbury
Hunyak . . . . Mindy Cooper
Mona . . . . Caitlin Carter
Matron "Mama" Morton . . . . Roz Ryan †4
Billy Flynn . . . . Brent Barrett †5
Mary Sunshine . . . . R. Bean
Go-To-Hell-Kitty . . . . Mary Ann Hermansen
Harry . . . . Sebastian LaCause
Aaron . . . . David Warren-Gibson
Judge . . . . Gregory Butler
Martin Harrison/Doctor . . . . Denis Jones
Court Clerk . . . . John Mineo
The Jury . . . . Michael Kubala
UNDERSTUDIES/STANDBYS: Nancy Hess (Velma/Roxie), Caitlin Carter (Roxie), Amy Spanger, Donna Marie Asbury (Roxie/Velma), John Mineo (Amos), Mamie Duncan-Gibbs (Mama/Velma), Michael Berresse (Billy), Michael Kubala (Billy/Amos), J. Loeffelholz (Mary), Luis Perez (Billy/Fred), Denis Jones (Amos/Fred), Michelle M. Robinson (Mama), Eric L. Christian, Rocker Verastique (Fred), Randy Slovacek (Amos), Deidre Goodwin (Mama), Gregory Butler (Billy/Fred), Mark Anthony Taylor (Fred), Sebastian LaCause (Fred).

MUSICAL NUMBERS: All That Jazz, Funny Honey, Cell Block Tango, When You're Good to Mama, Tap Dance, All I Care About, A Little Bit of Good, We Both Reached for the Gun, Roxie, I Can't Do It Alone, My Own Best Friend, Entr'acte, I Know a Girl, Me and My Baby, Mister Cellophane, When Velma Takes the Stand, Razzle Dazzle, Class, Nowadays, Hot Honey Rag, Finale

Brent Barrett and the Merry Murderesses

A new production of the 1975 musical in two acts. This production is based on the staged concert presented by City Center Encores. The action takes place in Chicago, late 1920s. Winner of 1997 Tony Awards for Revival of a Musical, Leading Actor in a Musical (James Naughton), Leading Actress in a Musical (Bebe Neuwirth), Direction of a Musical, Choreography, and Lighting. For original Broadway production with Gwen Verdon, Chita Rivera, and Jerry Orbach, see *Theatre World* Vol. 32.

*Still playing May 31, 2002. Moved to the Shubert Theatre on February 12, 1997.

†Succeeded by: 1. Vicki Lewis, Jasmine Guy, Bebe Neuwirth, Donna Marie Asbury, Deidre Goodwin, Vicki Lewis, Deidre Goodwin, Anna Montanero, Deidre Goodwin, Donna Marie Asbury, Roxanne Carrasco, Deidre Goodwin 2. Charlotte d'Amboise, Belle Calaway, Nana Visitor, Petra Nielsen, Nana Visitor, Belle Callaway, Denise Van Outen, Belle Calaway 3. Tom McGowan, P.J. Benjamin, Ray Bokhour, P.J. Benjamin 4. Marcia Lewis, Jennifer Holliday, Marcia Lewis, Roz Ryan, Michele Pawk, Alix Korey 5. Chuck Cooper, Clarke Peters, George Hamilton, Eric Jordan Young, Ron Raines, George Hamilton

Photo by Carol Rosegg

CONTACT

By Susan Stroman (Director/Choreography) and John Weidman (Writer); Set, Thomas Lynch; Costumes, William Ivey Long; Lighting, Peter Kaczorowski; Sound, Scott Stauffer; Casting, Johnson-Liff Associates, Tara Rubin, Daniel Swee; Production Stage Manger, Thom Widmann; Recording, RCA; Presented by Lincoln Center Theater (André Bishop, Artistic Director; Bernard Gersten, Executive Producer). Press, Philip Rinaldi/Miller Wright, James A. Babcock; Previewed from Thursday, March 2, 2000; Opened in the Vivian Beaumont on Thursday, March 30, 2000*

CAST

Jason Antoon †1	Nina Goldman	Stephanie Michels †2
John Bolton	Peter Gregus	Mayumi Miguel
Tomé Cousin	Shannon Hammons	Dana Stackpole
Holly Cruikshank	Jack Hayes	Scott Taylor
Pascale Faye	Seán Martin Hingston	Rocker Verastique
Boyd Gaines †3	Stacey Todd Holt	Robert Wersinger
Steve Geary	Angelique Ilo	Deborah Yates †4
David MacGillivray	Joanne Manning	Karen Ziemba †5

UNDERSTUDIES: John Bolton, Steve Geary, Stacey Todd Holt, Robert Wersinger (Frenchmen), Holly Cruikshank, Shannon Hammons, Angelique Ilo, Joanne Manning (Girl on a Swing), Holly Cruikshank, Nina Goldman, Angelique Ilo (Wife), John Bolton, Peter Gregus, Stacey Todd Holt (Husband), Steve Geary, Scott Taylor, Rocker Verastique (Headwaiter), Scott Taylor (Michael Wiley), Joanne Manning (Girl in a Yellow Dress), John Bolton, Stacey Todd Holt (Bartender)

STANDBYS: John Bolton (Michael Wiley), Holly Cruikshank (Girl in a Yellow Dress)

SWINGS: Steve Geary, Stacey Todd Holt; Angelique Ilo, Joanne Manning

A dance play in three short parts: Swinging, Did You Move?, and Contact. Winner of 2000 Tony Awards for Best Musical, Featured Actor in a Musical (Boyd Gaines), Featured Actress in a Musical (Karen Ziemba), and Choreography.

*Closed September 1, 2002 after 1,009 performances. Prior to Broadway, the production played in Off-Broadway's Mitzi E. Newhouse Theatre from September 9, 1999 – January 2, 2000.

†Succeeded by: 1. Danny Mastrogiorgio 2. Joanne Manning 3. D.W. Moffet 4. Colleen Dunn 5. Charlotte d'Amboise

Photos by Paul Kolnik

Stephanie Michels, Seán Martin Hingston

The Company

42nd STREET

Music, Harry Warren; Lyrics, Al Dubin; Book, Michael Stewart and Mark Bramble; Based on a Novel by Bradford Ropes; Director, Mark Bramble; Musical Staging/New Choreography, Randy Skinner; Musical Director, Todd Ellison; Musical Adaptation/Arrangements, Donald Johnston; Orchestrations (original), Philip J. Lang; Set, Douglas W. Schmidt; Costumes, Roger Kirk; Lighting, Paul Gallo; Sound, Peter Fitzgerald; Hair/Wigs, David H. Lawrence; Company Manager, Sandra Carlson; General Manager, Robert C. Strickstein; Production Stage Manager, Frank Hartenstein; Stage Manager, Karen Armstrong; Casting, Jay Binder; Original Direction/Dances, Gower Champion; Presented by Dodger Theatricals, Joop Van Den Ende and Stage Holding; Press, Chris Boneau–Adrian Bryan-Brown/Susanne Tighe, Amy Jacobs, Adriana Douzos. Previewed from Wednesday, April 4, 2001; Opened in the Ford Center for the Performing Arts on Wednesday, May 2, 2001*

CAST

Andy Lee . . . . Michael Arnold
Maggie Jones . . . . Mary Testa
Bert Barry . . . . Jonathan Freeman
Mac . . . . Allen Fitzpatrick
Phyllis . . . . Catherine Wreford
Lorraine . . . . Megan Sikora
Diane . . . . Tamlyn Brooke Shusterman
Annie . . . . Mylinda Hull
Ethel . . . . Amy Dolan
Billy Lawlor . . . . David Elder
Peggy Sawyer . . . . Kate Levering †1
Oscar . . . . Billy Stritch
Julian Marsh . . . . Michael Cumpsty
Dorothy Brock . . . . Christine Ebersole †2
Abner Dillon . . . . Michael McCarty
Pat Denning . . . . Richard Muenz
Waiters . . . . Brad Aspel, Mike Warshaw, Shonn Wiley
Thugs . . . . Allen Fitzpatrick, Jerry Tellier
Doctor . . . . Allen Fitzpatrick
ENSEMBLE: Brad Aspel, Becky Berstler, Randy Bobish, Chris Clay, Michael Clowers, Maryam Myika Day, Alexander de Jong, Amy Dolan, Isabelle Flachsmann, Jennifer Jones, Dontee Kiehn, Renée Klapmeyer, Jessica Kostival, Keirsten Kupiec, Todd Lattimore, Melissa Rae Mahon, Michael Malone, Jennifer Marquardt, Meredith Patterson, Darin Phelps, Wendy Rosoff, Megan Schenck, Kelly Sheehan, Tamlyn Brooke Shusterman, Megan Sikora, Jennifer Stetor, Erin Stoddard, Yasuko Tamaki, Jonathan Taylor, Jerry Tellier, Elisa Van Duyne, Erika Vaughn, Mike Warshaw, Merrill West, Shonn Wiley, Catherine Wreford

UNDERSTUDIES/STANDBYS: Beth Leavel (Dorothy Brock/Maggie Jones), Brad Aspel (Andy Lee, Bert Barry), Becky Berstler (Annie), Randy Bobish (Andy Lee), Amy Dolan (Annie, Maggie Jones), Allen Fitzpatrick (Abner Dillon/Pat Denning), Renée Klapmeyer (Diane), Jessica Kostival (Dorothy Brock), Richard Muenz (Julian Marsh), Meredith Patterson (Peggy Sawyer), Darin Phelps (Doctor/Mac/Thug), Erin Stoddard (Lorraine/Peggy Sawyer), Jerry Tellier (Julian Marsh/Pat Denning), Elisa Van Duyne (Phyllis), Luke Walrath (Doctor/Mac/Thug), Shonn Wiley (Billy Lawlor)

Christine Ebersole

MUSICAL NUMBERS: Overture, Audition, Young and Healthy, Shadow Waltz, Go into Your Dance, You're Getting to Be a Habit with Me, Getting Out of Town, Dames, Keep Young and Beautiful, Dames, I Only Have Eyes for You (not in orig production), We're in the Money, Keep Young and Beautiful (not in orig production), Entr'acte, Sunny Side to Every Situation, Lullaby of Broadway, Getting Out of Town, Montage, About a Quarter to Nine, With Plenty of Money and You (not in orig. production), Shuffle Off to Buffalo, 42nd Street, Finale

A new production of the 1980 musical in two acts. The action takes place in New York City and Philadelphia, 1933. Winner of 2001 Tony Award for Best Revival/Musical and Best Actress in a Musical (Christine Ebersole). For original Broadway production with Jerry Orbach and Tammy Grimes, see *Theatre World* Vol. 37.

Variety tallied 11 favorable, 1 mixed, and 4 negative reviews. *Times* (Brantley): "…premature revival…a faded fax of the last musical staged by the fabled Gower Champion…" *News* (Kissel) "…loaded with talent. And you know it as soon as the curtain rises on 24 pairs of tap-dancing feet." *Post* (Barnes): "…cast with exquisite care…everyone is superb…" *Variety* (Isherwood): "…gaudy, relentless production…pays tribute to the Gower Champion original…"

*Still playing May 31, 2002

†Succeeded by 1. Meredith Patterson 2. Beth Leavel, Christine Ebersole

Photo by Joan Marcus

THE FULL MONTY

Music/Lyrics, David Yazbek; Book by Terrence McNally; Based on the 1997 British film; Director, Jack O'Brien; Choreography, Jerry Mitchell; Orchestrations, Harold Wheeler; Set, John Arnone; Costumes, Robert Morgan; Lighting, Howell Binkley; Sound, Tom Clark; Musical Director/Vocal/Incidental Arrangements, Ted Sperling; Dance Arrangements, Zane Mark; General Manager, The Charlotte Wilcox Company; Company Manager, Dave Harris; Production Supervisor, Gene O'Donovan; Production Stage Manager, Nancy Harrington; Stage Manager, Julie Baldauff; Conductor, Kimberly Grigsby; Casting, Liz Woodman; Cast Recording, RCA; Presented by Fox Searchlight Pictures, Lindsay Law and Thomas Hall; Press, John Barlow–Michael Hartman/Wayne Wolfe, Shellie Shovanec. Previewed from Monday, September 25, 2000; Opened in the Eugene O'Neill Theatre on Thursday, October 26, 2000*

CAST

Georgie Bukatinsky	Annie Golden
Buddy "Keno" Walsh	Denis Jones
Reg Willoughby	Todd Weeks
Jerry Lukowski	Patrick Wilson †1
Dave Bukatinsky	John Ellison Conlee †2
Malcolm MacGregor	Jason Danieley †3
Ethan Girard	Romain Frugé †4
Nathan Lukowski	Nicholas Cutro, Thomas Michael Fiss
Susan Hershey	Laura Marie Duncan
Joanie Lish	Jannie Jones
Estelle Genovese	Liz McConahay
Pam Lukowski	Lisa Datz
Teddy Slaughter	Angelo Fraboni
Molly MacGregor	Patti Perkins
Harold Nichols	Marcus Neville †5
Vicki Nichols	Emily Skinner
Jeanette Burmeister	Kathleen Freeman †6
Noah "Horse" T. Simmons	André De Shields †7
Police Sergeant	C.E. Smith
Minister	Jay Douglas
Tony Giordano	Jimmy Smagula

UNDERSTUDIES: Jay Douglas (Jerry Lukowski/Malcolm MacGregor), Laura Marie Duncan (Estelle Genovese/Georgie Bukatinsky/Pam Lukowski/Vicki Nichols), Angelo Fraboni (Buddy "Keno" Walsh), Denis Jones (Ethan Girard), Jannie Jones (Georgie Bukatinsky), Liz McConahay (Vicki Nichols), Sue-Anne Morrow (Estelle Genovese/Georgie Bukatinsky/Pam Lukowski), Jason Opsahl (Ethan Girard/Malcolm MacGregor), Patti Perkins (Jeanette Burmeister), Jimmy Smagula (Dave Bukatinsky), C.E. Smith, Ronald Wyche (Noah "Horse" T. Simmons), Matthew Stocke (Jerry Lukowski), Todd Weeks (Harold Nichols)

MUSICAL NUMBERS: Overture, Scrap, It's a Woman's World, Man, Big-Ass Rock, Life with Harold, Big Black Man, You Rule My World, Michael Jordan's Ball, Entr'acte, Jeanette's Showbiz Number, Breeze off the River, The Goods, You Walk with Me, You Rule My World (reprise), Let It Go

A musical comedy in two acts. The action takes place in Buffalo, New York.

The Company

Times (Brantley): "The Eugene O'Neill Theater won't have to look for a new tenant for a long, long time … With a winning, ear-catching pop score by David Yazbek and a lively gallery of performers who seem truly in love with the people they're playing …" *News* (Hinckley): "… delightful and more than occasionally poignant story of blue-collar pals who in desperation decide the only way to lift the crushing weight of unemployment and restore their dignity is to take their clothes off … a full-fledged dance musical … songs range from joyous to pensive …" *Post* (Barnes): "… the most daring, yet successful, Broadway adaptation of a movie script … masterly kind of book that gives the chance for a musical to slide to heaven … extraordinary, witty lyrics …" *Variety* (Isherwood): "A working-class musical aimed at an accordingly broad audience …"

*Still playing May 31, 2002

†Succeeded by: 1. Will Chase 2. Daniel Stewart Sherman 3. Danny Gurwin 4. Chris Diamantopoulos 5. Steven Skybell 6. Jane Connell 7. Larry Marshall

Photos by Craig Schwartz

Denis Jones, John Ellison Conlee, Patrick Wilson

LES MISERABLES

By Alain Boublil and Claude-Michel Schonberg; Based on the Novel by Victor Hugo; Music, Mr. Schonberg; Lyrics, Herbert Kretzmer; Original French Text, Mr. Boublil and Jean-Marc Natel; Additional Material, James Fenton; Direction/Adaptation, Trevor Nunn and John Caird; Orchestration Score, John Cameron; Musical Supervisor/Director, Dale Rieling; Executive Musical Director, David Caddick; Design, John Napier; Lighting, David Hersey; Costumes, Andreane Neofitou; Sound, Andrew Bruce/Autograph; Casting, Johnson-Liff & Zerman; Resident Director, Ron LaRosa, Jason Moore; Cast Recording, Geffen; General Manager, Alan Wasser; Company Manager, Robert Nolan; Production Supervisor, Marybeth Abel; Stage Managers, Karen Carpenter, Greg Kirsopp, Bryan Landrine, Tom Schilling, Brent Peterson; Associate Producer, Martin McCallum; Executive Producers, David Caddick, Peter Lawrence; Presented by Cameron Mackintosh; Press, Publicity Office/Marc Thibodeau, Bob Fennell, Michael S. Borowski, Brett Oberman; Previewed from Saturday, February 28, 1987; Opened in the Broadway Theatre on Thursday, March 12, 1987*

CAST

PROLOGUE: J. Mark McVey †1 (Jean Valjean), Gregg Edelman †2 (Javert), Gary Moss, David McDonald, Paul Truckey, Christopher Eid, Chris Diamantopoulos, Joe Paparella, Stephen R. Buntrock, Peter Lockyer, Nick Wyman (Chain Gang), Mr. Paparella (Farmer), Kurt Kovalenko (Labourer), Ann Arvia (Innkeeper's Wife), Andrew Varela (Innkeeper), David Benoit (Bishop), Kevin Kern, Kevin Earley, Christopher Mark Peterson (Constables)

MONTREUIL-SUR-MER 1823: Jane Bodle †3 (Fantine), Mr. McDonald (Foreman), Mr. Varela, Mr. Diamantopoulos (Workers), Dana Meller, Erika MacLeod, Gina Lamparella, Alexandra Foucard, Catherine Brunell (Women Workers), Holly Jo Crane (Factory Girl), Mr. Eid, Mr. Moss, Mr. Diamantopoulos (Sailors), Ms. Arvia, Ms. MacLeod, Ms. Foucard, Ms. Brunell, Ms. Meller, Ms. Crane, Megan Lawrence, Tobi Foster (Whores), Becky Barta (Old Woman), Ms. Lamparella (Crone), Mr. Peterson (Pimp), Mr. Truckey (Bamatabois), Mr. Kern (Fauchelevent), Mr. Moss (Champmathieu)

MONTFERMEIL 1823: Christiana Anbri, Ashley Rose Orr, Cristina Faicco, Lisa Musser (Young Cosette/Young Eponine), Betsy Joslyn (Mme. Thenardier), Nick Wyman (Thenardier), Mr. Varela (Drinker), Mr. Eid, Ms. Foucard (Young Couple), Mr. Kern (Drunk), Mr. Benoit, Ms. MacLeod (Diners), Mr. Paparella, Mr. Peterson, Mr. Truckey (Drinkers), Mr. Moss (Young Man), Ms. Meller, Ms. Lamprella (Young Girls), Ms. Brunell, Mr. Diamantopoulos (Old Couple), Mr. McDonald, Mr. Kovalenko (Travelers)

PARIS 1832: Patrick J.P. Duffey, Cameron Bowen (Gavroche), Ms. Barta (Beggar Woman), Ms. Meller (Young Prostitute), Mr. McDonald (Pimp), Catherine Brunell †4 (Eponine), Mr. Benoit (Montparnasse), Mr. Kovalenko (Babet), Mr. Moss (Brujon), Mr. Paprella (Claquesous), Mr. Peterson (Enjolras), Peter Lockyer (Marius), Tobi Foster †5 (Cosette), Mr. McDonald (Combeferre), Mr. Eid (Feuilly), Mr. Varela (Courfeyrac), Mr. Diamantopoulos (Joly), Mr. Truckey (Grantaire), Mr. Earley (Lesgles), Mr. Kern (Jean Prouvaire), Mr. Diamantopoulos (Major Domo)

The Company

UNDERSTUDIES: Mr. Moss, Mr. Varela (Valjean), Mr. McDonald, Mr. Truckey (Javert), Mr. Brandt, Mr. Watkins (Bishop), Ms. Crane, Ms. Foucard, Ms. MacLeod, Ms. Zimmerman (Fantine), Mr. Benoit, Mr. Colella, Mr. McDonald, Mr. Paparella (Thenardier), Ms. Arvia, Ms. Barta, Ms. Doherty, Ms. Glushak, Ms. Tolpegin (Mme. Thenardier), Ms. Brunell, Ms. Sutton Foster, Ms. Lawrence, Ms. Meller (Eponine), Diane DiCroce, Ms. Lamparella, Ms. Meller, Ms. Nichols (Cosette), Mr. Diamantopoulos, Mr. Foster, Mr. Kern (Marius), Mr. Brandt, Mr. Early, Mr. Kovalenko, Mr. Peterson, Mr. Thorn (Enjolras), Mr. Duffey (Gavroche), Ms. Kalehoff, Ms. Morton (Young Eponine)

SWINGS: Greggory Brandt, Angela DeCicco, Julia Haubner, Pete Herber, Dave Hugo, Cathy Nichols, Clif Thorn, Jeffrey Scott Watkins

MUSICAL NUMBERS: Prologue, Soliloquy, At the End of the Day, I Dreamed a Dream, Lovely Ladies, Who Am I?, Come to Me, Castle on a Cloud, Master of the House, Thenardier Waltz, Look Down, Stars, Red and Black, Do You Hear the People Sing?, In My Life, A Heart Full of Love, One Day More, On My Own, A Little Fall of Rain, Drink with Me to Days Gone By, Bring Him Home, Dog Eats Dog, Soliloquy, Turning, Empty Chairs at Empty Tables, Wedding Chorale, Beggars at the Feast, Finale

A dramatic musical in two acts with four scenes and a prologue. Winner of 1987 Tony Awards for Best Musical, Best Score, Best Book, Best Featured Actor and Actress in a Musical (Michael Maguire, Frances Ruffelle), Direction of a Musical, Scenic Design, and Lighting.

*Still playing May 31, 2002. Moved to the Imperial Theatre on October 18.

†Succeeded by: 1. Ivan Rutherford, J. Mark McVey 2. Shuler Hensley, Philip Hernandez, 3. Jacquelyn Piro 4. Dana Meller, Diana Kaarina 5. Sandra Turley

Photo by Joan Marcus

THE LION KING

Music, Elton John; Lyrics, Tim Rice; Additional Music/Lyrics, Lebo M, Mark Mancina, Jay Rifkin, Julie Taymor, Hans Zimmer; Book, Roger Allers and Irene Mecchi adapted from screenplay by Ms. Mecchi, Jonathan Roberts and Linda Woolverton; Director, Julie Taymor; Choreography, Garth Fagan; Orchestrations, Robert Elhai, David Metzger, Bruce Fowler; Music Director, Joseph Church; Set, Richard Hudson; Costumes, Julie Taymor; Lighting, Donald Holder; Masks/Puppets, Julie Taymor and Michael Curry; Sound, Tony Meola; Vocal Arrangements/Choral Director, Lebo M; Cast Recording, Disney; Company Manager, Steven Chaikelson; Stage Manager, Jeff Lee; Presented by Walt Disney Theatrical Productions (Peter Schneider, President; Thomas Schumacher, Executive VP); Press, Chris Boneau–Adrian Bryan-Brown/Jackie Green, Patty Onagan, Colleen Hughes. Previewed from Wednesday, October 15, 1997; Opened in the New Amsterdam Theatre on Thursday, November 13, 1997*

Sheila Gibbs

CAST

Rafiki	Sheila Gibbs
Mufasa	Samuel E. Wright
Sarabi	Denise Marie Williams †1
Zazu	Tony Freeman
Scar	Derek Smith
Young Simba	Mykel Bath
Young Nala	Leovina Charles
Shenzi	Vanessa A. Jones †2
Banzai	Leonard Joseph †3
Ed	Timothy Gulan
Timon	John E. Brady
Pumba	Tom Alan Robbins
Simba	Christopher Jackson
Nala	Sharon L. Young

ENSEMBLE SINGERS: Eugene Barry-Hill, Gina Breedlove, Ntomb'khona Dlamini, Sheila Gibbs, Lindiwe Hlengwa, Christopher Jackson, Vanessa A. Jones, Faca Kulu, Ron Kunene, Anthony Manough, Philip Dorian McAdoo, Sam McKelton, Lebo M, Nandi Morake, Rachel Tecora Tucker

ENSEMBLE DANCERS: Camille M. Brown, Iresol Cardona, Mark Allan Davis, Lana Gordon, Timothy Hunter, Michael Joy, Aubrey Lynch II, Karine Plantadit-Bageot, Endalyn Taylor-Shellman, Levensky Smith, Ashi K. Smythe, Christine Yasunaga

UNDERSTUDIES/SWINGS: Sheila Gibbs, Lindiwe Hlengwa (Rafiki), Eugene Barry-Hill, Philip Dorian McAdoo (Mufasa), Camille M. Brown, Vanessa A. Jones (Sarabi), Kevin Cahoon, Danny Rutigliano (Zazu/Timon), Kevin Bailey (Scar), Kai Braithwaite (Young Simba), Jennifer Josephs (Young Nala), Lana Gordon, Vanessa A. Jones (Shenzi), Philip Dorian McAdoo, Levensky Smith (Banzai), Frank Wright II (Ed), Philip Dorian McAdoo, Danny Rutigliano (Pumba), Timothy Hunter, Christopher Jackson (Simba), Lindiwe Hlengwa, Sonya Leslie (Nala)

MUSICAL NUMBERS: Circle of Life, Morning Report, I Just Can't Wait to Be King, Chow Down, They Live in You, Be Prepared, Hakuna Matata, One by One, Madness of King Scar, Shadowland, Endless Night, Can You Feel the Love Tonight, King of Pride Rock/Finale

A musical in two acts. Winner of 1998 Tony Awards for Best Musical, Direction of a Musical, Scenic Design, Costume Design, Lighting, and Choreography.

*Still playing May 31, 2002

†Succeeded by: 1. Meena T. Jahi 2. Lana Gordon 3. Curtiss I' Cook

Photo by Joan Marcus

THE PHANTOM OF THE OPERA

Music, Andrew Lloyd Webber; Lyrics, Charles Hart; Additional Lyrics, Richard Stilgoe; Book, Mr. Stilgoe, Mr. Lloyd Webber; Director, Harold Prince; Musical Staging/Choreography, Gillian Lynne; Orchestrations, David Cullen, Mr. Lloyd Webber; Based on the novel by Gaston Leroux; Design, Maria Björnson; Lighting, Andrew Bridge; Sound, Martin Levan; Musical Direction/Supervision, David Caddick; Conductor, Jack Gaughan; Cast Recording (London), Polygram/Polydor; Casting, Johnson-Liff & Zerman; General Manager, Alan Wasser; Company Manager, Michael Gill; Stage Managers, Steve McCorkle, Bethe Ward, Richard Hester, Barbara-Mae Phillips; Presented by Cameron Mackintosh and The Really Useful Theatre Co.; Press, Merle Frimark, Marc Thibodeau. Previewed from Saturday, January 9, 1988; Opened in the Majestic Theatre on Tuesday, January 26, 1988*

CAST

The Phantom of the Opera	Howard McGillin
Christine Daae	Sarah Pfisterer †1, Adrienne McEwan †1 (alternate)
Raoul, Vicomte de Chagny	Gary Maurer †2
Carlotta Giudicelli	Liz McCartney
Monsieur Andre	Jeff Keller
Monsieur Firmin	George Lee Andrews
Madame Giry	Leila Martin
Ubaldo Piangi	Larry Wayne Morbitt
Meg Giry	Geralyn Del Corso
M. Reyer	Richard Poole
Auctioneer	Richard Warren Pugh
Porter/Marksman	Maurizio Corbino
M. Lefevre	Kenneth H. Waller
Joseph Buquet	Joe Gustern
Don Attilio	John Kuether
Passarino	Thomas Sandri
Slave Master	Daniel Rychlec
Solo Dancer	Paul B. Sadler Jr.
Flunky/Stagehand	Jack Hayes
Hairdresser/Marksman	Gary Lindemann
Policeman	Thomas Sandri
Page	Patrice Pickering
Porter/Fireman	Maurizio Corbino
Spanish Lady	Wren Marie Harrington
Wardrobe Mistress/Confidante	Mary Leigh Stahl
Princess	Elizabeth Southard
Madame Firmin	Melody Johnson
Innkeeper's Wife	Johanna Wiseman
Ballet Chorus of the Opera Populaire	Emily Addona, Teresa DeRose, Nina Goldman, Elizabeth Nackley, Erin Brooke Reiter, Christine Spizzo, Kate Wray

UNDERSTUDIES: Jeff Keller (Phantom), James Romick (Phantom/Raoul/Firmin/Andre), Elizabeth Southard (Christine), John Schroeder, Jim Weitzer (Raoul), Richard Warren Pugh (Firmin/Piangi), John Kuether (Firmin), Richard Warren Pugh (Firmin/Piangi), George Lee Andrews, Richard Poole (Andre), Wren Marie Harrington, Johanna Wiseman, Melody Johnson (Carlotta), Susan Russell, Patrice Pickering, Mary Leigh Stahl (Giry), Maurizio Corbino (Piangi), Teresa DeRose, Kate Wray (Meg), Paul B. Sadler Jr. (Master), Daniel Rychlec (Dancer)

Howard McGillin, Sarah Pfisterer

SWINGS: Susan Russell, James Romick, Jim Weitzer

MUSICAL NUMBERS: Think of Me, Angel of Music, Little Lotte/The Mirror, Phantom of the Opera, Music of the Night, I Remember/Stranger Than You Dreamt It, Magical Lasso, Notes/Prima Donna, Poor Fool He Makes Me Laugh, Why Have You Brought Me Here?/Raoul I've Been There, All I Ask of You, Masquerade/Why So Silent?, Twisted Every Way, Wishing You Were Somehow Here Again, Wandering Child/Bravo Bravo, Point of No Return, Down Once More/Track Down This Murderer, Finale

A musical in two acts with nineteen scenes and a prologue. The action takes place in and around the Paris Opera House, 1881–1911. Winner of 1988 Tony Awards for Best Musical, Leading Actor in a Musical (Michael Crawford), Featured Actress in a Musical (Judy Kaye), Direction of a Musical, Scenic Design, and Lighting Design. The title role has been played by Michael Crawford, Timothy Nolen, Cris Groendaal, Steve Barton, Jeff Keller, Kevin Gray, Marc Jacoby, Marcus Lovett, Davis Gaines, Thomas J. O'Leary, Hugh Panaro, and Howard McGillin.

*Still playing May 31, 2002.

†Succeeded by: 1. Sandra Joseph, Adrienne McEwan, Sarah Pfisterer, Beth Southard, Lisa Vroman 2. Jim Weitzer, Michael Shawn Lewis

Photo by Joan Marcus

THE PRODUCERS

Music/Lyrics, Mel Brooks; Book, Mr. Brooks and Thomas Meehan; Based on the 1967 film; Director/Choreography, Susan Stroman; Director, Patrick S. Brady; Musical Arrangements/Supervision, Glen Kelly; Orchestrations, Douglas Besterman, Larry Blank (uncredited); Musical Director/Vocal Arrangements, Patrick S. Brady; Set, Robin Wagner; Costumes, William Ivey Long; Lighting, Peter Kaczorowski; Sound, Steve Canyon Kennedy; Hair/Wigs, Paul Huntley; General Manager, Richard Frankel/Laura Green; Company Manager, Kathy Lowe; Production Stage Manager, Steven Zweigbaum; Stage Manager, Ira Mont; Cast Recording, Sony; Casting, Johnson-Liff Associates; Advertising, Serino Coyne, Inc.; Presented by Rocco Landesman, SFX Theatrical Group, The Frankel-Baruch-Viertel-Routh Group, Bob and Harvey Weinstein, Rick Steiner, Robert F.X. Sillerman and Mel Brooks, in association with James D. Stern/Douglas L. Meyer; Press, John Barlow–Michael Hartman/Bill Coyle, Shellie Schovanec. Previewed from Wednesday, March 21, 2001; Opened in the St. James Theatre on Thursday, April 19, 2001*

CAST

The Usherettes	Bryn Dowling, Jennifer Smith
Max Bialystock	Nathan Lane †1
Leo Bloom	Matthew Broderick †2
Hold-me Touch-me	Madeleine Doherty
Mr. Marks	Ray Wills
Franz Liebkind	Brad Oscar †3
Carmen Ghia	Roger Bart
Roger De Bris	Gary Beach
Bryan/Judge/Jack Lepidus	Peter Marinos
Scott/Guard/Donald Dinsmore	Jeffry Denman
Ulla	Cady Huffman
Lick-me Bite-me	Jennifer Smith
Shirley/Kiss-me Feel-me/Jury Foreman	Kathy Fitzgerald
Kevin/Jason Green/Trustee	Ray Wills
Lead Tenor	Eric Gunhus
Sergeant/Baliff	Abe Sylvia
O'Rourke	Matt Loehr
O'Houlihan	Robert H. Fowler

ENSEMBLE: Jeffry Denman, Madeleine Doherty, Bryn Dowling, Kathy Fitzgerald, Robert H. Fowler, Ida Gilliams, Eric Gunhus, Kimberly Hester, Naomi Kakuk, Matt Loehr, Peter Marinos, Angie L. Schworer, Jennifer Smith, Abe Sylvia, Tracy Terstriep, Ray Wills

UNDERSTUDIES: Jim Borstelmann (Franz Liebkind/Roger De Bris), Jeffry Denman (Franz Liebkind/Leo Bloom), Ida Gilliams (Ulla), Jamie LaVerdiere (Carmen Ghia/Leo Bloom), Brad Musgrove (Carmen Ghia/Roger De Bris), Brad Oscar (Max Bialystock/Roger De Bris), Angie L. Schworer (Ulla), Ray Wills (Max Bialystock).

SWINGS: Jim Borstelmann, Adrienne Gibbons, Jamie LaVerdiere, Brad Musgrove, Christina Marie Norrup

MUSICAL NUMBERS: Opening Night, The King of Broadway, We Can Do It, I Wanna Be a Producer, In Old Bavaria, Der Guten Tag Hop Clop, Keep It Gay, When You Got It Flaunt It, Along Came Bialy, Act One Finale, That Face, Haben Sie Gehoert das Deutsche Band?, You Never Say "Good Luck" On Opening Night, Springtime for Hitler, Where Did We Go Right?, Betrayed, 'Til Him, Prisoners of Love, Leo and Max, Goodbye!

Matthew Broderick and The Company

A musical comedy in two acts. The action takes place in New York City, 1959. Winner of 2001 Tony Awards for Best Musical, Best Score, Best Book of a Musical, Best Actor in a Musical (Nathan Lane), Best Featured Actor in a Musical (Gary Beach), Best Featured Actress in a Musical (Cady Huffman), Best Director/Musical, Best Choreography, Best Sets, Best Costumes, Best Lighting, Best Orchestrations

Variety tallied 18 favorable and 1 mixed review. *Times* (Brantley): "… the real thing: a big Broadway book musical that is so ecstatically drunk on its powers to entertain that it leaves you delirious, too…. Mr. Lane and Mr. Broderick… have the most dynamic stage chemistry since Natasha Richardson met Liam Neeson in Anna Christie…" *News* (Kissel): "Nathan Lane does his funniest work in years… Matthew Broderick sings and dances with suitably forlorn charm… No new musical in ages has offered so much imagination, so much sheer pleasure." *Post* (Barnes): "… a cast-iron, copper-bottomed, super-duper, mammoth old-time Broadway hit." *Variety* (Isherwood): "… the material is inherently terrific. But Brooks and his collaborators go further, capitalizing on the new medium in ways that add immensely to its appeal… the first Broadway smash of the new century."

*Still playing May 31, 2002.

†Succeeded by: 1. Ray Wills (during illness), Henry Goodman, Brad Oscar 2. Jamie LaVerdiere (during illness), Steven Weber 3. John Treacy Egan

Photo by Paul Kolnik

PROOF

By David Auburn; Director, Daniel Sullivan; Set, John Lee Beatty; Costumes, Jess Goldstein; Lighting, Pat Collins; Music/Sound, John Gromada; General Manager, Stuart Thompson; Company Manager, James Triner; Production Stage Manager, James Harker; Stage Manager, Heather Cousens; Presented by Manhattan Theatre Club (Lynne Meadow, Artistic Director; Barry Grove, Executive Producer), Roger Berlind, Carole Shorenstein Hays, OSTAR Enterprises, Daryl Roth, Stuart Thompson; Press Representative, Chris Boneau–Adrian Bryan-Brown/Steven Padla, Rachel Applegate; Previewed from Tuesday, October 10, 2000; Opened in the Walter Kerr Theatre on Tuesday, October 24, 2000*

CAST

Robert . . . . Larry Bryggman †1
Catherine . . . . Mary-Louise Parker †2
Hal . . . . Ben Shenkman †3
Claire . . . . Johanna Day †4
UNDERSTUDIES: Caroline Bootle (Catherine/Claire), Adam Dannheisser (Hal), Ron Parady (Robert)

A drama in two acts. The action takes place in Chicago. Winner of the 2001 Tony Award for Best Play, New York Drama Critics Circle (Best American Play) and the Pulitzer Prize. Winner of 2001 Tony Awards for Best Actress in a Play (Mary Louise Parker) and Best Direction of a Play. This production originated last season Off-Broadway, where it played 80 performances and 24 previews. For original Off-Broadway production, see *Theatre World* Vol. 56.

Variety tallied 9 favorable, and 2 mixed reviews. *Times* (Weber): "…exhilarating and assured…as accessible and compelling as a detective story." *News* (O'Toole): "It proves that it's still possible for an intelligent new play by a young American dramatist to make it onto Broadway…Parker…an electrifying performance…" *Post* (Barnes): "All four actors are pitch-perfect, but the one you'll remember is Parker." *Variety* (Hofler): "…managed to improve upon this remarkable play in its transfer to Broadway from the Manhattan Theatre Club…Together Bryggman and Parker hit enough emotional highs to sustain a dozen lesser plays."

*Still playing May 31, 2002

†Succeeded by: 1. Patrick Tovatt 2. Jennifer Jason Leigh 3. Josh Hamilton 4. Seana Kofoed

Photos by Joan Marcus

Johanna Day, Mary-Louise Parker

Mary-Louise Parker

RENT

Music/Lyrics/Book by Jonathan Larson; Director, Michael Greif; Arrangements, Steve Skinner; Musical Supervision/Additional Arrangements, Tim Weill; Choreography, Marlies Yearby; Original Concept/Additional Lyrics, Billy Aronson; Set, Paul Clay; Costumes, Angela Wendt; Lighting, Blake Burba; Sound, Kurt Fischer; Cast Recording, Dreamworks; General Management, Emanuel Azenberg, John Corker; Company Manager, Brig Berney; Stage Managers, John Vivian, Crystal Huntington; Presented by Jeffrey Seller, Kevin McCollum, Allan S. Gordon, and New York Theatre Workshop; Press, Richard Kornberg/ Don Summa; Ian Rand; Previewed from Tuesday, April 16, 1996; Opened in the Nederlander Theatre on Monday, April 29, 1996*

CAST

Roger Davis .... Norbert Leo Butz †1,
Richard H. Blake (alternate)
Mark Cohen .... Trey Ellett †2
Tom Collins .... Alan Mingo Jr. †3
Benjamin Coffin III .... Stu James
Joanne Jefferson .... Natalie Venetia Belcon †4
Angel Schunard .... Jai Rodriguez †5
Mimi Marquez .... Loraine Velez †6
Maureen Johnson .... Cristina Fadale †7
Mark's Mom/Alison/Others .... Maggie Benjamin
Christmas Caroler/Mr. Jefferson/Pastor/Others .... Byron Utley
Mrs. Jefferson/Woman with Bags/Others .... Aisha de Haas
Gordon/The Man/Mr. Grey/Others .... Chad Richardson
Steve/Man with Squeegee/Waiter/Others .... Owen Johnston II
Paul/Cop/Others .... Robert Glean
Alexi Darling/Roger's Mom/Others .... Kim Varhola
UNDERSTUDIES: Dean Balkwill (Roger), Richard H. Blake, Will Chase (Roger/Mark), Byron Utley (Tom), Calvin Grant, Robert Glean (Tom/ Benjamin), Darryl Ordell (Benjamin), Shelly Dickinson, Aisha de Haas (Joanne), Shayna Steele, Sharon Leal (Joanne/Mimi), Juan Carlos Gonzalez, Mark Setlock, Jai Rodriguez (Angel), Jessica Boevers, Maggie Benjamin, Kristen Lee Kelly (Maureen), Owen Johnston II (Roger/Angel), Chad Richardson, Peter Matthew Smith (Roger/Mark), Yassmin Alers, Karen Olivo, Julie P. Danao (Mimi/Maureen)

SWINGS: Mr. Blake, Ms. Danao, Mr. Gonzalez, Mr. Grant, Ms. Leal, Ms. Steele

Musical Numbers: Tune Up, Voice Mail (#1–#5), Rent, You Okay Honey?, One Song Glory, Light My Candle, Today 4 U, You'll See, Tango: Maureen, Life Support, Out Tonight, Another Day, Will I?, On the Street, Santa Fe, We're Okay, I'll Cover You, Christmas Bells, Over the Moon, La Vie Boheme/I Should Tell You, Seasons of Love, Happy New Year, Take Me or Leave Me, Without You, Contact, Halloween, Goodbye Love, What You Own, Finale/Your Eyes

A musical in two acts. The action takes place in New York City's East Village. Winner of 1996 Tony Awards for Best Musical, Best Original Score, Best Book of a Musical and Featured Actor in a Musical (Wilson Jermaine Heredia). *Rent* passed its 2,000th Broadway performance during this season. Tragedy occurred when the 35-year-old author, Jonathan Larson, died of an aortic aneurysm after watching the final dress rehearsal of his show on January 24, 1996.

Manley Pope, Loraine Velez

*Still playing May 31, 2002.

†Succeeded by: 1. Manley Pope 2. Matt Caplan 3. Mark Leroy Jackson, Mark Richard Ford 4. Myiia Watson-Davis 5. Andy Senor, Jai Rodriguez 6. Karmine Alers 7. Maggie Benjamin

Photo by Joan Marcus

THE TALE OF THE ALLERGIST'S WIFE

By Charles Busch; Director, Lynne Meadow; Set, Santo Loquasto; Costumes, Ann Roth; Lighting, Christopher Akerlind; Sound, Bruce Ellman, Brian Ronan; Hairstylist, J. Roy Helland; Casting, Nancy Piccione, David Caparelliotis; General Manager, Stuart Thompson; Company Manager, Sean Free; Production Stage Manager, William Joseph Barnes; Stage Manager, Laurie Goldfeder; Presented by Manhattan Theatre Club (Lynne Meadow, Artistic Director; Barry Grove, Executive Producer), Carole Shorenstein Hays, Daryl Roth, Stuart Thompson and Douglas S. Cramer; Press Representative, Chris Boneau–Adrian Bryan-Brown/Jackie Green, Rachel Applegate. Previewed from Wednesday, October 11, 2000; Opened in the Ethel Barrymore Theatre on Thursday, November 2, 2000*

CAST

Mohammed . . . . Anil Kumar †1
Marjorie . . . . Linda Lavin †2
Ira . . . . Tony Roberts †3
Frieda . . . . Shirl Bernheim †4
Lee . . . . .Michele Lee †5
UNDERSTUDIES/STANDBYS: Rose Arrick (Frieda), Jana Robbins (Lee/Marjorie), Jamie Ross (Ira), Deep Katdare (Mohammed)

A comedy in two acts. The action takes place in New York City. This production originated last season at Off-Broadway's Manhattan Theatre Club where it played 56 performances and 24 previews. For original Off-Broadway production, see *Theatre World* Vol. 56.

Variety tallied 7 favorable, 1 mixed, and 2 negative reviews. *Times* (Brantley): "…Mr. Busch demonstrates a sure gift for turning gimlet-eyed social observation into hearty comedy." *News* (O'Toole): "…the theater has a long and brilliant history of high camp…*The Allergist's Wife* simply isn't in that league." *Post* (Barnes): "…the play is really all about Linda Lavin…And rightly so, for Lavin gives a performance that makes virtuosity into a natural human condition…" *Variety* (Isherwood): "The only bad news is…the second act is still muddled…But in Lavin's assured hands … the funniest play to be seen thereabouts in several seasons."

*Still Playing May 31, 2002

†Succeeded by: 1. Charles Daniel Sandoval 2. Valerie Harper, Rhea Perlman 3. Richard Kind 4. Chevi Colton, Rose Arrick (alternate) 5. Marilu Henner

Photos by Joan Marcus

The Company

Tony Roberts, Linda Lavin, Michelle Lee

Tony Roberts, Valerie Harper, Michelle Lee

BROADWAY

Productions from past seasons that closed during this season

A CLASS ACT
The Company (Joan Marcus)
Opened March 11, 2001
Closed June 10, 2001
105 performances; 30 previews

ANNIE GET YOUR GUN
Jenny Rose Baker, Reba McIntyre,
Eddie Brandt, Blaire Restanco (Joan Marcus)
Opened March 4, 1999
Closed September 1, 2001
1,046 performances; 35 previews

BELLS ARE RINGING
Faith Prince (Lois Greenfield)
Opened April 12, 2001
Closed June 10, 2001
69 performances; 35 previews

BLAST!
The Company
Opened April 17, 2001
Closed September 23, 2001
176 performances; 13 previews

THE DINNER PARTY
The Company (Carol Rosegg)
Opened October 19, 2000
Closed September 1, 2001
366 performances; 20 previews

FOSSE
The Company (Joan Marcus)
Opened January 14, 1999
Closed August 25, 2001
1,100 performances; 22 previews

FOLLIES
The Company (Joan Marcus)
Opened April 5, 2001
Closed July 14, 2001
116 performances; 31 previews

GEORGE GERSHWIN ALONE
Hershey Felder (Carol Rosegg)
Opened April 30, 2001
Closed July 24, 2001
96 performances; 16 previews

THE INVENTION OF LOVE
Robert Sean Leonard, Richard Easton (Paul Kolnik)
Opened March 29, 2001
Closed June 30, 2001
108 performances; 31 previews

JANE EYRE
Marla Shaffel, James Barbour (Joan Marcus)
Opened December 10, 2000
Closed June 10, 2001
210 performances; 36 previews

KING HEADLEY
Charles Brown, Leslie Uggams (Joan Marcus)
Opened May 1, 2001
Closed July 1, 2001
72 performances; 24 previews

KISS ME, KATE
Burke Moses, Carolee Carmello (Joan Marcus)
Opened November 18, 1999
Closed December 30, 2001
885 performances; 28 previews

THE MUSIC MAN
Rebecca Luker, Craig Bierko, Michael Phelan
(Joan Marcus)
Opened April 27, 2000
Closed December 30, 2001
698 performances; 24 previews

ONE FLEW OVER THE CUCKOO'S NEST
Gary Sinise, Tim Sampson (Tristram Kenton)
Opened April 8, 2001
Closed July 29, 2001
121 performances; 24 previews

RIVERDANCE ON BROADWAY
The Company (E.J. Camp)
Opened March 16, 2000
Closed August 26, 2001
605 performances; 13 previews

THE ROCKY HORROR SHOW
The Company (Carol Rosegg)
Opened November 15, 2000
Closed January 6, 2002
437 performances; 30 previews

STONES IN HIS POCKETS
Conleth Hill, Seán Campion (Joan Marcus)
Opened April 1, 2001
Closed September 23, 2001
201 performances; 11 previews

OFF-BROADWAY

Productions that opened June 1, 2001 – May 31, 2002

Keith Baxter, Jared Reed in *The Woman in Black* (Craig Schwartz)

THE WOMAN IN BLACK

Adapted by Stephen Mallatratt from the Novel by Susan Hill; Director, Patrick Garland; Sets, James Noone; Costumes, Noel Taylor; Lighting, Ken Billington, Brian P. Monahan; Sound, Christopher Walker; Production Stage Manager, J.P. Elins; Press, Bill Evans; Opened at the Minetta Lane Theatre June 4, 2001*

CAST

Arthur Kipps . . . . Keith Baxter
The Actor . . . . Jared Reed

A play in two acts. An actor attempts to aid a lawyer in exorcising a ghostly female presence from a play within the play.

*Closed July 8, 2001, after 40 performances

EAT THE RUNT

By Avery Crozier; Director, Matthew von Waaden; Sets, Jerome Martin; Costumes, Courtney McClain; Lighting, Michele Disco; Sound and Music, Timothy Cramer; Associate Producer, Margaret Perry; Production Stage Manager, Adam Crosswirth; Press, Pat Dale; Opened at the American Place Theatre on June 5, 2001*

CAST

Kelli K. Barnett	Weil Richmond	Keesha Sharp
Linda Cameron	Thom Rivera	Curtis Mark Williams
LaKeith Hoskin		Jama Williamson

UNDERSTUDIES: Andrew Robbins, Joy Styles

A play in to acts. The action takes place in an art museum in the present. The audience chooses which actor plays which role.

*Closed October 7, 2001, after 125 performances

Keesha Sharp, Linda Cameron, Weil Richmond, LaKeith Hoskin, Kelli K. Barnett, Thom Rivera, Jama Williamson, Curtis Mark Williams in *Eat The Runt* (Mark Fisher)

TICK, TICK...BOOM!

Book, Music and Lyrics by Jonathan Larson; Director, Scott Schwartz; Choreography, Christopher Gattelli; Sets, Anna Louizos; Costumes, David Zinn; Lights, Kenneth Posner; Sound, Jon Weston; Musical Director, Orchestrator and Arranger, Stephen Oremus; Script Consultant, David Auburn; Casting, David Caparelliotis; Production Stage Manager, Ed Fitzgerald; Press, Richard Kornberg and Associates, Richard Kornberg, Don Summa; Producers, Victoria Leacock, Robyn Goodman, Dede Harris, Lorie Cowen Levy, Beth Smith; Associate Producers, Ruth and Stephen Hendel, Stephen Semlitz, Cathy Glaser; Opened at the Jane Street Theatre, June 13, 2001*

CAST
Jonathan . . . . Raúl Esparza
Susan, Karessa . . . . Amy Spanger
Michael . . . . Jerry Dixon
MUSICAL NUMBERS: 30/90, Green Green Dress, Johnny Can't Decide, Sunday, No More, Therapy, Play Game, Real Life, Sugar, See Her Smile, Come to Your Senses, Why, 30/90 (reprise), Louder Than Words

A musical performed without intermission. The action takes place at the edge of Soho in 1990. Musical revue by Mr. Auburn comprised of solo shows originally performed by Mr. Larson.

*Closed January 6, 2002, after 215 performances.

Jerry Dixon, Raúl Esparza, Amy Spanger in *Tick, Tick...Boom!* (Joan Marcus)

Deirdre O'Connell, Mark Johannes, Victor Slezak in *World of Mirth* (Carol Rosegg)

WORLD OF MIRTH

By Murphy Guyer; Director, Dona D. Vaughn; Producers, Amy Danis and Mars Theatricals Inc.; Sets, Michael Brown; Costumes, Tracy Christensen; Lights, James Vermeulen; Sound, Bruce Ellman; Fight Director, B.H. Barry; Production Stage Manager, Matthew Lacey; Press, Cromarty and Company, Peter Cromarty, Alice Cromarty; Opened at Theatre Four June 21, 2001*

CAST
Sweeney . . . . Mark Johannes
Buffy Starr . . . . Deirdre O'Connell
Emmett . . . . George Bartenieff
Augie . . . . Kieran Campion
Patch . . . . Jack Willis
Ken Harley . . . . John Elsen
Kaspar Kelly . . . . Victor Slezak
Marcey . . . . Angela Gots

A drama viewed through the eyes of a carnival clown about the dark side of life.

*Closed July 29, 2001, after 45 performances.

QUARTETT

By Heiner Muller; Translated by Marc von Henning; Director, Gabriella Maione; Sets, Jean Paul Chambs; Costumes, Catherine Zuber; Lights, Robert Wierzel; Sound, Peter Cerone, Michael Galasso; Music, Michael Galasso; Dramaturg, Aruthur Holmberg; Production Stage Manager, James Mountcastle; Press, Barlow-Hartman Public Relations, Joe Perotta; Producer, RPN Globe; Opened at the BAM Harvey Theater June 28, 2001*

CAST
Daniel McDonald . . . . Omar Mewally
Chandler Vinton . . . . Suzanne Packer

A piece performed without intermission.

*Closed July 1, 2001, after 5 performances.

SAINT LUCY'S EYES

By Bridgette A. Wimberly; Director, Billie Allen; Producers, Angelina Fiordellisi and Cherry Lane Theatre Company, in association with Women's Project and Productions; Sets, Beowulf Boritt; Costumes, Alvin B. Perry; Lights, Jane Reisman; Music and Sound, Michael Wimberly; Stage Manager, John Handy; Press, Springer/Chicoine; Public Relations, Susan Chicoine, Joe Trentacosta; Opened at the Cherry Lane Theatre July 26, 2001*

CAST
Grandma . . . . Ruby Dee
Young Woman . . . . Toks Olagundoye
Bay . . . . Willis Burks II
Woman . . . . Sally A. Steward

A play in two acts. A woman who performs illegal abortions struggles to survive as times change. Originally produced Off-Off-Broadway April 5, 2001, by Women's Project and Productions.

*Closed September 2, 2001, after 45 performances.

Leslie Lorusso, Kevin Pariseau, Kristie Dale Sanders, Larry Cahn, Jimmy Spadola in *Hello Muddah, Hello Fadduh!* (Carol Rosegg)

Kristie Dale Sanders, Jimmy Spadola, Larry Cahn, Leslie Lorusso, Kevin Pariseau in *Hello Muddah, Hello Fadduh!* (Carol Rosegg)

HELLO MUDDAH, HELLO FADDUH!

Revival of the Musical Revue of Doug Bernstein and Rob Krausz; Director, Mr. Krausz; Sets, William Barclay; Music and Lyrics by Allan Sherman; Lighting, Phil Monat; Costumes, Michael Louis; Directed by Rob Krausz; Produced by Jennifer Dumas and Jack Cullen; Production Stage Manager, Jason Cohen; Press, Keith Sherman and Associates, Miller Wright; Opened at the Triad Theatre on August 2, 2001*

CAST
Harvey . . . . Larry Cahn
Sarah . . . . Leslie Lorusso
Barry . . . . Kevin Pariseau
Sheila . . . . Kristie Dale Sanders
Phil . . . . Jimmy Spadola

A musical in two acts. For original Off-Broadway production which opened December 5, 1992, at the Circle in the Square, see *Theatre World*, Vol. 49, 1992–1993.

*Closed November 18, 2001, after 124 performances.

Simon Morley, David Friend in *Puppetry of the Penis*

RUDE ENTERTAINMENT

By Paul Rudnick; Director, Christopher Ashley; Sets, Allen Moyer; Lighting, Kirk Bookman; Costumes, Gregory A. Gale; Sound, Laura Grace Brown; Stage Manager, Sarah Bittenbender; Produced by the Drama Dept.; Press, Boneau/Bryan-Brown, Chris Boneau, Steven Padla, Aaron Meier; Opened at the Greenwich House Theatre on October 3, 2001*

CAST

Mr. Charles	Peter Bartlett
Shane	Neal Huff
Timmy	Neal Huff
Trent	Peter Bartlett
Katinka	Harriet Harris
Matthew	Neal Huff
Elaeanor	Harriet Harris
Paul	Peter Bartlett

Performed without intermission. Comic sketches spoofing modern life

*Closed October 28, 2001, after 31 performances

PUPPETRY OF THE PENIS

By David Friend and Simon Morley; Produced by David J. Foster and Ross Mollison, in assocation with Johnson Temple Productions; Associate Producer, Thomas Milazzo; Production Design, Andrew Dunne, Thomas Milazzo; Production Stage Manager, Janey Rainey; Opened at the John Houseman Theatre on October 5, 2001*

CAST

Wendy Vousden	David "Friendy" Friend
Simon Morley	Justin Morley

A "piece" performed in two acts.

*Still playing May 31, 2001.

REEFER MADNESS

Book by Kevin Murphy and Dan Studney; Music, Mr. Studney; Lyrics, Mr. Murphy; Director, Andy Fickman; Producers, James Nederlander, Verna Harrah; Associate Producers, Nathaniel Kramer, Terry Allen Kramer, Dead Old Man Productions; Choreography, Paula Abdul; Sets, Walt Spangler; Lighting, Robert Perry; Costumes, Dick Magnanti; Sound, Lew Mead; Music Direction, David Manning; Orchestrations, Nathan Wang, Mr. Manning; Fight Direction, Rick Sordelet; Stage Manager, Richard Druther; Casting, Jim Carnahan; Press, Richard Kornberg & Associates, Tom D'Ambrosio, Don Summa; Opened at the Variety Arts Theatre on October 7, 2001*

CAST

Lecturer	Gregg Edelman
Jimmy	Christian Campbell
Mary	Kristen Bell
Jack, Jesus	Robert Torti
Mae	Michele Pawk
Sally	ErinMatthews
Placard Girl	Roxane Barlow
Ralph	John Kassir
Ensemble	Andrea Chamberlain, Jennifer Gambatese, Paul Leighton, Michael Seelbach

UNDERSTUDIES: Robert Gallager, Paul Leighton, Michael Seelbach, Jennifer Gambatese, Molly Zimpfer, Robert Gallagher, Andrea Chamberlain, Erin Matthews

MUSICAL NUMBERS: Reefer Madness, Romeo & Juliet, The Stuff, Down at the Ol' Five & Dime, Jimmy Takes a Hit, The Orgy, Lonely Pew, Listen to Jesus Jimmy, Lullabye, Dead Old Man, Jimmy on the Lam, The Brownie Song, Little Mary Sunshine, Murder, Tell 'Em the Truth

Musical parody of the 1936 anti-marijuana propaganda film. The action takes place in 1936 in the United States.

*Closed October 28, 2001, after 25 performances.

THE SHAPE OF THINGS

By Neil LaBute; Director, Mr. LaBute; Sets, Giles Cadle; Lighting, James Vermeulen; Costumes, Lynette Meyer; Sound, Fergus O'Hare; Production Stage Manager, Jane Grey; Producers, Susan Aquint Gallin, Sandy Gallin, Stuart Thompson, Ben Sprecher, USA Ostar Theatricals; Press, Richard Kornberg & Associates, Richard Kornberg, Don Summa; Opened at the Promenade Theatre on October 10, 2001*

CAST

Evelyn . . . . Rachel Weisz
Adam . . . . Paul Rudd
Jenny . . . . Gretchen Mol
Philip . . . . Frederick Weller

A play performed without intermission.

*Closed January 20, 2002, after 118 performances

Rachel Weisz, Gretchen Mol in *The Shape of Things* (Joan Marcus)

Paul Rudd, Rachel Weisz in *The Shape of Things* (Joan Marcus)

David Turner, Jeremy Shamos, Peter Ackerman in *The Complete Works of William Shakespeare: Abridged* (Carol Rosegg)

THE COMPLETE WORKS OF WILLIAM SHAKESPEARE: ABRIDGED

Revival of Shakespearean Parody by Adam Long, Daniel Singer, Jess Winfield; Producers, Jeffrey Richards, Christopher Gould, Raymond Greenwald, Norma Langworthy, Jamie deRoy; Associate Producer, Howard Berlin; Director, Jeremy Dobrish; Sets, Steven Capone; Lighting, Michael Gottlieb; Costumes, Markas Henry; Sound and Original Music, Lewis Finn; Slide Projections, Richard Fahey; Movement and Fight Choreography, Tony Stevens; Production Stage Manager, Katherine Lee Boyer; Casting, Bernard Telsey Casting; Press, Jeffrey Richards Associates; Opened at The Century Center for the Performing Arts on October 15, 2001*

CAST

Peter Ackerman   Jamie Inglehart   Brian Shoaf
Mark Fish   Jeremy Shamos   David Turner

Performed in two acts.

*Closed May 26, 2002, after 256 performances.

T. Ryder Smith in *Underneath the Lintel* (Gilles DeCamps)

UNDERNEATH THE LINTEL

By Glen Berger; Director, Randy White; Produced by the Soho Playhouse, Scott Morfee, Tom Wirtshafter, Dana Matthow; Sets, Lauren Helpren; Lighting, Tyler Micoleau; Costumes, Miranda Hoffman; Sound, Paul Adams; Production Design, Elaine J. McCarthy; Production Stage Manager, Richard A. Hodge; Press, Shirley Herz Associates; Opened at the Soho Playhouse on October 23, 2001*

A one-person play performed without intermission starring T. Ryder Smith as the librarian.

UNDERSTUDY: Glen Berger

*Still playing May 31, 2002

HAVANA IS WAITING

By Eduardo Marchado; Director, Michael John Garcés; Producers, Barbara Ligeti, Angelina Fiordellisi; Associate Producer, Annette Tappert; Sets, Troy Hourie; Lighting, Kirk Bookman; Costumes, Elizabeth Hope Clancy; Sound, David Lawson; Production Stage Manager, Charles M. Turner III; Press, Springer/Chicoine Public Relations, Susan Chicoine, Joe Trentacosta; Opened at the Cherry Lane Theatre on October 24, 2001.*

CAST

Federico . . . . Bruce MacVittie
Fred . . . . Ed Vassallo
Ernesto . . . . Felix Solis
Percussion . . . . Richard Marquez

The action takes place in New York City as well as Havana, Cuba, in December, 1999.

A Cuban native searches for his roots, returning to Cuba forty years after being airlifted to the United States.

*Closed November 25, 2002, after 38 performances

Felix Solis, Bruce MacVittie, Ed Vassallo in *Havana Is Waiting* (Carol Rosegg)

Richard Marquez, Felix Solis, Bruce MacVittie, Ed Vassallo in *Havana Is Waiting* (Carol Rosegg)

TRUE LOVE

By Charles L. Mee; Director, Daniel Fish; Sets, Christine Jones; Lighting, Jane Cox; Costumes, Kaye Voyce; Sound, Robert Kaplowitz; Choreography, Peter Pucci; Musical Direction, Crispin Cloe; Casting, Janet Foster; Production Stage Manager, Babette Roberts; Producer, Jeannne Donovan; Co-producer, Tessa Blake; Press, Richard Kornberg and Associates, Don Summa, Tom D'Ambrosio, Erin Dunn; Opened at the Zipper Theatre on November 27, 2001*

CAST

Polly . . . . Laurie Williams
Edward . . . . Jeremiah Miller
Shirley . . . . Laura Esterman
Red Dicks . . . . Paul Mullins
Bonnie . . . . Jane Houdyshell
Phil . . . . Dallas Roberts
Jim . . . . Christopher McCann
Alicia . . . . Halley Wegryn Gross
Richard . . . . Roy Thinnes
MUSICIANS: Crispin Cloe, keyboard, saxophone, vocals; George Gilmore, guitar, vocals; Charles Giordano, keyboard, accordian; Robin Gould III, drums

Presented without intermission.

*Closed January 20, 2002, after 61 performances

Laurie Williams in *True Love* (Carol Rosegg)

MARC SALEM'S MIND GAMES, TOO

Produced by Marc Salem, Anita Waxman, Elizabeth Williams; Sets, Ray Brecht; Opened at the Duke on 42nd Street on December 3, 2001*

A solo mentalist act performed by Marc Salem; performed without intermission.

*Closed January 13, 2002, after 48 performance

CRISS ANGEL: MINDFREAK

By Criss Angel; Director, Mr. Angel; Choreography, Deanne Lay; Sets, John Farrell; Costumes, Barak Stribling; Lighting, Jules Fisher, Peggy Eisenhauer; Music, Mr. Angel, Klayton; Creature Design, Steve Johnson; Special Effects, Thaine Morris, Peter Cappadocia, Elia Popov; Production Stage Manager, Larry Baker; Opened at the World Underground Theatre at the World Wrestling Federation on December 13, 2001*

CAST

Criss Angel . . . . Tatyana Senchihina
Kirk McGee . . . . Ken Romo
Svetlana Alexandra . . . . Costa Sarantakos

Mentalist act with special effects.

*Closed January 6, 2003

Christopher McCann in *True Love* (Carol Rosegg)

SUMMER OF '42

Book by Hunter Foster; Music and Lyrics by David Kirshenbaum; Based on the Novel by Herman Raucher; Director and Choreographer, Gabriel Barre; Sets, James Youmans; Lighting, Tim Hunter; Costumes, Pamela Scofield; Sound, Jim Van Bergen; Orchestration, Vocal Arrangements and Music Direction, Lynne Shankel; Associate Choreographer, Jennifer Cody; Casting, Jim Carnahan, Warren Pincus; Production Stage Manager, Gail Eve Malatesta; Produced by Mitchell Maxwell, Victoria Maxwell, Robert Eckert, Michael Jenkins, Kumiko Yoshii, James L. Simon, Mark Goldberg, Andrea Pines, in association with Robert Bernstein and Sibling Entertainment; Press, Springer/Chicoine Public Relattions; Opened at the Variety Arts Theatre on December 18, 2001*

CAST

Hermie . . . . Ryan Driscoll
Dorothy . . . . Kate Jennings Grant
Pete . . . . Greg Stone
Aggie . . . . Celia Keenan-Bolger
Gloria . . . . Erin Webley
Oscy . . . . Brett Tabisel
Benjie . . . . Jason Marcus
Mr. Sanders, Walter Winchell . . . . Bill Kux
UNDERSTUDIES: Joe Gallagher, Kelli Sawyer, Buddy Crutchfield

ORCHESTRA: Lynne Shankel, conductor, keyboard; John DiPinto, associate conductor, keyboard; Chris MacDonnell, reeds; Peter Prosser, cello; MaryAnn McSweeney, bass; Joe Mowatt, percussion

MUSICAL NUMBERS: Here and Now, Will That Ever Happen to Me?, You're Gonna Miss Me, Little Did I Dream, The Walk, Like They Used To, I Think I Like Her, The Heat, The Movies, Man Around the House, Someone to Dance with Me, Unfinished Business, Make You Mine, The Drugstore, The Campfire, Promise of the Morning, Oh Gee, I Love My GI, The Dance

Musical based on the novel and movie of the same name; a young man's social and sexual awakening in a summer during World War II.

*Closed January 27, 2002, after 47 performances.

Greg Stone, Kate Jennings Grant, Ryan Driscoll in *Summer of '42* (Kevin Byrne)

Megan Valerie Walker, Brett Tabisel, Celia Keenan-Bolger, Ryan Driscoll in *Summer of '42* (Kevin Byrne)

WHAT'S ON THE HEARTS OF MEN

By Malik Yoba and A. Rahman Yoba; Directors, Malik Yoba, George Faison; Sets, Felix Cochren; Lighting, Marshall Williams; Costumes, A. Rahman Yoba; Sound, Sound of Authority; Produced by Peforming Arts Productions, Dia Theatricals and Malik Yoba; Opened at the Beacon Theatre on January 29, 2002*

CAST

Jerome Jones . . . . Malik Yoba
Al Washington . . . . BeBe Winans
Charles Ramsey (aka BOO) . . . . Michael LeMelle
Carmen . . . . Stephanie Mills
Trina . . . . Julie Dickens
Vanessa . . . . Patricia Cuffie

*Closed February 3, 2002, after 8 performances

THE MATCHMAKER

By Phyllis Ryan; Adapted from the Novella *Letters of a Matchmaker* by John B. Keane; Director, Michael Scott; Sets, Michael McCafferty; Costumes, Synan O'Mahoney; Original Music, Mr. Scott; Associate Producer, Matthew Gale; Production Stage Manager, John Brophy; Produced by The Machine Theatre Company and the Irish Repertory Theatre; Press, Barlow Hartman Public Relations; Opened on February 10, 2002*

Featuring Anna Manahan and Des Keogh. A play in two acts.

*Closed March 31, 2002, after 57 performances

GOLDEN LADDER

By Donna Spector; Director, Thomas Waites; Sets and Lighting, Barry Arnold; Costumes, Laura Frecon; Sound, David Gilman; Stage Manager, Terri Mintz; Press, Media Blitz; Produced by Donald Goldman; Opened at the Players Theatre on February 12, 2002*

CAST

Cathy Bronson . . . . Amy Redford
Aaron Feldman . . . . Michael Anderson
Carol Havens, Hotel Clerk . . . . Christi Kelsey
Bernard Bronson . . . . Neal Lerner
Laura Bronson . . . . Annie McGovern
Mary Scaccia . . . . Marjan Neshat

Comedy about a Christian girl who discovers she has Jewish ancestors.

*Closed March 10, 2002, after 32 performances.

Maria Thayer, Alyssa Bresnahan, Catherine Kellner, Sally Parrish in *Necessary Targets* (Joan Marcus)

Sherie René Scott, Norbert Leo Butz in *The Last Five Years* (Joan Marcus)

NECESSARY TARGETS

By Eve Ensler; Director, Michael Wilson; Sets, Jeff Cowie; Costumes, Susan Hilferty; Lighting, Howell Binkley; Music and Sound, John Gromada; Casting, Cindy Tolan; Production Stage Manager, Pamela Edington; Produced by Harriet Newman Leve, Willa Shalit, Bob Biyett, in association with Suze Orman, Melissa Howden, Beth Dozoretz/Jane Fonda/Pat Mitchell, Dori Berinstein/Douglas Teitelbaum; Press, The Publicity Office; Opened at the Variety Arts Theatre on February 28, 2002*

CAST

J.S. . . . . Shirley Knight
Melissa . . . . Catherine Kellner
Jelena . . . . Alyssa Bresnahan
Seada . . . . Mirjana Jokovic
Azra . . . . Sally Parrish
Nuna . . . . Maria Thayer

Performed without intermission. Seven women become unwitting comrades in war-torn Central Europe, after much conflict and discord

*Closed on April 21, 2002, after 61 performances.

THE LAST FIVE YEARS

Music and Lyrics by Jason Robert Brown; Director, Daisy Prince; Sets and Costumes, Beowulf Britt; Lighting, Christine Binder; Sound, Duncan Edwards; Orchestrations, Mr. Brown; Musical Director, Thomas Murray; Casting, Mark Simon; Production Stage Manager, Patty Lyons; Produced by Arielle Tepper, Marty Bell, in Association with Libby Adler Mages/Mari Glick, Rose/Land Productions; Press, Barlow-Hartman Public Relations; Opened at the Minetta Lane Theatre on March 3, 2002*

Featuring Sherie René Scott and Northbert Leo Butz

UNDERSTUDIES: Nicole Van Geisen and D.B. Bonds

ORCHESTRA: Jason Robert Brown, conductor, piano; Dorothy Lawson, associate conductor, cello I, percussion; Gary Seiger, acoustic guitar; Mairi Dorman, cello II, percussion; Randy Landau, electric bass; Christian Hebel, violin, percussion

MUSICAL NUMBERS: Still Hurting, Jamie's Song, See? I'm Smiling, Moving Too Fast, A Part of That, The Schmuel Song, A Summer in Ohio, The Next Ten Minutes, A Miracle Would Happen, Climbing Uphill, If I Didn't Believe in You, I Can Do Better Than That, Nobody Needs to Know, Goodbye Until Tomorrow

A musical performed without intermission

*Closed May 5, 2002, after 73 performances.

SURVIVING GRACE

By Trish Vradenberg; Director, Jack Hofsiss; Sets and Lighting, Russell H. Champa; Costumes, Ann Hould-Ward; Music and Sound, Guy Sherman/Aural Fixation; Casting, Jay Binder Casting; Production Stage Manager, Joshua Halperin; Produced by Nina Benton; Opened at the Union Square Theatre on March 12, 2002*

CAST

Kati Griswald . . . . .Illeana Douglas
Grace Griswald . . . . .Doris Belack
Jack Griswald . . . . .Jerry Grayson
Sam Gelman . . . . .Armand Schultz
Lorna . . . . .Cynthia Darlow
Madge Wellington, Nurse Pam . . . . .Linda Hart
UNDERSTUDIES: Lois Markle, Jennifer Reagan, Richard Davidson, Peter Bradbury

A play in two acts about a family dealing with the matriarch's progressive Alzheimer's disease.

*Closed June 16, 2002, after 92 performances

Alan King in *Mr. Goldwyn* (Carol Rosegg)

MR. GOLDWYN

By Marsha Lebby and John Lollos; Director, Gene Saks; Sets, David Gallo; Lighting Michael Lincoln; Costumes, Joseph Aulisi; Sound, T. Richard Fitzgerald; Casting, Deborah Brown; Production Stage Manager; Daniel Rosokoff; Produced by David Brown/The Manhattan Project Ltd. and Ben Sprecher/Emma Luke Productions, LLC in association with Michael Gardener; Associate Producers, David Jaroslawicz, Carol Fleisig, Aaron Levy; Press, The Publicity Office, Bob Fennell; Opened at the Promenade Theatre on March 12, 2002*

CAST

Sam Goldwyn . . . . Alan King
Helen . . . . Lauren Klein
UNDERSTUDY: Jan Leslie Harding

A play in two acts about the movie mogul, regarding his professional and love life. The action takes place in Hollywood, California, in 1952.

*Closed June 9, 2002, after 93 performances.

Seth Isler in *The Godfadda Workout* (Joan Marcus)

THE GODFADDA WORKOUT

Solo Performance by Seth Isler; Director, Susan Jane Sullivan; Lighting and Costumes, Mr. Isler and Ms. Sullivan; Sound, Jerry Houser; Produced by East of Doheny, in association with Woody Fraser; Press, Springer/Chicoine Public Relations; Opened at the American Place Theatre on March 25, 2002*

Featuring Seth Isler

A spoof of the *Godfather* movies.

*Closed June 2, 2002, after 76 performances.

MENOPAUSE: THE MUSICAL

Book and Lyrics by Jeannie Linders; Director, Kathleen Lindsay; Sets, Jesse Poleshuck; Lighting, Michael Gilliam; Costumes, Martha Bromelmeier; Sound, Johnna Doty; Musical Direction, Corinne Aquilina; Production Stage Manager, Christine Catti; Producers, Mark Schwartz and TOC Productions; in association with Brent Peek; Press, Shirley Herz Associates; Opened at Theatre Four on April 4, 2002*

CAST

Power Woman . . . . Joy Lynn Matthews
Soap Star . . . . Mary Jo McConnell
Earth Mother . . . . Joyce Presutti
Iowa Housewife . . . . Carolanne Page
UNDERSTUDIES: Nancy Slusser, Wanda Houston

ORCHESTRA: Jane Zieonka, piano, keyboard; Diana Herald, drums; Audry Perry, bass guitar

A musical presented without intermission. The action takes place in Bloomingdale's department store, in the present.

*Still playing May 31, 2002

Carolanne Page, Joy Lynn Matthews, Sally Ann Swarm, Lynn Eldredge in
Menopause: The Musical

THE ODYSSEY

Adapted from Homer by Derek Wolcott; Director, Edward Berkeley; Sets, Beowulf Boritt; Lighting, Matthew McCarthy; Costumes, Hilary Rosenfeld; Cesar Manzano; Produced by Willow Cabin Theatre Company; opened at the Theatre at St. Clement's on May 30, 2002*

CAST

John Bolger	Novella Nelson	Adriana Sevan
Jim Butz	Chuck Patterson	Jed Sexton
Michael Hunsaker	Michael Pemberton	Lou Sumrall
Caralyn Kozlowski	Andrew Polk	Sullivan Walker
Liza Lapira	Linda Powell	Cornell Womack
	Joanna Rhinehart	

A new perspective on Ulysses' travels after the Trojan War.

*Closed June 1, 2002.

RED HOT MAMA

Solo Performance by Sharon McKnight; Based on career of Sophie Tucker; Director, Jay Berkow; Sets, Mary Houston; Lighting, Mary Jo Dondlinger; Costumes, Patti Whitlock; Music Director, Louis Goldberg; Arrangements, Stan Freeman; Production Stage Manager, Scott F. de la Cruz; Produced by the York Theatre Company; Press, Keith Sherman and Associates; Opened at the Theatre at St. Peter's on May 8, 2002*

Featuring Sharon McKnight, performing the repertoire of Sophie Tucker.

*Closed August 4, 2002, after 27 performances

Sharon McKnight in *Red Hot Mama* (Larry Laszlo Comedia)

21 DOG YEARS: DOIN' TIME @ AMAZON.COM

Solo Performance by Mike Daisey; Director, Jean-Michele Gregory; Sets, Louisa Thompson; Lighting, Russell H. Champa; Produced by David Foster, Martian Entertainment and Peter Cane; Associate Producers, Steve Farbman, Tom Lightburn, Adam Weinstock; Press, Boneau/Bryan-Brown; Opened at the Cherry Lane Theatre on May 9, 2002*

Featuring Mike Daisey.

A former dot-com employee monologues about his experiences in the cyber world and how it is impacting our society.

*Closed August 31, 2002, after 27 performances.

CAPITOL STEPS:
WHEN BUSH COMES TO SHOVE

By Bill Strauss, Elaina Newport, Mark Eaton; Director, Mr. Strauss, Ms. Newport, Mr Eaton; Sets, RJ Matson; Lighting, Krista Martocci; Costumes, Lindarose Payne; Sound, Jill B.C. DuBoff; Produced by Eric Krebs in association with Capitol Steps; Press, Jeffrey Richards and Associates; Opened at the John Houseman Theatre on May 16, 2002*

With Mike Carruthers, Ann Johnson, Tracey Stephens, Mike Tilford, Jamie Zemarel.

Our government seen through satire and parody.

*Closed August 31, 2002, after 18 performances.

ONE SHOT, ONE KILL

By Richard Vetere; Director, Joe Brancato; Sets, Tony Straiges; Costumes, Curtis Hay; Lighting, Jeff Nellis; Music and Sound, Johnna Doty; Casting, Stephanie Klapper; Production Stage Messenger, Tanya Gillette; Produced by Primary Stages; Press, Barlow-Hartman Public Relations. Opened on May 20, 2002*

With Michael Cullen, Robert Montano, Andrea Maulella

Presented without intermission. A drama about a sniper whose world unravels around him performed without intermission.

*Closed June 23, 2002, after 12 performances.

Mike Daisey in *21 Dog Years: Doin' Time @ Amazon.com*

OFF-BROADWAY

Productions from past seasons that played through this season

DE LA GUARDA: VILLA VILLA

Created/Directed by Pichon Baldinu and Diqui James; Music/Musical Director, Gabriel Kerpel; Presented by Kevin McCollum, Jeffrey Seller, David Binder, Daryl Roth; Press, Richard Kornberg/Don Summa; Opened in the Daryl Roth Theatre on Tuesday, June 9, 1998*

CAST

Valerie Alonso	Carlos Casella	Alejandro Garcia
Pichon Baldinu	Fabio D'Aquila	Diqui James
Gabriela Barberio	Julieta Dentone	Tomas James
Martin Bauer	Rafael Ferro	Gabriel Kerpel
Mayra Bonard	Ana Frenkel	Maria Ucedo

Performance art presented (in an old bank) without intermission. "Villa Villa" translates roughly, as "by the seat of your pants."

*Still playing May 31, 2002.

De La Guarda: Villa Villa

THE DONKEY SHOW

Created/Directed by Diane Paulus and Randy Weiner; Conception, Mr. Weiner; Set, Scott Pask; Costumes, David C. Woolard; Lighting, Kevin Adams; Sound, Brett Jarvis; Specialty Dances, Maria Torres; Stage Manager, Jim Atens; Press, Karpel Group/Bridget Klapinski, Brian Carmody; Judy Jacksina/Aryn DeKaye, Molly Shaffer; Presented by Jordan Roth; Opened August 10, 1999, at Club El Flamingo*

CAST

Oberon/club owner . . . . Rachel Benbow Murdy
Tytania/disco-diva girlfriend . . . . Anna Wilson
Rollerena/Puck on Roller Skates . . . . Roman Pietrs
Helen, in love with Dimitri . . . . Jordin Ruderman
Dimitri, in love with Mia . . . . Emily Hellstrom
Mia, beloved of Sander . . . . Rachel Benbow Murdy
Sander, beloved of Mia . . . . Anna Wilson
Vinnie 1, a rude mechanical . . . . Jordin Ruderman
Vinnie 2, a rude mechanical . . . . Emily Hellstrom
Mustard Seed, Tytania's Fairy . . . . Oscar Estevez
Cob Web, Tytania's Fairy . . . . Luke Miller
Moth, Tytania's Fairy . . . . Dan Cryer
Peasebottom, Tytania's Fairy . . . . Quinn
Rico Suave, bouncer . . . . Orlando Santana
Disco Lady . . . . Barbara Resstab
DJ Hernando Pacheski . . . . Kevin Shand
MUSICAL NUMBERS: A Fifth of Beethoven, Also Sprach Zarathustra, Car Wash, Dance with Me, Disco Circus, Don't Leave Me This Way, I Love the Nightlife, Never Knew Love Like This Before, I'm Your Boogie Man, Knock on Wood, Ring My Bell, Salsation, That's the Way of the World, You Sexy Thing, We Are Family

A disco adaptation of Shakespeare's *A Midsummer Night's Dream* performed in a dance club.

*Still playing May 31, 2002.

I LOVE YOU, YOU'RE PERFECT, NOW CHANGE

Music/Arrangements, Jimmy Roberts; Lyrics/Book, Joe DiPietro; Director, Joel Bishoff; Musical Director, Tom Fay; Set, Neil Peter Jampolis; Costumes, Candice Donnelly; Lighting, Mary Louise Geiger; Sound, Duncan Edwards; Cast Recording, Varese Sarabande; Production Supervisor, Matthew G. Marholin; Stage Manager, William H. Lang; Presented by James Hammerstein, Bernie Kukoff, Jonathan Pollard; Press, Bill Evans/Jim Randolph; Previewed from July 15, 1996; Opened in the Westside Theatre/Upstairs on Friday, August 1, 1996*

CAST
Andrea Chamberlain
Jordan Leeds
Kevin Pariseau
Cheryl Stern

SUCCEEDING CAST: Marylee Graffeo, Lori Hammel, Mylinda Hull, Bob Walton, Adam Hunter, Evy O'Rourke

SWINGS: Ray Roderick, Karyn Quackenbush

MUSICAL NUMBERS: Cantata for a First Date, Stud and a Babe, Single Man Drought, Why Cause I'm a Guy, Tear Jerk, I Will Be Loved Tonight, Hey There Single Guy/Gal, He Called Me, Wedding Vows, Always a Bridesmaid, Baby Song, Marriage Tango, On the Highway of Love, Waiting Trio, Shouldn't I Be Less in Love with You?, I Can Live with That, I Love You You're Perfect Now Change

A two-act musical revue for hopeful heterosexuals. On January 7, 2001, the production played its 1,848th performance and became the longest running musical revue in Off-Broadway history (besting *Jacques Brel Is Alive and Well and Living in Paris*).

*Still playing May 31, 2002.

Andrea Chamberlain, Marylee Graffeo, Jordan Leeds, Adam Hunter in *I Love You, You're Perfect, Now Change* (Carol Rosegg)

LATE NITE CATECHISM

By Vicki Quade and Maripat Donovan; Director, Patrick Trettenero; Design, Marc Silvia; Lighting, Tom Sturge; Stage Manager, Stephen Sweeney; Presented by Entertainment Events and Joe Corcoran Productions; Press, David Rothenberg/David Gersten; Opened in St. Luke's on Thursday, September 26, 1996*

CAST
Sister . . . . Patti Hannon
Fr. Martinez . . . . George Bass

An interactive comedy in two acts. The setting is an adult catechism class.

*Still playing May 31, 2002.

Patti Hannon in *Late Night Catechism* (Carol Rosegg)

NAKED BOYS SINGING!

By Stephen Bates, Marie Cain, Perry Hart, Shelly Markham, Jim Morgan, David Pevsner, Rayme Sciaroni, Mark Savage, Ben Schaechter, Robert Schrock, Trance Thompson, Bruce Vilanch, Mark Winkler; Conceived/Directed by Robert Schrock; Choreography, Jeffry Denman; Musical Direction/Arrangements, Stephen Bates; Set/Costumes, Carl D. White; Lighting, Aaron Copp; Stage Manager, Christine Catti; Presented by Jamie Cesa, Carl D. White, Hugh Hayes, Tom Smedes, Jennifer Dumas; Press, Peter Cromarty; Previewed from Friday, July 2, 1999; Opened in the Actors' Playhouse on Thursday, July 22, 1999*

CAST

Glenn Allen †1	Tom Gualtieri	Sean McNally †5
Jonathan Brody †2	Patrick Herwood	Adam Michaels †6
Tim Burke †3	Daniel C. Levine †4	Trance Thompson †7

MUSICAL NUMBERS: Gratuitous Nudity, Naked Maid, Bliss, Window to Window, Fight the Urge, Robert Mitchum, Jack's Song, Members Only, Perky Little Porn Star, Kris Look What You've Missed, Muscle Addiction, Nothin' but the Radio on, The Entertainer, Window to the Soul, Finale/Naked Boys Singing!

A musical revue in two acts.

*Still playing May 31, 2002.

†Succeeded by: 1. Trevor Richardson, Eric Dean Davis 2. Richard Lear, Steve Sparagen 3. Kristopher Kelly 4. George Livengood 5. Luis Villabon 6. Glen Allen, Patrick Herwood 7. Dennis Stowe, Ralph Cole Jr., Stephan Alexander, Eric Potter

The Company of *Naked Boys Singing!* (Joan Marcus)

Eric Comstock, Hilary Cole, Christopher Gines in *Our Sinatra: A Musical Celebration* (James J. Kriegsmann)

OUR SINATRA: A MUSICAL CELEBRATION

Conceived by Eric Comstock, Christopher Gines, Hilary Kole; Director, Kurt Stamm; Production Supervisor, Richard Maltby Jr.; Set, Troy Hourie; Lighting, Jeff Nellis; Sound, Matt Berman; Stage Manager, Marian DeWitt; Presented by Jack Lewin and Scott Perrin; Press, Tony Origlio/David Lotz; Previewed from Wednesday, December 8, 1999; Opened in the Blue Angel on Sunday, December 19, 1999*

CAST

Eric Comstock †1	Christopher Gines	Hilary Kole

MUSICAL NUMBERS: These Foolish Things, Where or When, Come Rain or Come Shine, I Like to Lead When I Dance, A Lovely Way to Spend An Evening, I Fall in Love Too Easily, Time After Time, All the Way, The Tender Trap, Frome Here to Eternity, You're Sensational, Well Did You Evah?, My Kind of Town, As Long as There's Music, Nice 'n' Easy, I'm a Fool to Want You, Everything Happens to Me, Day In Day Out, Ol' Man River, Without a Song, One for My Baby, Angel Eyes, In the Wee Small Hours, It Never Entered My Mind, Last Night When We Were Young, At Long Last Love, How Do You Keep the Music Playing, I've Got the World on a String, To Love and Be Loved, The One I Love Belongs to Somebody Else, I Have Dreamed, If You Are But a Dream, The Song Is You, Day by Day, Night and Day, The Way You Look Tonight, They Can't Take That Away, Guess I'll Hang My Tears Out to Dry, I'll Never Smile Again, Come Fly with Me, East of the Sun, Fly Me to the Moon, Lady Is a Tramp, Luck Be a Lady, Here's That Rainy Day, All or Nothing At All, I've Got You Under My Skin, High Hopes, Best Is Yet to Come, I've Got a Crush on You, All My Tomorrows, How Little We Know, Witchcraft, I Get a Kick Out of You, Saturday Night, Strangers in the Night, Come Dance with Me, I Won't Dance, Summer Wind, Second Time Around, Young at Heart, You Make Me Feel So Young, My Way, The Song Is You, Put Your Dreams Away

A two-act musical revue of songs associated with Frank Sinatra. Performed at the Algonquin Hotel's Oak Room prior to this Off-Broadway engagement.

*Closed July 28, 2002, after 1,096 performances. Moved to The Reprise Room on August 13, 2000.

†Succeeded by: 1. Billy Stritch (during vacation)

James Farrell, Catherine Russell in *Perfect Crime* (Joe Bly)

PERFECT CRIME

By Warren Manzi; Director, Jeffrey Hyatt; Set, Jay Stone, Mr. Manzi; Costumes, Nancy Bush; Lighting, Jeff Fontaine; Sound, David Lawson; Stage Manager, Julia Murphy; Presented by The Actors Collective in association with the Methuen Company; Press, Debenham Smythe/Michelle Vincents, Paul Lewis, Jeffrey Clarke; Opened in the Courtyard Playhouse on April 18, 1987*

CAST

Margaret Thorne Brent . . . . Catherine Russell
Inspector James Ascher . . . . Michael Minor
W. Harrison Brent . . . . Don Leslie †1
Lionel McAuley . . . . Chris Lutkin †2
David Breuer . . . . Patrick Robustelli
UNDERSTUDIES: Lauren Lovett (Females), J.R. Robinson (Males)

A mystery in two acts. The action takes place in Windsor Locks, Connecticut.

*Still playing May 31, 2002. After opening at the Courtyard Playhouse, the production transferred to the Second Stage, 47th St. Playhouse, Intar 53 Theater, Harold Clurman Theatre, Theatre Four, and currently, The Duffy Theatre.

†Succeeded by: 1. Peter Ratray 2. Brian Hotaling

STOMP

Created/Directed by Luke Cresswell and Steve McNicholas; Lighting, Mr. McNicholas, Neil Tiplady; Production Manager, Pete Donno; General Management, Richard Frankel/Marc Routh; Presented by Columbia Artists Management, Harriet Newman Leve, James D. Stren, Morton Wolkowitz, Schuster/Maxwell, Galin/Sandler, and Markley/Manocherian; Press, Chris Boneau/Adrian Bryan-Brown, Jackie Green, Bob Fennell; Previewed from Friday, February 18, 1994; Opened in the Orpheum Theatre on Sunday, February 27, 1994*

CAST

Taro Alexander	Stephanie Marshall	R.J. Samson
Morris Anthony	Keith Middleton	Henry W. Shead Jr.
Maria Emilia Breyer	Jason Mills	Mario Torres
Marivaldo Dos Santos	Mikel Paris	Davi Vieira
Mindy Haywood	Raymond Poitier	Sheilynn Wactor
Raquel Horsford	Ray Rodriguez Rosa	Fiona Wilkes

An evening of percussive performance art. The ensemble uses everything but conventional percussion to make rhythm and dance.

*Still playing May 31, 2002.

Pamela Gien in *The Syringa Tree* (Michael Lamont)

THE SYRINGA TREE

By Pamela Gien; Director, Larry Moss; Set, Kenneth Foy; Costumes, William Ivey Long; Lighting, Jason Kantrowitz; Sound, Tony Suraci; Stage Manager, Frederick H. Orner; Press, Bill Evans/Jim Randolph, Jonathan Schwartz; Presented by Matt Salinger; Opened September 14, 2000, at Playhouse 91*

CAST

Pamela Gien (all 28 characters) †1

A drama performed without intermission. The action takes place in Johannesburg, South Africa, beginning in 1963.

*Still playing May 31, 2002

†Succeeded by: 1. Kate Elumberg

TONY 'N' TINA'S WEDDING

By Artificial Intelligence; Conception, Nancy Cassaro (Artistic Director); Director, Larry Pellegrini; Supervisory Director, Julie Cesari; Musical Director, Lynn Portas; Choreography, Hal Simons; Design/Decor, Randall Thropp; Costumes/Hairstyles/Makeup, Juan DeArmas; General Manager, Leonard A. Mulhern; Company Manager, James Hannah; Stage Manager, Larry S. Piscador; Presented by Joseph Corcoran & Daniel Cocoran; Press, David Rothenberg/Terence Womble; Opened in the Washington Square Church & Carmelita's on Saturday, February 6, 1988*

CAST

Valentia Lynne Nunzio, the bride . . . . . Domenica Cameron-Scorsese †1
Anthony Angelo Nunzio, the groom . . . . Scott Bielecky
Connie Mocogni, maid of honor . . . . Sophia Antonini
Barry Wheeler, best man . . . . Joe Dallo
Donna Marsala, bridesmaid . . . . Lisa Casillo
Dominick Fabrizzi, usher . . . . Sal Marino
Marina Gulino, bridesmaid . . . . Susan Ann Davis
Johnny Nunzio, usher/brother of groom . . . . Michael Perri
Josephine Vitale, mother of the bride . . . . Jacqueline Carol
Joseph Vitale, brother of the bride . . . . Michael Gargani
Luigi Domenico, great uncle of the bride . . . . Frankie Waters
Rose Domenico, aunt of the bride . . . . Susan Varon
Sister Albert Maria, cousin of bride . . . . Renae Patti
Anthony Angelo Nunzio, Sr., father of groom . . . . Mark Nassar
Madeline Monroe, Mr. Nunzio's girlfriend . . . . Denise Fennell
Grandma Nunzio, grandmother to groom . . . . Letty Serra
Michael Just, Tina's ex-boyfriend . . . . Patrick Holder
Father Mark, parish priest . . . . James J. Hendricks
Vinnie Black, caterer . . . . Henry Caplan
Loretta Black, wife of the caterer . . . . Rebecca Weitman
Nikki Black, daughter of the caterer . . . . Alyson Silverman
Pat Black, sister of the caterer . . . . Joanne Newborn
Mikey Black, son of the caterer . . . . Eric Gutman
Mike Black, brother of the caterer . . . . Matthew Bonifacio
Rick Demarco, the video man . . . . Anthony Barone
Sal Antonucci, the photographer . . . . John DiBenedetto

An environmental theatre production. The action takes place at a wedding and reception.

*Still playing May 31, 2002. After the opening, the production later transferred to St. John's Church & Vinnie Black's Coliseum (reception), and currently shows at St. Luke's Church and Vinnie Black's Vegas Room Coliseum in the Edison Hotel (reception).

†Succeeded by: 1. Kelly Cinnante

TUBES

Created and Written by Matt Goldman, Phil Stanton, Chris Wink; Director, Marlene Swartz and Blue Man Group; Artistic Coordinator, Caryl Glaab; Artistic/Musical Collaborators, Larry Heinemann, Ian Pai; Set, Kevin Joseph Roach; Costumes, Lydia Tanji, Patricia Murphy; Lighting, Brian Aldous, Matthew McCarthy; Sound, Raymond Schilke, Jon Weston; Computer Graphics, Kurisu-Chan; Stage Manager, Lori J. Weaver; Presented by Blue Man Group; Press, Manuel Igrejas; Opened at the Astor Place Theatre on Thursday, November 7, 1991*

BLUE MAN CASTS

Chris Bowen	Gen. Fermon Judd Jr.	Phil Stanton
Michael Cates	Matt Goldman	Pete Starrett
Wes Day	John Grady	Steve White
Jeffrey Doornbos	Randall Jaynes	Chris Wink
	Pete Simpson	

An evening of performance art presented without intermission.

*Still playing May 31, 2002.

Blue Man Group: Tubes (Martha Swope)

Eve Ensler in *The Vagina Monologues* (Joan Marcus)

THE VAGINA MONOLOGUES

By Eve Ensler; Production Supervisor, Joe Mantello; Set, Loy Arcenas; Lighting, Beverly Emmons; General Management, EGS; Stage Manager, Barnaby Harris; Press, Publicity Office/Bob Fennell, Marc Thibodeau; Presented by David Stone, Willa Shalit, Nina Essman, Dan Markley/Mike Skipper, and The Araca Group; Previewed from Tuesday, September 21, 1999; Opened in the Westside Theatre/Downstairs on Sunday, October 3, 1999*

THIS SEASON'S CASTS

Joy Behar, Hazelle Goodman, and Holland Taylor; Linda Ellerbee, Calista Flockhart, and Lisa Gay Hamilton; Carol Kane, Melissa Joan Hart, and Phylicia Rashad; Teri Hatcher, Ricki Lake, and Regina Taylor; Gloria Reuben, Julia Stiles, and Mary Testa; Brett Butler, Kimberly Williams, and Tonya Pinkins; Terri Garr, Sanaa Lathan, and Juliana Margulies; Brooke Shields, Mercedes Ruehl, and Ana Gasteyer; Kathleen Chalfant, Nell Carter, and Annabella Sciorra; Donna Hanover, Robin Givens, and Susie Essman; Erica Jong, Angelica Torn, and Lauren Velez; Ann Magnuson, Sarah Jones, and Lolita Davidovitch; Carolee Carmello, Roma Maffia, and Rue McClanahan; Julie Halston, Lisa Leguillou, and Lois Smith; Becky Ann Baker, Cynthia Garrett, and Ruthie Henshall; Kim Coles, Judy Gold, and Patricia Kalember; Katherine Helmond, Joie Lee, and Hayley Mills

Monologues based on interviews with a diverse group of women. Performed without intermission.

*Still playing May 31, 2002.

OFF-BROADWAY

Productions from past seasons that closed during this season

BAT BOY: THE MUSICAL
Deven May, Kerry Butler (Joan Marcus)
Opened March 21, 2001
Closed December 2, 2001
260 performances

BLUR (not pictured)
Opened May 17, 2001
Closed June 24, 2001
46 performances

THE FANTASTICKS
The Company
Opened May 3, 1960
Closed January 13, 2002
17,162 performances
The world's longest continuously playing musical,
it played for 42 years at the Sullivan Street
Playhouse in Greenwich Village.

FORBIDDEN BROADWAY: 2001:
A SPACE ODYSSEY (not pictured)
Opened November 18, 2000
Closed February 6, 2002
552 performances

GLIMMER, GLIMMER AND SHINE
Brian Kerwin, John Spencer,
Scott Cohen, Seana Kofoed (Joan Marcus)
Opened May 24, 2001
Closed July 8, 2001
54 performances

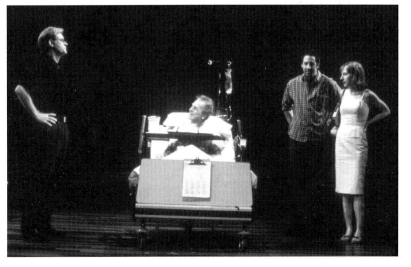

HAMLET (BAM & RNT)
Elizabeth Keefe, Dennis Turney (Brett Singer)
Opened May 30, 2000
Closed June 2, 2001
5 performances

LOBBY HERO (not pictured)
Opened May 8, 2001
Closed September 2, 2001
136 prformances

MADAME MELVILLE
Macaulay Culkin, Joely Richardson (Joan Marcus)
Opened May 3, 2001
Closed June 24, 2001
61 performances

MAYBE BABY, IT'S YOU
Charlie Shanian, Shari Simpson (Gerry Goodstein)
Opened November 9, 2000
Closed June 30, 2001
163 performances

NOCTURNE (not pictured)
Opened May 16, 2001
Closed June 17, 2001
38 performances

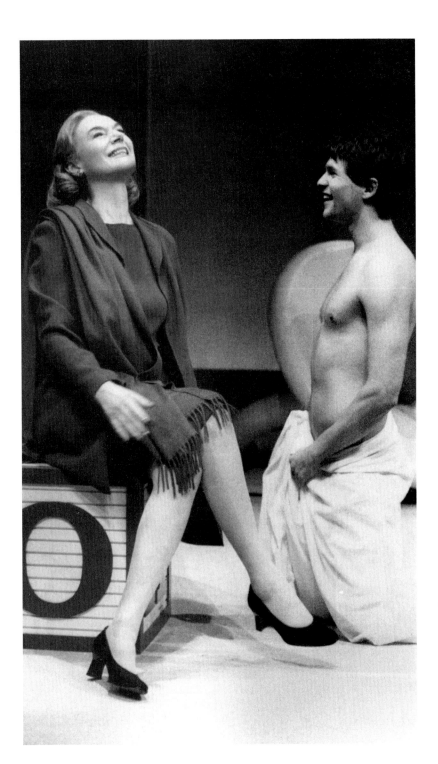

THE PLAY ABOUT THE BABY
Marian Seldes, David Burtka (Carol Rosegg)
Opened February 2, 2001
Closed September 1, 2001
245 performances

SIX GOUMBAS AND A WANNABE
(not pictured)
Opened May 10, 2001
Closed December 9, 2001
241 performances

UNCLE BOB
Joseph Gordon-Levitt, George Morfogen
(Yasuyuki Takagi)
Opened April 23, 2001
Closed July 1, 2001
80 performances

URINETOWN
The Company (Joan Marcus)
Opened May 6, 2001
Closed June 25, 2001
58 performances

OFF-BROADWAY
Company Series

BROOKLYN ACADEMY OF MUSIC

Chairman of the Board, Bruce C. Ratner; President, Karen Brooks Hopkins; Executive Producer, Joseph V. Melillo

THE GHOST SONATA by August Strindberg; Director, Ingmar Bergman; Choreography, Virpi Pahkinen; Sets, Goran Wassberg; Costumes, Anna Bergman; Lights, Pierre Leveau; Stage Manager, Tomas Wennerberg; Press, Elena Park, Melissa Cusick, Fateema Jones, Tamara McCaw, Kila Packett; Cast: Jan Malmsjo (The Old Man), Jonas Malmsjo (The Student), Virpi Pahkinen (The Milkmaid), Gertrud Mariano (The Doorman's Wife), Nils Eklund (The Dead Man), Gerthi Kulle (The Dark Lady), Elin Klinga (The Young Lady), Per Myrberg (The Colonel), Gunnel Lindblom (Mummy), Orjan Ramberg (Johannson), Ingvar Kjellson (Bengtsson), Anders Beckman (Posh Man), Margareta Hallin (The Cook), Margreth Weivers-Norstrom (The Fiancée), Maria Alm-Norell, Sven-Erik Eriksson, Carl-Lennart Frobergh, Per Hedefalk, Henrik Sjogren, Ulf Strandberg (Ensemble); (Harvey Theater) June 20–23, 2001 (5 performances)

A drama performed in Swedish with simultaneous English translation, without intermission.

CYMBELINE by William Shakespeare; Director, Mike Alfreds; Lighting, Donald Holder; Costumes and Properties, Jenny Tiramani; Choreography, Glynn McDonald; Music, Claire Van Kampen; Stage Manager, Kim Beringer; Prensented by the Brooklyn Academy of Music; Press, Sandt Sawotka, Melissa Cusick, Fateema Jones; Cast: Jane Arnfield, Terry McGinty, Fergus O'Donnell, John Ramm, Mark Rylance, Abigail Thaw; Musicians, Irita Kutchmy, Claire Van Kampen; (Harvey Theater) March 5–17, 2002 (14 performances)

Revival of Shakespeare's Globe Theatre production

CITY CENTER ENCORES!

President and Executive Director, Judith E. Daykin; Artistic Director, Jack Viertel

CARNIVAL Book, Michael Stewart; Music and Lyrics, Bob Merrill; Based on Material by Helen Deutsch; Director and Choreographer, Kathleen Marshall; Sets, John Lee Beatty; Lighting, Peter Kaczorowski; Costumes, Martin Pakledinaz; Sound, Scott Lehrer; Concert Adaptation, Wendy Wasserstein; Puppets, Jim Henson Company; Orchestrations, Philip Lang; Music Coordinator, Seymour Red; Production Stage Manager, Peter Hanson; Cast: Brian Stokes Mitchell, Anne Hathaway, Debbie Gravitte, David Margulies, David Costabile, Douglas Sills, Peter Jacobson, Philip LeStrange, Lloyd Culbreath, Angelo Fraboni, Peter Gregus, Julio Monge, Timothy Robert Blevins, Sara Gettelfinger, Liz McCartney, William Ryall, Enrique Brown, Blake Hammond, Carol Lee Meadows, Cynthia Sophiea, Jessia Leigh Brown, Emily Hsu, Tina Ou, Rebecca Spencer, Stephanie D'Abruzzo, Kevin Ligon, Andrew Pacho, John Tartaglia; Coffee Club Orchestra, Rob Fisher, Musical Director; February 7–10, 2002 (5 performances)

Concert version of the musical.

GOLDEN BOY by Clifford Odets; Music, Charles Strouse; Lyrics, Lee Adams; Book, Mr. Odets, William Gibson; Director, Walter Bobbie; Sets, John Lee Beatty; Lighting, Peter Kaczorowski; Costumes, William Ivey Long; Sound, Acme Sound Partners; Concert Adaptation, Suzan-Lori Parks; Choreographer, Wayne Cilento; Fight Direction, Michael Olajide; Music Coordinator, Seymour Red Press; Orchestrations, Ralph Burns, Don Sebesky; Production Stage Manager, Peter Hanson; Cast: Alfonso Ribiero, Anastasia Barzee, Norm Lewis, William McNulty, Paul Butler, Wayne Pretlow, Thursday Farrar, Michael Potts, Rob Bartlett, Joseph R. Sicari, Morgan Burke, Kamar de los Reyes, Karine Plantadit-Bageot, Julio Monge, Eric Anthony, Kristine Bendul, Chaundra Cameron, Kyra DaCosta, Manuel Herrera, Erik Houg, Terace Jones, Gelan Lambert Jr., Vicky Lambert, Sharon Moore, April Nixon, Devin Richards, Angela Robinson, Janelle Anne Robinson, J.D. Webster, Patrick Wetzel; The Coffee Club Orchestra, Rob Fisher, Musical Director; March 21–24, 2002 (5 performances)

Concert version of the Odets play originally produced on Broadway.

THE PAJAMA GAME Book by Richard Bissell and George Abbott; Music and Lyrics by Richard Adler and Jerry Ross; Based on the Novel *7 cents* by Richard Bissell; Director, John Rando; Sets, John Lee Beatty; Lighting, Ken Billington; Costumes, David C. Woolard; Sound, Scott Lehrer; Concert Adaptation, David Ives; Orchestrations, Don Walker; Music Coordinator, Seymour Red Press; Production Stage Manager, Peter Hanson; Cast: Brent Barrett, Karen Ziemba, Daniel Jenkins, Ken Page, Deidre Goodwin, Mark Linn-Baker, Gian Ferrall, Fred Burnell, Jennifer Cody, Katie Harvey, Edgar Goodineaux, Herman Payne, Rebecca Baxter, Timothy Reese, Tony Capone, Caitlin Carter, Susan Derry, Joe Farrell, Anne Hawthorne, Joy Hermalyn, Ann Kittredge, Kirk McDonald, April Nixon, Mark Oka, Tina Ou, Jessica Perrizo, Josh Prince, Devin Richards, Rebecca Robbins, Angela Robinson, J.D. Webster, Patrick Wetzel; With The Coffee Club Orchestra; May 2–5, 2002 (5 performances)

Concert version of the 1954 Broadway musical.

LINCOLN CENTER THEATER

Seventeenth season

Artistic Director, Andre Bishop; Executive Producer, Bernard Gersten

CHAUCER IN ROME by John Guare; Director, Nicholas Martin; Sets, Alexander Dodge; Costumes, Michael Krass; Lighting, Donald Holder, Original Music and Sound, Mark Bennett; Casting, Daniel Swee, Amy Christopher; Stage Manager, Michael Brunner; Press, Philip Rinaldi, Brian Rubin; CAST: Jon Tenney (Matt), Carrie Preston (Sarah), Bruce Norris (Pete), Umit Celebi (Renzo), Polly Holliday (Dolo), Dick Latessa (Ron, Il Dottore, Father Shapiro, Joe), Lee Wilkof (Charlie), Antonio Edwards Suarez (Il Tassinaro), Umit Celebi, Susan Finch, Mark Fish, Nancy McDaniel, William McGeever, Antonio Edwards Suarez (Pilgrims, Fellows); UNDERSTUDIES: Mr. Tenney (Baylen Thomas); Ms. Preston (Claire Lautier); Messrs. Noris, Wilkof [Joe], Suarez (Tim McGeever); Messrs. Latessa, Wilkof [Father Shapiro, Charlie] (Bill Cwikowski); Ms. Holiday (Nancy McDoniel); Mr. Wilkof [Il Dottore] (Umit Celebi); Mr. Celebi (Antonio Edwards Suarez); Pilgrims, Fellows (Claire Lautier, Baylen Thomas, Bill Cwikowski); (Mitzi E. Newhouse Theatre) June 7–July 29, 2001 (61 performances)

A comedy performed without intermission. The action takes place in Rome in 2000.

EVERETT BEEKIN by Richard Greenberg; Director, Evan Yionoulis; Sets, Christopher Barreca; Lighting, Donald Holder; Costumes, Teresa Snider-Stein; Sound and Music, Mike Yionoulis; Casting, Daniel Swee; Stage Manager, Denise Yaney; Press, Philip Rinaldi; CAST: Marcia Jean Kurta (Ma, Waitress), Robin Bartlett (Sophie, Celia, Anna's Older Daughter), Bebe Neuwirth (Anna, Nell, Anna's Younger Daughter), Jeff Allin (Jack, Bee), Jennifer Carpenter (Miri, Laurel), Kevin Isola (Jimmy, Ev); (Mitzi E. Newhouse Theatre) November 14, 2001–January 6, 2002 (62 performances)

A comedy. The action takes place in the late 1940s, 1990s on New York's Lower East Side.

THE CARPETBAGGER'S CHILDREN by Horton Foote; Director, Michael Wilson; Sets, Jeff Cowle; Lighting, Rui Rita; Costumes, David Woolard; Sound, John Gromada; Casting, Cindy Tolan, Daniel Swee; Stage Manager, Michael Brunner; Collaborative Production of Lincoln Center, the Alley Theatre, Guthrie Theatre and the Hartford Stage; Press, Philip Rinaldi; CAST: Roberta Maxwell (Cornelia), Jean Stapleton (Grace Anne), Hallie Foote (Sissie); UNDERSTUDIES: Jennifer Harmon and Sandra Shipley; (Mitzi E. Newhouse Theatre) March 7–June 2, 2002 (77 performances)

A play performed without intermission. The action takes place in the mid-twentieth century.

Jon Tenney, Carrie Preston in *Chaucer in Rome* (Paul Kolnik)

The Company of *Everett Beekin* (Joan Marcus)

Jean Stapleton in *The Carpetbagger's Children* (T. Charles Erickson)

MANHATTAN THEATRE CLUB

Thirtieth season

Artistic Director, Lynne Meadow; Executive Producer, Barry Grove

WONDER OF THE WORLD by David Lindsay-Abaire; Director, Christopher Ashley; Sets, David Gallo; Lighting, Ken Billington; Costumes, David C. Woolard; Sound and Music, Mark Bennett; Fight Director, Rick Sordelet; Casting, Nancy Piccione/David Caparelliotis; Production Stage Manager, Kate Broderick; Press, Boneau/Bryan-Brown, Chris Boneau, Steven Padla, Jackie Green, Aaron Meier; CAST: Sarah Jessica Parker (Cass Harris), Alan Tudyk (Kip Harris), Kristine Nielsen (Lois Coleman), Marylouise Burke (Karla), Bill Raymond (Glen), Kevin Chamberlin (Captain Mike), Amy Sedaris (Barbara, Helicopter Pilot, Three Waitresses, Janie); (City Center Stage I) November 1, 2001–January 5, 2002 (76 performances)

A play in two acts.

WHERE'S MY MONEY? by John Patrick Shanley; Director, Mr. Shanley; Sets, Michelle Malavet; Lighting, Sarah Sidman; Costumes, Mimi O'Donnell; Sound, Eric DeArmon; Fight Direction, Blaise Corrigan; Casting, Nancy Piccione/David Caparelliotis; Production Stage Manager, Dawn M. Wagner; Press, Boneau/Bryan-Brown, Chris Boneau, Steven Padla, Jackie Green, Aaron Meier; CAST: David Deblinger (Sidney), Yetta Gottesman (Celeste), Erik LaRay Harvey (Henry), Florencia Lozano (Marcia Marie), Chris McGarry (Tommy), Paula Pizzi (Natalie); (Labyrinth Theatre) November 7, 2001–January 13, 2002 (79 performances)

A play in two acts

Nicholas Woodeson, Veanne Cox in *House and Garden*

FURTHER THAN THE FURTHEST THING by Zinnie Harris; Director, Neil Pepe; Sets, Loy Arcenas; Lighting, James Ingalls; Costumes, Laura Bauer; Music and Sound, Scott Myers; Dramaturg, Paige Evans; Production Stage Manager, Harold Goldfaden; Press, Boneau/Bryan-Brown; CAST: Jennifer Dundas (Rebecca Rogers), Dan Futterman (Francis Swain), Peter Gerety (Mr. Hansen), Robert Hogan (Bill Laverello), Jenny Sterlin (Mill Laverello); UNDERSTUDIES: Marcus Chalt, Mikel Sarah Lambert, Aidan Sullivan, Kenneth Ryan; (City Center) on February 5–March 31, 2002 (64 performances)

A play in two acts. The action takes place in the 1960s on a remote island in the Atlantic.

FOUR by Christopher Shinn; Director, Jeff Cohen; Sets, Lauren Helpren; Costumes, Veronica Worts; Lighting, Traci Klainer; Sound, Paul Adams; Music, David Van Tiegham; Casting, Nancy Piccione/David Caparelliotis; Production Stage Manager, Jason Scott Eagan; Produced by Manhattan Theatre Club in association with the Worth Street Theatre Company; Press, Boneau/Bryan-Brown; CAST: Pascale Armand (Abigayle), Keith Nobbs (June), Armando Riesco (Dexter), Isiah Whitlock, Jr. (Joe); (City Center Stage II) February 19–March 31, 2002 (48 performances)

A play performed without intermission.

HOUSE AND GARDEN by Alan Ayckbourn; Director, John Tillinger; Sets, John Lee Beatty; Costumes, Jane Greenwood; Lighting, Duane Schuler; Sound, Bruce Ellman; Music, John Pattison; Fight Direction, Rick Sordelet; Casting, Nancy Piccione/David Caparelliotis; Production Stage Manager, (*House*) James Fitzsimmons, (*Garden*) Barclay Stiff; Press, Boneau/Bryan-Brown; HOUSE CAST: Patricia Connolly (Izzie Truce), Michael Countryman (Giles Mace), Veanne Cox (Joanna Mace), John Curless (Barry Love), Laura Marie Duncan (Pearl Truce) Carson Elrod (Jake Mace) Daniel Gerroll (Gavin Ryng-Mayne); GARDEN CAST: Bryce Dallas Howard (Sally Platt) Jan Maxwell (Trish Platt), Ellen Parker (Lindy Love), Olga Sosnovska (Lucille Cadeau), James A. Stephens (Warn Coucher), Sharon Washington (Fran Briggs), Nicholas Woodeson (Teddy Platt), Children: Alla Carpenter-Walker, Edie Feinstein, Ronan Greenwood, Aliza Goldberg, Madeline Hamingson, Matthew Hollis, Gillian Jakab, Sofia Kelley Johnson, Hillary Jost, Josh Marmer, Chandler Rosenthal, Emma Sadler, Daniel Stern; (City Center Stage II) May 21–July 28, 2002 (12 performances)

Two comedies performed simultaneously, each presented in two acts. The action takes place on a summer day in an English house and its garden.

NEW YORK SHAKESPEARE FESTIVAL/ JOSEPH PAPP PUBLIC THEATRE

Forty-seventh season

Producer, George C. Wolfe; Executive Director, Fran Reiter; Artistic Producer, Rosemarie Tichler

MEASURE FOR MEASURE by William Shakespeare; Director, Mary Zimmerman; Sets, Daniel Ostling; Costumes, Mara Blumenfeld; Light, T.J. Gerckens; Sound, Acme Sound Partners; Original Music, Michael Bodeen; Production Stage Manager, Charles Means; Press, Carol R. Fineman, Tom Naro; Producer, George C. Wolfe; CAST: Joe Morton (Vincentio), Herb Foster (Escalus), Billy Crudup (Angelo), John Pankow (Lucio), Darren Pettie, Victor Quinaz, Eric Alperin (Gentlemen), Julia Gibson (Mistress Overdone, Francsca), Christopher Evan Welch (Pompey), Daniel Pino (Claudio), Cote de Pablo (Juliet), Christopher Donahue (Provost), Robert Colston (Friar Peter), Sanaa Lathan (Isabella), Tom Aulino (Elbow), Daniel Pearce (Froth), Traber Burns (Justice, Barnadine), Dennis Michael Hall (Boy), Felicity Jones (Mariana), Glenn Fleshler (Abhorson), Eric Alperin, Gregory Bratman, Bryan Cogman, Sanjit De Silva, Dale Ho, Nicole Lowrance, Jenn Perkins, John Livingston Rolle (Ensemble); (Delacorte Theater) June 17–28, 2001 (10 performances)

Presented in two acts.

TOPDOG/UNDERDOG by Suzan-Lori Parks; Director, George C. Wolfe; Sets, Riccardo Hernandez; Lighting, Scott Zielinski; Costumes, Emilio Sosa; Sound, Dan Moses Schreier; Casting, Jordan E. Thaler, Heidi Griffiths; Production Stage Manager, Rick Steiger; Producer, Mr. Wolfe; Associate Producers, Bonnie Metzgar, John Dias; Press, Carol R. Fineman, Tom Naro, Kris Diaz; CAST: Don Cheadle (Booth), Jeffrey Wright (Lincoln); (Aspacher Space in the Public Theatre) July 26–September 2, 2001 (45 performances)

A play in two acts. Time: Now. Place: Here.

Winner of the Pulitzer Prize for Drama in 2002.

THE SEAGULL by Anton Chekov; Director, Mike Nichols; Adapted by Tom Stoppard; Sets and Costumes, Bob Crowley; Lighting, Jennifer Tipton; Sound, Acme Sound Partners; Music, Mark Bennett; Production Stage Manager, Peter Lawrence; Producer, George C. Wolfe; Press, Carol Fineman, Tom Naro; CAST: Meryl Streep (Arkadina), Kevin Kline (Trigorin), Christopher Walken (Sorin), Natalie Portman (Nina), Philip Seymour Hoffman (Konstantin), Steven Spinella (Medvedenko), Marcia Gay Harden (Masha), Debra Monk (Polina), Larry Pine (Dorn), John Goodman (Shamrayev), Henry Gummer (Yakov), Morena Baccarin, Vitali Baganov, Craig Bockhorn, Mark H. Dold, Sharon Scruggs (Servants); (Delacorte Theater) August 12–26, 2001 (12 performances)

A play in two acts. A modern adaptation of the Chekov classic. The action takes place in Russia in the nineteenth century.

Billy Crudup, Joe Morton in *Measure for Measure* (Michal Daniel)

Jeffrey Wright, Don Cheadle in *Topdog/Underdog* (Michal Daniel)

Meryl Streep, Kevin Kline in *The Seagull* (Michal Daniel)

ELAINE STRITCH AT LIBERTY Musical revue by Elaine Stritch and John Lahr; Director, George C. Wolfe; Sets, Riccardo Hernandez; Lighting, Jules Fisher, Peggy Eisenhower; Costumes, Paul Tazewell; Sound, Acme Sound Partners; Orchestrations, Jonathan Tunick; Music Direction, Rob Bowman; Music Coordinator, Seymour Red Press; Production Stage Manager, Rick Steiger; Produced by George C. Wolfe; Press, Carol Fineman, Tom Naro, Ian Rand; Featuring Elaine Stritch; (Newman Theatre) November 6, 2001–January 13, 2002 (50 performances)

MUSICAL NUMBERS: All in Fun, Broadway Baby, But Not For Me, If Love Were All, Can You Use Any Money Today, Civilization, Hurray for Hollywood, I'm Still Here, I've Been to a Marvelous Party, I Want a Long Time Daddy, The Little Things You Do Together, Something Good, The Ladies Who Lunch, The Party's Over, There Never Was a Baby Like My Baby, There's No Business Like Show Business, This Is All Very New to Me, Why Do the Wrong People Travel, Zip

The life of Elaine Stritch, told through song and monologue.

OTHELLO by William Shakespeare; Director, Doug Hughes; Sets, Neil Patel; Lighting, Robert Wierzel; Costumes, Catherine Zuber; Music and Sound, David Van Tieghem; Production Stage Manager, Buzz Cohen; Press, Carol Fineman, Tom Naro, Ian Rand; CAST: Christopher Evan Welch (Roderigo), Liv Schreiber (Iago), Jack Ryland (Barbantio), Keith David (Othello), Jay Goede (Cassio), George Morfogen (Duke of Vneice), Dan Snook (Lodovico), Thomas Schall (Gratiano), Kate Forbes (Desdemona), Thom Sesma (Montano), Becky Ann Baker (Emilia), Natacha Roi (Bianca), Corey Behnke, Paul Vincent Black, Mark H. Dold, Robert Steffen, Remy Auberjonois, Lea Coco, Gregory Derelian (Ensemble); (Anspacher Theatre) December 9–30, 2001 (24 performances.)

A play in two acts

36 VIEWS by Naomi Izuka; Director, Mark Wing-Davey; Sets, Douglas Stein; Lighting, David Weiner; Costumes, Myung Hee Cho; Sound, Matthew Spiro; Projections, Ruppert Bohle; Casting, Jordan Thaler/Heidi Griffiths Casting; Production Stage Manager, John C. McNamara; A Joseph Papp Public Theatre/New York Shakespeare Festival Production, George C. Wolfe, Producer in Association with Berkeley Repertory Theatre; Associate Producers, Bonnie Metzgar, John Dias; Press, Carol Fineman, Tom Naro, Elizabeth Wehrle; CAST: Stephen Lang (Darius Wheeler), Liana Pai (Setsuko Hearn), Ebon Moss-Bachrach (John Bell), Elaine Tse (Claire Tsong), Rebecca Wisocky (Elizabeth Newman-Orr), Richard Clarke (Owen Matthissen); (Newman Theatre) March 28–April 4, 2002 (22 performances)

HELEN by Ellen McLaughlin; Director, Tony Kushner; Sets, Michael Yeargan; Lighting, Scott Zeilinski; Costumes, Susan Hilferty; Sound, Gina Leishman; Casting, Jordan Thaler/Heidi Griffiths; Production Stage Manager, C.A. Clark; Associate Producers, Bonnie Metzgar, John Dias; Press, Carol R. Fineman, Tom Naro, Elizabeth Wehrle; CAST: Donna Murphy (Helen), Marian Seldes (Servant), Johanna Day (Io), Phylicia Rashad (Athena), Denis O'Hare (Meneleus); (Martinson Hall) April 8–22, 2002 (16 performances)

A play in two acts. The action takes place in an Egyptian hotel room seventeen years after the end of the Trojan War.

BLUE SURGE by Rebecca Gilman; Director, Robert Falls; Sets, Walt Spangler; Lighting, Michael Philippi; Sound, Richard Woodbury; Costumes, Birgit Rattenborg Wise; Casting, Jordan Thaler/Heidi Griffiths; Associate Producers, Bonnie Metzgar, John Dias; Press, Carol R. Fineman, Tom Naro, Elizabeth Wehrle; CAST: Rachel Miner (Sandy), Joe Murphy (Curt), Colleen Werthman (Heather), Steve Key (Doug), Amy Landecker (Beth); (Anspacher Theatre) April 22–May 12, 2002 (25 performances)

A play in two acts. The action takes place in the Midwest in the present.

Donna Murphy, Marian Seldes in *Helen* (Michal Daniel)

NEW YORK THEATRE WORKSHOP

Twenty-second season

Artistic Director, James C. Nicola; Managing Director, Lynn Moffat

SLANGUAGE by Universes (Gamal Abdel Chasten, Lemon, Flaco Navaja, Mildred Ruiz and Steven Sapp); Director, Jo Bonney; Sets, Scott Pask; Lights, James Vermeulen; Sound, Darron L. West; Projections, Batwin and Robin Productions; Production Stage Manager, Katherine Lee Boyer; CAST: Universes: Gamal Abdel Chasten, Lemon, Flaco Navaja, Mildred Ruiz and Steven Sapp; July 23–August 5, 2001 (16 performances)

An evening of performance art/poetry slam performed without intermission.

FIRST LOVE by Charles Mee; Director, Erin Mee; Sets, Klara Zieglerova; Lighting, Christopher Akerlind; Costumes, Christine Jones; Sound, Bo Bell; Production Stage Manager, Judith Schoenfeld; Press, Richard Kornberg and Associates, Don Summa; CAST: Frederick Neumann (Harold), Ruth Maleczech (Edith), Jennifer Hall (Melody); September 9–30, 2001 (26 performances)

A play performed without intermission.

Robert Parnell, Joan Mankin in *First Love* (David Allen)

Joan Mankin, Robert Parnell in *First Love* (David Allen)

EVERYTHING THAT RISES MUST CONVERGE by Flannery O'Connor; Director, Karin Coonrod; Sets, Marina Draghici; Lighting, Christopher Akerlind; Costumes, P.J. Wish; Sound, Tony Geballe; Production Stage Manager, Jennifer Rae Moore; Richard Kornberg and Associates, Don Summa; CAST: Isiah Whitlock, Jr. (Actor One), Michael Moran (Actor Two), Kelli Rae Powell (Actor Three), Ayeje Lavonne Feamster (Actor Four) Laura Hicks (Actor Five), Michael Rogers (Actor Six), John McAdams (Actor Seven), Ledlie Borgerhoff (Actor Eight); October 30–November 18, 2001 (24 performances)

A play in three acts.

HOMEBODY/KABUL by Tony Kushner; Director, Declan Donnellan; Sets, Nick Ormerod; Lighting, Brian McDevitt; Sound, Dan Moses Schreier; Production Stage Manager, Martha Donaldson; Press, Richard Kornberg and Associates; CAST: Linda Edmond (The Homebody), Joseph Kamal (Dr. Qari Shah), Firdous Bamji (Mullah Ali aftar Durrani), Dylan Baker (Milton Ceiling), Bill Campo (Quango Twistleton), Kelly Hutchinson (Priscilla Ceiling), Dariush Kashani (A Munkrat), Yusef Bulos (Khwaja Aziz Mondanabosh), Sean T. Krishnan (Zai Garshi, The Marabout), Rita Wolf (Mahala), Jay Charan (A Border Guard); UNDERSTUDIES: Edmund C. Davys, Joseph Kamal, Dariush Kashani, Autumn Dornfeld; December 19, 2001–March 3, 2002 (86 performances)

The action takes place in London and Kabul, just after the American bombing of terrorist camps in Khost, Afghanistan, in 1998.

Firdous Bamji, Dylan Baker in *Homebody/Kabul* (Joan Marcus)

Linda Edmond in *Homebody/Kabul* (Joan Marcus)

THROW PITCHFORK Solo performance by Alexander Thomas; Director, Leonora Pace; Sets, Troy Hourie; Lighting, Ben Stanton; Sound, Jerry Yager; Production Stage Manager, Jonathan Donahue; Press, Richard Kornberg and Associates; March 12–24, 2002 (16 performances)

Presented without intermission.

VIENNA: LUSTHAUS (REVISITED) by Martha Clarke; Director, Ms. Clarke; Sets and Costumes, Robert Israel; Lighting, Paul Gallo; Music Direction, Jill Jaffee; Production Stage Manager, Jennifer Rae Moore; Press, Richard Kornberg and Associates; CAST: Vivienne Benesch, Erica Berg, Elzbieta Czyzewska, Mark DeChiazza, George de la Pena, Philip Gardner, Richmond Hoxie, James Lorenzo, Denis O'Hare, Jimena Paz, Andrew Robinson, Paola Styron, Julia Wilkins; MUSICIANS: Jill Jaffee, violin; Daniel Barrett, cello; Steven Silverstein, woodwinds; Stewart Schuele, French horns; Nina Kellman, harp; STANDBYS: Mark DeChiazza, James Lorenzo; May 8–July 21, 2002 (27 performances)

PLAYWRIGHTS HORIZONS

Thirty-first season

Artistic Director, Tim Sanford; Managing Director, Leslie Marcus; General Manager, William Russo

THE CREDEAUX CANVAS by Keith Bunin; Director, Michael Mayer; Sets, Derek McLane; Costumes, Michael Krass; Lighting, Kenneth Posner; Sound, Scott Myers; Fight Direction, J. Steven White; Casting, James Calleri; Production Stage Manager, J. Philip Bassett; Press, Publicity Office, Bob Fennell, Marc Thibodeau, Michael S. Borowski, Candi Adams; CAST: Annie Parisse (Amelia), Glenn Howerton (Jamie), Lee Pace (Winston), E. Katherine Kerr (Tess); June 5–17, 2001 (16 performances)

A play in two acts. The action takes place in an attic Apartment on East 10th St. in New York City in the present.

BREATHE, BOOM by Kia Corthron; Director, Marion McClinton; Sets and Lighting, Michael Philippi; Costumes, Katherine Roth; Sound, Ken Travis; Fight Direction, David Leong; Casting, James Calleri; Production Stage Manager, Jane Pole; Press, Publicity Office, Bob Fennell, Marc Thibodeau, Michael S Borowski, Candi Adams; CAST: Russell Andres (Jerome), Pascale Armand (Jupiter), Dena Atlantic (Shondra, Pepper, Jo), Kalimi A. Baxter (Malika, Socks), Caroline S. Clay (Mother), Rosalyn Coleman (Angel), Donna Duplantier (Cat, Girl with Pepper, Jo's Friend), Yvette Ganier (Prix), Abigail Lopez (Fuego, Denise), Heather Alicia Simms (Comet); June 10–July 1, 2001 (25 performances)

A drama in two acts.

Lee Pace, Annie Parisse, in *The Credeaux Canvas* (Joan Marcus)

Liz Callaway, Phyllis Somerville, Garrett Long in *The Spitfire Grill* (Joan Marcus)

Rosalyn Coleman, Yvette Ganier in *Breath, Boom* (Carol Rosegg)

THE SPITFIRE GRILL Book by James Valcq and Fred Alley; Director, David Saint; Music, Mr. Valcq; Lyrics, Mr. Alley; Based on the Movie by Lee David Zlotoff; Sets, Michael Anania; Lighting, Howell Binkley; Costumes, Theoni V. Aldredge; Sound, Scott Stauffer; Musical Director, Andrew Wilder; Orchestrations, Mr. Valcq; Music Coordinator, John Miller; Casting, James Calleri; Production Stage Manager, Thomas Clewell; A Playwrights Horizons Production; Associate Producer, Ira Weitzman; Press, Publicity Office, Bob Fennell, Marc Thibodeau, Michael Borowski, Candi Adams; CAST: Garrett Long (Percy Talbott), Steven Pasquale (Sheriff Joe Sutter), Phyllis Somerville (Hannah Ferguson), Armand Schultz (Caleb Thorpe), Mary Gordon Murray (Effy Krayneck), Liz Callaway (Shelby Thorpe), Steven Sinclair (The Visitor); ORCHESTRA: Andrew Wilder, conductor, keyboard; Antoine Silverman, violin; Deborah Sepe, cello; Greg Utzig, guitar, mandolin; Charles Giordano, accordian; MUSICAL NUMBERS: A Ring Around the Moon, Something's Cooking at the Spitfire Grill, Out of the Frying Pan, When Hope Goes, Ice and Snow, The Colors of Paradise, Digging Stone, This Wide Woods, Forgotten Lullaby, Shoot the Moon, Come Alive Again, Forest for the Trees, Wild Bird, Shine, Way Back Home; (the Duke 42nd Street) October 2–14, 2001 (15 performances)

A musical in two acts. The action takes place in Wisconsin in the recent past.

LIGHT YEARS by Billy Aronson; Director, Jamie Richards; Sets, Narelle Sissons; Lighting, Michael Lincoln; Costumes, Amela Baksic; Sound, Laura Grace Brown; Fight Direction and Dance Consultant, Luis Perez; Production Stage Manager, Michael Schleifer; Press and Publicity Office, Bob Fennell, Marc Thibodeau, Michael Borowski, Candi Adams; CAST: Anne Marie Nest (Courtney), Sarah Rose (Daphne), Paul Bartholomew (Doug), Reed Kessler (Michael); October 21–November 4, 2001

A play in three acts. The action takes place on a college campus during four students' freshman, sophomore, and senior years, respectively.

PSYCH by Evan Smith; Director, Jim Simpson; Sets, Kyle Chepulis; Lighting, Frances Aaronson; Costumes, Claudia Brown; Music and Sound, Scott Myers; Production Stage Manager, James Fitzsimmons; Press, The Publicity Office, Bob Fennell, Michael Borowski; CAST: Danny Burstein (Bill, Michael, Gar, Advocate), Marissa Copeland (Dominique, Jana, Barbara Stafford, Therapist), Heather Goldenhersh (Sunny Goldfarb), Enid Graham (Molly Salter), Katie Kreisler (Desiree, Karen, Jennifer) Damien Young (Todd Cox, Profound Psychotic); (Peter Norton Space) December 16–30, 2001 (17 performances)

A play presented without intermission

Malcolm Gets, Robert Sella in *Boys and Girls* (Joan Marcus)

Katie Kreisler, Heather Goldenhersh in *Psych* (Joan Marcus)

FRANNY'S WAY by Richard Nelson; Director, Mr. Nelson; Sets, Thomas Lynch; Lighting, Jennifer Tipton; Costumes, Susan Hilferty, Linda Ross; Sound, Scott Lehrer; Casting, James Calleri; Production Stage Manager; Jane Pole; Press, The Publicity Office, Bob Fennell; CAST: Kathleen Widdoes (Older Franny), Elizabeth Moss (Franny, age 17), Domenica Cameron-Scorsese (Dolly), Yvonne Woods (Sally), Jesse Pennington (Phil), Kathleen Widdoes (Marjorie); (Atlantic Theatre) March 26–April 21, 2002 (32 performances)

The action takes place in a Greenwich Village apartment, following World War II.

BOYS AND GIRLS by Tom Donaghy; Director, Gerald Gutierrez; Sets, Douglas Stein, Costumes, Catherine Zuber; Lighting, David Weiner; Sound, Aural Fixation; Fight Director, Rick Sordelet; Casting, James Calleri; Production Stage Manager, Marjorie Horn; Press, The Publicity Office, Bob Fennell; CAST: Robert Sella (Reed) Malcolm Gets (Jason) Carrie Preston (Shelley), Nadia Dajani (Bev); (The Duke on 42nd Street) May 28–June 9, 2002

Jesse Pennington, Yvonne Woods in *Franny's Way* (Joan Marcus)

ROUNDABOUT THEATRE COMPANY

Artistic Director, Todd Haimes; Managing Director, Ellen Richard; Executive Director of External Affairs, Julia C. Levy

BLUE by Charles Randolph-Wright; Director, Sheldon Epps; Sets, James Leonard Joy; Costumes, Debra Bauer; Lights, Michael Gilliam; Sound, Kurt Eric Fischer; Music, Nona Hendryx; Lyrics, Nona Hendryx, Charles Randolph-Wright; Casting, Jeremy Rich, Pat McCorkle; Production Stage Manager, Jay Adler; Press, Boneau/Bryan-Brown, Adrian Bryan-Brown, Matt Polk, Jackie Green, Karalee Dawn, Cindy Valk; CAST: Hill Harper (Reuben Clark, adult), Chad Tucker (Reuber Clark, young), Chad Tucker (Blue Williams Jr.), Phylicia Rashad (Peggy Clark), Michael McElroy (Blue Williams), Howard W. Overshown (Sam Clark III), Messeret Stromann (LaTonya Dinkins), Randal Sheppard (Samuel Clark Jr.), Jewell Robinson (Tillie Clark); STANDBYS: Elizabeth Van Dyke; Robert Tyree; Jennifer Hunter; (Gramercy Theatre) June 28–September 23, 2001 (98 performances)

A play in two acts. The action takes place in the late 1970s in Kent, South Carolina.

Michael McElroy, Phylicia Rashad in *Blue* (Carol Rosegg)

Peter Frechette, Reg Rogers in *The Dazzle* (Joan Marcus)

SPEAKING IN TONGUES by Andrew Bovell; Director, Mark Clements; Sets, Richard Hoover; Lighting, Brian MacDevitt; Costumes, Jess Goldstein; Music and Sound, Scott Myers; Casting, Amy Christopher; Production Stage Manager, Jay Adler; Stage Manager, Leslie Lyter; Press, Boneau/Bryan-Brown, Adrian Bryan-Brown, Matt Polk, Jackie Green, Karalee Dawn, Cindy Valk; CAST: Karen Allen (Jane, Valerie), Kevin Anderson (Leon, Nick), Margaret Colin (Sonja, Sarah), Michael Gill (Pete, Neil, John); (Gramercy Theatre) November 15, 2001–January 20, 2002 (77 performances)

The action takes place in a coastal city in the United States in the present.

THE DAZZLE by Richard Greenberg; Director, David Warren; Sets, Allen Moyer; Lighting, Jeff Croiter; Choreography, Karen Azenberg; Costumes, Gregory Gale; Sound, Robert Murphy; Music, Lawrence Yurman; Casting, Amy Chrostopher and Bernard Telsey Casting; Production stage manager, Jay Adler; Press, Boneau/Bryan-Brown; CAST: Peter Frechette (Homer Collyer), Reg Rogers (Langley Collyer), Francie Swift (Milly Ashmore); (Gramercy Theatre) March 5–May 12, 2002 (80 performances)

Karen Allen, Kevin Anderson in *Speaking in Tongues* (Joan Marcus)

SECOND STAGE THEATRE

Twenty-third season

Artistic Director, Carole Rothman; Managing Director, Carol Fishman

ONCE AROUND THE CITY Book and Lyrics by Willie Reale; Music by Robert Real; Director, Mark Linn-Baker; Choreography, Jennifer Muller; Sets, Adrianne Lobel; Costumes, Paul Tazewell; Lighting, Donald Holder; Sound, Jon Weston; Music Direction and Orchestrations, Rick Fock; Music Coordinator, Seymour Red Press; Production Manager, Alexander Lyu Volckhausen; Stage Manager, Megan Schneid; Press, Richard Kornberg and Associates, Richard Kornberg, Tom D'Ambrosio; CAST: William Parry (Charlie, Brandebaine), Anna Stone (Phyllis, Eve), Peter Jay Fernandez (Luis), Patrick Garner (John), Joe Grifasi (Mario), Brandy Zarle (Elizabeth), Harry Althaus (Nicky), John Bowman (Ernie), Michael Potts (Rudy), Geoffrey Nauffts (Hank), Anne Torsiglieri (Margaret, Dolores), Michael Mandell (Bill), Michael Magee (David), Jane Bodle (Gwen), Sandra Shipley (Mrs. Merkin); July 10–22, 2001 (16 performances)

A musical in two acts.

Charlayne Woodard, Judith Light, John Glover, Marcy Harriell in *Sorrows and Rejoicings* (Bruce Davidson)

METAMORPHOSES by Mary Zimmerman; Based on the Work by Ovid; Director, Ms. Zimmerman; Sets, Daniel Ostling; Lighting, T.J. Gerckens; Costumes, Mara Blumenfeld; Sound, Andre Pluess; Composer, Willy Schwarz; Stage Manager, Brian Klevan Schneider; Production Stage Manager, Anjali Bidani; Press, Richard Kornbeg and Associates, Richard Kornberg, Tom D'Ambrosio, Don Summa; CAST: Anjali Bhimani (Myrrha and others), Raymond Fox (Midas and others), Kyle Hall (Hermes and others), Doug Hara (Phaeton and others), Felicity Jones (Aphrodite), Chris Kipiniak (Erysichthon and others), Louise Lamson (Alcyon and others), Erik Lochtefeld (Orpheus and others), Heidi Stillman (Eurydice and others), Lisa Tejero (Therapist and others); October 9–December 30, 2001 after 96 performances

Presented without intermission. Adaptation of Ovid's *Metamorphoses*; with inspiration from Rainier Maria Rilke's *Orpheus, Eurydice, Hermes*, Joseph Campbell, Carl Jung, Sigmund Freud, and James Hillman

Transferred to Broadway's The Circle in the Square Theatre on March 4, 2002

SORROWS AND REJOICINGS by Athol Fugard; Director, Mr. Fugard; Sets and Costumes, Susan Hilferty; Lighting, Dennis Parichy; Production Stage Manager, Alison Cote; Stage Manager, Amy Patricia Stern; Press, Richard Kornberg and Associates; CAST: Judith Light (Allison), Charlayne Woodard (Marta), Marcy Hariell (Rebecca), John Glover (David); February 4–March 3, 2002 (32 performances)

Presented without intermission. The action takes place in South Africa in the present.

RICKY JAY ON THE STEM Solo Performance by Ricky Jay; Director, David Mamet; Sets, Peter Larkin; Lighting, Jules Fisher, Peggy Eisenhauer; Effects, Jim Steinmeyer; Production Stage Manager, Matthew Silver; Press, Richard Kornberg and Associates; Featuring Ricky Jay; May 2–September 1, 2002 (30 performances)

John Glover, Judith Light in *Sorrows and Rejoicings* (Bruce Davidson)

YORK THEATRE COMPANY

Thirty-third season

PRODIGAL Book and Lyrics by Dean Bryant; Music, Matthew Frank; Director, James Morgan; Sets, Mr. Morgan; Lighting, Edward Pierce; Costumes, Daniel Lawson; Casting, Norman Meranus; Production Stage Manager, Scott F. Dela Cruz; Produced by York Theatre Company; Press, Keith Sherman and Associates; CAST: Christian Borle (Kane Flannery, Zach Marshall), Kerry Butler (Maddy Sinclair), Alison Fraser (Celia Flannery), David Hess (Harry Flannery), Joshua Park (Luke Flannery), Matthew Frank (Piano); (Theatre at St. Mark's) March 12–31, 2002 (24 performances)

Presented without intermission. The action takes place in Australia in the present.

ROADSIDE Book and Lyrics by Tom Jones; Music, Harvey Schmidt; Based on the Play *Roadside* by Lynn Riggs; Director and Choreographer, Drew Scott Harris; Sets, James Morgan; Lighting, MaryJo Dondlinger; Costumes, Suzy Benzinger; Orchestrations, Joseph Brent, Peter Larson; Musical Direction, John Mulcahy; Casting, Norman Meranus; Production Stage Manager, Scott F. Dela Cruz; Press, Keith Sherman and Associates, Dan Fortune; CAST: Jennifer Allen (Miz Foster), Ryan Appleby (Red Ike), G.W. Bailey (Pap Raider), Steve Barcus (Black Ike), Tom Flagg (Neb the Jailer), James Hindman (Amos K. Buzzey Hale), Julie Johnson (Hannie Raider), Jonathan Beck Reed (Texas), William Ryall (The Verdigree Marshal); MUSICIANS: John Mulcahy, conductor, piano; Joe Brent, fiddle, guitar, banjo, mandolin; Mike Kennan, bass; Barry Mitterhoff, guitar, banjo, mandolin, harmonica; (Lyric Stage Theatre at St. Peter's Church) November 29–December 23, 2001 (29 performances)

A musical in two acts. The action takes place in Oklahoma Territory in the early 1900s.

OFF-OFF-BROADWAY

Productions that opened June 1, 2001 – May 31, 2002

Liz Morton, Debrah Waller in *The Mooncalf* (Tom Bloom)

ABINGDON THEATRE COMPANY

THE MOONCALF by Elizabeth Karlin; October 24, 2001; Director, Sturgis Warner; CAST: Michael Chernus, Kit Flanagan, Liz Morton, Barbara Rosenblat, Guy Strobel, Debrah Waller

THE PARKER FAMILY CIRCUS by Jan Buttram; February 13, 2002; Director, Taylor Brooks; CAST: Lori Gardner, Rita Gardner, Debbie Jaffe, Carole Monferdi, Michael Pemberton, Brian Schany

THE ACTING COMPANY

THE TAMING OF THE SHREW by William Shakespeare; May 9, 2002; Director, Eve Shapiro

PUDD'NHEAD WILSON by Mark Twain, adapted by Charles Smith; May 15, 2002; Director, Walter Dallas; CAST: Coleman Zeigen, Roslyn Ruff, Michael Lluberes, Michael Abbott Jr., Jordan Simmons, Christen Simon, Jimmon Cole

THE ACTING SHAKESPEARE COMPANY

MEASURE FOR MEASURE by William Shakespeare; April 21, 2002; Director, Nona Shepphard; CAST: Joanna Bonaro, Tali Friedman, Anna Kepe, Demetrius Martin, Ian Bok, Alice Brickwood, Garth Hewitt, Kerri Ann Murphy, Joe Paulik, Kristin Proctor, Michael Anthony Rizzo, Benjamin Rosen, Benjamin Woodlock, Samantha Wright, Amy English, Trey Zeigler

THE ACTORS COMPANY THEATRE (TACT)

THE WALTZ OF THE TOREADORS by Jean Anouilh; October 5, 2001; Director, Alan Scott Evans; CAST: Cynthia Darlow, Francesca DiMauro, Cynthia Harris, Simon Jones, Greg McFadden, Eve Michelson, James Murtaugh, Margaret Nichols, Gregory Salata, Lyn Wright

TIME AND THE CONWAYS by J.B. Priestly; January 18, 2002; Director, Will Pomerantz; CAST: Delphi Harrington, Simon Jones, Eve Michelson, Margaret Nichols, John Plumpis, Scott Schafer, Lyn Wright, Mary Bacon, Allison Cimmet, Andrew Dolan

LOOK HOMEWARD ANGEL by Thomas Wolfe, adapted by Ketti Frings; March 8, 2002; CAST: Mary Bacon, Simon Billig, Nora Chester, Cynthia Darlow, Jack Koenig, Darrie Lawrence, James Murtaugh, Margaret Nichols, Joseph Siravo, Lyn Wright, Jamie Bennett, Ken Bolden, Paul DeBoy, Kathryn Phillip, James Prendergast, William Wise

WIDOWER'S HOUSES by George Bernard Shaw; March 8, 2002; Director, Simon Jones; CAST: Greg McFadden, Gregory Salata, Scott Schaffer, Genevieve Elam, Michael Frederic, Gretchen Michelfeld, James Prendergast

LONG ISLAND SOUND by Noël Coward; May 13, 2002; Director, Scott Allan Evans; CAST: Cynthia Darlow, Kyle Fabel, Delphi Harrington, Cynthia Harris, Simon Jones, Jack Koenig, Darrie Lawrence, Greg McFadden, James Murtaugh, Margaret Nichols, Scott Schafer, Rob Breckenridge, Suzanna Geraghty, Julie Halston, Brent Harris, Darren Kelly, Barbara Marineau, Patricia O'Connell, Patricia Randell, Charles Tuthill, Rebecca Wisocky

THE ACTOR'S PLAYGROUND

GRACE'S CURSE by Jolie Jalbert; November 4, 2001; Director, Jose Element; CAST: Heather Aldridge, Ms. Jalbert, Brook Marie Procida, Mary Holmstrom, Rob Maitner, Michael Goldfried, Cynthia Pierce

BRILLIANT TRACES by Cindy Lou Johnson; February 14, 2002; Director, Guido Venitucci; CAST: Heather Aldridge, Robert Harriell

ALTERED STAGES

SINGLE BULLET THEORY by Mike Bencivenga; April 9, 2002; Director, John McDermott

AMERICAN PLAYWRIGHTS THEATRE

CHAMPAGNE AND CAVIAR by Frances Galton; August 18, 2001; CAST: Alice Gold, Kerry Prep, Jacqueline Sydney

DISSONANT DOUBLES:
AN EVENING OF SHORT PLAYS CELEBRATING WOMEN'S HISTORY MONTH; MARCH 14, 2002
   SINCERITY written and directed by Mario Fratti

   PLACES WE'VE LIVED by Milan Stitt; Director, Richard Harden

   MIMI AND ME by Kitty Dubin; Director, Andrea Andresakis

   STAR COLLECTOR by Sally Carpenter; Director, Jeff Davolt; CAST: Emails Alexandra, Barney Fitzpatrick, Alice Gold, Clarisse Guild, Melissa Hurst, Effie Johnson, Chuck Muckle, Jeff O'Malley, Jacqueline Sydney, Louis Viola

AQUILA THEATRE COMPANY

MUCH ADO ABOUT NOTHING by William Shakespeare; June 28, 2001; Adapted and Directed by Robert Richmond; CAST: Alex Webb, Shirleyann Kaladjian, Lisa Carter, Richard Willis, Anthony Cochrane, Louis Butelli, Nathan Flower, Cameron Blair

ARCLIGHT THEATRE

HOMECOMING by Lauren Weedman; January 21, 2002; Director, Maryann Lombardi; with Ms. Weedman

BANK STREET THEATRE

EDWARD III by William Shakespeare; July 10, 2001; Director, Heather Anne McAllister and Kelly McAllister; CAST: Jessica Colley, Jamison Lee Driscoll, John Margliano, Emory Rose, Sara Thigpen, John Patrick Moore, Stacey Plaskett, Matthew Rankin

THE CONTENTS OF YOUR SUITCASE by Daphne R. Hull; Director, Donna Jean Fogel

LETTUCE SPRAY by Jim Doyle; Director, Tony Hamilton

THE FACES OF ANTS by Chay Yew; Director, James McLaughlin

WASTING TIME by Peter Mercurio; Director, John Jay Buol

AUNTIE MAYHEM by David Pumo; Director, Donna Jean Fogel

ST. ANTHONY AND THE APPENDIX by Robin Rice Lichtig; Director, James McLaughlin

F2F by Linda Eisenstein; Director, Donna Jean Fogel

REFRESHMENTS by Peter Mercurio; Director, Brenda D. Cook

NOT EXACTLY STRANGERS by Andreas J. Wrath; Director, Brenda D. Cook

STACKED: A DEVIANT DOCTORAL DISSERTATION by Lisa Haas; Director, James McLaughlin

BLOW by Chay Yew; Director, Dennis Smith

RUG STORE COWBOY by Gary Garrison; Director, Courtney A. Wendell

EVERGREEN by Amy A. Kirk; Director, Baca Lindstrom

PICK-UP TIMES by Anton Dudley; Director, Courtney A. Wendell

NEVER SAID by Kim Yawed; Director, Anton Dudley

CLASS DISMISSED by Rich Orloff; Director, Donna Jean Smith

WHITE By Chay Yew; Director, Anton Dudley

FALLING TO PIECES: THE PATSY CLINE MUSICAL Book and Lyrics by Ellis Nassour; Score, George Leonard; Director, Dan Wackerman

BREAKDOWN by Bill Bozzonen; Director, Keno Rider

IN THE GARDEN AT ST. LUKE'S by Stan Lachow; Director, Leann Walker

THE SPELLING BEE by Philip Vassallo; Director, Leann Walker

BLUE HERON THEATRE

KINGS by Christopher Logue; June 7, 2001; Director, James Milton; Cast: James Doherty, Michael Ringer

A PROPHET AMONG THEM by Wesley Brown; June 25, 2001; Director, Marie Thomas; Cast: Reggie Montgomery, Harvy Blanks, Perri Gaffney, Tom Titone, Dina Comoli, Marlon Cherry

TWO ROOMS by Lee Blessing; November 4, 2001; Director, Roger Danforth; Cast: Thomas James O'Leary, Monica Koskey, Beth Dixon, Steve Cell

THE CURE AT TROY by Seamus Heany; February 4, 2002; Director, Kevin Osborne; Cast: Jolie Garrett, Rainard Rachelle, Ian Oldaker, Sue Berch, Karla Hendrich, Margot White

BROKEN BOUGHS by Clay McCleod Chapman; March 3, 2002; Director, Charles Loffredo; Cast: Patricia Randell, Heather Grayson, Matt Tomasino, Hanna Cheek, Joe Sangillo

Harvy Banks, Perri Gaffney, Reggie Montgomery in *A Prophet Among Them* (Richard Termine)

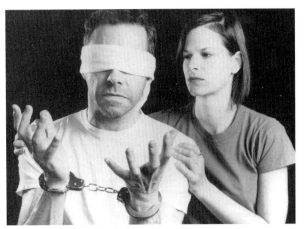

Thomas James O'Leary, Monica Koskey in *Two Rooms* (Richard Termine)

THE MOONCALF by Elizabeth Karlin; November 6, 2001; Director, Sturgis Warner; Cast: Guy Strobel, Kathy Lichter, Debrah Waller, Liz Morton, Stephen Boyer, Barbara Rosenblat

TWELVE BROTHERS by Jeffrey M. Jones and Camila Jones; Director, Page Burkeholder

RAPUNZEL by Melissa James Gibson; Director, David Levine

THE LITTLE MATCHGIRL by Lynn Nottage; Director, Daniela Varon

SNOW WHITE by Onome Ekeh; Director, Dave Simonds

LUCKY HANS by Margie Duffield; Director, Jean Wagner

HANNAH AND GRETEL by Creative Theatre Performance Team and John Istel; Director, Welker White; Cast: Amie Bermowitz, Rayme Cornell, Robert Hatcher, Tony Reilly, Christian Rummel, Jackie Sutton, Kathryn Velvel

Patricia Randell in *Broken Boughs* (Carl Sturmer)

Leo Lauer, Jeremy Koch in *Boys Life* (Karen Burger)

Jeslyn Kelly, Jeremy Koch in *Boys Life* (Karen Burger)

BROKEN WATCH PRODUCTIONS

BOYS LIFE by Howard Korder; September 10, 2001; Director, Drew DeCorleto; CAST: Leo Lauer, Andrew Hoff, Jeremy Koch, Jeslyn Kelly, Danielle Savin, Alli Steinberg, Teresa Goding

THE BUILDERS ASSOCIATION

XTRAVAGANZA Compiled and Directed by Marianne Weems; April 20, 2002; CAST: Moe Angelos, Aimee Guillot, Peter A. Jacobs, Heaven Phillips, Jeff Webster, Brahms LaFortune

CAP 21 THEATER

I LOVE MY WIFE by Book and Lyrics, Michael Stewart; Composer and Arranger, Cy Coleman; May 28, 2002; Director and Choreographer, John Znidarsic; CAST: Julie Beckham, Matt Kuehl, J. Brandon Savage, Elizabeth Shaw, Jared Stein, Spiff Weigand

CENTER STAGE

3 SISTERS LOUNGE based on *The Three Sisters* by Anton Chekov; September 6, 2001; Director, John Issendorf; CAST: Browne Smith, Becca Greene, Paula Ehrenberg, Barbara Sauerman, Steve Sherling, Roger Nasser, Jason St. Sauver, Tom Bartos, Jenny Bold

Steve Sherling, Becca Greene in *3 Sisters Lounge* (John Issenndorf)

CENTURY CENTER FOR THE PERFORMING ARTS

STAGED READINGS:

HEARTBREAK HOUSE by George Bernard Shaw; June 5, 2001; Director, Alfred Christie; Cast: Kier Dullea, Mia Dillon.

MAJOR BARBARA by George Bernard Shaw; June 6, 2001; Director, Marco Capalbo. "Mrs. Warren's Profession" by George Bernard Shaw; June 12, 2001; Director, Sue Lawless; with Tammy Grimes.

BLITHE SPIRIT by Noël Coward; June 13, 2001; Director, Alfred Christie; with Tammy Grimes.

PEER GYNT (PART I) by Henrik Ibsen; June 14, 2001; Director, Alex Lippard.

LOOK AFTER LULU by Noël Coward; Director, Steve Ramshur.

PRESENT LAUGHTER by Noël Coward; June 20, 2001; Director, Emily Hill.

PEER GYNT (PART II) by Henrik Ibsen.

LADY WINDEMERE'S FAN by Oscar Wilde; Director Alex Lippard.

SALOME by Oscar Wilde; Director, Joel Friedman.

HEDDA GABLER by Henrik Ibsen; Director, Alex Lippard; with Blake Lindsley, Blake Vogler, Barbara Haas, Nick Stannard, Maxine Prescott, Jessica Damrow, Christopher Mullern.

LITTLE EYOLF by Henrik Ibsen; Director, Steve Ramshur.

THE MASTER BUILDER by Henrik Ibsen; Director, J.C. Compton; with George Cavey, Harmony Shuttler, Padden Fallis, Dennis Parlato, Wendy Barrie-Wilson, David Jones, Tami Dixon.

JOHN GABRIEL BORKMAN by Henrik Ibsen; Director, Max Montel; with Eric Frandsen, Amber Gross, Charlotte Hampden, Richard Leighton, Cecelia Riddett, Kate Suber, Robert Thompson

CHASHAMA THEATRE

THE WITCH OF EDMONTON by William Rowley, Thomas Dekker, John Ford; November 1, 2001; Director, Rosey Hay; CAST: Susan Moses, Christiana Cobean, R. Paul Hamilton, James Hay, Daniel Huston, Patrick Lacey, Brad Lemons, Nicole Marsh, Tracey Paleo, Sonda Staley, Adam Swiderski, Anthony Vitrano, Peter Zazzali

MRS. FEURSTEIN by Murray Mednick; January 8, 2002; Director, Roxanne Rogers; CAST: Maria O'Brien, Lynnda Ferguson, Dan Ahearn, David Little, Samantha Quan, Kevin Shinick

Maria O'Brien in *Mrs. Feurstein* (Carol Rosegg)

Nada Rowand, Michael Graves in *Embers* (Carol Rosegg)

Joey Arias, Jason Scott in *Christmas with the Crawfords* (Billy Douglas)

CHELSEA PLAYHOUSE

CHRISTMAS WITH THE CRAWFORDS Created by Richard Winchester; Written by Wayne Buidens and Mark Sargent; November 20, 2001; Director, Donna Drake; CAST: Joey Arias, Connie Champagne, Trauma Flintstone, Max Grenyo, Chris March, Matthew Martin, Mr. Sargent, Jason Scott

EMBERS by Catherine Gropper; January 30, 2002; Director, Helena Webb; with Nada Rowand, Michael Graves, Kenneth Wilson-Harrington, Melissa Wolff

CHERRY LANE ALTERNATIVE

2001 MENTOR PROJECT
STRANGE ATTRACTORS by David Adjimi (Craig Lucas, mentor); June 6, 2001; Director, Richard Caliban; with Joanna P. Adler, Andrew Heckler, Michael Marisi, Adrienne Shelley

THE ALLEGORY OF PAINTING by Cybele Pascal (Marsha Norman, mentor); June 20, 2001; Director, Leigh Silverman; with Janine Barris-Gerstl, Angel Desai, Cody Nickel, Caitlin Gibbon, Tony Hoty, Jerusha Klemperer, John Leone, Annie McAdams, Michael T. Ringer, Garrett Savage

SPECIAL PROJECT
SIXTY MINUTES IN NEGROLAND Written and Performed by Margot Jefferson

YOUNG PLAYWRIGHTS FESTIVAL 2001
JOHNNY LIKABOOT KILLS HIS FATHER by Yelena Elkind; Director, Richard Caliban; with Michael Mosley, Steven Hauck, Cynthia Hood

CONFERENCE TIME by Jeb G. Havens; Director, Padraic Lillis; with Michael Mosley, Brad Malow, Ann Hu, Geoffrey Molloy, Sarah Bragin

GORGEOUS RAPTORS by Lucy Alibar-Harrison; Director, Beth Miles; with Geoffrey Molloy, Shannon Emerick, Sarah Bragin, Cynthia Hood, Anne Hu, Steven Hauck, Robin L. Taylor

NURSERY by Julia Jarcho; Director, Brett Reynolds; with Cynthia Hood, Shannon Emerick, Geoffrey Malloy, Brad Malow, Robin L. Taylor

BLACK HISTORY MONTH
PICKLING by Suzan-Lori Parks; Director, Allison Eve Bell; with Jaye Austin-Williams

HARRIET'S RETURN by Karen Jones-Meadows; Director, Saundra McClain; with Denise Burse-Fernandez

WOMEN'S HISTORY MONTH
FUENTE by Cusi Cram; Director, Shilarna Stokes; with Vanessa Aspillaga, Sanjiv Jhaveri, James Martin, Nathan Perez

ETHEL ROSENBERG by Lu Hauser; Director, Joan Micklin Silver

2002 MENTOR PROJECT
OUT OF STERNO by Deborah Zoe Laufer (Marsha Norman, mentor) April 2, 2002; Director, Eleanor Reissa; with Charles Borland, Dale Carman, Debbie Gravitte, Emily Loesser

99 HISTORIES by Julia Cho (David Henry Hwang, mentor) April 23, 2002; Director, Maria Mileaf; with Elaina Erika Davis, Joel de la Fuente, Ann Hu, Mia Katigbak, Darren Pettie, Mia Tagano

SIXTEEN WOUNDED by Eliam Kraiem (Michael Weller, mentor); Director, Matt August; with Mia Barron, Jane Burd, Edward Hajj, Dylan Dawson, Jonathan Hova, Jim Mole, Martin Rayner, Chime Serra, John Phillips

CLASSICAL THEATRE OF HARLEM

HAMLET by William Shakespeare; July 27, 2001; Director, Alfred Preisser; with J. Kyle Manzay, Quonta Shanell Beasley, Arthur French, Brian Homer, Damon Kinard, Rome Neal, Adam Wade, Lanette Ware

NATIVE SON by Richard Wright; Adapted and Directed by Christopher McElroen; with Johnnie May, Ben Rivers, Jim Ganser, Arlene Nadel, Sulai Lopez, Dana Watkins, Robert Heller, Damien Smith, George C. Hosmer

MEDEA by Euripides; Adapted by Alfred Preisser; Director, Mr. Preisser; with Arthur French, April Thompson

CLEMENTE SOTO VELEZ CULTURAL CENTER

THE FOUR LITTLE GIRLS by Pablo Picasso; October 17, 2001; Directors, R. Michael Blanco, Carol Blanco; with Joan Luno, Mary Murphy, Ms. Blanco, Kathryn Gayner

ANNA BELLA EEMA by Lisa D'Amour; September 30, 2001; Director, Katie Pearl

MIDNIGHT BRAINWASH REVIVAL by Kirk Wood Bromley; Director, Joshua Spafford

THE BOMB by Josh Fox; February 28, 2002; Director, Mr. Fox; with Sophie Amieva, Gina Hirsch, Peter Lettre, Patrick McCaffrey, Aya Ogawa, Robert Saietta, Aaron Mostkoff

SOON MY WORK by Josh Fox; Director, Mr. Fox; with Jason Fisher, Patrick McCaffrey, Alex Fox, Joe Sanchez

ICARUS AND ARTIST by Kirk Wood Bromley; Director, Joshua Spafford

CONNELLY THEATRE

CHEKOV NOW FESTIVAL: NOVEMBER 2001–FEBRUARY 2002
  UNCLE VANYA Director, Cynthia Croot; with C. Andrew Bauer, Margot Ebeling, Ed Jewett, Harriet Koppel, John Lenartz, Gail Neil, April Sweeny, Gary Wilmes

  AUNT VANYA Director, David Karl Lee; with Zoe Jenkin, C.S. Lee, Debra Ann Byrd, T.L. Lee, Alan Nebelthau, Amanda Allen, Craig Schoenbaum, Veronika Duka, Sondra Gorney, Eric Michael Kockmer

  BLOODY POETRY by Howard Brenton; Director, David Travis

  OUR TOWN by Thornton Wilder; Director, Jack Cummings III; with Barbara Andres, Tom Ligon, Emma Orelove, Jeff Edgerton, Robyn Hussa, Mark Ledbetter, Joanna Lee, Richard Martin, Matt Nowosielski, Carl Palmer, Monica Russell, Julie Siefkes, Jonathan Uffelman, James Weber, John Wellmann, Chuck Wilson, Matt Yaeger, Van Zeiler

CULTURE CLUB

BIRDY'S BACHELORETTE PARTY by Mark Nassar with Suzanna Melendez; May 17, 2002; Director, Ms. Melendez; with Maria Barrata, Wass Stevens, Melissa Short, Jamie Sorrentini, Alice Moore, Michael Gargani, Frank Rempe, Ms. Fennel, Christopher Campbell Scott Bilecky, Reed Hutchins

CURRICAN THEATRE

SEX AND OTHER COLLISIONS by Trista Baldwin; June 7, 2001; Director, Nela Wagman; with Sarah Buff, Whitney Buss, Anna Cody, Joe Fuer, Peter Humer, Matt Neely, Mike Szeles

THE DIRECTORS COMPANY

KILT by Jonathan Wilson; April 10, 2002; Director, Jack Hofsiss; with Chris Payne Gilbert, Tovah Feldshuh, Herb Foster, Jamie Harris, Kathleen Doyle

DIXON PLACE

THE MOON IN VAIN inspired by Anton Chekov's *The Seagull*; Director, Lee Gundersheimer; with Rae Wright, Ethan Cohen

UPPA CREEK by Keli Garrett; Director, Dominic Taylor; with Ms. Garrett, Amy Fellers, Yvonne Jung, Bradford Olson, Kaipo Schwab, Ron Riley, Rodney Owens, Gwen Mulumba

FIVE 'TIL by Edwin Lee Gibson; Director, Daphne Richards; with Mr. Gibson, Robert Blumenthal, Lynnard Williams, Terrence Williams, Amatusami Kari, Keisha Spraggin

ROSA by George Emilio Sanchez; Directed and Performed by Mr. Sanchez

SOPPIN' JUICE by Mark Holt; Director James Busby; with Coby Koehl, Ken Kincaid

DOUGLAS FAIRBANKS THEATRE

MR. PRESIDENT Book, Howard Lindsay and Russell Crouse; Music and Lyrics, Irving Berlin; Adaptation, Gerard Alessandrini; August 2, 2002; Directed and Musical Staging by John Znidarsic and Mr. Alessandrini; with Jono Mainelli, Clif Thorn, Michael West, Amanda Naughton, Whitney Allen, Eric Jordan Young, Stuart Zagnit

Michael Ryan, Matthew Maguire in *Nighttown* (Steve Kahn)

EDGE THEATRE COMPANY

LIFE IS A DREAM by Pedro Calderon de la Barca; January 31, 2002; Director, Paul Zablocki; with Sturgis Adams, Andrew Grusetkie, Guiseppe Jones, Andres Munar, Dustin Tucker, Kathryn Zamora-Benson, Arthur Aulisi, Jenn Harris, Omar Metwally, Ben Schenkkan, Aliza Waksal

FLATIRON THEATRE

NOT IN FRONT OF THE BABY by Stephen Gaydos; April 8, 2002; Director, Paul Zablocki; with Joe Fuer, Jeremy Peter Johnson, Rana Kazkaz, Jenna Kalinowski, Kelly McAndrew, Matt Neely, Jeannie Noth, Christopher Swift

THE FLEA THEATRE

NO MOTHER TO GUIDE HER by Lillian Mortimer; August 23, 2001; Director, Jim Simpson; with Joe Holt, Leila Howland, Jennifer McKenna, Cori Clark Nelson, Beth Tapper, Sam Marks, Dean Strange

AJAX (POR NOBODY) by Alice Tuan; Director, Jim Simpson; with Joanie Ellen, Sam Marka, Alfredo Narcisco, Kristin Stewart, Sioban Towey

THE GUYS by Anne Nelson; Director, Jim Simpson; with Bill Murray, Sigourney Weaver

NIGHTTOWN by Susan Moskaowski; Director, Ms. Moskaowski; with Matthew Maguire, Michael Ryan

45th ST. THEATRE

A MAGIC PLACE IN A NEW TIME by Robert Lesser; Director, Robert Armin; with Susan Gordon, Kaitlin O'Neal, Dean Fiore, Michael Karp, Celia Howard, John O'Creagh, Chuck Ardezzone, Eloise Iliff, George Santana

THE NINTH CIRCLE by Edward Musto; March 26–April 6, 2002; Director, Tom Herman; Sets, Rick Juliano; Costumes, Antonio Villarreal; Lighting, Michael Abrams; Sound, Mark Cannistraro; Stage Manager, Wendy Patten; Presented by CreZZle Productions; CAST: Gene Forman (Tom), Andrea Maybaum (Alley), Ann Rutter (Jane), Whalen J. Laurence (Bartender, Projectionist, Policeman, Ian), Heidi James (Lara), Rick Lawrence (Marvin, Curtis), John D. McNally (Hite), Darren Kelly (Upton), Sarah Schoenberg (Stevens, Baby, Doctor), Stephen Innocenzi (Score), Jay Greenberg (Jo-Jo), Rodrigo Lopresti (Julio), Beth Beyer (Catherine)

Dean Fiore, Kaitlin O'Neal in *A Magic Place in a New Time* (Steven Mosher)

45 BLEEKER

THREE DARK TALES by Theatre O.; Director, Joseph Alford; with Mr. Alford, Sarah Coxon, Lucien MacDougall, Carolina Valdes

MEASURE FOR MEASURE by William Shakespeare; Director, Nona Shepphard, with Joanna Bonaro, Tali Freedman, Anna Kepe, Demetrius Martin, Ian Bok, Alice Brickwood, Garth Hewitt, Kerri Ann Murphy, Joe Paulik, Kristin Proctor, Michael Anthony Rizzo

FOUNDRY THEATRE

TALK by Carl Hancock; Director, Marion McClinton; with Karen Kandel, Maria Tucci, Reg E. Cathey, James Himelsbach, Anthony Mackie, John Seitz

GENE FRANKEL THEATRE

SANTA CLAUS IS COMING OUT by Jeffrey Solomon; Director, Emily Weiner; with Mr. Solomon

UNEQUILIBRIUM by Alexander Lyrus and Robert McCaskill; Director, Mr. McCaskill; with Mr. McCaskill, Mr. Lyrus

GORILLA REPERTORY THEATRE

OTHELLO by William Shakespeare; Director, Christopher Carter Anderson; with John Roque, Joel de la Fuente, Mel Duane Gionson, Andrew Pang, Joshua Spafford, James Saito, Ariel Estrada, Tina Horti, Joel Carino, Tess Lina, Jennifer Kato

CYMBELINE by William Shakespeare; Director, Christopher Carter Anderson; with Michael Colby Jones, Katherine Gooch, Tim Moore, Rohana Kenin, Tom Staggs, Brian O'Sullivan, Sean Elias Reyes, Greg Petroff

UBU IS KING! by Alfred Jarry; Adaptation, Christopher Carter Anderson; Director, Mr. Anderson

A MIDSUMMER NIGHT'S DREAM by William Shakespeare

THE DEATH OF KING ARTHUR by Matthew Freeman; Director, Christopher Carter Anderson; with Sean Elias Reyes, Sarah Dandridge, Michael Colby Jones, Tom Staggs, Aubrey Chamberlain, Tim Moore, Rohana Kenin

GREENWICH STREET THEATRE

SOME VOICES by Joe Penhall; Director, Kevin Kittle; with Victor Villar-Hauser, Patrick Tull, Mike Finesilver, David Costelloe, Laoisa Sexton

SCAB by Sheila Callaghan; Director, Hayley Finn; with Shannon Burkett, Sasha Eden, David Wheir, Anne Carney, Flora Diaz

THE DOCTOR OF ROME by Nat Colley; Director, Ralph Carhart

THE MERCHANT OF VENICE by William Shakespeare; Director, Ralph Carhart; with Susan Hyon, Derek Johnsen, Juliet King, Rob Langeder, Brian Linden, Lanie MacEwan, Michael Mendelson, Lawrence Merritt, Matthew Pendergast, John Peterson, Miles Phillips, Dara Seitzman, Lou Tally, Franklin John Westbrooks

SYNDROME by Kirk Wood Bromley; Concept, Joshua Lewis Berg; Director, Rob Urbinati; with Joshua Lewis Berg

GROVE STREET PLAYHOUSE

HELLO HERMAN by John Buffalo Mailer; Director, Thomas Kail; with Jim Isler, John Newman, Nafeesa Monroe, Christina Pabst, Jonathan Mosley, Kady Duffy, Peter Cambor, Alexis Raben, Bob LaVelle, Neil Stewart, Anthony Veneziale, Sidney Williams

HENRY STREET SETTLEMENT

DEAD END by Sidney Kingsley; Director, David Gaard

THE HAPPY JOURNEY by Thornton Wilder; Director, Seth Sharp

AND WHERE WAS PANCHO VILLA WHEN YOU REALLY NEEDED HIM? By Silviana Wood; Director, Alexandra Lopez

URBAN TRANSITION: LOOSE BLOSSOMS by Ron Milner; Director, Woodie King Jr.; with Jerome Preston Bates; Chadwick Boseman, Joseph Edward, Diane Kirksey, Sade Lythcott, George Newton, Monica Soyemi

HERE ARTS CENTER

U.S. DRAG by Gina Giofriddo; Director, Pam McKinnon; with Ian Helfer, Effie Johnson, Vin Knight, Meg McCary, Annie McNamara, Maria Striar, Erich Strom, Mather Zickel

WOMAN KILLER by Chiori Miyagawa; Director, Sonoko Kawahara; with Krispin Freeman

THE BLAKKHAI by Euripides; Director, Rene Migliaccio; with Dana Marie Abbatiello, Noelle Adamoschek, Maya Alexander, Suzanne Aptman, Cecelia Biagini, Vanessa Eichler, Bertie Ferdman, Cheryl Fidelman, Jay Gaussoin, Rob Grace

TIMESLIPS by Anne Basting; Director, Christopher Bayes; with Hope Clarke, John Freimann, Jodie Lynne McClintock, Michael Shelle, Sheridan Thomas, Judith Van Buren

THE STAR PLAY by Michael Arthur; Director, Sonet Blanton; with Lisa Hargus, Rebekkah Ross, Janelle Schremmer, Troy Shcremmer

NOVEL by Nick Belitto; Director, Lorca Peress

CONFESSIONS OF A RELUCTANT BUDDHA by Daniel Levy

DESK by Aaron Landsman; Directed and Performed by Mr. Landsman

JUST LIKE A MAN by Fernando Maneca; Director, Mr. Maneca; Featuring Mr. Maneca

MARGARET by Damon Kiley/Real Time Theatre

THE DON QUIXOTE PROJECT by Peculiar Works Project

STARS OF THE SWEET DECLINE by Paul Warner Performance Group

COMEDIAN FROM A CRUMBLING EMPIRE by Kristin Page Stuart

RADIO WONDERLAND by Joshua Frid

Peter Reznikoff, Gena Bardwell, Michael Citriniti in *Novel* (MultiStages)

Mather Zickle, Maria Striar in *U.S. Drag* (Frank Ouderman)

SUITE DEVO by Created and Performed by Troika Ranch

THE UNHIDDEN AND UNHINGED by Aviva Geisman/Drastic Action

PSYCHOTHERAPY LIVE! by Lisa Levy; Featuring Ms. Levy

LAPIS BLUE, BLOOD RED by Cathy Caplan; Director, Paul Smithyman; with Natalie Arkus, Erica Berg, Peter Blomquist, Michael Dempsey, Meg Gibson, Dustin Smith, Scott Sowers, C.J. Wilson, Chandler Vinton

FANATICS Created and Performed by Ellen Beckerman & Company; Director, Ms. Beckerman

CALABI-YAU by Susanna Spier; Director, Tony Torn; with Michael Craskin, Hai Ting Chinn, John S. Hall, Rob Grace, James Urbaniak

DEAD TECH, based on Henrik Ibsen's *The Master Builder*; by Kristin Marting and Celise Kalk; Director, Ms. Marting; with Dmetrius Conley-Williams, Daphne Gaines, Trey Lyford, Holly Twining, Richard Toth, Zishan Urguria

HATCHED based on Angela Carter's *Nights at the Circus*, Director, Richard Crawford

AND THEN YOU GO ON by Bob Jaffee; Director, Peter Wallace

LIFE DURING WARTIME by Dominic Orlando; Director, Karin Bowersock; with Mark Leydorf, Carla Tessara, Kimberly Jay Thomas, Gerald Marsini, Darius Stone

THE RIGHT WAY TO SUE by Ellen Melaver; Director, Anne Kauffman; with Kelly AuCoin, Stepahnie Brooke, Robert English, T.R. Knight, Caitlin Miller, Jennifer Morris

SELF DEFENSE by Carson Kretizer; Director, Randy White; with Lynne McCollough, Carolyn Baeumler, Stephen Bradbury, Carolyn DeMerice, Dan Illian, Dee Pelletier, Melle Powers, Mark Zeisler

HUDSON GUILD THEATRE

A COMEDY OF EROS by Paul Firestone; Director, Harlan Meltzer; with Jordan Charney, Joan Copeland, Andrea Leigh, Paul Romero, Jennifer Dorr White, Travis Wood

ILLYRIA based on William Shakespeare's *Twelfth Night*; Music by Peter Mills; with Ames Adamson, Rich Affannato, Kate McKenzie, Kate Bradner, Matthew Alexander, Sarah Corey, Arik Luck, Jason Mills, Leon Land Gersing, Courter Simmons

IMMIGRANTS' THEATRE PROJECT

CRACKING MUD IS PINCHING ME by Haya Husseini; Director, Marcy Arlin

THE BERMUDA TRIANGLE by Nora Amin; Director, Lucinda Kidder

THE BLACK-EYED by Betty Shamieh; Director, Hayley Finn

THE BOAT PEOPLE by Nashed Nayla Naguib; Director, Kiebpoli Calnek

AHAGA by Torange Yeghiazarian

PORTRAIT OF A MARRIAGE by Fatma Durmush; Director, Shilarna Stokes

EDEWEDE by Juliana Okah; Director, Bridgit Evans

LULU LOLO TAKES HER HAT OFF TO THE FAIR SEX—UNFAIR VICTIMS Written and Performed by Lulu Lolo

THE INDEPENDENT THEATRE

SEX, DRUGS, ROCK & ROLL by Eric Bogosian; Director, Jason Summers; with Luis-Daniel Morales

INNOCENT THEATRE

THE VORTEX by Noël Coward; Director, Trip Cullman; with Nick Merritt, Dean Nolen, Alexandra Oliver, Tessa Auberjonois, Kathryn Gracey, Louis Cancelmi, James Kaliardos, Andrew Schulman, Elisabeth Waterson

Joan Copeland, Andrea Leigh in *A Comedy of Eros* (Carol Rosegg)

INSIDE ARTS

DRINKS BEFORE DINNER by E.L. Doctorow; Director, Darcelle Marta; with Todd Bazzini, Karin Bowersock, David Palmer Brown, Bethany Caputo, Nancy Collins, DeeDee Friedman, Sean Geoghan, Gerald Marsini, Gabriella Tapcov, Veronica Venture

IRISH ARTS CENTER

THE REVENGE TOUR with Niall Tobin

THE KINGS OF THE KILBURN HIGH ROAD by Jimmy Murphy; Director, Jim Nolan; with Sean Lawlor, Eamonn Hunt, Brendon Conroy, Noel O'Donovan, Frank O'Sullivan

JOHN HOUSEMAN THEATRE

GOOD TIME BLUES Concept and Direction, Eric Krebs; with Genovis Albright, Madame Pat Tandy

Barry Kaplan in *A Gilbert and Sullivan Christmas Carol* (James McNicholas)

JOHN MONTGOMERY THEATRE COMPANY

SEX ED by Suzanne Bachner; Director, Trish Minskoff; with John Houfe, Alex McCord, Danny Wiseman

CIRCLE by Suzanne Bachner; Director, Trish Minskoff; with Bob Celli, Judy Charles, Thaddeus Daniels, Felicia Scarangello, Judy Charles, Danny Wiseman

JOSE QUINTERO THEATRE

A GILBERT & SULLIVAN CHRISTMAS CAROL based on Charles Dickens' *A Christmas Carol*; Book and Lyrics, Gayden Wren; Music, Arthur Sullivan; Director, Mr. Wren; with Jonathan Baldwin, Hayley Chapple, Jonathan Demar, Kenneth Finegan, Kenneth Gartman, Hannah Hammel, Barry Kaplan, Cecily Kate, Jim Luddy, Kaia Monroe, Jermel Nakia, Matthew Nelson, Robert Charles Rhodes, Jill Skivington, Heather Thompson

THE SUICIDE BOMBER by Tuvia Tenebom; Director, Mr. Tenebom; with Lameese Isaaq, James Sears, Run Shayo, David Sitler

TAPE by Stephen Belber; Director, Geoffrey Nauffts

DAMIEN by Aldyth Morris; Director, Peter John Cameron; with Dominic Fumusa, Josh Stamberg, Alison West

CLOUD NINE by Caryl Churchill; Director, Mina Hartong; with Sam Hurlbut, Frances Anderson, Jason Woodruff, Elissa Lash, Jamie Watkins

RICHARD III, HENRY IV, PARTS I & II by William Shakespeare; Director; Joanne Zipay and Ivanna Cullinan; with Leese Wlaker, Jane Titus, Laurie Bannister-Colon, Sheridan Thomas, Lea Franklin, Vicki Hirsch, Vince Gatton, Bill Galarno, David Huber, Peter Zazzali, Rachel O'Neill, Claudia Peyton, Vanessa Elder, Kevin Till, Richard Kass, Christopher Bell, David Godbey, Jennifer Jonassen

RIVA COMPANY

MARISOL by Jose Rivera; Director, Melissa Boxwell; with Ariel Brooke, Tracey Renee Mathis, Emily Parker, Jessica Ramirez-Turner, Brian Turner, Brain Sacca, Hilary Ward

KRAINE THEATRE

MANAGERS by Kevin Mandel; Director, Lily Warren; Jennifer Carta, Steve Cell, Norma Fire, Benim Foster, Kelly Overton, Mandy Steckelberg, Dustin Tucker

LABYRINTH THEATRE COMPANY

WHERE'S MY MONEY? by John Patrick Shanley; Director, Mr. Shanley; with David Deblinger, Yetta Gottesman, Florencia Lozano, Chris McGarry, John Ortiz, Paula Pizzi

A WINTER PARTY by John Patrick Shanley; Director, John Gould Rubin; with the company

AUGUST IS A THIN GIRL by Julie Marie Myatt; Director, Joe Salvatore

MÉMOIRE by Tomoko Miyagi; Director, John Gould Rubin

LIKE IT WAS YESTERDAY by Daniel Harnett; Director, David Anzuelo

HOW TO CATCH A MONKEY by Michael Puzzo; Director, Chris McGarry

HARLEM AIN'T NUTTIN' BUT A WORD by Russell Jones; Director, Beresford Bennett

F*ING LOVE** by Justin Reinsilber

CULTURE BANDIT by Written and Performed by Vanessa Hidary; Director, Mariana Hellmund

DARWAZA by Written and Performed by Ajay Naidu; Director, David Anzuelo

MANHATTAN ENSEMBLE THEATRE

THE CASTLE by Franz Kafka; Director, Scott Schwartz; Adapted by David Fishelson; with William Atherton, E.J. Carroll, Catherine Curtin, Mireille Enos, Gina Farrell, Sean McCourt, Jim Parsons, Steven Rosen, Raynor Scheine, Grant James Varjas, Dan Zizski

THE GOLEM by H. Leivick; Director, Lawrence Sacharow; Adapted by David Fishelson; with Michael Milligan, Joseph McKenna, Robert Prosky, David Little, Jeff Ware, Ian Pfister, Steven Rosen, David Heuvelman, Ben Hammer, Brandon Demery, Lynn Cohen, Norma Fire, Stuart Rudin, Rosemary Garrison

MAVERICK THEATRE

I SING! by Eli Bolin, Sam Forman, Benjamin Salka; Director, Mr. Salka; with Billy Eichner, Jeff Juday, Jodie Langel, Michael Raine, Meredith Zeitlin

COLORED CONTRADICTIONS by Danny Boyd Beaty; Director, Leonora Pace

MA-YI THEATRE COMPANY

WATCHER by Han Ong; Director, Loy Arcenas; with Mia Katigbak, Marty Zentz, Orlando Pabotoy, Gilbert Cruz, Virginia Wing, Jojo Gonzalez, Anthony Ruivivar, Ching Valdes-Aran, Harvey Perr

THE SQUARE by Bridget Carpenter, Ping Chong, Constance Congdon, Kia Corthron, Maria Irene Fornes, Phillip Kan Gotanda, Jessica Hagedorn, David Henry Hwang, Craig Lucas, Robert O'Hara, Han Ong, Jose Rivera, Diana Son, Alice Tuan, Mac Wellman, Chay Yew; Director, Lisa Peterson; with David Wilson Barnes, Joel de la Fuente, Saidah Arrika Ekulona, Michael Ray Escamilla, Fiona Gallagher, Wai Ching Ho, Ken Leung, Hamish Linklater, Ching Valdes-Aran, Henry Yuk, Janet Zarish

MCGINN/CAZALLE THEATRE

KEY WEST by Dan O'Brien; Director, Daniel Gerroll

MONSIEUR AND THE FLOWERS OF THE KORAN by Eric Emmanual Schmitt; Director, Maria Mileaf

THE BREAD OF WINTER by Victor Lodato; Director, Loy Arcenas

SMASHING by Brook Berman; Director, Michael John Garcés

NO. 11 (BLUE & WHITE) by Alexandra Cunningham; Director, David Aukin with Hilary Edson, Liza Lapira, Arthur McDonald, Shauna Miles, Nell Mooney, Armando Reisco, Joey Shea, Robin Taylor, Katie Walder

MISS EVERS' BOYS by David Feldshuh; Director, Kent Gash; with Adrians Lenox, Daryl Edwards, Byron Easley, Chad Coleman, Helmar Augustus Cooper, J. Paul Boehmer, Terry Alexander

IN THE ABSENCE OF SPRING by Joe Calarco; Director, Mr. Calarco; with Sophie Hayden, Jason Trevor Oswalt, Gene Farber, Lizzy Cooper Davis, Minda Harden, Michelle Federer, Chris Stack

Catherine Wolf, Anne Jackson, Kim Hunter in *The Madwoman of Chaillot*
(David Rodgers)

METROPOLITAN PLAYHOUSE

THE WOMEN by William C. DeMille; Adaptation, David Zarko; Director, Mr. Zarkin; Kristen Stewart, Russell Hamilton, David Heckel, Leo Bertelsen, Annette Previti, Tod Mason, Tom Staggs, Sam Kitchin, Ken Bolden, Mike Nowak

OEDIPUS REX by Sophocles; Director, Ian Marshall; with Andy Stewart-Jones, Matt Daniels, Casey Grove

SALEM Written and Directed by Alex Roe; with David Carson, DeBanne Brown

THE FAITH HEALER by William Vaughn Moody; Director, Keith Oncale; with Henry Afro-Bradley, Roy Bacon, Scott Barrow, Katherine Brecka, Darra Herman, Michael Karp, Tod Mason, Colleen Russell, Jenni Tooley, Susan Willerman

DON JUAN by Molière; Director, Alex Roe; with Tom Staggs, George Sheffey, Stephanie Dorian, Sean Dill, Stephanie Cervellino

MOONWORK THEATRE

JULIUS CAESAR by William Shakespeare; Director, Gregory Wolfe

VOICES FROM THE HILL Adaptation from *Spoon River Anthology*; Director, Gregory Wolfe; Music, Andrew Sherman; with Mason Pettit, Aloysius Gigl, Lynn Eldredge, Elizabeth Zins, Noel Velez, Jeannie Goodman, Victoria Adams, Christopher Yates

NEIGHBORHOOD PLAYHOUSE

THE MADWOMAN OF CHAILLOT by Jean Giraudoux; Director, Roy Steinberg; with Anne Jackson, Kim Hunter, Alvin Epstein, Roger Serbagi, Ben Hammer, Catherine Wolf, Sloane Shelton

NUYORICAN POETS CAFÉ

SHOWING OUT by Timothy Reed; Director, Rome Neal; with Christiana Blain, Cassandra Hume, Michael A. Jones, Nikki Bell, Letha Rose, Jaymie Garner, Maxx

NEW DIRECTORS THEATRE

RANDOM HARVEST by Richard Willet; Director, Elizabeth Beckwith; with Patricia Randell, Ann Talman, Patrick Welsh, Kate Downing, Jay Alvarez, Jonathan Kandel

NEW DRAMATISTS

An organization devoted exclusively to playwrights; facilities available to members for private readings and open, script-in-hand readings. Artistic director, Todd London; Director of Administration and finance, Joel Ruark; Executive director, Paul A. Slee; Readings Open to the Public:

GOODBYE MY ISLAND by Deborah Brevoort; June 1, 2001; Composed by David Friedman; CAST: Chuck Cooper, Merwin Foard, James Fall, Peter Cormican, Allison Fischer, Eleanor Glockner, Virginia Ann Woodruff, Luisa Tedoff, Joan Barber, Lilli Cooper, Shelby Wong, Chris Valiando

UMKOVU by Eisa Davis; June 6, 2001; Director, Michael John Garcés; CAST: Rob Campbell, Laura Flanagan, Bertrand Wang, J. Kyle Manzay, Nilaja Sun, Michole White, Joe Latimore, Reyes Escamilla

ROAR by Betty Shamieh; June 7, 2001; Director, Emily Morse; CAST: Yusef Bulos, Dariush Kashani, Liza Lapira, Sabrina Le Beauf, Shaheen Vaaz, Lindsay Soson

KEEPERS by J. Holtham; June 8, 2001; Director, Tom Rowan; CAST: Mandy Seigfried, Chris Messina, Anthony Mackie, Nancy Wu

WHEATLEY by Lonnie Carter; June 11, 2001; Director, Sharon Scruggs; CAST: Mr. Carter, Matthew Korahais, Jill Kotler, Oni Faida Lampley, April Matthis, Forrest McClendon, Michael Rodgers

BIRTHMARKS by Sarah Treem; June 12, 2001; Director, Kirsten Kelly; CAST: Lynn Cohen, John Daggett, Addie Johnson, Maria Thayer

IN THE PIGEON HOUSE by Honour Kane; June 14, 2001; CAST: Ms. Kane, Elizabeth Whyte, Paul Vincent Black, Caroline Winterson

SPOTLIGHT ON A GIRL by Cnadice Baugh; June 15, 2001; Director, Linsay Firman

IF HE CHANGED MY NAME by Edgar Nkosi White; June 20, 2001; Director, Walter Jones; CAST: Waliek Crandall, Glenda Dixon, Fryday, Amy Leonard, Bobbi Owens, Andrew Platner, Lisa White, Paul J. Winston

SLOW FAST WALKING ON THE RED EYE by Caridad Svich; June 21, 2001; Director, Rebecca Brown; CAST: Carla Harting, Bryant Richards, Todd Cerveris, Gretchen Lee Krich, Carolina McNeely

TRANSMISSION 0500 / TO THE BLUE PENINSULA by Caridad Svich; September 19, 2001; Director, Anne Kauffman; CAST: Michael Bakkensen, Carla Harting, Jonathan Tindle, Nina Hellman, Michael McCartney, Jennifer Morris

DOG ACT by Liz Duffy Adams; October 1, 2001; Director, Rebecca Patterson; CAST: Keith Davis, Isabel Keating, Sarah Lord, Erica Schaeffer (stage directions), Myra Lucretia Taylor, Jonathan Trindle, Rufus Tureen

(900) by Zakiyyah Alexander; October 4, 2001; Director, Seret Scott; CAST: Eric Martin Brown, Caroline S. Clay, Donna Duplantier, Gretchen Lee Krich, Curtis McClarin, Angela Pietropinto, Randy Reyes, Shaheen Vaaz

I'D GO TO HEAVEN IF I WERE GOOD by Carole Thompson; October 10, 2001; Director, Ben Harney; CAST: Nathan Dyer, Yvonne Facey, Amaris Harney, Robin Johnson, Devry Robinson, Pawnee Sills

BIOGRAPHY by Don Wollner; October 11, 2001; Director, Mr. Wollner; CAST: Reed Birney, Joel Colodner, Cidele Curo

SALT by Peta Murray; October 15, 2001; Director, Debbie Saivitz; CAST: Paul Vincent Black, Judith Roberts, Kate Skinner

THE WOMEN OF LOCKERBIE by Deborah Brevoort; October 22, 2001; Director, Ms. Brevoort; CAST: Traber Burns, Kathleen Chalfant, Lynn Cohen, Jurian Hughes, Patrick Husted, Angela Pietropinto, Judith Roberts, Erica Sheffer

DON'T PROMISE by Silvia Gonzales; Director, Kim Rubenstein; CAST: Laura Flanagan, Gary Brownlee, Jilian Crane, Patrick Brinker, Ron Riley, Jay Edwards, Autumn Dornfeld, Welker White

EAST OF THE SUN AND WEST OF THE MOON: THE LOVE SONG FOR LANGSTON HUGHES by Edgar Nkosi White; October 24, 2001; Director, Dana Manno; CAST: Eric McLendon, Brenda Thomas, Arthur French, Abba Elethea, Gabriel Walsh, Lazaro Perez, Mike Smith, Chenana Manno, Von Jacobs, David Salvesdrive, Sean Schulich, Herman Chavez, Jezebel Montero, Aleta LaFarge, Jim Moody, Marcia McBroom

LORCA IN A GREEN DRESS by Nilo Cruz; October 25, 2001; Director, Mr. Cruz; CAST: George de la Pena, Isabel Keating, David Zayas, Carlos Orizondo, Mercedes Herrero, Simeon Moore, Gary Perez, La Conja

THE POET'S HOUR by Dmitry Lipkin; October 29, 2001; Director, Mark Brokaw; CAST: Helen Stenborg, Leslie Ayvazian, Tom Mardirosian, Thomas Schall, Meg Gibson, Irma St. Paule, Larry Bryggman, Kelly Hutchinson

SMITH AND BROWN by Carlyle Brown; October 30, 2001; Director, Mr. Brown; CAST: Louise Smith, Keith Davis, Melinda Wade

EL GRITO DEL BRONX by Migdalia Cruz; November 2, 2001; Director, Michael John Garcés; CAST: David Anzuelo, Carlos Molina, Amarelys Perez, Priscilla Lopez, Zabryna Guevara, Michael Ray Escamilla, Akili Prince

THE SUNGATHERERS by Tim Acito; November 15, 2001; Director, David Levine; CAST: Laila Robins, George de la Pena, Jim True Frost, Jodie Markell, David Turner, Nicole Alifante, Jeremy Shamos

JUSTICE by Herman Daniel Farrell III; November 15, 2001; Director, Seret Scott; CAST: Marissa Matrone, Jillian Crane, Eunice Wong, Myra Lucretia Taylor, Charles Randall, Ian August, Armando Riesco, Ari Edelson, Irma St. Paule

2B4U by Mark Druck; November 27, 2001; Director, Mr. Druck; CAST: Jay Stuart, Betty Miller, Polly Lee, Canan Erguder, Susan McCallum, Shade Vaughn, Howard Ross

ARRIVALS AND DEPARTURES by Rogelio Martinez; December 4, 2001; Director, David Levine; CAST: Florencia Lozano, Tony Gillan, John Ortiz

THE WOUNDED BODY by Bruce Walsh; December 4, 2001; Director, Christopher Damonte; CAST: Billie Roe, Jerry Zellers, Sarah Rome, Todd Allen Durkin, Josh Liveright, Gregg Weiner

THE SILENT CONCERTO by Alejandro Morales; December 6, 2001; Director, Lisa Portes; CAST: Christopher Rivera, Sarah Dandridge, Scott Ebersold, Chris Henry Coffey, Nate Mooney

INBETWEEN by J. Holtham; December 7, 2001; Director, Sarah Elsasef; CAST: Kim Donovan, Chris Wight, Amy Staats, Eric Scott, Ian Reed Kesler

BOLLYWOOD by Lonnie Carter; December 10, 2001; Director, Loy Arcenas; CAST: Oni Faida Lampley, Tanya Selvaratnam

HENRY FLAMETHROWA by John Belluso; December 12, 2001; Director, Mark Brokaw; CAST: Jessica Hecht, Daniel Jenkins, Keith Nobbs

GOODBYE MY ISLAND by Deborah Brevoort; January 8, 2002; CAST: Chuck Cooper, James Fall, Allison Fisher, Bill McKinley, Scott Johnson, Joan Barber, Eleanor Glockner, Peter Cormican, Katie Gessinger, Stephanie Weems, Christian Valiando, Lilli Cooper, Aaron Schweitzer

BROOKLYN BRIDGE by Melissa James Gibson; January 9, 2002; Director, Melissa Kievman; Music, Barbara Brousal; CAST: Elizabeth Bunch, William Badgett, Joanna P. Adler, Patrick Husted, Michelle Rios, Ms. Brousal, Livia Scott, Skip Ward, Adam Sorenson

TENNESSEE DESCENDING by Leslie Kramer; Director, Ethan McSweeney; CAST: Sam Tsoutsouvas, Jenna Lamia, Nance Williamson, Kurt Rhoads, Jack Ferver, Patrick McMenamin (stage direction)

MARSUPIAL GIRL by Lisa D'Amour; January 11, 2002; Director, Katie Pearl; Music, Skip Shirey; CAST: April Matthis, Babo Harrison, Ben Schneider, Sarah K. Chalmers, Maria Elena Ramirez

TRICK OF FATE by Stuart Vaughn; January 15, 2002; CAST: Robert Lavelle, Jennifer Chudy, John Fitzgibbon, Lauren Lovett, Joseph Culliton, Michael Milligan, Anne Vaughn (stage direction)

HIGH CEILINGS by Jillian Crane; January 30, 2002; Director, Mayra Cohen; CAST: Robert O'Gorman, Steve Cell, Jennifer Morris, Kevin Tomas, Lou Liberatore, Judith Hawking, Gareth Saxe, Celia Howard, Gerry Goodstein, Larry Bull, Alex Kranz (stage direction)

4 YOUR LOVE by Mary Gallagher; January 7, 2002; Director, David Levine; CAST: Gretchen Lee Krich, John McAdams, Tertia Lynch, Ron Riley, Donna Duplantier, Chris McKinney, Laura Kindred

COYOTE GOES SALMON FISHING by Deborah Brevoort; February 12, 2002; Director, Ms. Brevoort; CAST: Natalie Venetia Belcon, Culver Casson, Will Erat, J.D. Webster, James Sasson

LAUGHING PICTURES by Matthew McGuire; February 15, 2002; CAST: Florencia Lozano, Victoire Charles, Paula Pizzi, Donan Whelan, Steven Ratazzi, Fattah Dihann, T. Ryder Smith, Ben Masur, Edward O'Blenis

COURSE MAJURE by Gordon Dahlquist; February 20, 2002; CAST: Annie McAdams, Molly Powell, Gary Brownlee, Alana Jerins, John McAdams

BROWN UNIVERSITY MFA READINGS Artistic director, Ruth Margraff; February 2002: "Getting Away" by Kamili Feelings; Director, Dominic Taylor; with Erica N. Tazel, Akili Prince, Saidah Arrika Ekkulona, Danyon Davis, Ron Brice; "Weightless" by Christine Evans; Director, Tim Farrell; with Duane Boutte, Keith Nobbs, Lynne McCullough, Brian Delate, Katie Kreisler; "The Accident" by Kelly Doyle; Director, David Levine; with Laura Kindred, Edmund C. Davys, Kit Flanagan, Josh Stark, Marin Ireland, Armando Reisco, Jack Ferver, Kelly Doyle; "Stop Motion" by Robert Quillen Camp; Director, Steve Cosson; with Christina Kirk, Cam Kornman, James Urbaniak, Brian Sgambati, Ron Riley, Damian Baldet, Travis York, Mia Barron

SOMETHING SIMPLE, PLAIN SPOKEN by Caridad Svich; March 13, 2002; Director, Hayley Finn; Cast: Carolyn Baeumler, Michael J.X. Gladis, Gretchen Lee Krich, Chris Messina

PENETRATE THE KING by Gordon Dahlquist; March 22, 2002; Director, David Levine; Cast: Laura Kindred, John McAdams, Molly Ward, Michael Stuhlbarg, Ron Riley, Joseph Goodrich, Laurie Williams

COMPOSER/LIBRETTIST STUDIO by Eisa Davis, Melissa James Gibson, Keith Glover, Joseph Goodrich, Karen Hartman; March 23, 2002; Composer, Peter Knell, Elodie Lauten, Jeffrey Lependorf, Graham Reynolds, Jeffrey Stock; Music Director, Roger Ames; Cast: Ron Bagden, Angel Desai, Naomi Gurt Lind, Tracey Moore, James Stovall

MEDEA by Joseph Goodrich; April 12, 2002; Director, Nick Faust; Cast: Vanessa Skantze, Matthew Morgan, Ron Gural, David Johnson, Molly Powell, Dale Soules

VAN LIER READINGS; April 16, 2002: "Inbetween" by J. Holtham; Director, Seret Scott; Cast: Joanna Liao, Patrick Darragh, Vanessa Aspillaga, Danyon Davis, Armando Reisco; "The Black-Eyed" by Betty Shamieh; Director, Seret Scott; Cast: Roxanne Raja, Jenny Bacon, Vanessa Aspillaga, Sabrina LeBeauf; "Umkovu" by Eisa Davis; Director, Michael John Garcés; Cast: Rob Campbell, Kevin Carroll, Donna Duplantier, Jennifer Gibbs, Tim Kang, Joe Latimore, Alfredo Narciso, Michole White

AUTODELETE:// BEGINNING DUMP OF PHYSICAL MEMORY// by Honour Kane; April 22, 2002; Director, David Levine; CAST: Gretchen Lee Krich, Matthew Stadelmann, John Daggett, Fergus Loughnane

FLIGHT by Patrick White; April 26, 2002; Director, David Levine; CAST: David Johann, Ron Simons, John Andrew Morrison, Donna Duplantier, Jim Iorio, Jay Alvarez, Matthew Francisco Morgan, Erin McLaughlin, Danny Boyd Beatty, Amarelys Perez

ILLUMINATING VERONICA by Rogelio Martinez; April 29, 2002; Director, Ted Sod; CAST: Eduardo Machado, Octavio Stolis, Antonia Rey, KJ Sanchez, Vivia Font, Victor Argo

THE LUCIFER PLAY by JoSelle Vanderhooft; April 29, 2002; Director, Clare Lundberg; CAST: Yael Teplow, Celia Peters, Louis Cancelmi, Michael Bell, Andrew Dudek

RESTORING THE SUN by Joe Sutton; May 3, 2002; Director, Ethan McSweeney; CAST: Ken Marks, Helen Coxe, Ned Eisenberg, Tim Jerome

SPIN by Karl Gajdusek; May 6, 2002; Director, Pam McKinnon; CAST: Peggy Scott, Charles Hyman, Michael Stulbarg, Jenna Stern, Anne Dudek

THE HALF-LIFE OF MEMORY by Jason Lindner; May 6, 2002; Director, Karin Coonrod; CAST: Tom Pearl, Ned Eisenberg, David Patrick Kelly, Mia Barron, Tom Nelis, Vivienne Benesch, Gary Brownlee, Ed Vassallo

EARTHQUAKE CHICA by Anne Garcia Romero; May 8, 2002; Director, Leah C. Gardiner; CAST: Judy Reyes, Al Espinosa

NEW GEORGES

THE HOLY MOTHER OF HADLEY NEW YORK by Barbara Weichmann; Director, Rachel Dickstein; with Mary Shultz, Gretchen Lee Krich, Nicole Halmos, Maria Striar, Gary Brownlee, Andrea Maulella, Alan Benditt, Malachy Cleary, Christopher Mattox, Julia Prud'homme, Richard Toth

NEW YORK INTERNATIONAL FRINGE FESTIVAL

August 2001

THE BALLAD OF LARRY THE FLYER Written and Performed by Lexington Group; Director, David Reidy; at the Cherry Lane Theatre; with Chris Belden, Kathryn Gayner, Holli Harms, Tom Paitson Kelly, Sonya Rokes, Cole Wheeler

21 DOG YEARS by Written and Performed by Mike Daisey; Director, Jean-Michele Gregory; at the Cherry Lane Theatre

THE ADDING MACHINE by Elmer Rice; Director, Jonathan Silver; with Cynthia Carroll, Paul Marcarelli, Jessamyn Blakeslee, Joshua Dickens, Dan De Silva

DEBBIE DOES DALLAS Adapted by Susan L. Schwartz from the Screenplay by Maria Minestra; Director, Brock Enright; with Ms. Schwartz, Allison du Val, Ariel Sheldon, Renata Hinrichs, Theresa Young, Tonya Canada, Jill Madeo, Marian Heller, Gary Widlund, Tim Beemer, Matthew Armstrong, Ross Steeves, Bryant MacMillan, Jonathan Hyland, Adam Chandler, Theodore Bouloukos

EINSTEIN'S DREAMS by Alan Lightman; Adaptation by Raf Remshardt, David Gardiner, and Paul Stancato; Director, Mr. Stancato; with Charlie Coniglio, Drew D'Andrea, Leigh Elliott, Jennifer Sorika Horng, Joe LaRue, Rebecca Olympia, Brian Rhinehart, Tamar Schoenberg, Elizabeth Wolf

LOADER*26 by Roberto Marinas; Director, Vijay Mathew

EQUAL PROTECTION Written and Directed by Ann Warren; with Darcy Bledsoe, Lisa Catherine Clark, Joe Rejeski, Lynn Clayton, Helen Galek

PREVIEW OF MURDER Story by Robert Leslie Bellem; Adapted by Dawn Seifert; with Matt Wagner, Jon Hemingway, Robert Watts, Mike Gold, Ms. Seifert, John Dowgin, Terry Burch

THE ELEPHANT MAN: THE MUSICAL Book, Jeff Hylton and Tim Warenko; Lyrics, Mr. Hylton; Music, Paul Jones; Director, James Riggs; with Kenneth Dine, D.P. Duffy III, Mr. Hylton, Jenna Morris

FIFTY MINUTES by Lucas Rockwood; Director, Sherri Kronfeld; with Tigran Eldred, Jessica Faller, Raymond Hamlin, Guy Larkin, Mick Preston, Dawn Vicknair

A PIECE OF MY HEART by Shirley Lauro; Director, Nancy S. Chu; with Marc Diraison, Amy McKenna, Marco Jo Clate, Robin Dawn Arocha, Sarah Sims, Christine Rodgers, Gisela Adisa

JIM CARROLL'S THE BASKETBALL DIARIES by Jim Carroll; Adapted, Directed, and Performed by Pascal Ulli

DOING JUSTICE by Adina Taubman; Director, Beth Manspeizer

SNAPSHOT by Samantha Swan; Director, Christopher Comrie; with Swergio Gallinaro, Joanne Latimer, Steven Puchalski, Ms. Swan

ZOO by Margarita Manwelyan and Jessica Rotondi; Director, Ms. Rotondi; with Tiffany May, Alva French, Jay Curtis, Haskell King, M. Donelson Renda, Jeremy Barber, Crystal Williamson, Michael Andrews, Jimmy Bopp, Myhorah Middleton, Andy Brown, Alyson Riffey, Emily Gustafson, Mia Lottringer

FUCK YOU OR DEAD PEE HOLES by Written and Directed by John Bowman; Co-director, Raymond Sanchez; with Jeff Dickenson, Marc Landers, Ranya Ritchie, Nicole Marshall, Vanessa Meryn-Cohn, Jodie Fletcher, Raymond Sanchez, Kellie Starowski, Joel Freidrich, Rob McDonald, Rigo Irizarry, Jae Henson, Nick Nace, Diane Langan, Johanna Buccola, Brion Vytlacil, Brian Corr, McCready Baker, Ann Enzminger

OHIO THEATRE

THE TRAIN PLAY by Liz Duffy Adams; Director, Jonathan Silverstein; with Quincy Tyler Berstine, Keith Davis, Gibson Frazier, Nicole Halmos, Austin Jones, Mark Leydorf, Ryan Shogren, Ami Shukla

DANCE MY DARLING, DANCE by Stephanie Gilman and K. Tanzer; Directors, Ms. Gilman, Ms. Tanzer

GLAMOUR by John O'Keefe; Director, Katherine Owens

RED DEATH by Lisa D'Amour; Director, Anne Kauffman; with Mel Jurdem, Meghan Love, John McAdams; Robert Alexander Owens, Mary Schultz, Maria Striar

Mark Leydorf, Ryan Shogren, Gibson Frazier in *The Train Play* (Amanda Alik)

ONTOLOGICAL-HYSTERIC THEATRE

MARIA DEL BOSCO by Richard Foreman; Director, Mr. Foreman; with Juliana Francis, Okwul Okpokwasili, Funda Dayal, Frank Boudreaux, Ryan Holsopple, Youssef Kerkour, Zachary Oberzan, Thom Sibbit

PARADISE THEATRE COMPANY

WHAT THE HELL'S YOUR PROBLEM? AN EVENING WITH DR. BOB NATHELSON by Tom Noonan; Director, Mr. Noonan; with Grant James Varjas, Jay DiPietro, John Goode, Cellis Mills, Rhonda Keyser, Eileen O'Connell, Kendall Pigg, Hollis Welsh, Mr. Noonan

PHIL BOSAKOWSKI THEATRE

THE NORMAN CONQUESTS: ROUND AND ROUND THE GARDEN; TABLE MANNERS; LIVING TOGETHER by Alan Ayckbourne; Director, Lisa McDermott; with Dan Patrick Brady, Christina Cas, Ledger Free, Kathryn Gayner, Nick Mouyiaris, Chrisitine Verleny

PRESENT COMPANY THEATORIUM

LEO OSCAR'S BACKYARD by Leslie Bramm; Director, Pamela Butler; with Christopher Yeatts, Hadas Gil-Bar, George Colucci, Bart Mallard, Reggie Barton, Kymberly Harris Riggs

PROSPECT THEATRE COMPANY

THE THREE SISTERS by Anton Chekov; Director, John-Martin Green; with Joyce Lee, Robin Miles, Carolyn Roberts, Kalimi Baxter, Daniel Carlton, Rafael Clements, Benard Cummings, Michael Early, Arthur French, Jesse Kearney, Rudy Marsalis, Rhonda Akanke McLean-Nur, Gregory Mikell, Dennis Reid

PROVINCETOWN PLAYHOUSE

JOHAN PADAN AND THE DISCOVERY OF THE AMERICAS by Dario Fo; Director, Ron Jenkins; with Thomas Derrah

Rob Sedgwick, Linda Powell, Christopher Duva in *Finder's Fee* (Carol Rosegg)

PULSE EMSEMBLE THEATRE

OUTDOOR SHAKESPEARE SERIES:
MACBETH directed by Alexa Kelly; with Brian Richardson, Natalie Wilder, Bryan Brendle, Jayne Corey, Amanda Dubois, Aaron J. Fill, Nicole Godino, Molly Harrington, Tom Jasorka, Mark Vaughn, Nathan White, Pamela Anne Wild, Jim Wiznieweski

A MIDSUMMER NIGHT'S DREAM directed by Alexa Kelly; with Kolwole Ugundiran, Becky Leonard, Danielle Stille, Jim Wiznieweski, Steve Abbruscato, Joseph Capone, Jay Colligan, Oscar de la Colon, David Gosso, Christian Desmond, Gretchen Greaser, Linda Past

THE TEMPEST directed by Alexa Kelly; with Nalina Mann, Brian Richardson, Joy Jones, Andrew Stuart Jones, Oberon K A Adjepong, Jeremy Beck, Joshua Billig, Evermore Black, Mark Cirnigliaro, Ellen Hayes, Leslie Jones, Andrew Narston, Nicholas Paczar, Linda Past, Noelle Teagno, Adam Wyler

RATTLESTICK PRODUCTIONS

DOWN SOUTH by Doug Field; Director, Rick Sparks; with Alice Vaughn, Anthony de Santis, Erin McLaughlin, Dean Fortunato, Audrey Rapoport, David Bicha

NEIL'S GARDEN by Geoffrey Hassman; Director, Rod Kaats; with William Bogert, Michael Warren Powell

FINDER'S FEE by Wesley Moore; Director, Leigh Silverman; with Christopher Duva, Linda Powell, Tom Reynolds, Rob Sedgwick

SANFORD MESINER THEATRE

HABEAS CORPUS by Alan Bennett; Directed; Steven Keihn; with Neal Arluck, Mary Aufman, Carrie Brewer, Denise DeMirjiam, David Godbey, Anne F. Kavanagh, Brian Linden, Brad Makarowski, Robert Meksin, Kelly Miller, Kimberley Reiss

BELLY UP by Tom Bondi and Mark Holt; Director, James Busby; with Tom Bondi, Mark Holt

STARFISH THEATREWORKS

BUILDING by Gail Noppe-Brandon; Director, Ms. Noppe-Brandon; with Robert Jason Jackson, Keith Crowningsheild, Kathleen Murphy Jackson, James Doberman, Rosemary Loar, James Rich, Jennifer Mudge Tucker, Blanca Camacho, Nicki Walker, Joe O'Brien

78th ST. THEATRE LAB

SNATCHES by Laura Strausfeld; August 2001; Director, Ms. Strausfeld; with Jean Taylor, Patricia A. Chilsen

LIBIDOFF by Dawson Moore; with Paul Kropft, Sarah Lewis, Michael Lopez, Kira Onodera, Matthew Porter

PERMANENT VISITOR:
FESTIVAL OF PLAYS BY DAWN POWELL, APRIL 2002
  JIG SAW Director, Donna Lindermann

  AN ARTIST'S LIFE AND OTHER CAUTIONARY TALES ABOUT THE THEATRE by Kira Obolensky; Director, Will Pomerantz

  AS WE WERE SAYING (OR WERE WE?) by Laura Strausfeld; Director, Eileen Phelan

  WOMEN AT FOUR O'CLOCK by Ms. Powell; Director, Eric Nightengale

THE SERVICE PROJECT: AN EVENING OF SHORT PLAYS, APRIL 2002
  DOWN HERE by Melody Cooper

  KUWAIT by Vincent Delaney

  MCINTYRE'S by Suzanne Bradbeer

  THE REGULAR by Joanna Cherensky

  A PERFECT WORLD by Carol Scudder

  MUTANT SEX PARTY by Edward Manning

  SERVICE ORDER by Brian Dykstra

  SATISFACTION GUARANTEED by Kerry Logan

LAMOUCHE by Stephen Bittrich; with Julie Alexander, Scott Baker, Magamy Colimon, Colleen Cosgrove, James Davies, Tom Demenkoff, Phil Douglas, Bill Green, Melora Griffis, Carol Halstead, Karen Kitz, John Lewis, Bradford Olson, Oz Phillips, Dan Teachout, Erik Van Wyck, Stacy Wallace, Rob Wilson

BUMBERSHOOT by P. Seth Bauer

SHOW WORLD THEATRE CENTER

WORLDLY ACTS: FIVE ONE-ACT PLAYS, JUNE 2001
THE MYSTERY AT THE MIDDLE OF ORDINARY LIFE by Don deLillo; Director, Anastasia Traina; with Ali Marsh, Joe LoTruglio

  WHO'S ON TOP by Elizabeth Dewberry; Director, Shira-Lee Shalit; with Daniella Rich, Matthew Rauch

  BOISE, IDAHO by Sean Michael Welch; Director, Lizzie Gottlieb; with Jennifer Dundas, Peter Jacobson, Glenn Kessler, Daniel Baker

  DANIEL ON A THURSDAY by Garth Wingfield; Director, Anna Katherine Rutledge; with Jack Merrill, Matthew Del Negro

  THE STOLEN CHILD by Amanda Beesly; Director, Laramie Dennis; with Mike Weaver, Linda Powell

IN THE BOOM BOOM ROOM by David Rabe; Director, Renee Phillips; with Eileen O'Connell, John D'Arcangelo, Vera Beren, Meghan Love, Alison Saltz, Masha Sapron, JB Becton, Peter Lewis, Conn Horgan, Carlo Adinolfi, Joanne Gibson, Willie Caldwell

PORTIA COUGHLIN by Marina Carr; Director, Aaron Beall; with Mercedes McAndrew, Paul Obedzinski, Marina McCreery, Joseph Small, Fergus Loughnane, Caraid O'Brien, Dorothy Stasney, Ruth Kullerman, Kevin Hagan, Benn Stovall

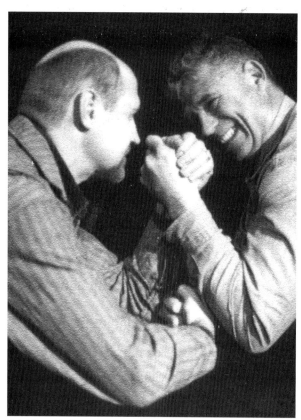

Kevin Villers, John Riggins in *Gillette* (Charles Cameron)

STORM THEATRE COMPANY

HENRY IV by Luigi Pirandello; October 2001; Director, John Regis; with Dan Berkey, Evangelia Costantakos, Laurence Drozd, Carl Pasbjerg, Paul Burns, Stephen Logan Day, Adriane Urdos, Brett Hemmerling, Hugh Brandon Kelly, Bill Roulet, Cary Seward, Eric Thorne, Brian Whisenant

GILLETTE by William Hauptman; Director, Peter Dobbins; with John Riggins, Eric Alperin, Kevin Villers, Shaula Chambliss, Genia Michaela, Eric Thorne

SYNAPSE THEATRE COMPANY

BLOODY POETRY by Howard Brenton; October 2001; Director, David Travis; with Adrian LaTourelle, Erik Steele, Adrienne Dreiss, Lael Logan, Omar Metwally, Michelle Federer

TARGET MARGIN THEATRE

CRAZY DAY, OR THE MARRIAGE OF FIGARO by Beaumarchais; November 2001; Director, David Herskovitz; with Rinne Groff, Robert Alexander Owens, Paul Vincent Black, Yuri Skujins, Kwana Martinez, Alvaro Hening, Joyce Lee

THE RING: THE OPERATIC ERA LABORATORY by Richard Wagner

RING CYCLE Directors, the Rattazzi Brothers

SIEGFRIED'S NERVE Director, Jyana S. Gregory; Adaptation, Lucas Hnath

BOCA Director, Yuri Skujins

VALKYRIE, OR WHAT HAPPENS WHEN A GOOD-NATURED GODDESS GOES BAD Director, Susanna Gellert

THE SANDMAN by E.T.A. Hoffman; May 2002; Director, David Herskovitz; with Rachel Mondanaro, Jay Johnson, Byron Singleton, Gregory Rahming, Violetta Zambetti, Christian Sebek

THEATRE AT ST. CLEMENTS CHURCH

SOMETHING CLOUDY, SOMETHING CLEAR by Tennessee Williams; Director, Anatole Fourmantchouk; October 2001; with Stass Klassen, Elissa Piszel, Joe Mihalchick, Chandler Vinton, Richard Guerreiro

GOOD THING by Jessica Goldberg; December 2001; Director, Jo Bonney; with Betsy Aidem, John Rothman, Alicia Goranson, Chris Messina, Cara Buono, Hamish Linklater

Chandler Vinton, Stass Klassen in *Something Cloudy, Something Clear*

THEATRE FOR A NEW AUDIENCE

CYMBELINE by William Shakespeare; Director, Bartlett Sher; with Robert Setttel, Andrew Weems, Michael Stuhlbarg, Earl Hindman, Boris McGiver, Pete Starrett, Roderick Hill, Randy Danson, Erica N. Tazel, Peter Francis James, Phillip Goodwin, Thomas M. Hammond

ANDORRA by Max Frisch; April 2002; Director, Liviu Ciulei; with David Barlow, Bill Buell, Justin Campbell, Jeffrey Fierson, Rafael Kalichstein, Laurie Kennedy, Nicholas Kepros, Peter Kybart, Maggie Lacey, Andrew McGinn, Boris McGiver, David Don Miller, Simeon Moore, Pamela Nyberg, Chip Persons, Jesse Steccato, Henry Strozier, Chandler Williams

THEATRE OF THE RIVERSIDE CHURCH

THE CREATION OF THE WORLD AND OTHER BUSINESS by Arthur Miller; October 2001; Director, Oleg Kheyfets; with Paul Sparks, Tony Torn, Tom Pearl, Kent Alexander, Valerie Stanford, Preston Dane

TRIBECA PLAYHOUSE

THE FEIGN'D COURTESANS by Aphra Behn; March 29, 2002; Director, Rebecca Patterson; with Lauren Jill Arnold, Virginia Baeta, Fatima Bazzy, Valentina McKenzie, Maureen Porter, Beverley Prentice, Jill Repplinger, Gisele Richardson, Ami Shukla, Cary Urban, DeeAnn Weir, Tessa Zugmeyer

SHAKESPEARE AND MRS. BEHN: LOVE ARM'D, APHRA BEHN & HER PEN by Karen Eterovich; with Ms. Eterovich

MRS. SHAKESPEARE (WILL'S FIRST & LAST LOVE) by Yvonne Hudson; April 2, 2002; Director, Robert Edward Burns; with Ms. Hudson

TARTUFFE by Molière; Adapted and Directed by Jeff Cohen; with Gerald Anthony, Keith Reddin, Jen Ryan, Crista Moore

TRILOGY THEATRE

TALLBOY WALKIN' by Joshua James; September 8, 2001; Director, Nick Corley; with Lou Carbonneau, Sharif Rashed, Ato Essandoh, James McCauley, Garrison Phillips

JAPA-RICA by Masayasu Nakanishi and Robert Baumgardner; February 7, 2002; Director, Mr. Baumgardner with Mr. Nakanishi

28th STREET THEATRE

BLUE WINDOW by Craig Lucas; July 11, 2001; Director, Julia Gibson; with Hope Chernov, Marcia DeBonis, Katy Hansz, Marin Hinkle, Neal Huff, Jason Kolotournos, Josh Stamberg

Jeff Taylor and Company in *Tartuffe* (Kate Raudenbush)

Gerald Anthony, Crista Moore in *Tartuffe* (Kate Raudenbush)

Peyton Thomas, Elizabeth Elkins, Leo Farley, Barbara Meyers, Moira MacDonald in *The Last Barbecue* (G. Alexander)

29th STREET REP

THE LAST BARBEQUE by Brett Neveu; September 22, 2001; Director, Tim Corcoran; with Peyton Thomas, Elizabeth Elkins, Leo Farley, Barbara Meyers, Moira MacDonald

FOOL FOR LOVE by Sam Shepard; May 2, 2002; Director, Tim Corcoran; with David Morgentale, Elizabeth Elkins, Stephen Payne, Tony de Vito

UPSTAIRS AT 54

DRAGAPELLA STARRING THE KINSEY SICKS by Ben Schatz, Irwin Keller, Maurice Kelly, Chris Dilley; October 17, 2001; Director, Glenn Casale; featuring the authors

URBAN STAGES

CIRCUMFERENCE OF A SQUIRREL by John Walch; February 19, 2002; Director, T.L. Reilly; with Paul Sparks

THE SWEEPERS by John C. Picardi; April 2, 2002; Director, Frances Hill; with Dana Smith, Brigitte Viellieu-Davis, Donna Davis, Ivy Vahanian, Matt Walton

VERSE THEATRE MANHATTAN

WAR MUSIC by Christopher Logue; Adapted from Homer's *Illiad*; September 8, 2001; Directed by James Milton; with Jo Barrick, Angela Moore, Marybeth Bentwood

WALKERSPACE

BLUEBEARD AND OTHER LESS GRISLY TALES OF LOVE by Liz Steinberg; September 9, 2001; Director, Ms. Steinberg; with Kate Baldwin, Erin Cardillo, Deanna Pacelli, Kate Arrington, Melissa Creighton, Lucia Rich, Aaron Clayton, Daniel Goldstein, Peter Russo, Ailsa Muir

WESTBETH THEATRE CENTER

ARE YOU DAVE GORMAN? by Dave Gorman; October 4, 2001; with Mr. Gorman

KIKI AND HERB; THERE'S A STRANGER IN THE MANGER! by Justin Bond and Kenny Mehlman; November 29, 2001; featuring the authors

HOMECOMING by Lauren Weedman; January 21, 2002; Director, Maryann Lombardi; with Ms. Weedman

BEWILDERNESS by Bill Bailey; March 7, 2002; with Mr. Bailey

WINGS THEATRE COMPANY

TANGO MASCULINO by Clint Jeffries; April 11, 2002; Director, Jeffrey Corrick; Music, Mr. Jeffries; with Miguel Belmonte, Stephen Cabral, Roberto Cambeiro, Samantha Clarke, Angel Comas, Ivan Davila, Mickey Goldhaber, Maureen Griffin, JoHary Ramos, Gustavo Santamarina, Karen Stanion, Paul Taylor

THE WOMEN'S SHAKESPEARE COMPANY

'TIS A PITY SHE'S A WHORE by John Ford; adapted by R.J. Tolan; March 18, 2002; Director, Mr. Tolan

WOOSTER GROUP

TO YOU THE BIRDIE Based on Racine's *Phaedra*; Translated by Paul Schmidt; February 19, 2002; Director, Elizabeth LeCompte; with Frances McDormand, Kate Vlak, Willem Dafoe, Ari Fliakos, Scott Shepherd, Suzzy Roche, Koosil-ja Hwang, Dominique Bousquet

WORKING THEATRE

**FREE MARKET (EIGHT SHORT WORKS);
ALL DIRECTED BY JOSEPH MEGEL; JUNE 2001**
  FIRE DRILL by William Wise; with Geoffrey Simmons

  20/20 SEX CARE by Karen Sunde; with Eunice Wong, Lourdes Martin, Geoffrey Simmons

  DAY OF OUR DEAD by Elaine Romero; with Lourdes Martin, Constance Boardman

  KICKIN SUMMIT by OyamO; with Geoffrey Simmons, Constance Boardman, Arthur French, Eunice Wong, Felix Solis, Lourdes Martin

  FREE MARKET by Jim Grimsley; with Geoffrey Simmons, Eunice Wong

  GIVE US THIS DAY by Julie Jenson; with Arthur French, Eunice Wong

  POODLES by Sachi Oyama; with Felix Solis, Constance Boardman, Geoffrey Simmons

  THE BORDERS CROSSERS LOUNGE by Guillermo Reyes; with Felix Solis, Geoffrey Simmons, Lourdes Martin, Constance Boardman, Eunice Wong, Arthur French

Felix Solis, Lourdes Martin, Eunice Wong in *Free Market* (Nick Andrews)

WORTH STREET THEATRE

FOUR by Christopher Shin; July 1, 2001; Director, Jeff Cohen; with Keith Nobbs, Vinessa Antoine, Isiah Whitlock Jr., Armando Reisco

TARTUFFE by Molière; adapted by Jeff Cohen; January 16, 2002; with Jennifer Bassey, Crista Moore, Adam Hirsch, Liam Christopher O'Brien, Sarah Lippman, Jim Hazzard, Jen Ryan, Keith Reddin, James Rana, Gerald Anthony, Jeff Taylor

ZIPPER THEATRE

TRUE LOVE by Charles L. Mee; November 28, 2001; Director, Daniel Fish; with Laurie Williams, Jeremiah Miller, Laura Esterman, Paul Mullins, Chrisopher McCann, Jayne Haudeyshell, Dallas Roberts, Halley Wegryn Gross, Roy Thinnes

RENO: REBEL WITHOUT A PAUSE by Reno; featuring Reno

DOWNTOWN DYSFUNCTIONALS, EPISODE 2: BABY BUDDHA Book by Richard Sheinmel, C. Colby Sachs; Music and Lyrics, Randy Lake, Davia Sacks, Mr. Scheinmel, Clay Zambo; April 25, 2002; with Todd Butera, Jennifer Houston, James Lawson, Gregory Marcel, Mardie Millit, Jim Taylor McNickle, Allison Mulrain, Erika Beth Phillips, Sunrize Highway

Keith Nobbs, Isiah Whitlock, Jr. in *Four* (Kate Raudenbush)

OFF-OFF-BROADWAY

Company Series

AMAS MUSICAL THEATRE

Rosetta Lenoire, Founder; Donna Trinkoff, Producing Artistic Director

LITTLE HAM based on Langston Hughes' play of the same name; Book, Dan Owen; based on a concept by Eric Krebs; Director, Eric Riley; Music, Judd Woldin; Lyrics, Richard Engquist and Judd Woldin; Choreography, Leslie Dockery; Sets, Edward T. Gianfrancesco; Lighting, Richard Latta; Costumes, Bernard Grenier; Music Direction, David Alan Bunn; Orchestrations and Arrangements, Luther Henderson; CAST: Ben Blake, D'Ambrose Boyd, Venida Evans, Carmen Ruby Floyd, Jerry Gallagher, André Garner, Danielle Lee Greaves, Julia Lema, Kevyn Morrow, Stacey Sargeant, Joy Styles, Lee Summers, Richard Vida, Joe Wilson Jr. Opened on November 28, 2001

ATLANTIC THEATRE COMPANY

Seventeenth Season

Artistic Director, Neil Pepe; Managing Director, Hillary Hinckle

THE DOG PROBLEM by David Rabe; Director, Scott Ellis; Sets, Allen Moyer; Lighting, Brian Nason; Costumes, Michael Krass; Sound, Eileen Tague; Fight Director, Rick Sordelet; Production Stage Manager, Darcy Stephens; CAST: Joe Pacheco, Larry Clarke, David Wike, Victor Argo, Tony Cucci, Andrea Gabriel, Robert Bella. Opened June 6, 2001

AN ADULT EVENING OF SHEL SIVERSTEIN by Shel Silverstein; Director, Karen Kohlhaas; Sets, Walt Spangler; Lighting, Robert Perry; Costumes, Miguel Angel Huidor; CAST: Jordan Lage, Alicia Goranson, Jody Lambert, Josh Stamberg, Maryann Urbano, Kelly Maurer. Opened October 17, 2001

HOBSON'S CHOICE by Harold Brighouse; Director, David Warren; CAST: Brian Murray, Martha Plimpton, David Aaron Baker, Peter Maloney, Amy Wilson, Katie Carr, Darren Pettie, Jim Fragione, Christopher Wynkoop, Aedin Moloney, Austin Lysy. Opened January 13, 2002

THIS THING OF DARKNESS by Craig Lucas and David Schulner; Director, Mr. Lucas; Sets, John McDermott; Lighting, Christopher Akerlind; Costumes, Candice Donnelly; Sound, Scott Myers; CAST: Daniel Eric Gold, Larry Keith, Nary McCann, Chris Messina, Thomas J. Ryan, Ralph Waite. Opened May 30, 2002

André Garner, Richard Vida in *Little Ham* (Carol Rosegg)

Larry Clarke in *The Dog Problem* (Carol Rosegg)

BROOKLYN ACADEMY OF MUSIC: NEXT WAVE FESTIVAL

Chairman, Bruce C. Ratner; President, Karen Brooks Hopkins; Executive Producer, Joseph V. Melillo.

CLOUDSTREET by Tim Winston; Adapted by Nick Enright and Justin Monjo; Director, Neil Armfield; Sets, Robert Cousins; Lighting Mark Howett; Costumes, Tess Schofield; Sound, Gavin Tempany; Choreography, Kate Champion; CAST: Wayne Blair, Roy Billing, John Gaden, Claire Jones, Gillian Jones, Kris McQuade, Christopher Pittman, Daniel Wylie. Opened October 2, 2001

THE THEFT OF SITA by Nigel Jamieson; Music composed by Paul Grabowsky in association with I Wayan Gde Yudane from an original idea by Nigel Jamieson and Paul Grabowsky; Director, Mr. Jamieson; Sets, Julian Crouch; Lighting, Damien Cooper; CAST: I Made Sidia, Peter Wilson, Paul Moore, Puppeteers, Steve Howarth, Udo Foerster; Vocalists, Shelly Scown, I Gusti Putu Sudarta. Opened October 17, 2001

CORROBOREE Composer David Page and Steve Francis; Director and Choreographer, Stephen Page; Sets, Stephen Page, Peter England and John Marcovic; Lighting, Karen Norris and Joseph Mercurio; Costumes, Jennifer Irwin. Opened October 24, 2002

NEED COMPANY'S KING LEAR by William Shakespeare; Director, Jan Lauwers; Sets, Mr. Lauwers; Lighting, Dries Vercruysse; Costumes, Lot Lemm; Choreography, Carlotta Sagna; Sound, Dré Schneider; CAST: Tom Jansen; Josse de Pauw; Simon Versnel, Grace Ellen Barkey, Anneke Bonnema, Carlotta Sagna, Hans Petter Dahl, Misha Downey, Dick Crane, Tijen Lawton, Timothy Couchman. Opened October 31, 2001

ONE UPON A TIME IN CHINESE AMERICA by Fred Ho and Ruth Margraff; Director, Mira Kinsley; Sets, Michael Forrest Kurtz, Kun-Feng "Tony" Cheng; Lighting, Allen Hahn; Music and Concept, Mr. Ho; Costumes, Kenneth Chu; CAST: Chen Jack, Gee Shin, Miao Hin, Li Wen Mao, Ng Mui

MASCURA FOGO by Pina Bausch; Director and Choreographer, Ms. Bausch; Sets, Peter Pabst; Costumes, Marion Cito. Opened November 8, 2001

POETRY BOOK, Music and Lyrics by Lou Reed; Director and Designer, Robert Wilson; Music Direction, Mr. Reed; Lighting, Mr. Wilson and Heinrich Brunke; Costume and Mask Design, Jacques Reynaud. Opened November 27, 2001

BIG LOVE by Charles L. Mee; an Adaptation of Aeshylus' *The Suppliant Women*; Director, Les Waters; Sets, Ann Smart; Lighting, Robert Wierzel; Costumes, James Schuette; Sound, Robert Milburn, Michael Bodeen; CAST: Carolyn Baeumler, Tony Speciale, Aimée Guillot, KJ Sanchez, Lauren Klein, J. Michael Flynn, Bruce McKenzie, Mark Zeisler, J. Matthew Jenkins, Amy Landecker, Luisa Strus, Adrian Danzig, Chuck Stubbings

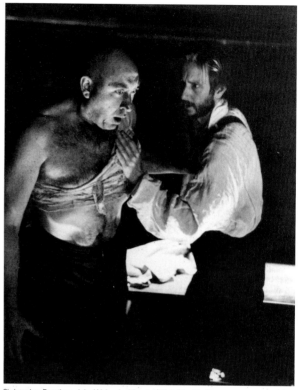

Christopher Donahue, Jake Weber in *Monster* (Dixie Sheridan)

CLASSIC STAGE COMPANY

Twenty-Fourth Season

Artistic Director, Barry Edelstein; Producing Director, Beth Emelson

IN THE PENAL COLONY by Philip Glass; Based on the Story by Franz Kafka; Director, Joanne Akalaitis; Sets, John Conklin; Lighting, Jennifer Tipton; Costumes, Susan Hilferty; Sound, Dominic Cody Kramers; CAST: Tony Boutée, Sterling K. Brown, John Duykers, Jesse J. Perez, Eugene Perry, Herbert Perry, Steven Rishard. Opened June 14, 2001

MONSTER by Neal Bell, Based on Mary Shelley's *Frankenstein*; Director, Michael Greif; Sets, Robert Brill; Lighting, Kenneth Posner; Costumes, Jess Goldstein; Sound, Erika H. Sellin; CAST: Jake Weber, Michael Cullen, Christopher Donahue, Annie Parisse, Michael Pitt, Jonno Roberts, Christen Clifford

THE UNDERPANTS by Carl Stearnheim, Adapted by Steve Martin; Director, Barry Edelstein; Sets, Scott Pask; Lighting, Russell H. Champa; Costumes, Angela Wendt; Sound, Elizabeth Rhodes; CAST: Patrick Boll, Cheryl Lynn Bowers, Christian Camargo, William Duell, Bryon Jennings, Kristine Nielsen, Lee Wilkof

DRAMA DEPT.

MUSIC FROM A SPARKLING PLANET Director, Mark Brokaw; Sets, Allen Moyer; Lighting, Kenneth Posner; Costumes, Michael Krass; Sound, Janet Kalas; Original Music, Lewis Flinn; Cast: J. Smith-Cameron, T. Scott Cunningham, Ross Gibby, Josh Hamilton and Michael Gaston

ENSEMBLE STUDIO THEATRE

MARATHON 2001 (SERIES C): Sets, Warren Karp; Lighting, Greg MacPherson; Costumes, Christopher Peterson; Sound, Robert Gold

    GRIEF by Craig Lucas; Director, Tom Rowan; Cast: Delphi Harrington, Neal Huff, Christopher Orr

    LARRY'S CHARM by Edward Allen Baker; Director, Ron Statson; Cast: Lynn Cohen, Tessa Gyhlin, Maria Gabriele

    LATE NIGHT IN THE WOMEN'S RESTROOM OF THE JUNGLE BAR by David Reidy; Director, Eileen Myers; Cast: Melinda Page Hamilton, Jen Drohan, Diana LaMar, Kevin Shinick

    INVITATION TO A FUNERAL by Julai McKee; Director, Deborah Hedwall; Cast: Kathleen Doyle, Susan Pelligrino

THE SECRET ORDER by Bob Clyman; Director, Jamie Richards; Sets, Bruse Goodrich; Lighting, Michael Lincoln; Costumes, Amelia Baksie; Sound, Robert Gould; Cast: Liam Craig, James Murtaugh, Amy Love, Joe Rooks

MARATHON 2002 (SERIES A): Sets, Jennifer Varbalow; Lighting, Michael Lincoln; Costumes, Amela Baksie; Sound, Robert Gould

    LARK by Romulus Linney

    WHY I FOLLOWED YOU by Lisa-Marie Radano

    REUNIONS by Billy Aronson

    SALVAGE BAAS by Brian Silbeman

MARATHON 2002 (SERIES B)
    AM LIT OR HIBERNOPHILIA by Dan O'Brien; Director, Kevin Confoy; with Tom Bloom

    THE PRISONER'S SONG by Horton Foote; Director, Harris Yulin; Cast: Mary Catherine Garrison, Tim Guinee, Merceline Hugot, Michael Moran

    ADAPTATION by Roger Hedden; Director, Billy Hopkins; Cast: Ian Reed Kesler, Fiona Gallagher, Dennis Boutsikaris, Brooke Smith, Spencer Garrett

    SALVATION by Bill Bozzone; Director, Keith Reddin; Cast: Katie Walder, Rishi Mehta, Alex Feldman

INTAR

THE ALAMO PIECE by Sigfrido Aguilar and Jim Calder; Cast: Mr. Aguilar and Mr. Calder

TIES THAT BIND (three plays in rep): *Young Valiant* by Oliver Mayer; Director, Michael John Garcés; Cast: Romi Dias, Alain Rivas, Donald Silva. *Cuchifrito* by Eduardo Andino; Director Angel David; with Carlo Alban, Ana Maria Correa, Joel Friedman, Henry Leyva, Marilyn Sanabria. *A to B* by Ricardo A. Bracho; Director, Ela Troyano; Cast: Leith Burke, Carlos Valencia

TWO by Ron Elisha, Director, Bernice Rohret; with Mark Hammer, Tibor Feldman, Irene Glezos

Jim Calder, Sigfrido Aguilar in *The Alamo Piece* (Laura Ochoa)

Sigfrido Aguilar, Jim Calder in *The Alamo Piece* (Laura Ochoa)

IRISH REPERTORY THEATER

Artistic Director, Charlotte Moore; Producing Director, Ciarán O'Reilly

A LIFE by Hugh Leonard; Director, Charlotte Moore; Sets, Dan Kuchar; Lighting, Gregory Cohen; Costumes, Linda Fisher; Sound, Murmod, Inc.; CAST: Jarlath Conroy, David Costelloe, Paddy Croft, Pauline Flanagan, John Keating, Heather O'Neill, Derdriu Ring, Fritz Weaver

THE IRISH…AND HOW THEY GO THAT WAY by Frank McCourt; Director, Charlotte Moore; CAST: Peter Cormican, Terry Donnelly, Bob Green, Mark Hartman, Donna Kane and Ciarán O'Reilly

SAVE IT FOR THE STAGE: THE LIFE OF REILLY by Charles Nelson Reilly and Paul Linke; Director, Mr. Linke; Sets, Patrick Hughes; Lighting, Gregory Cohen; Costumes, Noel Taylor; Sound, Murmod, Inc.; with Mr. Reilly

THE STREETS OF NEW YORK by Dion Boucicault; Directed and Adapted for the Stage by Charlotte Moore; Sets, Hugh Landwehr; Lighting, Clifton Taylor; Costumes, Linda Fisher; Sound, Murmod, Inc.; CAST: Peter Cormican, Ray DeMattis, Terry Donnelly, Danielle Ferland, Margaret Hall, Donna Kane, John Keating, Christopher Lynn, Kristin Maloney, Ciarán O'Reilly, Joshua Park

THAT…AND A CUP OF TEA; AN EVENING WITH CARMEL QUINN conceived and performed by Mr. Quinn

PIGTOWN by Mike Finn; Director, Charlotte Moore; Sets, James Morgan; Lighting, Kirk Bookman; Costumes, Robin L. McGee; CAST: Jarlath Conroy, Dara Coleman, David Costelloe, Terry Connelly, Rosemary Fine, Laura James Flynn, Christopher Joseph Jones, John Keating, Aedin Moloney, Declan Mooney, Anto Nolan

JEAN COCTEAU REPERTORY

Thirty-First Season

ARMS AND THE MAN by George Bernard Shaw; Director, Ernest Johns; with Manda Jones, Marlene May, Carey Van Driest, Jason Crowl, Edward Griffin, Michael Surabian, Mark Rimer, Harris Berlinsky

OEDIPUS THE KING by Sophocles

DANCE OF DEATH by August Strindberg; Director, Karen Lordi; with Craig Smith, Elise Stone, Jason Crowl, Kathryn Foster

THE MARRIAGE OF FIGARO by Beaumarchais; Director, David Fuller; with Christopher Black, Amanda Jones, Mark Rimer, Kathryn Foster, Michael Surabian

JEWISH REPERTORY THEATRE

Artistic Director, Ran Avni

A NAUGHTY KNIGHT Musical with Book by William Martin; Music and Lyrics by Chick Strand; Based on a Fable by Mark Twain; Director, Mr. Martin; Sets and Costumes, Frank Boros; Lighting, Jason Kankel; Sound, Randy Hansen; CAST: Rebecca Kupka, Mark Manley, Christopher J. Hanke, Gordon Joseph Weiss, Rebecca Rich, Kurt Domoney, John Michael Coppola

LA MAMA EXPERIMENTAL THEATRE CLUB (ETC.)

Fortieth Season

Founder and Director, Ellen Stewart

BITTERROOT Book by Paul Zimet, Based on the Life of Merriweather Lewis; Composer, Peter Gordon; Director, Mr. Zimet; Sets, Christine Jones; Lighting, Leonore Doxsee; Costumes, Kiki Smith; CAST: William Badgett, Ellen Maddow, Isaac Maddow-Zimet, Tina Shepard, Jeffrey Reynolds, Ryan Dietz, Randy Reyes, Michelle Rios, Hunyup Lee

FERDYDURKE by Witlod Gombrowitz; Adapted by Allen J. Kuharski; Director, Witold Mazurkiewicz, Janusz Oprynski; Sets, Jerry Rudzki; Lighting and Sound, Mr. Oprynski, Jan Szamryk; Music, Boris Somerschaf; CAST: Jacek Brzezkinski, Mr. Mazurkiewicz, Jaroslaw Tomica, Michael Zget

STAR MESSENGERS Book by Paul Zimet; Composer, Ellen Maddow; Director, Mr. Zimet, Sets, Nic Ularu; Choreography, Karrine Keithley; Lighting, Carol Mullins; Costumes, Kiki Smith; CAST: William Badgett, Court Dorsey, David Greenspan, Christine Ciccone, Ryan Dietz, Marcy Jellison, Ms. Keithley, Ms. Maddow, Randy Reyes, Michelle Rios

THE SOUND OF THE SUN by Arthur Maxmillian Adair; CAST: Mr. Adair, Einy Aam, Lara Benusir, Alta L. Bode, Marissa Buffone, Antonio Cerezo, Aundré Chin, Richard Cohen, Evaleena Dann, S-Dog, Brian Duggan, Foster, Sara Galassini, Ximena Garnica, Denise Greber, Tim Herlihy, Jake Incao, Jiyang Kim, Tom Lee, Julia Martin, Juan Merchan, La Nena, Scott Gannon Patton, Rolando Politti, Eugene the Poogene, Federico Restrepo, James Rowland, Paul Savas, Maeve Shelton, Sara Wilson Sherwin, Yukio Tsiji, Nella Vinci, Angela Wendt, Saria Young, Stefano Zazzera, Hadaaz Zucker

EROTIC ADVENTURES IN VENICE by Mario Fratti; Director, Dan Friedman; Sets, Floyd Gumble; CAST: Dave DeChristopher, Mika Duncan, Jennifer Herzog, Zenobia Shroff, Ross Stoner, Caroline Strong

DOUBLE AGENCY by Peggy Shaw and Lois Weaver, in collaboration with Suzy Willson and Paul Clark; "Miss Risqué" Director, Ms. Willson; Associate Director, Stormy Brandenberger; Sets, Annabel Lee; Lighting, Aideen Malone; Costumes, Susan Young; "It's a Small House and We've Lived in it Always" Director, Ms. Willson; Lyrics, Ms. Shaw and Ms. Weaver; Costumes, Sarah Blenkinsop; Lighting, Ms. Malone

THE HAMLET PROJECT by William Electric Black (a.k.a. Ian James); Music, Valerie Ghent; Arrangements, Mr. Black, Tony Mann, Giselle Hamburg; Choreography, Treiban Pollard; Costumes, Beth Leward; Fight Choreography, James Manley; CAST: Oberon Adjepong, Chris Brady, Eamonn Farrell, Michael Noon, Walter Pagan, Stephen Reyes, Sean Seibert, George Sosa, Brian Walker, Vanessa Burke, Liz Davito, Susanna Harris, Lauren Jacobs, Melissa Leiter, Erin Logemann, Mikey McCue, William Pagan, Lauren Porter, Eily Tuckman, Joni Weisfeld, Kathryn Yew

TUMOR BRAINOWICZ by Stanislaw Ignacy Witkiewicz, translated by Daniel Gerould; Director, Brooke O'Harra; Music, Brendan Connelly; CAST: Brian Bickerstaff, Mary Bonner-Baker, Rob Marcato, Matt Shapiro, Mary Regan, Nicky Paraiso, Zakia-Babb Bornstein, and the voices of Isaac Zimet-Maddow, Misako Takashima

THE RISE AND FALL OF TIMUR THE LAME by Theodora Skipitares; Composer, David First; Lighting, Pat Dignan; CAST: Sanjeeva Poojary, Lisa Kerrer; Narrators, Michael Moran, George Drance

PI = 3.14 Concept and Text by Yoshiko Chuma; Additional Text by Bonniesue Stein and the Company; Director, Ms. Chuma; Sets, Tom Lee; Lighting, Pat Dignan; Costumes, Gabriel Berry; Sound, Jacob Burckhardt; CAST: Tea Alagic, Jim DiBiasio, Ms. Chuma, Wazhmah Osman, Ivan Talijancic, Maggie McBrien, Jenny Smith

HOWLING Created by Virlana Tkacz, Sayan Zhambalov, Erzhena Zhambalov, Watoku Ueno; Director, Ms. Tkacz; Sets and Lighting, Mr. Ueno; Movement, Katja Kolcio; Music, Erzhena Zhambalov; CAST: Eunice Wong, Meredith Wright, Angela Lewis, Stephanie Summerville, Anais Alexandria Tekerian

KISS SHOT Musical by Jim Neu and Neal Kirkwood; Director, Keith McDermott; Sets, Donald Eastman; Lighting, Carol Mullins; CAST: Monte Blanc, Belle Russe, Mr. Neu, Charles Allcroft

BOW DOWN by Joe Brady; Director, Raine Bode; Sets, Arthur Adair; Lighting, Federico Restrepo; Costumes, Denise Greber; CAST: Mark Gallop, Paul Savas, Anne Moore, Uma Incrocci, Tommy Lonardo, Brian Glover, Neely Hepner, Tate Henderson, Mo Pula, Andy Rothkin, Antonio Cerezo, Melissa Glassman, Charlie Berfield

Lois Weaver, Peggy Shaw in *Double Agency* (Francis Keller)

Zenobia Shroff, Jennifer Herzog, Mika Duncan, Caroline Strong in *Erotic Adventures in Venice* (Jonathan Slaff)

CRACKS Direction, Choreography and Sets by Issey "Itzik" Nini; Costumes, Mr. Nini, Susan Lazar; Music, Mr. Nini, Stefano Zazzera, Greg Christo; CAST: Mr. Nini, Amanda LePore, Jonathan Nosan

SEGUIRIYA, THE HEART BEATS Conceived by Shigeko Suga; Director, Ms. Suga; Sets, Jun Maeda; Costumes, Denise Greber; CAST: Mieko Seto, Naomi Shibata, Minouche Waring, Kumi Kuwahata, Aundré Chin, Bret Boyle, Lisa Ann Williamson, Antonio Cerezo, Mitsunari Sakamoto

ONE NIGHT STANDS "The Book of Job" Book, Music and Lyrics by Danny Ashkenasi; CAST: Julie Alexander, Mr. Ashkenasi, Ian August, Joel Briel, Ryan Connolly, Allison Easter, Darra Herman, Anita Hollander, Jennie Im, Jamie Matthews. "Miss Mobile" by Emil Hrvatin. "Uncle Moon and Auntie Angus" with Trey Kay, Fritz Van Orden, Scott Selig, Carl Riehl, Jane Young, Henry Tenney, Bryan Costello, Doug Safranek, Christopher Caines

LINCOLN CENTER FESTIVAL

Director, Nigel Redden

2001 HAROLD PINTER FESTIVAL

A KIND OF ALASKA by Mr. Pinter; Director, Karel Reisz; Sets and Costumes, Liz Ascroft; Lighting, Mick Hughes; CAST: Brid Brennan, Stephen Brennan, Penelope Wilton

ONE FOR THE ROAD by Mr. Pinter; Director, Robin LeFevre; Sets and Costumes, Liz Ascroft; Lighting, Mick Hughes; CAST: Mr. Pinter, Lloyd Hutchinson, Indira Varma, Rory Copus

THE HOMECOMING by Mr. Pinter; Director, Robin LeFevre; Sets, Eileen Diss; Lighting, Mick Hughes; Costumes, Dany Everett; CAST: Ian Holm, Ian Hart, John Kavanagh, Jason O'Mara, Lia Williams, Nick Dunning

MONOLOGUE by Mr. Pinter; Director, Gari Jones; Sets, Eileen Diss; Costumes, Dany Everett; Lighting, Mick Hughes; with Henry Woolf

CELEBRATION by Mr. Pinter; Director, Mr. Pinter; Sets, Eileen Diss; Lighting, Mick Hughes; Costumes, Dany Everett; Sound, John Leonard; CAST: Keith Allen, Lindsay Duncan, Dani Dyer, Stephen Pacey, Nina Raine, Emily Strawson, Andy de la Tour, Indira Varma, Thomas Wheatley, Lia Williams, Susan Woodridge

LANDSCAPE by Mr. Pinter; Director, Karel Reisz; Sets, Eileen Diss; Lighting, Mick Hughes; Costumes Dany Everett; CAST: Stephen Brennan, Penelope Wilton

MOUNTAIN LANGUAGE by Mr. Pinter; Director, Kate Mitchell; Sets, Vicki Mortimer; Lighting, Paule Constable; Sound, Gareth Fry; CAST: Daniel Cerqueria, Neil Dudgeon, Gabrielle Hamilton, Anastasia Hille, Paul Hilton, Geoffrey Streatfield, Tim Treloar

ASHES TO ASHES by Mr. Pinter; Director, Katie Mitchell; Sets, Vicki Mortimer; Lighting, Paule Constable; Sound, Gareth Fry; CAST: Neil Dudgeon, Anastasia Hille

MABOU MINES

Artistic Directors: Lee Breuer, Sharon Fogarty, Ruth Maleczech, Frederick Neumann, Terry O'Reilly

PETER AND WENDY by J.M. Barrie, Adapted by Liza Lorwin; Director, Lee Breuer; Sets, Julie Archer; Costumes, Sally Thomas; Sound, Edward Cosla; Music, Jonny Cunningham; CAST: Karen Kandel; Puppeteers, Basil Twist, Jane Catherine Shaw, Sam Kack, Lute Ramblin', Sarah Provost, Jessica Chandlee Smith, Jenny Subjack

MANHATTAN CLASS COMPANY THEATRE (MCC)

Sixteenth Season

Artistic Directors, Robert LuPone and Bernard Telsey; Associate Artistic Director, William Cantler

THE GLORY OF LIVING by Rebecca Gilman; November 15, 2001; Director, Philip Seymour Hoffman; Sets, Michelle Malavet; Lighting, James Vermeulen; Costumes, Mimi O'Donnell; Original Music and Sound, David Van Tiegham; CAST: Anna Paquin, Jeffrey Donovan, David Aaron Baker, Erika Rolfsrud, Brittany Slattery, Alicia Van Couvering, Jenna Lamia, Larry Clarke, Andrew McGinn, Myk Watford; Finalist for the Pulitzer Prize in Drama

A LETTER FROM ETHEL KENNEDY by Christopher Gorman; May 16, 2002; Director, Joanna Gleason; Sets, Jeff Cowie; Lighting, Michael Chybowski; Costumes, Martin Pakledinaz; Original Music, David Van Tiegham; Sound, Jill B.C. DuBoff; CAST: Jay Goede, Anita Gillette, Randy Harrison, Stephen Baker Turner, Bernie McInerney

RUNT OF THE LITTER by Bo Eason; January 31, 2002; Director, Larry Moss; Sets, Neil Patel; Lighting, David Gipson; Sound, Bruce Ellman; with Mr. Eason

Bo Eason in *Runt of the Litter* (Joan Marcus)

Michele Ragusa, Mark Lotito, Josh Alexander, Christine Rea, Johmaalya Adelekan in *Tintypes* (Kevin Fox)

MELTING POT THEATRE COMPANY

TINTYPES A musical conceived by Mary Kyte, Mel Marvin, Gary Pearle; November 28, 2001; Director, Nick Corley; Sets, Michael Brown, Lighting, Jeff Croiter; Costumes, Daryl Stone; Choreography, Jennifer Paulson Lee; CAST: Johmaalya Adelekan, Josh Alexander, Mark Lotito, Michele Ragusa, Christine Rea

MISS EVERS' BOYS by David Feldshuh; March 13, 2002; Director, Kent Gash; Sets, Emily Beck; Lighting, William Grant III; Costumes, Earl Jerome Battle; Sound, Abe Jacob; CAST: Adriane Lenox, Daryl Edwards, Byron Easley, Chad L. Coleman, Helmar Augustus Cooper, J. Paul Boehmer, Terry Alexander

MINT THEATRE COMPANY

Tenth Season

Artistic Director, Jonathan Bank

MACBETH by William Shakespeare; July 31, 2001; Director, Rebecca Patterson; Sets, Louisa Thompson; Lighting, Mark Barton; Fight Direction, Deborah S. Keller, DeeAnn Weir; CAST: Virginia Baeta, Sheila Lynn Buckley, Aysan Celik, Heather Grayson, Jacqueline Gregg, Stacie Hirsch, Lisette Merenciana, Jina Oh, Karen Pruis, Ami Shukla, Katlan Walker, DeeAnn Weir, Tessa Zugmeyer

THE VOICE OF THE TURTLE by John Van Druten; November 23, 2001; Director, Carl Forsman; Sets, Nathan Heverin; Lighting, Josh Bradford; Costumes, Theresa Squire; Sound, Stephan Jacob; CAST: Elizabeth Bunch, Megan Byrne, Nick Toren

MURDER ON BAKER STREET by Judd Woldin; February 27, 2002; Director, Ike Schambelan; Sets, Merope Vachlioti; Lighting, Marc Janowitz; Costumes, Bryen Shannon; Sound, Gary Bergman; CAST: Melanie Boland, Jerry Lee, George Ashiotos, Richard Simon, Michael Dee, Nicholas Viselli

NO TIME FOR COMEDY by S.N. Behrman; March 19, 2002; Director, Kent Paul; Sets, Tony Andrea; Lighting, Peter West; Costumes, Jayde Chabot; Sound, Jane Shaw; CAST: Simon Booking, Hope Chernov, Diane Ciesla, Leslie Deniston, Ted Pejovich, Shawn Sturnick, Jason Summers

NEW YORK SHAKESPEARE FESTIVAL / THE JOSEPH PAPP PUBLIC THEATER

Forty-Seventh Season

Special projects, in addition to Off-Broadway productions:

NEW WORK NOW!! FESTIVAL OF NEW PLAY READINGS
GIRL SCOUTS OF AMERICA by Andrea Berloff and Mona Mansour; April 28, 2002

TALE OF 2 CITIES: AN AMERICAN JOYRIDE ON MULTIPLE TRACKS by Heather Woodbury; April 29, 2002

THE RATS ARE GETTING BIGGER by Julia Edwards; May 1, 2002

THE MUCKLE MAN by Roberto Aguirre-Sacasa; May 2, 2002

ORANGE LEMON EGG CHERRY by Rinne Groff

80 TEETH, 4 FEET AND 500 POUNDS by Gustavo Orr; Translated by Heather McKay; May 4, 2002

A HUMAN INTEREST STORY, OR THE GORY DETAILS AND ALL by Carlos Murillo; May 5, 2002

WELL by Lisa Kron; May 7, 2002

PYRETOWN by John Belluso; May 8, 2002

HAZELLE ON EDGE by Hazelle Goodman; May 9, 2002

LATE by Sara Ruhl; May 10, 2002

SEBASTIAN by Alejandro Morales; May 11, 2002

THE BEAUTY OF THE FATHER by Nilo Cruz; May 12, 2002

NEW COMPOSERS NOW!! THIRTY-MINUTE EXCERPTS FROM WORKS-IN-PROGRESS
FLORIDA by Randall Eng and Donna di Novelli; May 6, 2002

THE TUTOR by Andrew Gerle and Maryrose Wood; May 6, 2002

SUNDAY, A MUSICAL FABLE by Bruce Monroe and Alva Rogers; May 6, 2002

NEW FEDERAL THEATER

EVERY DAY A VISITOR by Richard Abrons; June 7, 2001; Director, Arthur Strimling; Sets, Robert Joel Schwartz; Lighting, Shirley Prendergast; Costumes, Dawn Robyn Petrlik; CAST: Lisa Bostnar, Tom Brennan, John Freimann, Sylvia Gassell, Kenneth Gray, Helen Hanft, Joe Jamrog, Jerry Matz, Anthony Spins, Fiona Walsh

URBAN TRANSITION: LOOSE BLOSSOMS by Ron Milner; April 7, 2002; Director, Woodie King; Sets, Robert Joel Schwartz; Lighting, Shirley Prendergast; Costumes, Evelyn Nelson; CAST: Jerome Preston Bates, Chadwick Aharon Boseman, Joseph Edward, Dianne Kirksey, Sade Lythcott, George Newton, Monica Soyemi

NEW GROUP

Eighth Season

Producing Director, Elizabeth Timperman

GOOD THING by Jessica Goldberg; December 16, 2001; Director, Jo Bonney; Sets, Neil Patel; Lighting, James Vermeulen; Costumes, Mimi O'Donnell; Sound, Ken Travis; CAST: Betsy Aidem, John Rothman, Alicia Goranson, Chris Messina, Cara Buono, Hamish Linklater

SMELLING A RAT by Mike Leigh; May 19, 2002; Director, Scott Elliott; Sets, Kevin Price; Lighting, Jason Lyons; Costumes, Eric Becker; Composer, Tom Kochan; CAST: Terence Rigby, Brian F. O'Byrne, Gillian Foss, Eddie Kaye Thomas, Michelle Williams

Barbara Suter in *Finally Flannery* (Joan Marcus)

NEW YORK THEATRE WORKSHOP

Twenty-Second Season

FINALLY FLANNERY by Barbara Suter; Director, Michael Sexton; with Ms. Suter and Nancy Robinette

PAN ASIAN REPERTORY THEATRE

Twenty-Fifth Season

Artistic Producing Director, Tisa Chang

FORBIDDEN CITY BLUES Book and Lyrics, Alexander Woo; Music, Ken Weiler; March 30, 2002; Director, Ron Nakahara; Sets, Eric Renschler; Lighting, Victor En Yu Tan; Costumes, Ingrid Maurer; Sound, Peter Griggs; CAST: Jose Ramon Rosario, Rick Ebihara, Kate Chaston, Perry Yung, Fay Ann Lee, Julia McLaughlin, Peter Von Berg, Les J.N. Mau, Scott Reeves

PEARL THEATRE COMPANY

Eighteenth Season

EXIT THE KING by Eugene Ionesco; Director, Joseph Hardy; with Celeste Ciulla, Robert Hock, Michael Nichols, Carol Schultz, Sue Jin Song, Ray Virta

IPHIGENEIA AT AULIS by Euripides; Director, Shepard Sobel; with Dan Daily, Carol Schultz, Sue Jin Song, Robert Hock, Albert Jones, Melissa Maxwell, Celeste Ciulla, Michael Nichols, Scott Whitehurst

THE PHANTOM LADY by Pedro Calderon de la Barca; Director, Rene Buch; with Ray Virta, Dominic Cuskern, Celeste Ciulla, Robin Leslie Brown, Jason Manuel Olazabal, Aaron Ganz, Dan Daily, Rachel Botchan, Emily Gray

ROMEO AND JULIET by William Shakespeare; Director, Shepard Sobel; with Edward Seamon, Dominic Cuskern, Celeste Ciulla, Robin Leslie Brown, Rachel Brown, Joanna Camp, Andy Prosky, Matt Mundy, Scott Whitehurst, Eric Sheffer Stevens, Evan Robertson, Ray Virta, Christopher Moore, Christopher Rivera, Andrew Firda, Robert Hock, John Wylie, James Doherty

MUCH ADO ABOUT NOTHING by William Shakespeare; Director, J.R. Sullivan; with Edward Seamon, Dominic Cuskern, Celeste Ciulla, Robin Leslie Brown, Rachel Brown, Joanne Camp, Andy Prosky, Matt Mundy, Scott Whitehurst, Eric Sheffer Stevens, Evan Robertson, Ray Virta, Christopher Moore, Christopher Rivera, Andrew Firda, Robert Hock, John Wylie, James Doherty

Carol Schultz, Robert Hock, Celeste Ciulla in *Exit the King* (Tom Bloom)

PERFORMANCE SPACE 122

IN ON IT by Daniel MacIvor; October 2, 2001; Director, Mr. MacIvor; Lighting, Kimberly Purrell; Sound and Music, Richard Feren; with Mr. MacIvor, Darreb O'Donnell

DRUMMER WANTED by Richard Maxwell; November 15, 2001; Director, Mr. Maxwell; Songs, Mr. Maxwell; Sets, Angela Moore; Lighting, Michael Schmelling; Costumes, Tony Vazquez; with Ellen LeCompte, Peter Simpson

ECCO PORCO Book by Lee Breuer; January 16, 2002; Director, Mr. Breuer; Composer Bob Telson, Eve Beglarian, Casey Neel; Sets, Manuel Lutgenhorst; Lighting, Kevin Taylor; Costumes, Elizabeth Bourgeois; Sound, Eric Shim; CAST: Black-eyed Susan, Honora Fergusson, Clove Galilee, Karen Kandel, Ruth Maleczech, Maude Mitchell, Frederick Neumann, Terry O'Reilly, Barbara Pollitt

PRIMARY STAGES

Seventeenth Season

Artistic Director, Casey Childs

BYRD'S BOY by Bruce J. Robinson; June 11, 2001; Director, Arthur Masella; sets, Narelle Sissons; Lighting, Peter West; Costumes, Judith Dolan; Original Music and Sound, Donald DiNicola; with David McCallum, Myra Lucretia Taylor

AN IMMACULATE MISCONCEPTION by Carl Djerassi; October 1, 2001; Director, Margaret Booker; Sets, G.W. Mercier; Lighting, Deborah Constantine; Costumes, Laura Crow; Sound and Music, Lewis Flinn; CAST: David Adkins, Ann Dowd, Adam Rose, Thomas Schall

Ann Dowd, Thomas Schall in *An Immaculate Misconception* (Marvin Einhorn)

PUERTO RICAN TRAVELING THEATER

Founder and Producer, Miriam Colon Valle

LA LUPE: MY LIFE, MY DESTINY by Carmen Rivera; June 27, 2001; Director, Luis Caballero; Translation, Raul Davila; Sets, Salvatory Tagliarino; Lighting, Maria Cristina Fuste; Costumes, A. Christina Gianni; Sound, Frank Rodriguez; CAST: Sally Diaz, Gilberto Arribas, Eddie Marrero, Monica Perez-Brandes, Marly Rivera, Hector Maximo Rodriguez, Jimmy Delgado, Johnny Rivero

SIGNATURE THEATRE COMPANY

Eleventh Season

THE LATE HENRY MOSS by Sam Shepard; September 24, 2001; Director, Joseph Chaikin; Sets, Christine Jones; Lighting, Michael Chybowski; Choreography, Peter Pucci; Costumes, Teresa Snider-Stein; Music and Sound, David Van Tieghem, Jill DuBoff; CAST: Guy Boyd, Sheila Tousey, Arliss Howard, Ethan Hawke, Jose Perez, Clark Middleton, Michael Aronov, Tim Michael, Luke Notary

A FEW STOUT INDIVIDUALS by John Guare; May 12, 2002; Director, Michael Greif; Sets, Allen Moyer; Lighting, James Vermeulen; Costumes, Gabriel Berry; Sound and Music, David Van Tieghem; CAST: James Yaegashi, Donald Moffat, William Sadler, Polly Holliday, Tom McGowan, Michi Barall, Umit Celebi, Charles Brown, Amy Hohn, TJ Kenneally, Mark Fish, Clark Middleton, Cheryl Evans

SOHO REP

Artistic Director, Daniel Aukin

[SIC] by Melissa James Gibson; November 20, 2001; Director, Daniel Aukin; Sets, Louisa Thompson; Lighting, Matt Frey; Costumes, Kim Gill; Sound, Robert Murphy; Cast: James Urbaniak, Dominic Fumusa, Christina Kirk, Jennifer Morris, Trevor Williams

ATTEMPTS ON HER LIFE by Martin Crimp; April 22, 2002; Director, Steve Cosson; Sets, Robert Pyzocha; Lighting, Thomas Dunne; Costumes, Kaye Voyce; Sound, Ken Travis; Cast: Christopher McCann, Sara Barnett, T. Ryder Smith, Tracey A. Leight, Damian Balder, Aysan Celik, Jayne Houdyshell

Elizabeth Ruf, Michael Vazquez in *Dream Star Café* (Jonathan Slaff)

THEATRE FOR THE NEW CITY

Developmental theatre and new experimental works. Executive Director, Crystal Field

CANDIDA AND HER FRIENDS by Mario Fratti; June 7, 2001; Director, Michael Hillyer; Sets, Mark Symczak; Lighting, Jason A. Cina; Costumes, Roi "Bubi" Escudero; Cast: Brian Runbeck, Caroline Strong, Neil Levine, Alex McCord, Toks Olagundoye

THE PATIENTS ARE RUNNING THE ASYLUM by Crystal Field; August 4, 2001; Director, Ms. Field; Music Composed and Arranged by Joseph Vernon Banks; Designers, Mary Blanchard, Walter Gurbo; Sound, Joy Linscheid, David Nolan; Costumes, Alexandra Nichols, Ruth Muzio

BABES IN AMERICA by Carole Clement; September 13, 2001; Director, Max Daniels; Cast: Kate Lunsford, Paula Nance, Alexandra Leeper, Lisa Rock, Samuel Ward, Ryan Paulsen, Joseph Jude Zito

PETER PAN by J.M. Barrie; November 22, 2001; Director, Jim Neisen; Sets, Ken Rothschild; Choreography, Sarah Adams; Lighting, Randy Glickman; Costumes, Christianne Myers; Cast: Danny Bacher, Josh Bacher, Rezelle Caravaca, Michael-David Gordon, Missy Jayme, Jack Lush, Sven Miller, Patrena Murray, Damen Scranton

THE INSURRECTION MASS WITH FUNERAL MARCH FOR A ROTTEN IDEA (A special mass for the aftermath of the events of Sept. 11th) December 18, 2001; Director, Peter Schumann; Cast: Strawberry Cantubo, Adam Cook, Susie Dennison, Vasilos Gletsos, Susan Hirschmugl, Jason Norris, Michael Romanyshyn, Maria Schumann, Lydia Stein

DREAM STAR CAFÉ by Jack Agueros; January 31, 2002; Director, Crystal Field; Cast: Elizabeth Ruf, Dalia Ruiz, Michael Vazquez, Primy Rivera

THE SHORT VIOLENT LIFE OF MARGIE GOOD by Jimmy Camicia; April 6, 2002; Director, Harvey Tavel; Sets, Mark Marcante; Lighting, Alexander Bartenieff; Cast: Crystal Field, Craig Meade, Irma St. Paule, Mary Tierney, Althea Vythuys, Dorothy Cantwell, Darby Dizard, Marian Sarach

THE MURALS OF ROCKEFELLER CENTER by Jim Neisen and Members of the Irondale Ensemble Project; April 24, 2002; Director, Mr. Neisen; Sets, Ken Rothchild; Lighting, Randy Glickman; Costumes, T. Michael Hall; Music, Walter Thompson; Cast: Danny Bacher, Josh Bacher, Michael-David Gordon, Missy Jayme, Jack Lush, Sven Miller, Patrena Murray, Damen Scranton

CHOCOLATE IN HEAT: GROWING UP ARAB IN AMERICA by Betty Shamieh; August 24, 2001; Director, Damen Scranton; Cast: Ms. Shamieh, Piter Fattouche

THE VINEYARD THEATRE

Twenty-First Season

Artistic Director, Douglas Aibel; Executive Director, Barbara Zinn Kreiger; Managing Director, Jeffrey Solis

UNWRAP YOUR CANDY Four one acts written and directed by Doug Wright; October 8, 2001; Sets, Michael Brown; Lighting, Phil Monat; Costumes, Ilona Somogyi; Sound, David Van Tieghem, Jill DuBoff; Music, Mr. Van Tieghem; Cast: Reg Rogers, Leslie Lyles, Michi Barall, Henry Stram, Darren Pettie. Also on the bill: "Lot 13: The Bone Violin," "Wildwood Park," "Baby Talk"

BRUTAL IMAGINATION Musical adaptation, Cornelius Eady and Diane Paulus from Mr. Eady's poem; Music, Dierdre Murray; January 9, 2002; Director, Ms. Paulus; Sets, Mark Wendland; Lighting, Kevin Adams; Costumes, Ilona Somogyi; Sound, Brett Jarvis, David A. Gilman; Cast: Joe Morton, Sally Murphy

SWIMMING WITH WATERMELONS by Randy Weiner, Diane Paulus and Members of Project 400; April 11, 2002; Director, Mr. Weiner; Sets, Myung Hee Cho; Lighting, Michael Chybowski; Costumes, Ilona Somogyi; Sound, Brett Jarvis; Cast: Emily Hellstrom, Rachel Benbow Murdy, Anna Wilson, Jordin Ruderman

WOMEN'S PROJECT & PRODUCTIONS

Twenty-Fourth Season

Artistic Director, Julia Miles; Managing Director, Georgia Buchanan

THE STRANGE CASE OF MARY LINCOLN Book, June Bingham; Music and Lyrics, Carmel Owen; Director, Victoria Pero; Cast: Chris Clavelli; David Hess, Mark Ledbetter; Karen Murphy, Peter Samuel, Gayle Turner

CARSON MCCULLERS (HISTORICALLY: INACCURATE) by Sarah Schulman; January 20, 2002; Director, Marion McClinton; Sets, Neil Patel; Lighting, Donald Holder; Costumes, Toni-Leslie James; Sound, Janet Kalas; Cast: Michi Barall, Rosalyn Coleman, Barbara Eda-Young, Leland Gantt, Tim Hopper, Rick Stear, Anne Torsiglieri

Reg Rogers, Leslie Lyles in *Unwrap Your Candy* (Carol Rosegg)

Sally Murphy, Joe Morton in *Brutal Imagination* (Carol Rosegg)

PROFESSIONAL REGIONAL COMPANIES

Highlights

AHMANSON THEATRE/ CENTER THEATRE GROUP

Los Angeles, California

Thirty-Fifth Season

Artistic Director/Producer, Gordon Davidson; Managing Director, Charles Dillingham; General Manager, Douglas C. Baker; Associate Producer, Madeline Puzo; Press Director, Tony Sherwood; Press Associate, Ken Werther; Associate Manager, Jennifer Oliver; Assistant Producer, Susan Obrow; Director of Marketing & Communications, Jim Royce; Casting Director, Amy Lieberman, C.S.A.; Development Director, Yvonne Carlson Bell; Chief Financial Officer, Edward L. Rada

THE CAR MAN by Matthew Bourne; Director and Choreographer, Mr. Bourne; Production Design, Lez Brotherston; Lighting, Chris Davey; Sound, Matt McKenzie and Autograph; Music, Terry Davies & Rodin Schedrin's *Carmen Suite* (after Bizet's *Carmen*); Composer and Arranger, Terry Davies; Musical Director, Brett Morris; Conductors, Benjamin Pope, Gavin Sutherland; Production Managers, David Evans, O'Donovan & Bradford; Production Stage Manager, Marina Kilby; General Management, Douglas C. Baker, Jennifer Oliver; Company Managers, Simon Lacey, Frank Lott, Margaret Irwin; General Press Representative, Tony Sherwood; Press Associate, Ken Werther; Associate Producer, Madeline Puzo; Associate Directors, Scott Ambler, Etta Murfitt; Produced by Center Theatre Group/Ahmanson Theatre with Katherine Doré for Adventures Motion Pictures; September 6–October 28, 2001; CAST: Scott Ambler, Sam Archer, Stephen Berkeley-White, Belinda Lee Chapman, Andrew Corbett, Suzanne Curtin, Vicky Evans, Darren J. Fawthrop, Valentina Formenti, Adam Galbraith, Nina Goldman, Heather Habens, Paulo Kadow, Will Kemp, Nanette Kincaid, Rachel Lancaster, James Leece, Etta Murfitt, Kevin Muscat, Neil Penlington, Emily Piercy, Arthur Pita, Lee Smikle, Alan Vincent, Ewan Wardrop, Shelby Williams, Richard Winsor

Will Kemp in *The Car Man, An Auto-Erotic Thriller* (Bill Cooper)

Saranne Curtin, Alan Vincent in *The Car Man, An Auto-Erotic Thriller* (Bill Cooper)

THE ALLIANCE THEATRE COMPANY

Atlanta, Georgia

Artistic Director, Susan V. Booth; Managing Director, Gus Stuhlreyer

DINAH WAS by Oliver Goldstick; Sets, Michael Yeargan; Lighting, John Lasiter; Costumes, Paul Tazewell; Sound, Rob Milburn; Musical Arrangements and Orchestrations, Jason Robert Brown; Choreography, George Faison; CAST: Dan Bollinger (Bellhop), Chandra Currelley (Dinah Washington), Matt de Caro (Spinelli/Sam), Jeffrey Hutchinson (Frick/Rollie), Tim Rohze (Boss/Chase), Saycon Sengbloh (Maye/Mama/Violet)

Sonja Lanzener in *Lovely Sunday for Creve Coeur* (Michelle Hollberg)

A LOVELY SUNDAY FOR CREVE COEUR by Tennessee Williams; Director, Kent Gash; Sets, Emily Beck; Lighting, William Grant III; Costumes, Andre Harrington; Sound, Clay Benning; CAST: Genevieve Elam (Dorothea), Felicity La Fortune (Helena), Sonja Lanzener (Bodey), Heather Robison (Miss Gluck)

BELOW THE BELT by Richard Dresser; Director, B.J. Jones; Sets, Michael Philippi; Lighting, Liz Lee; Costumes, English Toole; Sound, Clay Benning; CAST: Kyle Colerider-Krugh (Merkin), Larry C. Larson (Hanrahan), Quint Von Canon (Dobbitt)

Chandra Currelley in *Dinah Was* (Jonathan Burnette)

Kyle Colerider-Krugh, Larry Larson, Quint Von Canon in *Below the Belt* (Michelle Hollberg)

A CHRISTMAS CAROL by Charles Dickens; Adapted and Directed by David H. Bell; Sets, D. Martyn Bookwalter; Lighting, Diane Ferry Williams; Costumes, Mariann Verheyen; Sound, Clay Benning; CAST: Jessie Andary, Hunter Ballard, Rebekah Baty, Taurean Blacque, Crista Nicole Brown, Terry Burrell, Ritchie Crownfield, Jeremy Cudd, Thomas Neal Antwon Ghant, Schafer Gray, Gavin Gregory, Kenya Hamilton, Charles Horton, Matthew Johnson, Chris Kayser, Noelle Kayser, Katie Kneeland, Briana Leigh Leech, Daniel May, Michael McClain, Megan McFarland, Wendy Melkonian, Chris Moses, Elisabeth Omilami, Courteney Patterson, Allen Read, Kendrick Young, Laparee Young

JAR THE FLOOR by Cheryl West; Director, Andrea Frye; Sets, Dex Edwards; Lighting, Kathy Perkins; Costumes, Earl Jerome Battle; Sound, Clay Benning; CAST: Pat Bowie (Madear), Terry Burrell (Maydee), Margo Moorer (Lola), Saycon Sengbloh (Vennie), Laurie Strickland (Raisa)

THE GAME OF LOVE AND CHANCE by Marivaux; Director, Stephen Wadsworth; Sets, Robert Andrew Dahlstrom; Lighting, Adam Silverman; Costumes, David Zinn; Sound, Clay Benning; CAST: Christopher Baker (Dorante), Julia Sion (Silvia), Patty Foster (Commedia), Pamela Gold (Commedia/Valet), William McNulty (Orgon), David Pichette (Harlequin), Jeff Portell (Mario), Michelle Six (Lisette), Jennifer Smiles (Commedia)

PROOF by David Auburn; Director, Susan V. Booth; Sets, Todd Rosenthal; Lighting, Michael Philippi; Costumes, Linda Roethke; Sound, Clay Benning; Original Music, Rob Milburn and Michael Bodeen; CAST: Brik Berkes (Hal), William Bogert (Robert), Rhoda Griffis (Claire), Susan Pourfar (Catherine)

SLEEPWALKERS by Jorge Ignacio Cortinas; Director, Ruben Polendo; Sets, Scott Spahr; Lighting, Dawn Chiang; Costumes, Carol Bailey; Sound, Clay Benning; CAST: Nick Bixby (Tito), Mateo Gomez (Soldier), Michelle Rios (Skinny Woman), Sophia Salguero (Pionera, age 12), Rafael Sardina (Charley), Liam Torres (Orderly/Bloody Butcher/Tourist)

Brik Berkes, Susan Pourfar in *Proof* (Jonathan Burnette)

WOODY GUTHRIE'S AMERICAN SONG Songs and Writings by Woody Guthrie; Conceived and Adapted by Peter Glazer; Director, Susan V. Booth; Sets, G.W. Mercier; Lighting, Robert Wierzel; Costumes, Susan E. Mickey; Sound, Clay Benning; CAST: Rebekah Baty (Young Woman), Brian Gunter (Second Young Woman), Jahi Kearse (First Young Man), Tom Key (Man), Bernadine Mitchell (Woman)

IN THE ALLIANCE CHILDREN'S THEATRE:
ANDROCLES AND THE LION by Aesop, adapted by Aurand Harris; Director, Rosemary Newcott; Sets, Rochelle Barker; Lighting, Liz Lee; Costumes, Sydney Roberts; Sound, Clay Benning; CAST: Hope Chatham, Thomas Neal Antwon Ghant, Christine L. Horn, Jim Hubbert, Jahi Kearse, Heather Ward

PINNOCHIO by Carlo Collodi; Original Adaptation, Eric Coble; Director, Rosemary Newcott; Sets, Kevin Landon Raper; Lighting, Jason Scott Foster; Costumes, Susan Mickey; Sound, Clay Benning; CAST: Cheri Christian, Rita Dolphin, Jen Harper, Jahi Kearse, Keland Scher, Pete Turner

Mateo Gomez, Nick Bixby, Sophia Salguero in *Sleepwalkers* (Jonathan Burnette)

BARTER THEATRE

Abingdon, Virginia

Sixty-Ninth Season

Producing Artistic Director, Richard Rose

IDOLS OF THE KING by Ronnie Claire Edwards and Allen Crowe; Director, John Briggs; Musical Director, Wm. Perry Morgan; Scenic Design, Daniel Ettinger; Costumes, Amanda Aldridge; Lighting, David Friedl; Sound, Bobby Beck; Props, Cheri Prough DeVol; Technical Director, Mark J. DeVol; Stage Manager, Karen N. Rowe; Barter Theatre, February 6–March 17, 2002; CAST: Tom Angland (All Men Parts), Christine Rowan (All Women Parts), Scot Bruce (Elvis)

MACBETH by William Shakespeare adapted by Richard Rose; Director, Richard Rose; Original Music, Peter Yonka; Scenic Design, Mark J. DeVol; Costumes, Amanda Aldridge; Lighting, David Friedl; Sound, Bobby Beck; Props, Cheri Prough DeVol; Technical Director, Mark J. DeVol; Dramaturg, Peter Yonka; Fight Choreographer, Robert Walsh; Fight Captain, Will Bigham; Stage Manager, John Keith Hall; Assistant Stage Manager, Karen N. Rowe; Barter Stage II, March 13–May 19, 2002; CAST: John Hedges (Macbeth), Karen Sabo (Lady Macbeth), Will Bigham, Catherine Gray, John Hardy, Mike Ostroski, Peter Yonka

SOMETHING'S AFOOT Book, Music, and Lyrics by James McDonald, David Vos and Robert Gerlach, Additional Music by Ed Linderman; Director, John Hardy; Choreographer, Amanda Aldridge; Music Director, Wm. Perry Morgan; Scenic Design, Gary English; Costumes, Amanda Aldridge; Lighting, Trevor Maynard; Sound, Bobby Beck; Props, Cheri Prough DeVol; Technical Director, Mark J. DeVol; Stage Manager, John Keith Hall; Assistant Stage Managers, John Hardy, Karen N. Rowe; Assistant to Scenic Designer, Cully Long; Barter Theatre, March 22–May 18, 2002; CAST: Karen Sabo (Lettie), Will Bigham, (Flint), James Pritchett (Clive), Catherine Gray (Hope Langdon), John Hedges (Dr. Grayburn), Mike Ostroski (Nigel Rancour), Josephine Hall (Lady Grace Manley-Prowe), Michael Poisson (Colonel Gillweather), Evalyn Baron (Miss Tweed), Peter Yonka (Geoffrey)

Scot Buce in *Idols of the King*

Jessi Nunley, Michael Poisson in *To Kill a Mockingbird*

ON GOLDEN POND by Ernest Thompson; Director, Kate Musgrove; Scenic Design, Charlie Morgan; Costumes, Karen Brewster; Lighting, Trevor Maynard; Sound, Bobby Beck; Props, Cheri Prough DeVol; Technical Director, Mark J. DeVol; Stage Manager, Karen N. Rowe; Assistant Stage Managers, John Keith Hall, John Hardy; Barter Theatre, March 28–May 18, 2002; CAST: James Pritchett (Norman Thayer, Jr.), Evalyn Baron (Ethel Thayer), Wm. Perry Morgan (Charlie Martin), Josephine Hall (Chelsea Thayer Wayne), Michael Poisson (Billy Ray), Ryan Cury, Joseph Grantham (Billy Ray as a boy)

OKLAHOMA! Music by Richard Rodgers; Book and Lyrics by Oscar Hammerstein II, based on the play *Green Grow the Lilacs* by Lynn Riggs; Original Dances by Agnes de Mille; Director, Evalyn Baron; Musical Director, Wm. Perry Morgan; Choreographer, Amanda Aldridge; Scenic Design, Dale Jordan; Costumes, Amanda Aldridge; Lighting, Dale Jordan; Sound, Bobby Beck; Props, Cheri Prough DeVol; Technical Director, Mark J. DeVol; Stage Manager, Karen N. Rowe; Assistant Stage Manager, John Hardy, John Keith Hall; Assistant to the Choreographer, Katy Brown; Fight Choreographer, Will Bigham; Dance Captain, Sandra Murphy; Barter Theatre, May 23–August 11, 2002; CAST: Peter Yonka (Curly McClain), Elizabeth Bauer (Laurey Williams), Mike Ostroski (Will Parker), Josephine Hall (Aunt Eller Murphy), John Hedges (Jud Frye), Michael Poisson (Ali Hakim), Karen Sabo (Ado Annie Carnes), Will Bigham, Paige Brown, Juliana Caycedo, Mackenzie Demaree, Russ Hicks, Jennifer J. Katz, Janine Kyanko, Craig Larkin, Catherine E. Matthews, Greg McMillan, Rebecca Miller, Sandra Murphy, J.J. Musgrove, Brandon Roberts, Willoughby Smith, Tony Smithey, Ali Squitieri, Eugene Sumlin, Gavin Waters

TALLEY'S FOLLY by Lanford Wilson; Director Kate Musgrove; Scenic Design, Cheri Prough DeVol; Costumes, Jennifer Gibson; Lighting, Trevor Maynard; Sound, Bobby Beck; Technical Director, Mark J. DeVol; Stage Manager, John Keith Hall; Assistant Stage Manager, Karen N. Rowe; Barter Stage II, May 30–August 17, 2002; CAST: Catherine Gray (Sally Talley), John Hardy (Matt Friedman)

THE IMPORTANCE OF BEING EARNEST by Oscar Wilde; Director, Richard Rose; Scenic Design, Dale Jordan; Costumes, Amanda Aldridge; Lighting, Dale Jordan; Sound, Bobby Beck; Props, Cheri Prough DeVol; Technical Director, Mark J. DeVol; Stage Manager, John Keith Hall; Assistant Stage Managers, Karen N. Rowe, John Hardy; Dramaturg, Mike Ostroski; Barter Theatre, June 5–August 10, 2002; CAST: Wm. Perry Morgan (Manservant, Butler), Peter Yonka (Algernon Moncrieff), John Hedges (Jack Worthing), Evalyn Baron (Lady Bracknell), Josephine Hall (Gwendolen Fairfax), Catherine Gray (Cecily Cardew), Will Bigham (Wilhelmina Bigham, Miss Prism), J.J. Musgrove (Reverend Canon Chausible)

TALES FROM BLAIR MOUNTAIN by Victor Depta; Director, John Hardy; Scenic Design, D.R. Mullins; Costumes, Jennifer Gibson; Lighting, Trevor Maynard; Sound, Bobby Beck; Props, Cheri Prough DeVol; Technical Director, Mark J. DeVol; Stage Manager, Karen N. Rowe; Assistant Stage Managers, John Hardy, John Keith Hall; Barter Stage II, June 12–August 4, 2002; CAST: Elizabeth Bauer, Jennifer J. Katz, Mike Ostroski, Michael Poisson, Miles Polaski, Brandon Roberts, Karen Sabo, Eugene Sumlin

MY WAY Conceived by David Grapes and Todd Olson, book by Todd Olson, Original production directed by David Grapes; Musical Director, Vince di Mura, Choreographer, John Fredo; Lighting, Todd O. Wren; Costumes, Amanda Aldridge; Sound, Bobby Beck; Props, Cheri Prough DeVol; Technical Director, Mark J. DeVol; Stage Manager, Karen N. Rowe; Barter Theatre, August 15–September 14, 2003; CAST: John Fredo, Douglas Kampsen, Ginger Newman, Kathy Weese

TO KILL A MOCKINGBIRD by Christopher Sergel, based upon the novel by Harper Lee; Director, Richard Rose; Original Music Composer, Wm. Perry Morgan; Assistant Director, Evalyn Baron; Scenic Design, Daniel Ettinger; Costumes, Amanda Aldridge; Lighting, E. Tonry Lathroum; Sound, Bobby Beck; Props, Cheri Prough DeVol; Technical Director, Mark J. DeVol; Stage Manager, John Keith Hall; Assistant Stage Manager, Karen N. Rowe; Barter Theatre, September 19–November 23, 2002; CAST: Michael Poisson (Atticus Finch), Jessi Nunley/Annie Grace Surber (Scout), Ryan Cury (Jeremy Finch), John Hardy (Bob Ewell), Catherine Gray (Mayella Ewell), Charles Baker Harris (Luke Daniel Bart), Eugene Sumlin (Tom Robinson), Mike Ostroski (Boo Radley), Evalyn Baron, Frank Green, Josephine Hall, John Hedges, Janine Kyanko, Alicia Laws, Jasper McGruder, Marcus Montgomery, Wm. Perry Morgan, Rebecca Newton, Miles Polaski, Elizabeth P. McKnight, Karen Sabo, Matthew Ryan Smith, Willoughby Smith, Jon Vandertholen, Ronnie Williams, Virginia Wing, Peter Yonka

SOUTH PACIFIC Book by Oscar Hammerstein II and Joshua Logan, Music by Richard Rodgers, Lyrics by Oscar Hammerstein II, Adapted from the Pulitzer Prize–winning novel *Tales of the South Pacific* by James A. Michener; Director, Richard Rose; Musical Director, Wm. Perry Morgan; Choreographer, Amanda Aldridge; Scenic Design, Daniel Ettinger; Costumes, Amanda Aldridge; Lighting, E. Tonry Lathroum; Sound, Bobby Beck; Props, Cheri Prough DeVol; Technical Director; Mark J. DeVol; Dramaturg, Carrie Clare; Stage Manager, Karen N. Rowe; Assistant Stage Managers, John Keith Hall, John Hardy; Dance Captain, Catherine E. Matthews; Barter Theatre, October 3–November 23, 2002; CAST: Peter Yonka (Lt. Joseph Cable), Katy Brown (Liatt), Jon Vandertholen (Emile de Becque), Catherine Gray (Ensign Nellie Forbush), Virginia Wing (Bloody Mary), Catherine E. Matthews, John Hedges, J.J. Musgrove, Eugene Sumlin, Elizabeth P. McKnight, Miles Polaski, Wendy Catherine Mitchell, Matthew Ryan Smith, Willoughby Smith, Michael Poisson, Jasper McGruder, Juliana Caycedo, Karthik Venkataraman

THE MEMORY OF WATER by Shelagh Stephenson; Director, John Hardy; Scenic Design, Cheri Prough DeVol; Costumes, Amanda Aldridge; Lighting, Trevor Maynard; Sound, Miles Polaski; Props, Cheri Prough DeVol; Technical Director, Mark J. DeVol; Stage Manager, John Keith Hall; Barter Stage II, October 8–November 17, 2002; CAST: Karen Sabo (Mary), Evalyn Baron (Vi), Josephine Hall (Teresa), Janine Kyanko (Catherine), Mike Ostroski (Mike), Frank Green (Frank)

HOLIDAY MEMORIES by Truman Capote, adapted for the stage by Russell Vandenbroucke; Director, Katy Brown; Music Composer, Matthew M. Stone; Additional Music, Wm. Perry Morgan; Scenic Design, D.R. Mullins; Costumes, Amanda Aldridge; Lighting, Trevor Maynard; Sound, Bobby Beck; Props, Cheri Prough DeVol; Technical Director, Mark J. DeVol; Stage Manager, Karen N. Rowe; Assistant Stage Managers, John Keith Hall, John Hardy; Fight Choreographer, Mike Ostroski; Barter Stage II, November 26–December 22, 2002; CAST: Mike Ostroski (Truman), Miles Polaski (Buddy), Josephine Hall (Miss Sook), J.J. Musgrove (Man), Catherine Gray (Woman)

A CHRISTMAS CAROL by Charles Dickens, adapted by Richard Rose; Director, Richard Rose; Musical Director, Peter Yonka; Choreographer, Amanda Aldridge; Scenic Director, Daniel Ettinger; Costumes, Amanda Aldridge; Lighting, Richard Rose; Sound, Bobby Beck; Technical Director, Mark J. DeVol; Stage Manager, John Keith Hall; Assistant Stage Manager, Karen N. Rowe; Barter Theatre, November 29–December 29, 2002; CAST: John Hedges (Scrooge), John Hardy (Mr. Cratchit), Michael Poisson (Jacob Marley), Jessi Nunley/Mackenzie Demarre (Tiny Tim), Evalyn Baron, Emily Blevins, Chase Helton, Russ Hicks, Mindy Miller, Anita Ostrovsky, Karen Sabo, Kirstie Sensky, Eugene Sumlin, Peter Yonka

Karen Sabo, Evalyn Baron in *The Memory of Water*

BERKELEY REPERTORY THEATRE

Berkeley, California

In association with the Joseph Papp Public Theater/New York Shakespeare Festival

Artistic Director, Tony Taccone; Managing Director, Susan Medak

36 VIEWS by Naomi Iizuka; Director, Mark Wing-Davey; Sets, Douglas Stein; Lighting, David Weiner; Costumes, Myung Hee Cho; Sound, Matthew Spiro; September 7, 2001–October 28, 2001; CAST: Darius Wheeler, Setsuko Hearn, John Bell, Claire Tsong, Owen Mattiassen, Elizabeth Newman-Orr, Bill Camp, Liana Pai, Ebon Moss-Bachrach, Elaine Tse, Peter Donat, Rebecca Wisocky

Rebecca Wisocky, Elaine Tse in *36 Views* (Kevin Berne)

NOCTURNE by Adam Rapp; Director, Mark Brokaw; Sets, Neil Patel; Lighting, Mark McCullough; Costumes, Donna Marie; Sound and Original Music, David Van Tieghem; October 12, 2001–November 11, 2001; CAST: Anthony Rapp as the Son

MUCH ADO ABOUT NOTHING by William Shakespeare; Director, Brian Kulick; Sets, Mark Wendland; Lighting, Michael R. Chybowski; Costumes, Ann Hould-Ward; Sound, Matthew Spiro; November 16, 2001–January 8, 2002; CAST: Elijah Alexander (Don John), Atosa Babanoff (Ursula), Sterling Brown (Benedick), Michael Brusasco (Verges), Hector Correa (Conrad/Friar), Nathan Darrow (Claudio), Francesca Faridany (Beatrice), Geoff Hoyle (Dogberry), Julian Lopez-Morillas (Leonato), Andy Murray (Borachio), Charles Shaw Robinson (Don Pedro), Stacy Ross (Margaret), Noel True (Hero)

RHINOCEROS by Eugene Ionesco; Translated and Adapted by Allen Kuharski and Georges Moskos; Director, Barbara Damashek; Sets, Christopher Barreca; Lighting, York Kennedy; Costumes, Beaver Bauer; Sound, Matthew Spiro; January 18–March 10, 2002; CAST: Margaret Schenck (The Housewife), Geoff Hoyle (Berenger), Jason Monroe (Jean), Hector Correa (Café Proprietor), Jennifer Taggert (The Waitress), Wilma Bonet (The Grocer's Wife), W. Frances Walters (The Grocer), Warren Keith (The Logician), Gerald Hiken (The Old Gentleman), Susan Marie Brecht (Daisy), Andrew Hurteau (Dudard), Gerald Hiken (Botard), Warren Keith (Mr. Papillon), Wilma Bonet (Mrs. Boeuf), Paul Finocchiaro (Fireman)

Susan Marie Brecht, Geoff Hoyle, Andrew Hurteau, Wilma Bonet, Gerald Hiken, Warren Keith in *Rhinoceros* (Ken Friedman)

CULTURE CLASH IN AMERICCA Written, Created, and Performed by Culture Clash: Richard Montoya, Ric Salinas, Herbert Siguenza; Director, Tony Taccone; Sets and Lighting, Alexander V. Nichols; Costumes, Donna Marie; Sound, Matthew Spiro; February 1–March 3, 2002

HOMEBODY/KABUL by Tony Kushner; Director, Tony Taccone; Sets, Kate Edmunds; Lighting, Peter Maradudin; Costumes, Lydia Tanji; Sound, Matthew Spiro; April 9–June 9, 2002; Cast: Michelle Morain, Julian Lopez-Morillas, Hector Correa, Charles Shaw Robinson, Bruce McKenzie, Heidi Dippold, Rahul Gupta, Harsh Nayyar, Waleed Zuaiter, Jacqueline Antaramian

CLOUD NINE by Caryl Churchill; Director, Tony Taccone; Sets, Loy Arcenas; Lighting, James Vermeulen; Costumes, William Lane; Sound, Matthew Spiro; June 7–July 28, 2002; Cast: Matthew Boston, Angela Brazil, Timothy Crowe, Stacy Ross, Danny Scheie, Cynthia Strickland, Fred Sullivan, Jr.

Ric Salinas, Herbert Siguenza in *Culture Clash in AmeriCCa* (Kevin Berne)

Michelle Morain in *Homebody/Kabul* (Kevin Berne)

CAPITAL REPERTORY THEATRE

Albany, New York

Producing Artistic Director, Maggie Mancinelli-Cahill; Managing Director, Jeff Dannick

A RAISIN IN THE SUN by Lorraine Hansberry; Director, Reggie Life; Sets, Ruben Arana-Downs; Lighting, Michael Gianetti; Costumes, Isabel Rubio; Sound, Christopher St. Hilaire; CAST: Regina H. Bain (Ruth Younger), Christopher M. Huntley (Travis Younger), Omar Sterling McGill (Travis Younger), Kim Sullivan (Walter Lee Younger), Schantelle Cason (Beneatha Younger), Betty Vaughn (Mama Lena Younger), Kevin Merrill Wilson (Joseph Asagai), Daver Morrison (George Murchison), Michael Hayes (Karl Linder), Marlon Morrison (Bobo), Kofi Candela (Mover)

WOODY GUTHRIE'S AMERICAN SONG Songs and Lyrics by Woody Guthrie; Conceived and Adapted by Peter Glazer; Director and Musical Director, David M. Lutken; Sets, Ted Simpson; Lighting, Deborah Constantine; Costumes, Denise Dygert; Sound, Christopher St. Hilaire

DINNER WITH FRIENDS by Donald Margulies; Director, Jane Page; Sets, Donald Eastman; Lighting, Stephen Quandt; Costumes, Gail Brassard; Sound, Steve Stevens; CAST: Richard Edward Long, Elizabeth Hess, Patricia Dalen, Mark Elliot Wilson

TRIPLE ESPRESSO—a highly caffeinated comedy by Bill Arnold, Michael Pearce Donley and Bob Stromberg; Director, William Partlan; CAST: Michael Pearce Donley, Bob Stromberg, Bill Arnold

THE SMELL OF THE KILL by Michele Lowe; Director, Maggie Mancinelli-Cahill; Sets, Donald Eastman; Lighting, Deborah Constantine; Costumes, Isabel Rubio; Sound, Jane Shaw; CAST: Corinna May, Shelley Delaney, Pamela Hart

Elizabeth Hess, Patricia Dalen, Richard E. Long in *Dinner with Friends* (Joe Schuyler)

Corinna May, Pamela Hart, Shelley Delaney in *The Smell of the Kill* (Joe Schuyler)

CENTER STAGE

Baltimore, Maryland

Thirty-Ninth Season

Artistic Director, Irene Lewis; Managing Director, Thomas Pechar

THE PAJAMA GAME Book by George Abbott and Richard Bissell; Music and Lyrics by Richard Adler and Jerry Ross; Director, Irene Lewis; Choreographer, Willie Rosario; Music Director, Milton Granger; Set Designer, Walt Spangler; Lighting Designer, Mimi Jordan Sherin; Costumes, Catherine Zuber; Sound Designer, Janet Kalas; Stage Manager, Linda Marvel; Head Theater, October 12–December 2, 2001; CAST: Robert Dorfman (Hines), Michael Brian (Prez), Sarah Anderson (Virginia), Jason Weston (Joe), Merwin Goldsmith (Hasler), Meg Gillentine (Gladys), Tina Johnson (Mabel), Albert Macklin (First Helper), Justin Patterson (Second Helper), Ann Harada (Brenda), Zoie Morris Quinde (Mary), Katie Harvey (Mae), Katie Barrett (Poopsie), Robert Bartley (Sid Sorokin), Dennis Kenney (Charley), Derric Harris (Eddie), Christianne Tisdale (Babe Williams), Laurence O'Dwyer (Max/Pop)

A RAISIN IN THE SUN by Lorraine Hansberry; Director, Marion McClinton; Set Designer, Michael Philippi; Costume Designer, Toni-Leslie James; Lighting Designer, Tom Sturge; Sound Designers, Rob Milburn and Michael Bodeen; Stage Management, Karen Shepherd; Pearlstone Theater, November 15–December 23, 2001; CAST: Linda Powell (Ruth Younger), Keith Glover (Walter Lee Younger), Sylvester Lee Kirk and Robert M. Harley (Travis Younger), Tracie Thomas (Beneatha Younger), Trezana Beverley (Lena Younger/Mama), Curtis McClarin (Joseph Asagai), Harvey Gardner Moore (George Murchison), Darrill Rosen (Karl Lindner), Clayton LeBouef (Bobo)

THREE TALL WOMEN by Edward Albee; Director, Tim Vasen; Set Designer, John Coyne; Costume Designer, Meg Neville; Lighting Designer, Matthew Frey; Sound, Michael Creason; Stage Manager, Mike Schleifer; Pearlstone Theater; January 11–February 10, 2002; CAST: Scotty Bloch (A), Patricia Hodges (B), Anne Louise Zachry (C), Jacob Zahniser (The Boy)

THE WINTER'S TALE by William Shakespeare; Director, Irene Lewis; Set Designer, Christine Jones; Costume Designer, Candice Donnelly; Lighting Designer, Pat Collins; Sound Designer, David Budries; Stage Manager, Karen Shepherd; Pearlstone Theater, February 22–March 31, 2002; CAST: Mark Elliot Wilson (Polixenes), Jon De Vries (Leontes), Olivia Birkelund (Hermione), James E. Bonilla, Sam Hulsey (Mamillius), Conan McCarty (Camillo), Diana LaMar (Emilia/Mopsa), Karen Hansen (Lady), Robert Alexander Owens (A Lord of Sicilia), Stephen Patrick Martin (An Officer of Sicilia), Stephen F. Schmidt (Antigonus/Sicilian Gentleman), Caitlin O'Connell (Paulina), Carlos J. Gonzalez (Jailer/Cleomenes), Marc Anthony Nelson (Servant of Leontes), Warren Snipe (Dion/Bear), B. Thomas Rinaldi (Bodyguard), Laurence O'Dwyer (Time), Tom Mardirosian (Autolycus), Derek Phillips (Florizel), Tina Jones (Perdita), Karen Hansen (Dorcas), David J. Steinberg (Bohemian Servant), Jacob Riggs (Bodyguard/Shepherd)

BLITHE SPIRIT by Noël Coward; Director, Tim Vasen; Set Designer, Michael Vaughn Sims; Costume Designer, David Burdick; Lighting Designer, Michael Chybowski; Sound Designer, David Budries; Stage Manager, Julianne Franz; Pearlstone Theater, April 12–May 19, 2002; CAST: Lise Bruneau (Ruth), Catherine Weidner (Edith), David Adkins (Charles), Patrick Husted (Dr. Bradman), Becky London (Mrs. Bradman), Randy Danson (Madame Arcati), Lynnda Ferguson (Elvira)

CINCINNATI PLAYHOUSE IN THE PARK

Cincinnati, Ohio

Artistic Director, Edward Stern; Executive Director, Buzz Ward

SMOKE ON THE MOUNTAIN by Connie Ray; Director, Alan Bailey; Sets, Peter Harrison; Lighting, Susan Terrano; Costumes, Jeanette deJong; July 5–August 19, 2001; CAST: David Hemsley Caldwell, Jonah Marsh, Constance Barron, Bobby Taylor, Dionne McGuire Gardner, Jason Edwards, Chad Borden

KING LEAR by William Shakespeare; Director, Edward Stern; Sets, Karen TenEyck; Lighting, Thomas Hase; Costumes, Susan Tsu; September 4–October 5, 2001; CAST: Christopher McHale, Philip Pleasants, Conan McCarty, Joneal Joplin, Pamela Nyberg, Rachel Botchan, Robin Moseley, Bruce Cromer, John Rensenhouse, Steve Cirbus, Phillip Christian, Michael Milligan, Todd Cerveris, Dale Hodges, Andrew Burkhart, Alex Domeyko, A. Jackson Ford, John Edward Goodnow, Mark Sage Hamilton, Jason Huysman, Aaron Simms, Patrick Toon, Gary Warden, Adam Ziemkiewicz, Akiko Hashimoto, Christine S. Williams

GOD'S MAN IN TEXAS by David Rambo; Director, Stephen Rothman; Sets, Klara Zieglerova; Lighting, Betsy Adams; Costumes, Gordon DeVinney; Sound, Matt Briganti Kelly; September 22–October 21, 2001; CAST: Bob Burrus, Robert Elliott, William Cain

William Cain, Robert Elliott in *God's Man in Texas* (Sandy Underwood)

John Woodson, Pamela Myers in *Gypsy* (Sandy Underwood)

GYPSY Book, Arthur Laurents; Music, Julie Styne; Lyrics, Stephen Sondheim; Director, Victoria Bussert; Sets, John Ezell; Lighting, Peter F. Sargeant; Costumes, Suzy Benzinger; Choreographer, Janet Watson; October 16–November 16, 2001; CAST: Kathleen France (Mom, Mazeppa, Showgirl), Carol Schulberg (Mom, Electra, Showgirl), Rebecca Spencer (Mom, Miss Cratchitt, Tessie, Showgirl), Jerry Vogel (Uncle Jocko, Weber, Mr. Goldstone, Patsey), Meghan Weber (Musician), Erin McCamley (Balloon Gril), Jacqueline Probst (Baby June), Jamie Anderson (Baby Louise), Pamela Myers (Rose), Hardy Rawls (Pop, Kringelein, Cigar, Phil), John Woodson (Herbie), Robert Breslin IV, Michael Carr, Eric Myers (Newsboys), Emily Rabon Hall (June), Joan Hess (Louise), Hunter Bell (Tulsa), Pierre Jacques Brault (Angie, Cow, Showboy, Georgie), Andrew Hansen (L.A.), Jim Lash (Yonkers, Cow, Showboy, Georgie), Jodi Dominick (Thelma, Sign Girl, Showgirl, Cow, Renee), Julie Hogan (Agnes, Showgirl), Faith Sandberg (Dolores, Sign Girl), Holly Kristen Thomas (Marjorie May, Showgirl, Cow)

Michael Milligan, Joneal Joplin, in *King Lear* (Sandy Underwood)

BEEHIVE Created by Larry Gallagher; Director and Choreographer, Pamela Hunt; Sets, James Morgan; Lighting, Mary Jo Dondlinger; Costumes, John Carver Sullivan; November 3, 2001–January 6, 2002; CAST: Heather Ayers, Ashanti Johnson, Laiona Michelle, Joye Ross, Rachel Stern, Kirsten Wyatt

A CHRISTMAS CAROL by Charles Dickens; Adaptation, Howard Dallin; Director, Michael Evan Haney; Sets, James Leonard Joy; Lighting, Kirk Bookman; Costumes, David Murin; Sound/Composer, David B. Smith; November 30–December 30, 2001; CAST: Joneal Joplin, Mark Mocahbee, Larry Bates, Bruce Cromer, Jake Storms, Gregory Procaccino, Raye Lankford, A.J. Grubbs, Ali Breneman, Mark Mineart, Dale Hodges, Jeremiah Wiggins, Eva Kaminsky, Regina Pugh, Dustin Hicks, K. McKenzie Miller, Julia Mendelsohn, Evan Martin, Andrea Auten, Adam Ziemkiewicz, Amber K. Browning, Damon Gravina, Nathan Wallace, Aaron Mayo, Sarah M. White, Joan Jankowski, Akiko Hashimoto, Maha McCain, Mark Sage Hamilton, Jason Huysman, A. Jackson Ford

The Company of *Beehive* (Sandy Underwood)

Walter Hudson, Karen Radcliffe, Tony Campisi in *Men on the Take* (Sandy Underwood)

BLUES FOR AN ALABAMA SKY by Pearl Cleage; Director, Harold Scott; Sets, Joseph Tilford; Lighting, Frances Aaronson; Costumes, David Kay Mickelson; January 15–February 15, 2002; CAST: Brenda Pressley, Ray Ford, Lawrence Ballard, Lisa Renee Pitts, Marcus Naylor

MEN ON THE TAKE by Carter W. Lewis; Director, Edward Stern; Sets, Paul Shortt; Lighting, John Lasiter; Costumes, Gordon DeVinney; Sound, Jill B.C. DuBoff; February 9–March 10, 2002; CAST: Tony Campisi, Walter Hudson, Karen Radcliffe

Brenda Pressley in *Blues for an Alabama Sky* (Sandy Underwood)

Lori Fischer in *Barbara's Blue Kitchen* (Sandy Underwood)

TEN LITTLE INDIANS by Agatha Christie; Director, John Going; Sets, James Wolk; Lighting, Dennis Parichy; Costumes, Elizabeth Covey; Composer, Joe Payne; March 5–April 5, 2002; CAST: Stephen Temperley, Drew Fracher, Dale Hodges, Jennifer Erin Roberts, Kurt Rhoads, Jeffries Thaiss, John Tillotson, Frank Lowe, Jill Tanner, Thomas Carson, Anderson Matthews

BARBARA'S BLUE KITCHEN by Lori Fischer; Director, Martha Banta; Sets, Eric Renschler; Lighting, Matthew Frey; Costumes, Gordon DeVinney; March 23–April 28, 2002; CAST: Lori Fischer, Kurt Ziskie

Kurt Rhoads, Jennifer Erin Roberts in *Ten Little Indians* (Sandy Underwood)

KING O'THE MOON by Tim Dudzick; Director, Terence Lamude; Sets, Bill Clarke; Lighting, Tom Sturge; Costumes, Martha Hally; Sound, Tom Gould; April 21–May 24, 2002; CAST: Geoffrey Molloy, Christopher Drescher, Charlie Pollock, Cheryl Giannini, Kelly Mares, Rachel Fowler, Steve Brady

DIRTY BLONDE by Claudia Shear; Conceived by Claudia Shear and James Lapine; Director, Loretta Greco; Sets, Myung Hee Cho; Lighting, James Vermeulen; Costumes, Elizabeth Hope Clancy; Sound, Robert Kaplowitz; May 11–June 16, 2002; CAST: Jeffrey Kuhn, Adinah Alexander, Darrin Baker

CLEVELAND PLAYHOUSE

Cleveland, Ohio

Artistic Director, Peter Hackett; Managing Director, Dean Gladden

CYRANO Adaptation of Edmond Roston's *Cyrano de Bergerac* by Frank Langella; Director, Peter Hackett; Sets, Ariel Goldberger; Lighting, Rick Paulsen; Costumes, David Kay Mickelsen; Sound, Robin Heath; September 25–October 28, 2001; Cast: David Furr, Melinda Page Hamilton, Darrie Lawrence, Brad Bellamy, Suzanne Mignanelli, Mike Hartman, Andrew May, Ross Williams, Jamie Horton, Erik Andrews, Kevin Brewer, Joe Saraceno, Erin Hurley, Laura Caslin

I HATE HAMLET by Paul Rudnick; Director, David Colacci; Sets, Bill Clarke; Lighting, Tracy Odishaw; Costumes, David Kay Mickelsen; Sound, Brian McQueen; November 6–December 2, 2001; Cast: Portia Johnson, David Furr, Heidi Dippold, Darrie Lawrence, Andrew May, Kevin Orton

THE TIN PAN ALLEY RAG by Mark Saltzman; Music and Lyrics, Scott Joplin and Irving Berlin; Director and Choreographer, Lynne Taylor-Corbett; Musical Arrangements, Brad Ellis; Sets, Christine Jones; Lighting, Michael Korsch; Costumes, Judanna Lynn; Sound, Jeremy Lee; November 27–December 30, 2001; Cast: Bob Ader, Fred Berman, Betsey DiLellio, Karen Gardner, Robert Jason Jackson, Allie Laurie, Janelle Anne Robinson, Tom Souhrada, Dathan B. Williams, David Lemoyne, Tina Tompkins, James Workman

THE AMEN CORNER by James Baldwin; Director, Chuck Patterson; Sets, Felix E. Cochren; Lighting, William H. Grant III; Costumes, Myrna Colley-Lee; Sound, Brian MacQueen; January 8–February 10, 2002; Cast: Elizabeth Van Dyke, Diane Weaver, Mariama Whyte, RaSheryl McCreary, Cecelia Antoinette, Glenn Turner, LaShawn Banks, Wiley Moore, Kelly Chapman, Leathia J. Williams, Millette Wright, Paul Hobson Sadler, Carlton Fellows, Daniel Spearman, Ruthie Spearman, Natalie Chapman, Caleb Wright

THE INFINITE REGRESS OF HUMAN VANITY by Murphy Guyer; Director, David Colacci; Sets, Robert Schmidt; Lighting, Michael Roesch; Costumes, Mary Schilling-Martin; February 5–March 3, 2002; Cast: Steve McCue, Jonathan Partington, Ben Nordstrom, Paul Fioriano, Mary Hammett, Torrey Hanson, Rondi Reed, Kevin Hogan, Andrew May, Kevin Brewer, Erik Andrews

THE WAVERLEY GALLERY by Kenneth Lonergan; Director, Peter Hackett; Sets, Felix Cochren; Lighting, Richard Winkler; Costumes, James Scott; Sound, Brian MacQueen; March 12–April 7, 2002; Cast: Ann Guilbert, Andrew Katz, Gregory Northrop, Darrie Lawrence, Mike Hartman

BETRAYAL by Harold Pinter; Director, Peter Hackett; Sets, Costumes and Lighting, Pavel Dobrusky; Sound, Brian MacQueen; April 9–May 5, 2002; Cast: Anne Torsiglieri, Andrew May, Paul Vincent Black, Erik Andrews

DINNER WITH FRIENDS by Donald Margulies; Director, Seth Gordon; Sets/Lighting, Kent Dorsey; Costumes, Jeffrey Van Curtis; Sound, Brian MacQueen; May 7–June 2, 2002; Cast: Susan Eriksen, David Colacci, Kate Hodge, Wayne Maugans

Andrew May in *The Infinite Regress of Human Vanity* (Roger Mastroianni)

FLORIDA STAGE

Manalapan, Florida

Producing Director, Louis Tyrrell

THIEF RIVER by Lee Blessing; Director, Louis Tyrrell; Sets, Paul Owen; Lighting, Jim Fulton; Costumes, Suzette Pare; Sound, Matt Kelly; October 26–December 2, 2001; CAST: Paul Whitthorne, David McNamara, Michael MacCauley, Joseph Adams, John Newton, David Bailey

BLACK SHEEP by Lee Blessing; Director, Michael Bigelow Dixon; Sets and Lighting, Victor Becker; Costumes, Lynda Peto; Original Music and Sound, Michael Roth; December 14, 2001–January 20, 2002; CAST: Jonathan Bustle, Brandon Morris, Angie Radosh, Paul Tei, Caitlin Miller

RED HERRING by Michael Hollinger; Director, Lou Jacob; Sets and Lighting, Richard Crowell; Costumes, Ilona Somogyi; Sound, Matt Kelly; February 1–March 10, 2002; CAST: Patricia Dalen, Stephen G. Anthony, Kendra Kassebaum, Johnathan F. McClain, Suzanne Grodner, Gordon McConnell

BEE-LUTHER HATCHEE by Thomas Gibbons; Director, Seret Scott; Sets, Kent Goetz, Lighting, Jim Fulton; Costumes, Nelson Fields; Sound, Matt Kelly; March 22–April 28, 2002; CAST: Brenda Thomas, Karen Stephens, Barbara Sloan, John Fionte, Randall Newsome

WOMEN WHO STEAL by Carter F. Lewis; Director, Louis Tyrrell; Sets, Klara Zieglerova; Lighting, Suzanne M Jones; Costumes, Don Mangone; Sound, Matt Kelly; CAST: Peggy Cosgrave, Annie Fitzpatrick, Robert Elliott

Paul Tei, Jonathan Bustle, Caitlin Miller in *Black Sheep* (Susan Green)

Gordon McConnell, Stephen G. Anthony, Suzanne Grodner in *Red Herring* (Susan Green)

Karen Stephens, John Fionte, Randall Newsome, Brenda Thomas in *Bee-Luther Hatchee* (Susan Green)

GEORGIA SHAKESPEARE FESTIVAL

Atlanta, Georgia

Artistic Director, Richard Garner; Managing Director, Philip J. Santora

AMADEUS by Peter Schaffer; Director, Karen Robinson; Sets, Rochelle Barker; Lighting, Liz Lee; Costumes, Christine Turbitt; Sound, Brian Kettler; June 15–August 12, 2001; CAST: John Ammerman, James Andrew Butz, Jessie Andary, Jonathan Davis, Rob Cleveland, Tim McDonough, Allen O'Reilly, Joe Knezevich, Chris Kayser, John M. Tufts, Cary Donaldson, Hudson Adams, Bruce Evers, Suzanne Jordan Roush, Denita J. Linnertz, Maria Gabriela Parra

AS YOU LIKE IT by William Shakespeare; Director, Jessica Phelps West; Sets, Crawford C. Pratt; Lighting, Liz Lee; Costumes, Stan Poole; Sound and Music, Thom Jenkins; June 29–August 11, 2001; CAST: Tim McDonough, Brad Sherill, Rob Cleveland, Anthony Irons, Hudson Adams, Suzanne Jordan Rousch, Michele McCullough, Jonathan Davis, John M. Tufts, Bruce Evers, Chris Kayser, James Andrew Butz, Cary Donaldson, Allen O'Reilly, John Ammerman, Maria Gabriela Parra, Kathleen McManus, Denita Linnertz

THE WINTER'S TALE by William Shakespeare; Director, Richard Garner; Sets, Charlie Caldwell; Lighting, Liz Lee; Costumes, Miranda Hoffman; July 13–August 10, 2001; CAST: Allen O'Reilly, Carolyn Cook, Evan O'Reilly, Tim McDonough, John Ammerman, Brad Sherrill, Hudson Adams, Janice Akers, Suzanne Jordan Rousch, Rob Cleveland, Anthony Irons, Jessie Andary, Bruce Evers, Jonathan Davis, Chris Kayser, James Andrew Butz, Denita Linnertz, Maria Gabriela Parra

JULIUS CAESAR by William Shakespeare; Director, John Dillon; Sets, Paul Owen; Lighting, Mike Post; Costumes, Sam Fleming; Sound, Brian Kettler; October 12–November 4, 2001; CAST: Bruce Evers, Teresa DeBerry, Charles Horton, Chris Kayser, Damon Boggess, Scot Mann, Brik Berkes, David Harrell, Gregory Thomas Isaac, Joe Knezevich, Anthony Irons, Barry Stoltze, Daniel Burnley, Saxon Palmer, Lisa Paulsen, Brian Husky, Randy Cohlmia, Neal Hazard, Helen Beattie, Kara Blanton, Colin Gray, Blair Hoover, Jillian Martin, Bernard Moore, Melissa Shipman, Christina Riley, Ayesha Siddique, Emily Whitworth

Allen O'Reilly, Carolyn Cook, Rob Cleveland in *The Winter's Tale* (T.W. Meyer)

GOODSPEED OPERA HOUSE

East Haddam, Connecticut

BRIGADOON Book and Lyrics, Alan J. Lerner; Music, Frederick Loewe; Director, Greg Ganakas; Sets, Howard Jones; Lighting, Kirk Bookman; Costumes, John Carver Sullivan; March 30–June 23, 2001; CAST: David Barron, Nili Bassman, Lisa Brescia, Paul Carlin, James Clow, Robyn Cohen, Brian J. Cooper, Elizabeth Ferrell, Paul Gallagher, Dale Hensley, Natalie Hill, Kevin Loreque, Patrick Mullaney, Daniel Reichard, Greg Roderick, David Rossmer, James Santos, Amanda Serkasevich, Adam Souza, James Tabeek, Jennifer Taylor, Melanie Vaughn, Anna Winthrop

THEY ALL LAUGHED! The New Gershwin Musical: Music and Lyrics by George and Ira Gershwin; Book, Joe DiPietro; Director, Christopher Ashley; Sets, John Lee Beatty; Lighting, Ken Billington; Costumes, Jess Goldstein; June 29–October 22, 2001; CAST: Kevin Crewell, David Dollase, Donna English, Matthew Farver, Lori Ann Ferrari, Diane J. Findlay, Kate Fisher, Jessica Hartman, Ethan Jones, Dennis Kelly, Mark Lotito, James Ludwig, Mike McGowan, Michael McGrath, Karina Michaels, Laurie Mitchell, Mary Beth Peil, Marla Schaffel, Laura Schutter, Amanda Watkins

A LITTLE NIGHT MUSIC Music and Lyrics, Stephen Sondheim; Book, Hugh Wheeler; Director, Darko Tresnjak; Sets, David P. Gordon; Lighting, Christopher J. Landy; Costumes, Linda Cho; October 28–December 16, 2001; CAST: Nora Blackwell, Lisa Brescia, Eric Briarley, Leslie Denniston, M'el Dowd, Joe Farrell, José "Chach" Francisco, John Herrera, Cristin Hubbard, Kristin Huxhold, T. Doyle Leverett, Brad Little, Stephanie Lynge, Amanda Naughton, Greg Roderick, Matt Stokes, Jennifer Sharon Taylor, Melanie Vaughn

DOUBLE TROUBLE, A Musical Tour de Farce: Music, Book, and Lyrics by Bob Walton and Jim Walton; Director, Ray Broderick; Sets, Edward T. Gianfrancesco; Lighting, Eric T. Haugen; Costumes, Martha Bromelmeier; Sound, Tony Meola; May 17–June 10, 2001; CAST: Merwin Garner, Millie Ferber, Jimmy Martin, Bobby Martin, Bix Minky, Seymour Beckley, Rebecca LeFleurdelemaganis, Swifty Morris, Preston Creest, Shuster, Jenna Jumper

GREAT EXPECTATONS, The Musical Book and Lyrics, John Jakes; Music, Mel Marvin; Director, Kent Thompson; Sets, Emily Beck; Lighting, Mark Stanley; Costumes, Pamela Scofield; August 2–26, 2001; CAST: Michael Winther, Andrew Blau, Robert Aronson, Terence Goodman, Elizabeth Arnold, Jamie Jackson, David B. Heuvelman, Ken Krugman, Ben Arvan, Colin Stokes, Kristin Woodbury, Annah Rozelle, Rita Gardner, William Ryall, Cary Barker, Ben Baxley, Rachael Warren, Jonathan Prager, Jason Dula, Jamey McGaugh, Brooks Rozelle

LIZZIE BORDEN Books and Lyrics, Christopher McGovern and Amy Powers; Music, Mr. McGovern; Director, Bill Castellino; Sets, Michael Anania; Lighting, Paul Miller; Costumes, Dale diBernardo; Sound, Jay Hilton; November 1–25, 2001; CAST: Bridget Beirne, Danica Connors, Brenda Cummings, Andy Gale, Eleanor Glockner, Tim Jerome, Mischa Kischkum, Darren Matthias, Mackenzie Mauzy, Christiane Noll, Tally Stafford, Melinda Tanner, Gwendolyn Walker

David Rossmer, James Clow, Amanda Serkasevich in *Brigadoon* (Diane Sobolewski)

Marla Schaffel, James Ludwig in *They All Laughed!* (Diane Sobolewski)

Kristin Huxhold, Lisa Brescia in *A Little Night Music* (Diane Sobolewski)

THE GUTHRIE THEATRE

Minneapolis, Minnesota

Artistic Director, Joe Dowling; Managing Director, Susan B. Trapnell

ONCE IN A LIFETIME by Moss Hart and George S. Kaufman; Director, Douglas Wager; Sets/Costumes, Zack Brown; Lighting, Allen Lee Hughes; Sound, Scott Edwards; June 2–July 1, 2001; CAST: Richard Kind, Kathryn Meisle, Marcus Giamatti, Jim Lichtscheidl, Sally Wingert, Julie Lund, Jennifer Blagen, Marvette Knight, Emily Dooley, Kelly Bertenshaw, Cliff Rakerd, Natalie Moore, John Patrick Fitzgibbons, Barbara Kinglsey, Paul de Cordova, Virginia Burke, Richard Iglewski, John Schuman, Amy McDonald, Lewis J. Stadlen, Kris Nelson, Michael Kissin, Anthony Ciaravino, Kelly Bertenshaw, Jennifer Blagen, Marvette Knight

AMADEUS by Peter Shaffer; Director, Joe Dowling; Sets, Patrick Clark; Lighting, Christopher Akerlind; Costumes, Paul Tazewell; July 21–August 26, 2001; CAST: Charles Janasz, T.R. Knight, Amanda Detmer, Richard Iglewski, Nathaniel Fuller, John Tillotson, Richard Ooms, Jim Lichtscheidl, Kris L. Nelson, Robert O. Berdahl, Michael Booth, Michael Tezla, Paul Doepke, Suzanne Warmanen, Laura Esping

THE CARPETBAGGER'S CHILDREN by Horton Foote; Director, Michael Wilson; Sets, Jeff Cowie; Lighting, Rui Rita; Costumes, David Woolard; Sound, John Gromada; August 3–September 2, 2001; CAST: Robert Maxwell, Jean Stapleton, Hallie Foote

Stephen Pelinski, Tony Mockus in *Da* (Michal Daniel)

DA by Hugh Leonard; Director, Doug Hughes; Sets/Costumes, Monica Frawley; Lighting, Michael Chybowski; Sound, Timothy Knox; September 22–October 21, 2001; CAST: Stephen Pelinski, Michael Booth, Tony Mockus, Barbara Bryne, Joe Delafield, Jarlath Conroy, Fiona Walsh, Sally Wingert

MERRILY WE ROLL ALONG Music and Lyrics by Stephen Sondheim; Book, George Furth; Director, John Miller-Stephany; Sets/Costumes, Mathew J. LeFebvre; Lighting, Charles D. Craun; Sound, Scott Edwards; October 11–December 2, 2001; CAST: Ken Barnett, Bob Beverage, Adena Brumer, Brian Grandison, David Hawkanson, Steve Hendrickson, Nate Irvin, Michael Mayer, Christa Justus, Jim Lichtscheidl, Molly Sue McDonald, Natalie Moore, Tinia Moulder, Juan Rivera-LeBron, Mark Rosenwinkel, Tony Vierling, Shannon Warne, Carla Woods, Mimi Wyche

A CHRISTMAS CAROL by Charles Dickens; Adaptation, Barbara Field; Director, Gary Gisselman; Sets, Neil Patel; Lighting, Marcus Dilliard; Costumes, Jess Goldstein; November 16–December 30, 2001; CAST: Erin Anderson, Michael Booth, Barbara Bryne, Gerald Drake, Nathaniel Fuller, Peter Michael Goetz, Kathleen Humphrey, Richard Iglewski, Michael Kissin, Wendy Lehr, Angela Mannella, Bill McCallum, Isabell Monk, Kris Nelson, Togba Norris

Charles Janasz in *Amadeus* (Michal Daniel)

Robert Cuccioli, Laila Robins, Tess Lina, Tracey Maloney in *Antony and Cleopatra* (T. Charles Erickson)

ANTONY AND CLEOPATRA by William Shakespeare; Director, Mark Lamos; Sets, Ming Cho Lee; Lighting, Stephen Strawbridge; Costumes, Jane Greenwood; Sound, Scott Edwards; January 19–February 24, 2002; CAST: Robert Cuccoli, Leith Burke, Mark Rosenwinkel, Laila Robins, Stephen Pelinski, Stephen Yoakam, Bob Davis, Paris Remillard, Bill McCallum, Bob Davis, Arnell Powell, Kate Nowlin, Michael Tezla, Steve Hendrickson, Anthony Ciaravino, David Charles Mann, Barton Tinapp, Tess Lina, Tracey Maloney, Richard Iglewski, Kris Nelson, Bruce Bohne

THIEF RIVER by Lee Blessing; Director, Ethan McSweeny; Sets, Michael Sims; Lighting, Jane Cox; Costumes, Rich Hamson; Sound, Michael Roth; February 15–March 10, 2002; CAST: Alex Podulke, Bard Goodrich, James Shanklin, William Whitehead, Bernie Sheredy, Richard Ooms

The Company of *Merrily We Roll Along* (T. Charles Erickson)

AH! WILDERNESS by Eugene O'Neill; Director, Douglas Wager; Sets, Ming Cho Lee; Lighting, Allen Lee Hughes; Costumes, Zack Brown; Sound, Scott Edwards; February 21–May 12, 2002; CAST: Nathaniel Fuller, Margo Skinner, Sean Michael Dooley, Joe Delafield, Tara White, Jack Davis, Maggie D'Ambrose, Brian Reddy, Laura Esping, Martin Ruben, Piper Brooks, Charles Fraser, Natalie Moore, Mary Alette Davis, Casey Lewis, Paul de Cordova

THE CANTERBURY TALES Based on the Stories by Geoffrey Chaucer; Adaptations, Michael Bogdanov; Additional Material, Kevin Kling; Director, Mr. Bogdanov; Sets/Costumes, Ulrike Engelbrecht; Lighting, Ann Wrightson; Sound, Scott Edwards; March 30–April 28, 2002; CAST: Richard Iglewski, Jim Lichtscheidl, Sarah Jane Nelson, Evan Pappas, Leenya Rideout, Matthew Saldivar, Brandon Williams, Sally Wingert

Helen Carey, Peter Michael Goetz in *All My Sons* (T. Charles Erickson)

ALL MY SONS by Arthur Miller; Director, Joe Dowling; Sets, John Lee Beatty; Lighting, Matthew Reinert; Costumes, Devon Painter; Sound, Scott Edwards; May 11–June 9, 2002; CAST: Peter Michael Goetz, Helen Carey, Todd Gearhart, Michelle O'Neill, Bill McCallum, Stephen Pelinski, Marquetta Senters, Jim Lichtscheidl, Jennifer Blagen, Derek Farnam, Jordan Pressman

ILLINOIS THEATRE CENTER

Park Forest, Illinois

Twenty-Sixth Season: September 2001–May 2002

Producing Director, Etel Billig; Associate Directors, Jonathan Billig, Alexandra Murdoch, James Corey

THE HEIRESS by Ruth and August Goetz; Director, Etel Billig; CAST: Elizabeth Dwyer, Gary Rayppy, James Wm. Joseph, Judy Rossignuolo-Rice, Alexandra Murdoch, Lisa Fontana, Donna Blanchard, Patrick Van Ort, Rachel Rozycki

BUBBE MEISES by Ellen Gould and Holly Gewandter; Director, Tim Rezash; CAST: Mary Mulligan, Dawn DeVries, Etel Billig

THE TIN PAN ALLEY RAG Book, Mark Saltzman; Songs and Lyrics, Irving Berlin and Scott Joplin; Director, Pete Thelen; CAST: John S. Crowley, Alan Ball, Sam Nykaza-Jones, Katherine Keberlien, Kristin Stennis, J. Michael Jones, Laura Colins, Peter Vamvakis, Byron Glenn Willis

HOW I LEARNED TO DRIVE by Paula Vogel; Director, David Perkovich; CAST: Melissa Carlson, Michael Lasswell, Wendi Weber, Will Clinger, Rachael Rozycki

THE OLD SETTLER by John Henry Redwood; Director, Luther Goins; CAST: Laura Collins, Paulette McDaniels, Craig Boyd, Makeba Pace

THE ENTERTAINER by John Osborne; Director, Etel Billig; CAST: Robert Browning, Iris Lieberman, Larry McCauley, Georgina Stoyles, Robert Fagin, Bill Kirksey, Jeff Grafton

THE RINK Book, Terrence McNally; Music, John Kander; Lyrics, Fred Ebb; Director, Pete Thelen; CAST: Shelley Crosby, Erin Crosby, Peter Robel, Tim Rezash, Bernard Rice, Bradford Cummings, Bryan McElroy, David Tibble, Emily Longo, Megan Rademacher

James Wm. Joseph, Judy Rossignuolo-Rice in *The Heiress*

Robert Browning, Iris Lieberman in *The Entertainer*

Bernard Rice, Brian McElroy, Tim Rezash, Peter Robel, Bradford Cummings, David Tibble in *The Rink*

MARK TAPER FORUM/ CENTER THEATRE GROUP

Los Angeles, California

October 2, 2001–September 1, 2002

Artistic Director, Gordon Davison; Managing Director, Charles Dillingham

FLOWER DRUM SONG by Richard Rogers and Oscar Hammerstein; Book, David Henry Hwang; Director, Robert Longbottom; Sets, Robin Wagner; Lighting, Brian Nason; Costumes, Gregg Barnes; Sound, Jon Gottlieb; CAST: Sandra Allen, Mayumi Legaspi Ando, Ronald M. Banks, Charlene Carabeo, Rich Ceraulo, Eric Chan, Marcus Choi, Michael Dow, Alvin Ing, Thomas Kouo, Keri Lee, Allen Liu, Jose Llana, Jodi Long, Tzi Ma, Blythe Matsui, Liz Paw, Jennifer Paz, Robert Pendilla, Lea Salonga, Chloe Stewart, Kim Varhola, Diane Veronica Phelan, Christine Yasunaga

Eric Chan, Sandra Allen, Robert Pendilla in *Flower Drum Song* (Craig Schwartz)

Jan Maxwell, Peter Friedman in *My Old Lady* (Craig Schwartz)

Katie MacNichol, Patricia Conolly, Anna Belknap in *The School for Husbands* (Craig Schwartz)

COPENHAGEN by Michael Frayn; Director, Michael Blakemore; Sets and Costumes, Peter J. Davison; Lighting, Mark Huntley; Sound, Tony Meola; CAST: Len Cariou, Mariette Hartley, Hank Stratton

MY OLD LADY by Israel Horovits; Director, David Esbjornson; Sets, John Lee Beatty; Lighting, Scott Zielinski; Costumes, Elizabeth Hope Clancy; Sound, Jon Gottlieb; CAST: Peter Friedman, Sian Phillips, Jan Maxwell

THE MOLIÈRE COMEDIES "The School for Husbands" and "The Imaginary Cuckhold"; Director, Brian Bedford; Sets, Ming Cho Lee; Lighting, Robert Wierzel; Costumes, Jane Greenwood; Sound, Jon Gottlieb; CAST: Brian Bedford, Anna Belknap, Patricia Conolly, Jerry Kernion, Jeff Klein, Katie MacNichol, Don Reilly, Ned Schmidtke, Graham Sheils, Erik Sorenson

Judith Light, John Glover in *Sorrows and Rejoicings* (Craig Schwartz)

SORROWS AND REJOICINGS by Athol Fugard; Director, Mr. Fugard; Sets/Costumes, Susan Hilferty; Lighting, Dennis Parichy; Cast: Brienin Nequa Bryant, John Glover, Judith Light, Cynthia Martells

THE HOUSE OF BERNARDA ALBA by Federico García Lorca; Director, Lisa Peterson; Sets, Rachel Hauck; Lighting, Christopher Akerlind; Costumes, Joyce Kim Lee; Sound, Mark Bennett; Cast: Adrianne Avey, Christine Avila, Marissa Chibas, Tsai Chin, Aixa Clemente, Anita Dashiell, Eileen Galindo, Karen Huie, Carla Jiminez, Lydia Look, Sandra Oh, Chita Rivera, Jeanne Sakata, Camille Saviola, Rita Wolf

Sandra Oh in *The House of Bernarda Alba* (Craig Schwartz)

AWARDS

2002 THEATRE WORLD AWARD WINNERS

Justin Bohon of *Oklahoma!*

Simon Callow of *The Mystery of Charles Dickens*

Mos Def of *Topdog/Underdog*

Emma Fielding of *Private Lives*

Adam Godley of *Private Lives*

Martin Jarvis of *By Jeeves*

Spencer Kayden of *Urinetown*

Gretchen Mol of *The Shape of Things*

Anna Paquin of *The Glory of Living*

Louise Pitre of *Mamma Mia!*

David Warner of *Major Barbara*

Rachel Weisz of *The Shape of Things*

58TH ANNUAL THEATRE WORLD AWARDS PRESENTATION

Studio 54

Monday, June 3, 2002

Created in 1944 by *Theatre World* founders Daniel Blum, Norman MacDonald, and John Willis to coincide with the first release of *Theatre World*, the now fifty-eight-year-old definitive pictorial and statistical record of the American theatre, the Theatre World Awards are the oldest awards given for debut performances in New York City, as well as one of the oldest honors bestowed on New York actors.

A committee of New York drama critics currently joins longtime *Theatre World* editor John Willis in choosing six actors and six actresses for the Theatre World Awards, who have distinguished themselves in Broadway and Off-Broadway productions during the past theatre season. Occasionally, Special Theatre World Awards are also bestowed on performers, casts, or others who have made a particularly lasting impression on the New York theatre scene.

The Theatre World Award "Janus" statuette is an original bronze sculpture in primitive-modern style created by internationally recognized artist Harry Marinsky. It is adapted from the Roman myth of Janus, god of entrances, exits, and all beginnings, with one face appraising the past and the other anticipating the future. It is cast and mounted on marble in the Del Chiaro Foundry in Pietrasanta, Italy.

Theatre World Awards Board members: Tom Lynch, President; Marianne Tatum, Vice President; Patricia Elliot, Secretary; Peter Filichia, Treasurer; David Birney; Ben Hodges; Walter Willison

The Theatre World Awards are voted on by the following committee of New York drama critics:

Clive Barnes (*New York Post*), Peter Filichia (*Theatermania.com*), Harry Haun (*Playbill*), Ben Hodges (*Theatre World*), Frank Scheck (*The Hollywood Reporter*), Michael Sommers (*Newark Star Ledger*), Douglas Watt (*The Daily News*), John Willis (*Theatre World*), and Linda Winer (*Newsday*)

Master of Ceremonies, Peter Filichia; Executive Producer, Ben Hodges

Master of Ceremonies Peter Filichia

2002 TWA winner Spencer Kayden (*Urinetown*) and 1945 TWA winner John Raitt

1993 Special TWA winner Rosetta LeNoire

1992 TWA winner and 2002 presenter Laura Linney

2002 TWA winner Louise Pitre (*Mamma Mia!*) with the Schubert Organization chairman Gerald Schoenfeld

TWA founder and *Theatre World* editor in chief John Willis

2002 presenters and previous TWA winners Kate Burton, Laura Linney, Lindsay Duncan

1976 TWA winner Tovah Feldshuh

2002 TWA winner Martin Jarvis (*By Jeeves*)

Previous TWA winner Andrea Martin and fellow *Oklahoma!* cast member and 2002 TWA winner Justin Bohon

Previous TWA winners Walter Willison, Judy Kaye and John Raitt with TWA founder John Willis, previous TWA winner Bambi Linn, and 2002 winner Louise Pitre

2002 TWA winner Gretchen Mol (*The Shape of Things*) with Laura Linney

Previous TWA winners Juliette Koka and Lucie Arnaz

Presenter and 1995 TWA winner Billy Crudup

1963 TWA winner and presenter Estelle Parsons

Previous TWA winners Lindsay Duncan and Rosemary Harris

TWA winner Justin Bohon

1983 TWA winner Kate Burton presents to TWA
Winner Spencer Kayden

2002 TWA winner Mos Def (*Topdog/Underdog*)

Previous TWA winners Patricia Elliot and Kate Burton

Screen World editor Barry Monush, John Willis, and
Theatre World former editor Tom Lynch

2002 TWA winner Kathleen Freeman

2002 TWA winner Louise Pitre and previous winner Judy Kaye

2002 TWA winner Martin Jarvis and previous winner
Joanna Gleason

Previous TWA winners Laura Linney and Andrea Martin

Actor Theodore Bikel

John Willis with 1979 TWA winner Lucie Arnaz

Presenter and 1953 TWA winner Rosemary Harris

1953 TWA winner Eileen Heckart

Theatre World associate editor and TWA executive producer Ben Hodges with John Willis

1945 TWA winners and original *Oklahoma!* cast members John Raitt and Bambi Linn

1986 TWA winner Julie Hagerty

Presenter and 1977 TWA winner Joanna Gleason

PREVIOUS THEATRE WORLD AWARD RECIPIENTS

1944–45: Betty Comden, Richard Davis, Richard Hart, Judy Holliday, Charles Lang, Bambi Linn, John Lund, Donald Murphy, Nancy Noland, Margaret Phillips, John Raitt

1945–46: Barbara Bel Geddes, Marlon Brando, Bill Callahan, Wendell Corey, Paul Douglas, Mary James, Burt Lancaster, Patricia Marshall, Beatrice Pearson

1946–47: Keith Andes, Marion Bell, Peter Cookson, Ann Crowley, Ellen Hanley, John Jordan, George Keane, Dorothea MacFarland, James Mitchell, Patricia Neal, David Wayne

1947–48: Valerie Bettis, Edward Bryce, Whitfield Connor, Mark Dawson, June Lockhart, Estelle Loring, Peggy Maley, Ralph Meeker, Meg Mundy, Douglass Watson, James Whitmore, Patrice Wymore

1948–49: Tod Andrews, Doe Avedon, Jean Carson, Carol Channing, Richard Derr, Julie Harris, Mary McCarty, Allyn Ann McLerie, Cameron Mitchell, Gene Nelson, Byron Palmer, Bob Scheerer

1949–50: Nancy Andrews, Phil Arthur, Barbara Brady, Lydia Clarke, Priscilla Gillette, Don Hanmer, Marcia Henderson, Charlton Heston, Rick Jason, Grace Kelly, Charles Nolte, Roger Price

1950–51: Barbara Ashley, Isabel Bigley, Martin Brooks, Richard Burton, Pat Crowley, James Daley, Cloris Leachman, Russell Nype, Jack Palance, William Smithers, Maureen Stapleton, Marcia Van Dyke, Eli Wallach

1951–52: Tony Bavaar, Patricia Benoit, Peter Conlow, Virginia de Luce, Ronny Graham, Audrey Hepburn, Diana Herbert, Conrad Janis, Dick Kallman, Charles Proctor, Eric Sinclair, Kim Stanley, Marian Winters, Helen Wood

1952–53: Edie Adams, Rosemary Harris, Eileen Heckart, Peter Kelley, John Kerr, Richard Kiley, Gloria Marlowe, Penelope Munday, Paul Newman, Sheree North, Geraldine Page, John Stewart, Ray Stricklyn, Gwen Verdon

1953–54: Orson Bean, Harry Belafonte, James Dean, Joan Diener, Ben Gazzara, Carol Haney, Jonathan Lucas, Kay Medford, Scott Merrill, Elizabeth Montgomery, Leo Penn, Eva Marie Saint

1954–55: Julie Andrews, Jacqueline Brookes, Shirl Conway, Barbara Cook, David Daniels, Mary Fickett, Page Johnson, Loretta Leversee, Jack Lord, Dennis Patrick, Anthony Perkins, Christopher Plummer

1955–56: Diane Cilento, Dick Davalos, Anthony Franciosa, Andy Griffith, Laurence Harvey, David Hedison, Earle Hyman, Susan Johnson, John Michael King, Jayne Mansfield, Sara Marshall, Gaby Rodgers, Susan Strasberg, Fritz Weaver

1956–57: Peggy Cass, Sydney Chaplin, Sylvia Daneel, Bradford Dillman, Peter Donat, George Grizzard, Carol Lynley, Peter Palmer, Jason Robards, Cliff Robertson, Pippa Scott, Inga Swenson

1957–58: Anne Bancroft, Warren Berlinger, Colleen Dewhurst, Richard Easton, Tim Everett, Eddie Hodges, Joan Hovis, Carol Lawrence, Jacqueline McKeever, Wynne Miller, Robert Morse, George C. Scott

1958–59: Lou Antonio, Ina Balin, Richard Cross, Tammy Grimes, Larry Hagman, Dolores Hart, Roger Mollien, France Nuyen, Susan Oliver, Ben Piazza, Paul Roebling, William Shatner, Pat Suzuki, Rip Torn

1959–60: Warren Beatty, Eileen Brennan, Carol Burnett, Patty Duke, Jane Fonda, Anita Gillette, Elisa Loti, Donald Madden, George Maharis, John McMartin, Lauri Peters, Dick Van Dyke

1960–61: Joyce Bulifant, Dennis Cooney, Sandy Dennis, Nancy Dussault, Robert Goulet, Joan Hackett, June Harding, Ron Husmann, James MacArthur, Bruce Yarnell

1961–62: Elizabeth Ashley, Keith Baxter, Peter Fonda, Don Galloway, Sean Garrison, Barbara Harris, James Earl Jones, Janet Margolin, Karen Morrow, Robert Redford, John Stride, Brenda Vaccaro

1962–63: Alan Arkin, Stuart Damon, Melinda Dillon, Robert Drivas, Bob Gentry, Dorothy Loudon, Brandon Maggart, Julienne Marie, Liza Minnelli, Estelle Parsons, Diana Sands, Swen Swenson

1963–64: Alan Alda, Gloria Bleezarde, Imelda De Martin, Claude Giraud, Ketty Lester, Barbara Loden, Lawrence Pressman, Gilbert Price, Philip Proctor, John Tracy, Jennifer West

1964–65: Carolyn Coates, Joyce Jillson, Linda Lavin, Luba Lisa, Michael O'Sullivan, Joanna Pettet, Beah Richards, Jaime Sanchez, Victor Spinetti, Nicolas Surovy, Robert Walker, Clarence Williams III

1965–66: Zoe Caldwell, David Carradine, John Cullum, John Davidson, Faye Dunaway, Gloria Foster, Robert Hooks, Jerry Lanning, Richard Mulligan, April Shawhan, Sandra Smith, Leslie Ann Warren

1966–67: Bonnie Bedelia, Richard Benjamin, Dustin Hoffman, Terry Kiser, Reva Rose, Robert Salvio, Sheila Smith, Connie Stevens, Pamela Tiffin, Leslie Uggams, Jon Voight, Christopher Walken

1967–68: David Birney, Pamela Burrell, Jordan Christopher, Jack Crowder (Thalmus Rasulala), Sandy Duncan, Julie Gregg, Stephen Joyce, Bernadette Peters, Alice Playten, Michael Rupert, Brenda Smiley, Russ Thacker

1968–69: Jane Alexander, David Cryer, Blythe Danner, Ed Evanko, Ken Howard, Lauren Jones, Ron Leibman, Marian Mercer, Jill O'Hara, Ron O'Neal, Al Pacino, Marlene Warfield

1969–70: Susan Browning, Donny Burks, Catherine Burns, Len Cariou, Bonnie Franklin, David Holliday, Katharine Houghton, Melba Moore, David Rounds, Lewis J. Stadlen, Kristoffer Tabori, Fredricka Weber

1970–71: Clifton Davis, Michael Douglas, Julie Garfield, Martha Henry, James Naughton, Tricia O'Neil, Kipp Osborne, Roger Rathburn, Ayn Ruymen, Jennifer Salt, Joan Van Ark, Walter Willison

1971–72: Jonelle Allen, Maureen Anderman, William Atherton, Richard Backus, Adrienne Barbeau, Cara Duff-MacCormick, Robert Foxworth, Elaine Joyce, Jess Richards, Ben Vereen, Beatrice Winde, James Woods

1972–73: D'Jamin Bartlett, Patricia Elliott, James Farentino, Brian Farrell, Victor Garber, Kelly Garrett, Mari Gorman, Laurence Guittard, Trish Hawkins, Monte Markham, John Rubinstein, Jennifer Warren; Special Award: Alexander H. Cohen

1973–74: Mark Baker, Maureen Brennan, Ralph Carter, Thom Christopher, John Driver, Conchata Ferrell, Ernestine Jackson, Michael Moriarty, Joe Morton, Ann Reinking, Janie Sell, Mary Woronov; Special Award: Sammy Cahn

1974–75: Peter Burnell, Zan Charisse, Lola Falana, Peter Firth, Dorian Harewood, Joel Higgins, Marcia McClain, Linda Miller, Marti Rolph, John Sheridan, Scott Stevensen, Donna Theodore; Special Award: Equity Library Theatre

1975–76: Danny Aiello, Christine Andreas, Dixie Carter, Tovah Feldshuh, Chip Garnett, Richard Kelton, Vivian Reed, Charles Repole, Virginia Seidel, Daniel Seltzer, John V. Shea, Meryl Streep; Special Award: *A Chorus Line*

1976–77: Trazana Beverley, Michael Cristofer, Joe Fields, Joanna Gleason, Cecilia Hart, John Heard, Gloria Hodes, Juliette Koka, Andrea McArdle, Ken Page, Jonathan Pryce, Chick Vennera; Special Award: Eva LeGallienne

1977–78: Vasili Bogazianos, Nell Carter, Carlin Glynn, Christopher Goutman, William Hurt, Judy Kaye, Florence Lacy, Armelia McQueen, Gordana Rashovich, Bo Rucker, Richard Seer, Colin Stinton; Special Award: Joseph Papp

1978–79: Philip Anglim, Lucie Arnaz, Gregory Hines, Ken Jennings, Michael Jeter, Laurie Kennedy, Susan Kingsley, Christine Lahti, Edward James Olmos, Kathleen Quinlan, Sarah Rice, Max Wright; Special Award: Marshall W. Mason

1979–80: Maxwell Caulfield, Leslie Denniston, Boyd Gaines, Richard Gere, Harry Groener, Stephen James, Susan Kellermann, Dinah Manoff, Lonny Price, Marianne Tatum, Anne Twomey, Dianne Wiest; Special Award: Mickey Rooney

1980–81: Brian Backer, Lisa Banes, Meg Bussert, Michael Allen Davis, Giancarlo Esposito, Daniel Gerroll, Phyllis Hyman, Cynthia Nixon, Amanda Plummer, Adam Redfield, Wanda Richert, Rex Smith; Special Award: Elizabeth Taylor

1981–82: Karen Akers, Laurie Beechman, Danny Glover, David Alan Grier, Jennifer Holliday, Anthony Heald, Lizbeth Mackay, Peter MacNicol, Elizabeth McGovern, Ann Morrison, Michael O'Keefe, James Widdoes; Special Award: Manhattan Theatre Club

1982–83: Karen Allen, Suzanne Bertish, Matthew Broderick, Kate Burton, Joanne Camp, Harvey Fierstein, Peter Gallagher, John Malkovich, Anne Pitoniak, James Russo, Brian Tarantina, Linda Thorson; Special Award: Natalia Makarova

1983–84: Martine Allard, Joan Allen, Kathy Whitton Baker, Mark Capri, Laura Dean, Stephen Geoffreys, Todd Graff, Glenne Headly, J.J. Johnston, Bonnie Koloc, Calvin Levels, Robert Westenberg; Special Award: Ron Moody

1984–85: Kevin Anderson, Richard Chaves, Patti Cohenour, Charles S. Dutton, Nancy Giles, Whoopi Goldberg, Leilani Jones, John Mahoney, Laurie Metcalf, Barry Miller, John Turturro, Amelia White; Special Award: Lucille Lortel

1985–86: Suzy Amis, Alec Baldwin, Aled Davies, Faye Grant, Julie Hagerty, Ed Harris, Mark Jacoby, Donna Kane, Cleo Laine, Howard McGillin, Marisa Tomei, Joe Urla; Special Award: Ensemble Studio Theatre

1986–87: Annette Bening, Timothy Daly, Lindsay Duncan, Frank Ferrante, Robert Lindsay, Amy Madigan, Michael Maguire, Demi Moore, Molly Ringwald, Frances Ruffelle, Courtney B. Vance, Colm Wilkinson; Special Award: Robert DeNiro

1987–88: Yvonne Bryceland, Philip Casnoff, Danielle Ferland, Melissa Gilbert, Linda Hart, Linzi Hately, Brian Kerwin, Brian Mitchell, Mary Murfitt, Aidan Quinn, Eric Roberts, B.D. Wong; Special Awards: Tisa Chang, Martin E. Segal

1988–89: Dylan Baker, Joan Cusack, Loren Dean, Peter Frechette, Sally Mayes, Sharon McNight, Jennie Moreau, Paul Provenza, Kyra Sedgwick, Howard Spiegel, Eric Stoltz, Joanne Whalley-Kilmer; Special Awards: Pauline Collins, Mikhail Baryshnikov

1989–90: Denise Burse, Erma Campbell, Rocky Carroll, Megan Gallagher, Tommy Hollis, Robert Lambert, Kathleen Rowe McAllen, Michael McKean, Crista Moore, Mary-Louise Parker, Daniel von Bargen, Jason Workman; Special Awards: Stewart Granger, Kathleen Turner

1990–91: Jane Adams, Gillian Anderson, Adam Arkin, Brenda Blethyne, Marcus Chong, Paul Hipp, LaChanze, Kenny Neal, Kevin Ramsey, Francis Ruivivar, Lea Salonga, Chandra Wilson; Special Awards: Tracey Ullman, Ellen Stewart

1991–92: Talia Balsam, Lindsay Crouse, Griffin Dunne, Larry Fishburne, Mel Harris, Jonathan Kaplan, Jessica Lange, Laura Linney, Spiro Malas, Mark Rosenthal, Helen Shaver, Al White; Special Awards: *Dancing at Lughnasa* Company, Plays for Living

1992–93: Brent Carver, Michael Cerveris, Marcia Gay Harden, Stephanie Lawrence, Andrea Martin, Liam Neeson, Stephen Rea, Natasha Richardson, Martin Short, Dina Spybey, Stephen Spinella, Jennifer Tilly. Special Awards: John Leguizamo, Rosetta LeNoire

1993–94: Marcus D'Amico, Jarrod Emick, Arabella Field, Adam Gillett, Sherry Glaser, Michael Hayden, Margaret Illman, Audra Ann McDonald, Burke Moses, Anna Deavere Smith, Jere Shea, Harriet Walter

1994–95: Gretha Boston, Billy Crudup, Ralph Fiennes, Beverly D'Angelo, Calista Flockhart, Kevin Kilner, Anthony LaPaglia, Julie Johnson, Helen Mirren, Jude Law, Rufus Sewell, Vanessa Williams; Special Award: Brooke Shields

1995–96: Jordan Baker, Joohee Choi, Karen Kay Cody, Viola Davis, Kate Forbes, Michael McGrath, Alfred Molina, Timothy Olyphant, Adam Pascal, Lou Diamond Phillips, Daphne Rubin-Vega, Brett Tabisel; Special Award: *An Ideal Husband* Cast

1996–97: Terry Beaver, Helen Carey, Kristin Chenoweth, Jason Danieley, Linda Eder, Allison Janney, Daniel McDonald, Janet McTeer, Mark Ruffalo, Fiona Shaw, Antony Sher, Alan Tudyk; Special Award: *Skylight* Cast

1997–98: Max Casella, Margaret Colin, Ruaidhri Conroy, Alan Cumming, Lea Delaria, Edie Falco, Enid Graham, Anna Kendrick, Ednita Nazario, Douglas Sills, Steven Sutcliffe, Sam Trammel; Special Awards: Eddie Izzard, *Beauty Queen of Leenane* Cast

1998–99: Jillian Armenante, James Black, Brendan Coyle, Anna Friel, Rupert Graves, Lynda Gravatt, Nicole Kidman, Ciaran Hinds, Ute Lemper, Clarke Peter, Toby Stephens, Sandra Oh; Special Award: Jerry Herman

1999–2000: Craig Bierko, Everett Bradley, Gabriel Byrne, Ann Hampton Callaway, Toni Collette, Henry Czerny, Stephen Dillane, Jennifer Ehle, Philip Seymour Hoffman, Hayley Mills, Cigdem Onat, Claudia Shear

2000–2001: Juliette Binoche, Macaulay Culkin, Janie Dee, Raúl Esparza, Kathleen Freeman, Devin May, Reba McEntire, Chris Noth, Joshua Park, Rosie Perez, Joely Richardson, John Ritter; Special Awards: Seán Campion, Conleth Hill

2001–2002 ANTOINETTE PERRY "TONY" AWARDS

BEST PLAY (award goes to both author as well as producer): *The Goat, or Who is Sylvia?* by Edward Albee; produced by Elizabeth Ireland McCann, Daryl Roth, Carole Shorenstein Hays, Terry Allen Kramer, Scott Rudin, Bob Boyett, Scott Nederlander, Jeffrey Sine/ZPI **Nominees:** *Fortune's Fool* by Ivan Turgenev, adapted by Mike Poulton; produced by Julian Schlossberg, Roy Furman, Ben Sprecher, Ted Tulchin, Aaron Levy, Peter May, Bob Boyett, James Fantaci; *Metamorphoses* by Mary Zimmerman; produced by Roy Gabay, Robyn Goodman, Allan S. Gordon, Élan V. McAllister, Dede Harris/Morton Swinsky, Ruth Hendel, Sharon Karmazin, Randall L. Wreghitt/Jane Bergére, Second Stage Theater, Carole Rothman, Carol Fishman; *Topdog/Underdog* by Suzan-Lori Parks; produced by Carole Shorenstein Hays, Waxman Williams Entertainment, Bob Boyett, Freddy De Mann, Susan Dietz/Ina Meibach, Scott Nederlander, Ira Pittelman, *Hits* magazine, Kelpie Arts, Rick Steiner/Frederic H. Mayerson, The Joseph Papp Public Theater/New York Shakespeare Festival

BEST MUSICAL (award goes to producer): *Thoroughly Modern Millie* produced by Michael Leavitt, Fox Theatricals, Hal Luftig, Stewart F. Lane, James L. Nederlander, Independent Presenters Network, Libby Adler Mages/Mari Glick, Dori Berinstein/Jennifer Manocherian/Dramatic Forces, John York Noble, Whoopi Goldberg **Nominees:** *Mamma Mia!* produced by Judy Craymer, Richard East and Björn Ulvaeus for Littlestar, Universal; *Sweet Smell of Success* produced by Clear Channel Entertainment, David Brown, Ernest Lehman, Marty Bell, Martin Richards, Roy Furman, Joan Cullman, Bob Boyett, East of Doheny, Bob and Harvey Weinstein; *Urinetown* produced by the Araca Group and Dodger Theatricals, TheaterDreams, Inc., Lauren Mitchell

BEST BOOK OF A MUSICAL Greg Kotis, *Urinetown* **Nominees:** Catherine Johnson, *Mamma Mia!*; John Guare, *Sweet Smell of Success*; Richard Morris and Dick Scanlan, *Thoroughly Modern Millie*

BEST ORIGINAL SCORE (music and lyrics): Mark Hollmann (music), Mark Hollmann and Greg Kotis (lyrics), *Urinetown* **Nominees:** Marvin Hamlisch (music) and Craig Carnelia (lyrics), *Sweet Smell of Success*; Jeanine Tesori (music) and Dick Scanlan (lyrics), *Thoroughly Modern Millie*; Harry Connick Jr. (music and lyrics), *Thou Shall Not*

BEST REVIVAL OF A PLAY (award goes to producer): *Private Lives* produced by Emanuel Azenberg, Ira Pittelman, Scott Nederlander, Frederick Zollo, Nicholas Paleologos, Dana Broccoli/Jeffrey Sine, James Nederlander, Kevin McCollum, Jeffery Seller, Duncan C. Weldon and Paul Elliott for Triumphant Entertainment Partners, Ltd. **Nominees:** *The Crucible* produced by David Richenthal, Manocherian/Leve/Boyett, Max Cooper, Allan S. Gordon, Roy Furman, Us Productions, Élan V. McAllister, Adam Epstein, Margo Lion, Dede Harris/Morton Swinsky, Clear Channel Entertainment, Old Ivy Productions, Jujamcyn Theaters, Jeffrey Ash, Dori Berinstein/Roni Selig, Margaret McFeeley Golden/Michael Skipper, Gene Korf, Roundabout Theater Company; *Morning's at Seven* produced by Lincoln Center Theater under the direction of André Bishop and Bernard Gersten; *Noises Off* produced by Ambassador Theater Group and Act Productions, Waxman Williams Entertainment, Dede Harris/Morton Swinsky, USA Ostar Theatricals and Nederlander Presentations, Inc., The Royal National Theatre

BEST REVIVAL OF A MUSICAL (award goes to producer): *Into the Woods* produced by Dodger Theatricals, Stage Holding/Joop van den Ende and TheaterDreams, Inc. **Nominee:** *Oklahoma!* Produced by Cameron Mackintosh, The Royal National Theatre

BEST SPECIAL THEATRICAL EVENT *Elaine Stritch at Liberty* produced by John Schreiber, Creative Battery, Margo Lion, Robert Cole, Dede Harris/Morton Swinsky, Cheryl Wiesenfeld, The Joseph Papp Public Theater/New York Shakespeare Festival **Nominees:** *Bea Arthur on Broadway, Just Between Friends* produced by Daryl Roth, M. Beverly Bartner, USA Ostar Theatricals; *Barbara Cook in Mostly Sondheim* produced by Lincoln Center Theater under the direction of André Bishop and Bernard Gersten; *Sexaholix...a Love Story* produced by Tate Entertainment Group, Inc.

BEST PERFORMANCE BY A LEADING ACTOR IN A PLAY Alan Bates, *Fortune's Fool* **Nominees:** Billy Crudup, *The Elephant Man*; Liam Neeson, *The Crucible*; Alan Rickman, *Private Lives*; Jeffrey Wright, *Topdog/Underdog*

BEST PERFORMANCE BY A LEADING ACTRESS IN A PLAY Lindsay Duncan, *Private Lives* **Nominees:** Kate Burton, *Hedda Gabler*; Laura Linney, *The Crucible*; Helen Mirren, *Dance of Death*; Mercedes Ruehl, *The Goat, or Who is Sylvia?*

BEST PERFORMANCE BY A LEADING ACTOR IN A MUSICAL John Lithgow, *Sweet Smell of Success* **Nominees:** Gavin Creel, *Thoroughly Modern Millie*; John Cullum, *Urinetown*; John McMartin, *Into the Woods*; Patrick Wilson, *Oklahoma!*

BEST PERFORMANCE BY A LEADING ACTRESS IN A MUSICAL Sutton Foster, *Thoroughly Modern Millie* **Nominees:** Nancy Opel, *Urinetown*; Louise Pitre, *Mamma Mia!*; Jennifer Laura Thompson, *Urinetown*; Vanessa Williams, *Into the Woods*

BEST PERFORMANCE BY A FEATURED ACTOR IN A PLAY Frank Langella, *Fortune's Fool* NOMINEES: William Biff McGuire, *Morning's at Seven*; Brian Murray, *The Crucible*; Sam Robards, *The Man Who Had All the Luck*; Stephen Tobolowsky, *Morning's at Seven*

BEST PERFORMANCE BY A FEATURED ACTRESS IN A PLAY Katie Finneran, *Noises Off* NOMINEES: Kate Burton, *The Elephant Man*; Elizabeth Franz, *Morning's at Seven*; Estelle Parsons, *Morning's at Seven*; Frances Sternhagen, *Morning's at Seven*

BEST PERFORMANCE BY A FEATURED ACTOR IN A MUSICAL Shuler Hensley, *Oklahoma!* NOMINEES: Norbert Leo Butz, *Thou Shalt Not*; Gregg Edelman, *Into the Woods*; Brian d'Arcy James, *Sweet Smell of Success*; Marc Kudisch, *Thoroughly Modern Millie*

BEST PERFORMANCE BY A FEATURED ACTRESS IN A MUSICAL Harriet Harris, *Thoroughly Modern Millie* NOMINEES: Laura Benanti, *Into the Woods*; Spencer Kayden, *Urinetown*; Judy Kaye, *Mamma Mia!*; Andrea Martin, *Oklahoma!*

BEST SCENIC DESIGN Tim Hatley, *Private Lives* NOMINEES: John Lee Beatty, *Morning's at Seven*; Daniel Ostling, *Metamorphoses*; Douglas W. Schmidt, *Into the Woods*

BEST LIGHTING DESIGN Brian MacDevitt, *Into the Woods* NOMINEES: Paul Gallo, *The Crucible*; David Hersey, *Oklahoma!*; Natasha Katz, *Sweet Smell of Success*

BEST COSTUME DESIGN Martin Pakledinaz, *Thoroughly Modern Millie* NOMINEES: Jenny Beavan, *Private Lives*; Susan Hilferty, *Into the Woods*; Jane Greenwood, *Morning's at Seven*

BEST CHOREOGRAPHY Rob Ashford, *Thoroughly Modern Millie* NOMINEES: John Carrafa, *Into the Woods*; John Carrafa, *Urinetown*; Susan Stroman, *Oklahoma!*

BEST DIRECTION OF A PLAY Mary Zimmerman, *Metamorphoses* NOMINEES: Howard Davies, *Private Lives*; Richard Eyre, *The Crucible*; Daniel Sullivan, *Morning's at Seven*

BEST DIRECTION OF A MUSICAL John Rando, *Urinetown* NOMINEES: James Lapine, *Into the Woods*; Michael Mayer, *Thoroughly Modern Millie*; Trevor Nunn, *Oklahoma!*

BEST ORCHESTRATIONS Doug Besterman and Ralph Burns, *Thoroughly Modern Millie* NOMINEES: Benny Anderson, Björn Ulvaeus, and Martin Koch, *Mamma Mia!*; William David Brohn, *Sweet Smell of Success*; Bruce Coughlin, *Urinetown*

SPECIAL TONY AWARD FOR LIFETIME ACHIEVEMENT IN THE THEATRE Julie Harris; Robert Whitehead

REGIONAL THEATRE TONY AWARD Williamstown Theatre Festival, Williamstown, Massachusetts

AMERICAN THEATRE WING ANTOINETTE PERRY (TONY) PAST AWARD-WINNING PRODUCTIONS

Awards listed are Best Play followed by Best Musical, and as awards for Best Revival and the subcategories of Best Revival of a Play and Best Revival of a Musical were instituted, they are listed respectively.

1947: No award given for musical or play. 1948: Mister Roberts (play) 1949: Death of a Salesman, Kiss Me, Kate (musical) 1950: The Cocktail Party, South Pacific 1951: The Rose Tattoo, Guys and Dolls 1952: The Fourposter, The King and I 1953: The Crucible, Wonderful Town 1954: The Teahouse of the August Moon, Kismet 1955: The Desperate Hours, The Pajama Game 1956: The Diary of Anne Frank, Damn Yankees 1957: Long Day's Journey into Night, My Fair Lady 1958: Sunrise at Campobello, The Music Man 1959: J.B., Redhead 1960: The Miracle Worker, Fiorello! tied with The Sound of Music 1961: Becket, Bye Bye Birdie 1962: A Man for All Seasons, How to Succeed in Business Without Really Trying 1963: Who's Afraid of Virginia Woolf?, A Funny Thing Happened on the Way to the Forum 1964: Luther, Hello Dolly! 1965: The Subject Was Roses, Fiddler on the Roof 1966: The Persecution and Assassination of Marat as Performed by the Inmates of the Asylum of Charenton Under the Direction of the Marquis de Sade, Man of La Mancha 1967: The Homecoming, Cabaret 1968: Rosencrantz and Guildenstern Are Dead, Hallelujah Baby! 1969: The Great White Hope, 1776 1970: Borstal Boy, Applause 1971: Sleuth, Company 1972: Sticks and Bones, Two Gentlemen of Verona 1973: That Championship Season, A Little Night Music 1974: The River Niger, Raisin 1975: Equus, The Wiz 1976: Travesties, A Chorus Line 1977: The Shadow Box, Annie 1978: Da, Ain't Misbehavin', Dracula (innovative musical revival) 1979: The Elephant Man, Sweeney Todd 1980: Children of a Lesser God, Evita, Morning's at Seven (best revival) 1981: Amadeus, 42nd St., The Pirates of Penzance 1982: The Life and Adventures of Nicholas Nickelby, Nine, Othello 1983: Torch Song Trilogy, Cats, On Your Toes 1984: The Real Thing, La Cage aux Folles, Death of a Salesman 1985: Biloxi Blues, Big River, Joe Egg 1986: I'm Not Rappaport, The Mystery of Edwin Drood, Sweet Charity 1987: Fences, Les Misérables, All My Sons 1988: M. Butterfly, The Phantom of the Opera, Anything Goes 1989: The Heidi Chronicles, Jerome Robbins' Broadway, Our Town 1990: The Grapes of Wrath, City of Angels, Gypsy 1991: Lost in Yonkers, The Will Rogers' Follies, Fiddler on the Roof 1992: Dancing at Lughnasa, Crazy for You, Guys and Dolls 1993: Angels in America: Millenium Approaches, Kiss of the Spider Woman, Anna Christie 1994: Angels in America: Perestroika (play), Passion (musical), An Inspector Calls (play revival), Carousel (musical revival) 1995: Love! Valour! Compassion!, Sunset Boulevard, Show Boat, The Heiress 1996: Master Class, Rent, A Delicate Balance, King and I 1997: Last Night of Ballyhoo, Titanic, A Doll's House, Chicago 1998: Art, The Lion King, View from the Bridge, Cabaret 1999: Side Man, Fosse, Death of a Salesman, Annie Get Your Gun 2000: Copenhagen, Contact, The Real Thing, Kiss Me, Kate 2001: Proof, The Producers, One Flew Over the Cuckoo's Nest, 42nd Street 2002: Edward Albee's The Goat, or Who is Sylvia?, Thoroughly Modern Millie, Private Lives, Into the Woods

47th ANNUAL VILLAGE VOICE OBIE AWARDS

For outstanding achievement in Off- and Off-Off-Broadway theater

PERFORMANCE: Bill Camp, *Homebody/Kabul*; Reg E. Cathey, James Himelsbach, Karen Kandel, Anthony Mackie, John Seitz, Maria Tucci, *Talk*; Christopher Donahue, *Monster*; Linda Emond, *Homebody/Kabul*; Raúl Esparza, *tick, tick...BOOM!*; Peter Frechette, Reg Rogers, *The Dazzle*; Yvette Ganier, *Breath, Boom*; Martha Plimpton, *Hobson's Choice*; Jeffrey Wright, *Topdog/Underdog* **DIRECTION:** George C. Wolfe, *Topdog/Underdog*; Mary Zimmerman, *Metamorphoses* **SUSTAINED EXCELLENCE IN LIGHTING DESIGN:** Kevin Adams **SET AND LIGHTING DESIGN:** Angela Moore, Michael Schmelling, *Drummer Wanted* **VIDEO:** Marilys Ernst, *Talk* **SOUND DESIGN:** Whit MacLaughlin, *The Fab 4 Reach the Pearly Gates* **PLAYWRIGHTING:** Melissa James Gibson, *[sic]*; Tony Kushner, *Homebody/Kabul* **SUSTAINED ACHIEVEMENT:** Caryl Churchill **SPECIAL CITATION:** ART/NY, for support of Off-Broadway theater; Daniel Aukin and Louisa Thompson, direction and set design of *[sic]*; Ingmar Bergman and The Royal Dramatic Theatre of Sweden, *The Ghost Sonata*; Daniel MacIvor, *In on It*; Charles L. Mee and Les Waters, playwriting and direction of *Big Love*; Elaine Stritch, *Elaine Stritch at Liberty*; The Wooster Group, *To You, the Birdie!* **GRANTS:** Ma-Yi Theater Company; Salt Theater Company **ROSS WETZSTEON AWARD:** P.S. 122

OBIE AWARDS—BEST NEW PLAY AWARD–WINNING PRODUCTIONS

1956: Absalom, Absalom **1957:** A House Remembered **1958:** no award given **1959:** The Quare Fellow **1960:** no award given **1961:** The Blacks **1962:** Who'll Save the Plowboy? **1963:** no award given **1964:** Play **1965:** The Old Glory **1966:** The Journey of the Fifth Horse **1967:** no award given **1968:** no award given **1969:** no award given **1970:** The Effect of Gamma Rays on Man-in-the-Moon Marigolds **1971:** House of Blue Leaves **1972:** no award given **1973:** The Hot L Baltimore **1974:** Short Eyes **1975:** The First Breeze of Summer **1976:** American Buffalo, Sexual Perversity in Chicago **1977:** Curse of the Starving Class **1978:** Shaggy Dog Animation **1979:** Josephine **1980:** no award given **1981:** FOB **1982:** Metamorphosis in Miniature, Mr. Dead and Mrs. Free **1983:** Painting Churches, Andrea Rescued, Edmond **1984:** Fool for Love **1985:** The Conduct of Life **1986:** no award given **1987:** The Cure, Film Is Evil, Radio Is Good **1988:** Abingdon Square **1989:** no award given **1990:** Prelude to a Kiss, Imperceptible Mutabilities in the Third Kingdom, Bad Benny, Crowbar, Terminal Hip **1991:** The Fever **1992:** Sight Unseen, Sally's Rape, The Baltimore Waltz **1993:** no award given **1994:** Twilight: Los Angeles 1992 **1995:** Cyrptogram **1996:** Adrienne Kennedy **1997:** One Flea Spare **1998:** Pearls for Pigs and Benita Canova **1999:** no award given **2000:** no award given **2001:** The Syringa Tree **2002:** no award given

47th ANNUAL DRAMA DESK AWARDS

For outstanding achievement in the 2001–2002 season, voted on by an association of New York drama reporters, editors and critics from nominations made from a committee.

NEW PLAY: (tie) *Metamorphoses* and *The Goat, or Who is Sylvia?* **NEW MUSICAL:** *Thoroughly Modern Millie* **REVIVAL OF A PLAY:** *Private Lives* **REVIVAL OF A MUSICAL:** *Into the Woods* **BOOK:** Elaine Stritch and John Lahr, *Elaine Stritch at Liberty* **COMPOSER:** Jason Robert Brown, *The Last Five Years* **LYRICIST:** Jason Robert Brown, *The Last Five Years* **MUSIC IN A PLAY:** Willy Schwarz, *Metamorphoses* **ACTOR IN A PLAY:** Alan Bates, *Fortune's Fool* **ACTRESS IN A PLAY:** Lindsay Duncan, *Private Lives* **FEATURED ACTOR IN A PLAY:** Frank Langella, *Fortune's Fool* **FEATURED ACTRESS IN A PLAY:** Katie Finneran, *Noises Off* **ACTOR IN A MUSICAL:** John Lithgow, *Sweet Smell of Success* **ACTRESS IN A MUSICAL:** Sutton Foster, *Thoroughly Modern Millie* **FEATURED ACTOR IN A MUSICAL:** Shuler Hensley, *Oklahoma!* **FEATURED ACTRESS IN A MUSICAL:** Harriet Harris, *Thoroughly Modern Millie* **SOLO PERFORMANCE:** Elaine Stritch, *Elaine Stritch at Liberty* **DIRECTOR OF A PLAY:** Mary Zimmerman, *Metamorphoses* **DIRECTOR OF A MUSICAL:** Michael Mayer, *Thoroughly Modern Millie* **CHOREOGRAPHY:** Susan Stroman, *Oklahoma!* **ORCHESTRATIONS:** Doug Besterman and Ralph Burns, *Thoroughly Modern Millie* **SET DESIGN OF A PLAY:** Tim Hatley, *Private Lives* **SET DESIGN OF A MUSICAL:** Douglas W. Schmidt, *Into the Woods* **COSTUME DESIGN:** Isaac Mizrahi, *The Women* **LIGHTING DESIGN:** T.J. Gerckens, *Metamorphoses* **SOUND DESIGN:** Dan Moses Schreier, *Into the Woods* **SPECIAL AWARDS:** Paul Huntley, lifetime achievement in hair and wig design; Billy Rosenfield, contributions to the preservation of musical theatre recordings; Mint Theater Company, presenting and preserving little known classics; Worth Street Theater Company, for its Stage Door Canteen shows for workers at Ground Zero.

52nd ANNUAL OUTER CRITICS CIRCLE AWARDS

For outstanding achievement in the 2001–2002 season, voted on by critics on out-of-town periodicals and media

BROADWAY PLAY: *The Goat, or Who is Sylvia?* **OFF-BROADWAY PLAY:** *The Dazzle* **REVIVAL:** *Morning's at Seven* **ACTOR IN A PLAY:** Alan Bates, *Fortune's Fool* **ACTRESS IN A PLAY:** Mercedes Ruehl, *The Goat, or Who is Sylvia?* **FEATURED ACTOR IN A PLAY:** Frank Langella, *Fortune's Fool* **FEATURED ACTRESS IN A PLAY:** Katie Finneran, *Noises Off* **DIRECTOR OF A PLAY:** Mary Zimmerman, *Metamorphoses* **BROADWAY MUSICAL:** *Urinetown* **OFF-BROADWAY MUSICAL:** *tick, tick...Boom!* **REVIVAL OF A MUSICAL:** *Oklahoma!* **ACTOR IN A MUSICAL:** John Lithgow, *Sweet Smell of Success* **ACTRESS IN A MUSICAL:** Sutton Foster, *Thoroughly Modern Millie* **FEATURED ACTOR IN A MUSICAL:** Shuler Hensley, *Oklahoma!* **FEATURED ACTRESS IN A MUSICAL:** Spencer Kayden, *Urinetown* **DIRECTOR OF A MUSICAL:** John Rando, *Urinetown* **CHOREOGRAPHY:** Susan Stroman, *Oklahoma!* **SCENIC DESIGN:** Anthony Ward, *Oklahoma!* **COSTUME DESIGN:** Isaac Mizrahi, *The Women* **LIGHTING DESIGN:** David Hersey, *Oklahoma!* **SOLO PERFORMANCE:** Elaine Stritch, *Elaine Stritch at Liberty* **JOHN GASSNER PLAYWRITING AWARD:** Suzan-Lori Parks, *Topdog/Underdog* **SPECIAL ACHIEVEMENT AWARD:** Mos Def and Jeffrey Wright, *Topdog/Underdog*

PULITZER PRIZE
AWARD–WINNING PRODUCTIONS

1918: Why Marry? 1919: no award 1920: Beyond the Horizon 1921: Miss Lulu Bett 1922: Anna Christie 1923: Icebound 1924: Hell-Bent fer Heaven 1925: They Knew What They Wanted 1926: Craig's Wife 1927: In Abraham's Bosom 1928: Strange Interlude 1929: Street Scene 1930: The Green Pastures 1931: Alison's House 1932: Of Thee I Sing 1933: Both Your Houses 1934: Men in White 1935: The Old Maid 1936: Idiot's Delight 1937: You Can't Take It with You 1938: Our Town 1939: Abe Lincoln in Illinois 1940: The Time of Your Life 1941: There Shall Be No Night 1942: no award 1943: The Skin of Our Teeth 1944: no award 1945: Harvey 1946: State of the Union 1947: no award 1948: A Streetcar Named Desire 1949: Death of a Salesman 1950: South Pacific 1951: no award 1952: The Shrike 1953: Picnic 1954: The Teahouse of the August Moon 1955: Cat on a Hot Tin Roof 1956: The Diary of Anne Frank 1957: Long Day's Journey into Night 1958: Look Homeward, Angel 1959: J.B. 1960: Fiorello! 1961: All the Way Home 1962: How to Succeed in Business Without Really Trying 1963: no award 1964: no award 1965: The Subject Was Roses 1966: no award 1967: A Delicate Balance 1968: no award 1969: The Great White Hope 1970: No Place to Be Somebody 1971: The Effect of Gamma Rays on Man-in-the-Moon Marigolds 1972: no award 1973: That Championship Season 1974: no award 1975: Seascape 1976: A Chorus Line 1977: The Shadow Box 1978: The Gin Game 1979: Buried Child 1980: Talley's Folly 1981: Crimes of the Heart 1982: A Soldier's Play 1983: 'night, Mother 1984: Glengarry Glen Ross 1985: Sunday in the Park with George 1986: no award 1987: Fences 1988: Driving Miss Daisy 1989: The Heidi Chronicles 1990: The Piano Lesson 1991: Lost in Yonkers 1992: The Kentucky Cycle 1993: Angels in America: Millenium Approaches 1994: Three Tall Women 1995: Young Man from Atlanta 1996: Rent 1997: no award 1998: How I Learned to Drive 1999: Wit 2000: Dinner with Friends 2001: Proof 2002: Topdog/Underdog

NEW YORK DRAMA CRITICS
AWARD–WINNING PRODUCTIONS

Awards listed are in the following order: Best American Play, Best Foreign Play, Best Musical, and Best Regardless of Category, which was instituted during the 1962–1963 award season.

1936: Winterset 1937: High Tor 1938: Of Mice and Men, Shadow and Substance 1939: The White Steed 1940: The Time of Your Life 1941: Watch on the Rhine, The Corn Is Green 1942: Blithe Spirit 1943: The Patriots 1944: Jacobowsky and the Colonel 1945: The Glass Menagerie 1946: Carousel 1947: All My Sons, No Exit, Brigadoon 1948: A Streetcar Named Desire, The Winslow Boy 1949: Death of a Salesman, The Madwoman of Chaillot, South Pacific 1950: The Member of the Wedding, The Cocktail Party, The Consul 1951: Darkness at Noon, The Lady's Not for Burning, Guys and Dolls 1952: I Am a Camera, Venus Observed, Pal Joey 1953: Picnic, The Love of Four Colonels, Wonderful Town 1954: Teahouse of the August Moon, Ondine, The Golden Apple 1955: Cat on a Hot Tin Roof, Witness for the Prosecution, The Saint of Bleecker Street 1956: The Diary of Anne Frank, Tiger at the Gates, My Fair Lady 1957: Long Day's Journey into Night, The Waltz of the Toreadors, The Most Happy Fella 1958: Look Homeward Angel, Look Back in Anger, The Music Man 1959: A Raisin in the Sun, The Visit, La Plume de Ma Tante 1960: Toys in the Attic, Five Finger Exercise, Fiorello! 1961: All the Way Home, A Taste of Honey,

Carnival 1962: Night of the Iguana, A Man for All Seasons, How to Succeed in Business without Really Trying 1963: Who's Afraid of Virginia Woolf? 1964: Luther, Hello Dolly! 1965: The Subject Was Roses, Fiddler on the Roof 1966: The Persecution and Assassination of Marat as Performed by the Inmates of the Asylum of Charenton under the Direction of the Marquis de Sade, Man of La Mancha 1967: The Homecoming, Cabaret 1968: Rosencrantz and Guildenstern Are Dead, Your Own Thing 1969: The Great White Hope, 1776 1970: The Effect of Gamma Rays on Man-in-the-Moon Marigolds, Borstal Boy, Company 1971: Home, Follies, The House of Blue Leaves 1972: That Championship Season, Two Gentlemen of Verona 1973: The Hot L Baltimore, The Changing Room, A Little Night Music 1974: The Contractor, Short Eyes, Candide 1975: Equus, The Taking of Miss Janie, A Chorus Line 1976: Travesties, Streamers, Pacific Overtures 1977: Otherwise Engaged, American Buffalo, Annie 1978: Da, Ain't Misbehavin' 1979: The Elephant Man, Sweeney Todd 1980: Talley's Folley, Evita, Betrayal 1981: Crimes of the Heart, A Lesson from Aloes, Special Citation to Lena Horne, The Pirates of Penzance 1982: The Life and Adventures of Nicholas Nickleby, A Soldier's Play, (no musical) 1983: Brighton Beach Memoirs, Plenty, Little Shop of Horrors 1984: The Real Thing, Glengarry Glen Ross, Sunday in the Park with George 1985: Ma Rainey's Black Bottom, (no musical) 1986: A Lie of the Mind, Benefactors, (no musical), Special Citation to Lily Tomlin and Jane Wagner 1987: Fences, Les Liaisons Dangereuses, Les Misérables 1988: Joe Turner's Come and Gone, The Road to Mecca, Into the Woods 1989: The Heidi Chronicles, Aristocrats, Largely New York (special), (no musical) 1990: The Piano Lesson, City of Angels, Privates on Parade 1991: Six Degrees of Separation, The Will Rogers Follies, Our Country's Good, Special Citation to Eileen Atkins 1992: Two Trains Running, Dancing at Lughnasa 1993: Angels in America: Millenium Approaches, Someone Who'll Watch Over Me, Kiss of the Spider Woman 1994: Three Tall Women, Anna Deavere Smith (special) 1995: Arcadia, Love! Valour! Compassion!, Special Award: Signature Theatre Company 1996: Seven Guitars, Molly Sweeny, Rent 1997: How I Learned to Drive, Skylight, Violet, Chicago (special) 1998: Pride's Crossing, Art, Lion King, Cabaret (special) 1999: Wit, Parade, Closer, David Hare (special) 2000: Jitney, James Joyce's The Dead, Copenhagen 2001: The Invention of Love, The Producers, Proof 2002: Edward Albee's The Goat, or Who is Sylvia?, Special citation to Elaine Stritch for Elaine Stritch at Liberty

LUCILLE LORTEL AWARDS

Awards given by the League of Off-Broadway Theatres and Producers

PLAY: *Metamorphoses,* by Mary Zimmerman **MUSICAL:** *Urinetown,* music and lyrics by Mark Hollmann, book and lyrics by Greg Kotis **REVIVAL:** *Cymbeline,* by William Shakespeare, produced by Theatre for a New Audience **ACTOR:** Reg Rogers, *The Dazzle* **ACTRESS:** Linda Emond, *Homebody/Kabul* **FEATURED ACTOR:** Keith Nobbs, *Four* **FEATURED ACTRESS:** Kathleen Widdoes, *Franny's Way* **DIRECTION:** Mary Zimmerman, *Metamorphoses* **CHOREOGRAPHY:** John Carrafa, *Urinetown* **SCENERY:** Douglas Stein, *36 Views* **COSTUMES:** Elizabeth Caitlin Ward, *Cymbeline* **LIGHTING:** T.J. Gerckens, *Metamorphoses* **SOUND:** Scott Lehrer, *Franny's Way* **BODY OF WORK:** Second Stage Theatre **LIFETIME ACHIEVEMENT:** Edward Albee **EDITH OLIVIER AWARD:** Ruby Dee **UNIQUE THEATRICAL EXPERIENCE:** *Elaine Stritch at Liberty* **2002 INDUCTEE, PLAYWRIGHTS' SIDEWALK:** Romulus Linney

LUCILLE LORTEL PAST AWARD-WINNING PRODUCTIONS

Awards listed are Outstanding Play and Outstanding Musical, respectively, since inception

1986: *Woza Africa!*; no musical award **1987:** *The Common Pursuit*; no musical award **1988:** no play or musical award **1989:** *The Cocktail Hour*; no musical award **1990:** no play or musical award **1991:** *Aristocrats*; *Falsettoland* **1992:** *Lips Together, Teeth Apart*; *And the World Goes 'Round* **1993:** *The Destiny of Me*; *Forbidden Broadway* **1994:** *Three Tall Women*; *Wings* **1995:** *Camping with Henry & Tom*; *Jelly Roll!* **1996:** *Molly Sweeney*; *Floyd Collins* **1997:** *How I Learned to Drive*; *Violet* **1998:** *Gross Indecency*, and *The Beauty Queen of Leenane* (tie); no musical award **1999:** *Wit*; no musical award **2000:** *Dinner With Friends*; *James Joyce's The Dead* **2001:** *Proof*; *Bat Boy: The Musical* **2002:** *Metamorphoses*; *Urinetown*

AMERICAN THEATRE CRITICS/STEINBERG NEW PLAY AWARDS AND CITATIONS

NEW PLAY CITATIONS: **1977:** *And the Soul Shall Dance* by Wakako Yamauchi **1978:** *Getting Out* by Marsha Norman **1979:** *Loose Ends* by Michael Weller **1980:** *Custer* by Robert E. Ingham **1981:** *Chekhov in Yalta* by John Driver and Jeffrey Haddow **1982:** *Talking With* by Jane Martin **1983:** *Closely Related* by Bruce MacDonald **1984:** *Wasted* by Fred Gamel **1985:** *Scheherazade* by Marisha Chamberlain

NEW PLAY AWARD: **1986:** *Fences* by August Wilson **1987:** *A Walk in the Woods* by Lee Blessing **1988:** *Heathen Valley* by Romulus Linney **1989:** *The Piano Lesson* by August Wilson **1990:** *2* by Romulus Linney **1991:** *Two Trains Running* by August Wilson **1992:** *Could I Have This Dance* by Doug Haverty **1993:** *Children of Paradise: Shooting a Dream* by Steven Epp, Felicity Jones, Dominique Serrand, and Paul Walsh **1994:** *Keely and Du* by Jane Martin **1995:** *The Nanjing Race* by Reggie Cheong-Leen **1996:** *Amazing Grace* by Michael Cristofer **1997:** *Jack and Jill* by Jane Martin **1998:** *The Cider House Rules, Part II* by Peter Parnell **1999:** *Book of Days* by Lanford Wilson

ATCA/STEINBERG NEW PLAY AWARD AND CITATIONS

2000: *Oo-Bla-Dee* by Regina Taylor
CITATIONS: *Compleat Female Stage Beauty* by Jeffrey Hatcher; *Syncopation* by Allan Knee

2001: *Anton in Show Business* by Jane Martin
CITATIONS: *Big Love* by Charles L. Mee; *King Hedley II* by August Wilson

2002: *The Carpetbagger's Children* by Horton Foote
CITATIONS: *The Action Against Sol Schumann* by Jeffrey Sweet; *Joe and Betty* by Murray Mednick

21st ANNUAL ASTAIRE AWARDS

For excellence in dance and choreography, administered by the Theatre Development Fund and selected by a committee comprising Douglas Watt, Clive Barnes, Howard Kissel, Michael Kuchwara, Donald McDonagh, Richard Philip, Charles L. Reinhart, and Linda Winer.

CHOREOGRAPHY: Susan Stroman, *Oklahoma!* **FEMALE DANCER:** Sutton Foster, *Thoroughly Modern Millie* **MALE DANCER:** Justin Bohon, *Oklahoma!* **DANCE TEACHERS:** Frank Hatchett, Luigi, Phil Black, Gabriela Taub-Darvash

57TH ANNUAL CLARENCE DERWENT AWARDS

Given to a female and male performer by Actors Equity Association, based on work in New York that demonstrates promise.

Anne Hathaway; Sam Robards

12th ANNUAL CONNECTICUT CRITICS CIRCLE AWARDS

For outstanding achievement in Connecticut theater during the 2001–2002 season.

PRODUCTION OF A PLAY: (tie) Hartford Stage, *Seascape* and Long Wharf Theatre, *Yellowman* **PRODUCTION OF A MUSICAL:** Downtown Cabaret Theatre, *Smokey Joe's Café* **ACTRESS IN A PLAY:** Dael Orlandersmith, *Yellowman* **ACTOR IN A PLAY:** Howard W. Overshown, *Yellowman* **ACTRESS IN A MUSICAL:** (tie) Florence Lacey, *Wings* and Lovena Fox, *Jekyll and Hyde* **ACTOR IN A MUSICAL:** Michael McGrath, *They All Laughed* **DIRECTION OF A PLAY:** Rob Ruggiero, *The Laramie Project* **DIRECTION OF A MUSICAL:** Semina DeLaurentis, *My Way: A Musical Tribute to Frank Sinatra* **CHOREOGRAPHY:** Jamie Rocco, *Smokey Joe's Café* **SET DESIGN:** John Coyne, *You Never Can Tell* **LIGHTING DESIGN:** Mimi Jordan Sherin, *Seascape* **COSTUME DESIGN:** Mirena Rada, *Pera Palas* **SOUND DESIGN:** David Budries, *Seascape* **ENSEMBLE PERFORMANCE:** Michael Anderson, Mary Bacon, Natalie Brown, Matthew J. Cody, Antoinette LaVecchia, Duane Noch, Susan Patrick and Jeremy Webb, *The Laramie Project* **DEBUT AWARD:** Patrick O'Sullivan and Philip Parrot, *Lost in Yonkers* **SPECIAL AWARD:** International Festival of Arts and Ideas, *Translations* **TOM KILLEN MEMORIAL AWARD:** Steve Campo, artistic director of TheaterWorks

68th ANNUAL DRAMA LEAGUE AWARDS

For distinguished achievement in the American theater.

PLAY: *Metamorphoses* **MUSICAL:** *Urinetown* **REVIVAL OF A PLAY OR MUSICAL:** *The Crucible* **DISTINGUISHED PERFORMANCE:** Liam Neeson, *The Crucible* **JULIA HANSEN AWARD FOR EXCELLENCE IN DIRECTING:** Richard Eyre **ACHIEVEMENT IN MUSICAL THEATRE:** Elaine Stritch **UNIQUE CONTRIBUTION TO THEATER:** Julia Hansen

2001 DRAMATIST GUILD AWARDS

To the playwright whose work deals with social, political or religious mores of the time, selected by the Dramatist Guild Council.

2001 ELIZABETH HULL-KATE WARRINER AWARD: Tony Kushner, *Homebody/Kabul* **FREDERICK LOEWE AWARD FOR DRAMATIC COMPOSITION:** Cy Coleman **FLORA ROBERTS AWARD:** Neal Bell **LIFETIME ACHIEVEMENT:** Betty Comden and Adolph Green

2002 M. ELIZABETH OSBORN AWARD

Presented to an emerging playwright by the American Theatre Critics Association; Mia McCullough, *Chagrin Falls.*

20th ANNUAL ELLIOTT NORTON AWARDS

For outstanding contribution to the theater in Boston, voted by a Boston Theater Critics Association selection committee comprising Terry Byrne, Carolyn Clay, Iris Fanger, Joyce Kullhawik, Jon L. Lehman, Bill Marx, Ed Siegel and Caldwell Titcomb.

NEW PLAY: Adam Rapp, *Nocturne* **NORTON PRIZE:** Barbara Meek Productions **VISITING COMPANIES:** *The Glass Menagerie*, Hartford stage **LARGE RESIDENT COMPANY:** *Homebody/Kabul*, produced by Trinity Repertory Theater Company **SMALL RESIDENT COMPANY:** *Twelfth Night*, produced by Commonwealth Shakespeare Company **LOCAL FRINGE COMPANY:** *The Laramie Project*, produced by Boston Theater Works **SOLO PERFORMANCE:** Catherine Samie, *The Last Supper* **MUSICAL PRODUCTIONS:** Large Company: *Contact*, produced by Broadway in Boston; Small Company: *Sunday in the Park with George*, produced by Lyric Stage Company **ACTOR:** Large company: Simon Russell Beale, *Hamlet*; Small company: Robert Pemberton, *Much Ado About Nothing, Lobby Hero, Shel's Shorts* **ACTRESS:** Large company: Andrea Martin, *Betty's Summer Vacation*; Small company: Nancy E. Carroll, *Bailegangaire* **DIRECTOR:** Large company: Nicholas Martin, *Betty's Summer Vacation*; Small company: Carmel O' Reilly, *The Lonesome West, Bailegangaire* **SET DESIGN:** Alexander Dodge, *Twelfth Night, Heartbreak House* **COSTUME DESIGN:** Gail Astrid Buckley, *Curse of the Bambino, Twelfth Night, Much Ado About Nothing, Shel's Shorts* **GUEST OF HONOR:** Julie Harris **20th ANNIVERSARY AWARD:** Robert Brustein **SPECIAL CITATION:** Eliza Rose Fichter, *A Russian Tea Party, One Flea Spare, The Miracle Worker, Reason*

18th ANNUAL HELEN HAYES AWARDS

Presented by the Washington Theatre Awards Society in recognition of excellence in Washington, D.C., theater.

RESIDENT PRODUCTIONS

PLAY: *Home*, produced by Round House Theatre **MUSICAL:** *Blues in the Night*, produced by Arena Stage **LEAD ACTRESS, MUSICAL:** Bernardine Mitchell, *Blues in the Night* **LEAD ACTOR, MUSICAL:** Brian Childers, *Danny & Sylvia: A Musical Love Story* **LEAD ACTRESS, PLAY:** Jenifer Deal, *The Muckle Man* **LEAD ACTOR, PLAY:** Nigel Reed, *The Judas Kiss* **SUPPORTING ACTRESS, MUSICAL:** Kadejah Oni Higdon, *Spunk* **SUPPORTING ACTOR, MUSICAL:** Michael Sharp, *Grand Hotel* **SUPPORTING ACTRESS, PLAY:** Mia Wing, *Far East* **SUPPORTING ACTOR, PLAY:** Helmar Augustus Cooper, *Jitney* **DIRECTOR, PLAY:** Thomas W. Jones II, *Home* **DIRECTOR, MUSICAL:** Mary Hall Surface, *Perseus Bayou* **SET DESIGN, PLAY OR MUSICAL:** (tie) Tony Cisek, *The Judas Kiss*; Ming Cho Lee, *Don Carlos* **COSTUME DESIGN, PLAY OR MUSICAL:** Robert Perdziola, *Don Carlos* **LIGHTING DESIGN, PLAY OR MUSICAL:** Chris Perry, *Don Carlos* **SOUND DESIGN, PLAY OR MUSICAL:** Daniel Portaix, *Les Cloisons (Partitions)* **MUSICAL DIRECTION, PLAY OR MUSICAL:** Jon Kalbfleisch, *Grand Hotel* **CHOREOGRAPHY:** Ilona Kessell, *Damn Yankees*

NON-RESIDENT PRODUCTIONS

PRODUCTION: *Mill on the Floss*, produced by the Kennedy Center **LEAD ACTRESS:** Jodi Capeless, *Late Nite Catechism* **LEAD ACTOR:** Jason Watkins, *A Servant to Two Masters* **SUPPORTING PERFORMER:** Tom Riis Farrell, *Dirty Blonde* **CHARLES MACARTHUR AWARD FOR OUTSTANDING NEW PLAY:** *In the Garden*, Norman Allen

2001 GEORGE FREEDLEY MEMORIAL AWARD

For the best book about live theater published in the United States the previous year.

Harlequin Unmasked: The Commedia Dell'Arte and Porcelain Sculpture, Meredith Chilton

2000–2001 GEORGE JEAN NATHAN AWARD

For dramatic criticism; Laurence Senelick.

2002 GEORGE OPPENHEIMER AWARD

To the best new American playwright, presented by Newsday; Cornelius Eady, Brutal Imagination.

2002 HEWES DESIGN AWARDS

For outstanding design originating in the U.S., selected by a committee comprising Tish Dace (chair), Glenda Frank, Mario Fratti, Randy Gener, Mel Gussow, Henry Hewes, Jeffrey Eric Jenkins and Joan Ungaro

SCENIC DESIGN: Louisa Thompson, *[sic]* **LIGHTING DESIGN:** T.J. Gerckens, *Metamorphoses* **COSTUME DESIGN:** Susan Hilferty, *Into the Woods* **UNUSUAL EFFECTS:** David Gallo, *Wonder of the World* (repeating clouds against blue sky)

33rd ANNUAL JOSEPH JEFFERSON AWARDS

For achievement in Chicago theater during the 2000–2001 season, given by the Jefferson Awards Committee in 28 competitive categories.

RESIDENT PRODUCTIONS

NEW WORK: *The Pagans*, Ann Noble; *The Ballad of Little Jo*, Mike Reid and Sarah Schlesinger **NEW ADAPTATION:** *Hard Times*, Heidi Stillman **PRODUCTION OF A PLAY:** Lookingglass Theatre Company in association with Actors Gymnasium, *Hard Times* **PRODUCTION OF A MUSICAL:** Marriott Theatre in Lincolnshire, *The King and I* **DIRECTOR OF A PLAY:** Heidi Stillman, *Hard Times* **DIRECTOR OF MUSICAL:** Gary Griffin, *Big* **DIRECTOR OF A REVUE:** Marc Robin, *And the World Goes 'Round* **ACTOR IN A PRINCIPAL ROLE, PLAY:** Greg Vinkler, *King Lear* **ACTRESS IN A PRINCIPAL ROLE, PLAY:** Carmen Roman, *Wit* **ACTOR IN A SUPPORTING ROLE, PLAY:** David Darlow, *Endgame* **ACTRESS IN A SUPPORTING ROLE, PLAY:** Laura T. Fisher, *Early and Often* **ACTOR IN A PRINCIPAL ROLE, MUSICAL:** Rod Thomas, *Big* **ACTRESS IN A PRINCIPAL ROLE, MUSICAL:** Mary Ernster, *The King and I* **ACTOR IN A SUPPORTING ROLE, MUSICAL:** Gordon McClure, *Being Beautiful* **ACTRESS IN A SUPPORTING ROLE, MUSICAL:** Alene Robertson, *Mame* **ACTOR IN A REVUE:** Mark Townsend, *The Nat King Cole Story* **ACTRESS IN A REVUE:** E. Faye Butler, *Could It Be Magic?* **ENSEMBLE:** *The Incident*, produced by Next Theatre **SCENIC DESIGN:** Linda Buchanan, *House* **COSTUME DESIGN:** Nancy Missimi, *The King and I* **LIGHTING DESIGN:** Brian Sidney Bembridge, *Hard Times* **SOUND DESIGN:** Mike Frank and Andre Pluess, *Macbett* **CHOREOGRAPHY:** Sylvia Hernandez-DiStasi, *Hard Times* **ORIGINAL MUSIC:** Alaric Jans, *The Two Gentleman of Verona* **MUSICAL DIRECTION:** Patrick Vaccariello, *The Ballad of Little Jo*

NON-RESIDENT PRODUCTIONS

PRODUCTION: Marshall Cordell, Q Brothers, and Mary Lu Roffe, *The Bomb-Itty of Errors* **ACTOR IN A PRINCIPAL ROLE:** Nick Garrison, *Hedwig and the Angry Inch* **ACTRESS IN A PRINCIPAL ROLE:** Marilu Henner, *Annie Get Your Gun*

SPECIAL AWARDS:

IRV KUPCIENT and the late **ESSEE KUPCIENT** for "six decades of working together to make Chicago a fertile ground for careers in the arts and for nurturing the talents of Chicago actors and artists."

ARTBEAT CHICAGO, a program of WTTW television, for "its intelligent, witty and compassionate celebration of the depth, diversity and talent in Chicago theatre."

29th ANNUAL JOSEPH JEFFERSON CITATIONS WING AWARDS

For outstanding achievement in professional productions during the 2001–2002 season of Chicago theaters not operating under union contracts.

PRODUCTIONS: *The Crucible*, produced by Timeline Theatre Company; *Who's Afraid of Virginia Woolf?*, produced by Shattered Globe Theatre **ENSEMBLE:** *Corpus Christi*; *The Crucible*; *The Life and Times of Tulsa Lovechild*; *Who's Afraid of Virginia Woolf?* **DIRECTORS:** Nick Bowling, *The Crucible*; Louis Contey, *Who's Afraid of Virginia Woolf?*; Nathaniel Swift, *2* **NEW WORK:** Mia McCullough, *Chagrin Falls*; Jim O'Connor, *Rosemary* **NEW ADAPTATION:** Page Hearn, *Jeeves and the Mating Season*; Michael Thomas, *With or Without Wings* **ACTRESS IN A PRINCIPAL ROLE:** Kati Brazda, *The Life and Times of Tulsa Lovechild*; Michelle Courvais, *Rosemary*; Linda Reiter, *Who's Afraid of Virginia Woolf?* **ACTOR IN A PRINCIPAL ROLE:** Darrell W. Cox, *Some Voices*; Steven Fedoruk, *2* **ACTRESS IN A SUPPORTING ROLE:** Jennifer Kern, *Who's Afraid of Virginia Woolf?*; Beth Lackey, *The Life and Times of Tulsa Lovechild* **ACTOR IN A SUPPORTING ROLE:** Marc Jab Lon, *Sexual Perversity in Chicago*; Jim Sonia, *Fortinbras*; Joseph Wycoff, *Jeeves and the Mating Season* **SCENIC DESIGN:** Heather Graff and Richard Peterson, *The Crucible*; Stephanie Nelson, *Unbinding Isaac* **COSTUME DESIGN:** Michelle Lynette Bush, *Les Liaisons Dangereuses*; Jeffrey Kelly; *Nine* **LIGHTING DESIGN:** Heather Graff and Richard Peterson, *The Crucible* **SOUND DESIGN:** Joseph Fosco, *The Return of the King* **ORIGINAL MUSIC:** Pho'ro and the Ministers of the New Super Heavy Funk, *Kosi Dasa* **MUSICAL DIRECTION:** Chris Staton, *Pippin*

2002 FRANCESCA PRIMUS PRIZE

Presented by the Francesca Primus Foundation and the Denver Center Theatre Company; Alexandra Cunningham, Pavane.

24th ANNUAL KENNEDY CENTER HONORS

For distinguished achievement by individuals who have made significant contributions to American culture through the arts.

Julie Andrews; Van Cliburn; Quincy Jones; Jack Nicholson; Luciano Pavarotti

5TH ANNUAL KENNEDY CENTER– MARK TWAIN PRIZE

For American humor; Bob Newhart.

2001 NATIONAL MEDALS OF THE ARTS

For individuals and organizations who have made outstanding contributions to the excellence, growth, support, and availability of the arts in the Untied States, selected by the President of the United States from nominees presented by the National Endowment for the Arts.

Alvin Ailey Dance Foundation; Rudolfo Anaya; Johnny Cash; Kirk Douglas; Helen Frankenthaler; Judith Jamison; Yo-Yo Ma; Mike Nichols

2002 NEW DRAMATISTS LIFETIME ACHIEVEMENT AWARD

To an individual who has made an outstanding artistic contribution to the American theater; Barbara Cook.

13th ANNUAL OSCAR HAMMERSTEIN AWARD

For lifetime achievement in musical theater; Cameron Mackintosh.

2002 RICHARD ROGERS AWARDS

For staged readings of musicals in nonprofit theaters, administered by the American Academy of Arts and Letters and selected by a jury including Stephen Sondheim (chairman), Lynn Ahrens, Jack Beeson, Sheldon Harnick, R.W.B. Lewis and Richard Maltby Jr.

The Fabulist, David Spencer and Stephen Witkin; *The Tutor*, Maryrose Wood and Andrew Gerle

24th ANNUAL SUSAN SMITH BLACKBURN PRIZE

For women who have written works of outstanding quality for the English-speaking theater.

Gina Gionfriddo, *U.S. Drag*; Susan Miller, *A Map of Doubt and Rescue*; HONORABLE MENTION: Julia Jordan, *Our Boy*

21st ANNUAL WILLIAM INGE THEATRE FESTIVAL AWARD

For distinguished achievement in American theater.

John Kander and Fred Ebb; NEW VOICE: Dana Yeaton

THE THEATER HALL OF FAME

The Theater of Hall of Fame was created in 1971 to honor those who have made outstanding contributions to the American theater in a career spanning at least twenty-five years, with at least five major credits.

George Abbott; Maude Adams; Viola Adams; Stella Adler; Edward Albee; Theoni V. Aldredge; Ira Aldridge; Jane Alexander; Mary Alice; Winthrop Ames; Judith Anderson; Maxwell Anderson; Robert Anderson; Julie Andrews; Margaret Anglin; Jean Anouilh; Harold Arlen; George Arliss; Boris Aronson; Adele Astaire; Fred Astaire; Eileen Atkins; Brooks Atkinson; Lauren Bacall; Pearl Bailey; George Balanchine; William Ball; Anne Bancroft; Tallulah Bankhead; Richard Barr; Philip Barry; Ethel Barrymore; John Barrymore; Lionel Barrymore; Howard Bay; Nora Bayes; Samuel Beckett; Brian Bedford; S.N. Behrman; Norman Bel Geddes; David Belasco; Michael Bennett; Richard Bennett; Robert Russell Bennett; Eric Bentley; Irving Berlin; Sarah Bernhardt; Leonard Bernstein; Earl Blackwell; Kermit Bloomgarden; Jerry Bock; Ray Bolger; Edwin Booth; Junius Brutus Booth; Shirley Booth; Philip Bosco; Alice Brady; Bertolt Bercht; Fannie Brice; Peter Brook; John Mason Brown; **Robert Brustein**; Billie Burke; Abe Burrows; Richard Burton; Mrs. Patrick Campbell; Zoe Caldwell; Eddie Cantor; Morris Carnovsky; Mrs. Leslie Carter; Gower Champion; Frank Chanfrau; Carol Channing; Ruth Chatterton; Paddy Chayefsky; Anton Chekhov; Ina Claire; Bobby Clark; Harold Clurman; Lee. J. Cobb; Richard L. Coe; George M. Cohan; Alexander H. Cohen; Jack Cole; Cy Coleman; Constance Collier; **Alvin Colt**; Betty Comden; Marc Connelly; Barbara Cook; Katherine Cornell; Noel Coward; Jane Cowl; Lotta Crabtree; Cheryl Crawford; Hume Cronym; Russel Crouse; Charlotte Cushman; Jean Dalrymple; Augustin Daly; E.L. Davenport; Gordon Davidson; Ossie Davis; Ruby Dee; Alfred De Liagre Jr.; Agns DeMille; Colleen Dewhurst; Howard Deitz; Dudley Digges; Melvyn Douglas; Eddie Dowling; Alfred Drake; Marie Dressler; John Drew; Mrs. John Drew; William Dunlap; Mildred Dunnock; Charles Durning; Eleanora Duse; Jeanne Eagles; Fred Ebb; Florence Eldridge; Lehman Engel; Maurice Evans; Abe Feder; Jose Ferber; Cy Feuer; Zelda Fichandler; Dorothy Fields; Herbert Fields; Lewis Fields; W.C. Fields; Jules Fischer; Minnie Maddern Fiske; Clyde Fitch; Geraldine Fitzgerald; Henry Fonda; Lynn Fontanne; Horton Foote; Edwin Forrest; Bob Fosse; Rudolf Friml; Charles Frohman; Robert Fryer; Athol Fugard; John Gassner; **Peter Gennaro**; Grace George; George Gershwin; Ira Gershwin; John Gielgud; W.S. Gilbert; Jack Gilford; William Gillette; Charles Gilpin; Lillian Gish; John Golden; Max Gordon; Ruth Gordon; Adolph Green; Paul Green; Charlotte Greenwood; Joel Grey; **George Grizzard**; John Gaure; Otis L. Guernsey Jr.; Tyrone Guthrie; Uta Hagan; Lewis Hallam; **T. Edward Hambleton**; Oscar Hammerstein II; Walter Hampden; Otto Harbach; E.Y. Harburg; Sheldon Harnick; Edward Harrigan; Jed Harris; Julie Harris; Rosemary Harris; Sam H. Harris; Rex

Harrison; Kitty Carlisle Hart; Lorenz Hart; Moss Hart; Tony Hart; June Havoc; Helen Hayes; Leland Hayward; Ben Hecht; Eileen Heckart; Theresa Helburn; Lillian Hellman; Katherine Hepburn; Victor Herbert; Jerry Herman; James A. Herne; **Henry Hewes**; Al Hirschfeld; Raymond Hitchcock; Hal Holbrook; Celeste Holm; Hanya Holm; Arthur Hopkins; De Wolf Hopper; John Houseman; Eugene Howard; Leslie Howard; Sidney Howard; Willie Howard; Barnard Hughes; Henry Hull; Josephine Hull; Walter Huston; Earle Hyman; Henrik Ibsen; William Inge; Bernard B. Jacobs; Elise Janis; Joseph Jefferson; Al Jolson; James Earl Jones; Margo Jones; Robert Edmond Jones; Tom Jones; Jon Jory; Raul Julia; John Kander; Garson Kanin; George S. Kaufman; Danny Kaye; Elia Kazan; Gene Kelly; George Kelly; Fanny Kemble; Jerome Kern; Walter Kerr; Michael Kidd; Richard Kiley; Sidney Kingsley; Florence Klotz; Joseph Wood Krutch; Bert Lahr; Burton Lane; Lawrence Langner; Lillie Langtry; Angela Lansbury; Charles Laughton; Arthur Laurents; Gertrude Lawrence; Jerome Lawrence; Eva Le Gallienne; Ming Cho Lee; Robert E. Lee; Lotte Lenya; Alan Jay Lerner; Sam Levene; Robert Lewis; Beatrice Lillie; Howard Lindsay; Frank Loesser; Frederick Loewe; Joshua Logan; Pauline Lord; Lucille Lortel; Alfred Lunt; Charles MacArthur; Steele McKaye; Rouben Mamoulian; Richard Mansfield; Robert B. Mantell; Frederic March; Nancy Marchand; Julia Marlowe; Ernest H. Martin; Mary Martin; Raymond Massey; Siobhan McKenna; Terrence McNally; Helen Menken; Burgess Meredith; Ethel Merman; David Merrick; Jo Mielziner; Arthur Miller; Marilyn Miller; Liza Minnelli; Helena Modjeska; Ferenc Molnar; Lola Montez; Victor Moore; Robert Morse; Zero Mostel; Anna Cora Mowatt; Paul Muni; Tharon Musser; George Jean Nathan; Mildred Natwick; Nazimova; James M. Nederlander; Mike Nichols; Elliot Norton; Sean O'Casey; Clifford Odets; Donald Oenslager; Laurence Olivier; Eugene O'Neill; Jerry Orbach; Geraldine Paige; Joseph Papp; Osgood Perkins; Bernadette Peters; Molly Picon; Harold Pinter; Luigi Pirandello; Christopher Plummer; Cole Porter; Robert Preston; Harold Prince; Jose Quintero; Ellis Rabb; John Raitt; Tony Randall; Michael Redgrave; Ada Rehan; Elmer Rice; Lloyd Richards; Ralph Richardson; Chita Rivera; Jason Robards; Jerome Robbins; Paul Robeson; Richard Rodgers; Will Rogers; Sigmund Romberg; Harold Rome; Lillian Russell; Donald Saddler; Gene Saks; William Saroyan; Joseph Schildkraut; Harvey Schmidt; Alan Schnider; Gerald Shoenfeld; Arthur Schwartz; Maurice Schwartz; George C. Scott; Marian Seldes; Irene Sharaff; George Bernard Shaw; Sam Shepard; Robert F. Sherwood; J.J. Shubert; Lee Shubert; Herman Shumlin; Neil Simon; Lee Simonson; Edmund Simpson; Otis Skinner; Maggie Smith; Oliver Smith; Stephen Sondheim; E.H. Sothern; Kim Stanley; Maureen Stapleton; Frances Sternhagen; Roger L. Stevens; **Isabelle Stevenson**; Ellen Stewart; Dorothy Stickney; Fred Stone; Tom Stoppard; Lee Strasburg; August Strindberg; Elaine Stritch; **Charles Strouse**; Jule Styne; Margaret Sullivan; Arthur Sullivan; Jessica Tandy; Laurette Taylor; Ellen Terry; Tommy Tune; Gwen Verdon; Robin Wagner; Nancy Walker; Eli Wallach; James Wallack; Lester Wallack; Tony Walton; Douglas Turner Ward; David Warfield; Ethel Waters; Clifton Webb; Joseph Weber; Margaret Webster; Kurt Weill; Orson Welles; Mae West; Robert Whitehead; Oscar Wilde; Thorton Wilder; Bert Williams; Tennessee Williams; Landford Wilson; P.G. Wodehouse; Peggy Wood; Alexander Woollcott; Irene Worth; Teresa Wright; Ed Wynn; Vincent Youmans; Stark Young; Florenz Zeigfeld; Patricia Zipprodt

Honorees inducted January 28, 2002.

THE THEATER HALL OF FAME FOUNDERS AWARD

Established in 1993 in honor of Earl Blackwell, James M. Nederlander, Gerald Oestreicher and Arnold Weissberger, the Theater Hall of Fame Founders Award is voted by the Hall's board of directors to an individual for his of her outstanding contribution to the theater.

1993 James M. Nederlander; **1994** Kitty Carlisle Hart; **1995** Harvey Sabinson; **1996** Henry Hewes; **1997** Otis L. Guernsey Jr.; **1998** Edward Colton; **1999** no award; **2000** Gerard Oestreicher, Arnold Weissberger; **2001** Tom Dillon

MARGO JONES CITIZEN OF THE THEATER MEDAL

Presented annually to a citizen of the theater who has made a lifetime commitment to theater in the United States and has demonstrated an understanding and affirmation of the craft of playwriting.

1961 Lucille Lortel; **1962** Michael Ellis; **1963** Judith Rutherford Marechal; George Savage (university award); **1964** Richard Barr, Edward Albee & Clinton Wilder; Richard A. Duprey (university award); **1965** Wynn Handman; Marston Balch (university award); **1966** Jon Jory; Arthur Ballet (university award); **1967** Paul Baker; George C. White (workshop award); **1968** Davey Marlin-Jones; Ellen Stewart (workshop award); **1969** Adrian Hall; Edward Parone & Gordon Davidson (workshop award); **1970** Joseph Papp; **1971** Zelda Fichandler; **1972** Jules Irving; **1973** Douglas Turner Ward; **1974** Paul Weidner; **1975** Robert Kalfin; **1976** Gordon Davidson; **1977** Marshall W. Mason; **1978** Jon Jory; **1979** Ellen Stewart; **1980** John Clark Donahue; **1981** Lynne Meadow; **1982** Andre Bishop; **1983** Bill Bushnell; **1984** Gregory Mosher; **1985** John Lion; **1986** Lloyd Richards; **1987** Gerald Chapman; **1988** no award; **1989** Margaret Goheen; **1990** Richard Coe; **1991** Otis L. Guernsey Jr.; **1992** Abbot Van Nostrand; **1993** Henry Hewes; **1994** Jane Alexander; **1995** Robert Whitehead; **1996** Al Hirschfield; **1997** George C. White; **1998** James Houghton; **1999** George Keathley; **2000** Eileen Heckart; **2001** Mel Gussow

MUSICAL THEATRE HALL OF FAME

This organization was established at New York University on November 10, 1993.

Harold Arlen; Irving Berlin; Leonard Bernstein; Eubie Blake; Abe Burrows; George M. Cohan; Dorothy Fields; George Gershwin; Ira Gershwin; Oscar Hammerstein II; E.Y. Harburg; Larry Hart; Jerome Kern; Burton Lane; Alan Jay Lerner; Frank Loesser; Frederick Loewe; Cole Porter; Ethel Merman; Jerome Robbins; Richard Rogers; Harold Rome

LONGEST RUNNING SHOWS ON BROADWAY

Whsen the musical or play version of a production is in question, it is so indicated, as are revivals. *Plays that were still playing as of May 31, 2001.

CATS (7,485 Performances)
Opened October 7, 1982
Closed September 10, 2000

LES MISÉRABLES* (6,281 Performances)
Opened March 12, 1987

A CHORUS LINE (6,137 Performances)
Opened July 25, 1975
Closed April 28, 1990

PHANTOM OF THE OPERA* (5,984 Performances)
Opened January 26, 1988

OH! CALCUTTA (REVIVAL) (5,959 Performances)
Opened September 24, 1976
Closed August 6, 1989

MISS SAIGON (4,097 Performances)
Opened April 11, 1991
Closed January 28, 2001

42nd STREET (3,486 Performances)
Opened August 25, 1980
Closed January 8, 1989

GREASE (3,388 Performances)
Opened February 14, 1972
Closed April 13, 1980

FIDDLER ON THE ROOF (3,242 Performances)
Opened September 22, 1964
Closed July 2, 1972

LIFE WITH FATHER (3,224 Performances)
Opened November 8, 1939
Closed July 12, 1947

TOBACCO ROAD (3,182 Performances)
Opened December 4, 1933
Closed May 31, 1941

BEAUTY AND THE BEAST* (2,891 Performances)
Opened April 18, 1994

HELLO, DOLLY! (2,844 Performances)
Opened January 16, 1964
Closed December 27, 1970

MY FAIR LADY (2,717 Performances)
Opened March 15, 1956
Closed September 29, 1962

Carole Demas, Barry Bostwick in *Grease*, 1972

RENT* (2,540 Performances)
Opened April 29, 1996

ANNIE (2,377 Performances)
Opened April 21, 1977
Closed January 22, 1983

MAN OF LA MANCHA (2,328 Performances)
Opened November 22, 1965
Closed June 26, 1971

ABIE'S IRISH ROSE (2,327 Performances)
Opened May 23, 1922
Closed October 21, 1927

CHICAGO (MUSICAL, REVIVAL)* (2,311 Performances)
Opened November 14, 1996

OKLAHOMA! (2,212 Performances)
Opened March 31, 1943
Closed May 29, 1948

SMOKEY JOE'S CAFÉ (2,036 Performances)
Opened March 2, 1995
Closed January 16, 2000

PIPPIN (1,944 Performances)
Opened October 23, 1972
Closed June 12, 1977

THE LION KING* (1,932 Performances)
Opened November 13, 1997

Michael Rennie, Barbara Bel Geddes in *Mary, Mary,* 1961 (Friedman-Abeles)

SOUTH PACIFIC (1,925 Performances)
Opened April 7, 1949
Closed January 16, 1954

THE MAGIC SHOW (1,920 Performances)
Opened May 28, 1974
Closed December 31, 1978

DEATHTRAP (1,793 Performances)
Opened February 26, 1978
Closed June 13, 1982

GEMINI (1,788 Performances)
Opened May 21, 1977
Closed September 6, 1981

HARVEY (1,775 Performances)
Opened November 1, 1944
Closed January 15, 1949

DANCIN' (1,774 Performances)
Opened March 27, 1978
Closed June 27, 1982

LA CAGE AUX FOLLES (1,761 Performances)
Opened August 21, 1983
Closed November 15, 1987

HAIR (1,750 Performances)
Opened April 29, 1968
Closed July 1, 1972

CABARET (REVIVAL)* (1,707 Performances)
Opened March 19, 1998

THE WIZ (1,672 Performances)
Opened January 5, 1975
Closed January 29, 1979

BORN YESTERDAY (1,642 Performances)
Opened February 4, 1946
Closed December 31, 1949

THE BEST LITTLE WHOREHOUSE IN TEXAS (1,639 Performances)
Opened June 19, 1978
Closed March 27, 1982

CRAZY FOR YOU (1,622 Performances)
Opened February 19, 1992
Closed January 7, 1996

AIN'T MISBEHAVIN' (1,604 Performances)
Opened May 9, 1978
Closed February 21, 1982

MARY, MARY (1,572 Performances)
Opened March 8, 1961
Closed December 12, 1964

EVITA (1,567 Performances)
Opened September 25, 1979
Closed June 26, 1983

THE VOICE OF THE TURTLE (1,557 Performances)
Opened December 8, 1943
Closed January 3, 1948

JEKYLL & HYDE (1,543 Performances)
Opened April 28, 1997
Closed January 7, 2001

The Company of *Hair,* 1968 (Martha Swope)

BAREFOOT IN THE PARK (1,530 Performances)
Opened October 23, 1963
Closed June 25, 1967

BRIGHTON BEACH MEMOIRS (1,530 Performances)
Opened March 27, 1983
Closed May 11, 1986

DREAMGIRLS (1,522 Performances)
Opened December 20, 1981
Closed August 11, 1985

MAME (MUSICAL) (1,508 Performances)
Opened May 24, 1966
Closed January 3, 1970

GREASE (REVIVAL) (1,503 Performances)
Opened May 11, 1994
Closed January 25, 1998

SAME TIME, NEXT YEAR (1,453 Performances)
Opened March 14, 1975
Closed September 3, 1978

ARSENIC AND OLD LACE (1,444 Performances)
Opened January 10, 1941
Closed June 17, 1944

THE SOUND OF MUSIC (1,443 Performances)
Opened November 16, 1959
Closed June 15, 1963

ME AND MY GIRL (1,420 Performances)
Opened August 10, 1986
Closed December 31, 1989

HOW TO SUCCEED IN BUSINESS WITHOUT REALLY TRYING
(1,417 Performances)
Opened October 14, 1961
Closed March 6, 1965

HELLZAPOPPIN' (1,404 Performances)
Opened September 22, 1938
Closed December 17, 1941

THE MUSIC MAN (1,375 Performances)
Opened December 19, 1957
Closed April 15, 1961

FUNNY GIRL (1,348 Performances)
Opened March 26, 1964
Closed July 15, 1967

MUMMENSCHANZ (1,326 Performances)
Opened March 30, 1977
Closed April 20, 1980

ANGEL STREET (1,295 Performances)
Opened December 5, 1941
Closed December 30, 1944

LIGHTNIN' (1,291 Performances)
Opened August 26, 1918
Closed August 27, 1921

PROMISES, PROMISES (1,281 Performances)
Opened December 1, 1968
Closed January 1, 1972

THE KING AND I (1,246 Performances)
Opened March 29, 1951
Closed March 20, 1954

CACTUS FLOWER (1,234 Performances)
Opened December 8, 1965
Closed November 23, 1968

SLEUTH (1,222 Performances)
Opened December 8, 1965
Closed October 13, 1973

TORCH SONG TRILOGY (1,222 Performances)
Opened June 10, 1982
Closed May 19, 1985

1776 (1,217 Performances)
Opened March 16, 1969
Closed February 13, 1972

EQUUS (1,209 Performances)
Opened October 24, 1974
Closed October 7, 1977

SUGAR BABIES (1,208 Performances)
Opened October 8, 1979
Closed August 28, 1982

GUYS AND DOLLS (1,200 Performances)
Opened November 24, 1950
Closed November 28, 1953

AMADEUS (1,181 Performances)
Opened December 17, 1980
Closed October 16, 1983

CABARET (1,165 Performances)
Opened November 20, 1966
Closed September 6, 1969

MISTER ROBERTS (1,157 Performances)
Opened February 18, 1948
Closed January 6, 1951

ANNIE GET YOUR GUN (1,147 Performances)
Opened May 16, 1946
Closed February 12, 1949

GUYS AND DOLLS (REVIVAL) (1,144 Performances)
Opened April 14, 1992
Closed January 8, 1995

Timothy Jerome, Jane Krakowski in *Grand Hotel*, 1989 (Martha Swope)

THE SEVEN YEAR ITCH (1,141 Performances)
Opened November 20, 1952
Closed August 13, 1955

BRING IN 'DA NOISE, BRING IN 'DA FUNK (1,130 Performances)
Opened April 25, 1996
Closed January 19, 1999

BUTTERFLIES ARE FREE (1,128 Performances)
Opened October 21, 1969
Closed July 2, 1972

PINS AND NEEDLES (1,108 Performances)
Opened November 27, 1937
Closed June 22, 1940

PLAZA SUITE (1,097 Performances)
Opened February 14, 1968
Closed October 3, 1970

FOSSE (1,092 Performances)
Opened January 14, 1999
Closed August 25, 2001

THEY'RE PLAYING OUR SONG (1,082 Performances)
Opened February 11, 1979
Closed September 6, 1981

GRAND HOTEL (MUSICAL) (1,077 Performances)
Opened November 12, 1989
Closed April 25, 1992

KISS ME, KATE (1,070 Performances)
Opened December 30, 1948
Closed July 25, 1951

DON'T BOTHER ME, I CAN'T COPE (1,065 Performances)
Opened April 19, 1972
Closed October 27, 1974

THE PAJAMA GAME (1,063 Performances)
Opened May 13, 1954
Closed November 24, 1956

Janis Paige, John Raitt, Carol Haney in *The Pajama Game*, 1954 (Talbot)

John Cullum, Donna Theodore in *Shenandoah*, 1975 (Friedman-Abeles)

SHENANDOAH (1,050 Performances)
Opened January 7, 1975
Closed August 7, 1977

ANNIE GET YOUR GUN (REVIVAL) (1,046 Performances)
Opened March 4, 1999
Closed September 1, 2001

THE TEAHOUSE OF THE AUGUST MOON (1,027 Performances)
Opened October 15, 1953
Closed March 24, 1956

DAMN YANKEES (1,019 Performances)
Opened May 5, 1955
Closed October 12, 1957

NEVER TOO LATE (1,007 Performances)
Opened November 26, 1962
Closed April 24, 1965

BIG RIVER (1,005 Performances)
Opened April 25, 1985
Closed September 20, 1987

THE WILL ROGERS FOLLIES (983 Performances)
Opened May 1, 1991
Closed September 5, 1993

ANY WEDNESDAY (982 Performances)
Opened February 18, 1964
Closed June 26, 1966

SUNSET BOULEVARD (977 Performances)
Opened November 17, 1994
Closed March 22, 1997

A FUNNY THING HAPPENED ON THE WAY TO THE FORUM
(964 Performances)
Opened May 8, 1962
Closed August 29, 1964

THE ODD COUPLE (964 Performances)
Opened March 10, 1965
Closed July 2, 1967

ANNA LUCASTA (957 Performances)
Opened August 30, 1944
Closed November 30, 1946

KISS AND TELL (956 Performances)
Opened March 17, 1943
Closed June 23, 1945

SHOW BOAT (REVIVAL) (949 Performances)
Opened October 2, 1994
Closed January 5, 1997

ANNIE GET YOUR GUN (REVIVAL)* (938 Performances)
Opened March 4, 1999

DRACULA (REVIVAL) (925 Performances)
Opened October 20, 1977
Closed January 6, 1980

BELLS ARE RINGING (924 Performances)
Opened November 29, 1956
Closed March 7, 1959

THE MOON IS BLUE (924 Performances)
Opened March 8, 1951
Closed May 30, 1953

BEATLEMANIA (920 Performances)
Opened May 31, 1977
Closed October 17, 1979

THE ELEPHANT MAN (916 Performances)
Opened April 19, 1979
Closed June 28, 1981

AIDA* (910 Performances)
Opened March 23, 2000

KISS OF THE SPIDER WOMAN (906 Performances)
Opened May 3, 1993
Closed July 1, 1995

CONTACT (903 Performances)
Opened March 30, 2000

LUV (901 Performances)
Opened November 11, 1964
Closed January 7, 1967

THE WHO'S TOMMY (900 Performances)
Opened April 22, 1993
Closed June 17, 1995

CHICAGO (MUSICAL) (898 Performances)
Opened June 3, 1975
Closed August 27, 1977

APPLAUSE (896 Performances)
Opened March 30, 1970
Closed July 27, 1972

CAN-CAN (892 Performances)
Opened May 7, 1953
Closed June 25, 1955

CAROUSEL (890 Performances)
Opened April 19, 1945
Closed May 24, 1947

I'M NOT RAPPAPORT (890 Performances)
Opened November 19, 1985
Closed January 17, 1988

HATS OFF TO ICE (889 Performances)
Opened June 22, 1944
Closed April 2, 1946

FANNY (888 Performances)
Opened November 4, 1954
Closed December 16, 1956

CHILDREN OF A LESSER GOD (887 Performances)
Opened March 30, 1980
Closed May 16, 1982

FOLLOW THE GIRLS (882 Performances)
Opened April 8, 1944
Closed May 18, 1946

KISS ME, KATE (MUSICAL, REVIVAL) (881 Performances)
Opened November 18, 1999
Closed December 30, 2001

CITY OF ANGELS (878 Performances)
Opened December 11, 1989
Closed January 19, 1992

CAMELOT (873 Performances)
Opened December 3, 1960
Closed January 5, 1963

I LOVE MY WIFE (872 Performances)
Opened April 17, 1977
Closed May 20, 1979

THE BAT (6,281 Performances)
Opened August 23, 1920
Closed Unknown

MY SISTER EILEEN (864 Performances)
Opened December 26, 1940
Closed January 16, 1943

NO, NO, NANETTE (REVIVAL) (861 Performances)
Opened January 19, 1971
Closed February 3, 1973

RAGTIME (861 Performances)
Opened January 18, 1998
Closed January 16, 2000

SONG OF NORWAY (860 Performances)
Opened August 21, 1944
Closed September 7, 1946

CHAPTER TWO (857 Performances)
Opened December 4, 1977
Closed December 9, 1979

A STREETCAR NAMED DESIRE (855 Performances)
Opened December 3, 1947
Closed December 17, 1949

BARNUM (854 Performances)
Opened April 30, 1980
Closed May 16, 1982

COMEDY IN MUSIC (849 Performances)
Opened October 2, 1953
Closed January 21, 1956

RAISIN (847 Performances)
Opened October 18, 1973
Closed December 7, 1975

BLOOD BROTHERS (839 Performances)
Opened April 25, 1993
Closed April 30, 1995

YOU CAN'T TAKE IT WITH YOU (837 Performances)
Opened December 14, 1936
Closed Unknown

LA PLUME DE MA TANTE (835 Performances)
Opened November 11, 1958
Closed December 17, 1960

THREE MEN ON A HORSE (835 Performances)
Opened January 30, 1935
Closed January 9, 1937

THE SUBJECT WAS ROSES (832 Performances)
Opened May 25, 1964
Closed May 21, 1966

BLACK AND BLUE (824 Performances)
Opened January 26, 1989
Closed January 20, 1991

THE KING AND I (REVIVAL) (807 Performances)
Opened April 11, 1996
Closed February 22, 1998

INHERIT THE WIND (806 Performances)
Opened April 21, 1955
Closed June 22, 1957

ANYTHING GOES (REVIVAL) (804 Performances)
Opened October 19, 1987
Closed September 3, 1989

TITANIC (804 Performances)
Opened April 23, 1997
Closed March 21, 1999

NO TIME FOR SERGEANTS (796 Performances)
Opened October 20, 1955
Closed September 14, 1957

FIORELLO! (795 Performances)
Opened November 23, 1959
Closed October 28, 1961

WHERE'S CHARLEY? (792 Performances)
Opened October 11, 1948
Closed September 9, 1950

THE LADDER (789 Performances)
Opened October 22, 1926
Closed Unknown

FORTY CARATS (780 Performances)
Opened December 26, 1968
Closed November 7, 1970

LOST IN YONKERS (780 Performances)
Opened February 21, 1991
Closed January 3, 1993

THE PRISONER OF SECOND AVENUE (780 Performances)
Opened November 11, 1971
Closed September 29, 1973

M. BUTTERFLY (777 Performances)
Opened March 20, 1988
Closed January 27, 1990

OLIVER! (774 Performances)
Opened January 6, 1963
Closed November 14, 1964

THE PIRATES OF PENZANCE (REVIVAL, 1981) (772 Performances)
Opened January 8, 1981
Closed November 28, 1982

WOMAN OF THE YEAR (770 Performances)
Opened March 29, 1981
Closed March 13, 1983

MY ONE AND ONLY (767 Performances)
Opened May 1, 1983
Closed March 3, 1985

SOPHISTICATED LADIES (767 Performances)
Opened March 1, 1981
Closed January 2, 1983

BUBBLING BROWN SUGAR (766 Performances)
Opened March 2, 1976
Closed December 31, 1977

INTO THE WOODS (765 Performances)
Opened November 5, 1987
Closed September 3, 1989

STATE OF THE UNION (765 Performances)
Opened November 14, 1945
Closed September 13, 1947

STARLIGHT EXPRESS (761 Performances)
Opened March 15, 1987
Closed January 8, 1989

THE FIRST YEAR (760 Performances)
Opened October 20, 1920
Closed Unknown

BROADWAY BOUND (756 Performances)
Opened December 4, 1986
Closed September 25, 1988

YOU KNOW I CAN'T HEAR YOU WHEN THE WATER'S RUNNING
(755 Performances)
Opened March 13, 1967
Closed January 4, 1969

TWO FOR THE SEESAW (750 Performances)
Opened January 16, 1958
Closed October 31, 1959

JOSEPH AND THE AMAZING TECHNICOLOR DREAMCOAT (REVIVAL)
(747 Performances)
Opened January 27, 1982
Closed September 4, 1983

DEATH OF A SALESMAN (742 Performances)
Opened February 10, 1949
Closed November 18, 1950

FOR COLORED GIRLS WHO HAVE CONSIDERED SUICIDE/WHEN THE RAINBOW IS ENUF (742 Performances)
Opened September 15, 1976
Closed July 16, 1978

SONS O' FUN (742 Performances)
Opened December 1, 1941
Closed August 29, 1943

CANDIDE (MUSICAL VERSION, REVIVAL) (740 Performances)
Opened March 10, 1974
Closed January 4, 1976

GENTLEMEN PREFER BLONDES (740 Performances)
Opened December 8, 1949
Closed September 15, 1951

THE MAN WHO CAME TO DINNER (739 Performances)
Opened October 16, 1939
Closed July 12, 1941

NINE (739 Performances)
Opened May 9, 1982
Closed February 4, 1984

CALL ME MISTER (734 Performances)
Opened April 18, 1946
Closed January 10, 1948

VICTOR/VICTORIA (734 Performances)
Opened October 25, 1995
Closed July 27, 1997

WEST SIDE STORY (732 Performances)
Opened September 26, 1957
Closed June 27, 1959

HIGH BUTTON SHOES (727 Performances)
Opened October 9, 1947
Closed July 2, 1949

FINIAN'S RAINBOW (725 Performances)
Opened January 10, 1947
Closed October 2, 1948

CLAUDIA (722 Performances)
Opened February 12, 1941
Closed January 9, 1943

THE GOLD DIGGERS (720 Performances)
Opened September 30, 1919
Closed Unknown

JESUS CHRIST SUPERSTAR (720 Performances)
Opened October 12, 1971
Closed June 30, 1973

CARNIVAL! (719 Performances)
Opened April 13, 1961
Closed January 5, 1963

THE DIARY OF ANNE FRANK (717 Performances)
Opened October 5, 1955
Closed June 22, 1955

A FUNNY THING HAPPENED ON THE WAY TO THE FORUM (REVIVAL)
(715 Performances)
Opened April 18, 1996
Closed January 4, 1998

I REMEMBER MAMA (714 Performances)
Opened October 19, 1944
Closed June 29, 1946

TEA AND SYMPATHY (712 Performances)
Opened September 30, 1953
Closed June 18, 1955

JUNIOR MISS (710 Performances)
Opened November 18, 1941
Closed July 24, 1943

FOOTLOOSE (708 Performances)
Opened October 22, 1998
Closed July 2, 2000

LAST OF THE RED HOT LOVERS (706 Performances)
Opened December 28, 1969
Closed September 4, 1971

THE SECRET GARDEN (706 Performances)
Opened April 25, 1991
Closed January 3, 1993

COMPANY (705 Performances)
Opened April 26, 1970
Closed January 1, 1972

SEVENTH HEAVEN (704 Performances)
Opened October 30, 1922
Closed Unknown

GYPSY (MUSICAL) (702 Performances)
Opened May 21, 1959
Closed March 25, 1961

THE MIRACLE WORKER (700 Performances)
Opened October 19, 1959
Closed July 1, 1961

THAT CHAMPIONSHIP SEASON (700 Performances)
Opened September 14, 1972
Closed April 21, 1974

THE MUSIC MAN (MUSICAL, REVIVAL) (698 Performances)
Opened April 27, 2000
Closed December 30, 2001

DA (697 Performances)
Opened May 1, 1978
Closed January 1, 1980

CAT ON A HOT TIN ROOF (694 Performances)
Opened March 24, 1955
Closed November 17, 1956

LI'L ABNER (693 Performances)
Opened November 15, 1956
Closed July 12, 1958

THE CHILDREN'S HOUR (691 Performances)
Opened November 20, 1934
Closed Unknown

PURLIE (688 Performances)
Opened March 15, 1970
Closed November 6, 1971

DEAD END (687 Performances)
Opened October 28, 1935
Closed June 12, 1937

THE LION AND THE MOUSE (686 Performances)
Opened November 20, 1905
Closed Unknown

WHITE CARGO (686 Performances)
Opened November 5, 1923
Closed Unknown

DEAR RUTH (683 Performances)
Opened December 13, 1944
Closed July 27, 1946

Shorty Long, Susan Johnson, and the Company of *The Most Happy Fella*, 1956, (Arthur Cantor)

EAST IS WEST (680 Performances)
Opened December 25, 1918
Closed Unknown

COME BLOW YOUR HORN (677 Performances)
Opened February 22, 1961
Closed October 6, 1962

THE MOST HAPPY FELLA (676 Performances)
Opened May 3, 1956
Closed December 14, 1957

DEFENDING THE CAVEMAN (671 Performances)
Opened March 26, 1995
Closed June 22, 1997

THE DOUGHGIRLS (671 Performances)
Opened Dec. 30, 1942
Closed July 29, 1944

THE IMPOSSIBLE YEARS (670 Performances)
Opened October 13, 1965
Closed May 27, 1967

IRENE (670 Performances)
Opened November 18, 1919
Closed Unknown

BOY MEETS GIRL (669 Performances)
Opened November 27, 1935
Closed Unknown

THE TAP DANCE KID (669 Performances)
Opened December 21, 1983
Closed August 11, 1985

BEYOND THE FRINGE (667 Performances)
Opened October 27, 1962
Closed May 30, 1964

PROOF* (665 Performances)
Opened October 24, 2000

THE FULL MONTY* (664 Performances)
Opened October 26, 2000

WHO'S AFRAID OF VIRGINIA WOOLF? (664 Performances)
Opened October 13, 1962
Closed May 16, 1964

BLITHE SPIRIT (657 Performances)
Opened November 5, 1941
Closed June 5, 1943

A TRIP TO CHINATOWN (657 Performances)
Opened November 9, 1891
Closed Unknown

THE WOMEN (657 Performances)
Opened December 26, 1936
Closed Unknown

THE TALE OF THE ALLERGIST'S WIFE* (654 Performances)
Opened November 2, 2000

BLOOMER GIRL (654 Performances)
Opened October 5, 1944
Closed April 27, 1946

THE FIFTH SEASON (654 Performances)
Opened January 23, 1953
Closed October 23, 1954

RAIN (648 Performances)
Opened September 1, 1924
Closed Unknown

WITNESS FOR THE PROSECUTION (645 Performances)
Opened December 16, 1954
Closed June 30, 1956

CALL ME MADAM (644 Performances)
Opened October 12, 1950
Closed May 3, 1952

JANIE (642 Performances)
Opened September 10, 1942
Closed January 16, 1944

THE GREEN PASTURES (640 Performances)
Opened February 26, 1930
Closed August 29, 1931

AUNTIE MAME (PLAY VERSION) (639 Performances)
Opened October 31, 1956
Closed June 28, 1958

A MAN FOR ALL SEASONS (637 Performances)
Opened November 22, 1961
Closed June 1, 1963

JEROME ROBBINS' BROADWAY (634 Performances)
Opened February 26, 1989
Closed September 1, 1990

THE FOURPOSTER (632 Performances)
Opened October 24, 1951
Closed May 2, 1953

THE MUSIC MASTER (627 Performances)
Opened September 26, 1904
Closed Unknown

TWO GENTLEMEN OF VERONA (MUSICAL VERSION)
(627 Performances)
Opened December 1, 1971
Closed May 20, 1973

THE TENTH MAN (623 Performances)
Opened November 5, 1959
Closed May 13, 1961

THE HEIDI CHRONICLES (621 Performances)
Opened March 9, 1989
Closed September 1, 1990

IS ZAT SO? (618 Performances)
Opened January 5, 1925
Closed July 1926

ANNIVERSARY WALTZ (615 Performances)
Opened April 7, 1954
Closed September 24, 1955

THE HAPPY TIME (PLAY VERSION) (614 Performances)
Opened January 24, 1950
Closed July 14, 1951

SEPARATE ROOMS (613 Performances)
Opened March 23, 1940
Closed September 6, 1941

AFFAIRS OF STATE (610 Performances)
Opened September 25, 1950
Closed March 8, 1952

OH! CALCUTTA! (610 Performances)
Opened June 17, 1969
Closed August 12, 1972

STAR AND GARTER (609 Performances)
Opened June 24, 1942
Closed December 4, 1943

THE MYSTERY OF EDWIN DROOD (608 Performances)
Opened December 2, 1985
Closed May 16, 1987

THE STUDENT PRINCE (608 Performances)
Opened December 2, 1924
Closed Unknown

SWEET CHARITY (608 Performances)
Opened January 29, 1966
Closed July 15, 1967

BYE BYE BIRDIE (607 Performances)
Opened April 14, 1960
Closed October 7, 1961

RIVERDANCE ON BROADWAY (605 Performances)
Opened March 16, 2000
Closed August 26, 2001

IRENE (REVIVAL) (604 Performances)
Opened March 13, 1973
Closed September 8, 1974

SUNDAY IN THE PARK WITH GEORGE (604 Performances)
Opened May 2, 1984
Closed October 13, 1985

ADONIS (603 Performances)
Opened ca. 1884
Closed Unknown

BROADWAY (603 Performances)
Opened September 16, 1926
Closed Unknown

PEG O' MY HEART (603 Performances)
Opened December 20, 1912
Closed Unknown

MASTER CLASS (601 Performances)
Opened November 5, 1995
Closed June 29, 1997

STREET SCENE (PLAY) (601 Performances)
Opened January 10, 1929
Closed Unknown

ART (600 Performances)
Opened March 1, 1998
Closed August 8, 1999

FLOWER DRUM SONG (600 Performances)
Opened December 1, 1958
Closed May 7, 1960

KIKI (600 Performances)
Opened November 29, 1921
Closed Unknown

A LITTLE NIGHT MUSIC (600 Performances)
Opened February 25, 1973
Closed August 3, 1974

AGNES OF GOD (599 Performances)
Opened March 30, 1982
Closed September 4, 1983

DON'T DRINK THE WATER (598 Performances)
Opened November 17, 1966
Closed April 20, 1968

WISH YOU WERE HERE (598 Performances)
Opened June 25, 1952
Closed November 28, 1958

SARAFINA! (597 Performances)
Opened January 28, 1988
Closed July 2, 1989

A SOCIETY CIRCUS (596 Performances)
Opened December 13, 1905
Closed November 24, 1906

ABSURD PERSON SINGULAR (592 Performances)
Opened October 8, 1974
Closed March 6, 1976

A DAY IN HOLLYWOOD/A NIGHT IN THE UKRAINE (588 Performances)
Opened May 1, 1980
Closed September 27, 1981

THE ME NOBODY KNOWS (586 Performances)
Opened December 18, 1970
Closed November 21, 1971

THE TWO MRS. CARROLLS (585 Performances)
Opened August 3, 1943
Closed February 3, 1945

KISMET (MUSICAL VERSION) (583 Performances)
Opened December 3, 1953
Closed April 23, 1955

GYPSY (MUSICAL VERSION, REVIVAL) (582 Performances)
Opened November 16, 1989
Closed July 28, 1991

BRIGADOON (581 Performances)
Opened March 13, 1947
Closed July 31, 1948

DETECTIVE STORY (581 Performances)
Opened March 23, 1949
Closed August 12, 1950

NO STRINGS (580 Performances)
Opened March 14, 1962
Closed August 3, 1963

BROTHER RAT (577 Performances)
Opened December 16, 1936
Closed Unknown

BLOSSOM TIME (576 Performances)
Opened September 29, 1921
Closed Unknown

PUMP BOYS AND DINETTES (573 Performances)
Opened February 4, 1982
Closed June 18, 1983

SHOW BOAT (572 Performances)
Opened December 27, 1927
Closed May 4, 1929

THE SHOW-OFF (571 Performances)
Opened February 5, 1924
Closed Unknown

SALLY (570 Performances)
Opened December 21, 1920
Closed April 22, 1922

JELLY'S LAST JAM (569 Performances)
Opened April 26, 1992
Closed September 5, 1993

GOLDEN BOY (MUSICAL VERSION) (568 Performances)
Opened October 20, 1964
Closed March 5, 1966

ONE TOUCH OF VENUS (567 Performances)
Opened October 7, 1943
Closed February 10, 1945

THE REAL THING (566 Performances)
Opened January 5, 1984
Closed May 12, 1985

HAPPY BIRTHDAY (564 Performances)
Opened October 31, 1946
Closed March 13, 1948

LOOK HOMEWARD, ANGEL (564 Performances)
Opened November 28, 1957
Closed April 4, 1959

MORNING'S AT SEVEN (REVIVAL) (564 Performances)
Opened April 10, 1980
Closed August 16, 1981

THE GLASS MENAGERIE (561 Performances)
Opened March 31, 1945
Closed August 3, 1946

Nancy Marchand, Elizabeth Wilson, Maureen O'Sullivan, Teresa Wright in *Morning's at Seven*, 1980 (Martha Swope)

I DO! I DO! (560 Performances)
Opened December 5, 1966
Closed June 15, 1968

WONDERFUL TOWN (559 Performances)
Opened February 25, 1953
Closed July 3, 1954

THE LAST NIGHT OF BALLYHOO (557 Performances)
Opened February 27, 1997
Closed June 28, 1998

ROSE MARIE (557 Performances)
Opened September 2, 1924
Closed Unknown

STRICTLYDISHONORABE (557 Performances)
Opened Sept. 18, 1929
Closed Unknown

SWEENEY TODD, THE DEMON BARBER OF FLEET STREET
(557 Performances)
Opened March 1, 1979
Closed June 29, 1980

THE GREAT WHITE HOPE (556 Performances)
Opened October 3, 1968
Closed January 31, 1970

A MAJORITY OF ONE (556 Performances)
Opened February 16, 1959
Closed June 25, 1960

THE SISTERS ROSENSWEIG (556 Performances)
Opened March 18, 1993
Closed July 16, 1994

SUNRISE AT CAMPOBELLO (556 Performances)
Opened January 30, 1958
Closed May 30, 1959

TOYS IN THE ATTIC (556 Performances)
Opened February 25, 1960
Closed April 8, 1961

JAMAICA (555 Performances)
Opened October 31, 1957
Closed April 11, 1959

STOP THE WORLD—I WANT TO GET OFF (555 Performances)
Opened October 3, 1962
Closed February 1, 1964

FLORODORA (553 Performances)
Opened November 10, 1900
Closed January 25, 1902

NOISES OFF (553 Performances)
Opened December 11, 1983
Closed April 6, 1985

Dolores St. Amand, James Earl Jones, Joanna Featherstone, Hilda Haynes in *The Great White Hope*, 1968 (Friedman-Abeles)

ZIEGFELD FOLLIES (1943) (553 Performances)
Opened April 1, 1943
Closed July 22, 1944

DIAL "M" FOR MURDER (552 Performances)
Opened October 29, 1952
Closed February 27, 1954

GOOD NEWS (551 Performances)
Opened September 6, 1927
Closed Unknown

PETER PAN (REVIVAL) (551 Performances)
Opened September 6, 1979
Closed January 4, 1981

HOW TO SUCCEED IN BUSINESS WITHOUT REALLY TRYING (REVIVAL)
(548 Performances)
Opened March 23, 1995
Closed July 14, 1996

LET'S FACE IT (547 Performances)
Opened October 29, 1941
Closed March 20, 1943

MILK AND HONEY (543 Performances)
Opened October 10, 1961
Closed January 26, 1963

WITHIN THE LAW (541 Performances)
Opened September 11, 1912
Closed Unknown

PAL JOEY (REVIVAL) (540 Performances)
Opened January 3, 1952
Closed April 18, 1953

THE SOUND OF MUSIC (REVIVAL) (540 Performances)
Opened March 12, 1998
Closed June 20, 1999

WHAT MAKES SAMMY RUN? (540 Performances)
Opened February 27, 1964
Closed June 12, 1965

THE SUNSHINE BOYS (538 Performances)
Opened December 20, 1972
Closed April 21, 1974

WHAT A LIFE (538 Performances)
Opened April 13, 1938
Closed July 8, 1939

CRIMES OF THE HEART (535 Performances)
Opened November 4, 1981
Closed February 13, 1983

DAMN YANKEES (REVIVAL) (533 Performances)
Opened March 3, 1994
Closed August 6, 1995

THE UNSINKABLE MOLLY BROWN (532 Performances)
Opened November 3, 1960
February 10, 1962

THE RED MILL (REVIVAL) (531 Performances)
Opened October 16, 1945
Closed January 18, 1947

RUMORS (531 Performances)
Opened November 17, 1988
Closed February 24, 1990

A RAISIN IN THE SUN (530 Performances)
Opened March 11, 1959
Closed June 25, 1960

GODSPELL (527 Performances)
Opened June 22, 1976
Closed September 4, 1977

FENCES (526 Performances)
Opened March 26, 1987
Closed June 26, 1988

THE SOLID GOLD CADILLAC (526 Performances)
Opened November 5, 1953
Closed February 12, 1955

BILOXI BLUES (524 Performances)
Opened March 28, 1985
Closed June 28, 1986

IRMA LA DOUCE (524 Performances)
Opened September 29, 1960
Closed December 31, 1961

THE BOOMERANG (522 Performances)
Opened August 10, 1915
Closed Unknown

FOLLIES (521 Performances)
Opened April 4, 1971
Closed July 1, 1972

ROSALINDA (521 Performances)
Opened October 28, 1942
Closed January 22, 1944

THE BEST MAN (520 Performances)
Opened March 31, 1960
Closed July 8, 1961

CHAUVE-SOURIS (520 Performances)
Opened February 4, 1922
Closed Unknown

BLACKBIRDS OF 1928 (518 Performances)
Opened May 9, 1928
Closed Unknown

THE GIN GAME (517 Performances)
Opened October 6, 1977
Closed December 31, 1978

SUNNY (517 Performances)
Opened September 22, 1925
Closed December 11, 1926

VICTORIA REGINA (517 Performances)
Opened December 26, 1935
Closed Unknown

FIFTH OF JULY (511 Performances)
Opened November 5, 1980
Closed January 24, 1982

HALF A SIXPENCE (511 Performances)
Opened April 25, 1965
Closed July 16, 1966

THE VAGABOND KING (511 Performances)
Opened September 21, 1925
Closed December 4, 1926

THE NEW MOON (509 Performances)
Opened September 19, 1928
Closed December 14, 1929

THE WORLD OF SUZIE WONG (508 Performances)
Opened October 14, 1958
Closed January 2, 1960

THE ROTHSCHILDS (507 Performances)
Opened October 19, 1970
Closed January 1, 1972

ON YOUR TOES (REVIVAL) (505 Performances)
Opened March 6, 1983
Closed May 20, 1984

SUGAR (505 Performances)
Opened April 9, 1972
Closed June 23, 1973

SHUFFLE ALONG (504 Performances)
Opened May 23, 1921
Closed July 15, 1922

UP IN CENTRAL PARK (504 Performances)
Opened January 27, 1945
Closed January 13, 1946

CARMEN JONES (503 Performances)
Opened December 2, 1943
Closed February 10, 1945

SATURDAY NIGHT FEVER (502 Performances)
Opened October 21, 1999
Closed December 30, 2000

THE MEMBER OF THE WEDDING (501 Performances)
Opened January 5, 1950
Closed March 17, 1951

PANAMA HATTIE (501 Performances)
Opened October 30, 1940
Closed January 13, 1942

PERSONAL APPEARANCE (501 Performances)
Opened October 17, 1934
Closed Unknown

BIRD IN HAND (500 Performances)
Opened April 4, 1929
Closed Unknown

ROOM SERVICE (500 Performances)
Opened May 19, 1937
Closed Unknown

SAILOR, BEWARE! (500 Performances)
Opened September 28, 1933
Closed Unknown

TOMORROW THE WORLD (500 Performances)
Opened April 14, 1943
Closed June 17, 1944

LONGEST RUNNING SHOWS OFF-BROADWAY

*Plays that were still playing as of May 31, 2001.

THE FANTASTICKS (17,162 Performances)
Opened May 3, 1960
Closed January 13, 2002

PERFECT CRIME* (6.254 Performances)
Opened April 5, 1987

TUBES* (5,212 Performances)
Opened November 17, 1991

TONY 'N' TINA'S WEDDING* (4,654 Performances)
Opened May 1, 1987

NUNSENSE (3,672 Performances)
Opened December 12, 1985
Closed October 16, 1994

STOMP* (3,464 Performances)
Opened February 27, 1994

THE THREEPENNY OPERA (2,611 Performances)
Opened September 20, 1955
Closed December 17, 1961

I LOVE YOU, YOU'RE PERFECT, NOW CHANGE* (2,448 Performances)
Opened August 1, 1996

FORBIDDEN BROADWAY 1982–87 (2,332 Performances)
Opened January 15, 1982
Closed August 30, 1987

LITTLE SHOP OF HORRORS (2,209 Performances)
Opened July 27, 1982
Closed November 1, 1987

GODSPELL (2,124 Performances)
Opened May 17, 1971
Closed June 13, 1976

VAMPIRE LESBIANS OF SODOM (2,024 Performances)
Opened June 19, 1985
Closed May 27, 1990

JACQUES BREL (1,847 Performances)
Opened October 1, 1992
Closed February 7, 1997

FOREVER PLAID (1,811 Performances)
Opened May 20, 1990
Closed June 12, 1994

VANITIES (1,785 Performances)
Opened August 6, 1928
Closed Unknown

Thais Clark, Topsy Chapman, Sylvia "Kuumba" Williams in *One Mo' Time*, 1979

Jane Galloway, Susan Merson, Kathy Bates in *Vanities*, 1976

YOU'RE A GOOD MAN, CHARLIE BROWN (1,597 Performances)
Opened March 7, 1967
Closed February 14, 1971

DE LA GUARDA* (1,549 Performances)
Opened June 16, 1998

THE BLACKS (1,408 Performances)
Opened May 4, 1961
Closed September 27, 1964

ONE MO' TIME (1,372 Performances)
Opened October 22, 1979
Closed 1982–83 season

GRANDMA SYLVIA'S FUNERAL (1,360 Performances)
Opened October 9, 1994
Closed June 20, 1998

LET MY PEOPLE COME (1,327 Performances)
Opened January 8, 1974
Closed July 5, 1976

NAKED BOYS SINGING (1,206 Performances)
Opened July 22, 1999

DRIVING MISS DAISY (1,195 Performances)
Opened April 15, 1987
Closed June 3, 1990

THE HOT L BALTIMORE (1,166 Performances)
Opened September 8, 1973
Closed January 4, 1976

I'M GETTING MY ACT TOGETHER AND TAKING IT ON THE ROAD
(1,165 Performances)
Opened May 16, 1987
Closed March 15, 1981

LITTLE MARY SUNSHINE (1,143 Performances)
Opened November 18, 1959
Closed September 2, 1962

STEEL MAGNOLIAS (1,126 Performances)
Opened November 17, 1987
Closed February 25, 1990

LATE NITE CATECHISM* (1,115 Performances)
Opened October 4, 1995

EL GRANDE DE COCA-COLA (1,114 Performances)
Opened February 13, 1973
Closed April 13, 1975

THE PROPOSITION (1,109 Performances)
Opened March 24, 1971
Closed April 14, 1974

THE VAGINA MONOLOGUES (1,105 Performances)
Opened October 3, 1999

BEAU JEST (1,069 Performances)
Opened October 10, 1991
Closed May 1, 1994

OUR SINATRA* (1,037 Performances)
Opened December 8, 1999

TAMARA (1,036 Performances)
Opened November 9, 1989
Closed July 15, 1990

ONE FLEW OVER THE CUCKOO'S NEST (REVIVAL) (1,025 Performances)
Opened March 23, 1971
Closed September 16, 1973

THE BOYS IN THE BAND (1,000 Performances)
Opened April 14, 1968
Closed September 29, 1985

FOOL FOR LOVE (1,000 Performances)
Opened November 27, 1983
Closed September 29, 1985

OTHER PEOPLE'S MONEY (990 Performances)
Opened February 7, 1989
Closed July 4, 1991

CLOUD 9 (971 Performances)
Opened May 18, 1981
Closed September 4, 1983

SECRETS EVERY SMART TRAVELER SHOULD KNOW
(953 Performances)
Opened October 30, 1997
Closed February 21, 2000

SISTER MARY IGNATIUS EXPLAINS IT ALL FOR YOU & THE ACTOR'S NIGHTMARE (947 Performances)
Opened October 21, 1981
Closed January 29, 1984

YOUR OWN THING (933 Performances)
Opened January 13, 1968
Closed April 5, 1970

CURLEY MCDIMPLE (931 Performances)
Opened November 22, 1967
Closed January 25, 1970

LEAVE IT TO JANE (REVIVAL) (928 Performances)
Opened May 29, 1959
Closed 1961–62 season

Nicolas Surovy, John Pankow in *Cloud 9*, 1981 (Peter Cunningham)

THE DONKEY SHOW* (862 Performances)
Opened January 26, 1999

HEDWIG AND THE ANGRY INCH (857 Performances)
Opened February 14, 1998
Closed April 9, 2000

FORBIDDEN BROADWAY STRIKES BACK (850 Performances)
Opened October 17, 1996
Closed September 20, 1998

WHEN PIGS FLY (840 Performances)
Opened August 14, 1996
Closed August 15, 1998

THE MAD SHOW (831 Performances)
Opened January 9, 1966
Closed September 10, 1967

SCRAMBLED FEET (831 Performances)
Opened June 11, 1979
Closed June 7, 1981

THE EFFECT OF GAMMA RAYS ON MAN-IN-THE-MOON MARIGOLDS
(819 Performances)
Opened April 7, 1970
Closed June 1, 1973

OVER THE RIVER AND THROUGH THE WOODS (800 Performances)
Opened October 5, 1998
Closed September 3, 2000

A VIEW FROM THE BRIDGE (REVIVAL) (780 Performances)
Opened November 9, 1965
Closed December 11, 1966

THE BOY FRIEND (REVIVAL) (763 Performances)
Opened January 25, 1958
Closed 1961–62 season

TRUE WEST (762 Performances)
Opened December 23, 1980
Closed January 11, 1981

FORBIDDEN BROADWAY CLEANS UP ITS ACT! (754 Performances)
Opened November 17, 1998
Closed August 30, 2000

ISN'T IT ROMANTIC (733 Performances)
Opened December 15, 1983
Closed September 1, 1985

DIME A DOZEN (728 Performances)
Opened June 13, 1962
Closed 1963–64 season

THE POCKET WATCH (725 Performances)
Opened November 14, 1966
Closed June 18, 1967

THE CONNECTION (722 Performances)
Opened June 9, 1959
Closed June 4, 1961

THE PASSION OF DRACULA (714 Performances)
Opened September 28, 1977
Closed July 14, 1979

ADAPTATION & NEXT (707 Performances)
Opened February 10, 1969
Closed October 18, 1970

OH! CALCUTTA! (704 Performances)
Opened June 17, 1969
Closed August 12, 1972

SCUBA DUBA (692 Performances)
Opened November 11, 1967
Closed June 8, 1969

THE FOREIGNER (686 Performances)
Opened November 2, 1984
Closed June 8, 1986

THE KNACK (685 Performances)
Opened January 14, 1964
Closed January 9, 1966

FULLY COMMITTED (675 Performances)
Opened December 14, 1999
Closed May 27, 2001

THE CLUB (674 Performances)
Opened October 14, 1976
Closed May 21, 1978

THE BALCONY (672 Performances)
Opened March 3, 1960
Closed December 21, 1961

PENN & TELLER (666 Performances)
Opened July 30, 1985
Closed January 19, 1992

DINNER WITH FRIENDS (654 Performances)
Opened November 4, 1999
Closed May 27, 2000

AMERICA HURRAH (634 Performances)
Opened November 7, 1966
Closed May 5, 1968

OIL CITY SYMPHONY (626 Performances)
Opened November 5, 1987
Closed May 7, 1989

THE COUNTESS (618 Performances)
Opened September 28, 1999
Closed December 30, 2000

HOGAN'S GOAT (607 Performances)
Opened March 6, 1965
Closed April 23, 1967

BEEHIVE (600 Performances)
Opened March 30, 1986
Closed August 23, 1987

TROJAN WOMEN (600 Performances)
Opened December 23, 1963
Closed May 30, 1965

THE SYRINGA TREE* (583 Performances)
Opened September 14, 2000

THE DINING ROOM (583 Performances)
Opened February 24, 1982
Closed July 17, 1982

KRAPP'S LAST TAPE & THE ZOO STORY (582 Performances)
Opened August 29, 1960
Closed May 21, 1961

THREE TALL WOMEN (582 Performances)
Opened April 13, 1994
Closed August 26, 1995

THE DUMBWAITER & THE COLLECTION (578 Performances)
Opened January 21, 1962
Closed April 12, 1964

FORBIDDEN BROADWAY 1990 (576 Performances)
Opened January 23, 1990
Closed June 9, 1991

DAMES AT SEA (575 Performances)
Opened April 22, 1969
Closed May 10, 1970

THE CRUCIBLE (REVIVAL) (TRANSFER) (571 Performances)
Opened March 14, 1990
Closed May 13, 1990

THE ICEMAN COMETH (REVIVAL) (565 Performances)
Opened May 8, 1956
Closed 1957–58 season

FORBIDDEN BROADWAY 2001: A SPOOF ODYSSEY*
(552 Performances)
Opened December 6, 2000

THE HOSTAGE (REVIVAL) (TRANSFER) (545 Performances)
Opened October 16, 1972
Closed October 8, 1973

WIT (545 Performances)
Opened October 6, 1998
Closed April 9, 2000

WHAT'S A NICE COUNTRY LIKE YOU DOING IN A STATE LIKE THIS?
(543 Performances)
Opened July 31, 1985
Closed February 9, 1987

FORBIDDEN BROADWAY 1988 (534 Performances)
Opened September 15, 1988
Closed December 24, 1989

GROSS INDECENCY: THE THREE TRIALS OF OSCAR WILDE
(534 Performances)
Opened September 5, 1997
Closed September 13, 1998

FRANKIE AND JOHNNY IN THE CLAIRE DE LUNE (533 Performances)
Opened December 4, 1987
Closed March 12, 1989

SIX CHARACTERS IN SEARCH OF AN AUTHOR (REVIVAL)
(529 Performances)
Opened March 8, 1963
Closed June 28, 1964

ALL IN THE TIMING (526 Performances)
Opened November 24, 1993
Closed February 13, 1994

OLEANNA (513 Performances)
Opened October 3, 1992
Closed January 16, 1994

MAKING PORN (511 Performances)
Opened June 12, 1996
Closed September 14, 1997

THE DIRTIEST SHOW IN TOWN (509 Performances)
Opened June 26, 1970
Closed September 17, 1971

HAPPY ENDING & DAY OF ABSENCE (504 Performances)
Opened June 13, 1965
Closed January 29, 1967

GREATER TUNA (501 Performances)
Opened October 21, 1982
Closed December 31, 1983

A SHAYNA MAIDEL (501 Performances)
Opened October 29, 1987
Closed January 8, 1989

THE BOYS FROM SYRACUSE (REVIVAL) (500 performances)
Opened April 15, 1963
Closed June 28, 1964get

BIOGRAPHICAL DATA

Hayden Adams

Wendy Allegaert

Michael Anderson

Todd Anthony-Jackson

Aaron, Jack Born May 1, 1933 in New York, NY. Attended Hunter Col., Actors Workshop. OB in *Swim Low Little Goldfish*, followed by *Journey of the 5th Horse, The Nest, One Flew Over the Cuckoo's Nest, The Birds, The Pornographer's Daughter, Love Death Plays, Unlikely Heroes, Taking Steam, Mark VIII:xxxvi, Made in Heaven, No Niggers No Jews No Dogs,* Bdwy in *Sunshine Boys* (1998).

Ackroyd, David Born May 30, 1940 in Orange, NJ. Graduate Bucknell, Yale U. Bdwy debut 1971 in *Unlikely Heroes* followed by *Full Circle, Hamlet, Hide and Seek, Children of a Lesser God,* OB in *Isadora Duncan Sleeps with the Russian Navy, It Just Catches.*

Acuña, Arthur T. Born Dec. 11, 1961 in Manila, Philippines. Attended De La Salle U., Philippines. OB debut 1993 in *The Hounded & Possessed,* followed by *Santos & Santos, Mother Courage, Dogeater.*

Adams, Hayden Born in Northbrook, IL. Graduate IN U., U. of DE. OB debut in *Strictly Personal.*

Adams, Mason Born Feb. 26, 1919 in New York, NY. Graduate U. WI. Bdwy credits include *Get Away Old Man, Public Relations, Career Angel, Violet, Shadow of the Enemy, Tall Story, Inquest, Trial of the Catonsville 9, The Sign in Sidney Brustein's Window,* OB in *Meegan's Game, Shortchanged Review, Checking Out, The Sop Touch, Paradise Lost, The Time of Your Life, Danger: Memory, The Day Room, Rose Quartet, The Ryan Interview, Last of Thorntons.*

Agustin, Julio Born Oct. 16, 1967 in Bronx, NY. Graduate FL St. U. Bdwy debut 1997 in *Steel Pier,* followed by *Fosse, Bells Are Ringing.*

Ahearn, Daniel Born Aug. 7, 1948 in Washington, DC. Attended Carnegie Mellon U. OB debut 1981 in *Woyzek* followed by *Brontosaurus Rex, Billy Liar, Second Prize, Two Months in Leningrad, No Time Flat, Hollywood Scheherazade, Better Days, Joy Solution, Making Book, Flight, As You Like It.*

Aidem, Betsy Born Oct. 28, 1957 in East Meadow, NY. Graduate NYU. OB debut 1981 in *The Trading Post,* followed by *A Different Moon, Balm in Gilead, Crossing the Bar, Our Lady of the Tortilla, Steel Magnolias, Road, 5 Women Wearing the Same Dress, Pera Palas, Ghost on Fire, Tamicanfly, The Butterfly Collection.*

Aldredge, Tom Born Feb. 28, 1928 in Dayton, OH. Attended Dayton U., Goodman Theatre. Bdwy debut 1959 in *Nervous Set,* followed by *UTBU, Slapstick Tragedy, Everything in the Garden, Indians, Engagement Baby, How the Other Half Loves, Sticks and Bones, Where's Charley?, Leaf People, Rex, Vieux Carré, St. Joan, Stages, On Golden Pond, The Little Foxes, Into the Woods, Two Shakespearean Actors, Inherit the Wind, Boys from Syracuse* (Encores), *1776, Tom Sawyer,* OB in *The Tempest, Between Two Thieves, Henry V, The Premise, Love's Labour's Lost, Troilus and Cressida, The Butter and Egg Man, Ergo, Boys in the Band, Twelfth Night, Colette, Hamlet, The Orphan, King Lear, The Iceman Cometh, Black Angel, Getting Along Famously, Fool for Love, Neon Psalms, Richard II, Last Yankee, Incommunicado, La Terrasse, Time of the Cuckoo.*

Allegaert, Wendy Born in New York, NY. Graduate Barnard Col. Debut OB in *Saved.*

Ancheta, Susan Born Jan. 1 in Honolulu, HI. Graduate SMU. 1997 Debut OB in *Shanghai Lil's,* Bdwy debut 1997 in *Miss Saigon,* followed by *Flower Drum Song.*

Anderman, Maureen Born Oct. 26, 1946 in Detroit, MI. Graduate UMI. Bdwy debut 1970 in *Othello,* followed by *Moonchildren,* for which she received a 1972 Theatre World Award, *An Evening with Richard Nixon…, The Last of Mrs. Lincoln, Seascape, Who's Afraid of Virginia Woolf?, A History of the American Film, The Lady from Dubuque, The Man Who Came to Dinner, Einstein and the Polar Bear, You Can't Take It With You, Macbeth, Benefactors, Social Security,* OB in *Hamlet, Elusive Angel, Out of Our Father's House, Sunday Runners, Ancestral Voices, The Waverly Gallery, Passion Play.*

Anderson, Michael Born June 23, 1972 in Denver, CO. Attended Whitman Col. OB debut in *Making Peter Pope.*

Anderson, Nancy . Born April 22, 1972 in Boston, MA. Attended Smith Col, Tufts U. OB debut in *Fables in Slang,* followed by *Jolson & Co,* Bdwy debut *A Class Act* (also OB).

Anthony, Eric Born Dec. 10 in Baltimore, MD. Graduate Carver Center for the Arts and Technology. Bdwy debut 2001 in *Lion King,* followed by *Hairspray,* OB debut 2002 in City Center Encores! *Golden Boy.*

Anthony, Gerald Born July 31, 1951 in Pittsburgh, PA. Graduate USCS, CA State. OB debut in *Uncle Jack*, followed by *Snapshots* 2000.

Anthony-Jackson, Todd Born in Hartford, CT. Attended Cornell U., American Conservatory Theatre. OB in *A Lesson from Aloes*.

Aranas, Raul Born Oct. 1, 1947 in Manila, Philippines. Graduate Pace U. OB debut 1976 in *Savages*, followed by *Yellow is My Favorite Color*, 49, *Bullet Headed Birds*, *Tooth of the Crime*, *Teahouse*, *Shepard Sets*, *Cold Air*, *La Chunga*, *The Man Who Turned into a Stick*, *Twelfth Night*, *Shogun Macbeth*, *Boutique Living*, *Fairy Bones*, *In the Jungle of Cities*, *Dogeaters*, Bdwy in *Loose Ends* (1978), followed by *Miss Saigon*, *King and I*, *Flower Drum Song*.

Ari, Robert (Bob) Born July 1, 1949 in New York, NY. Graduate Carnegie Mellon U. OB debut 1976 in *Boys from Syracuse*, followed by *Gay Divorce*, *Devour the Snow*, *Carbondale Dreams*, *Show Me Where the Good Times Are*, *CBS Live*, *Picasso at the Lapin Agile*, *Twelfth Night*, *Baby Anger*, *Names*, *June Moon*, *Pieces of the Sky*, *Wish You Were Here*, *Jolson & Co.*, Bdwy in *Bells Are Ringing*.

Armitage, Robert Born Sept. 18, 1970 in Bristol, CT. Attended Central CT St. U. Bdwy debut 1996 *Victor/Victoria*, followed by *Aida*, OB in *A Connecticut Yankee in King Arthur's Court* (CC).

Asquith, Ward Born March 21 in Philadelphia, PA. Graduate U. PA, Columbia U. OB debut 1979 in *After the Rise*, followed by *Kind Lady*, *Incident at Vichy*, *Happy Birthday Wanda June*, *Another Part of the Forest*, *Little Foxes*, *Sherlock Holmes & the Hands of Othello*, *Macbeth*, *Real Inspector Hound*, *Uncle Vanya*, *Cyrano de Bergerac*, *What the Butler Saw*, *The Professional*, *Welcome to Our City*.

Atkins, Eileen Born June 16, 1934 in London, England. Attended Guildhall Schl. Bdwy debut 1966 in *The Killing of Sister George*, followed by *The Promise*, *Viva! Vivat Regina!*, *The Night of the Tribades*, *Indiscretions*, OB in *Prin*, *A Room of One's Own*, *Vita and Virginia*, *The Unexpected Man*.

Atkinson, Jayne Born Feb. 18, 1959 in Bournemouth, England. Graduate Northwestern U., Yale U. Debut 1986 OB in *Bloody Poetry* followed by *Terminal Bar*, *Return of Pinocchio*, *The Art of Success*, *The Way of the World*, *Appointment with a High Wire Lady*, *Why We Have a Body*, *How I Learned to Drive*, Bdwy in *All My Sons* (1987) followed by *Ivanov*, *Our Town*.

Auberjonois, Rene Born June 1, 1940 in NYC. Graduate Carnegie Inst. With LC Rep in *A Cry of Player*, *King Lear*, and *Twelfth Night*, Bdwy in *Fire* (1969), *Coco*, *Tricks*, *The Good Doctor*, *Break a Leg*, *Every Good Boy Deserves Favor*, *Big River*, *Metamorphosis*, *City of Angels*, *Don Juan in Hell in Concert*, *The New York Idea* (BAM), *Three Sisters*, *The Play's the Thing*, *Julius Caesar*, *Dance of the Vampires*.

Baker, Becky Ann (formerly Gelke) Born Feb. 17, 1953 in Ft. Knox, KY. Graduate W. KY. U. Bdwy debut 1978 in *Best Little Whorehouse in Texas* followed by *Streetcar Named Desire* (1988), *Titanic*, OB in *Altitude Sickness*, *John Brown's Body*, *Chamber Music*, *To Whom It May Concern*, *Two Gentlemen of Verona*, *Bob's Guns*, *Buzzsaw Berkeley*, *Colorado Catechism*, *Jeremy Rudge*, *Laura Dennis*, *June Moon*, *The Most Fabulous Story Ever Told*, *Shanghai Moon*.

Baker, Dylan Born in Lackey, VA. Graduate William and Mary Col., Yale U. OB debut 1985 in *Not About Heroes*, followed by *Two Gentlemen of Verona*, *The Common Pursuit*, *Much Ado About Nothing*, *WolfMan*, *Dearly Departed*, *Pride's Crossing*, *That Championship Season*, *Tartuffe*, *What the Butcher Saw*, Bdwy debut 1989 in *Eastern Standard* (also OB), for which he received a 1989 Theatre World Award.

Baldwin, Alec Born April 3, 1958 in Massapequa, NY. Attended George Washington U., NYU. Bdwy debut 1986 in *Loot*, for which he received a 1986 Theatre World Award, followed by *Serious Money*, *A Streetcar Named Desire*, OB in *Prelude to a Kiss*, *Macbeth Voices!*, *Arsenic and Old Lace* (CC).

Banderas, Antonio (Jose Antonio Dominguiz Bandera) Born Aug. 8, 1960 in Malaga, Spain. Attended Art Dramatic National School. Bdwy debut 2003 in *Nine* for which he received a Theatre World Award.

Barbour, James Born April 25, 1966 in Cherry Hill, NJ. Graduate Hofstra U. OB debut 1990 in *Class Clown*, followed by *The Merry Wives of Windsor*, *Tom Sawyer*, *Harold and the Purple Crayon*, *Milk and Honey*, Bdwy in *Cyrano*, *The Musical* (1993) followed by *Carousel*, *Jane Eyre*, *Beauty and the Beast*.

Bareikis, Arija Born July 21, 1966 in Bloomington, IN. Bdwy debut 1997 in *Last Night of Ballyhoo*, OB in *The Moment When*, *Hotel Universe*, *Alice in Bed*.

Barnes, Ezra Born Jan. 22, 1963 in Brooklyn, NY. Graduate Amherst Col. Natl. Theatre Cons. Debut 1998 OB in *Richard II*, followed by *Far and Wide*.

Barnes, Lisa Born March 5, 1957 in Pasadena, CA. Graduate USC. Debut 1983 OB in *Midsummer Night's Dream* followed by *Domino Courts*, *Life on Earth*, *Quick-Change Room*, *Rapt*.

Barnett, Ken Born July 24, 1972 in Memphis, TN. Graduate Wesleyan U. OB in *A Christmas Carol* (MSG), *Imperfect Chemistry*, Bdwy in *The Green Bird* (2000).

Barrett, Brent Born Feb. 28, 1957 in Quinter, KS. Graduate Carnegie Mellon U. Bdwy debut 1980 in *West Side Story*, followed by *Dance a Little Closer*, *Grand Hotel*, *Candide* (1997), *Chicago*, *Annie Get Your Gun*, OB in *March of the Falsettos*, *Portrait of Jenny*, *Death of Von Richthofen*, *Sweethearts*, *What's a Nice Country Like You Doing in a State Like This?*, *Time of the Cuckoo*, *Swan Song*, *Closer Than Ever*, *Marry Me a Little*, *On a Clear Day You Can See Forever* (CC).

Barrie-Wilson, Wendy Born June 9 in Loveland, OH. Graduate Denison UNC. Bdwy debut 1987 in *All My Sons*, followed by *Our Town* (2002), OB in *The Voice of the Prairie*.

Bart, Roger Born Sept. 29, 1962 in Norwalk, CT. Graduate Rutgers U. OB debut 1984 in *Second Wind*, followed by *Lessons*, *Up Against It*, *Henry IV Parts 1 and 2*, *Fully Committed*, *On A Clear Day You Can See Forever* (CC), Bdwy in *Big River* (1987), *King David*, *Triumph of Love*, *You're a Good Man*, *Charlie Brown*, *The Producers*.

Barta, Becky Born Dec. 27, 1962 in Kansas City, MO. Graduate U. of KS. OB debut in *Always*, *Patsy Cline*, followed by *Forbidden Broadway Cleans Up It's Act*.

Ward Asquith

James Barbour

Ken Barnett

Becky Barta

Bartenieff, George Born Jan. 24, 1933 in Berlin, Germany. Bdwy debut 1947 in *The Whole World Over*, followed by *Venus Is, All's Well That Ends Well, Quotations from Chairman Mao Tse-Tung, Death of Bessie Smith, Cop-Out, Room Service, Unlikely Heroes*, OB in *Walking in Waldheim, Memorandum, Increased Difficulty of Concentration, Trelawny of the Wells, Charley Chestnut Rides the IRT, Radio (Wisdom): Sophia Part I, Images of the Dead, Dead End Kids, The Blonde Leading the Blonde, The Dispossessed, Growing Up Gothic, Rosetti's Apologies, On the Lam, Samuel Beckett Trilogy, Quartet, Help Wanted, Matter of Life and Death, Heart That Eats Itself, Coney Island Kid, Cymbeline, Better People, Blue Heaven, He Saw His Reflection, Sabina, Beekeeper's Daughter, Desire Under the Elms, I Love Dick, I Will Bear Witness.*

Bartlett, Peter Born Aug. 28, 1942 in Chicago, IL. Attended Loyola U., LAMDA. Bdwy debut 1969 in *A Patriot for Me*, followed by *Gloria and Esperanza, Beauty and the Beast, Voices in the Dark*, OB in *Boom Boom Room, I Remember the House Where I was Born, Crazy Locomotive, A Thurber Carnival, Hamlet, Buzzsaw Berkeley, Learned Ladies, Jeffrey, The Naked Truth, Mr. Charles, The Most Fabulous Story Ever Told, A Connecticut Yankee in King Arthur's Court* (CC).

Bast, Stephanie Born Oct. 4, 1972 in Seoul, Korea. Graduate Allentown Col. Debut 1995 OB in *Schoolhouse Rock*, Bdwy 1995 in *Christmas Carol* (MSG) followed by *Miss Saigon, King David, Scarlet Pimpernel, Nine.*

Bates, Jerome Preston Born July 20, 1954 in Augusta, GA. Attended Knoxville Col., U. of TN, LAMDA. Debut 1985 OB in *Jonin* followed by *Amulets Against the Dragon Force, Burning Blue, Daisy in Dreamtime.*

Batt, Bryan Born March 1, 1963 in New Orleans, LA. Graduate Tulane U. OB debut 1987 in *Too Many Girls*, followed by *Golden Apple, Jeffrey, Forbidden Bdwy, Forbidden Bdwy Strikes Back, Ascendancy, Forbidden Bdwy Cleans Up Its Act!*, Bdwy in *Starlight Express* (1987), *Sunset Blvd., Saturday Night Fever, Seussical.*

Beach, David Born Feb. 20, 1964 in Dayton, OH. Attended Dartmouth Col., LAMDA. OB debut 1990 in *Big Fat and Ugly with a Moustache*, followed by *Modigliani, Octoberfest, Pets, That's Life!, Message to Michael, Urinetown*, Bdwy in *Moon Over Buffalo* (1995), *Beauty and the Beast., Sweet Adeline* (Encores).

Beach, Gary Born Oct. 10, 1947 in Alexandria, VA. Graduate NC Sch. of Arts. Bdwy debut 1971 in *1776*, followed by *Something's Afoot, Mooney Shapiro Songbook, Annie, Doonesbury, Beauty and the Beast*, OB in *Smile Smile Smile, What's a Nice Country Like You Doing in a State Like This?, Ionescapade, By Strouse, A Bundle of Nerves.*

Bean, Reathel Born Aug. 24, 1942 in Missouri. Graduate Drake U. OB in *America Hurrah, San Francisco's Burning, Love Cure, Henry IV, In Circles, Peace, Journey of Snow White, Wanted, The Faggot, Lovers, Not Back with the Elephants, The Art of Coarse Acting, The Trip Back Down, Hunting Cockroaches, Smoke on the Mountain, Avow*, Bdwy in *Doonesbury* (1983), *Big River, Inherit the Wind, Chicago, Our Town.*

Bean, Shoshana Born Sept. 1, 1977 in Olympia, WA. Graduate U. of Cincinnati, College Conservatory of Music. OB debut 2000 in *Godspell*, Bdwy. Debut 2002 in *Hairspray.*

Becker, Rob Born in San Jose, CA in 1956. Bdwy debut 1995 in *Defending the Caveman.*

Beddow, Margery Born Dec. 13, 1937 in Grosse Point, MI. Attended HB Studio. Bdwy debut 1959 in *Redhead* followed by *Fiorello!, Show Boat, The Conquering Hero, We Take the Town, Take Me Along, Little Me, Here's Love, Ulysses in Nighttown*, OB in *Sing Melancholy Baby, Anyone Can Whistle, 24 Evenings of Wit and Wisdom.*

Bedford, Brian Born Feb. 16, 1935 in Morley, England. Attended RADA. Bdwy debut 1960 in *Five Finger Exercise* followed by *Lord Pengo, The Private Ear, The Astrakhan Coat, Unknown Soldier and His Wife, Seven Descents of Myrtle, Jumpers, Cocktail Party, Hamlet, Private Lives, School for Wives, The Misanthrope, Two Shakespearean Actors, Timon of Athens, Moliere Comedies, London Assurance, Tartuffe* OB in *The Knack, The Lunatic the Lover and the Poet, Much Ado About Nothing, The Miser*

Bell, Glynis Born July 30, 1947 in London, England. Attended Oakland U., AADA. OB debut 1975 in *The Devils*, followed by *The Time of Your Life, The Robber Bridegroom, Three Sisters, Sleep Deprivation Chamber, Diana of Dobson's, Blithe Spirit*, Bdwy debut 1993 in *My Fair Lady*, followed by *Amadeus.*

Bryan Batt

Brian Belovitch

Shirl Bernheim

Ian Blackman

Bellamy, Brad Born June 18, 1951 in Marshall, MO. Graduate Westminster Col. OB debut 1974 in *Little Tips*, followed by *Crocodiles in the Potomac, Man Who Shot Jesse James, Andorra, Caine Mutiny Court Marshall, Flight, District of Columbia, Proof, If It Was Easy.*

Belovitch, Brian Born April 10, 1956 in Fall River, MA. Attended RI Col. OB debut in *Boys Don't Wear Lipstick.*

Benanti, Laura Born 1980 in Kinnelon, NJ. Attended NYU. Bdwy debut 1999 in *Sound of Music*, followed by *Nine.*

Bern, Mina Born May 5, 1920 in Poland. Bdwy debut 1967 in *Let's Sing Yiddish* followed by *Light Lively and Yiddish, Sing Israel Sing, Those Were the Days*, OB in *The Special, Old Lady's Guide to Survival, Blacksmith's Folly, Yentl.*

Bernheim, Shirl Born Sept. 21, 1921 in New York, NY. OB debut 1967 in *A Different World*, followed by *Stage Movie, Middle of the Night, Come Back, Little Sheba, One-Act Festival, EST Marathon 93, Old Lady's Guide to Survival.*

Bertrand, Jacqueline Born June 1, 1939 in Quebec, Canada. Attended Neighborhood Playhouse, Actors Studio, LAMDA. OB debut 1978 in *Unfinished Woman*, followed by *Dancing for the Kaiser, Lulu, War and Peace, Nest of the Wood Grouse, Salon, When She Danced, Antigone, Bravo Ubu, In Transit.*

Billman, Sekiya Born April 18, 1968 in Los Angeles, CA. Graduate UCLA. Bdwy debut 1996 in *Miss Saigon*. OB in *Shanghai Moon.*

Binoche, Juliette Born March 9, 1964 in Paris, France. Bdwy debut 2000 in *Betrayal*, for which she received a 2001 Theatre World Award.

Birdsong, Mary Born April 18th in Tallahassee, FL. Graduate NYU. OB debut 2002 in *Adult Entertainment.*

Birkelund, Olivia Born April 26, 1963 in New York, NY. Graduate Brown U. OB debut 1990 in *Othello*, followed by *Cowboy in His Underwear, Misanthrope, Aimee and Hope, Servicemen.*

Birney, Reed Born Sept. 11, 1954 in Alexandria, VA. Attended Boston U. Bdwy debut 1977 in *Gemini*, OB in *Master and Margarita, Bella Figura, Winterplay, Flight of the Earls, Filthy Rich, Lady Moonsong, Mr. Monsoon, Common Pursuit, Zero Positive, Moving Targets, Spare Parts, Murder of Crows, 7 Blowjobs, Loose Knot, The Undertaker, An Imaginary Life, Family of Mann, Dark Ride, Minor Demons, Volunteer Man, Knee Desires the Dirt, With and Without, The Exact Center of the Universe, The Butterfly Collection.*

Biton, Joshua Born Dec. 19, 1973 in Queens, NY. Graduate SUNY Albany and Rutgers U. OB debut 2000 in *The Crumple Zone.*

Blackman, Ian Born Sept. 2, 1959 in Toronto, Canada. Attended Bard Col. OB debut 1982 in *Herself as Lust*, followed by *Sister Mary Ignatius Explains It All, The Actor's Nightmare, The Bone Ring*, Bdwy debut 1986 in *The House of Blue Leaves*, followed by *The Man Who Came to Dinner.*

Blankenbuehler, Andy Born March 7, 1970 in Cincinnati, OH. Attended SMU. Bdwy debut 1993 in *Guys and Dolls* followed by *Steel Pier, Big, Fosse, Man of La Mancha.*

Blanchard, Steve Born Dec. 4, 1958 in York, PA. Attended U. MD. Bdwy debut 1984 in *The Three Musketeers*, followed by *Camelot, Christmas Carol, Beauty and the Beast*, OB in *Moby Dick.*

Blazer, Judith Born Oct. 22, 1956. OB in *Oh Boy!*, followed by *Roberta, A Little Night Music, Company, Babes in Arms, Hello Again, Jack's Holiday, Louisiana Purchase, Hurrah At Last, The Torchbearers, A Connecticut Yankee in King Arthur's Court* (CC), Bdwy in *Me and My Girl, A Change in the Heir, Titanic.*

Bloch, Scotty Born Jan. 28 in New Rochelle, NY. Attended AADA. OB debut 1945 in *Craig's Wife*, followed by *Lemon Sky, Battering Ram, Richard III, In Celebration, An Act of Kindness, The Price, Grace, Neon Psalms, Other People's Money, Walking The Dead, EST Marathon '92, The Stand-In, Unexpected Tenderness, Brutality of Fact, What I Meant Was, Scotland Road The Waverly Gallery, Saved or Destroyed*, Bdwy in *Children of a Lesser God* (1980).

Block, Larry Born Oct. 30, 1942, in NYC. Graduate URI. Bdwy debut 1966 in *Hail Scrawdyke*, followed by *La Turista*, *Wonderful Town* (NYCO), OB in *Eh?*, *Fingernails Blue as Flowers*, *Comedy of Errors*, *Coming Attractions*, *Henry IV Part 2*, *Feuhrer Bunker*, *Manhattan Love Songs*, *Souvenirs*, *The Golem*, *Responsible Parties*, *Hit Parade*, *Largo Desolato*, *The Square Root of 3*, *Young Playwrights Festival*, *Hunting Cockroaches*, *Two Gentlemen of Verona*, *Yello Dog Contract*, *Temptation*, *Festival of 1 Acts*, *Faithful Brethern of Pitt Street*, *Loman Family Picnic*, *One of the All-Time Greats*, *Pericles*, *Comedy of Errors*, *The Work Room*, *Don Juan in Chicago*, *Him*, *Devil Inside*, *Uncle Philip's Coat*, *Evolution* .

Bloom, Tom Born November 1, 1944 in Washington, D.C. Graduate Western MD Col., Emerson Col. OB debut 1989 in *Widow's Blind Date*, followed by *A Cup of Coffee*, *Major Barbara*, *A Perfect Diamond*, *Lips Together Teeth Apart*, *Winter's Tale*, *The Guardsman*, *Stray Cats*, *Arms and the Man*, Bdwy in *Racing Demon* (1995), *Winter's Tale* (2003).

Blum, Joel Born May 19, 1952 in San Francisco, CA. Attended Marin Col., NYU. Bdwy debut 1976 in *Debbie Reynolds on Broadway*, followed by *42nd Street*, *Stardust*, *Radio City Easter Show*, *Show Boat* (1994), *Steel Pier*, OB in *And the World Goes Round*, *Game Show*.

Blum, Mark Born May 14, 1950 in Newark, NJ. Graduate U. PA, U. MN. OB debut 1976 in *The Cherry Orchard*, followed by *Green Julia*, *Say Goodnight Gracie*, *Table Settings*, *Key Exchange*, *Loving Reno*, *Messiah*, *It's Only a Play*, *Little Footsteps*, *Cave of Life*, *Gus & Al*, *Laureen's Whereabouts*, *Mizlansky*, *Zilinksy*, *Gore Vidal's The Best Man*, *The Waverly Gallery*, Bdwy in *Lost in Yonkers* (1991), *My Thing of Love*, *A Thousand Clowns*.

Blumenkrantz, Jeff Born June 3, 1965 in Long Branch, NJ. Graduate Northwestern U. OB debut 1986 in *Pajama Game*, Bdwy debut 1987 in *Into the Woods*, followed by *3 Penny Opera*, *South Pacific*, *Damn Yankees*, *How to Succeed in Business Without Really Trying* (1995), *A Class Act*.

Bobbie, Walter Born Nov. 18, 1945 in Scranton, PA. Graduate U. Scranton, Catholic U. Bdwy debut 1971 in *Frank Merriwell*, followed by *The Grass Harp*, *Grease*, *Tricks*, *Going Up*, *History of the American Film*, *Anything Goes*, *Getting Married*, *Guys and Dolls*, OB in *Drat!*, *She Loves Me*, *Up from Paradise*, *Goodbye Freddy*, *Cafe Crown*, *Young Playwrights '90*, *Polish Joke*.

Bobby, Anne Marie Born Dec. 12, 1967 in Paterson, NJ. Attended Oxford U. OB debut 1983 in *American Passion*, followed by *Class I Acts*, *Godspell*, *Progress*, *Groundhog*, *Misconceptions*, *Merrily We Roll Along*, *Strictly Personal*, Bdwy in *The Human Comedy* (1984), *The Real Thing*, *Hurlyburly*, *Precious Sons*, *Smile*, *Black Comedy*.

Bockhorn, Craig Born May 30, 1961 in New York, NY. Graduate Emerson Col. OB debut 1989 in *You Can't Think of Everything*, followed by *Truth Teller*, *Third Millennium*, *As You Like It*, *Loveliest Afternoon of the Year*, *Women of Manhattan*, *Runyon on Wry*, *Bard Silly*, *Hope Zone*, *Kit Marlowe*, Bdwy debut 1990 in *Prelude to a Kiss* (also OB).

Bodle, Jane Born November 12th in Lawrence, KS. Attended U. UT. Bdwy debut 1983 in *Cats*, followed by *Les Miserables*, *Miss Saigon*, *Sunset Blvd*, OB in *Once Around the City*.

Boevers, Jessica Born Aug. 25, 1972 in Highland Park, IL. Graduate Cincinnati Cons. of Music, U. of Cincinnati. Bdwy debut 1994 in *Beauty and the Beast*, followed by *A Funny Thing Happened on the Way to the Forum*, OB in *The It Girl*.

Bogardus, Stephen Born March 11, 1954 in Norfolk, VA. Graduate Princeton U. Bdwy debut 1980 in *West Side Story* followed by *Les Miserables*, *Grapes of Wrath*, *Falsettos*, *Allegro*, (Encores), *Love! Valour! Compassion!* (also OB), *Sweet Adeline*, *King David*, *High Society*, *Man of La Mancha*, OB in *Genesis*, *March of the Falsettos*, *In Trousers*, *Feathertop*, *No Way to Treat a Lady*, *Falsettoland*, *Umbrellas of Cherbourg*.

Bosco, Philip Born Sept. 26, 1930 in Jersey City, NJ. Graduate Catholic U. Credits: *Auntie Mame*, *Rape of the Belt*, *Ticket of Leave Man*, *Donnybrook*, *A Man for All Seasons*, *Mrs. Warren's Profession*, with LC Rep in *A Great Career*, *In the Matter of J. Robert Oppenheimer*, *The Miser*, *The Time of Your Life*, *Camino Real*, *Operation Sidewinder*, *Amphitryon*, *Enemy of the People*, *Playboy of the Western World*, *Good Woman of Setzuan*, *Antigone*, *Mary Stuart*, *Narrow Road to the Deep North*, *The Crucible*, *Twelfth Night*, *Enemies*, *Plough and the Stars*, *Merchant of Venice*, *A Streetcar Named Desire*, *Henry V*, *Threepenny Opera*, *Streamers*, *Stages*, *St. Joan*, *The Biko Inquest*, *Man and Superman*, *Whose Life Is It Anyway?*, *Major Barbara*, *A Month in the Country*, *Bacchae*, *Hedda Gabler*, *Don Juan in Hell*, *Inadmissible Evidence*, *Eminent Domain*, *Misalliance*, *Learned Ladies*, *Some Men Need Help*, *Ah, Wilderness!*, *The Caine Mutiny Court Martial*, *Heartbreak House*, *Come Back Little Sheba*, *Loves of Anatol*, *Be Happy for Me*, *Master Class*, *You Never Can Tell*, *Devil's Disciple*, *Lend Me a Tenor*, *Breaking Legs*, *Fiorello* (Encores), *An Inspector Calls*, *The Heiress*, *Moon Over Buffalo*, *Strike Up the Band* (Encores), *Twelfth Night*, *Copenhagen*, *Ancestral Voices*, *Bloomer Girl* (CC).

Bostnar, Lisa Born July 19th in Cleveland, OH. Attended Case Western U. OB in *It's Far and Wide*.

Boston, Gretha Born April 18, 1959 in Crossett, AR. Attended U. No. TX, U. IL. Bdwy debut 1994 in *Show Boat*, for which she received a 1995 Theatre World Award, OB in *Tea Time*, *Far and Wide*.

Bourne, Bette Born Sept. 22, 1939 in the United Kingdom. Graduate Central Sch. London. OB in *Resident Alien*.

Bove, Mark Born Jan. 9, 1960 in Pittsburgh, PA. Bdwy debut in *West Side Story* (1980) followed by *Woman of the Year*, *Chorus Line*, *Kiss of the Spider Woman*, *The Life*, *Urban Cowboy*.

Bowen, Andrea Born March 4, 1990 in Columbus, OH. Bdwy debut 1997 in *Les Miserables*, followed by *Sound of Music*, *Jane Eyre*.

Bradley, Brad Born Dec. 9, 1971 in San Diego, CA. Graduate USC. Bdwy debut 1995 in *Christmas Carol*, followed by *Steel Pier*, *Strike Up the Band* (Encores), *Annie Get Your Gun*, OB in *Coconuts*.

Bradley, Everett Born March 16, 1963 in Greenwood, SC. Graduate IN U. OB debut in *Stomp*, followed by *Bloomer Girl*, Bdwy in *Swing* (1996).

Brennan, Maureen Born Oct.11, 1952 in Washington, DC. Attended U Conn. Bdwy debut 1974 in *Candide* for which she received a Theatre World Award, followed by *Going Up*, *Knickerbocker Holiday*, *Little Johnny Jones*, *Stardust*, *Our Town*, OB in *Shakespeare's Cabaret*, *Cat and the Fiddle*, *Nuts and Bolts: Tightened*, *Hart & Hammerstein Centennial*.

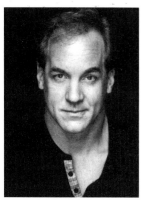

Steve Blanchard

Everett Bradley

Joel Briel

Eric Martin Brown

Briel, Joel Born Aug. 7, 1960 in San Francisco, CA. Graduate AZ St. U. Bdwy debut 1990 in *Cats*, OB in *That's Life*, followed by *Bearded Iris*.

Brightman, Julian Born March 5, 1964 in Philadelphia, PA. Graduate U. PA. OB debut 1987 in 1984, followed by *Critic, Leaves of Grass, Songbox, Look Ma, I'm Dancing, Watch Your Step*, Bdwy in *Peter Pan* (1990/1991), *Hello, Dolly!* (1995).

Broderick, Matthew Born March 21, 1963 in New York, NY. OB debut 1981 in *Torch Song Trilogy*, followed by *The Widow Claire, A Christmas Memory*, Bdwy debut 1983 in *Brighton Beach Memoirs*, for which he received a 1983 Theatre World Award, followed by *Biloxi Blues, How to Succeed in Business Without Really Trying* (1995), *Night Must Fall, Taller Than a Dwarf, The Producers*.

Broderick, William Born Oct. 19, 1954 in Queens, NY. Graduate Hunter Col. OB debut 1986 in *Pere Goriot*, followed by *The Real Inspector Hound, Iolanthe, Teasers and Tormentors, Dorian, White Widow, Rosmersholm*.

Brown, P.J. Born Nov.5, 1956 in Staten Island, New York, NY. Graduate Boston Col. Debut 1990 OB in *Othello* followed by *America Dreaming, Waiting for Lefty, Soldier's Play*, Bdwy in *Grapes of Wrath* (1990), *Burning Blue*.

Brown, Ann Born Dec. 1, 1960 in Westwood, NJ. Graduate Trinity Col. OB debut 1987 in *Pacific Overtures*, followed by *Side by Side by Sondheim, Stages, Golden Apple, 20 Fingers 20 Toes, Salute to Tom Jones and Harvey Schmidt*, Bdwy in *Once Upon a Mattress* (1996), *Sound of Music, Music Man, Tom Sawyer*.

Brown, David, Jr. Born November 15, 1971 in Flushing, NY. Attended CCNY. OB debut in *Y2K*, followed by *Up Against the Wind*.

Brown, Eric Martin Born May 20th in Syracuse, NY. Graduate NYU, Yale. Debut OB in *Servicemen*.

Brown, Jeb Born Aug. 11, 1964 in New York, NY. Graduate Yale U. Bdwy debut 1974 in *Cat on a Hot Tin Roof*, followed by *Bring Back Birdie, I'm Not Rappaport* (2002),OB in *A Walk on the Wild Side, Game Show*.

Brown, Robin Leslie Born Jan. 18th in Canandaigua, NY. Graduate LIU. OB debut 1980 in *Mother of Us All*, followed by *Yours Truly, Two Gentlemen of Verona, Taming of the Shrew, The Mollusc, The Contrast, Pericles, Andromache, Macbeth, Electra, She Stoops to Conquer, Berneice, Hedda Gabler, Midsummer Night's Dream, Three Sisters, Major Barbara, Fine Art of Finesse, Two by Schnitzler, As You Like It, Ghosts, Chekhov Very Funny, Beaux' Strategem, God of Vengeance, Good Natured Man, Twelfth Night, Little Eyolf, Venetian Twins, King Lear, Doll's House, Antigone, Venice Preserv'd, Hard Times, The Country Wife, The Miser, Merry Wives of Windsor, The Way of the World, The Oresteia, Mirandolina, John Gabriel Borkman, The Cherry Orchard*.

Brummel, David Born November 1, 1942 in Brooklyn, NY. Bdwy debut 1973 in *The Pajama Game*, followed by *Music Is, Oklahoma!, Bells Are Ringing*, OB in *Cole Porter, The Fantasticks, Prom Queens Unchained, Camilla, Carmelina, Kuni-Leml*.

Bunch, Elizabeth Born Oct. 23, 1975 in Huntington, WV. Graduate NYU. OB debut 1997 in *Water Children*, followed by *The Light Outside*.

Bundy, Laura Bell Born April 10, 1981 in Euclid, OH raised in Lexington, KY. Graduate Lexington Catholic H.S., attending NYU. Broadway debut 2002 in Hairspray, OB in *Ruthless The Musical*.

Burkett, Shannon Born in New Jersey. Graduate NYU. Bdwy debut 2000 in *The Ride Down Mt. Morgan*, OB in *Endpapers* followed by *Cavedwellers*.

Burks, Willis II Born Oct. 25, 1935 in Birmingham, AL. Attended Columbia Col. OB debut 1994 in *East Texas Hot Links*, followed by *Jitney, Saint Lucy's Eyes*.

David Burtka

Seán Campion

Len Cariou

Dana Chaifetz

Burrell, Fred Born Sept. 18, 1936. Graduate UNC, RADA. Bdwy debut 1964 in *Never Too Late*, followed by *Ilya Darling, Cactus Flower, On Golden Pond, Inherit the Wind, Judgment at Nuremberg*, OB in *The Memorandum, Throckmorton, Texas, Voices in the Head, Chili Queen, The Queen's Knight, In Pursuit of the Song of Hydrogen, Unchanging Love, More Fun Than Bowling, Woman Without a Name, Sorrows of Fredrick, Voice of the Prairie, Spain, Democracy and Esther, Last Sortie, Rough/Play, Life is a Dream, Taming of the Shrew, Twelfth Night, Modest Proposal, Oedipus at Colonus, A Hamlet, 3 in the Back 2 in the Head, True Crimes, Rhinoceros, After-Dinner Joke, The Appearance of Impropriety, On the Middle Watch, God's Creatures.*

Burtka, David Born May 29, 1975 in Dearborn, MI. Graduate U. MI. OB debut 1998 in *Beautiful Thing*, followed by *The Play about the Baby*.

Burton, Arnie Born Sept. 22, 1958 in Emmett, ID. Graduate U. AZ. Bdwy debut 1983 in *Amadeus*, OB in *Measure for Measure, Major Barbara, Schnitzler One Acts, Tartuffe, As You Like It, Ghosts, Othello, Moon for the Misbegotten, Twelfth Night, Little Eyolf, Mollusc, Venetian Twins, Beaux Stratagem, King Lear, Winter's Tale, When Ladies Battle, Barber of Seville, Mere Mortals, Cymbeline, A Will of His Own, Andromache, The Cherry Orchard, The Last Sunday in June.*

Busch, Charles Born Aug. 23, 1954 in Hartsdale, NY. Graduate Northwestern U. Debut OB 1985 in *Vampire Lesbians of Sodom* followed by *Times Square Angel, Psycho Beach Party, Lady in Question, Red Scare on Sunset, Charles Busch Revue, You Should Be So Lucky, Flipping My Wig*, all of which he also wrote, *Swingtime Canteen* (co-writer), *Shanghai Moon.*

Butler, Dan Born Dec. 2, 1954 in Huntington, IN. Attended IN U. Purdue, San Jose St. Bdwy debut 1982 in *The Hothouse*, followed by *Biloxi Blues*, OB in *True West* (1983), *Walk the Dog Whistle, Domino, Wrestlers, Emerald City, Lisbon Traviata, Much Ado about Nothing, Early One Evening at the Rainbow Bar & Grill, Only Thing Worse You Could Have Told Me* which he wrote, *Old Money.*

Butler, Kerry Born in Brooklyn, NY. Graduate Ithaca Col. Bdwy debut 1993 in *Blood Brothers*, followed by *Beauty and the Beast, Hairspray*, OB in *The "I" Word: Interns, The Folsom Head, King of Hearts, Bat Boy.*

Butz, Norbert Leo Born Jan. 30, 1967 in St. Louis, MO. Graduate Webster U., U. of AL. Bdwy debut 1996 in *Rent*, OB in *Juno and the Paycock, Saved.*

Cain, William Born May 27, 1931 in Tuscaloosa, AL. Graduate U. Wash., Catholic U. Debut 1962 OB in *Red Roses for Me*, followed by *Jericho Jim Crow, Henry V, Antigone, Relatively Speaking, I Married an Angel in Concert, Buddha, Copperhead, Forbidden City, Fortinbras, Endpapers*, Bdwy in *Wilson in the Promise Land* (1970), *You Can't Take It with You, Wild Honey, The Boys in Autumn, Mastergate, A Streetcar Named Desire The Heiress, Delicate Balance.*

Callaway, Liz Born Apr. 13, 1961 in Chicago, IL. Debut 1980 OB in *Godspell*, followed by *The Matinee Kids, Brownstone, No Way to Treat a Lady, Marry Me a Little, 1-2-3-4-5, Merrily We Roll Along in Concert*, Bdwy in *Merrily We Roll Along* (1981), *Baby, The Three Musketeers, Miss Saigon, Cats, Fiorello (Encores).*

Camp, Joanne Born April 4, 1951 in Atlanta, GA. Graduate FL Atlantic U., George Washington U. OB debut 1981 in *The Dry Martini*, followed by *Geniuses*, for which she received a 1983 Theatre World Award, *June Moon, Painting Churches, Merchant of Venice, Lady from the Sea, The Contrast, Coastal Disturbances, The Rivals, Andromache, Electra, Uncle Vanya, She Stoops to Conquer, Hedda Gabler, Heidi Chronicles, Importance of Being Earnest, Medea, Three Sisters, Midsummer Night's Dream, School for Wives, Measure for Measure, Dance of Death, Two Schnitzler One-Acts, Tartuffe, Lips Together Teeth Apart, As You Like It, Moon for the Misbegotten, Phaedra, Little Eyolf, Beaux Strategem, King Lear, Life Is a Dream, Winter's Tale, When Ladies Battle, The Guardsman, Candida, The Country Wife, The Seagull, The Way of the World, The Oresteia, John Gabriel Borkman, Blithe Spirit, The Cherry Orchard*, Bdwy in *Heidi Chronicles* (1989), *Sisters Rosensweig, Last Night of Ballyhoo, Dinner at Eight.*

Campion, Seán Born Dec. 20, 1959 in Freshford, Co. Kilkenny, Ireland. OB debut in *Stones in His Pockets.*

Carl, Gordan Born Jan. 20, 1932 in Richmond, VA. Graduate Brooklyn College. Bdwy debut 1966 in *The Great White Hope*, followed by *Ain't Supposed to Die a Natural Death, The Piano Lesson, Ma Rainey's Black Bottom*, OB in *Day of Absence, Happy Ending, The Strong Breed, Trials of Brother Jero, Kongi's Harvest, Welcome to Black River, Shark, Orrin and Sugar Mouth, A Love Play, Black Girl, The Great MacDaddy, The Sty of the Blind Pig, The River Niger, The Death of Boogie Woogie, In an Upstate Motel, Zooman and The Sign, Do Lord Remember Me, The Piano Lesson, Checkmates*.

Cariou, Len Born Sept. 30. 1939 in Winnipeg, Canada. Bdwy debut 1968 in *House of Atrew*, followed by *Henry V, Applause*, for which he received a 1970 Theatre World Award, *Night Watch, A Little Night Music, Cold Storage, Sweeney Todd, Dance a Little Closer, Teddy and Alice, The Speed of Darkness, The Dinner Party*, OB in *A Sorrow Beyond Dreams, Up from Paradise, Master Class, Day Six, Measure for Measure, Mountain, Papa*.

Carley, Christopher Murphy Born May 31, 1978 in Suffern, NY. Attended NYU. Bdwy debut 1999 in *The Beauty Queen of Leenane, A Skull in Connemara*.

Carlisle, Kitty Born Sept. 3, 1915 in New Orleans, LA. Attended RADA. Bdwy debut 1932 in *Rio Rio* followed by *Champagne, Sec; White Horse Inn; Three Waltzes; Walk With Music; The Rape of Lucretia; Anniversary Waltz; Kiss Me, Kate* (CC'56); *On Your Toes*, OB in *24 Evenings of Wit and Wisdom*.

Carmello, Carolee Born in Albany, NY. Graduate SUNY Albany. Bdwy debut 1989 in *City of Angels*, followed by *Faslettos, 1776, Parade, Scarlet Pimpernel*, OB in *I Can Get it for You Wholesale* (1991), *Hello Again, Goose, The Case of the Dead Flamingo Dancer, A Class Act*.

Carter, Aaron Born Dec. 8, 1987 in Tampa, FL. Bdwy debut 2001 in *Seussical*.

Carter, Caitlin Born Feb. 1 in San Francisco, CA. Graduate Rice U., NC School of Arts. Bdwy debut 1993 in *Ain't Broadway Grand*, followed by *Chicago, Victor Victoria, Chicago, Swing, Bells Are Ringing*.

Casey, Shawna Born in San Diego, CA. OB in *Joe & Betty.*

Celli, Bob Born Feb. 4, 1958 in Princeton, NJ. Graduate Villanova U., Rider Col. OB debut 1985 in *Vinyl*, followed by *Two Birds with One Stone, Found in the Garden, Madmen Madame and Mayhem, Jesse and the Bandit Queen, Burn This, Circle.*

Ceraso, Chris Born Sept. 23, 1952 in Leechburg, PA. Graduate U. Notre Dame, FL St. U. OB in *Summer Cyclone.*

Chaifetz, Dana Born Sept. 1 in New York, NY. OB debut 1992 in *El Barrio*, followed by *Somewhere, Halfway There, Resurrection, The Survivor, Ghost on Fire, Sitting Pretty.*

Chalfant, Kathleen Born Jan. 14, 1945 in San Francisco, CA. Graduate Stanford U. Bdwy debut 1975 in *Dance with Me*, followed by *M. Butterfly, Angels in America, Racing Demon*, OB in *Jules Feiffer's Hold Me, Killings on the Last Line, The Boor, Blood Relations, Signs of Life, Sister Mary Ignatius Explains it All, Actor's Nightmare, Faith Healer, All the Nice People, Hard Times, Investigation of the Murder in El Salvador, 3 Poets, The Crucible, The Party, Iphigenia and Other Daughters, Cowboy Pictures, Twelve Dreams, Henry V, Endgame, When It Comes Early, Nine Armenians, Phaedra in Delirium, Wit, True History and Real Adventures, Bloomer Girl* (CC), *Far Away.*

Chalfy, Dylan Born June 22, 1970 in Sarasota, FL. OB debut 1994 in *Blood Guilty*, followed by *Cross Your Heart, Home of the Brave, Big Potato*, Bdwy debut 1995 in *Rose Tattoo*, followed by *Ah, Wilderness!.*

Chamberlain, Andrea Born June 5, 1972 in Fresno, CA. Bdwy debut 1998 in *Little Me*, OB in *I Love You, You're Perfect, Now Change.*

Chamberlin, Kevin Born November 25, 1963 in Baltimore, MD. Graduate Rutgers U., OB debut 1990 in *Neddy*, followed by *Smoke on the Mountain, Ziegfeld Follies of 1936, As 1000 Cheer, Dirty Blonde*, Bdwy in *My Favorite Year* (1992), *Abe Lincoln in Illinois, One Touch of Venus* (Encores), *Triumph of Love, Seussical.*

Chandler, David Born Feb. 3, 1950 in Danbury, CT. Graduate Oberlin Col. Bdwy debut 1980 in *The American Clock*, followed by *Death of a Salesman, Lost in Yonkers*, OB in *Made in Heaven, Black Sea Follies, The Swan, Watbanaland, Phaedra, Slavs!, Working Title, What You Get and What You Expect, The Trestle at Pope Lick Creek, Cellini.*

Charles, Walter Born April 4, 1945 in East Stroudsburg, PA. Graduate Boston U. Bdwy debut 1973 in *Grease*, followed by *1600 Pennsylvania Avenue, Knickerbocker Holiday, Sweeney Todd, Cats, La Cage Aux Folles, Aspects of Love, Me and My Girl, 110 in the Shade* (NYCO), *A Christmas Carol, Boys From Syracuse*, OB in *Wit, Tenderloin, The Immigrant.*

Charney, Jordan Born April 1, 1937 in New York, NY. Graduate Brooklyn Col. OB in *Harry, Noon and Night, A Place for Chance, Hang Down Your Head and Die, The Pinter Plays, Telemachus Clay, Zoo Story, Viet Rock, MacBird, Red Cross, Glorious Ruler, Waiting for Godot, Slow Memories, One Flew Over the Cuckoo's Nest, Boy Who Came to Leave, Cretan Bull, Naomi Court, Sublime Lives, Waste, Code of the West, Troilus and Cressida*, Bdwy in *Slapstick Tragedy* (1966), *The Birthday Party, Talley's Folly.*

Chernov, Hope Born June 13 in Philadelphia, PA. Graduate Temple U., U. CA Irvine. OB debut 1996 in *Barber of Seville*, followed by *Venice Preserv'd, As Bees in Honey Drown, Richard II, Miss Julie, School for Scandal, The Country Wife, The Seagull, Blithe Spirit, Julius Caesar.*

Chiasson, Gilles Born November 1, 1966 in Muskegon, MI. Graduate U. MI. OB debut 1992 in *Groundhog*, followed by *Fermat's Last Tango*, Bdwy 1996 in *Rent*, followed by *Scarlet Pimpernel, The Civil War, La Boheme.*

Christopher, Thom Born Oct. 5, 1940 in Jackson Heights, NY. Attended Ithaca Col., Neighborhood Playhouse. Debut 1972 OB in *One Flew Over the Cuckoo's Nest*, followed by *Tamara, Investigation of the Murder in El Salvador, Sublime Lives, Triumph of Love, The Changeling, Den of Thieves, Night Becoming Jasmine, Knepp*, Bdwy in *Emperor Henry IV* (1973), *Noel Coward in Two Keys*, for which he received a 1974 Theatre World Award, *Caesar and Cleopatra.*

Kevin Chamberlin

Tanya Clarke

Jennifer Cody

Lynn Cohen

Cissel, Charles Born July 31, 1956 in Denville, NJ. Attended CT. Col. of Dance. OB in *Period of Adjustment, The Country Girl, All Over.*

Ciulla, Celeste Born Sept. 10, 1967 in New York, NY. Graduate Northwestern U., Harvard. OB debut 1992 in *Othello*, followed by *The Good Natured Man, Phaedra, Fair Fight, A Will of His Own, Andromache.*

Clark, Phillip Born Aug. 12, 1941 in San Diego, CA. Attended USCal. Bdwy debut 1966 in *We Have Always Lived in the Castle*, followed by *Fifth of July*, OB in *The Boys in the Band, A Last Dance For Sybil.*

Clarke, Tanya Born Feb. 2, 1972, in Chicago, IL. OB debut in *The Director*, followed by *Bobbi Boland.*

Clayton, Lawrence Born Oct. 10, 1956 in Mocksville, NC. Attended NC Central U. Debut 1980 in *Tambourines to Glory*, followed by *Skyline, Across the Universe, Two by Two, Romance in Hard Times, Juba, Tapestry, Saturn Returns*, Bdwy in *Dreamgirls* (1984), *High Rollers, Once Upon a Mattress, The Civil War, Bells Are Ringing.*

Cody, Jennifer Born November 10, 1969 in Rochester, NY. Graduate SUNY Fredonia. OB debut 1992 in *Anyone Can Whistle*, followed by *The Wild Party*, Bdwy in *Cats* (1994), *Grease, Seussical.*

Cofield, Carl Jay Born Dec. 19 in Fulda, Germany. Attended U. of Miami, RADA. OB debut 1995 in *Henry V*, followed by *As You Like It, Mud River Stone, Desire Under the Elms, The In-Gathering.*

Cohen, Lynn Born Aug. 10 in Kansas City, MO. Graduate Northwestern U. OB debut 1979 in *Don Juan Comes Back From the Wars*, followed by *Getting Out, The Arbor, Cat and the Canary, Suddenly Last Summer, Bella Figura, The Smash, Chinese Viewing Pavilion, Isn't It Romantic, Total Eclipse, Angelo's Wedding, Hamlet, Love Diatribe, A Couple with a Cat, XXX Love Acts, Model Apt., The Devils, Knee Desires the Dirt, Paradise Island*, Bdwy in *Orpheus Descending* (1989), *Ivanov.*

Coleman, Rosalyn Born July 20, 1965 in Ann Arbor, MI. Graduate Harvard U., Yale U. Bdwy debut 1990 in *Piano Lesson*, followed by *Mule Bone, Seven Guitars*, OB in *Destiny of Me* (1992), *Major Crimes, Old Settler, Flight to Freedom, Wyoming, Bitter Tears of Petra Von Kant, Breath, Boom.*

Colin, Margaret Born May 26, 1957 in Brooklyn, NYC. OB in *Sight Unseen, Aristocrats, Psychopathia Sexualis*, Bdwy debut 1997 in *Jackie* for which she received a Theatre World Award, followed by *A Day in Death a Joe Egg.*

Comley, Bonnie Born in MA. Graduate Emerson Col. OB debut 1988 in *Noo Yawk Tawk*, followed by *Fortune's Fools, If It Was Easy.*

Cone, Michael Born Oct. 7, 1952 in Fresno, CA. Graduate U. WA. Bdwy debut 1980 in *Brigadoon*, followed by *Christmas Carol, La Boheme*, OB in *Bar Mitzvah Boy, The Rink, Commedia Tonite!, London Cuckolds.*

Conlin, Vanessa Born in Texas. Graduate Manhattan School of Music, Graduate B.U. Broadway debut 2002 in *La Boheme.*

Connell, Gordon Born March 19, 1923 in Berkeley, CA. Graduate U. CA., NYU. Bdwy debut 1961 in *Subways are for Sleeping*, followed by *Hello, Dolly!, Lysistrata, Human Comedy* (also OB), *Big River*, OB in *Beggars Opera, Butler Did It, With Love and Laughter, Deja Review, Good Doctor, Leave It to Me, Comedians.*

Connell, Jane Born Oct. 27, 1925 in Berkeley, CA. Attended U. CA. Bdwy debut in *New Faces of 1956*, followed by *Drat! The Cat!, Mame* (1966/83), *Dear World, Lysistrata, Me and My Girl, Lend a Tenor, Crazy For You, Moon Over Buffalo, Tom Sawyer*, OB in *Shoestring Revue, Threepenny Opera, Pieces of Eight, Demi-Dozen, She Stoops to Conquer, Drat!, Real Inspector Hound, Rivals, Rise and Rise of Daniel Rocket, Laughing Stock, Singular Dorothy Parker, No No Nanette in Concert, Good Doctor, 70 Girls 70.*

Conolly, Patricia Born Aug. 29, 1933 in Tabora, East Africa. Attended U. Sydney. With APA in *You Can't Take It With You, War and Peace, School for Scandal, Wild Duck, Right You Are, We Comrades Three, Pantagleize, Exit the King, Cherry Orchard, Misanthrope, Cocktail Party, Cock-a-doodle Dandy, Streetcar Named Desire, Importance of Being Earnest, The Circle, Small Family Business, Real Inspector Hound/15 Minute Hamlet, Heiress, Tartuffe: Born Again, Sound of Music, Waiting in the Wings, Judgment at Nuremberg*, OB in *Blithe Spirit, Woman in Mind, Misalliance.*

Bonnie Comley

Patricia Conolly

Joan Copeland

Joseph Costa

Conroy, Jarlath Born Sept. 30, 1944 in Galway, Ireland. Attended RADA. Bdwy debut 1976 in *Comedians*, followed by *The Elephant Man*, *Macbeth*, *Ghetto*, *The Visit*, *On the Waterfront*, *The Iceman Cometh*, OB in *Translations*, *The Wind that Shook the Barley*, *Gardenia*, *Friends*, *Playboy of the Western World*, *One-Act Festival*, *Abel & Bela/Architect*, *The Matchmaker*, *Henry V*, *Our Lady of Sligo*, *Bloomer Girl*, *A Man of No Importance*.

Conroy, Maryellen Born Aug. 31, 1947 in White Plains, NY. Graduate Pace U. Bdwy debut 1994 in *Inspector Calls*.

Converse, Frank Born May 22, 1938 in St. Louis, MO. Attended Carnegie Mellon U. Bdwy debut 1966 in *First One Asleep Whistle*, followed by *The Philadelphia Story*, *Brothers*, *Design for Living*, *A Streetcar Named Desire*, *Our Town*, OB in *House of Blue Leaves*, *Lady in the Dark in Concert*, *Thief River*.

Conway, Kevin Born May 29, 1941 in NYC. Debut 1968 in *Muzeeka* followed by *Saved*, *Plough and the Stars*, *One Flew Over the Cuckoo's Nest*, *When You Comin' Back Red Ryder*, *Long Day's Journey into Night*, *Other Places*, *King John*, *Other People's Money*, *Man Who Fell in Love with His Wife*, *Ten Below*, Bdwy in *Indians* (1969), *Moonchildren*, *Of Mice and Men*, *Elephant Man*, *On the Waterfront*, *Dinner at Eight*.

Cook, Victor Trent Born Aug. 19, 1967 in New York, NY. OB debut 1976 in *Joseph and the Amazing Technicolor Dreamcoat*, followed by *Haggadah*, *Moby Dick*, *Romance in Hard Times*, *Cinderella*, Bdwy in *Don't Get God Started* (1988), *Starmites* (also OB), *Smokey Joe's Cafe*, *Street Corner Symphony*, *St. Louis Woman* (Encores).

Copeland, Joan Born June 1, 1922 in New York, NY. Attended Brooklyn Col., AADA. OB debut 1945 in *Romeo and Juliet*, followed by *Othello*, *Conversation Piece*, *Delightful Season*, *End of Summer*, *The American Clock*, *The Double Game*, *Isn't it Romantic?* *Hunting Cockroaches*, *Young Playwrights Festival*, *The American Plan*, *Rose Quartet*, *Another Time*, *A Dybbuk*, *Over the River and Through the Woods*, *Fishkin Touch*, *The Torchbearers*, *Second Summer*, *24 Evenings of Wit and Wisdom*, Bdwy in *Sundown Beach*, *Detective Story*, *Not for Children*, *Hatful of Fire*, *Something More*, *The Price*, *Two by Two*, *Pal Joey*, *Checking Out*, *The American Clock*.

Corbett, Patricia Born Feb. 17, 1940 in North Hollywood, CA. Graduate UCLA Opera Dept. Bdwy debut in *La Boheme*.

Corbo, Georgina Born Sept. 21, 1965 in Havana, Cuba. Attended SUNY Purchase. OB debut 1988 in *Ariano*, followed by *Born to Rumba*, *Mambo Louie and the Dancing Machine*, *Ghost Sonata*, *You Can't Win*, *Dog Lady*, *The Bundle*, *Family Affair*, *The House Must be Dismantled*.

Costa, Joseph Born June 8, 1946 in Ithaca, NY. Graduate Gettysburg Col., Yale U. OB debut 1978 in *The Show Off*, followed by *The Tempest*, *The Changeling*, *A Map of the World*, *Julius Caesar*, *Titus Andronicus*, *Love's Labor's Lost*, *Macbeth*, *The Crucible*, *The Way of the World*, *The Clearing*, Bdwy in *Gore Vidal's The Best Man*.

Cover, Bradford Born Jan. 26, 1967 in New York, NY. Graduate Denison U., U. WI. OB debut 1994 in *King Lear*, followed by *Beaux Strategem*, *Venetian Twins*, *Oedipus at Colonus*, *Mrs. Warren's Profession*, *Winter's Tale*, *Life Is a Dream*, *When Ladies Battle*, *Antigone*, *Misalliance*, *The Forest*, *School for Scandal*, *Richard II*, Bdwy in *A Thousand Clowns*.

Cowan, Edwardyne Born July 23 in Queens, NY. Graduate New Rochelle Col. OB debut 1992 in *The Molly Maguires*, followed by *Anything Goes*, *Lakme*, Bdwy 1993 in *My Fair Lady*, *Fermat's Last Tango*.

Cox, Veanne Born Jan. 19, 1963 in VA. Bdwy debut 1986 in *Smile*, followed by *Company*, *The Dinner Party*, OB in *Nat'l Lampoon's Class of '86*, *Flora the Red Menace*, *Showing Off*, *Food Chain*, *Question of Mercy*, *Waiting Room*, *Batting Cage*, *Labor Day*, *Freedomland*, *The Altruists*.

Coxe, Helen P. Born Oct. 19, 1967 in Bryn Mawr, PA. Graduate U. of Hartford, ACT. Bdwy debut 1999 in *Sideman*, OB in *My Mother's a Baby Boy*.

Crain, Todd Alan Born May 16, 1972 in WI. Graduate Otterbien Col. OB debut in *Personals*.

Cravens, Pierce Born Jan. 8, 1986 in Dallas, TX. OB debut 1993 in *All's Well that Ends Well*, Bdwy debut 1994 in *Beauty and the Beast*, followed by *Tom Sawyer*.

Crawford, Michael Born Jan. 19, 1942 in Salisbury, Wiltshire, Eng. Bdwy debut 1967 in *Black Comedy* followed by *Phantom of the Opera*, *Dance of the Vampires*.

Todd Alan Crain

Joseph Culliton

Nicholas Cutro

Lisa Datz

Croft, Paddy Born in Worthing, England. Attended Avondale Col. OB debut 1961 OB in *The Hostage*, followed by *Billy Liar, Live Like Pigs, Hogan's Goat, Long Day's Journey into Night, Shadow of a Gunman, Pygmalion, Plough and the Stars, Kill, Starting Monday, Philadelphia Here I Come!, Grandchild of Kings, Fragments, Same Old Moon, Nightingale and Not the Lark, Da, James Joyce's The Dead, A Life*, Bdwy in *Killing of Sister George, Prime of Miss Jean Brodie, Crown Matrimonial, Major Barbara, Night Must Fall, The Dead*.

Crosby, B.J. Born November 23, 1952 in New Orleans, LA. Bdwy debut 1995 in *Smokey Joe's Café*, OB in *Tea Time*, followed by *Harlem Song*.

Crudup, Billy Born July 8, 1968 in Manhasset, NY. Graduate U. NC, NYU. OB debut 1994 in *America Dreaming*, followed by *Oedipus, Measure for Measure*, Bdwy debut 1995 in *Arcadia*, for which he received a 1995 Theatre World Award, followed by *Bus Stop, Three Sisters*.

Cruikshank, Holly Born June 18, 1973 in Scottsdale, AZ. Attended NC School of Arts. Bdwy debut in *Hello Dolly* (1995), followed by *Fosse, Movin' Out*.

Culkin, Macaulay Born Aug. 26, 1980 in New York, NY. OB debut 2001 in *Madame Melville*, for which he received a 2001 Theatre World Award.

Culliton, Joseph Born Jan. 25, 1948 in Boston, MA. Attended CA. St. U. OB debut 1982 in *Francis*, followed by *Flirtations, South Pacific* (LC), *Julius Caesar, King John, Company, On a Clear Day, Bald Soprano*, Bdwy debut 1987 in *Broadway*, followed by *Gore Vidal's The Best Man*.

Cullum, John Born March 2, 1930 in Knoxville, TN. Graduate U. TN. Bdwy debut 1960 in *Camelot*, followed by *Infidel Caesar, The Rehearsal, Hamlet, On a Clear Day You Can See Forever*, for which he received a 1966 Theatre World Award, *Man of La Mancha, 1776, Vivat! Vivat Regina!, Shenandoah* (1975/1989), *Kings, Trip Back Down, On the 20th Century, Deathtrap, Doubles, You Never Can Tell, Boys in Autumn, Aspect of Love, Show Boat*, OB in *3 Hand Reel, The Elizabethans, Carousel, In the Voodoo Parlor of Marie Leveau, King and 1, Whistler, All My Sons, Urinetown, Old Money*.

Cumpsty, Michael Born in England. Graduate UNC. Bdwy debut 1989 in *Artist Descending a Staircase*, followed by *La Bete, Timon of Athens, Translations, Heiress, Racing Demon, 1776, Electra, Copenhagen, 42nd Street*, OB in *Art of Success, Man and Superman, Hamlet, Cymbeline, Winter's Tale, King John, Romeo and Juliet, All's Well That Ends Well, Timon of Athens*.

Curless, John Born Sept. 16 in Wigan, England. Attended Central Sch. of Speech. OB debut 1982 in *The Entertainer*, followed by *Sus, Up 'n' Under, Progress, Prin, Nightingale, Absent Friends, Owners/Traps, Comic Potential, Passion Play*, Bdwy in *A Small Family Business* (1992), *Racing Demon, King and I, Sound of Music*.

Curtin, Catherine Born in New York, NY. Graduate Princeton U. Bdwy debut 1990 in *Six Degrees of Separation*, OB in *Gulf War, Making Book, Orphan Muses, Aimee and Hope, Love, Janis*.

Cutro, Nicholas Born April 28, 1988 in New York, NY. Bdwy debut 2000 in *The Time of the Cuckoo* (LC), followed by *The Full Monty*.

Cyr, Myriam Born in New Brunswick, Canada. Attended Cons. d'Art Dramatique de Montreal, Ecole Nat'l de Strasbourg, LAMDA. OB debut 1995 in *Floating Rhoda and the Glue Man*, followed by *Green Bird, Antigone, Brave Ubu, Cartas: A Nun in Love, In Transit*.

D'Abruzzo, Stephanie Born in Pittsburgh, PA. Graduate Northwestern U. OB debut 2002 in *Carnival* (Encores! 2002), followed by *Encores! 10th Anniversary Bash, Avenue Q*.

Dafoe, Willem (William). Born July 22, 1955. Has performed with OB's Wooster Group since 1977. OB in *Hairy Ape*, followed by *Brace Up!*

Danson, Randy Born April 30, 1950 in Plainfield NJ. Graduate Carnegie-Mellon U. Debut 1978 OB in *Gimme Shelter* followed by *Big and Little, Winter Dancers, Time Steps, Casualties, Red and Blue, Resurrection of Lady Lester, Jazz Poets at the Grotto, Plenty, Macbeth, Blue Window, Cave Life, Romeo and Juliet, One-Act Festival, Mad Forest, Triumph of Love, The Treatment, Phaedra, Arts & Leisure, The Devils, The Erinyes, First Picture Show, Portia Coughlan, Eight Days (Backwards)*.

Stephen DeRosa

Erik Devine

David de Vries

Cliff Diamond

Daily, Daniel Born July 25, 1955 in Chicago, IL. Graduate Notre Dame U., U. WA. OB debut 1988 in *Boy's Breath*, followed by *A Ronde, Iron Bars, Chekhov Very Funny, Macbeth, As You Like It, Free Zone, Scarlet Letter, Two Nikita, The Adoption, Tenth Man, Helmut Sees America, School for Scandal, Richard II, Angel Street, The Country Wife, The Seagull, The Way of the World, The Oresteia, Merry Wives of Windsor, Mirandolina, The Cherry Orchard.*

Danieley, Jason Born July 13, 1971 in St. Louis, MO. Attended So. IL U. OB debut 1994 in *Hit the Lights*, followed by *Floyd Collins, Trojan Women: A Love Story*, Bdwy in *Allegro* (Encores 1994), *Candide* (1997), for which he received a 1997 Theatre World Award, *Strike Up the Band* (Encores), *The Fully Monty*.

Danner, Blythe Born Feb. 3, 1944 in Philadelphia, PA. Graduate Bard Col. OB debut 1966 in *The Infantry*, followed by *Collision Course, Summertree, Up Eden, Someone's Comin' Hungry, Cyrano, Miser*, for which she received a 1969 Theatre World Award, *Twelfth Night, New York Idea, Much Ado About Nothing, Love Letters, Sylvia, Moonlight, Ancestral Voices*, Bdwy in *Butterflies are Free, Betrayal, Philadelphia Story, Blithe Spirit, Streetcar Named Desire, Deep Blue Sea, Follies* 2001.

Danson, Randy Born April 30, 1950 in Plainfield NJ. Graduate Carnegie Mellon U. OB debut 1978 in *Gimme Shelter*, followed by *Big and Little, Winter Dancers, Time Steps, Casualties, Red and Blue, Resurrection of Lady Lester, Jazz Poets at the Grotto, Plenty, Macbeth, Blue Window, Cave Life, Romeo and Juliet, One-Act Festival, Mad Forest, Triumph of Love, The Treatment, Phaedra, Arts & Leisure, The Devils, The Erinyes, First Picture Show, Portia Coughlan, The Winter's Tale, Saved.*

Darlow, Cynthia Born June 13, 1949 in Detroit, MI. Attended NC Sch of Arts, PA St. U. OB debut 1974 in *This Property Is Condemned*, followed by *Portrait of a Madonna, Clytemnestra, Unexpurgated Memoirs of Bernard Morgandigler, Actor's Nightmare, Sister Mary Ignatius Explains.., Fables for Friends, That's It Folks!, Baby with the Bath Water, Dandy Dick, Naked Truth, Cover of Life, Death Defying Acts, Mere Mortals, Once in a Lifetime, Til the Rapture Comes, Sex, Juno and the Paycock, Hank Williams: Lost Highway,* Bdwy in *Grease* (1976), *Rumors, Prelude to a Kiss* (also OB), *Sex and Longing, Taller Than a Dwarf.*

Datz, Lisa Born April 24, 1973 in Evanston, IL. Graduate U. of MI. Bdwy debut 1997 in *Titanic*, followed by *The Full Monty.*

David, Keith Born May 8, 1954 in New York, NY. Juilliard Graduate. OB debut 1979 in *Othello*, followed by *The Haggadah, Pirates of Penzance, Macbeth, Coriolanus, Titus Andronicus, The Winter's Tale, Euripides' Medea, Kit Marlowe,* Bdwy in *Jelly's Last Jam* (1992), *Seven Guitars.*

Davidson, Jack Born July 17, 1936 in Worcester, MA. Graduate Boston U. OB debut 1968 OB in *Moon for the Misbegotten*, followed by *Big and Little, Battle of Angels, A Midsummer Night's Dream, Hot L Baltimore, Tribute to Lili Lamont, Ulysses in Traction, Lulu, Hey Rube!, In the Recovery Lounge, Runner Stumbles, Winter Signs, Hamlet, Mary Stuart, Ruby Ruby Sam Sam, The Diviners, Marching to Georgia, Hunting Scenes from Lower Bavaria, Richard II, Great Grandson of Jedediah Kohler, Buck, Time Framed, Love's Labour's Lost, Bing and Walker, After the Dancing in Jericho, Fair Country, Twelfth Night,* Bdwy in *Capt. Brassbound's Conversion* (1972), *Anna Christie, The Price, Shimada, Ah, Wilderness!, Judgment at Nuremberg.*

Davis, Mary Bond Born June 3, 1958 in Los Angeles, CA. Attended Cal. State U./Northridge, LACC. Debut 1985 in *Trousers* followed by *Hysterical Blindness, Scapin,* Bdwy in *Mail* (1988), followed by *Jelly's Last Jam, Hairspray .*

Day, Jamie Born in Decatur, IL. Graduated from NKU. OB debut 2002 in *Debbie Does Dallas.*

Dee, Ruby Born Oct. 27, 1923 in Cleveland, OH. Graduate Hunter Col. Bdwy debut 1946 in *Jeb*, followed by *Anna Lucasta, Smile of the World, Long Way Home, Raisin in the Sun, Purlie Victorious, Checkmates* (1988), OB in *World of Sholom Aleichem, Boesman and Lena, Wedding Band, Hamlet, Take It from the Top, Checkmates* (1995), *My One Good Nerve, Saint Lucy's Eyes, A Last Dance for Sybil.*

de Jong, Alexander Born Oct. 2, 1962 in Holland. Attended Amsterdam Th. Sch. Bdwy debut 1993 in *My Fair Lady*, followed by *42nd Street.*

Delany, Dana Born March 13, 1956 in New York, NY. Graduate Wesleyan U. Bdwy debut 1980 in *A Life* (also 2000), followed by *Blood Moon, Translations,* OB in *Dinner with Friends.*

Natascia Diaz

Douglas Dickerman

Ed Dixon

Kathleen Early

Delaria, Lea Born 1962 in Belleville, IL. OB debut 1997 in *On the Town* (also Bdwy), for which she received a 1998 Theatre World Award, followed by *Mineola Twins*, Bdwy debut 1998 in *Li'l Abner* (Encores), followed by *The Rocky Horror Show*.

DeLavallade, Carmen Born March 6, 1931 in New Orleans, LA. Bdwy debut 1954 in *House of Flowers*, followed by *Josephine Baker and Company*, OB in *Othello*, *Departures*, *The Dreams of Clytemnestra*, *Island Memories*, *24 Evenings of Wit and Wisdom*.

DeMunn, Jeffrey Born April 15, 1947 in Buffalo, NY. Graduate Union Col. Debut 1975 OB in *Augusta* followed by *A Prayer for My Daughter*, *Modigliani*, *Chekhov Sketchbook*, *Midsummer Night's Dream*, *Total Abandon*, *Country Girl*, *Hands Of Its Enemy*, *One Shoe Off*, *Gun-Shy*, Bdwy in *Comedians* (1976), *Bent*, *K2*, *Sleight of Hand*, *Spoils of War*, *Our Town*.

Dennehy, Brian Born July 9, 1938 in Bridgeport, CT. Debut 1988 OB in *Cherry Orchard* followed by Bdwy 1995 in *Translations*, *Death of a Salesman*, *Long Day's Journey into Night*.

De Ocampo, Ramón Attended Carnegie Mellon U. OB debut in *The Taming of the Shrew*, followed by *Birth Marks*, *Middle-finger*.

DeRosa, Stephen Born June 10, 1968 in New York, NY. Graduate Georgetown U., Yale U. OB debut 1998 in *Love's Fire*, followed by *Mystery of Irma Vep*, *Do Re Mi*, *Wonderful Town*, *The It Girl*, *Newyorker*, Bdwy in *The Man Who Came to Dinner*.

DeShields, Andre Born Jan. 12, 1946 in Baltimore, MD. Graduate U. WI. Bdwy debut 1973 in *Warp*, followed by *Rachel Lily Rosenbloom*, *The Wiz*, *Ain't Misbehavin'* (1978/1988), *Harlem Nocturne*, *Just So*, *Stardust*, *Play On*, *The Full Monty*, OB in *2008-1/2 Jazzbo Brown*, *Soldier's Tale*, *Little Prince*, *Haarlem Nocturne*, *Sovereign State of Boogedy Boogedy*, *Kiss Me When It's Over*, *Saint Tous*, *Ascension Day*, *Casino Paradise*, *The Wiz*, *Angel Levine*, *Ghost Cafe*, *Good Doctor*.

Devine, Erik Born May 3, 1954 in Galveston, TX. Graduate U. Tulsa, Wayne St. U. Bdwy debut 1983 in *Cats*, followed by *Sid Caesar & Co.*, *Allegro in Concert*, *Seussical*, OB in *Plain and Fancy*, *Lucky Stiff*.

de Vries, David Born August 28, 1958 in Binghampton, NY. Graduate American U. Bdwy debut 1999 in *Beauty and the Beast*.

De Vries, Jon Born March 26, 1947 in New York, NY. Graduate Bennington Col. Pasadena Playhouse. OB debut 1977 in *Cherry Orchard*, followed by *Agamemnon*, *Ballad of Soapy Smith*, *Titus Andronicus*, *Dreamer Examines his Pillow*, *Sight Unseen*, *Patient A*, *Scarlet Letter*, *One Flea Spare*, *Red Address*, *Kit Marlowe*, Bdwy in *Inspector General*, *Devour the Snow*, *Major Barbara*, *Execution of Justice*.

Deyle, John Born in Rochester, NY. Graduate NC. Sch. of the Arts. OB debut 1986 in *The Pajama Game*, followed by *Pageant*, *Pal Joey* (Encores), *Urinetown*, Bdwy debut 1979 in *Annie*, followed by *Footloose*, *Camelot* (1980).

Diamond, Cliff Born April 21, 1965 in New York, NY. Graduate Colby Col., Col. of William and Mary. Debut OB in *The Soul of an Intruder*.

Diaz, Natascia Born Jan. 4, 1970 in Lugano, Switzerland. Graduate Carnegie Mellon U. OB debut 1993 in *Little Prince*, followed by *I Won't Dance*, *Bright Lights*, *Big City*, *Saturday Night Fever*, Bdwy in *Seussical*, followed by *Man of La Mancha*.

Dickerman, Douglas Born July 30, 1974 in Livingston, NJ. Graduate Ithaca Col. OB debut in *Never Swim Alone*.

Dickson, James Born Jan. 5, 1949 in Akron, OH. Attended NYATA. OB debut 1971 *in One Flew Over the Cuckoo's Nest*, followed by *Automatic Earth*, *Don't Blink*.

Dillane, Stephen Born March 27, 1957 in London, England. Bdwy debut 2000 in *The Real Thing*.

Christine Ebersole

Jennifer Ehle

Jennie Eisenhower

Jeremy Ellison-Gladstone

Dillon, Mia Born July 9, 1955 in Colorado Springs, CO. Graduate Penn State U. Bdwy debut 1977 in *Equus*, followed by *Da, Once a Catholic, Crimes of the Heart, The Corn is Green, Hay Fever, The Miser*, OB in *The Crucible, Summer, Waiting for the Parade, Crimes of the Heart, Fables for Friends, Scenes from La Ve de Boheme, Three Sisters, Wednesday, Roberta in Concert, Come Back Little Sheba, Venna Notes, George White's Scandals, Lady Moonsong, Mr. Monsoon, Almost Perfect, The Aunts, Approximating Mother, Remembrance, Lauren's Whereabouts, New England, With and Without, Cape Cod Souvenirs* .

Dilly, Erin Born May 12, 1972 in Royal Oak, MI. Graduate U. MI. OB debut 1999 in *Things You Shouldn't Say Past Midnight*, Bdwy in *Follies* 2001, *Boys from Syracuse*.

Dixon, Ed Born Sept. 2, 1948 in OK. Attended U. OK. Bdwy in *The Student Prince*, followed by *No, No, Nanette, Rosalie in Concert, The Three Musketeers, Les Miserables, Cyrano: The Musical, Scarlet Pimpernel, The Iceman Cometh, Gore Vidal's The Best Man*, OB in *By Bernstein, King of the Schnorrers, Rabboni, Hunchback of Notre Dame, Moby Dick, Shylock, Johnny Pye and the Foolkiller, America's Sweetheart, On a Clear Day You Can See Forever* (CC).

Dixon, MacIntyre Born Dec. 22, 1931 in Everett, MA. Graduate Emerson Col. Bdwy debut 1965 in *Xmas in Las Vegas*, followed by *Cop-Out, Story Theatre, Metamorphosis, Twigs, Over Here, Once in a Lifetime, Alice in Wonderland, 3 Penny Opera, A Funny Thing Happened on the Way to the Forum* (1996), *Tempest, 1776, Getting and Spending*, OB in *Quare Fellow, Plays for Bleecker Street, Stewed Prunes, The Cat's Pajamas, Three Sisters, 3 X 3, Second City, Mad Show, Meow!, Lotta, Rubbers, Conjuring an Event, His Majesty the Devil, Tomfoolery, A Christmas Carol, Times and Appetites of Toulouse Lautrec, Room Service, Sills and Company, Little Murders, Much Ado about Nothing, A Winter's Tale, Arms and the Man, Hamlet, Pericles, Luck Pluck Virtue, A Country Christmas Carol, Taming of the Shrew, Comic Potential*.

Dorfman, Robert Born Oct. 8, 1950 in Brooklyn, NY. Attended CCNY. OB debut 1979 in *Say Goodnight Gracie*, followed by *America Kicks, Winterplay, Normal Heart, Waving Goodbye, Richard II, When She Died, A Dybbuk, The Wax*, Bdwy in *Social Security* (1987).

Duell, William Born Aug. 30, 1923 in Corinth, NY. Attended Wesleyan U., Yale U. OB debut 1962 in *Portrait of the Artist as a Young Man/Barroom Monks*, followed by *A Midsummer Night's Dream, Henry IV, Taming of the Shrew, The Memorandum Threepenny Opera, Loves of Cass Maguire, Romance Language, Hamlet, Henry IV (I & II), On the Bum, Arsenic and Old Lace*, Bdwy in *A Cook for Mr. General, Ballad of the Sad Cafe, Ilya Darling, 1776, Kings, Stages, Inspector General, Marriage of Figaro, Our Town, A Funny Thing Happened on the Way to the Forum* (1996), *The Man Who Came To Dinner*.

Dutton, Charles S. Born Jan.30, 1951 in Baltimore, MD. Graduate Yale. Debut 1983 OB in *Richard III* followed by *Pantomime, Fried Chicken and Invisibility, Splendid Mummer*, Bdwy in *Ma Rainey's Black Bottom* for which he received a Theatre World Award, *Piano Lesson, St. Louis Woman (Encores), Ma Rainey's Black Bottom* .

Dys, Deanna Born April 23, 1966 in Dearborn, MI. Bdwy debut 1988 in *Legs Diamond*, followed by *Meet Me in St. Louis, Crazy for You, Candide* (1997), *Annie Get Your Gun*.

Dysart, Eric Born in Cleveland, OH. Bdwy debut 2002 in *Hairspray*.

Eagan, Daisy Born November 4, 1979 in Brooklyn, NY. Attended Neighborhood Playhouse. OB debut 1988 in *Tiny Tim's Christmas Carol*, followed by *The Little Prince, James Joyce's The Dead, Where Everything is Everything*, Bdwy debut 1989 in *Les Miserables*, followed by *The Secret Garden*.

Earle, Dottie Born Oct. 6, 1962 in Norwalk, CT. Graduate U. MA. OB debut 1989 in *Up Against It*, followed by *Radio City Christmas Spectacular*, Bdwy in *The Will Rogers Follies* (1993), *Follies* 2001.

Early, Kathleen Born Oct. 31 in Irving, TX. Graduate U. of OK. OB debut in *The Play about the Baby*.

Camilla Enders

Raúl Esparza

Katie Finneran

Thomas Michael Fiss

Easton, Richard Born March 22, 1933 in Montreal, Canada. Bdwy debut 1957 in *The Country Wife*, for which he received a 1958 Theatre World Award, followed by *Back to Methuselah*, with APA in *Anatol, Man and Superman, The Seagull, Exit the King, Pantagleize, The Cherry Orchard, Misanthrope, Cock-a-doodle Dandy*, and *Hamlet*, OB in *Salad Days, Murderous Angels, Waste, Hotel Universe, Give Me Your Answer, Do!, The Invention of Love*.

Ebersole, Christine Born Feb. 21, 1953 in Park Forest, IL. Attended AADA. Bdwy debut 1976 in *Angel Street*, followed by *I Love My Wife, On the 20th Century, Oklahoma, Camelot, Harrigan and Hart, Getting Away with Murder, Gore Vidal's The Best Man, 42nd Street*, OB in *Green Pond, Three Sisters, Geniuses, Ziegfeld Follies of 1936, Current Events, A Connecticut Yankee in King Arthur's Court* (CC).

Edelman, Gregg Born Sept. 12, 1958 in Chicago, IL. Graduate Northwestern U. Bdwy debut 1982 in *Evita*, followed by *Oliver!, Cats, Cabaret, City of Angels, Falsettos, Anna Karenina, Passion, Fiorello* (Encores), *Out of This World* (Encores), *1776, Les Miserables*, OB in *Weekend, Shop on Main Street, Forbidden Broadway, She Loves Me, Babes in Arms, Make Someone Happy, Greetings, Standing By, Round About, Thief River*.

Egan, John Treacy Born July 10, 1962 in New York, NY. Graduate SUNY Purchase, Attended Westchester Comm Col. OB debut 1990 in *Whatnot, followed by When Pigs Fly, Bat Boy*, Bdwy in *Jekyll & Hyde* (1997).

Ehle, Jennifer Born Dec. 29, 1969 in NC. Bdwy debut 2000 in *The Real Thing*.

Eisenberg, Ned Born Jan. 13, 1957 in New York, NY. Attended Acl. Inst. of Arts. OB debut 1980 in *Time of the Cuckoo*, followed by *Our Lord of Lynchville, Dream of a Blacklisted Actor, Second Avenue, Moving Targets, Claus, Titus Adronicus, Saturday Morning Cartoons, Antigone in NY, Green Bird, Red Address, Bloomer Girl* (CC), Bdwy in *Pal Joey* (Encores, 1995).

Eisenhower, Jennie Born Aug. 15, 1978 in San Clemente, CA. Graduate Northwestern U. OB debut 2000 in *Suburb*.

Elder, David Born July 7, 1966 in Houston, TX. Attended U. Houston. Bdwy debut 1992 in *Guys and Dolls*, followed by *Beauty and the Beast, Once Upon a Mattress, Titanic, Strike Up the Band* (Encores), *42nd Street*.

Elkins, Elizabeth Born July 24, 1967 in Ft. Lauderdale, FL. OB debut 1991 in *Blue Window*, followed by *Lion in the Streets, Never the Same Rhyme Twice, Night of Knave, Bobby Supreme, Vegetable Love, The Censor, South of No North*.

Ellison-Gladstone, Jeremy Born Oct. 20, 1976 in Concord, NH. Graduate Oberlin Col. OB debut 1999 in *Out of the Blue*, followed by *The Fantasticks, Game Show*.

Emery, Lisa Born Jan. 29 in Pittsburgh, PA. Graduate Hollins Col. OB debut 1981 in *In Connecticut, followed by Talley & Son, Dalton's Back, Grownups!, The Matchmaker, Marvin's Room, Watbanaland, Monogomist, Curtains, Far East, Dinner With Friends, What the Butler Saw*, Bdwy in *Passion* (1983), *Burn This, Rumors, Present Laughter, Jackie*.

Emick, Jarrod Born July 2, 1969 in Ft. Eustas, VA. Attended SD St. U. Bdwy debut 1990 in *Miss Saigon*, followed by *Damn Yankees*, for which he received a 1994 Theatre World Award, *The Rocky Horror Show*, OB in *America's Sweetheart*.

Enders, Camilla Born Sept. 6, 1967 in Boston, MA. Graduate Oberlin Col., U. London. Debut 1995 OB in *Sylvia*, followed by *Ivanov, Mississippi Nude, Wyoming*.

Engel, David Born Sept. 19, 1959 in Orange County, CA. Attended U. CA Irvine. Bdwy debut 1983 in *La Cage aux Folles*, followed by *Putting It Together, Seussical*, OB in *Forever Plaid*.

English, Robert Born Oct. 18, 1965 in Queens, NY. Graduate Northwestern U. OB debut 1995 in *Doll's House*, followed by *The Idiot, Brothers Karamazov, Antigone, Winter's Tale, The Right Way to Sue*.

Epperson, John Born 1956 in Hazelburst, MS. OB debut 1988 in *I Could Go on Lypsynching*, followed by *The Fabulous Lypsinka Show. Lypsinka! A Day in the Life!, As I Lay Lip-Synching, Messages for Gary, Lypsinka! The Boxed Set*.

Esparza, Raúl Born Oct. 24, 1970 in Wilmington, DE. Graduate NYU. Bdwy debut 2000 in *The Rocky Horror Show*.

Eugene Fleming

Mary Fogarty

Angelo Fraboni

Arthur French

Esterman, Laura Born April 12 in New York, NY. Attended Radcliffe Col., LAMDA. OB debut 1969 in *Time of Your Life*, followed by *Pig Pen*, *Carpenters*, *Ghosts*, *Macbeth*, *Sea Gull*, *Rubbers*, *Yankees 3 Detroit 0*, *Golden Boy*, *Out of Our Father's House*, *The Master and Margarita*, *Chinchilla*, *Dusa*, *Fish Stas and Vi*, *Midsummer Night's Dream*, *Recruiting Officer*, *Oedipus the King*, *Two Fish in the Sky*, *Mary Barnes*, *Tamara*, *Marvin's Room*, *Edith Stein*, *Curtains*, *Yiddish Trojan Women*, *Good as New*, *American Clock*, *Cranes*, *The Wax*, Bdwy in *Waltz of the Toreadors*, *The Show-off*.

Ewin, Paula Born Dec. 6, 1955 in Warwick, RI. Attended King's Col. Wilkes-Barre, PA, Graduate RI Col. OB debut 1991 in *Necktie Breakfast*, followed by *As You Like It*, *Lion in the Streets*, *Baptists*, *Night of Nave*, *Never the Same Rhyme Twice*, *Pig*, *Bobby Supreme*, *Vegetable Love*, *The Censor*, *South of No North*.

Ewing, Linda Born March 29, 1961 in Houston, TX. Graduate USC. OB debut 1996 in *Code of the West* (also 2000), followed by *Night They Burned Washington*.

Ferguson, Jesse Tyler Born Oct. 22, 1975 in Missoula, MT. Graduate Amer. Musical & Dramatic Arts. OB debut 1997 in *On the Town*, followed by *The Most Fabulous Story Ever Told*, *Kean*, *This Love*, *Hair* (CC), *Newyorkers*, Bdwy in *On The Town*.

Figueroa, Rona Born March 30, 1972 in San Francisco, CA. Attended UC Santa Cruz. Bdwy debut 1993 in *Miss Saigon*, OB in *Caucasian Chalk Circle*, *Dogeaters*.

Finneran, Katie Born Jan. 22, 1971 in Chicago, IL. Attended Carnegie Mellon. Bdwy in *Cabaret*.

Fiss, Thomas Michael Born Dec. 7, 1986 in San Diego, CA. Bdwy debut 2000 in *The Full Monty*.

Fitzpatrick, Allen Born Jan. 31, 1955 in Boston, MA. Graduate U. VA. OB debut 1977 in *Come Back Little Sheba*, followed by *Wonderful Town*, *Rothschilds*, *Group One Acts*, *Peephole*, *Jack's Holiday*, *Mata Hari*, *Carmelina*, *Annie Warbucks*, Bdwy debut 1991 in *Les Miserables*, followed by *Gentlemen Prefer Blondes* (1995), *Damn Yankees*, *Boys from Syracuse* (Encores), *Scarlet Pimpernel*, *42nd Street*.

Flanagan, Pauline Born June 29, 1925 in Sligo, Ireland. OB debut 1958 in *Ulysses in Nighttown*, followed by *Pictures in the Hallway*, *Later*, *Antigone*, *The Crucible*, *Plough and the Stars*, *Summer*, *Close of Play*, *In Celebration*, *Without Apologies*, *Yeats*, *A Celebration*, *Philadelphia Here I Come!*, *Grandchild of Kings*, *Shadow of a Gunman*, *Juno and the Paycock*, *Plough and the Stars*, *Portia Coughlan*, *A Life*, Bdwy in *God and Kate Murphy*, *The Living Room*, *The Innocents*, *The Father*, *Medea*, *Steaming*, *Corpse*, *Philadelphia Here I Come* (1994), *Prophets and Heroes*.

Fleming, Eugene Born April 26, 1961 in Richmond, VA. Attended NC Sch. of Arts. Bdwy debut in *Chorus Line*, followed by *Tap Dance Kid*, *Black and Blue*, *High Rollers*, *DuBarry Was a Lady* (Encores), *Swinging on a Star*, *Street Corner Symphony*, *Fosse*, OB in *Voorhas*, *Dutchman*, *Ceremonies in Dark Old Men*, *Freefall*.

Fogarty, Mary Born in Manchester, NH. OB debut 1959 in *The Well of Saints*, followed by *Shadow and Substance*, *Nathan the Wise*, *Bonjour La Bonjour*, *Fanrih Comedy*, *Steel Magnolias*, *Dearly Departed*, *Filumena*, *Mack*, *The Understanding*, *Hard Feelings*, Bdwy in *National Health* (1974), *Watch on the Rhine* (1980), *Of the Fields Lately*.

Foote, Hallie Born 1955 in New York, NY. OB in *Night Seasons*, *Roads to Home*, *Widow Claire*, *Courtship*, *1918*, *On Valentine's Day*, *Talking Pictures*, *Laura Dennis*, *Young Man from Atlanta*, *900 Oneonta*, *When They Speak of Rita*, *Last of the Thorntons*.

Foster, Herbert Born May 14, 1936 in Winnipeg, Canada. Bdwy in *Ways and Means*, *Touch of the Poet*, *Imaginary Invalid*, *Tonight at 8:30*, *Henry V*, *Noises Off*, *Me and My Girl*, *Lettice and Lovage*, *Timon of Athens*, *Government Inspector*, *Sacrilege*, *Getting Away with Murder*, *Herbal Bed*, OB in *Afternoon Tea*, *Papers*, *Mary Stuart*, *Playboy of the Western World*, *Good Woman of Setzuan*, *Scenes from American Life*, *Twelfth Night*, *All's Well That Ends Well*, *Richard II*, *Gifts of the Magi*, *Heliotrope Bouquet*, *Troilus and Cressida*, *Sympathetic Magic*, *Henry VIII*, *Timon of Athens*, *Skin of Our Teeth*, *Cymbeline*, *Measure for Measure*.

Fowler, Beth Born November 1, 1940 in NJ. Graduate Caldwell Col. Bdwy debut 1970 in *Gantry*, followed by *A Little Night Music*, *Over Here*, *1600 Pennsylvania Avenue*, *Peter Pan*, *Baby*, *Teddy and Alice*, *Sweeney Todd* (1989), *Beauty and the Beast*, *Bells Are Ringing*, OB in *Preppies*, *The Blessing*, *Sweeney Todd*.

Foxworth, Robert Born November 1, 1941 in Houston, TX. Graduate Carnegie Tech. Bdwy debut 1969 in *Henry V*, followed by *The Crucible*, for which he received a 1972 Theatre World Award, *Candida, Ivanov, Honour, Judgment at Nuremberg*, OB in *Terra Plova*.

Fraboni, Angelo Born Sept. 21, 1963 in Hibbing, MN. Bdwy in *The Full Monty*.

Franklin, Nancy Born in New York, NY. Debut 1959 OB in *Buffalo Skinner*, followed by *Power of Darkness, Oh Dad, Poor Dad, Mama's Hung You in the Closet and I'm Feeling So Sad, Theatre of Peretz, 7 Days of Mourning, Here Be Dragons, Beach Children, Safe Place, Innocent Pleasures, Loves of Cass McGuire, After the Fall, Bloodletters, Briar Patch, Lost Drums, Ivanov, Cat's Paw*, Bdwy in *Never Live Over a Pretzel Factory* (1964), *Happily Never After, The White House, Charlie and Algernon*.

Franz, Joy Born in 1944 in Modesto, CA. Graduate U. Mo. OB debut 1969 in *Of Thee I Sing*, followed by *Jacques Brel Is Alive is Alive and Well and Living in Paris, Out of This World Curtains, I Can't Sleep Running in Place, Tomfoolery, Penelope, Bittersuite, Assassins, New Yorkers, Bitter Tears of Petra Von Kant*, Bdwy in *Sweet Charity, Lysistrata, A Little Night Music, Pippin, Musical Chairs, Into the Woods*.

Frechette, Peter Born Oct. 3, 1956 in Warwick, RI. OB debut 1979 in *Hornbeam Maze*, followed by *Journey's End, In Cahoots, Harry Ruby's Songs My Mother Never Sang, Pontifications on Pigtails and Puberty, Scooter Thomas Makes It to the Top of the World, We're Home, Flora the Red Menace, Hyde in Hollywood, Absent Friends, And Baby Makes Seven, Destiny of Me, La Ronde, Raised in Captivity, Night and Her Stars, Hurrah at Last, What the Butler Saw*, Bdwy debut 1989 in *Eastern Standard* (also OB), for which he won a 1989 Theatre World Award, followed by *Our Country's Good, Any Given Day*.

Freed, Sam Born Aug. 29, 1948 in York, PA. Graduate PA. St. U. OB debut 1972 in *The Proposition*, followed by *What's a Nice Country Like You Doing in a State Like This?, Dance on a Country Grave, Morocco, BAFO, The Folsom Head*, Bdwy in *Candide* (1974), *Torch Song Trilogy, Brown*.

Freeman, Jonathan Born Feb. 5, 1950 in Bay Village, OH. Graduate Ohio U. OB debut 1974 in *The Miser*, followed by *Bil Baird Marionette Theatre, Babes in Arms, Confessions of Conrad Gerhardt, Bertrano, Clap Trap, In a Pig's Valise, A Class Act*, Bdwy in *Sherlock Holmes* (1974), *Platinum, 13 Days to Broadway, She Loves Me, How to Succeed in Business Without Really Trying, On the Town, Li'l Abner* (Encores), *An Empty Plate in the Café du Grand Boeuf, 42nd Street*.

French, Arthur Born in New York, NY. Attended Brooklyn Col. OB debut 1962 in *Raisin' Hell in the Sun*, followed by *Ballad of Bimshire, Day of Absence, Happy Ending, Brotherhood, Perry's Mission, Rosalee Pritchett, Moonlight Arms, Dark Tower, Brownsville Raid, Nevis Mountain Dew, Julius Caesar, Friends, Court of Miracles, The Beautiful LaSalles, Blues for a Gospel Queen, Black Girl, Driving Miss Daisy, The Spring Thing, George Washington Slept Here, Ascension Day, Boxing Day Parade, A Tempest, Hills of Massabielle, Treatment, As You Like It, Swamp Dwellers, Tower of Burden, Henry VI, Black Girl, Last Street Play, Out of the South, Fly, Living in the Wind*, Bdwy in *Ain't Supposed to Die a Natural Death, The Iceman Cometh, All God's Chillun Got Wings, Resurrection of Lady Lester, You Can't Take It with You, Design for Living, Ma Rainey's Black Bottom, Mule Bone, Playboy of the West Indies*.

Frugé, Romain Born March 4, 1959 in Los Angeles, CA. Graduate Allentown Col. Bdwy debut 1986 in *Big River*, followed by *Tommy, The Full Monty*, OB in *Shabbatai* (1995), *Last Sweet Days, Sam Shepard One-Acts*.

Fuller, Penny Born 1940 in Durham, NC. Attended Northwestern U. Bdwy in *Barefoot in the Park* (1965) followed by *Cabaret, Richard II, As You Like It, Henry IV, Applause, Rex, American Daughter, The Dinner Party*, OB in *Cherry Orchard, Three Viewings, New England, A New Brain, Ancestral Voices*.

Gam, Rita Born April 2, 1928 in Pittsburgh, PA. Attended Columbia, Actors Studio. Bdwy debut 1946 in *A Flag is Born* followed by *Temporary Island, Insect Comedy, The Young and the Fair, Montserrat, There's a Girl in My Soup*, OB in *Hamlet, Rasputin, 24 Evenings of Wit and Wisdom*.

Garner, Patrick Born March 16, 1958 in Dearborn, MI. Graduate U. of MI, SMU. OB debut 1984 in *Found a Peanut*, followed by *Marriage of Bette & Boo, Ubu, Tartuffe, Once Around the City*, Bdwy 1986 in *Front Page* (LC), *Laughter on the 23rd Floor, A Funny Thing Happened on the Way to the Forum*.

Garrick, Barbara Born Feb. 3, 1962 in New York, NY. OB debut 1986 in *Today I Am a Fountain Pen*, followed by *Midsummer Night's Dream, Rosencrantz and Guildenstern Are Dead*, Bdwy in *Eastern Standard* (1988, also OB), *Small Family Business, Stanley, A Thousand Clowns*.

Garrison, David Born June 30, 1952 in Long Branch, NJ. Graduate Boston U. OB debut 1976 in *Joseph and the Amazing Technicolor Dreamcoat*, followed by *Living at Home, Geniuses, It's Only a Play, Make Someone Happy, Family of Mann, I Do I Do* (1996), *The Torchbearers*, Bdwy in *History of the American Film* (1978), *Day in Hollywood/A Night in the Ukraine, Pirates of Penzance, Snoopy, Torch Song Trilogy, One Touch of Venus* (Encores), *Titanic, Strike Up the Band* (Encores), *Bells Are Ringing*.

Geller, Marc Born July 5, 1959 in RI. OB debut 1981 in *Butterflies are Free*, followed by *As Is, Marat/Sade, Equus, Cloud 9, Orphans, Bomber Jackets, Faustus, Box Office Poison, Unidentified Human Remains, Exit the King, Adjoining Trances, The Ballad of The Sad Café, Cloud 9, Naked Will, Dysteria*.

Gibson, Julia Born June 8, 1962 in Norman, OK. Graduate U. IA, NYU. OB debut 1987 in *Midsummer Night's Dream*, followed by *Love's Labor's Lost, Crucible, Man Who Fell in Love with His Wife, Learned Ladies, Machinal, Candide., Dracula, Arabian Nights, View of the Dome, Henry VIII, Da, Measure for Measure*.

Gibson, Meg Born Aug. 24 in Bridgeton, NJ. Graduate U. UT, Juilliard. OB debut 1983 in *Fen*, followed by *King Lear, Messiah, From Above, The Ride Down Mt. Morgan, Knepp*.

Giles, Nancy Born July 17, 1960 in Queens, NY. Graduate Oberlin Col. OB debut 1985 in *Mayor*, for which she received a 1985 Theatre World Award, followed by *Mother, Circus of Death, Pinky, Oh You Hostage, Snicker Factor, Tiny Mommy Sparks in the Park, Czar of Rock and Roll, Johnny Business, Urban Blight, Police Boys, Going To The River, The New Jack Paar Show*.

Joanna Glushak

Rita Glynn

Deidre Goodwin

Rahti Gorfien

Gillette, Anita Born Aug. 16, 1938 in Baltimore, MD. OB debut 1960 in *Russell Paterson's Sketchbook*, for which she received a 1960 Theatre World Award, followed by *Rich and Famous, Dead Wrong, Road Show, Class 1-Acts, The Blessing, Moving Targets, Juno, Able-Bodied Seaman, Decline of the Middle West*, Bdwy in *Carnival, Gypsy, Gay Life, All American, Mr. President, Kelly, Don't Drink the Water, Cabaret, Jimmy, They're Playing Our Song, Brighton Beach Memoirs, Chapter Two, Bloomer Girl* (CC).

Glushak, Joanna Born May 27, 1958 in New York, NY. Attended NYU. OB debut 1983 in *Lenny and the Heartbreakers*, followed by *Lies and Legends, Miami, Unfinished Song, A Little Night Music* (NYCO), *Just as If, Big Potato*, Bdwy in *Sunday in the Park with George* (1984), *Rags, Les Miserables*.

Glynn, Rita Born Dec. 27, 1991 in Durham, NC. Bdwy debut 2000 in *Jane Eyre*.

Goethals, Angela Born May 20, 1977 in New York, NY. Bdwy debut 1987 in *Coastal Disturbances*, followed by *Four Baboons Adoring the Sun, Picnic*, OB in *Positive Me, Approaching Zanzibar, The Good Times are Killing Me, True History and Real Adventure, Blur*.

Goetz, Peter Michael Born Dec. 10, 1941 in Buffalo, NY. Graduate SUNY Fredonia, So. IL U. OB debut 1980 in *Jail Diary of Albie Sacks*, followed by *Before the Dawn, Comic Potential*, Bdwy in *Ned and Jack* (1981), *Beyond Therapy, Queen and the Rebels, Brighton Beach Memoirs, Government Inspector, Sex and Longing, Last Night of Ballyhoo, Macbeth*.

Golden, Annie Born Oct. 19, 1951 in Brooklyn, NY. Bdwy debut 1977 in *Hair*, followed by *Leader of the Pack, The Full Monty*, OB in *Dementos, Dr. Selavy's Magic Theatre, A... My Name is Alice, Little Shop of Horrors, Class of '86, Assassins, Hit the Lights!, Sugar Bean Sisters, On the Town, Broadway '68, Saturn Returns, La Terrasse, On The Town, An Empty Plate in the Café du Grand Boeuf*.

Goldsmith, Merwin Born Aug. 7, 1937 in Detroit, MI. Graduate UCLA, Old Vic. Bdwy debut 1970 in *Minnie's Boys*, followed by *The Visit, Chemin de Fer, Rex, Leda Had a Little Swan, Trelawney of the Wells, Dirty Linen, 1940's Radio Hour, Slab Boys, Me and My Girl, Ain't Broadway Grand, Bloomer Girl* (CC), OB in *Naked Hamlet, Chickencoop Chinaman, Real Life Funnies, Wanted, Rubbers and Yanks, Chinchilla, Yours Anne, Big Apple Messengers, La Boheme, Learned Ladies, An Imaginary Life, Little Prince, Beau Jest, After-Play, Louisianna Purchase, Beauty Part*.

Goodwin, Deidre Born Sept. 15, 1969 in Oklahoma City, OK. Attended Southwest MI St. U. Bdwy debut 1998 in *Chicago*, followed by *Jesus Christ Superstar, The Rocky Horror Show*.

Gorfien, Rahti Born April 2, 1958 in New Haven, CT. Graduate NYU. OB in *Bearded Iris*.

Gorshin, Frank April 5, 1933 in Pittsburgh, PA. Bdwy debut 1969 in *Jimmy*, followed by *Whodunnit, Say Goodnight Gracie*.

Graff, Randy Born May 23, 1955 in Brooklyn, NY. Graduate Wagner Col. OB debut 1978 in *Pins and Needles*, followed by *Station Joy, A... My Name Is Alice, Once on a Summer's Day, Do Re Mi*, Bdwy in *Sarava, Grease, Les Miserables, City of Angels, Falsettos, Laughter on the 23rd Floor, Moon Over Buffalo, High Society, A Class Act*.

Graham, Enid Born Feb. 8 in TX. Graduate Juilliard. Bdwy debut 1998 in *Honour*, OB in *Look Back in Anger, Crimes of the Heart*.

Grant, Kate Jennings Born March 23, 1970 in Elizabeth, NJ. Graduate U. of PA, Juilliard. Bdwy debut 1997 in *American Daughter*, followed by *Hard Feelings*, OB in *Wonderland, Hard Feelings*.

Gray, Charles Born July 15, 1960 in Annapolis, MD. Attended Towson St. U. Bdwy debut 1995 in *Grease*, OB in *Long Road Home*.

Graybill, Kathryn Graduate SMU. OB in *King Lear*.

Kathryn Graybill   Justin Greer   Sylver Gregory   John Lyndsay Hall

Greenhill, Susan Born March 19 in New York, NY. Graduate U. PA., Catholic U. Bdwy debut 1982 in *Crimes of the Heart*, OB in *Hooters, Our Lord of Lynchville, September in the Rain, Seascape with Shark and Dancer, Murder of Crows, Better Days, Marathon '89, Tounges of Stone, Festival of One Acts, Watbanaland, The Increased Difficulty of Conversation, Brown.*

Greenspan, David Born 1956 In Los Angeles, CA. OB in *Phaedra, Education of Skinny Spyz, Boys in the Band, Moose Mating, Second Hand Smoke, Sueño, Alien Boy, Small Craft Warnings, Saved or Destroyed, Lipstick Traces, The Wax.*

Greer, Justin Born Jan. 25, 1973 in Buffalo, NY. Graduate Carnegie Mellon U. Bdwy debut 1999 in *Babes in Arms* (CC/Encores), followed by *Annie Get Your Gun, Seussical.*

Gregory, Sylver Born Oct. 14, 1980 in Fort-de-France, Martinique. OB debut 2000 in *Welcome to Our City.*

Grizzard, George Born April 1, 1928 in Roanoke, Rapids, VA. Graduate U. NC. Bdwy debut 1954 in *All Summer Long*, followed by *Desperate Hours, Happiest Millionaire*, for which he received a 1957 Theatre World Award, *The Disenchanted, Big Fish Little Fish, APA 1961-62, Who's Afraid of Virginia Woolf, Glass Menagerie, You Know I Can't Hear You When the Water's Running, Noel Coward's Sweet Potato, Gingham Dog, The Inquest, Country Girl, Creation of the World and Other Business, Crown Matrimonial, Royal Family, California Suite, Man and Superman, Delicate Balance* (1996), *Judgment at Nuremberg*, OB in *Beach House, Another Antigone, Ancestral Voices.*

Grollman, Elaine Born Oct. 22, 1928 in Bronx, NY. Debut 1974 OB in *Yentl the Yeshiva Boy*, followed by *Kaddish, The Water Hen, Millions of Miles, Come Back, Little Sheeba, Biography: A Game, House Music, The Workroom, Yentl* (2002) Bdwy in *Yentl.*

Grotke, Diane Born Nov. 15, 1953 in No. Tonawanda, NY. Attended U. FL, U. So. FL. OB debut 1987 in *Bird/Bear*, followed by *Reel to Real, Boar's Carcass, Pieces of the Sky, Horsey People.*

Guncler, Sam Born Oct. 17, 1955 in Bethlehem, PA. Graduate Lehigh U. OB debut 1983 in *Her Honor the Mayor*, followed by *The Racket, Sail Away, Winning, Clash By Night, It's My Party*, Bdwy in *The Gathering.*

Gurwin, Danny Born Nov. 14, 1972 in Detroit, MI. Graduate U. MI. OB debut 1998 in *R & J*, followed by *Kuni-Leml, The Scarlet Pimpernel, Forbidden Broadway.*

Guttman, Ronald Born Aug. 12, 1952 in Brussels, Belgium. Graduate Brussels U. OB debut 1986 in *Coastal Disturbances*, followed by *Modigliano, Free Zone, Escurial, Liliom, Philanthropist, Funky Crazy Bugaloo Boy, No Exit, Sabina, Price of Madness, Uncle Jack, Bravo Ubu*, Bdwy in *Coastal Disturbances* (1987).

Hadge, Michael Born June 6, 1932 in Greensboro, NC. Bdwy debut 1958 in *Cold Wind and the Warm*, followed by *Lady of the Camelias, Impossible Years*, OB in *Local Stigmata, Hunter, Night Seasons, Laura Dennis, Last of the Thorntons.*

Hadley, Jonathan Born May 6, 1964 in Charlotte, NC. Graduate NC Sch. of Arts. OB debut 1993 in *Theda Bara and the Frontier Rabbi*, followed by *Cincinnati Saint, Prime Time Prophet, Mayor Musicals, Sheba, Kuni-Leml, Reunion, A Class Act.*

Hall, Anthony Blair Born May 5, 1987 in Washington, DC. Bdwy debut 1997 in *A Christmas Carol*, followed by *A Christmas Carol* (1998), *Ragtime, Seussical.*

Hall, John Lyndsay Born in Baltimore, MD. Attended Morgan St. U. OB debut 2000 in *Welcome to Our City.*

Halstead, Carol Born Sept. 12 in Hempstead, NY. Graduate FL St. U., ACT. OB debut 1992 in *The Mask*, followed by *Bats, Margo's Party, Cucumbers*, Bdwy in *Gore Vidal's The Best Man.*

Halston, Julie Born Dec. 7, 1954 in NY. Graduate Hofstra U. OB debut 1985 in *Times Square Angel*, followed by *Vampire Lesbians of Sodom, Sleeping Beauty or Coma, The Dubliners, Lady in Question, Money Talks, Red Scare on Sunset, I'll Be the Judge of That, Lifetime of Comedy, Honeymoon Is Over, You Should Be So Lucky, This Is Not Going to Be Pretty, Saved or Destroyed*, Bdwy in *Boys from Syracuse* (Encores), *The Man Who Came to Dinner.*

Carol Halstead

Julie Halston

Delphi Harrington

Rich Hebert

Hammel, Lori Born in Minneapolis, MN. OB debut 1998 in *Forbidden Broadway Strikes Back*, followed by *Forbidden Broadway Cleans Up Its Act, I Love You, You're Perfect, Now Change.*

Hammer, Ben Born Dec. 8, 1925 in Brooklyn, NY. Graduate Brooklyn Col. Bdwy debut 1955 in *Creat Sebastians*, followed by *Diary of Anne Frank, Tenth Man, Mother Courage, The Deputy, Royal Hunt of the Sun, Colda, Broadway Bound, Three Sisters, The Gathering*, OB in *The Crucible, Murderous Angels, Richard III, Slavs!, The Gathering.*

Harada, Ann Born Feb. 3, 1964 in Honolulu, HI. Attended Brown U. OB debut 1987 in *1-2-3-4-5*, followed by *Hit the Lights!, America Dreaming, Dog and His Master, Falsettoland, The Moment When, A Tribute to Julie and Carol*, Bdwy in *M. Butterfly* (1988), *Seussical.*

Harner, Jason Butler Born Oct. 9 in Elmira, NY. Graduate VCU, NYU. OB debut in *Henry VIII*, followed by *Macbeth, An Experiment with an Air Pump, Juno and the Paycock, Crimes of the Heart.*

Harper, Valerie Born Aug. 22, 1940 in Suffern, NY. Bdwy debut in *Li'l Abner*, followed by *Destry Rides Again, Take Me Along, Wildcat, Subways are for Sleeping, Something Different, Story Theatre, Metamorphosis, Tale of the Allergist's Wife*, OB in *Death Defying Acts, All Under Heaven.*

Harrington, Delphi Born Aug. 26 in Chicago, IL. Graduate Northwestern U. OB debut 1960 in *Country Scandal*, followed by *Moon for the Misbegotten, Baker's Dozen, The Zykovs, Character Lines, Richie, American Garage, After the Fall, Rosencrantz and Guildenstern Are Dead, Good Grief, Hay Fever, Madwoman of Chaillot, Too Clever by Half, Beauty Part, Heartbreak House, Pirate's Lullaby, Blithe Spirit, The Admirable Crichton*, Bdwy in *Thieves* (1974), *Everything in the Garden, Romeo and Juliet, Chapter Two, Sea Gull.*

Harris, Jared Born 1962 in London. Attended Duke U. OB in *Henry IV, 'Tis a Pity She's a Whore, King Lear, Ecstacy, More Lies about Jerzy,*

Harrison, Gregory Born May 31, 1950 on Catalina Island, CA. Graduate Actors Studio. Bdwy debut 1997 in *Steel Pier, Follies* 2001.

Hart, Linda Born Aug. 1, 1950 in Dallas, TX. Attended LACC. Debut 1982 OB in *Livin' Dolls*, followed by *Sunday Serenade, Gospel Rocks the Ballroom, Sid Caesar & Company*, Bdwy in *Bette Midler's Divine Madness* (1979), *Anything Goes* (1987) for which she received a Theatre World Award.

Hartung, Billy Born June 21, 1971 in Pittsburgh, PA. Graduate Point Park Col. Bdwy debut in *Side Show* (1997), followed by *Footloose, Minnelli on Minnelli, Hair* (CC), OB 1995 in *The Rink.*

Harvey, Ellen Born Oct. 2 in Pomona, CA. Graduate Boston U. Bdwy debut 2000 in *Music Man.*

Hayden, Michael Born July 28, 1963 in St. Paul, MN. Graduate Juilliard. OB debut 1991 in *The Matchmaker*, followed by *Hello Again, Off-Key, Nebraska, All My Sons, Far East*, Bdwy debut 1994 in *Carousel*, for which he received a 1994 Theatre World Award, followed by *Judgment at Nuremberg.*

Heard, Cordis Born July 27, 1944 in Washington, DC. Graduate Chatham Col. Bdwy debut 1973 in *Warp*, followed by *Elephant Man, Macbeth*, OB in *Vanities, City Junket, Details without a Map, Inside Out, Jasper in Grammercy Park, Oh, My Dear Andersen.*

Hebert, Rich Born Dec. 14, 1956 in Quincy, MA. Graduate Boston U. OB debut 1978 in *Rimers of Eldritch*, followed by *110 in the Shade, Dazy, Easy Money, Ballad of Sam Grey*, Bdwy in *Rock 'n' Roll: First 5000 Years* (1982), *Cats, Les Miserables, Sunset Blvd, The Life, Saturday Night Fever.*

Hecht, Paul Born Aug. 16, 1941 in London, England. Attended McGill U. OB in *Sjt. Musgrave's Dance, Macbird, Phaedra, Enrico IV, Coriolanus, Cherry Orchard, Androcles and the Lion, Too Clever by Half, London Suite, Moonlight, Big Potato*, Bdwy in *Rosencrantz and Guildenstern Are Dead, 1776, Rothschilds, Ride Across Lake Constance, Great God Brown, Don Juan, Emperor Henry IV, Herzl, Caesar and Cleopatra, Night and Day, Noises Off, The Invention of Love, Euripides' Medea.*

Heredia, Wilson Jermaine Born 1972 in Brooklyn, NY. OB in *New Americans, Popal Vu, The Tower, Eli's Comin'*, Bdwy in *Rent* (1996-also OB).

George Heslin

Conleth Hill

Mark Hofmaier

Mylinda Hull

Herrera, John Born Sept. 21, 1955 in Havana, Cuba. Graduate Loyola U. Bdwy debut 1979 in *Grease*, followed by *Evita, Camelot, The Mystery of Edwin Drood, Shogun, Tom Sawyer, Man of La Mancha*, OB in *La Boheme, Lies and Legends, Do Re Mi*.

Heslin, George Born 1972. OB debut 2000 in *Juno and the Paycock*.

Hibbard, David Born June 21, 1965. Graduate Ohio St U. OB debut 1989 in *Leave It to Jane*, followed by *Chess, Forbidden Bdwy Strikes Back, A Class Act*, Bdwy in *Cats* (1993), *Once Upon a Mattress* (1996).

Hidalgo, Allen Born Dec. 15, 1967 in New York, NY. Attended Bard Col., NYU. OB debut 1992 in *Eating Raoul*, followed by *4 Guys Named Jose*, Bdwy in *Candide* (1997).

Hill, Conleth Born Nov. 24, 1964 in Ballycastle, Ireland. Attended St. MacNissis Col. Bdwy debut 2001 in *Stones in His Pockets*.

Hilliard, Ryan Born Jan. 20, 1945 in Ashtabula, OH. Graduate Kent State U. Debut 1971 OB in *Godspell*, followed by *The Bear, Under Milk Wood, the Madwoman of Chaillot, Behind a Mask*, One Act Festival, *What the Butler Saw, The Uninvited Guest*

Hines, John Born March 15, 1961 in Chicago, IL. Graduate U. IL, Yale U. OB debut 1998 in *Black Snow*, followed by *Arsenic and Old Lace* (CC).

Hingston, Seán Martin Born Dec. 16, 1965 in Melbourne, Australia. Bdwy debut 1994 in *Crazy for You*, followed by *Boys from Syracuse* (Encores), *Promises Promises* (Encores), *A Connecticut Yankee in King Arthur's Court* (CC), OB in *Contact*.

Hock, Robert Born May 20, 1931 in Phoenixville, PA. Graduate Yale U. OB debut 1982 in *Caucasian Chalk Circle*, followed by *Adding Machine, Romeo and Juliet, Edward II, Creditors, Two Orphans, Macbeth, Kitty Hawk, Heathen Valley, Comedy of Errors, Phaedra, Good Natur'd Man, Oedipus the King, Game of Love and Chance, Twelfth Night, Mrs. Warren's Profession, Oedipus at Colonus, King Lear, Beaux Stratagem, Life Is a Dream, Doll's House, Antigone, he Chairs, Venice Preserv'd, Misalliance, The Seagull, The Miser, The Country Wife, The Way of the World, The Oresteia, The Cherry Orchard*, Bdwy in *Some Americans Abroad* (1990).

Hodges, Patricia Born in Puyallup, WA. Graduate U. WA. OB debut 1985 in *The Normal Heart*, followed by *No End of Blame, On the Verge, Hard Times, One-Act Festival*, Bdwy in *Six Degrees of Separation* (1991), *Dancing at Lughnasa, Lion in Winter, Gore Vidal's The Best Man*.

Hoffman, Philip Seymour Born July 23, 1967 in Fairport, NY. Attended NYU. OB in *Food and Shelter, The Skriker, Defying Gravity, Shopping and Fucking, All in the Timing, The Treatment, The Author's Voice, In Arabia We'd All Be Kings, The Seagull* (CC), Bdwy in *True West*.

Hofheimer, Charlie Born April 17, 1981 in Detroit, MI. Bdwy debut 1995 in *On the Waterfront*, OB in *Minor Demons, Old Money*.

Hofmaier, Mark Born July 4, 1950 in Philadelphia, PA. Graduate U. AZ. OB debut 1978 in *Midsummer Night's Dream*, followed by *Marvelous Gray, Modern Romance, Relative Values, The Racket, Come as You Are, Global Village*.

Hollis, Tommy Born March 27, 1954 in Jacksonville, TX. Attended Lon Morris Col., U. Houston. OB debut 1985 in *Diamonds*, followed by *Secrets of the Lava Lamp, Paradise, Africanus Instructus, Colored Museum, Yip & Gershwin*, Bdwy debut 1990 in *Piano Lesson*, for which he received a 1990 Theatre World Award, followed by *Seven Guitars, Tom Sawyer*.

Holm, Celeste Born April 29, 1919 in New York, NY. Attended UCLA, U. Chicago. Bdwy debut 1938 in *Gorianna*, followed by *Time of Your Life, Another Sun, Return of the Vagabond, 8 O'Clock Tuesday, My Fair Ladies, Papa Is All, All the Comforts of Home, Damask Cheek, Oklahoma!, Bloomer Girl, She Stoops to Conquer, Affairs of State, Anna Christie, King and I, His and Hers, Interlock, Third Best Sport, Invitation to a March, Mame, Candida, Habeas Corpus, Utter Glory of Morrissey Hall, I Hate Hamlet, Allegro in Concert*, OB in *Month in the Country, Paris Was Yesterday, With Love and Laughter, Christmas Carol, The Brooch, Don Juan in Hell, Arsenic and Old Lace* (CC).

Holmes, Denis Born June 7, 1921 in Coventry, Eng. Graduate LAMDA. Bdwy debut 1955 in *Troilus and Cressida*, followed by *Homecoming, Merchant of Venice, Moliere Comedies, Hamlet, Ideal Husband, Major Barbara*, OB in *Dandy Dick* (1987).

Kelly Hutchinson

Bill Irwin

Jamie Jones

Jen Jones

Hopkins, Kaitlin/Kate Born Feb. 1, 1964 in New York, NY. Attended Carnegie Mellon U., RADA. OB debut 1984 in *Come Back Little Sheba*, followed by *Take Two, My Favorite Year, Johnny Pye and the Foolkiller, Bat Boy*.

Huff, Neal Born in New York, NY. Graduate NYU. Debut 1992 OB in *Young Playwrights Festival*, followed by *Joined at the Head, Day the Bronx Died, Macbeth, House of Yes, Class 1-Acts, Saturday Mourning Cartoons, Troilus and Cressida, Tempest, From Above, The Seagull: 1990 The Hamptons, Other People*.

Huffman, Cady Born Feb. 2, 1965 in Santa Barbara, CA. OB debut 1983 in *They're Playing Our Song*, followed by *Festival of 1 Acts, Oh Hell!, Love Soup*, Bdwy 1985 in *La Cage aux Folles*, followed by *Big Deal, Will Rogers Follies, The Producers*.

Hughes, Jurian Born Nov. 6 in Albany, NY. Graduate Williams Col., NYU. Bdwy debut 1996 in *Night of the Iguana*, followed by *Judgment at Nuremberg*, OB debut 1996 in *Grace and Glorie*, followed by *Never the Sinner, The Primary English Class*.

Hughes, Laura Born Jan. 28, 1959 in New York, NY. Graduate Neighborhood Playhouse. OB debut 1980 in *The Diviners*, followed by *A Tale Told, Time Framed, Fables for Friends, Talley and Son, Kate's Diary, Playboy of the Western World, Missing/Kissing, The Trail of Her Inner Thighs*.

Hull, Mylinda Born March 3 in San Diego, CA. Bdwy debut 2001 in *42nd Street*, OB in *I Love You, You're Perfect, Now Change*.

Hunt, Helen Born in Los Angeles, CA. Debut 1986 OB in *Been Taken*, followed by *The Taming of the Shrew, Three Sisters*, Bdwy in *Our Town* (1989), *Life(x)3*.

Hurt, Mary Beth Born Sept. 26, 1948 in Marshalltown, IA. Attended U. Iowa, NYU. OB debut 1972 in *More Than You Deserve*, followed by *As You Like It, Trelaway of the Wells, The Cherry Orchard, Love for Love, Member of the Wedding, Boy Meets Girl, Secret Service, Father's Day, Nest of the Wood Grouse, The Day Room, Secret Rapture, Othello, One Shoe Off, Arts and Leisure, Oblivion Postponed, Old Money*, Bdwy in *Crimes of the Heart* (1981), *The Misanthrope, Benefactors*.

Hutchinson, Kelly Born March 17, 1976 in New Brunswick, NJ. Graduate Boston U. Bdwy debut 2000 in *Macbeth*, followed by *Major Barbara*.

Hyams, Paul Born Feb. 14, 1959 in Paris, France. Bdwy debut 1981 in *Merrily We Roll Along*, OB in *Merrily We Roll Along in Concert*.

Ing, Alvin Born May 26, 1938 in Honolulu, HI. Graduate U. of HI, Columbia U. Bdwy debut 1959 in *World of Suzie Wong* followed by *Two Gentlemen of Verona, Pacific Overtures, Flower Drum Song* (2002), OB in *Tenth of an Inch, Cranes and Peonies, Coffins for Butterflies, Six*.

Irish, Mark Born Dec. 18, 1963 in Hartland, ME. Graduate Dartmouth Col. OB debut 1988 in *On Tina Tuna Walk*, followed by *Good Honest Food, The Littlest Clown, Lily Wong, Trophies, The Heidi Chronicles, Jig Saw*.

Irwin, Bill Born April 11, 1950 in Santa Monica, CA. Attended UCLA, Clown Col. OB debut 1982 in *Regard of Flight*, followed by *The Courtroom, Waiting for Godot, Scapin*, Bdwy in *5-6-7-8 Dance* (1983), *Accidental Death of an Anarchist, Regard of Flight, Largely New York, Fool Moon, Tempest*.

Ivey, Dana Born Aug. 12 in Atlanta, GA. Graduate Rollins Col., LAMDA. Bdwy debut 1981 in *Macbeth* (LC), followed by *Present Laughter, Heartbreak House, Sunday in the Park with George, Pack of Lies, Marriage of Figaro, Indiscretions, Last Night of Ballyhoo, Sex and Longing, Waiting in the Wings, Major Barbara*, OB in *Call from the East, Vivien, Candida, Major Barbara, Quartermaine's Terms, Baby with the Bath Water, Driving Miss Daisy, Wenceslas Square, Love Letters, Hamlet, Subject Was Roses, Beggars in the House of Plenty, Kindertransport, Li'l Abner, Tartuffe*.

Ivey, Judith Born Sept. 4, 1951 in El Paso, TX. Bdwy debut 1979 in *Bedroom Farce*, followed by *Steaming, Hurlyburly, Blithe Spirit, Park Your Car in Harvard Yard, Madhouse in Goa, Voices in the Dark, Follies 2001*, OB in *Dulsa Fish Stas and Vi, Sunday Runners, Second Lady, Mrs. Dally Has a Lover, Moonshot and Cosmos, A Fair Country, Noel Coward's Suite in 2 Keys*.

Catrice Joseph

Deep Katdare

Sylva Kelegian

Dennis Kelly

Jackson, Greg (formerly Greg Vallee). Born March 22, 1955 in NJ. Graduate Boston U. OB debut 1980 in *Times Square*, followed by *Loss of Roses, Ladies of the Odeon, Initiation Rites, Occasional Grace, Twelfth Night, Duet: A Romantic Fable, Dark of the Moon, Meanwhile, on the Other Side of Mt. Vesuvius, O Pioneers!*

Jacoby, Mark Born May 21, 1947 in Johnson City, TN. Graduate GA State U., FL. State U., St. John's U. Debut 1984 OB in *Bells Are Ringing, Enter the Guardsman, Sitting Pretty*, Bdwy debut in *Sweet Charity*, for which he received a 1986 Theatre World Award, followed by *Grand Hotel, The Phantom of the Opera, Show Boat*.

James, Brian D'Arcy Born 1968 in Saginaw, MI. Graduate Northwestern U. Bdwy in *Carousel, Blood Brothers, Titanic*, OB in *Public Enemy, Floyd Collins, Violet, The Good Thief*

James, Peter Francis Born Sept. 16, 1956 in Chicago, IL. Graduate RADA. OB debut 1979 in *Julius Caesar*, followed by *Long Day's Journey into Night, Antigone, Richard II, Romeo and Juliet, Enrico IV, Cymbeline, Hamlet, Learned Ladies, 10th Young Playwrights Festival, Measure for Measure, Amphitryon, Troilus and Cressida*, Bdwy debut 2000 in *Judgment at Nuremberg*.

Jennings, Ken Born Oct. 10, 1947 in Jersey City, NJ. Graduate St. Peter's Col. Bdwy debut 1975 in *All God's Chillun Got Wings*, followed by *Sweeney Todd*, for which he received a 1979 Theatre World Award, *Present Laughter, Grand Hotel, Christmas Carol, London Assurance, Side Show*, OB in *Once on a Summer's Day, Mayor, Rabboni, Gifts of the Magi, Carmilla, Sharon, Mayor, Amphigory, Shabbatai, Urinetown*.

Johnston, Nancy Born Jan. 15, 1949 in Statesville, NC. Graduate Carson Newman Col., UNC Greensboro. OB debut 1987 in *Olympus on My Mind*, followed by *Nunsense, Living Color, White Lies, You Can Be a New Yorker Too, Splendora, Doctor Doctor*, Bdwy in *Secret Garden, Allegro* (Encores), *The Music Man*.

Jones, Cherry Born Nov. 21, 1956 in Paris, TN. Graduate Carnegie Mellon U. OB debut 1983 in *The Philanthropist*, followed by *He and She, The Ballad of Soapy Smith, The Importance of Being Earnest, I Am a Camera, Claptrap, Big Time, A Light Shining in Buckinghamshire, The Baltimore Waltz, Goodnight Desdemona, And Baby Makes 7, Desdemona, Pride's Crossing, A Moon for the Misbegotten*, Bdwy in *Stepping Out* (1986), *Our Country's Good, Angels in America, The Heiress, Night of the Iguana, Major Barbara*.

Jones, Jamie Born Nov. 11, 1959 in Sacramento, CA. Graduate Amer. Acad. Of Dramatic Arts. OB debut in *Before Breakfast*, followed by *The Elephant Man*.

Jones, Jen Born March 23, 1927 in Salt Lake City, UT. OB debut 1960 in *Dreams Under the Window*, followed by *Long Voyage Home, Diff'rent, The Creditors, Look at Any Man, I Knock at the Door, Pictures in the Hallway, Grab Bag, Bo Bo, Oh Dad Poor Dad, Henhouse, Uncle Vanya, Grandma's Play, Distance from Calcutta, Good, Last of the Thorntons*, Bdwy in *Dr. Cook's Garden* (1967), *But Seriously, Eccentricities of a Nightingale, Music Man* (1980), *Octette Bridge Club*.

Jones, Simon Born July 27, 1950 in Wiltshire, England. Attended Trinity Hall. OB debut 1984 in *Terra Nova*, followed by *Magdalena in Concert, Woman in Mind, Privates on Parade, Quick-Change Room, You Never Can Tell, Passion Play, The Admirable Crichton*, Bdwy in *The Real Thing* (1984), *Benefactors, Getting Married Private Lives, Real Inspector Hound/5 Minute Hamlet, School for Scandal, Herbal Bed, Ring Round The Moon, Waiting in the Wings*.

Jones, Walker Born Aug. 27, 1956 in Pensacola, FL. Graduate Boston U., Yale U. OB debut 1989 in *Wonderful Town*, followed by *Scapin, Byzantium, Merry Wives of Windsor, Merchant of Venice, Henry VI, Just As If*.

Joseph, Catrice Born July 8 in New York, NY. Graduate NYU. OB debut in *Brief History of White Music*, Bdwy debut 2000 in *Seussical*.

Katdare, Deep Born July 4, 1970 in Buffalo, NY. Graduate MIT. Bdwy debut 2000 in *Tale of the Allergist's Wife*.

Michelle Kittrell

Ezra Knight

T. R. Knight

Swoosie Kurtz

Kelegian, Sylva Born Feb. 2, 1962 in New York, NY. OB debut 2000 in *The Soul of an Intruder*.

Kelly, Dennis Bdwy debut 1994 in *Damn Yankees*, followed by *Annie Get Your Gun*, OB in *Music in the Air*, *Suburb*.

Kelly, Kristen Lee Born 1968. OB in *Loved Less*, *Blaming Mom*, *Apollo of Bellac*, *After The Rain*, *American Passenger*, Bdwy in *Rent* (1996-also OB), *Rocky Horror Show*.

Kepros, Nicholas Born Nov. 8, 1932 in Salt Lake City, UT. Graduate U. UT, RADA. OB debut 1958 in *Golden Six*, followed by *Wars and Roses*, *Julius Caesar*, *Hamlet*, *Henry IV*, *She Stoops to Conquer*, *Peer Gynt*, *Octaroon*, *Endicott and the Red Cross*, *Judas Applause*, *Irish Hebrew Lesson*, *Judgment in Havana*, *The Millionairess*, *Androcles and the Lion*, *The Redempter*, *Othello*, *Times and Appetites of Toulouse-Lautrec*, *Two Fridays*, *Rameau's Nephew*, *Good Grief*, *Overtime*, *Measure for Measure*, *You Never Can Tell*, *Things You Shouldn't Say Past Midnight*, *Iphigenia Cycle*, *Troilus and Cressida*, Bdwy in *Saint Joan* (1968/1993), *Amadeus*, *Execution of Justice*, *Timon of Athens*, *Government Inspector*, *The Rehearsal*.

King, Nicolas Born July 26, 1991 in Westerly, RI. Bdwy debut 2000 in *Beauty and the Beast*, followed by *A Thousand Clowns*.

Kirk, Justin Born May 28, 1969 in Salem, OR. OB debut 1990 in *The Applicant*, followed by *Shardston*, *Loose Ends*, *Thanksgiving*, *Lovequest Live*, *Old Wicked Songs*, *June Moon*, *Ten Unknowns*, Bdwy in *Any Given Day* (1993), *Love! Valour! Compassion!* (also OB).

Kitt, Eartha Born Jan. 26, 1928 in North, SC. Appeared with Katherine Dunham before Bdwy debut in *New Faces of 1952*, followed by *Mrs. Patterson*, *Shinbone Alley*, *Timbuktu*, *Wizard of Oz* (MSG), *The Wild Party*, OB in *New Faces of 1952*, *Cinderella*.

Kittrell, Michelle Born Dec. 16, 1972 in Cocoa Beach, FL. OB debut 1993 in *Girl of My Dreams*, followed by *New Yorkers*, *Joseph and the Amazing Technicolor Dreamcoat*, Bdwy debut 2000 in *Seussical*.

Klavan, Scott Born June 5,1959 in Manhasset, NY. Graduate Kanyon Col. Debut 1982 OB in *War and Peace*, followed by *Williwaw*, *The Homesteaders*, *The Seagull*, *Marie and Bruce*, *Endpapers*.

Klein, Sally Born Jan. 21 in Toledo, OH. Graduate U of AZ. Bdwy debut 1981 in *Merrily We Roll Along* followed by *Agnes of God*, OB in *Merrily We Roll Along in Concert*.

Knight, Ezra Born July 7, 1962 in Atlanta, GA. OB debut 1995 in *Othello*, followed by *King Lear*, *You Say What I Mean*, *Julius Caesar*.

Knight, T.R. Born Minneapolis, MN. OB debut 1999 in *Macbeth*, followed by *This Lime Tree Bower*, *The Hologram Theory*, *The Right Way to Sue*.

Kofoed, Seana Born in IL. Graduate Northwestern U. OB debut 1997 in *The Disputation*, followed by *The Memory of Water*, *Mom and the Razorblades*, *An Experiment with an Air Pump*, *Hard Feelings*, Bdwy in *Night Must Fall*.

Kolinski, Joseph Born June 26, 1953 in Detroit, MI. Attended U. Detroit. Bdwy debut 1980 in *Brigadoon*, followed by *Dance a Little Closer*, *The Human Comedy* (also OB), *Three Musketeers*, *Les Miserables*, *Christmas Carol*, *Titanic*, OB in *HiJinks!*, *Picking up the Pieces*, *Time and Again*.

Korbich, Eddie Born Nov. 6, 1960 in Washington, DC. Graduate Boston Cons. OB debut 1985 in *A Little Night Music*, followed by *Flora the Red Menace*, *No Frills Revue*, *The Last Musical Comedy*, *Godspell*, *Sweeney Todd*, *Assassins*, *Casino Paradise*, *Gifts of the Magi*, *Eating Raoul*, *Taking a Chance on Love*, Bdwy in *Sweeney Todd* (1989), *Singin' in the Rain*, *Carousel* (1994), *Seussical*, *Bloomer Girl* (CC).

Korey, Alix (formerly Alexandra) Born May 14 in Brooklyn, NY. Graduate Columbia U. OB debut 1976 in *Fiorello!*, followed by *Annie Get Your Gun*, *Jerry's Girls*, *Rosalie in Concert*, *America Kicks Up Its Heels*, *Gallery*, *Feathertop*, *Bittersuite*, *Romance in Hard Times*, *Songs You Might Have Missed*, *Forbidden Broadway 10th Anniversary*, *Camp Paradox*, *Cinderella* (LC), *Best of the West*, *Jack's Holiday*, *No Way to Treat a Lady*, *Wonderful Town*, *The Wild Party*, *Suburb*, Bdwy in *Hello, Dolly!* (1978), *Show Boat* (1983), *Ain't Broadway Grand*, *Triumph of Love*.

Kudisch, Marc Born Sept. 22, 1966 in Hackensack, NJ. Attended FL. Atlantic U. OB debut 1990 in *Tamara*, followed by *Quiet on the Set*, *Beauty Part*, Bdwy in *Joseph and the Amazing Technicolor Dreamcoat* (1994), *Beauty and the Beast*, *Chicago* (Encores), *High Society*, *The Wild Party*, *The Scarlet Pimpernel*, *Bells Are Ringing*.

Tom Lacy

Debra Laws

Joel Leffert

Zoaunne LeRoy

Kuhn, Judy Born May 20, 1958 in New York, NY. Graduate Oberlin Col. OB debut 1985 in *Pearls*, followed by *Rodgers & Hart Revue, Dream True, As 1000 Cheer, Eli's Comin'*, Bdwy in *Mystery of Edwin Drood* (1985-also OB), *Rags, Les Miserables, Chess, Two Shakespearean Actors, She Loves Me, King David, Strike Up the Band* (Encores).

Kurtz, Swoosie Born Sept. 6, 1944 in Omaha, NE. Attended USC, LAMDA. Debut 1968 OB in *The Firebugs,* followed by *The Effect of Gamma Rays…, Life Class, Enter a Free Man, Children, Museum, Uncommon Women and Others, Wine Untouched, Summer, The Beach House, Lips Together Teeth Apart, The Mineola Twins, The Vagina Monologues, The Guys,* Bdwy in *Ah Wilderness!* (1975), *Tartuffe, A History of the American Film, 5th of July, House of Blue Leaves* (also OB), *Six Degrees of Separation* (also OB), *Imaginary Friends.*

Kybart, Peter Born Dec. 7, 1939 in Berlin, Germany. Attended Webber-Douglas Sch. Drama. OB debut 1966 in *The Parasite,* followed by *Trials of Oz, Cymbeline,* Bdwy debut 1997 in *Diary of Anne Frank,* followed by *Judgment at Nuremberg.*

Lacy, Tom Born Aug. 30, 1933 in New York, NY. OB debut 1965 in *Fourth Pig,* followed by *The Fantasticks, Shoemakers Holiday, Love and Let Love, The Millionairess, Crimes of Passion, Real Inspector Hound, Enemies, Flying Blind, Abel & Bela/Archtruc, Kingdom of Earth, Our Lady of Sligo, Tiny Alice,* Bdwy in *Last of the Red Hot Lovers* (1971), *Two Shakespearean Actors, Timon of Athens, Government Inspector, Holiday.*

Lage, Jordan Born Feb. 17, 1963 in Palo Alto, CA. Graduate NYU. OB debut 1988 in *Boy's Life,* followed by *Three Sisters, Virgin Molly, Distant Fires, Macbeth, Yes But So What?, Blue Hour, Been Taken, The Woods, Five Very Live, Hot Keys, As Sure as You Live, The Arrangement, The Lights, Shaker Heights, Missing Persons, Blaming Mom, Night and Her Stars, Dangerous Corner, Edmond, Joy of Going Somewhere Definite, Heart of Man, Mojo, Wolf Lullaby, The Hothouse, Force Continuum,* Bdwy debut 1989 in *Our Town,* followed by *Old Neighborhood, Gore Vidal's The Best Man.*

LaManna, Janine Born June 14 in Rochester, NY. Graduate Wagner Col. Bdwy debut 1998 in *Ragtime,* followed by *Seussical, Kiss Me, Kate.*

Lamb, Mary Ann Born July 4, 1959 in Seattle, WA. Attended Neighborhood Playhouse. Bdwy debut 1985 in *Song and Dance,* followed by *Starlight Express, Jerome Robbins' Broadway, Goodbye Girl, Fiorello!* (Encores), *Out of This World* (Encores), *Pal Joey* (Encores), *A Funny Thing Happened on the Way to the Forum* (1996), *Chicago, Promises Promises* (Encores), *Fosse, Seussical.*

Lambert, Mikel Sarah Born in Spokane, WA. Graduate Radcliffe Col., RADA. OB debut 1996, in *900 Oneonta,* followed by *Cyrano, Private Battles, The Way of the World, The Oresteia, Wit, Diana of Dobson's.*

Landers, Matt Born Oct. 21, 1952 in Mohawk Valley, NY. Attended Boston Cons. Debut OB 1974 in *Godspell* followed by *Mama's Little Angels, Telecast, Battle of Black and Dogs,* Bdwy in *Grease* (1975), *Working.*

Lane, Nathan Born Feb. 3, 1956 in Jersey City, NJ. Debut 1978 OB in *A Midsummer Night's Dream,* followed by *Love, Measure for Measure, Claptrap, Common Pursuit, In a Pig's Valise, Uncounted Blessings, Film Society, Lisbon Traviata, Bad Habits, Lips Together Teeth Apart, Mizlansky/ Zilensky,* Bdwy in *Present Laughter* (1982), *Merlin, Wind in the Willows, Some Americans Abroad, On Borrowed Time, Guys and Dolls, Laugher on the 23rd Floor, Love! Valour! Compassion!* (also OB), *A Funny Thing Happened on the Way to the Forum* (1996), *The Man Who Came to Dinner, The Producers.*

Lansbury, David Born Feb. 25, 1961 in New York, NY. Attended CT Col., Circle in the Square Theatre Sch., Central Sch. of Speech/Drama, London. OB debut 1989 in *Young Playwrights Festival,* followed by *Advice from a Caterpillar, Progress, Hapgood, Principality of Sorrows, Pride's Crossing, The Invisible Hand,* Bdwy in *Heidi Chronicles* (1990), *Major Barbara.*

LaPlatney, Martin Born Sept. 12, 1952 in Coos Bay, OR. Graduate Central WA St. U. Bdwy debut 1978 in *Crucifer of Blood,* followed by *Amadeus,* OB in *Passion of Dracula, Tartuffe, Private Battles, The Waverly Gallery, If It Was Easy, A Mind of It's Own, I'm Coming in Soon.*

Daniel C. Levine

Lorinda Lisitza

David Little

James W. Ludwig

Larsen, Liz Born Jan. 16, in Philadelphia, PA. Attended Hofstra U., SUNY Purchase. Bdwy debut 1981 in *Fiddler on the Roof*, followed by *Starmites*, *A Little Night Music*, (NYCO/LC), *Most Happy Fella*, *Damn Yankees*, *DuBarry Was a Lady* (Encores*)*, OB in *Kuni Leml*, *Hamlin*, *Personals*, *Starmites*, *Company*, *After These Messages*, *One Act Festival*, *Loman Family Picnic*, *Teibele and Her Demon*, *America's Sweetheart*, *The Adjustment*, *A New Brain*, *Little By Little*, *Newyorkers*.

Laurent, Wendell Born Dec. 1, 1961 in New Orleans, LA. Graduate Loyola U. OB debut 1991 in *You're a Good Man Charlie Brown*, followed by *My Sister Eileen*, *Holy Ghosts*, *Maderati*, *'Tis Pity She's a Whore*, *Chuppah*, *Rain from Heaven*.

Law, Mary Kate Born Sept. 12 in Harper, KS. Graduate Wichita St. U., Yale U. Bdwy debut 1989 in *Starmites*, followed by *Bloomer Girl* (CC), OB in *Key West*.

Laws, Debra Born in Houston, TX. Attended Houston Com. Col. Bdwy debut 1999 in *It Ain't Nothin' But the Blues*.

Leach, Nicole Born May 10, 1979 in NJ. OB debut 1994 in *Bring in the Morning*, followed by *Crumbs from the Table of Joy*, *UKIMWI*, *Starmites* 2001.

Leask, Katherine Born Sept. 2, 1957 in Munich, Germany. Graduate SMU. OB debut 1988 in *Man Who Climbed the Pecan Tree*, followed by *Cahoots*, *Melville Boys*, *Amphitryon*, *The Imposter*, *Stonewall Jackson's House*, *The "I" Word: Interns*, *The Way of the World*, *The Oresteia*, *Night Rules*.

Leavel, Beth Born Nov. 1, 1955 in Raleigh, NC. Graduate Meredith Col., UNC Greensboro. OB debut 1982 in *Applause*, followed by *Promises Promises*, *Broadway Juke Box*, *Unfinished Song*, *The Jazz Singer*, Bdwy in *42nd Street* (1984), *Crazy for You*, *Civil War*, *42nd Street*.

Lee, Jerry Born Jan. 23, 1946 in Oak Ridge, TN. Attended E. Mich. U. Debut 1974 OB in *The Gospel According to Mark Twain*, followed by *Ruby's Place*, *Midsummer*, *An Awfully Big Adventure*, *The Conversion*, *She Loves Me*, *The Overcoat*, *The Men's Group*, *Ten Little Indians*.

Lee, Darren Born June 8, 1972 in Long Beach, CA. Bdwy debut 1990 in *Shogun*, followed by *Miss Saigon*, *Victor Victoria*, *Boys from Syracuse* (Encores), *On The Town*, *Kiss Me Kate*, *Seussical*, OB in *Petrified Prince* (1994), *Chang Fragments*.

Lee, Karen Tsen Born in New York, NY. Graduate Hunter Col. OB debut 1991 in *Letters to a Student Revolutionary*, followed by *A Doll's House*, *Much Ado About Nothing*, *Macbeth*, *Desert Rites*, *Carry the Tiger to the Mountain*, *Fish-Eye View*.

Leeds, Jordan Born Nov. 29, 1961 in Queens, NY. Graduate SUNY Binghamton. Bdwy debut 1987 in *Les Miserables*, followed by *Sunset Blvd.*, OB in *Beau Jest*, *Angel Levine*, *Jest a Second*, *Fishkin Touch*, *I Love You You're Perfect Now Change*.

Leffert, Joel Born Dec. 8, 1951 in New York, NY. Graduate Brown U. OB debut 1976 in *Orphee*, followed by *Heroes*, *Last Burning*, *Relatively Speaking*, *The Bachelor*, *Scaramouche*, *Macbeth*, *Don Juan in Hell*, *Village Wooing*, *Long Smoldering*, *Loveplay*, *The Straw*, *Richard III*, *Hard Times*, *Gardens of Frau Hess*, Bdwy debut 1999 in *Not About Nightingales*.

Lehman, Ross Born Sept. 6, 1956 in State College, PA. Graduate PA St. Bdwy debut 1995 in *Tempest*, followed by *A Funny Thing Happened on the Way to the Forum*, *Epic Proportions*, *One Flew Over the Cuckoo's Nest*, OB in *'Tis a Pity She's a Whore*, *Wings*.

Leibman, Ron Born Oct. 11, 1937 in New York, NY. Attended Ohio Wesleyan Col., Actors Studio. Bdwy debut 1963 in *Dear Me the Sky is Falling*, followed by *Bicycle Ride to Nevada*, *The Deputy*, *We Bombed in New Haven*, for which he received a 1969 Theatre World Award, *Cop-Out*, *I Ought to Be in Pictures*, *Doubles*, *Rumors*, *Angels in America*, OB in *The Academy*, *John Brown's Body*, *Scapin*, *The Premise*, *Legend of Lovers*, *Dead End*, *Poker Session*, *Transfers*, *Room Service*, *Love Two*, *Rich and Famous*, *Children of Darkness*, *Non Pasquale*, *Give the Bishop My Faint Regards*, *Merchant of Venice*, *A Dybbuk*, *Adam Baum and the Jew Movie*, *A Connecticut Yankee in King Arthur's Court* (CC).

Charles Major

David Margulies

Stuart Marland

Jamahl Marsh

Leonard, Robert Sean Born Feb. 28, 1969 in Westwood, NJ. OB debut 1985 in *Sally's Gone She Left Her Name*, followed by *Coming of Age in Soho*, *Beach House*, *Young Playwrights Festival-And the Air Didn't Answer*, *When She Danced*, *Romeo and Juliet*, *Pitching to the Star*, *Good Evening*, *Great Unwashed*, *Principality of Sorrows*, *Below the Belt*, *You Never Can Tell*, Bdwy debut 1985 in *Brighton Beach Memoirs*, followed by *Breaking the Code*, *Speed of Darkness*, *Candida*, *Philadelphia Here I Come*, *Arcadia*, *The Iceman Cometh*, *The Music Man*, *The Invention of Love*.

LeRoy, Zoaunne Born Jan. 5, 1935 in Olympia, WA. Graduate U. of WA. OB debut 2001 in *A Skull in Connemara*.

LeStrange, Philip Born May 9, 1942 Bronx, NY. Graduate Catholic U., Fordham U. OB debut 1970 in *Getting Married*, followed by *Erogenous Zones*, *Quilling of Prue*, *Front Page*, *Six Degrees of Separation*, Bdwy in *A Small Family Business* (1992), *Guys and Dolls*, *Rose Tattoo*, *Last Night of Ballyhoo*, *Death of a Salesman*, *True West*, *Judgment at Nuremberg*.

Leverett, T. Doyle Born Jan. 19, 1954 in Kankakee, IL. Attended IL St. U., Vienna Music Academy. Bdwy debut 1992 in *The Most Happy Fella*, OB in *King of Hearts*.

Levine, Daniel C. Born July 30, 1972 in Boston, MA. Graduate Brandeis U., Tufts U. OB debut 1999 in *Naked Boys Singing!*, followed by *The Gorey Details*, Bdwy debut 2000 in *Jesus Christ Superstar*.

Linden, Hal Born March 20, 1931 in New York, NY. Attended CCNY, Amer. Theatre Wing. Bdwy debut 1956 in *Strip for Action*, followed by *Bells Are Ringing*, *Wildcat*, *On a Clear Day You Can See Forever*, *Subways are for Sleeping*, *Something More*, *The Apple Tree*, *Ilya Darling*, *The Education of H*Y*M*A*N K*A*P*L*A*N**, *The Rothschilds*, *The Sign in Sidney Brustein's Window*, *Pajama Game*, *Three Men on a Horse*, *I'm Not Rappaport*, *The Sisters Rosensweig*, OB debut in *Anything Goes*, followed by *Visiting Mr. Green*.

Linser, Bruce Born Nov. 1, 1967 in Menomonee Falls, WI. Attended UW Eau Claire, U. of MN Minneapolis. OB debut in *Naked Boys Singing*, followed by *The Performer's Confession*.

Lisitza, Lorinda Born March 8, 1970 in Porcupine Plain, Canada. Graduate U. of Saskatchewan, AMDA. OB debut 2000 in *Berlin to Broadway*.

Little, David Born March 21 in Wadesboro, NC. Graduate William & Mary Col., Catholic U. OB debut 1968 in *MacBird*, followed by *Iphigenia in Aulis*, *Antony and Cleopatra*, *Antigone*, *An Enemy of the People*, *The Wisteria Trees*, *Three Sons*, *Almost in Vegas*, *Sam and Itkeh*, *Bobbi Boland*, Bdwy in *Thieves* (1973), *Les Blancs*, *Zalmen or the Madness of God*, *Blood Knot*, *Six Degrees of Separation* (also OB).

Litzsinger, Sarah E. Born Oct. 22, 1971 in Indianapolis, IN. Bdwy debut 1983 in *Marilyn*, followed by *Oliver*, *Beauty and the Beast*, OB in *Nightmare Alley*.

Long, Jodi Born in New York, NY. Graduate SUNY Purchase. Bdwy debut 1962 in *Nowhere to Go But Up*, followed by *Loose Ends*, *Bacchae*, *Getting Away with Murder*, OB in *Fathers and Sons*, *Family Devotions*, *Rohwer*, *Tooth of the Crime*, *Dream of Kitamura*, *Midsummer Night's Dream*, *Madame de Sade*, *The Wash*, *Golden Child*, *Red*, *Old Money*.

Lopez, Carlos Born May 14, 1963 in Sunnyvale, CA. Attended CA St. U. Hayward. OB debut 1987 in *Wish You Were Here*, Bdwy in *The Pajama Game* (NYCO-1989), *A Chorus Line*, *Grand Hotel*, *Guys and Dolls*, *Grease*, *Wonderful Town* (NYCO), *Annie Get Your Gun*.

Lopez, Jonathan Born April 21, 1969 in Manila, Philippines. Graduate Cleveland St. U., Brooklyn Col. OB debut in *True Confessions of a Dogeater*, followed by *Dogeaters*.

Lopez, Priscilla Born Feb. 26, 1948 in The Bronx, NY. Bdwy debut 1966 in *Breakfast at Tiffany's*, followed by *Henry Sweet Henry*, *Lysistrata*, *Company*, *Her First Roman*, *Boy Friend*, *Pippin*, *Chorus Line* (also OB), *Day in Hollywood/Night in the Ukraine*, *Nine*, OB in *What's a Nice Country Like You Doing in a State Like This*, *Key Exchange*, *Buck*, *Extremities*, *Non Pasquak*, *Be Happy for Me*, *Times and Appetites of Toulouse-Lautrec*, *Marathon '88*, *Other People's Money*, *Antigone in NY*, *Newyorkers*.

Loud, David Born Nov. 28, 1961 in Cincinnati, OH. Attended Yale U. Bdwy debut 1981 in *Merrily We Roll Along*, OB in *Merrily We Roll Along in Concert*.

Michael Mastro

Kathryn Meisle

Gregory Mikell

Mark Nadler

Lovejoy, Deirdre Born June 30, 1962 in Abilene, TX. Graduate U. Evansville, NYU. OB debut 1988 in *Midsummer Night's Dream*, followed by *Henry IV Part 1, Hannah 1939, Machinal, Alice in Wonderland, Don Juan, Preservation Society, Water Children, Imperfect Chemistry*, Bdwy 1991 in *Six Degrees of Separation*, followed by *Getting and Spending, The Gathering.*

Lowe, Chad Born Jan. 15, 1968 in Dayton, OH. Debut 1990 OB in *Grotesque Lovesongs* followed by *Burning Blue.*

Ludwig, James W. Born Nov. 16, 1967 in Subic Bay Naval Base, Philippines. Graduate U. MI, U. WA. OB debut 1995 in *jon & jen*, followed by *Louisiana Purchase, After the Fair, Suburb.*

LuPone, Robert Born July 29, 1956 in Brooklyn, NY. Graduate Juilliard. Bdwy debut 1970 in *Minnie's Boys*, followed by *Jesus Christ Superstar, The Rothschilds, Magic Show, A Chorus Line, Saint Joan, Late Night Comic, Zoya's Apartment, View from the Bridge, True West, A Thousand Clowns*, OB in *Charlie Was Here, Twelfth Night, In Connecticut, Snow Orchid, Lemon, Black Angel, The Quilling of Prue, Time Framed, Class 1 Acts, Remembrance, Children of Darkness, Kill, Winter Lies, The Able-Bodied Seaman, Clothes for a Summer Hotel, The Light Outside.*

Lyles, Leslie Born in Plainfield, NJ. Graduate Monmouth Col., Rutgers U. OB debut 1981 in *Sea Marks*, followed by *Highest Standard of Living, Vanishing Act, I Am Who I Am, The Arbor, Terry by Terry, Marathon '88, Sleeping Dogs, Nebraska, My House Play, Life During Wartime, Angel of Death, Sam I Am, The Workroom, Dark Ride, Brutality of Fact, Scotland Road, The Perpetual Patient, Imperfect Love, Passion Play, Down the Garden Paths*, Bdwy in *Night and Day* (1979), *Hide and Seek, Real Thing, Garden District, Ah, Wilderness!.*

Ma, Rosanne Born Feb. 22, 1974 in Stockton, CA. Graduate International Actor Training Acad., UC Santa Barbara. OB debut 1999 in *The Joy Luck Club*, followed by *Rashomon.*

MacIntyre, Marguerite Born in Detroit, MI. Graduate USC, RADA. Debut 1988 OB in *Some Summer Night*, followed by *Weird Romance, Awakening of Spring, Annie Warbucks, Mata Hari, No Way to Treat a Lady*, Bdwy in *City of Angels* (1991), *Jane Eyre.*

Mackay, Lizbeth Born March 7 in Buffalo, NY. Graduate Adelphi U., Yale U. Bdwy debut 1981 in *Crimes of the Heart*, for which she received a 1982 Theatre World Award, followed by *Death and the Maiden, Abe Lincoln in Illinois, Heiress, The Price*, OB in *Kate's Diary, Tales of the Lost Formicans, Price of Fame, Old Boy, Durang Durang, The Seagull, Lips, Two-Headed More Lies About Jerzy.*

MacPherson, Lori Born July 23 in Albany, NY. Attended Skidmore Col. Bdwy debut 1988 in *The Phantom of the Opera*, followed by *Bloomer Girl* (CC).

Major, Charles Born March 19 in New York, NY. Attended Bates Col., Adelphi U., Neighborhood Playhouse. Bdwy debut 1967 in *Spofford*, followed by *Sly Fox*, OB in *Gloria and Esperanza, The Elizabethans, Sports Czar, The Iceman Cometh, Othello, Six Characters in Search of an Author, An Ordinary Man, Tribute, Better Living, Black Hat Karma, Queens!, Sitting Pretty.*

Malone, Michael Born April 3, 1968 in Nashville, TN. Graduate Harvard U., Amer. Rep Inst. OB debut 1993 in *Orestes*, followed by *Anything Cole, Stonewall: Night Variations, Message to Michael, Ascendancy*, Bdwy debut 2000 in *42nd Street.*

Mann, Terrence Born in 1951 in KY. Graduate NC Sch. Of Arts. Bdwy debut 1980 in *Barnum*, followed by *Cats, Rags, Les Miserables, Jerome Robbins' Broadway, Beauty and the Beast, Christmas Carol, Getting Away with Murder, Promises Promises* (Encores), *Scarlet Pimpernel, Rocky Horror Show*, OB in *Night at the Fights, Queen's Diamond, Assassins, Arsenic and Old Lace* (CC).

Marcum, Brian J. Born May 17, 1972 in Lexington, TN. Graduate OK City U. Bdwy debut 1999 in *The Gershwins' Fascinating Rhythm*, followed by *42nd Street.*

Marcus, Daniel Born May 26, 1955 in Redwood City, CA. Graduate Boston U. Bdwy debut 1981 in *Pirates of Penzance*, followed by *1776*, OB in *La Bohême, Kuni Leml, Flash of Lightning, Pajama Game, Gunmetal Blues, Merchant of Venice, Carmelina, Urinetown.*

Margulies, David Born Feb. 19, 1937 in New York, NY Graduate CCNY. OB debut 1958 in *Golden Six*, followed by *Six Characters in Search of an Author*, *Tragical Historie of Dr. Faustus*, *Tango*, *Little Murders*, *Seven Days of Mourning*, *La Analysis*, *An Evening with the Poet Senator*, *Kid Champion*, *The Man with the Flower in His Mouth*, *Old Tune*, *David and Paula*, *Cabal of Hypocrites*, *The Perfect Party*, *Just Say No*, *George Washington Dances*, *I'm with Ya Duke*, *The Treatment*, *Tales of I.B. Singer*, *In the Western Garden*, *Visiting Mr. Green*, *Cranes*, *Big Potato*, *In Dreams and Gimpel*, Bdwy in *Iceman Cometh* (1973), *Zalmen or the Madness of God*, *Comedians*, *Break a Leg*, *West Side Waltz*, *Brighton Beach Memoirs*, *Conversations with My Father*, *Angels in America*, *A Thousand Clowns*.

Marineau, Barbara Born Aug. 22 in Detroit, MI. Graduate W. MI U. Bdwy debut in *Shenandoah* (1977) followed by *The Best Little Whore House in Texas*, *Beauty and the Beast*, *Christmas Carol*, OB in *I'm Getting My Act Together* (1981), *Bittersuite*, *Witch of Wall Street*, *Our American Ballroom Theatre*, *Requiem for William*, *A Man of No Importance*..

Marks, Kenneth Born Feb. 17, 1954 in Harwick, PA. Graduate U. PA, Lehigh U. OB debut 1978 in *Clara Bow Loves Gary Cooper*, followed by *Canadian Cothic*, *Time and the Conways*, *Savoury Meringue*, *Thrombo*, *Fun*, *1-2-3-4-5*, *Manhattan Class I Acts*, *Bright Room Called Day*, *Pix*, *Sabina*, *Easter*, *First Picture Show*, *Brutality of Fact*, *Bright Lights Big City*, *When They Speak of Rita*, *Birdseed Bundles*, *Blur*, Bdwy in *Dancing at Lughnasa* (1992).

Marland, Stuart Born Feb. 28, 1959 in Montreal, Can. Attended UCLA. Bdwy debut 1993 in *Cyrano-The Musical*, followed by *Jekyll & Hyde*, OB in *Madison Avenue*, *Birdwatcher*, *The Brass Jackal*, *Scoundrel*.

Marsh, Jamahl Born Oct. 27, 1973 in Newark, NJ. Graduate Rutgers U. OB debut 2000 in *A Lesson Before Dying*.

Marshall, Donna Lee Born Feb. 27, 1958 in Mt. Holly, NJ. Attended AADA. OB debut 1987 in *By Strouse*, followed by *Human Comedy*, *Sidewalkin'*, *Charley's Tale*, Bdwy in *Pirates of Penzance*, *Christmas Carol*, *Footloose*, *Tom Sawyer*.

Martin, Lucy Born Feb. 8, 1942 in New York, NY. Graduate Sweet Briar Col. OB debut 1962 in *Electra*, followed by *Happy as Larry*, *Trojan Women*, *Iphigenia in Aulis*, *Wives*, *Cost of Living*, *Substance of Fire*, *Private Battles*, *Passion Play*, *Strictly Personal*, Bdwy in *Shelter* (1973) *Children of a Lesser God*, *Pygmalion*, *The Sisters Rosensweig*, *Major Barbara*.

Mastrantonio, Mary Elizabeth Born Nov. 17, 1958 in Chicago, IL. Attended U of IL. Bdwy debut in *West Side Story* (1980), followed by *Copperfield*, *Oh Brother*, *Human Comedy*, *Marriage of Figaro*, *Man of La Mancha*, OB in *Henry V*, *Christmas Carol*, *Measure for Measure*, *The Knife*, *Twelfth Night*, *Northeast Local*.

Mastro, Michael (formerly Mastrototaro) Born May 17, 1962 in Albany, NY. Graduate NYU. OB debut 1984 in *Victoria Station*, followed by *Submarines*, *Naked Truth/Name Those Names*, *Darker Purpose*, *Hot Keys*, *Crows in the Cornfield*, *City*, *Escape from Happiness*, *Naked Faith*, *Alone But Not Lonely*, *Water Children*, *Tamicanfly*, Bdwy debut 1995 in *Love! Valour! Compassion!*, followed by *Side Man*, *Judgment at Nuremberg*.

Mather, Leisa Born July 16, 2000 in Melbourne, Australia. OB debut 2000 in *Forbidden Broadway Cleans Up Its Act*.

Matsusaka, Tom Born Aug. 8 in Wahiawa, HI. Graduate MI St. U. Bdwy debut 1968 in *Mame*, followed by *Ride the Winds*, *Pacific Overtures*, *South Pacific*, OB in *Agamemnon*, *Chu Chem*, *Jungle of Cities*, *Santa Anita '42*, *Extenuating Circumstances*, *Rohwer*, *Teahouse*, *Song of a Nisei Fisherman*, *Empress of China*, *Pacific Overtures* (1984), *Eat a Bowl of Tea*, *Shogun Macbeth*, *The Imposter*, *Privates*, *Lucky Come Hawaii*, *Caucasian Chalk Circle*, *Carry the Tiger to the Mountain*, *The Joy Luck Club*, *The Teahouse of the August Moon*, *Rashomon*.

Mau, Les J.N. Born Jan. 8, 1954 in Honolulu, HI. Graduate U. of HI. OB debut 1983 in *Teahouse*, followed by *Empress of China*, *Eat a Bowl of Tea*, *Lucky Come Hawaii*, *Wilderness*, *Pacific Overtures*, *New Living Newspaper*, *Geniuses*, *Friends*, *Dog and His Master*, *The Gaol Gate/Purgatory*, *Tibet Does Not Exist*, *The Joy Luck Club*, *The Poet of Columbus Ave*, *Rashomon*.

Maxwell, Jan Born Nov. 20, 1956 in Fargo, ND. Graduate Moorhead St. U. Bdwy debut 1990 in *City of Angels*, followed by *Dancing at Lughnasa*, *Doll's House*, *Sound of Music*, *The Dinner Party*, OB in *Everybody Everybody*, *Hot Feet*, *Light Years to Chicago*, *Ladies of the Fortnight*, *Two Gentlemen of Verona*, *Marriage Fool*, *Oedipus Private Eye*, *Inside Out*, *The Professional*.

Maxwell, Roberta Born in Canada. OB debut 1968 in *Two Gentlemen of Verona*, followed by *A Whistle in the Dark*, *Slag*, *Plough and the Stars*, *Merchant of Venice*, *Ashes*, *Mary Stuart*, *Lydie Breeze*, *Before the Dawn*, *Real Estate*, *When I Was a Girl*, *Cripple of Inishmaan*, *June and the Paycock*, Bdwy in *Prime of Miss Jean Brodie*, *Henry V*, *House of Atreus*, *Resistible Rise of Arturo Ui*, *Othello*, *Hay Fever*, *There's One in Every Marriage*, *Equus*, *The Merchant*, *Our Town*, *Summer and Smoke*.

May, Deven Born April 3, 1971 in Whittier, CA. Attended Southern UT U. OB debut 2001 in *Bat Boy*, for which he received a 2001 Theatre World Award.

May, Seth Michael Born April 17, 1971 in New York, NY. OB debut in *Richard II/Richard III*, followed by *Middle Finger*.

McCallum, David Born Sept. 19, 1933 in Scotland. Attended Chapman Col. Bdwy debut 1968 in *Flip Side*, followed by *California Suite*, *Amadeus*, OB debut in *After the Prize*, followed by *The Philanthropist*, *Ghosts*, *Nasty Little Secrets*, *Communicating Doors*, *Julius Caesar*, *Time and Again*.

McCarthy, Jeff Born Oct. 16, 1954 in Los Angeles, CA. Graduate Amer. Conservatory. Bdwy debut 1982 in *Pirates of Penzance*, followed by *Zorba* (1983), *Beauty and the Beast*, *Side Show*, OB in *Gifts of the Magi*, *On the 20th Century*, *Sisters Rosensweig*, *Urinetown*.

McClintock, Jodie Lynne Born April 7, 1955 in Pittsburgh, PA. Graduate Westminster Col. Debut 1988 OB in *As You Like It* followed by *1984*, *The Art of Success*, *Free Zone*, *Daisy in the Dreamtime*, Bdwy in *Long Day's Journey into Night*.

McConahay, Liz Graduate U. WI, Attended Royal Nat. Theatre Sch. London. OB debut 1997 in *Secrets Every Smart Traveler Should Know*, Bdwy debut 2000 in *The Full Monty*.

McCormick, Carolyn Born Sept. 19, 1959 in TX. Graduate Williams Col. OB debut 1988 in *In Perpetuity Throughout the Universe*, followed by *Lips Together Teeth Apart*, *Laureen's Whereabouts*, *Donahue Sisters*, *Oedipus*, *Dinner with Friends*, Bdwy in *The Dinner Party*.

McCune, Rod Born Oct. 12, 1962 in Jasper, IN. Graduate Purdue U. Butler U. Bdwy debut 1993 in *Ain't Broadway Grand* followed by *Movin' Out.*

McCulloh, Barbara Born March 5 in Washington, DC. Attended Col. of William & Mary, U. of MD. OB debut 1984 in *Up in Central Park*, followed by *Kuni-Leml, On the 20th Century, 1-2-3-4-5, Life Forms, Leave It to Me*, Bdwy in *King and I, Peter Pan.*

McDonald, Daniel Born July 30 in Scranton, PA. OB debut 1994 in *First Night*, followed by *Chesterfield, The Personal Equation, Quartett* (BAM), Bdwy debut 1997 in *Steel Pier*, for which he won a 1997 Theatre World Award, followed by *High Society.*

McDonald, Tanny Born Feb. 13 in Princeton, NJ. Graduate Vassar Col. OB debut 1961 in *American Savoyards*, followed by *All in Love, To Broadway with Love, Carricknabauna, The Beggar's Opera, Brand, Goodbye, Dan Bailey, Total Eclipse, Gorky, Don Juan Comes Back from the War, Vera with Kate, Francis, On Approval, A Definite Maybe, Temptation, Titus Andronicus, Hamlet, June, Johnny Pye and the Foolkiller, Birdseed Bundles, Sitting Pretty*, Bdwy in *Fiddler on the Roof, Come Summer, The Lincoln Mask, Clothes for a Summer Hotel, Macbeth, Man of La Mancha.*

McDonough, J.M. Born April 1, 1946 in Baltimore, MD. Graduate U. of the South. OB debut 1999 in *The Made Man*, followed by *Descent, Sweeney Todd.*

McEntire, Reba Born March 28, 1955 in McAlester, OK. Graduate Southeastern St. U. Bdwy debut 2001 in *Annie Get Your Gun.*

McGiver, Boris Born Jan. 23, 1962 in Cobleskill, NY. Graduate Ithaca Col., SUNY Cobleskill, NYU. OB debut 1994 in *Richard II*, followed by *Hapgood, Troilus and Cressida, Timon of Athens, Henry VI, Anthony and Cleopatra, The Devils, Lydie Breeze, More Lies about Jerzy.*

McGrane, Paul Born in Dublin, Ireland. OB debut 1994 in *Brothers of the Brush*, followed by *Whistle in the Dark, Da, Plough and the Stars, Mass Appeal. Major Barbara, Long Day's Journey into Night, The Irish…and How They Got That Way, The Shaughraun, The Picture of Dorian Gray.*

McGrath, Michael Born Sept. 25, 1957 in Worcester, MA. OB debut 1988 in *Forbidden Bdwy*, followed by *Cocoanuts, Forbidden Hollywood, Louisiana Purchase, Secrets Every Smart Traveler Should Know, Exactly Like You, Game Show*, Bdwy in *My Favorite Year* (1992), *Goodbye Girl, DuBarry Was a Lady* (Encores), *Swinging on a Star*, for which he received a 1996 Theatre World Award, *Boys from Syracuse* (Encores), *Little Me.*

McRobbie, Peter Born Jan. 31, 1943 in Hawick, Scotland. Graduate Yale U. OB debut 1976 in *The Wobblies*, followed by *Devil's Disciple, Cinders, The Ballad of Soapy Smith, Rosmersholm, American Bagpipes, Richard III, Timon of Athens, Memory of Water*, Bdwy in *Whose Life Is It Anyway?* (1979), *Macbeth* (1981), *Mystery of Edwin Drood, Master Builder* (1992), *Saint Joan, Night Must Fall, The Invention of Love.*

Medina, Aixa M. Rosario Born July 5, 1965 in Rio Piedras, Puerto Rico. Graduate U. Puerto Rico. Bdwy debut 1995 in *Victor/Victoria*, followed by *Once Upon a Mattress* (1996), OB in *Ziegfeld Follies of 1936, A Connecticut Yankee in King Arthur's Court* (CC).

Meisels, Annie Born in Baltimore, MD. Graduate Rutgers U. OB debut 1992 in *Things That Should Be Said*, followed by *Little Women, Caught in the Act, Pera Palas, My Mother's a Baby Boy.*

Meisle, Kathryn Born June 7 in Appleton, WI. Graduate Smith Col., UNC Chapel Hill. OB debut 1988 in *Dandy Dick*, followed *by Cahoots, Othello, As You Like It* (CP), *Brutality of Fact, The Most Fabulous Story Ever Told, What You Get and What You Expect, Old Money*, Bdwy in *Racing Demon* (1995), *The Rehearsal, London Assurance.*

Menzel, Idina Born 1972 in Long Island, NY. Graduate NYU. OB debut 1996 in *Rent* (also Bdwy), followed by *The Wild Party, Hair* (CC).

Merediz, Olga Born Feb. 15, 1956 in Guantanamo, Cuba. Graduate Tulane U. Bdwy debut 1987 in *The Human Comedy*, OB in *El Bravo!, Women Without Men, El Grande de Coca-Cola, The Blessing, The Lady from Havana, 10th Young Playwrights Festival*, Bdwy in *Man of La Mancha.*

Michenner, Adam Born March 12, 1931 in London, England. Graduate CCNY, NYU. Debut 1988 OB in *Revenge of the Space Pandas*, followed by *Troilus and Cresida, King John, The Walk, Merry Wives of Windsor, The Illusionists, Dorian, Baked Meats, The Joneses, River Moves, Danton's Death, A Different Kind of Dog, Three Sisters, Trelawny of The Wells, Ten Little Indians.*

Mikell, Gregory Born June 18, 1966 in Statesboro, GA. Graduate Jacksonville St. U. OB debut in *Carnivore*, followed by *A Midsummer Night's Dream, Welcome to Our City.*

Miller, Andrew Born May 25 in Racine, WI. Attended U. of IL, Royal Nat. Theatre Studio. OB debut 1995 in *Blue Man Group: Tubes*, followed by *A Hamlet, Macbeth, Hunting Humans, In Betweens, Snapshots, The Folsom Head, The Bloomers, Sex, Troilus and Cressida.*

Miller, Betty Born March 27, 1925 in Boston, MA. Attended UCLA. OB in *Summer and Smoke, Cradle Song, La Ronde, Plays for Bleecker St., Desire Under the Elms, The Balcony, Power and the Glory, Beaux Stratagem, Gandhi, Girl on the Via Flammia, Hamlet, Summer, Before the Dawn, Curtains, Lake Hollywood, More Lies about Jerzy*, Bdwy in *You Can't Take It with You, Right You Are, Wild Duck, Cherry Orchard, Touch of the Poet, Eminent Domain, Queen and the Rebels, Richard III.*

Miller, William Marshall Born June 19, 1951 in Summit, NJ. OB debut 2001 in *If It Was Easy.*

Milligan, (Jacob) Tuck Born March 25, 1949 in Kansas City, MO. Graduate U. Kansas City. Bdwy debut 1976 in *Equus*, followed by *Crucifer of Blood, The Kentucky Cycle, Herbal Bed, A Moon for the Misbegotten*, OB in *Beowulf, Everybody's Gettin' into the Act, Arsenic and Old Lace* (CC).

Mills, Elizabeth Born Aug. 3, 1967 in San Jose, CA. Attended San Jose St. U. Bdwy debut 1993 in *Ain't Broadway Grand*, followed by *Crazy for You, DuBarry was a Lady* (Encores), *Kiss Me Kate*, OB in *A Connecticut Yankee in King Arthur's Court* (CC).

Montano, Robert Born April 22 in Queens, NY. Attended Adelphi U. Bdwy debut 1995 in *Cats*, followed by *Chita Rivera + Two, Legs Diamond, Kiss of the Spider Woman, On the Town*, OB in *The Chosen* (1987), *The Torturer's Visit, How Are Things in Costa del Fuego?, Picture Perfect, Young Playwrights Festival, On the Town, Knepp.*

Kathy Najimy   Casey Nicholaw   Marina Nichols   Julianne Nicholson

Moore, Christopher Born May 7, 1972 in Minneapolis, MN. Graduate Juilliard, U. St. Thomas. OB debut 1997 in *Measure for Measure*, followed by *Venice Preserv'd*, *Richard II*, *School for Scandal*, *The Forest*, *Candida*, *The Country Wife*, *The Miser*, *The Seagull*, *Merry Wives of Windsor*, *The Way of the World*, *The Oresteia*, *John Gabriel Borkman*, *A Will of His Own*, *Andromoche*, *The Cherry Orchard*.

Moore, Dana Born in Sewickley, PA. Bdwy debut 1982 in *Sugar Babies*, followed by *Dancin'*, *Copperfield*, *On Your Toes*, *Singin' in the Rain*, *Sweet Charity*, *Dangerous Games*, *A Chorus Line*, *Will Rogers Follies*, *Pal Joey* (Encores), *Fosse*, OB in *Petrified Prince*, *Camila*.

Moore, Lee Born Feb. 19, 1929 in Brooklyn, NY. OB debut 1978 in *Once More with Feeling*, followed by *The Caine Mutiny Court-Martial*, *Christopher Blake*, *Cat and Canary*, *Shrunken Heads*, *Raspberry Picker*, *Blessed Event*, *Before Dawn*, *Small Potatoes*, *Alison's House*, *Welcome to Our City*.

Moran, Martin Born Dec. 29, 1959 in Denver, CO. Attended Stanford U., Amer. Conservatory Theatre. OB debut 1983 in *Spring Awakening*, followed by *Once on a Summer's Day*, *1-2-3-4-5*, *Jacques Brel Is Alive* (1992), *Bed and Sofa*, *Floyd Collins*, *Fallen Angles*, Bdwy in *Oliver!* (1984), *Big River*, *How to Succeed in Business Without Really Trying* (1995), *Titanic*, *Cabaret*, *Bells Are Ringing*.

Morfogen, George Born March 30, 1933 in New York, NY. Graduate Brown U., Yale U. OB debut 1957 in *Trial of D. Karamazov*, followed by *Christmas Oratorio*, *Othello*, *Good Soldier Schweik*, *Cave Dwellers*, *Once in a Lifetime*, *Total Eclipse*, *Ice Age*, *Prince of Homburg*, *Biography: A Game*, *Mrs. Warren's Profession*, *Principia Scriptoriae*, *Tamara*, *Maggie and Misha*, *Country Girl*, *Othello*, *As You Like It* (CP), *Uncle Bob*, *Henry V*, *Hope Zone*, *The Disputation*, *Cyrano*, *Cymbeline*, *Hamlet*, *Uncle Bob*, Bdwy in *Fun Couple* (1962), *Kingdoms*, *Arms and the Man*, *An Inspector Calls*.

Morgan, Cass Born April 15 in Rochester, NY. Attended Adelphi U. OB debut 1984 in *La Boheme*, followed by *Another Paradise*, *The Knife*, *Catfish Loves Anna*, *Feast Here Tonight*, *Can Can*, *Merrily We Roll Along*, *Inside Out*, *Floyd Collins*, *The Immigrant*, Bdwy in *Hair* (1969), *Pump Boys and Dinettes*, *Human Comedy*, *Beauty and the Beast*, *1776*.

Moritz, Marc Born Feb. 4, 1956 in Cleveland, OH. Graduate Kent State U. Debut 1978 OB in *Androcles and the Lion* followed by *The House of Blue Leaves*, *Total Eclipse*, *Merrily We Roll Along in Concert*, Bdwy 1981 in *Merrily We Roll Along*.

Morris, Kenny Born Nov. 4, 1954 in Brooklyn, NY. Graduate UNC Chapel Hill. OB debut 1981 in *Francis*, followed by *She Loves Me*, *Half a World Away*, *Jacques Brel Is Alive and Well and Living in Paris*, *Quick-Change Room*, *Jayson*, *Death in England*, *Leave It to Me*, *I Married an Angel*, Bdwy 1983 in *Joseph and the Amazing Technicolor Dreamcoat*, followed by *Tenth Man*.

Morton, Joe Born Oct. 18. 1947 in New York, NY. Attended Hofstra U. OB debut 1968 in *A Month of Sundays*, followed by *Salvation*, *Charlie Was Here and Now He's Gone*, *G. R. Point*, *Crazy Horse*, *A Winter's Tale*, *Johnny on a Spot*, *A Midsummer Night's Dream*, *The Recruiting Officer*, *Oedipus the King*, *The Wild Duck*, *Rhinestone*, *Souvenirs*, *Cheapside*, *King John*, *Measure for Measure* (CP), Bdwy in *Hair*, *Two Gentlemen of Verona*, *Tricks*, *Raisin*, for which he received a 1974 Theatre World Award, *Oh Brother!*, *Honky Tonk Nights*, *Lady in the Dark in Concert*, *Art*.

Muenz, Richard Born in 1948 in Hartford, CT. Attended Eastern Baptist Col. Bdwy debut 1976 in *1600 Pennsylvania Avenue*, followed by *Most Happy Fella*, *Camelot*, *Rosalie in Concert*, *Chess*, *Pajama Game* (LC), *Nick and Nora*, *110 in the Shade* (LC), *Wonderful Town* (LC), *42nd Street*, OB in *Leading Men Don't Dance*.

Murney, Julia Born Jan. 14, 1969 in State College, PA. Graduate Syracuse U. OB debut 2000 in *The Wild Party*, followed by *A Class Act*, *Time and Again*, *Crimes of the Heart*.

Murphy, Karen Born Aug. 11, 1958 in White Plains, NY. Attended Boston Consv., UMA. Debut 1989 OB in *Forbidden Broadway* followed by *Hysterical Blindness*, *Greenwillow*, *Showtune*, Bdwy in *Christmas Carol* (1994).

Bill Nolte

Ben Nordstrom

Jim Norton

Thomas James O'Leary

Murray, Brian Born Oct. 9, 1939 in Johannesburg, SA. OB debut 1964 in *The Knack*, followed by *King Lear, Ashes, Jail Diary of Albie Sachs, Winter's Tale, Barbarians, The Purging, Midsummer Night's Dream, Recruiting Officer, Arcata Promise, Candide in Concert, Much Ado About Nothing, Hamlet, Merry Wives of Windsor, Travels with My Aunt, Entertaining Mr. Sloane, Molly Sweeney, The Entertainer, Da, Mud River Stone, Misalliance, Long Day's Journey into Night, Spreadeagle, The Butterfly Collection, The Play about the Baby*, Bdwy in *All in Good Time* (1965), *Rosencrantz and Guildenstern Are Dead, Sleuth, Da, Noises Off, Small Family Business, Black Comedy, Racing Demon, Little Foxes, Twelfth Nite, Uncle Vanya*.

Mydell, Joseph Born June 30, 1945 in Savannah, GA. Graduate NYU. Debut 1969 OB in *The Ofay Watcher*, followed by *Volpone, Henry IV, Please Don't Cry and Say No, Love's Labour's Lost, Lyrics of the Hearthside*, Bdwy in *Media*.

Nadler, Mark Born Oct. 14, 1961 in Waterloo, IA. Attended Interlochen Arts Academy. OB debut 1990 in *7 O'Clock at the Top of the Gate*, followed by *The Sheik of Avenue B, Nonstop Broadway Hootenany, Dame Edna's Royal Tour, Gershwin's American Rhapsody*

Najimy, Kathy Born in San Diego, CA. Attended San Diego St. U. Bdwy debut 2001 in *Dirty Blonde*.

Nakahara, Ron Born July 20, 1947 in Honolulu, HI. Attended U. HI, U. TN. OB debut 1981 in *Danton's Death*, followed by *Flowers and Household Gods, Rohwer, A Midsummer Night's Dream, Teahouse, Song for Nisei Fishermen, Eat a Bowl of Tea, Once Is Never Enough, Noiresque, Play Ball, Three Sisters, And the Soul Shall Dance. Earth and Sky, Cambodia Agonistes, A Doll's House, School for Wives, Ah, Wilderness!, Rashomon*, Bdwy in *A Few Good Men* (1989).

Nauffts, Geoffrey Born Feb. 3, 1961 in Arlington, MA. Graduate NYU. OB debut 1987 in *Moonchildren*, followed by *Stories from Home, Another Time Another Place, The Alarm, Jerusalem Oratorio, The Survivor, Spring Awakening, Summer Winds, Saturday Mourning Cartoons, Flyovers, June Moon, Maiden's Prayer, Snakebit, Once Around the City*, Bdwy in *A Few Good Men* (1989).

Naughton, Keira Born June 3, 1971 in New Haven, CT. Graduate Skidmore Col., NYU. Bdwy debut in *Three Sisters*, OB debut in *All My Sons*, followed by *Tesla's Letters, Hotel Universe, Uncle Jack, Snapshots 2000*.

Nicholaw, Casey Born Oct. 6. Attended UCLA. OB debut 1986 in *Pajama Game*, followed by *Petrified Prince*, Bdwy in *Crazy for You* (1992), *Best Little Whorehouse Goes Public, Victor Victoria, Steel Pier, Seussical*.

Nichols, Marina Born Nov. 20, 1972 in Lvov, Russia. OB debut 2000 in *A Taste of Honey*.

Nicholson, Julianne Born July 1, 1971 in Medford, MA. Attended Hunter Col. OB debut 2000 in *Stranger*.

Niebanck, Paul Born Sept. 22, 1964 in Philadelphia, PA. Graduate Boston U., Yale U. OB debut 1997 in *American Clock*, followed by *The Seagull, Leaving Queens*.

Nobbs, Keith Born 1979 in Kingswood, TX. Attended Columbia U. OB in *Stupid Kids, Fuddy Meers, Four*.

Nolen, Dean Born Oct. 5, 1964 in Dallas, TX. Graduate Hardin-Simmons U., Yale. OB debut 2000 in *Tabletop*.

Nolte, Bill Born June 4, 1953 in Toledo, OH. Graduate CCCM OB debut 1977 in *Wonderful Town*, followed by Bdwy in *Cats* (1985), *Me and My Girl, The Secret Garden, Joseph and the Amazing Technicolor Dreamcoat* (1993), *Christmas Carol* (MSG), *1776, Jane Eyre*.

Nordstrom, Ben Born Nov. 26, 1976 in Dallas, TX. Graduate Webster U. OB debut 2000 in *The Gorey Details*.

Norton, Jim Born Jan 4, 1938 in Dublin, Ireland. Bdwy debut 1999 in *The Weir*, OB 2000 in *Juno and the Paycock*.

Noth, Chris Born Nov. 13, 1957 in Madison, WI. Graduate Yale U., attended Marlborough Coll, Neighborhood Playhouse. OB in *Patronage, Arms and the Man, Kentucky Cycle*, Bdwy in *The Best Man* (2000).

O'Connor, Susan Born March 11, 1975 in Las Cruces, NM. Graduate U. of FL. OB debut 2000 in *Never Swim Alone*, followed by *See Bob Run*.

Björn Olsen

Kevin Pariseau

Robyne M. Parrish

Estelle Parsons

Ohama, Matsuko OB debut 2001 in *Straight as a Line.*

Ojeda, Perry Laylon Born April 25, 1968 in Tecumseh, MI. Graduate U of MI. Debut 1991 OB in *Jekyll and Hyde* followed by *Cute Boys… Prove How Good They Are, Geneology, Ben and Jerry, The Trick, Café Boys,* Bdwy in *Blood Brothers, Imaginary Friends..*

O'Kelly, Aideen Born in Dalkey, Ireland. Member Dublin's Abbey Theatre. Bdwy debut 1980 in *A Life,* followed by *Othello,* OB in *Killing of Sister George, Man Enough, Resistance, Remembrance, Somewhere I Have Never Traveled, Same Old Moon, Da, The Libertine, Philadelphia Here I Come, The Country Boy, Red Roses and Petrol.*

O'Leary, Thomas James Born June 21, 1956 in Windsor Locks, CT. Graduate U. CT. Bdwy debut 1991 in *Miss Saigon,* followed by *Phantom of the Opera,* OB in *Medal of Honor Rag.*

Olsen, Björn Born April 21 in Gothenburg, Sweden. OB debut 2000 in *Berlin to Broadway.*

O'Neill, Heather Born in Belfast, Northern Ireland. OB debut 1999 in *Eclipsed,* followed by *The Country Boy, A Life.*

Oreskes, Daniel Born in New York, NY. Graduate U. PA, LAMDA. OB debut 1990 in *Henry IV,* followed by *Othello, 'Tis Pity She's a Whore, Richard II, Henry VI, Troilus and Cressida, Quills, Missing/Kissing, The Devils, Mrs. Peter's Connections, Cellini,* Bdwy in *Crazy He Calls Me* (1992), *Electra, Aida.*

Oscar, Brad Born Sept. 22, 1964 in Washington, DC. Graduate Boston U. Bdwy debut 1990 in *Aspects of Love,* followed by *Jekyll & Hyde, The Producers,* OB in *Forbidden Broadway* (1993), *Do Re Mi, Jekyll & Hyde.*

O'Sullivan, Anne Born Feb. 6, 1952 in Limerick City, Ireland. OB debut 1977 in *Kid Champion,* followed by *Hello Out There, Fly Away Home, The Drunkard, Dennis, Three Sisters, Another Paradise, Living Quarters, Welcome to the Noon, Dreamer Examines His Pillow, Mama Drama, Free Fall, Magic Act, Plough and the Stars, Marathon '88, Bobo's Guns, Marathon '90, Festival of 1 Acts, Marathon '91, Murder of Crows, Cats and Dogs, Mere Mortals and Others, Mary McGregor, Arabian Nights.*

Overbey, Kellie Born Nov. 21, 1964 in Cincinnati, OH. Graduate Northwestern U. OB debut 1988 in *Debutante Ball,* followed by *Second Coming, Face Divided, Melville Boys, Betty's Summer Vacation, The Hologram Theory, Comic Potential,* Bdwy in *Buried Child* (1996), *Present Laughter, Judgment at Nuremberg.*

Page, Carolanne Born in Odessa, TX. Graduate Curtis Inst. of Music. Bdwy debut 1974 in *Candide,* followed by *Music Is, Allegro* (Encores), OB debut 1993 in *First Lady Suite,* followed by *Sondheim Celebration at Carnegie Hall, Fishkin Touch, Blood on the Dining Room Floor, Woof.*

Pankow, John Born 1955 in St. Louis, MO. Attended St. Nichols Sch. of Arts. OB debut 1980 in *Merton of the Movies,* followed by *Slab Boys, Forty Deuce, Hunting Scenes from Lower Bovaria, Cloud 9, Jazz Poets at the Crotto, Henry V, North Shore Fish, Two Gentlemen of Verona, Italian American Reconciliation Aristocrats, Ice Cream with Hot Fudge, EST Marathon '92, Tempest* (CP), *Baby Anger, Measure for Measure* (CP), Bdwy in *Amadeus* (1981), *The Iceman Cometh, Serious Money.*

Pappas, Evan Born Aug. 21, 1958 in San Francisco, CA. Attended CA Jr. Col. Bdwy debut 1982 in *A Chorus Line,* followed by *My Favorite Year,* OB debut 1991 in *I Can Get It for You Wholesale,* followed by *Pera Palace, The Wound of Love, The Immigrant.*

Pariseau, Kevin Born Jan. 23, 1963 in Providence, RI. Graduate Brown U. OB debut 1996 in *I Love You You're Perfect Now Change.*

Park, Joshua Born Nov. 26, 1976 in North Carolina. Attended NC Sch. of the Arts. Bdwy debut 2001 in *Tom Sawyer.*

Park, Michael Born July 20, 1968 in Canandaigua, NY. Graduate Nazareth Col. of Rochester. OB debut 1994 in *Hello Again,* followed by *Violet,* Bdwy in *Smokey Joe's Café* (1995), *Little Me, Bloomer Girl* (CC).

Parrish, Robyne M. Born in Middletown, OH. Attended NC Sch. of the Arts. OB debut 2000 in *Welcome to Our City.*

Jeff Patterson   Susan Pellegrino   Patti Perkins   Brocton Pierce

Parry, William Born Oct. 7, 1947 in Steubenville, OH. Graduate Mt. Union Col. Bdwy debut 1971 in *Jesus Christ Superstar*, followed by *Rockabye Hamlet, The Leaf People, Camelot* (1980), *Sunday in the Park with George, Into the Light, Passion,* OB in *Sgt. Pepper's Lonely Hearts Club Band, The Conjurer, Noah, The Misanthrope, Joseph and the Amazing Technicolor Dreamcoat, Agamemnon, Coolest Cat in Town, Dispatches, The Derby, The Knife, Cymbeline, Marathon '90, Den of Thieves, Once Around the City.*

Parsons, Estelle Born Nov. 20, 1927 in Lynn, MA. Attended Boston U., Actors Studio. Bdwy debut 1956 in *Happy Hunting*, followed by *Whoop Up, Beg Borrow or Steal, Mother Courage, Ready When You Are C.B., Malcolm, Seven Descents of Myrtle, And Miss Reardon Drinks a Little, Norman Conquests, Ladies at the Alamo, Miss Marguerida's Way, Pirates of Penzance, Shadow Box* (1994), OB in *DemiDozen, Pieces of Eight, Threepenny Opera, Automobile Graveyard, Mrs. Dally Has a Lover* (1963), for which she received a 1963 Theatre World Award, *Next Time I'll Sing to You, Come to the Palace of Sin, In the Summer House, Monopoly, The East Wind, Galileo, Peer Gynt, Mahagonny, People Are Living There, Barbary Shore, Oh Glorious Tintinnabulation, Mert and Paul, Elizabeth and Essex, Dialogue for Lovers, New Moon* (in concert), *Orgasmo Adulto Escapes from the Zoo, Unguided Missile, Baba Goya, Extended Forecast, Deja Revue, Grace and Gloria, The Forty-nine Years, First Picture Show, Last of the Thorntons.*

Pasekoff, Marilyn Born Nov. 7, 1949 in Pittsburgh, PA. Graduate of Boston U. Debut 1975 OB in *Godspell*, followed by *Maybe I'm Doing IT Wrong , Professionally Speaking, Forbidden Broadway, Showing Off, Forbidden Broadway 1990, Forbidden Broadway 1991, Shmulnik's Waltz, The Yiddish Trojan Women,* Bdwy in *Godspell* (1976), *The Odd Couple* (1985), *I Hate Hamlet, Taller Than a Dwarf.*

Patterson, Edwin Sean Born Aug. 25, 1968 in Arlington, TX. Graduate U. of OK. OB debut 1998 in *A Lie of the Mind*, followed by *Loot, Cock and Bull Story, Sweeney Todd.*

Patterson, Jeff OB in *Horsey People.*

Patterson, Meredith Born Nov. 24, 1975 in Concord, CA. Bdwy in *A Christmas Carol, 42nd Street,* OB in *The Increased Difficulty of Concentration.*

Patton, Charlotte Born June 12 in Danville, KY. Attended U. Cincinnati, OB in *The New Living Newspaper, The Problem, The Bad Penny, The Happy Journey from Trenton to Camden, You've Changed, Montage, Delicate Dangers, The Street, My Mother's a Baby Boy.*

Paul, Guy Born Sept. 12, 1949 in Milwaukee, WI. Attended U. MN. OB debut 1984 in *Flight of the Earls*, followed by *Frankenstein, The Underpants, Oresteia, Ever Afters, Oh Baby Oh Baby, Of Blessed Memory, Candida,* Bdwy in *Arms and the Man* (1985), *Wild Honey, Rumors, Private Lives, King and I* (1996), *1776, The Invention of Love.*

Pawk, Michele Born Nov. 16, 1961 in Pittsburgh, PA. Graduate CCCM. Bdwy debut 1988 in *Mail*, followed by *Crazy for You, Cabaret, Seussical,* OB in *Hello Again, Decline of the Middle West, john & jen, After the Fair.*

Pearthree, Pippa Born Sept., 23, 1956 in Baltimore, MD. Attended NYU. Bdwy debut 1977 in *Grease*, followed by *Whose Life is it Anyway?, Taking Steps,* OB in *American Days, Hunting Scenes from Lower Bavaria, And I Ain't Finished Yet, The Dining Room, The Singular Life of Albert Nobbs, Hamlet, Aunt Dan and Lemon, Nightingale, Endpapers.*

Pedi, Christine Born Oct. 24 in Yonkers, NY. Graduate Fordham U. OB debut 1993 in *Forbidden Bdwy*, followed by *Forbidden Bdwy Strikes Back,* Bdwy in *Little Me.*

Pellegrino, Susan Born June 3, 1950 in Baltimore, MD. Attended CC San Francisco, CA St. U. OB debut 1982 in *Wisteria Trees*, followed by *Steel on Steel, Master Builder, Equal Wrights, Come as You Are, Painting Churches, Marvin's Room, Glory Girls, Minor Demons, Blood Orange, I'm Coming in Soon,* Bdwy in *Kentucky Cycle* (1994), *Present Laughter, View from the Bridge.*

Perez, Rosie Born Sept. 4, 1966 in Brooklyn, NY. OB debut 2001 in *The Vagina Monologues*, followed by *References to Salvador Dali Make Me Hot.*

Perkins, Patti Born July 9 in New Haven, CT. Attended AMDA. OB debut 1972 in *The Contrast*, followed by *Fashion, Tuscaloosa's Calling Me, Patch, Shakespeare's Cabaret, Maybe I'm Doing It Wrong, Fabulous LaFontaine, Hannah 1939, Free Zone, New Yorkers,* Bdwy in *All Over Town* (1974), *Shakespeare's Cabaret, The Full Monty.*

Alice Playten

Ricardo Puente

John Quilty

Dan Remmes

Phillips, Amy Jo Born Nov. 15, 1958 in Brooklyn, NY. Graduate Ithaca Col. OB debut 1986 in *Little Shop of Horrors*, followed by *Burnscape*, *Pretty Faces*, Bdwy debut 1994 in *Show Boat*, followed *St. Louis Woman* (Encores), *Tom Sawyer*.

Pieche, Jennifer (Lynn) Born Jan. 25, 1967 in Camden, NJ. Graduate Col. of William and Mary. OB debut 1995 in *Lust*, followed by *After the Fair*, *As You Like It*.

Pierce, Brocton Born June 14 in Baltimore, MD. Graduate Frostburg St. Col. OB debut 1997 in *Grandma Sylvia's Funeral*, followed by *Welcome to Our City*.

Pietropinto, Angela Born Feb. 4 in New York, NY. Graduate NYU. OB in *Henry IV*, *Alice in Wonderland*, *Endgame*, *Sea Gull*, *Jinx Bridge*, *The Mandrake*, *Marie and Bruce*, *Green Card Blues*, *3 by Pirandello*, *Broken Pitcher*, *Cymbeline*, *Romeo and Juliet*, *Midsummer Night's Dream*, *Twelve Dreams*, *The Rivals*, *Cap and Bells*, *Thrombo*, *Lies My Father Told Me*, *Sorrows of Stephen*, *Between the Wars*, *Hotel Play*, *Rain Some Fish No Elephants*, *Young Playwrights 90*, *Tunnel of Love*, *Thanksgiving Day*, *Vilna's Got a Golem*, *Down the Garden Paths*, Bdwy in *The Suicide* (1980), *Eastern Standard*.

Pine, Larry Born March 3, 1945 in Tucson, AZ. Graduate NYU. OB debut 1967 in *Cyrano*, followed by *Alice in Wonderland*, *Mandrake*, *Aunt Dan and Lemon*, *Taming of the Shrew*, *Better Days*, *Dolphin Project*, *Treasure Island*, *Preservation Society*, *The Disputation*, *Mizlansky/Zilinsky*, *The Chemistry of Change*, *The Designated Mourner*, *Saved or Destroyed*, Bdwy in *End of the World* (1984), *Angels in America*, *Bus Stop*, *Wrong Mountain*.

Piro, Jacquelyn Born Jan. 8, 1965 in Boston MA. Graduate Boston U. OB debut 1987 in *Company*, followed by *Suburb*, Bdwy in *Les Miserables* (1990), *Sweet Adeline* (Encores).

Pitoniak, Anne Born March 30, 1922 in Westfield, MA. Attended U. NC Women's Col. Debut 1982 OB in *Talking With*, followed by *Young Playwrights Festival*, *Phaedra*, *Steel Magnolias*, *Pygmalion*, *The Rose Quartet*, *Batting Cage*, *Last of the Thorntons*, Bdwy debut 1983 in *'night, Mother*, for which she received a 1983 Theatre World Award, followed by *The Octette Bridge Club*, *Picnic*, *Amy's View*, *Uncle Vanya*.

Playten, Alice Born Aug. 28, 1947 in New York, NY. Bdwy debut 1960 in *Gypsy*, followed by *Oliver!*, *Hello Dolly!*, *Henry Sweet Henry*, for which she received a 1968 Theatre World Award, *George M.!*, *Spoils of War* (also OB), *Rumors*, *Seussical*, OB in *Promenade*, *The Last Sweet Days of Isaac*, *National Lampoon's Lemmings*, *Valentine's Day*, *Pirates of Penzance*, *Up from Paradise*, *A Visit*, *Sister Mary Ignatius Explains It All*, *An Actor's Nightmare*, *That's It Folks*, *1-2-3-4-5*, *Marathon '90 and '93*, *The Mysteries*, *First Lady Suite*, *Flea in Her Ear*.

Poe, Richard Born Jan. 25, 1946 in Portola, CA. Graduate U. San Francisco, UC Davis. OB debut 1971 in *Hamlet*, followed by *Seasons Greetings*, *Twelfth Night*, *Naked Rights*, *Approximating Mother*, *Jeffrey*, *View of the Dome*, *Til the Rapture Comes*, Bdwy in *Broadway* (1987), *M. Butterfly*, *Our Country's Good*, *Moon Over Buffalo*, *1776*, *Tom Sawyer*.

Pogrebin, Abby (Abigail) Born May 17, 1965 in New York, NY. Bdwy debut 1981 in *Merrily We Roll Along*, OB in *Behind the Heart*.

Potts, Michael Born Sept. 21, 1962 in Brooklyn, NY. Graduate Columbia U., Yale U. OB debut 1993 in *Playboy of the West Indies*, followed by *America Play*, *Rent*, *Overtime*, *Mud River Stone*, *Arms and the Man*, *Once Around the City*.

Preston, Corliss Born Feb. 3 in East Chicago, IN. Graduate IN. U., Bristol Old Vic. OB debut 1988 in *Hired Man*, followed by *The Cherry Orchard*, *Alive by Night*, *A Piece of My Heart*, *The Erotica Project's Cunning Stunts*, *Boss Grady's Boys*.

Price, Lonny Born March 9, 1959 in New York, New York. Attended Julliard. Debut 1979 OB in *Class Enemy* for which she received a Theatre World Award, followed by *Up from Paradise*, *Rommel's Garden*, *Times and Appetites of Toulouse-Lautrec*, *Room Service*, *Come Blow Your Horn*, *The Immigrant*, *A Quiet End*, *Falsettoland*, Bdwy in *The Survivor* (1980), *Merrily We Roll Along*, *Master Harold and the Boys*, *The Time of Your Life*, *Children of the Sun*, *Rage*, *Broadway*, *Burn This!*, *Merrily We Roll Along in Concert*.

Don Richard

Derdriu Ring

James Riordan

Jana Robbins

Prince, Faith Born Aug. 5, 1957 in Augusta, GA. Graduate U. of Cincinnati. OB debut 1981 in *Scrambled Feet*, followed by *Olympus on My Mind*, *Groucho*, *Living Color*, *Bad Habits*, *Falsettoland*, *3 of Hearts*, *The Torchbearers*, *Ancestral Voices*, Bdwy in *Jerome Robbins' Broadway* (1989), *Nick & Nora*, *Guys and Dolls* (1992), *Fiorello* (Encores), *What's Wrong with This Picture*, *DuBarry Was a Lady* (Encores), *King and I*, *Little Me*, *James Joyce's The Dead*, *Bells Are Ringing*.

Pruitt, Richard Born Jan. 20, 1950 in New Albany, IN. Graduate IN U. OB debut 1987 in *Wicked Philanthropy*, followed by *Bat Boy*, Bdwy in *On the Waterfront* (1995).

Puente, Ricardo Born March 1, 1962 in Brooklyn, NY. Attended AMDA. OB debut 2000 in *Four Guys Named Jose*.

Purl, Linda Born Sept. 2, 1955 in Greenwich, CT. Attended Toho Geino, NYU. Bdwy debut 1998 in *Getting and Spending*, followed by *Tom Sawyer*, OB debut 1991 in *The Baby Dance*.

Quilty, John Born Sept. 9, 1970 in Philadelphia, PA. OB debut 2000 in *The Countess*.

Quinn, Patrick Born Feb. 12, 1950 in Philadelphia, PA. Graduate Temple U. Bdwy debut 1976 in *Fiddler on the Roof*, followed by *Day in Hollywood/ Night in the Ukraine*, *Oh, Coward!*, *Lend Me a Tenor*, *Damn Yankees*, *Beauty and the Beast*, *Boys from Syracuse* (Encores), *A Class Act*, OB in *It's Better with a Bank*, *By Strouse*, *Forbidden Broadway*, *Best of Forbidden Broadway*, *Raft of Medusa*, *Forbidden Broadway's 10th Anniversary*, *A Helluva Town*, *After the Ball*, *Wonderful Town*.

Ragno, Joseph Born March 11, 1936 in Brooklyn, NY. Attended Allegheny Col. OB debut 1960 in *Worm in the Horseradish*, followed by *Elizabeth the Queen*, *Country Scandal*, *The Shrike*, *Cymbeline*, *Love Me Love My Children*, *Interrogation of Havana*, *The Birds*, *Armenians*, *Feedlot*, *Every Place in Newark*, *Modern Romance*, *Hunting Cockroaches*, *Just Say No*, *The Return*, *Black Marble Shoeshine Stand*, *Power Failure*, *The Vocal Lords*, Bdwy debut 1969 in *Indians*, followed by *Iceman Cometh*, *Sound of Music*.

Raiken, Lawrence/Larry Born Feb. 5, 1949 on Long Island, NY. Graduate William & Mary Col., UNC. Debut 1979 OB in *Wake Up It's Time to Go to Bed*, followed by *Rise of David Levinsky*, *Bells Are Ringing*, *Pageant*, *Talley's Folly*, Bdwy in *Woman of the Year* (1981), *Sheik of Avenue B*, *Follies* 2001.

Raiter, Frank Born Jan. 17, 1932 in Cloquet, MN. Graduate Yale U. Bdwy debut 1958 in *Cranks*, followed by *Dark at the Top of the Stairs*, *J.B.*, *Camelot*, *Salome*, *Sacrilege*, OB in *Soft Core Pornographer*, *Winter's Tale*, *Twelfth Night*, *Tower of Evil*, *Endangered Species*, *Bright Room Called Day*, *Learned Ladies*, *'Tis Pity She's A Whore*, *Othello*, *Comedy of Errors*, *Orestes*, *Marathon Dancing*, *Sudden Devotion*, *The Devils*, *Defying Gravity*, *Cymbeline*, *Troilus and Cressida*.

Ramos, Richard Russell Born Aug. 23, 1941 in Seattle, WA. Graduate U. MN. Bdwy debut 1968 in *House of Atreus*, followed by *Arturo Ui*, *Major Barbara*, OB in *Adaptation*, *Screens*, *Lotta*, *Tempest*, *Midsummer Night's Dream*, *Gorky*, *The Seagull*, *Entertaining Mr. Sloane*, *Largo Desolato*, *Henry I V Parts I and 2*, *Dog Opera*.

Ramsay, Remak Born Feb. 2, 1937 in Baltimore, MD. Graduate Princeton U. OB debut 1964 in *Hang Down Your Head and Die*, followed by *Real Inspector Hound*, *Landscape of the Body*, *All's Well That Ends Well* (CP), *Rear Column*, *Winslow Boy*, *Dining Room*, *Save Grand Central*, *Quartermaine's Terms*, *Misalliance*, *Thief River*, Bdwy in *Half a Sixpence*, *Sheep on the Runway*, *Lovely Ladies Kind Gentlemen*, *On the Town*, *Jumpers*, *Private Lives*, *Dirty Linen*, *Every Good Boy Deserves Favor*, *The Devil's Disciple*, *Woman in Mind*, *Nick and Nora*, *St. Joan*, *Moliere Comedies*, *Heiress*.

Rebhorn, James Born Sept. 1, 1948 in Philadelphia, PA. Graduate Wittenberg U. Columbia U. Debut 1972 OB in *Blue Boys* followed by *Are You Now...*, *Trouble with Europe*, *Othello*, *Hunchback of Notre Dame*, *Period Adjustment*, *The Freak*, *Half a Lifetime*, *Touch Black*, *To Gillian on Her 37th Birthday*, *Rain*, *Hasty Heart Husbandry*, *Isn't It Romantic*, *Blind Date*, *Cold Sweat*, *Spoils of War*, *Marathon '88*, *Ice Cream with Her Fudge*, *Life During Wartime*, *Innocents*, *Crusade*, *On the Bum*, *Oblivion*, *Postponed*, *Dinner at Eight*, Bdwy in *I'm Not Rappaport*, *Our Town* (1989).

Grant Rosenmeyer

Jamie Ross

Daphne Rubin-Vega

Amy Ryan

Remmes, Dan Born Aug. 19, 1966 in Stoughton, MA. Graduate AADA. OB debut 1989 in *I Love Lucy Who?*, followed by *Pvt. Wars, What Doesn't Kill Us, Waiting Women, Café Encounters, Bedlam.*

Richard, Don Born Aug. 30, 1959 in Lexington, KY. Graduate U. of KY, OK U. Bdwy debut 2000 in *Jane Eyre.*

Richardson, Joely Born Jan 9, 1965 in London, England. OB debut 2001 in *Madame Melville*, for which she received a 2001 Theatre World Award.

Rigby, Terence Born Jan. 2, 1937 in Birmingham, England. Graduate RADA. Bdwy debut 1967 in *The Homecoming*, followed by *No Man's Land, Hamlet, Amadeus*, OB in *Richard III, Troilus and Cressida, Saved.*

Ring, Derdriu Born April 11, 1973 in Cahirsiveen, Co. Kerry, Ireland. Attended U. Col. Cork. OB debut 2000 in *The Hostage*, followed by *A Life.*

Riordan, James Born Feb. 15, 1970. Graduate Temple U. OB debut 2000 in *The Countess.*

Ripley, Alice Born Dec. 14, 1963 in San Leandro, CA. Graduate Kent St. U. Bdwy debut 1993 in *Tommy*, followed by *Sunset Blvd, King David, Side Show, Li'l Abner* (Encores), *Les Miserables, James Joyce's The Dead, Rocky Horror Show.*

Ritter, John Born Sept. 17, 1948 in Los Angeles, CA. Graduate USC. Bdwy debut 2000 in *The Dinner Party.*

Rivera, Chita Born Jan. 23, 1933 in Washington, DC. Bdwy debut 1950 in *Guys and Dolls* followed by *Call Me Madam, Can-Can, Seventh Heaven, Mr. Wonderful, West Side Story, Bye Bye Birdie, Bajour, Chicago, Bring Back Birdie, Merlin, The Rink, Jerry's Girls, Kiss of the Spider Woman, Nine* (2002), OB in *Shoestring Revue.*

Rivera, Eileen Born March 3, 1970 in Queens, NY. Graduate Boston U. OB debut 1995 in *Cambodia Agonistes*, followed by *Portrait of the Artist as Filipino, Shanghai Lil's, He Who Says Yes/He Who Says No, Li'l Brown Brother/Nikimalika, Dogeaters.*

Robbins, Jana Born April 18, 1947 in Johnstown, PA. Graduate Stephens Col. Bdwy debut 1974 in *Good News*, followed by *I Love My Wife, Crimes of the Heart, Romance/Romance, Gypsy, The Tale of the Allergist's Wife*, OB in *Tickles by Tucholsky, Tip-Toes, All Night Strut, Colette Collage, Circus Gothic, Ad Hock, So Long 174th St.*

Roberts, Angela Born Oct. 25, 1961 in Pasadena, TX. Graduate Rice U., So. Methodist U. Debut 1990 OB in *Love's Labours Lost*, followed by *Twelfth Night, Extras, Spirit of Man.*

Robins, Laila Born March 14, 1959 in St. Paul, MN. Graduate U. WI, Yale U. Bdwy debut 1984 in *The Real Thing*, followed by *Herbal Bed*, OB in *Bloody Poetry, Film Society, For Dear Life, Maids of Honor, Extra Man, Merchant of Venice, Mrs. Klein, Tiny Alice.*

Rodriguez, Enrico Born July 18, 1980 in Warren, MI. Bdwy debut in *Big* (1996), OB in *Zanna Don't.*

Rogers, Gil Born Feb. 4, 1934 in Lexington, KY. Attended Harvard U. OB in *Ivory Branch, Vanity of Nothing, Warrior's Husband, Hell Bent for Heaven, Gods of Lighting, Pictures in a Hallway, Rose, Memory Bank, A Recent Killing, Birth, Come Back Little Sheba, Life of Galileo, Remembrance, Mortally Fine, Frankie, History of President JFK Part I, On Deaf Ears, Second Summer*, Bdwy in *Great White Hope, Best Little Whorehouse in Texas, Corn is Green* (1983).

Rogers, Michael Born Dec. 8, 1954 in Trinidad. Attended LIU, Yale U. OB debut 1974 in *Elena*, followed by *Chiaroscuro, Forty Deuce, Antigone, Julius Caesar, Insufficient Evidence, Othello, Young Playwrights '90, Salt, Troilus and Cressida.*

Roi, Natacha Born Dec. 9 in Lennoxville, Canada. Graduate Boston Conservatory, NYU. Bdwy debut in *Wait Until Dark*, followed by *Closer*, OB in *Three Birds Alighting on a Field, Passion Play.*

Roop, Reno Born Dec. 19 in Narva, Estonia. Graduate Goodman Theatre. Debut 1965 OB in *Medea*, followed by *Hamlet, Timon of Athens, How Far Is It to Babylon?*, Bdwy in *Emperor Henry IV, Freedom of the City, Sound of Music, Judgment at Nuremberg.*

Rosenmeyer, Grant Born July 3, 1991 in Manhasset, NY. OB debut 2000 in *Macbeth*.

Rosen-Stone, Mekenzie Born Jan. 12, 1988 in Baltimore, MD. Bdwy debut 1997 in *Annie*, followed by *Tom Sawyer*.

Ross, Jamie Born May 4, 1939 in Markinch, Scot. Attended RADA. Bdwy debut 1962 in *Little Moon of Alban*, followed by *Moon Besieged, Ari, Different Times, Woman of the Year, La Cage aux Folles, 42nd Street, Gypsy* (1990), *Gentlemen Prefer Blondes* (1995), OB in *Penny Friend, Oh Coward!, Approaching Zanzibar, Tale of the Allergist's Wife*.

Rothman, John Born June 3, 1949 in Baltimore, MD. Graduate Wesleyan U., Yale U. OB debut 1978 in *Rats Nest*, followed by *Impossible H.L. Mencken, Buddy System, Rosario and the Gypsies, Italian Straw Hat, Modern Ladies of Guanabacoa, Faith Hope Charity, Some Americans Abroad, EST Marathon '92, Death Defying Acts, Goodnight Children Everywhere, Arsenic and Old Lace* (CC), Bdwy in *End of the World...*(1984), *Some Americans Abroad*.

Rowe, Stephen Born June 3, 1948 in Johnstown, PA. Graduate Emerson Col., Yale U. Debut 1979 OB in *Jungle Coup* followed by *A Private View, Cinders, Coming of Age in Soho, The Normal Heart, Whispers, Terry by Terry, Macbeth*, Bdwy in *Serious Money* (1988)

Rubin-Vega, Daphne Born Nov. 18, 1968 in Panama. Bdwy debut 1996 in *Rent* (also OB), for which she received a 1996 Theatre World Award, followed by *Rocky Horror Show*, OB in *Two Sisters and a Piano, Gum*.

Rudd, Paul Born April 6, 1969 in Passaic, NJ. Graduate U. KS, AADA/West. OB debut 1993 in *Bloody Poetry*, followed by *Alice in Bed*, Bdwy debut 1996 in *Last Night of Ballyhoo*.

Ryall, William Born Sept. 18, 1954 in Binghamton, NY. Graduate AADA. OB debut 1979 in *Canterbury Tales*, followed by *Elizabeth and Essex, He Who Gets Slapped, Sea Gull, Tartuffe, Little Kit*, Bdwy debut 1986 in *Me and My Girl*, followed by *Grand Hotel, Best Little Whorehouse Goes Public, How to Succeed in Business Without Really Trying* (1995), *High Society, Amadeus, Seussical*.

Ryan, Amy Born May 3, 1968 in New York, NY. OB debut 1988 in *A Shayna Maidel*, followed by *Rimers of Eldritch, Eleemosynary, Marking, Hysterical Blindness, Imaging Brad, The Stumbling Tongue, Saved, Crimes of the Heart*, Bdwy in *Sisters Rosensweig* (1993), *Uncle Vanya*.

Ryan, Thomas Jay Born Aug. 1, 1962 in Pittsburgh, PA. Graduate Carnegie Mellon. OB debut 1992 in *Samuel's Major Problem*, followed by *Egypt, My Head was a Sledgehammer, Robert Zucco, Dracula, Venus, South, Juno and the Paycock*.

Salamandyk, Tim Born Feb. 25, 1967 in Minneapolis, MN. Graduate Wesleyan U. OB debut 1996 in *Food Chain*, followed by *Green Heart*, Bdwy in *Bloomer Girl* (CC).

Salata, Gregory Born July 21, 1949 in New York, NY. Graduate Queens Col. Bdwy debut 1975 in *Dance with Me*, followed by *Equus, Bent*, OB in *Piaf: A Remembrance, Sacraments, Measure for Measure, Subject of Childhood, Jacques and His Master, Androcles and the Lion, Madwoman of Chaillot, Beauty Part, Heartbreak House, Filumena, Boy Meets Girl, The Admirable Crichton*.

Salonga, Lea Born Feb. 22, 1971 in Manila, PI. Attended Manila U. Bdwy debut 1991 in *Miss Saigon* for which she received a Theatre World Award followed by *Flower Drum Song* (2002).

Samuel, Peter Born Aug. 15, 1958 in Pana, IL. Graduate E. IL. U. Bdwy debut 1981 in *The First*, followed by *Joseph and His Amazing Technicolor Dreamcoat, Three Musketeers, Rags, Les Miserables, The Secret Garden, Parade, Maria Christine*, OB in *Human Comedy, 3 Guys Naked from the Waist Down, Road to Hollywood, Elizabeth and Essex, Little Eyolf, King David, Old Money*.

Santiago-Hudson, Ruben Born 1957 in Lackawanna, NY. Attended SUNY Binghamton, Wayne St. U. OB debut in *Soldier's Play*, followed by *Measure for Measure, East Texas Hot Links, Ceremonies in Dark Old Men, Deep Down, Lackawanna Blues*, Bdwy in *Jelly's Last Jam* (1992), *Seven Guitars*.

Sayre, Clark Born March 3, 1960 in Santa Barbara, CA. Attended UCLA. Bdwy debut 1981 in *Merrily We Roll Along*, followed by *Oliver!*, OB in *Merrily We Roll Along in Concert*.

Schafer, Scott Born Aug. 26, 1958 in Chicago, IL. Graduate DePaul U. OB debut 1980 in *Aphrodite: The Witch Play*, followed by *Babes in Toyland, Sally, Beauty Thing, Boy Meets Girl, The Admirable Crichton*, Bdwy in *Raggedy Ann* (1986).

Sciotto, Eric Born March 18, 1975 in Altoona, PA. Cincinnati's Col.-Cons. of Music. Bdwy debut 1999 in *Annie Get Your Gun*.

Scott, Michael Born Jan. 24, 1954 in Santa Monica, CA. Attended CA St. U. Bdwy debut 1978 in *Best Little Whorehouse in Texas* (also OB), followed by *Happy New Year, Show Boat* (1994), OB in *Leave It to Me, A Country Christmas Carol*.

Seamon, Edward Born April 15, 1937 in San Diego, CA. Attended San Diego St. Col. OB debut 1971 in *Life and Times of J. Walter Smintheus*, followed by *The Contractor, The Family, Fishing, Feedlot, Cabin 12, Rear Column, Devour the Snow, Buried Child, Friends, Extenuating Circumstances, Confluence, Richard II, Great Grandson of Jedediah Kohler, Marvelous Gray, Time Framed, Master Builder, Fall Hookup, Fool for Love, The Harvesting, Country for Old Men, Love's Labour's Lost, Caligula, Mound Builders, Quiet in the Land, Talley & Son, Tomorrow's Monday, Ghosts, Of Mice and Men, Beside Herself, You Can't Think of Everything, Tales of the Last Formicans, Love Diatribe, Empty Hearts, Sandbox, Winter's Tale, Cymbeline, Barber of Seville, Venice Preserv'd, The Forest, Richard II, Candida, School for Scandal, The Country Wife, The Miser, The Seagull, Merry Wives of Windsor, The Cherry Orchard*, Bdwy in *The Trip Back Down* (1977), *Devour the Snow, American Clock*.

Sedgwick, Kyra Born Aug. 19, 1965 in New York, NY. Attended USC. OB debut 1981 in *Time Was*, followed by *Dakota's Belly Wyoming, Not Waving, Thicker Than Water, Twelfth Nite, Stranger*, Bdwy debut 1989 in *Ah, Wilderness!*, for which she received a 1989 Theatre World Award.

Segal, Holiday Born Aug. 28, 1987 in New York, NY. Bdwy debut 1998 in *High Society*, followed by *Bobbi Boland*.

James Sie

Emily Skinner

Pete Starrett

Cheryl Stern

Selby, William Born Nov. 22, 1961 in Melrose, MA. Graduate Emerson Col. OB debut 1987 in *Apple Tree,* followed by *Juba, Forbidden Bdwy, Forbidden Hollywood, Forbidden Bdwy Strikes Back, Forbidden Bdwy Cleans Up Its Act.*

Seldes, Marian Born Aug. 23, 1928 in New York, NY. Attended Neighborhood Playhouse. Bdwy debut 1947 in *Media,* followed by *Crime and Punishment, That Lady, Town Beyond Tragedy, Ondine, On High Ground, Come of Age, Chalk Garden, Milk Train Doesn't Stop Here Anymore, The Wall, Gift of Time, Delicate Balance, Before You Go, Father's Day, Equus, The Merchant, Deathtrap, Boys from Syracuse* (Encores), *Ivanov, Ring Round the Moon,* OB in *Different, Ginger Man, Mercy Street, Isadora Duncan Sleeps with the Russian Navy, Painting Churches, Gertrude Stein and Companion, Richard II, The Milk Train Doesn't Stop…, Bright Room Called Day, Another Time, Three Tall Women, The Torchbearers, Dear Liar, The Butterfly Collection, The Play about the Baby.*

Shakar, Martin Born Jan. 1, 1940 in Detroit, MI. Attended Wayne St. U. Bdwy debut 1969 in *Our Town,* OB in *Lorenzaccio, Macbeth, The Infantry, American Pastoral, No Place to Be Somebody, World of Mrs. Solomon, And Whose Little Boy Are You?, Investigation of Havana, Night Watch, Owners, Actors, Richard III, Transfiguration of Benno Blimpie, Jack Gelber's New Play, Biko Inquest, Second Story Sunlight, Secret Thighs of New England, After the Fall, Faith Healer, Hunting Cockroaches, Yellow Dog contract, Marathon '90, How to Sacrifice a Child, Redfest, Birth Marks, More Lies about Jerzy.*

Shine, David Born Sept. 21, 1960 in Dumont, NJ. Graduate NYU, AADA. Bdwy debut 1981 in *Merrily We Roll Along,* OB in *Merrily We Roll Along in Concert.*

Shipley, Sandra Born Feb. 1 in Rainham, Kent, Eng. Attended New Col. of Speech and Drama, London U. OB debut 1988 in *Six Characters in Search of an Author,* followed by *Big Time, Kindertransport, Venus, Backward Glance, Phaedra in Delirium, Arms and the Man, The Clearing, Once Around the City,* Bdwy 1995 in *Indiscretions,* followed by *Deep Blue Sea.*

Shue, Elizabeth Born in Delaware. Attended Wellesley Col., Harvard U. Debut 1990 off and on Bdwy in *Some Americans Abroad,* also OB in *Burn This* (2002).

Sie, James Born Dec. 18, 1962 in Summit, NJ. Graduate Northwestern U. OB debut 2000 in *Straight as a Line.*

Signor, Tari Born in PA. Graduate Juilliard. OB debut 1996 in *Death Defying Acts,* followed by *Trelawny of the Wells, Heartbreak House, Mr. Peter's Connections, Troilus and Cressida.*

Skinner, Emily Born June 29, 1970 in Richmond, VA. Graduate Carnegie Mellon U. Bdwy debut 1994 in *Christmas Carol* (MSG) followed by *Jekyll & Hyde, Side Show, The Full Monty,* OB in *Watbanaland, James Joyce's The Dead.*

Skinner, Margo Born Jan. 3, 1950 in Middletown, OH. Graduate Boston U. OB debut 1980 in *Missing Persons,* followed by *The Dining Room, Mary Barnes, The Perfect Party, Spare Parts, Oedipus the King, Game of Love and Chance, Durang Durang, Mrs. Warren's Profession, Boss Grady's Boys.*

Slezak, Victor Born July 7, 1957 in Youngstown, OH. OB debut 1979 in *Electra Myth,* followed by *Hasty Heart, Ghosts, Alice and Fred, Window Claire, Miracle Worker, Talk Radio, Marathon '88, One Act Festival, Briar Patch, Appointment with a High Wire Lady, Sam I Am, White Rose, Born Guilty, Naked Truth, Ivanov, Mafia on Prozac, Tesla's Letters, 24 Years, Bacchanalia, Other People,* Bdwy in *Any Given Day* (1993), *Garden District, Jackie.*

Smiar, Brian Born Aug. 27, 1937 in Cleveland, OH. Graduate Kent State U., Emerson Col. OB debut 1982 in *Edmund,* followed by *3X3, True to Life, Young Playwrights Festival, Marathon '90, Winter's Tale, Cellini,* Bdwy in *Mixed Emotions* (1993).

Snow, Dan Born April 24, 1951 in Pittsburgh, PA. Graduate Edinboro U. OB debut 1975 in *Salome,* followed by *Geneva, No Honey, The Cannibals, Richard III, W.E.B. DuBois Prophet in Limbo.*

Sophiea, Cynthia Born Oct. 26, 1954 in Flint, MI. Bdwy debut 1981 in *My Fair Lady,* followed by *She Loves Me, Victor Victoria,* OB in *Lysistrata, Sufragette, Golden Apple, Winter's Tale, Petrified Prince, Leaving Queens.*

Sorge, Joey Born July 28, 1969 in Washington, DC. Graduate U. of MD. OB debut 2000 in *Saturday Night Fever,* followed by *Follies* 2001.

Larry Swansen

Mary Testa

Clif Thorn

Jonathan Tindle

Spaisman, Zypora Born Jan. 2, 1920 in Lublin, Poland. OB debut 1955 in *Lonesome Ship*, followed by *My Father's Court, Thousand and One Nights, Eleventh Inheritor, Enchanting Melody, Fifth Commandment, Bronx Express, Melody Lingers On, Yoshke Musikant, Stempenya, Generation of Green Fields, Ship, Play for the Devil, Broome Street America, Flowering Peach, Riverside Drive, Big Winner, Land of Dreams, Father's Inheritance, At the Crossroads, Stempenyu, Mirele Efros, Double Identity, Maiden of Ludmir, Blacksmith's Folly, Green Fields.*

Spencer, Rebecca Born April 29, 1960 in Levittown, PA. Graduate Ithaca Col. OB debut 1986 in *Desert Song*, followed by *Watch Your Step, A Connecticut Yankee in King Arthur's Court* (CC), Bdwy in *Call Me Madam* (Encores/1995), *Jekyll & Hyde.*

Stanley, Dorothy Born Nov. 18 in Hartford, CT. Graduate Ithaca Col., Carnegie Mellon U. OB debut 1978 in *Gay Divorce*, followed by *Dames at Sea*, Bdwy in *Sugar Babies* (1980), *Annie, 42nd Street, Broadway, Jerome Robbins' Broadway, Kiss of the Spider Woman, Show Boat* (1984), *High Society, Follies* 2001.

Stark, Molly Born in New York, NY. Graduate Hunter Col.. OB debut 1969 in *Sacco-Vanzetti*, followed by *Riders to the Sea, Medea, One Cent Plain, Elisabeth and Essex, Principally Pinter, Toulouse, Winds of Change, The Education of Hyman Kaplan, The Land of Dreams, Beau Jest, Mamaleh!*, Bdwy in *Molly* (1973).

Starrett, Pete Born Nov. 4, 1970 in Fitchburg, MA. OB debut 1997 in *Blue Man Group: Tubes*, followed by *Letters From Cuba, Other People, Saved.*

Stein, Adam Born Jan. 28, 1972 in Ft. Knox, KY. Graduate Yale U., NYU. OB debut 1995 in *Uncle Bob*, followed by *Skin of Our Teeth, Hotel Universe, More Lies about Jerzy*, Bdwy in *Iceman Cometh.*

Stender, Doug Born Sept. 14, 1942 in Nanticoke, PA. Graduate Princeton U., RADA. Bdwy debut 1973 in *Changing Room*, followed by *Run for Your Wife, The Visit*, OB in *New England Elective, Hamlet, Second Man, How He Lied to Her Husband, Bhutan, Clothes for a Summer Hotel, The Libertine, John Gabriel Borkman, Blithe Spirit.*

Stern, Cheryl Born July 1, 1956 in Buffalo, NY. Graduate Northwestern U. OB debut 1984 in *Daydreams*, followed by *White Lies, Pets, That's Life!, I Love You You're Perfect, Now Change, Game Show.*

Sterner, Steve Born May 5, 1951 in New York, NY. Attended NYCC. Bdwy debut in *Clothes for a Summer Hotel* (1980) followed by *Oh Brother!*, OB in *Lovesong, Vagabond Stars, The Fabulous '50s, My Heart is in the East, Mandrake, The Special, Let it Ride, Encore!, Yiddle with a Fiddle, That's Life!, Cincinnati Saint, Double Identity, Yentl.*

Stevens, Gary Born Dec. 19, 1962 in NYC. Attended NYU. Bdwy debut 1971 in *Frank Merriwell*, followed by *Merrily We Roll Along*, OB in *Merrily We Roll Along in Concert.*

Stevenson, James Born Nov. 18, 1930 in New York, NY. Graduate Vanderbilt U. Bdwy debut 1957 in *Goodbye Again*, followed by *The Wall, Don't Drink the Water, Forty Carats, Hello Dolly*, OB in *Once Upon a Mattress* (1959), *Seascape, Period of Adjustment, The Country Girl, All Over.*

Stewart, Gwen Born Sept. 5, 1963 in Newark, NJ. OB debut 1986 in *Mama I Want to Sing*, followed by *God's Creation, Suds, Oedipus Private Eye, Starmites*, Bdwy debut 1989 in *Starmites*, followed by *Truly Blessed, Rent.*

Stiller, Jerry Born June 8, 1931 in New York, NY. Graduate Syracuse U. OB debut 1953 in *Coriolanus*, followed by *Power and the Glory, Golden Apple, Measure for Measure, Taming of the Shrew, Carefree Tree, Diary of a Scoundrel, Romeo and Juliet, As You Like It, Two Gentlemen of Verona, Passione, Prairie/Shawl, Much Ado about Nothing, After-Play, Down the Garden Paths*, Bdwy in *The Ritz* (1975), *Unexpected Guests, Passione, Hurlyburly* (also OB), *3 Men on a Horse, What's Wrong with This Picture?, Three Sisters.*

Stillman, Bob/Robert Born Dec. 2, 1954 in New York, NY. Graduate Princeton U. OB debut 1981 in *The Haggadah*, followed by *Street Scene, Lola, No Frills Revue, Six Wives, Last Session, Saturn Returns*, Bdwy in *Grand Hotel* (1989), *Dirty Blonde* (and OB).

Stone, Danton Born in Queens, NY. OB debut 1976 in *Mrs. Murray's Farm*, followed by *In This Fallen City, Say Goodnight Gracie, Angels Fall, Balm in Gilead, Fortune's Fools, Mere Mortals and Others*, Bdwy in *5th of July* (1980), *One Flew Over the Cuckoo's Nest.*

Storch, Larry Born Jan. 8, 1923 in New York, NY. Bdwy debut 1958 in *Who Was That Lady I Saw You With?*, followed by *Porgy and Bess* (1983), *Arsenic and Old Lace, Annie Get Your Gun*, OB in *The Littlest Revue* (1956), *Breaking Legs, Things You Shouldn't Say Past Midnight.*

Stout, Mary Born April 8, 1952 in Huntington, WV. Graduate Marshall U. OB debut 1980 in *Plain and Fancy*, followed by *The Sound of Music, Crisp, A Christmas Carol, Song for a Saturday, Prizes, Golden Apple, Identical Twins from Baltimore, Snapshots*, Bdwy in *Copperfield* (1981), *Change in the Heir, My Favorite Year, Jane Eyre.*

Stratton, Hank Born in Long Beach, CA. Attended LAMDA. OB debut 1993 in *Jeffrey*, followed by *Lady in the Dark* (CC), Bdwy 2000 in *Man Who Came to Dinner.*

Stuhlbarg, Michael Born in Long Beach, CA. Attended UCLA, Juilliard. Bdwy debut 1992 in *Saint Joan*, followed by *Three Men on a Horse, Timon of Athens, The Government Inspector, Taking Sides, Cabaret, The Invention of Love*, OB in *As You Like It*, followed by *Woyzeck, All's Well That Ends Well, Richard II, Henry VIII, A Dybbuk, The Winter's Tale.*

Sullivan, Kim Born July 21, 1952 in Philadelphia, PA. Graduate NYU. OB debut 1972 in *Black Terror*, followed by *Legend of the West, Deadwood Dick, Big Apple Messenger, Dreams Deferred, Raisin in the Sun, The Tempest, Ground People, Celebration, In My Father's House, Hundred Penny Box, The Missing Face.*

Sullivan, K.T. Born Oct. 31, 1953 in Coalgate, OK. Graduate OK U. Bdwy debut 1989 in *3 Penny Opera, followed by Gentlemen Prefer Blondes* (1995), OB debut 1992 in *A… My Name Is Still Alice*, followed by *Splendora, So Long 174th St, Gershwin's American Rhapsody.*

Sutcliffe, Steven Born Oct. 19 in Lindsay, Ontario, Canada. Attended Ryerson Theatre Sch. Bdwy debut 1998 in *Ragtime*, for which he received a 1998 Theatre World Award, OB in *A Connecticut Yankee in King Arthur's Court* (CC).

Swansen, Larry Born Nov. 10, 1930 in Roosevelt, OK. Graduate U. OK. Bdwy debut 1966 in *Those That Play the Clowns*, followed by *Great White Hope, King and I*, OB in *Dr. Faustus Lights the Lights, Thistle in My Bed, Darker Flower, Vincent, MacBird, Unknown Soldier and His Wife, Sound of Music, Conditioning of Charlie One, Ice Age, Prince of Homburg, Who's There?, Heart of a Dog, Grandma Pray for Me, Frankenstein, Knights of the Round Table, Returner, House of Mirth, On the Middle Watch, Welcome to Our City.*

Talman, Ann Born Sept. 13, 1957 in Welch, WV. Graduate PA St. U. OB debut 1980 in *What's So Beautiful about a Sunset over Prairie Avenue?*, followed by *Louisiana Summer, Winterplay, Prairie Avenue, Broken Eggs, Octoberfest, We're Home, Yours Anne, Songs on a Shipwrecked Sofa, House Arrest, One Act Festival, Freud's House, Random Harvest, Cat's Paw*, Bdwy in *Little Foxes* (1981), *House of Blue Leaves, Some Americans Abroad* (also OB), *Better Days.*

Taylor, Myra (Lucretia) Born July 9, 1960 in Ft. Motte, SC. Graduate Yale U. OB debut 1985 in *Dennis*, followed by *The Tempest, Black Girl, Marathon 86, Phantasie, Walking the Dead, I Am a Man, Marathon Dancing, Come Down Burning, American Clock, Force Continuum*, Bdwy in *A Streetcar Named Desire* (1987), *Mule Bone, Chronicle of a Death Foretold, Electra, Macbeth.*

Testa, Mary Born June 4, 1955 in Philadelphia, PA. Attended U. RI. OB debut 1979 in *In Trousers*, followed by *Company, Life Is Not a Doris Day Movie, Not-So-New Faces of 1982, American Princess, Mandrake, 4 One-Act Musicals, Next Please!, Daughters, One-Act Festival, The Knife, Young Playwrights Festival, Tiny Mommy, Finnegan's Funeral and Ice Cream Shop, Peter Breaks Through, Lucky Stiff, 1-2-3-4-5, Scapin, Hello Muddah Hello Faddah, Broken English, On the Town, A New Brain, From Above, Ziegfeld Follies of 1936, Haile, Mary!, Tartuffe, The Wax*, Bdwy in *Barnum* (1980), *Marilyn, The Rink, A Funny Thing Happened on the Way to the Forum* (1996), *On the Town, Marie Christine.*

Thomas, Ray Anthony Born Dec. 19, 1956 in Kentwood, LA. Graduate U. TX El Paso. OB debut 1981 in *Escape to Freedom*, followed by *Sun Gets Blue, Blues for Mr. Charlie, Hunchback of Notre Dame, Ground People, The Weather Outside, One Act Festival, Caucasian Chalk Circle, Virgin Molly, Black Eagles, Distant Fires, Shaker Heights, The Lights, Dancing on Moonlight, Volunteer Man, The Devils, Force Continuum, Saved or Destroyed, The Beginning of August.*

Thompson, Evan Born Sept. 3, 1931 in New York, NY. Graduate U. CA. Bdwy debut 1969 in *Jimmy*, followed by *1776, City of Angels, Ivanov*, OB in *Mahogonny, Treasure Island, Knitters in the Sun, HalfLife, Fasnacht Dau, Importance of Being Earnest, Under the Gaslight, Henry V, The Fantasticks, Walk the Dog Willie, Macbeth, 1984, Leave It to Me, Earth and Sky, No Conductor, Nightmare Alley, The Family Reunion, O'Neill, Buying Time.*

Thompson, Jennifer Laura Born Dec. 5, 1969 in Southfield, MI. Graduate U. MI, AADA. OB debut 1994 in *A Doll's Life*, followed by *Urinetown*, Bdwy debut 1998 in *Strike Up the Band* (Encores).

Thorn, Clif Born Aug. 11, 1964 in Little Rock, AK. Graduate USC. OB debut 1994 in *Forever Plaid*, followed by *Du Barry was a Lady* (CC), Bdwy 1998 in *Les Miserables.*

Tindle, Jonathan OB debut 2000 in *Welcome to Our City.*

Tirrell, Barbara Born Nov. 24, 1953 in Nahant, MA. Graduate Temple U., Webber-Douglas Acad. OB debut 1977 in *Six Characters in Search of an Author*, followed by *Cyrano, Romeo and Juliet, Louis Quinse, Day Out of Time, King Lear, Oedipus Texas, Father West, Leaving Queens*, Bdwy in *Annie* (1997).

Titone, Thomas Born March 24, 1959 in Secaucus, NJ. Attended NC Sch. of Arts. With Amer Ballet Th. before Bdwy debut 1992 in *Most Happy Fella*, followed by *My Favorite Year, Once Upon a Mattress* (1996), OB in *Hunchback of Notre Dame, A Prophet Among Them.*

Tomaino, Chris Born March 8, 1967 in Long Branch, NJ. Graduate IN U., Monmouth U. OB debut 1998 in *The Jello is Always Red*, followed by *Strictly Personal.*

Toner, Thomas Born May 25, 1928 in Homestead, PA. Graduate UCLA. Bdwy debut 1973 in *Tricks*, followed by *The Good Doctor, All Over Town, The Elephant Man, California Suite, A Texas Trilogy, The Inspector General, Me and My Girl, The Secret Garden*, OB in *Pericles, The Merry Wives of Windsor, A Midsummer Night's Dream, Richard III, My Early Years, Life and Limb, Measure for Measure, Little Footsteps, Saturday Mourning Cartoons, The Family Reunion, Boss Grady's Boys.*

Chris Tomaino

Thomas Toner

Jill Van Note

Colleen Smith Wallnau

Trammell, Sam Born May 15, 1971 in LA. Graduate Brown U. OB debut 1997 in *Wir Spielen Seechach*, followed by *Dealers Choice, My Night with Reg, Ancestral Voices, If Memory Serves, Kit Marlowe*, Bdwy debut 1998 in *Ah, Wilderness!*, for which he won a 1998 Theatre World Award.

Tucker, Allyson Born Aug. 14 in Milwaukee, WI. Graduate Brown U. OB debut 1985 in *De Obeah Man*, Bdwy debut 1989 in *Oh Kay!*, followed by *Will Rogers Follies, Ragtime, Follies* 2001.

Urbaniak, James Born Sept. 17, 1963 in Bayonne, NJ. OB debut 1988 in *Giants of the Mountain*, followed by *The Universe, Imaginary Invalid, South, Mamba's Daughters, Lipstick Traces.*

Vandenbussche, Jorre Born April 8, 1975 in Brugge, Belgium. Attended Royal Flemish Music Cons. OB debut 2000 in *Alice in Bed.*

Van Dyck, Jennifer Born Dec. 23, 1962 in St. Andrews, Scotland. Graduate Brown U. OB debut 1977 in *Gus and Al*, followed by *Marathon '88, Secret Rapture, Earth and Sky, Man in His Underwear, Cheever Evening, Arsenic and Old Lace* (CC), Bdwy in *Secret Rapture, Two Shakespearean Actors, Dancing at Lughnasa.*

Van Note, Jill Born April 1, 1961 in Houlton, ME. Graduate U. of ME, attended University Col. London. OB debut 1994 in *Landscape*, followed by *Murder in the Cathedral, Measure for Measure, As You Like It, A Midsummer Night's Dream, Seascape, All Over.*

Vereen, Ben Born Oct. 10, 1946 in Miami, FL. OB debut 1965 in *Prodigal Son*, Bdwy in *Sweet Charity, Golden Boy, Hair, Jesus Christ Superstar*, for which he received a 1972 Theatre World Award, *Pippin, Grind, Jelly's Last Jam, Christmas Carol* (MSG).

Vipond, Neil Born Dec. 24, 1929 in Toronto, Canada. Bdwy debut 1956 in *Tamburlain the Great*, followed by *Macbeth*, OB in *Three Friends, Sunday Runners, Hamlet, Routed, Mr. Joyce is Leaving Paris, The Time of Your Life, Children of the Sun, Romeo and Juliet, The Lark, The Crucible, Endpapers.*

Vivona, Jerome Born March 7, 1967 in Bayville, NY. Attended Quinnipac Col., IN U., Nassau CC. Bdwy debut 1994 in *Guys and Dolls*, followed by *How to Succeed in Business Without Really Trying* (1995), *Kiss Me Kate, Seussical.*

Wade, Adam Born March 17, 1935 in Pittwsburgh, PA. Attended Va. State U. Debut 1976 OB in *My Sister My Sister*, followed by *Shaded of Harlem, Falling Apart, The War Party, Staggerlee, Lifetimes, Burner's Frolic, Black Girl.*

Walbye, Kay Born Ft. Collins, CO. Attended KS St U. OB debut 1984 in *Once on a Summer's Day*, followed by *Majestic Kid, Urinetown*, Bdwy in *Run for Your Wife* (1989), *Secret Garden, Rose Tattoo, Titanic.*

Wallnau, Colleen Smith Born June 28, 1948 in Trenton, NJ. Graduate Emerson Col., Trenton St., Rutgers U. OB debut 1992 in *Thru Darkest Ohio*, followed by *Romeo and Juliet, On the Verge, Beggar on Horseback*, Bdwy in *Crazy for You* (1994).

Walton, Bob Born June 25, 1960 in Marion, IN. Graduate Cincinnati Cons. of Music. OB debut 1983 in *Preppies*, followed by *Forbidden Broadway Strikes Back, I Love You, You're Perfect, Now Change, Game Show*, Bdwy debut 1990 in *City of Angels*, followed by *Once Upon a Mattress, Ziegfeld Follies of 1936* (Encores/CC).

Ward, Lauren Born June 19, 1970 in Lincoln, NE. Graduate NC Sch. of Arts. Bdwy debut 1994 in *Carousel*, followed by *1776*, OB in *Jack's Holiday, Violet, Saturday Night Fever, Time and Again.*

Waring, Wendy Born Dec. 7, 1960 in Melrose, MA. Attended Emerson Col. OB debut 1987 in *Wish You Were Here*, followed by *Ziegfeld Follies of 1936*, Bdwy in *Legs Diamond* (1988), *Will Rogers Follies, Crazy for You, Follies* 2001.

Wasiniak, John Born June 12, 1962 in Cleveland, OH. Graduate UCCM, Xavier U. OB debut 1997 in *When Pigs Fly*, followed by *Leave It To Me.*

Watkins, Amanda Born Aug. 17, 1973 in Gainesville, GA. Graduate FL St. U. Bdwy debut 1996 in *Grease*, followed by *Beauty and the Beast, Cats*, OB debut 2000 in *The Wild Party*, followed by *Imperfect Chemistry.*

Bob Walton

Andrew Weems

C.J. Wilson

Weaver, Fritz Born Jan. 19, 1926 in Pittsburgh, PA. Graduate U. Chicago. Bdwy debut 1955 in *Chalk Garden*, for which he received a 1956 Theatre World Award, followed by *Protective Custody, Miss Lonelyhearts, All American, Lorenzo, The White House, Baker Street, Child's Play, Absurd Person Singular, Angels Fall, The Crucible* (1991), *A Christmas Carol, Ring Round The Moon*, OB in *The Way of the World, White Devil, Doctor's Dilemma, Family Reunion, Power and the Glory, Great God Brown, Peer Gynt, Henry IV, My Fair Lady* (CC), *Lincoln, Biko Inquest, The Price, Dialogue for Lovers, A Tale Told, Time Framed, Wrong Turn at Lungfish, The Professional, Don Juan in Hell, Ancestral Voices, A Life*.

Webb, Jeremy Born June 10, 1972 in Ithaca, NY. Attended NC Sch. of the Arts. OB debut 2000 in *Tabletop*.

Weems, Andrew Born July 18, 1961 in Seoul, S. Korea. Graduate Brown U., U. CA. OB debut 1993 in *A Quarrel of Sparrows*, followed by *Marathon Dancing, Mud Angel, Midsummer Night's Dream, Dolphin Position, Green Bird, Mere Mortals and Others*, Bdwy in *London Assurance, Troilus and Cressida, Don't Wink, Princess Turandot*.

Weiman, Kate Born Sept. 16, 1948 in Rockville Center, NY. Attended NYU, AADA. Debut 1981 OB in *Engaged*, followed by *A Thurber Carnival*.

Weiss, Jeff Born in 1940 in Allentown, PA. OB debut 1986 in *Hamlet*, followed by *Front Page, Casanova, Hot Keys, Henry V, The Wallenberg Mission, Mr. Peter's Connections*, Bdwy in *Macbeth*, (1988), *Our Town, Mastergate, Face Value, Real Inspector Hound/15 Minute Hamlet, Carousel* (1994), *Present Laughter, Ivanov, Iceman Cometh, The Invention of Love*.

Whelihan, Paul Born Nov. 22, 1961 in Philadelphia, PA. Graduate Montclair St. U. OB debut 2000 in *The Flame Keeper*.

White, Jane Born Oct. 30, 1922 in New York, NY. Attended Smith Col. Bdwy debut 1942 in *Strange Fruit*, followed by *Climate of Eden, Take a Giant Step, Jane Eyre, Once Upon a Mattress* (also OB), *Cuban Thing, Follies 2001*, OB in *Razzle Dazzle, Insect Comedy, Power and Glory, Hop Signor, Trojan Women, Iphigenia in Aulis, Cymbeline, Burnt Flowerbed, Rosmersholm, Jane White Who?, Ah Men, Lola, Madwoman of Chaillot, Vivat!Vivat!Regina!, King John, Tropical Breeze Hotel, Petrified Prince, Give the Man a Fish*.

Whitthorne, Paul Born Feb. 17, 1970 in Tucson, AZ. Graduate Juilliard. Bdwy debut 1995 in *The Tempest*, OB in *Orestes: I Murdered My Mother* (1996), *Getting In, Measure for Measure, Uncle Jack, Snapshots* 2000.

Wilkof, Lee Born June 25, 1951 in Canton, OH. Graduate U. of Cincinnati. OB debut 1977 in *Present Tense*, followed by *Little Shop of Horrors, Holding Patterns, Angry Housewives, Assassins, Born Guilty, Treasure Island, Golden Boy, Names, Waiting for Lefty, Mizlansky, Zilinsky, The Stumbling Tongue, Oy!, Do Re Mi, Arsenic and Old Lace* (CC), Bdwy in *Sweet Charity* (1986), *Front Page, She Loves Me, Kiss Me Kate*.

Willey, Charles Born Sept. 18, 1956 in Abington, PA. Graduate Syracuse U. OB debut 1991 in *Necktie Breakfast*, followed by *Battery, Single and Proud, Holy Note, The Firebugs, Blue Window, Lion in the Streets, Bobby Supreme, The Censor, South of No North*.

Williams, Dick Anthony Born Aug. 9, 1938 in Chicago, IL. Debut OB 1968 in *Big Time Buck White*, followed by *Jamimma, What the Winesellers Buy*, Bdwy in *Ain't Supposed to Die a Natural Death, We Interrupt This Program, The Poison Tree, Ma Rainey's Black Bottom*.

Williams, Treat Born Dec. 1, 1951 in Rowayton, CT. Bdwy debut 1974 in *Grease*, followed by *Over Here, Once in a Lifetime, Pirates of Penzance, Love Letters, Follies 2001*, OB in *Maybe I'm Doing It Wrong, Love Letters, Some Men Need Help, Oh Hell!, Oleanna, Captains Courageous*.

Wills, Ray Born Sept. 14, 1960 in Santa Monica, CA. Graduate Wichita St. U., Brandeis U. OB debut 1988 in *Side by Side by Sondheim*, followed by *Kiss Me Quick Before the Lava Reaches the Village, Grand Tour, The Cardigans, The Rothschilds, Hello Muddah Hello Faddah, Little Me, A Backers Audition, All in the Timing, Young Playwrights Festival/Guy World. Wonderful Town, A Class Act*, Bdwy 1993 in *Anna Karenina*, followed by *Big*.

Willis, Richard Born in Dallas, TX. Graduate Cornell U., Northwestern U. OB debut 1986 in *Three Sisters*, followed by *Nothing to Report, The Rivalry of Dolls, The Time of Your Life, Much Ado About Nothing*.

Wilson, C.J. OB debut 1994 in *The Merry Wives of Windsor*, Bdwy debut 2000 in *Gore Vidal's The Best Man*.

Wilson, Patrick Born July 3, 1973 in Norfolk, VA. Graduate Carnegie Mellon U. OB debut 1999 in *Bright Lights Big City*, followed by *Tenderloin* (CC), Bdwy in *The Gershwins' Fascinating Rhythm, The Full Monty.*

Wing, Virginia Born Nov. 9 in Marks, MS. Graduate MS. Col. OB debut 1989 in *Two by Two*, followed by *Food and Shelter, Cambodia Agonistes, America Dreaming, Caucasian Chalk Circle, You Can't Take It with You, Making Tracks, Watcher.*

Winkler, Henry Born Oct. 30, 1945 in New York, NY. Graduate Emerson Col., Yale U. OB debut 1973 in *42 Seconds from Broadway*, Bdwy debut 2000 in *The Dinner Party.*

Wise, William Born May 11 in Chicago, IL. Attended Bradley U., Northwestern U. OB debut 1970 in *Adaptation/Next*, followed by *Him, Hot l Baltimore, Just the Immediate Family, 36, For the Use of the Hall, Orphans, Working Theatre Festival, Copperhead, Early One Evening at the Rainbow Bar & Grill, Special Interests, Theme and Variations, Marathon '91, Drop in the Bucket, Hysterical Blindness, Quick-Change Room, Belmont Ave. Social Club, Little Airplanes of the Heart, Moving Bodies, Summer Cyclone.*

Wiseman, Joseph Born May 15, 1919 in Montreal, Canada. Attended CCNY. Bdwy in *Journey to Jerusalem, Abe Lincoln in Illinois, Candle in the Wind, The Three Sisters, Storm Operation, Joan of Lorraine, Anthony and Cleopatra, Detective Story, That Lady, King Lear, Golden Boy, The Lark, Zalmen or the Madness God, The Tenth Man, Judgment at Nuremberg*, OB in *Marco Millions, Incident at Vichy, In the Matter of J. Robert Oppenheimer, Enemies, Duchess of Malfi, Last Analysis, The Lesson, The Golem, Unfinished Stories, Slavs!, I Can't Remember Anything.*

Wolf, Catherine Born May 25 in Abington, PA. Attended Carnegie Tech. U., Neighborhood Playhouse. Bdwy debut 1976 in *The Innocents*, followed by *Otherwise Engaged, An Inspector Calls*, OB in *A Difficult Burning, I Can't Keep Running in Place, Cloud 9, The Importance of Being Earnest, Miami, American Plan, The Understanding, Second Summer.*

Woods, Carol Born Nov. 13, 1943 in Jamaica, NY. Graduate Ithaca Col. OB debut 1980 in *One Mo' Time*, followed by *Blues in the Night, Dreamstuff*, Bdwy in *Grind* (1985), *Big River, Stepping Out, The Crucible, A Little Hotel on the Side, Goodbye Girl, One Touch of Venus* (Encores), *Follies 2001.*

Worth, Irene Born June 23, 1916 in Nebraska. Graduate UCLA. Bdwy debut 1943 in *The Two Mrs. Carrolls*, followed by *Cocktail Party, Mary Stuart, Toys in the Attic, King Lear, Tiny Alice, Sweet Bird of Youth, Cherry Orchard, Lady from Dubuque, John Gabriel Borkman*, OB in *Happy Days, Letters of Love and Affection, Chalk Garden, Golden Age, Coriolanus, Edith Wharton, Gypsy and the Yellow Canary, Chère Maitre, Ancestral Voices, Euripides' Medea.*

Wright, Valerie Born in Las Vegas, NV. Graduate USC. Bdwy debut 1984 in *Cats*, followed by *Song and Dance, Sally Marr & Her Escorts, Damn Yankees* (1994), *Steel Pier, Annie Get Your Gun*, OB in *Showing Off, And the World Goes Round.*

Wylie, John Born Dec. 14, 1925 in Peacock, TX. Graduate No. TX St. U. OB debut 1987 in *Lucky Spot*, followed by *Life is a Dream, Winter's Tale, Venetian Turn, Cymbeline, Venice Preserv'd, Barber of Seville, School for Scandal, Skyscraper, Richard II, John Gabriel Borkman, Mirandolina, The Urn, The Way of the World, The Oresteia, A Will of His Own, Andromache, The Cherry Orchard*, Bdwy in *Born Yesterday* (1989), *Grand Hotel.*

Young, Karen Born Sept. 29, 1958 in Pequonnock, NJ. Attended Douglas Col., Rutgers U. OB debut 1982 in *Three Acts of Recognition*, followed by *A Lie of the Mind, Dog Logic, Wifey, Taxicab Chronicles, The Wax.*

Youngsman, Christopher Born Oct. 26, 1972 in Grand Rapids, MI. Bdwy debut 1996 in *Grease!*, OB debut 2000 in *The Gorey Details.*

Zagnit, Stuart Born March 28 in New Brunswick, NJ. Graduate Montclair St. Col. OB debut 1978 in *The Wager*, followed by *Manhattan Transference, Women in Tune, Enter Laughing, Kuni Leml, Tatterdemalion, Golden Land, Little Shop of Horrors, Lucky Stiff, Grand Tour, Majestic Kid, Made in Heaven, Encore!, A Trip to the Beach, Retribution , A Dybbuk, Good Doctor*, Bdwy in *The Wild Party, Seussical.*

Zorich, Louis Born Feb. 12, 1924 in Chicago, IL. Attended Roosevelt U. OB in *Six Characters in Search of an Author, Crimes and Crimes, Henry V, Thracian Horses, All Women Are One, The Good Soldier Schweik, Shadow of Heroes, To Clothe the Naked, A Memory of Two Mondays, They Knew What They Wanted, The Gathering, True West, The Tempest, Come Day Come Night, Henry IV Parts 1 & 2, The Size of the World, On A Clear Day You Can See Forever* (CC), Bdwy in *Beckett, Moby Dick, The Odd Couple, Hadrian VII, Moonchildren, Fun City, Goodtime Charley, Herzl, Death of a Salesman, Arms and the Man, The Marriage of Figaro, She Loves Me, Follies 2001.*

OBITUARIES

June 1, 2001 – May 31, 2002

Josephine Abady, 52, Richmond, VA–born director/producer, died May 25, 2002, in New York, NY, of breast cancer. After heading the Hampshire College Theater department for three years, she began her directorial career at the Berkshire Theater Festival, where her Off-Broadway production of *The Boys Next Door* garnered an Outer Critics Circle nomination. Her next appointment was as artistic director at the Cleveland Playhouse, where she developed, among other works, *Born Yesterday*, which opened on Broadway in 1989. Following six years at the Cleveland Playhouse, she was hired to run Circle in the Square in New York, where her productions included a revival of *Bus Stop* with Billy Crudup and Mary Louise Parker, for which she received a Tony nomination as producer, as well as a revival of *The Rose Tattoo* starring Mercedes Ruehl. Survivors include her husband, Michael Krawitz, sister, actress Caroline Aaron, and a brother.

Larry Adler, 87, Baltimore, MD–born harmonica player/composer, died on Aug. 7, 2001, in London, England. Broadway credits include *Smiles*, followed by *Flying Colors* and *Keep Off the Grass*, as well as several films. He is survived by his son, three daughters, two granddaughters, and two great-grandchildren.

Andrea Akers, 58, New York, NY–born actress/theater founder/philanthropist, died March 20, 2002. She made her Broadway debut in 1970 in *Charley's Aunt*, followed by *Perfectly Frank* and *Wanted* Off-Broadway. National tours include *A Little Night Music*, for which she received a Los Angeles Drama Critics Award for her performance as Charlotte. Also know for her work in television and film, she was a founding member of the Mark Taper Forum repertory theater in Los Angeles, CA, and served on a number of advisory boards, including the Center for Partnership Studies, the Mobius Group, and the Lindesfarne Fellows. She was also instrumental in founding the Nae-Tao Clinic on the Thailand-Burma border to aid victims of landmines in the area. Survivors include her mother, Jane Ridgeway, and a sister, Ellery.

Frieda Altman Gamzue, 97, Boston, MA–born actress, died Jan. 14, 2002. Broadway credits include *Another Language*, followed by *Counsellor-at-Law*, *Carry Nation*, *We the People*, *Hilda Cassidy*, *Picnic*, *Spring Song*, *Paradise Lost*, *Timber House*, *Days to Come*, *Marching Song*, *Your Obedient Husband*, *Pastoral*, *Gabrielle*, *Guest in the House*, *Ah, Wilderness*, *Hickory Stick*, *Days to Come*, *A Joy Forever*, *Little Brown Jug*, *The Naked Genius*, *Land's End*, *The Wanhope Building*, *Strange Bedfellows*, *The Young and Fair*, *Hilda Crane*, *The Southwest Corner*, *The Waltz of the Toreadors*, *The Visit*, *Chéri*, and *A Distant Bell*. She also appeared in several films.

Martin Aronstein, 65, Pittsfield, MA–born lighting designer, died May 3, 2002, in Van Nuys, CA, of heart failure. He assisted lighting on 1959's *Arturo Ui*, before making his Broadway debut in 1964 on *The Milk Train Doesn't Stop Here Anymore*, followed by *A Severed Head*, *I Was Dancing*, *Tiny Alice*, *The Impossible Years*, *The Royal Hunt of the Sun*, *Cactus Flower*, *The Condemned of Altona*, *Slapstick Tragedy*, *The Investigation*, *Those that Play the Clowns*, *Marat/Sade*, *The Astrakhan Coat*, *The East Wind*, *Galileo*, *Song of the Grasshopper*, *How Now, Dow Jones*, *The Guide*, *The Education of H*Y*M*A*N K*A*P*L*A*N*, *George M!*, *Her First Roman*, *Morning, Noon, and Night*, *Promises, Promises*, *Forty Carats*, *Play It Again, Sam*, *The Dozens*, *Billy*, *The Penny Wars*, *Buck White*, *La Strada*, *Paris Is Out!*, *The Chinese and Dr. Fish*, *Grin and Bare It!/Postcards*, *Park*, *The Gingerbread Lady*, *Four on a Garden*, *And Miss Reardon Drinks a Little*, *The Incomparable Max*, *Ain't Supposed to Die a Natural Death* (Tony nomination), *Moonchildren*, *Sugar*, *Promenade, All!*, *The Little Black Book*, *Different Times*, *Don't Play Us Cheap!*, *Hurry, Harry*, *Much Ado About Nothing* (Tony nomination), *Ambassador*, *Nash at Nine*, *Smith*, *In the Boom Boom Room* (Tony nomination), *Three Sisters*, *Measure for Measure*, *The au Pair Man*, *Scapin*, *Next Time I'll Sing to You*, *What the Wine-Sellers Buy*, *My Fat Friend*, *An American Millionaire*, *Short Eyes*, *Mert & Phil*, *Fame*, *The Ritz*, *A Doll's House*, *Little Black Sheep*, *Kennedy's Children*, *Hamlet*, *The Poison Tree*, *Mrs. Warren's Profession*, *De Journees Entieres Dans le Arbres*, *I Have a Dream*, *Bing Crosby on Broadway*, *Dirty Linen & New-Found-Land*, *Hello, Dolly!*, *Players*, *The Grand Tour*, *Home*, *Blackstone!*, *Division Street*, *Mixed Couples*, *Medea* (Tony nomination), *Ghosts*, *Whodunnit*, *Noises Off*, *Beethoven's Tenth*, *A Woman of Independent Means*, *Benefactors*, *Wild Honey* (Tony nomination), *Pygmalion*, *Broadway*, *Accomplice*, *The Twilight of the Golds*, *Peter Pan* (1998 and 1999). Off-Broadway credits include *As You Like It*, *Charlie Was Here and Now He's Gone*, *Hair*, *Hamlet*, *Henry V*, *King Lear*, *Measure for Measure*, *More Than You Deserve*, *Much Ado About Nothing*, *Once I Saw a Boy Laughing*, *Pericles, Prince of Tyre*, *The Basic Training of Pavlo Hummel*, *The Chalk Garden*, *The Comedy of Errors*, *The Merry Wives of Windsor*, *The Tales of Cymbeline*, *Ti-Jean and His Brothers*, *Timons of Athens*, and *Wedding Band*. He also designed regularly for the Mark Taper Forum and the Ahmanson Center in Los Angeles, CA, upon relocating to California in 1977. He received awards from the Pasadena Playhouse in 1983 and 1984 for distinguished achievement, and in 1996 he received the Los Angeles Critics Circle's Angstrom Award for career achievement in lighting. He also served as adjunct professor at the theater school of the University of Southern California. Design credits also include the San Francisco Ballet Company, the St. Louis Muny Opera, the Kennedy Center, and twenty seasons as a designer for the New York Shakespeare Festival. He is survived by his companion, Lawrence Metzler, and a niece, Rosemary Diglio, of Sunrise, FL.

Bridget Aschenberg, 73, Hamburg, Germany–born playwright's agent, died March 6, 2002, in New York, NY. Her clients included Tennessee Williams, Arthur Miller, William Inge, Arthur Kopit, and Steve Martin, in addition to representing the properties of Jane Bowles' *In the Summer House*, Mart Crowley's *The Boys in the Band*, Frederick Knott's *Wait Until Dark*, Clare Boothe Luce's *The Women*, and Jean Giraudoux's *The Mad Woman of Chaillot*, among many others. She had a longtime relationship with Circle Repertory Off-Broadway and worked for International Creative Management from 1975 until the time of her death.

Norman Atkins, 82, opera and musical theater performer, died Jan. 13, 2002, in Hackensack, NJ, from complications of heart surgery. A member of the New York City Opera from 1959 to 1962, he sang in many musical theater productions there, including *The Most Happy Fella* and the role of Escamillo in *The Golem*, which he also performed in 1965 for City Center. He also appeared in *Those Were the Days* on Broadway, in productions of *Silk Stockings* with Don Ameche, and as Tevye in *Fiddler on the Roof*. He is survived by a daughter, Andrea Atkins Hessekiel, two sons, Jay, of Wyckoff, NJ, and Bruce, of Woodcliff Lake, NJ, and six grandchildren.

Beverly Hope Atkinson, 66, New York, NY–born actress, died Dec. 11, 2001, in Los Angeles, CA, of cancer. A student of Lee Strasberg and a member of the Actors Studio, Café LaMama in New York, and Theater West in Los Angeles, CA, her career included international tours of *Skin of Our Teeth* and *Tom Paine* in London, England. She performed in *A Midsummer Night's Dream*, *Lysistrata*, and *The Blacks* at Seattle Rep. She taught acting later in life and is known for her television and film work. She is survived by her mother.

Milton Berle (Mendel Berlinger), 93, New York, NY–born actor/comedian, died March 27, 2002, in Los Angeles, CA, in his sleep. He made his New York debut on stage in *Floradora*, followed by credits including *Earl Carroll's Vanities*, *Saluta*, *Ziegfeld Follies*, *See My Lawyer*, and *The Goodbye People*. He also appeared on Broadway in several single- and multiple-billed comedy shows. Arguably the first television star, he made his start in vaudeville, night clubs and on the radio, before starring in *Texaco Star Theater*, which ran on NBC from 1948–1954, ruling Tuesday nights in America during the early years of live television. As a child actor, he appeared in more than fifty silent films and continued to make frequent television and film appearances after starring in his own shows regularly in the early 1960s. He received an Emmy Award for "Best Kinescoped Personality" in 1950 and received further Emmy nominations in 1961 and 1994 for guest appearances. He appeared regularly at celebrity roasts and in Las Vegas shows, and was an ardent supporter of charities, making appearances at thousands of benefits and performing at army hospitals during both World Wars. He is survived by his wife, Lorna, and daughter, Vicki Walton.

Buster Brown (James Brown), 88, Baltimore, MD–born dancer/choreographer/teacher, died May 7, 2002, in New York, NY. Broadway credits include *Bubblin' Brown Sugar* and *Black and Blue*, and he toured extensively with Cab Calloway, Count Basie, Dizzy Gillespie, and Duke Ellington. He was also a member of The Three Aces, Speed Kings, Original Hoofers, and Copasetics dance teams. His work was honored in the 1995 Broadway musical, *Bring in Da Noise, Bring in Da Funk*, and he made appearances in several films and documentaries. No reported survivors.

Ralph Burns, 79, Newton, MA–born composer/arranger/conductor/musician, died Nov. 21, 2001, in Los Angeles, CA, from complications of a recent stroke and pneumonia. Broadway credits include *Phoenix 55*, *Copper and Brass*, *No Strings*, *Little Me*, *Hot Spot*, *Funny Girl*, *Fade Out-Fade In*, *Golden Boy*, *Something More!*, *Do I Hear a Waltz?*, *Sweet Charity*, *Breakfast at Tiffany's*, *Ilya Darling*, *Darling of the Day*, *Minnie's Boy*, *No, No, Nanette*, *Pippin*, *Irene*, *Chicago*, *The Act*, *Dancin'*, *They're Playing Our Song*, *Peter Pan*, *Bring Back Birdie*, *Big Deal*, *Sweet Charity*, *Chicago*, *Fosse* (Tony Award), *Thoroughly Modern Millie* (Tony Award), and *Funny Girl* (special benefit). Also active in the adaptation and orchestration of film scores, he won Academy Awards for his work on *Cabaret* (1972) and *All That Jazz* (1979). He also received an Emmy Award for his work on *Baryshnikov on Broadway*. For fifteen years at the beginning of his career he played with Woody Herman's band, composing some of Herman's biggest hits. No reported survivors.

Jeffrey Alan Chandler (Jeffrey Allan Chandler), 56, Durham, NC–born actor, died Dec. 19, 2001, in Los Angeles, CA, from liver failure. He made his Off-Broadway debut in 1969 in *The People vs. Ranchman*, followed by *Your Own Thing* and *Penguin Touquet*. Broadway credits include *Elizabeth I* (1972), *The Dresser*, *Whodunit?*, *Two Shakespearean Actors*, *Timon of Athens*, and *The Government Inspector*. Upon relocating to the Los Angeles area in the 1980s, he appeared in *Arcadia* at the Mark Taper Forum, and in roles at South Coast Repertory and the Old Globe Theater. He also worked with the American Conservatory Theater and the Tyrone Guthrie Theater and appeared in many roles on television and film. Survivors include his partner, June Gable.

Imogene Coca, 92, Philadelphia, PA–born actress/comedian, died June 2, 2001, at her home in Westport, CT. Her numerous Broadway credits include *When You Smile*, *Garrick Gaieties*, *Shoot the Works*, *Flying Colors*, *New Faces of 1934*, *Who's Who*, *The Straw Hat Revue*, *All in Fun*, *Concert Varieties*, *The Girls in 509*, and *On the Twentieth Century* (Tony nomination). She is perhaps best known for her Emmy Award–winning pairing opposite Sid Caesar on the television series "Your Show of Shows." She appeared in several film roles. No reported survivors.

David Cogan, 78, Romania–born producer, died Feb. 7, 2002, in Bedford, NY, of lung cancer. Originally beginning his professional life as an accountant and then a theatrical manager, clients included Anne Bancroft, William Gibson, and Neil Simon, among others. In 1959 he produced *A Raisin in the Sun*, the first play produced on Broadway by a black playwright, as well as the first Broadway play to have a black director, Lloyd Richards. It received a Tony nomination for Best Play. Other Broadway credits include *In the Counting House*, *The Odd Couple*, *The Midnight Sun*, and *Caligula*. He purchased the Biltmore Theater in 1960, which housed such productions as *Hair*, *Brother Rat*, *Take Her, She's Mine*, and *Barefoot in the Park*, among others. He also owned the Eugene O'Neill Theater in the mid-1960s. He is survived by his wife, Arline, two daughters, Carol Savitsky and Sharon Cogan-Black, three stepchildren, Kim Snyder, Jill Snyder, and Gary Snyder, all of whom live in New York, NY.

Imogene Coca

Gloria Foster

Kathleen Freeman

Carrie Hamilton

Bert Conway, 87, Orange, NJ–born actor/director, died Feb. 7, 2002, in Mission Hills, CA, of heart failure. Broadway credits include *Golden Boy* (1937 and 1952), *Dance Night, Night Music, Cue for Passion, The Lovers, J.B., First Love, The Last Analysis, And Things That Go Bump in the Night*. He also appeared in Joseph Papp's New York Shakespeare Festival and in tours of *The Caine Mutiny Court Martial, On A Clear Day You Can See Forever, A Memory of Two Mondays*, and *Ah, Wilderness!* He began directing in 1947 at the Actors Lab in Hollywood and helmed the first interracial production of *Golden Boy*, as well as produced the Off-Broadway revival of *Deep Are the Roots*. He was also known for several film roles. He is survived by a son and two grandchildren.

Fred De Cordova, 90, New York, NY–born producer/director, died Sept. 15, 2001, in Los Angeles, CA. Broadway credits include *Elmer the Great, Hold Your Horses, Piper Paid, Ziegfeld Follies of 1936, Keep Off the Grass, Beverly Hills*, and *Ziegfeld Follies of 1943*. Best known as the long-running producer of *The Tonight Show Starring Johnny Carson*, he was nominated seventeen times for an Emmy Award for his efforts on that show, winning on seven occasions. He also served as director and producer of *The Jack Benny Show*, and *The Burns and Allen Show*, and directed numerous feature films. Survivors include his wife, Janet.

Angus Duncan, 90, New York, NY–born actor/Actors Equity executive, died April 21, 2002, of natural causes. Broadway credits include *The Dark Hours, John Ferguson*, and *So Proudly We Hail*, before embarking on a life-time of service to Actors Equity Association. He was a co-founder of the Actors Fund and served as executive secretary, remaining in that post for twenty years. He is survived by his wife, Dorothy, a son and daughter, three grandchildren, and one great grandson.

Barbara Erwin, Boston, MA–born actress, died April 5, 2001. She made her Off-Broadway debut in 1973 in *The Secret Life of Walter Mitty*, followed by *Broadway* and *One Way to Ulan Bator*. Broadway credits include *Annie, Ballroom, Animals*, and *Gypsy*.

Gloria Foster, 64, Chicago, IL–born actress, died Sept. 29, 2001, in New York, NY. A 1966 Theatre World Award winner for her role in *Medea*, she made her Broadway debut in 1961 in *Purlie Victorious*, followed by *A Hand is on the Gate, Yerma*, and *Having Our Say*. She made her Off-Broadway debut in 1963 in *In White America, The Forbidden City, The Cherry Orchard, Mother Courage and Her Children, Long Day's Journey Into Night, Coriolanus, Black Visions*, and *Agamemnon*. She is also known for her numerous roles in television and film. No reported survivors.

Janet Fox, 89, Chicago, IL–born actress, died April 22, 2002, in Palm Beach, FL. The niece of writer Edna Ferber, she made her Broadway debut in 1932 as Tina, the conniving maid in the Kaufman-Ferber comedy *Dinner at Eight*, and played Nurse Preen in USO tours of the Kaufman-Hart comedy *The Man Who Came to Dinner*, with Moss Hart in the title role. She later recreated the role in *Sherry!*, its 1967 Broadway musical version. Other Broadway credits include *Cross Ruff, Life's Too Short, Tomorrow's a Holiday, Stage Door, Having a Wonderful Time, The American Way, Higher and Higher, Cuckoos on the Hearth, Bravo!, The Tunnel of Love*, and *Tall Story*. She also toured in *Gigi* with George Hamilton, was a frequent player at the Bucks County Playhouse, including appearances in *The Matchmaker*, and appeared in numerous television and radio broadcasts. She played her aunt, Edna Ferber, in the 1963 film version of Moss Hart's autobiography, *Act One*. Survivors include her husband, publisher Henry Goldsmith, her daughter, playwright/author Julie Gilbert Daniel, and son-in-law, film and sound engineer/architectural acoustician Francis Daniel.

Kathleen Freeman, 78, Chicago, IL–born actress, died Aug. 23, 2001, in New York, NY, of lung cancer. She was appearing on Broadway in *The Full Monty* at the time of her death, for which she won a 2001 Theatre World Award. Other Broadway credits include *13 Tue de l'Amour*, as well as numerous film and television appearances. No reported survivors.

Luigi Gasparinetti (Louis Gasparinetti), 60, dancer, died May 16, 2002, in New York, NY, of a heart attack. Broadway credits include *Milk and Honey, Café Crown, Guys and Dolls, On a Clear Day You Can See Forever, Mame*, and *Sherry!*

Avril Gentles, 82, actress, died Nov. 21, 2001, in New York, NY. Broadway credits include *Present Laughter*, *My Mother, My Father, and Me*, *Grin and Bare It!/Postcards*, *Lysistrata*, *A Texas Trilogy: Lu Ann Hampton Laverty Oberlander*, *A Texas Trilogy: The Oldest Living Graduate*, and *Showboat*. She also appeared in many television and Off- and Off-Off-Broadway productions, as well as numerous regional and cabaret productions.

Leonard Gershe, 79, New York, NY–born writer, died March 9, 2002, in Beverly Hills, CA, of complications from a stroke. Broadway credits include *Alive and Kicking*, *Destry Rides Again*, and *Butterflies Are Free*. He adapted his best-known play, *Butterflies Are Free*, to the screen in 1972, and earned an Academy Award nomination for his 1957 script *Funny Face* (for which he also collaborated on two songs with Roger Edens). He is survived by a brother and a sister.

Ruth Goetz (Ruth Goodman), 93, Philadelphia, PA–born writer, who collaborated with her husband Augustus Goetz on the 1947 play *The Heiress* and adapted it to the screen two years later, died Oct. 12, 2001, in Englewood, NJ. Other Broadway credits include *One-Man Show*, *The Immoralist*, and *The Hidden River*. The Goetzes also wrote several screenplays. She is survived by her daughter, Judy Sanger, and a granddaughter.

Sally Gracie, 80, Little Rock, AR–born actress died Aug. 13, 2001, at her home in Manhattan. Broadway credits include *Six O'Clock Theatre*, *Dinosaur Wharf*, *Goodbye Again*, *Major Barbara*, *Fair Game*, *Venus at Large*, and *But Seriously*. Off-Broadway credits include *Naomi Court* and *A Lie of the Mind*; other stage credits include *Vickie* and *At War with the Army*. She was the first wife of actor Rod Steiger. She is survived by a son from her second marriage, a stepdaughter, stepson, and six grandchildren.

Carrie Hamilton, 38, actress/writer, died Jan. 21, 2002, in Los Angeles, CA, of cancer. She co-wrote the play *Hollywood Arms* with her mother, actress Carol Burnett. It appeared on Broadway in 2002. Along with Burnett, she is survived by her two sisters.

Elek Hartman, Canton, OH–born actor, died Jan. 12, 2002. Broadway credits include *We Bombed in New Haven*, followed by *Angel*. Off-Broadway credits include *Where People Gather*, *Goa*, *Loyalties*, *Matchmaker*, *Mirandolina*, *Cassett*, *Artists and Admirers*, *Barber of Seville*, and *Daydreams*.

Nigel Hawthorne, 72, Coventry, England–born actor, died Dec. 26, 2001, at his home in Baldock, Hertfordshire, England, of a heart attack. He made his Broadway debut in 1974 in *As You Like It*, followed by *Shadowlands*, for which he received a Tony Award for Best Actor in a Play. He is also known for numerous television and stage roles in England, and he appeared in many film roles later in his career. He received an Academy Award nomination as Best Actor for his performance in *The Madness of King George*. He is survived by his companion, Trevor Bentham.

Eileen Heckart (Anna Eileen Heckart), 82, Columbus, OH–born actress, died Dec. 31, 2001, at her home in Norwalk, CT, of cancer. A 1953 Theatre World Award winner for her role in *Picnic*, she made her Broadway debut in 1943 in *The Voice of the Turtle*, followed by *Brighten the Corner*, *Trial Honeymoon*, *Hilda Crane*, *In Any Language*, *The Bad Seed*, *A View from the Bridge*, *The Dark at the Top of the Stairs* (Tony nomination, Best Featured Actress in a Play), *Invitation to a March* (Tony nomination, Best Featured Actress in a Play), *Everybody Loves Opal*, *A Family Affair*, *Too True to Be Good*, *Barefoot in the Park*, *And Things that Go Bump in the Night*, *You Know I Can't Hear You When the Water's Running*, *The Mother Lover*, *Butterflies Are Free* (Tony Award, Best Featured Actress in a Play), *Veronica's Room*, *Ladies at the Alamo*, and *The Cemetery Club*. She made her Off-Broadway debut in 1942 in *Tinker's Dam*, followed by *Eleemosynary*, *Northeast Local*, *The Lisbon Traviata*, and *The Waverly Gallery* (also on Broadway). She won an Academy Award as Best Supporting Actress in 1973 for repeating her stage role as the protective mother of a young blind man in *Butterflies Are Free*, and in 2000 she was awarded a special Tony Award for her lifetime of work in the theater. Also known for her multiple television roles, she won an Emmy Award for her work in that medium. She is survived by three sons, two half-sisters, and two grandchildren.

Christopher Hewett, 80, Sussex, England–born actor, died Aug. 3, 2001, in Los Angeles, CA, following a period of declining health. He made his Broadway debut in 1957 in *My Fair Lady*, followed by *First Impressions*, *Unsinkable Molly Brown*, *Kean*, *The Affair*, *Hadrian VII*, *Sleuth*, *No Sex Please, We're British*, *Music Is*, *Peter Pan* (1980), and *Sweethearts in Concert*. Broadway directing credits include *Almost Crazy*, and *From A to Z*. Off-Broadway credits include *Tobias and Angel*, *Trelawny of the Wells* (also Broadway), *Finian's Rainbow*, and *New Jerusalem*. He was also known for his work in television and several notable film roles. Survivors include a nephew.

Jack Lemmon (John Uhler Lemmon, III), 76, Boston, MA–born actor, who became one of America's most popular and beloved performers in his nearly fifty-year career in theatre and film, died June 27, 2001, in Los Angeles, CA, of complications from cancer. He made his Broadway debut in 1953 in *Room Service*, followed by *Face of a Hero*, *Tribute* (Tony nomination, Best Actor in a Play), and *A Long Day's Journey Into Night* (Tony nomination, Best Actor in a Play). He went on to win Academy Awards for Best Supporting Actor for *Mister Roberts*, in 1955, and for Best Actor for *Save the Tiger*, in 1973. There were additional nominations for *Some Like It Hot*, *The Apartment*, *Days of Wine and Roses*, *The China Syndrome*, *Tribute*, and *Missing*. He was the recipient of such awards as the Kennedy Center Honors and the American Film Institute Life Achievement Award. He is survived by his second wife, actress Felicia Farr; their daughter; a son from his first marriage, actor Chris Lemmon; and three grandchildren.

Eileen Heckart

Jack Lemmon

Nobu McCarthy

Bill McCutcheon

Rosetta LeNoire, (Rosetta Burton), 90, New York, NY–born actress/producer, died March 17, 2002, in Teaneck, NJ, of natural causes. A recipient of a 1993 Special Theatre World Award for distinguished service to the theatre, she made her Broadway debut in 1939 in *The Hot Mikado*, followed by *Anna Lucasta, Four Twelves Are 48, Finian's Rainbow, Mister Johnson, Destry Rides Again, Sophie, Tambourines to Glory, Blues for Mr. Charlie, I Had a Ball, The Great Indoors, A Cry of Players, Lost in the Stars, The Sunshine Boys, A Streetcar Named Desire, God's Favorite, The Royal Family, Bubbling Brown Sugar, It's So Nice to Be Civilized, You Can't Take It With You*, and *Paul Robeson*. A pioneer in nontraditional casting, she was an early and effective advocate of expanding opportunities for minority performers to act in plays and musicals. She was the founder in 1968 of the AMAS theatre company, and eight years after its inception she added a children's theatrical course to its program. In 1989, Colleen Dewhurst, then the president of Actors Equity, chose her as the first recipient of the union's annual award for broadening participation in theater, and the award was then named for her. In 1999 she received the National Medal of the Arts. She is survived by her son, William, of Manahawkin, NJ; a sister, Mary A. Francis, of Palm Coast, FL; her brothers, Wilmote Burton of the Bronx and Warren Burton of Palm Coast, FL; two grandchildren; and two great-grandchildren.

Alan Manson, 83, actor, died March 5, 2002, in Jamaica, Queens, lived in Easthampton, NY. Broadway credits include *Journey to Jerusalem, Call Me Mister, Southern Exposure, Angels Kiss Me, The Ponder Heart, The Tenth Man, Gideon, Funny Girl, Forty Carats, A Place for Polly*, and *Broadway Bound*. He was one of the 310 real-life soldiers chosen by Irving Berlin to play in *This is the Army*, Berlin's 1942 tribute to the American armed forces, which ran on Broadway and toured around the world. He also made a variety of appearances in television and film. Survivors include his brother, Arthur, and his wife, Corey Rose Lang.

Nobu McCarthy (Nobu Atsumi), 67, Ottawa-born actress who became the artistic director of the first Asian American theatre company, East West Players, died after collapsing on a movie set on Apr. 6, 2002, in Londrina, Brazil, while on location for a film shoot. She is survived by two children from her first marriage and by three brothers.

Bill McCutcheon (Bill McCutchen), 77, Russell, KY–born actor, died Jan. 9, 2002 in Ridgewood, NJ, after a long illness. Broadway credits include *Out West of Eighth, New Faces of 1956, Dandelion Wine, West Side Story, The Front Page, My Daughter, Your Son, Hide and Seek, The Man Who Came to Dinner, You Can't Take It with You, Anything Goes* (Tony Award, Best Featured Actor in a Musical). Off-Broadway credits include *How to Steal and Election, Wet Paint, One's a Crowd, Shoestring Revue, Upstairs at the Downstairs, The Little Revue*, and *The Marriage of Bette and Boo* (Obie Award). He worked extensively in regional theatre, and had a long-running role on *Sesame Street*, which won him three Daytime Emmy Awards. Survived by his wife, Anne, a son, two daughters, and five grandchildren.

Dorothy McGuire, 85, Omaha, NE–born actress, died Sept. 13, 2001, in Santa Monica, CA, of arrhythmia resulting from a broken leg. Her Broadway credits include *Our Town, Swingin' the Dream, Medicine Show, Kind Lady, Claudia, Legend of Lovers, Winesburg, Ohio*, and *The Night of the Iguana*. Known for her extensive work in film, she was nominated for an Academy Award for Best Actress in 1947 for her work in *Gentleman's Agreement*. She also made many television appearances and was one of the founders of the LaJolla Playhouse. Survivors include her son, photographer Mark Swope, and a daughter.

Dorothy McGuire

Jason Miller

Dudley Moore

Carroll O'Connor

James B. Mckenzie, 76, Appleton, WI–born producer, died Feb. 20, 2002, in Norwalk, CT, of cancer and pneumonia. Serving as the executive producer of the Westport, CT, Country Playhouse for 41 years, he also served as the executive producer of San Francisco's American Conservatory Theater when it received the 1979 regional theater Tony Award, and was at various times executive producer of nine other regional theaters, including Florida's Royal Poinciana Playhouse in Palm Beach and the Peninsula Players Theater in Fish Creek, WI. Broadway producing credits include *The Girl in the Freudian Slip, And Miss Reardon Drinks a Little*, and *The Secret Affairs of Mildred Wild*, as well as three American Conservatory Theater plays in rep (*Tiny Alice, A Flea in Her Ear*, and *Three Sisters*), in 1969. Additionally, he produced or co-produced over sixty national and international tours, including *The Impossible Years, Cactus Flower*, and *Rosencrantz and Guildenstern Are Dead*. Also known for extensive television producing, he helped create more than 100 live television shows in the 1950s and was an active member of the League of American Theaters and Producers, Council of Stock Theaters, Council of Resident Summer Theaters, Actors Equity and its Pension and Health Fund, the Association of Theatrical Press Agents and Managers, and IATSE. Survivors include his wife, Philisse Barrows (who also served as his assistant for thirty years), two sons, two daughters, two brothers, and two sisters.

Jason Miller, 62, New York, NY–born actor/playwright, died May 13, 2001, in Scranton, PA, of a heart attack. A Pulitzer Prize winner in 1973 for his play *That Championship Season*, he is also known for his Academy Award–nominated performance in 1973's *The Exorcist*. He is survived by three sons, including actor Jason Patric, and a daughter.

Reggie Montgomery (Reginald Alexander Montgomery), 54, Tallahassee, FL–born actor/director, died Jan. 13, 2002, in New York, NY, of undetermined causes. The first black clown to perform with the Ringling Brothers and Barnum & Bailey Circus, his Broadway credits include *Mule Bone* and *The Green Bird*. Off-Broadway credits include *The Merry Wives of Windsor, The Colored Museum, The Caucasian Chalk Circle, The America Play, Spunk: Three Tales by Zora Neale Hurston, Short Eyes, Raft of the Medusa, Cold Sweat*, and *Black Eagles*. Establishing the Minority Repertory Company in Dallas, he also performed in regional theatre at the Hartford Stage Company, and worked extensively as a director at Center Stage in Baltimore, MD, the Dallas Theater Center, and the Hartford Stage Company, serving as the associate director at the latter for two years. He worked extensively in television and film. Survivors include a brother, Rodney Montgomery, of Wellington, FL, and a sister, Yvonne Montgomery-Curl, of Far Hills, NJ.

Dudley Moore, 66, Dagenham, Essex, England–born actor/writer/comedian, died March 27, 2002, at his home in Plainfield, NJ, of pneumonia as a complication from progressive supranuclear palsy. First known as a member of the satirical quartet Beyond the Fringe, with whom he premiered on Broadway in the early 1960s, he won a Special Tony Award for their performance. He had a fifteen-year professional relationship with one of the members, Peter Cook, with whom he often performed. He won a second Special Tony Award in 1974 for *Good Evening*, on Broadway. Off-Broadway credits include *Sergeant Musgrave's Dance*. Also known for his many film roles, he earned an Academy Award nomination and a Golden Globe Award for his performance for playing the perpetually soused millionaire in the 1981 comedy hit *Arthur*. He won a second Golden Globe in 1984 for *Micki and Maude*. He was also an accomplished concert pianist, scoring movies and making many concert appearances. He is survived by his sons Patrick (by actress Tuesday Weld) and Nicholas (by Nicole Rothschild), and sister, Barbara Stevens.

Bibi Osterwald

Anthony Quinn

Avery Schreiber

Kim Stanley

Harry Nederlander, 84, Detroit, MI–born theatre producer/mogul, died Jan. 5, 2002, in Rancho Mirage, CA, following a long illness. As one of six children of David Nederlander, who ran the Shubert and other legit theatres, he worked his way up through the family company, which grew to encompass theatres on Broadway, in London, as well as around the United States. He was best known for being in charge of the Birmingham Theatre, in suburban Detroit, a post he held for fifteen years, from 1979–1984. During his tenure, he brought many Off-Broadway and lesser-known shows to the theatre, many out of the usual range of Michigan audiences, such as *Agnes of God*, *Master Harold and the Boys*, *Crimes of the Heart*, and *Driving Miss Daisy*.

Carroll O'Connor, 76, New York, NY–born actor, died June 21, 2001, in Culver City, CA, of a heart attack brought on by complications from diabetes. Broadway credits include *God and Kate Murphy*, *Brothers* (also directed), and *Home Front*. He made numerous film appearances and is best known for his Emmy Award–winning characterization of Archie Bunker on the classic television series *All in the Family*. He is survived by his wife.

Bibi Osterwald (Margaret Osterwald), 83, New Brunswick, NJ–born actress, died Jan. 2, 2002, in Burbank, CA. Broadway credits include *Sing Out, Sweet Land*, *Three to Make Ready*, *Sally*, *Magnolia Alley*, *Gentleman Prefer Blondes*, *Bus Stop*, *The Golden Apple* (Outer Critics Award, 1953), *The Vamp*, *Look Homeward Angel*, *A Family Affair*, and *Hello, Dolly!*, for which she was the understudy for the title role for seven years, filling in for Ginger Rogers, Betty Grable, Phyllis Diller, Martha Raye, Ethel Merman, and others. She also appeared in national tours and in many television and film roles. She is survived by her husband, Justin Arndt, a son, Christopher Arndt, of San Clemente, CA, and two granddaughters.

Mary Grant Price, 85, Wales-born costume designer, died March 9, 2002, in Boston, MA. Broadway credits include *Two for the Show*, *Sons o' Fun*, *The Cat Screams*, *Ziegfeld Follies of 1943*, *Carmen Jones*, *Mexican Hayride*, *Seven Lively Arts*, *Marinka*, *Polonaise*, *Woman Bites Dog*, and *Big Fish, Little Fish*. She also costumed several notable films.

Anthony Quinn (Anthony Rudolph Oaxaca Quinn), 86, Chihuahua, Mexico–born actor, died June 3, 2001, in Boston, MA, of respiratory failure. He made his Broadway debut in 1947 in *The Gentleman from Athens*, followed by *A Streetcar Named Desire*, *Borned in Texas*, *Becket* (Tony nomination), *Tchin-Tchin*, and *Zorba*. Also known for a prolific film career which spanned more than sixty years, he won two Academy Awards for his work in that medium, for Best Supporting Actor in *Viva Zapata!* in 1950 and for Best Supporting Actor in *Lust for Life* in 1956. He is survived by thirteen children and his wife, Kathy Bevin Quinn.

Rod Rodgers, 64, Cleveland, OH–born choreographer, died March 24, 2002, from complications of a stroke. During a career that spanned more than forty years, he was known for being an articulate spokesperson for black artists, and created dances inspired by Dr. Martin Luther King, Jr., Malcolm X, Duke Ellington, Langston Hughes, and other black artists and activists. He was active with Dancemobile, which brought dance to communities with little or no exposure to the art form, and was the director of Mobilization of Youth, a popular lecture-demonstration program. The Rod Rodgers Dance Company, the troupe that he founded in 1969, is still in operation, and he also directed for the Syracuse Opera Company and the Harlem Opera at City Center, and helmed Off-Broadway productions which include *The Prodigal Sister*. He is survived by his partner, Kim Grier, two brothers, Ernest and Virgil, two sisters, Rhonda and LaJune Rodgers, all of Detroit; four sons, Jason, of Brooklyn; Kaldar, of Jersey City; Kalan, of Bayonne, NJ; and Jasmal, of Manhattan; and a grandson, Kyler Anthony, of Bayonne, NJ.

Polly Rowles, 87, Philadelphia, PA–born actress, died Oct. 7, 2001, in Concord, NH. Broadway credits include *Julius Caesar*, *Anne of the Thousand Days*, *King Richard III*, *Come Back, Little Sheba*, *The Golden State*, *Gertie*, *Time Out for Ginger*, *The Wooden Dish*, *Goodbye Again*, *Auntie Mame*, *Look after Lulu*, *A Mighty Man Is He*, *No Strings*, *The Best Laid Plans*, *The Killing of Sister George*, *Forty Carats*, *The Women*, and *Steaming*. She is also known for her work in television and film.

Beatrice Straight

Ray Stricklyn

Victor Wong

Irene Worth

Charles Rule, 74, St. Charles, MO–born actor, died Feb. 11, 2002, of esophageal cancer. Broadway credits over his forty-five-year career include *Courtin' Time, Happy Hunting, Oh, Captain!, The Conquering Hero, Donnybrook!, Bye Bye Birdie, Fiddler on the Roof, Henry, Sweet Henry, Maggie Flynn, 1776, Cry for Us All, Gypsy, Goodtime Charley, Rex, On the Twentieth Century,* and *The Phantom of the Opera.* Off-Broadway credits include *Family Portrait,* and he also appeared in numerous national tours, operas, and televisions shows.

Avery Schreiber, 66, Chicago, IL–born actor/comedian, died January 7, 2002, in Los Angeles, CA, of a heart attack. Broadway credits include *How to Be a Jewish Mother, Ovid's Metamorphoses, Dreyfus in Rehearsal, Can-Can,* and *Welcome to the Club.* Other stage credits include *A Funny Thing Happened on the Way to the Forum, Wally's Café, Strike up the Band,* and *Showboat.* Also known early in his career as one half of the often politically satirical comedy duo (Jack) Burns and Schreiber, he made numerous appearances on television in the 1960s and 1970s, and he made further television appearances by himself in the 1970s and 1980s. He also played several roles on film. He is survived by his wife, Rochelle Isaacs Schreiber, a daughter, and a son.

Anthony Joshua Shaffer, 75, Liverpool, England–born playwright, died of a heart attack on Nov. 6, 2001. A Tony Award winner for Best Play of 1970 for *Sleuth,* his other Broadway credit is *Whodunit* in 1982. Other plays include *The Case of the Oily Levantine* and *Murderer,* as well as several screenplays. He is survived by his wife, Diane Cilento, brother, playwright Peter Shaffer, and two daughters from a previous marriage.

Zypora Spaisman, 86, Lublin, Poland–born actress and longtime artistic director and then executive producer of the Folksbiene, New York's only surviving Yiddish theater, died May 18, 2002, in New York, NY. A staunch advocate of Yiddish theater in New York City, she was involved in its preservation for over forty years. Her numerous theater credits at the Folksbiene include *It's Hard to Be a Jew, The Memory Lingers On, The Blacksmith's Folly,* and *The Land of Dreams.* For her efforts, she received an Obie Award, a Drama Desk Award, and a New York City People's Choice Award. Survivors include her son, Ben Ami.

Kim Stanley (Patricia Kimberley Reid), 76, Tularosa, NM–born actress and one of the leading Broadway stars of the 1950s, died Aug. 20, 2001, in Santa Fe, NM, of uterine cancer. She made her Broadway debut in 1949 in *Montserrat,* followed by *The House of Bernarda Alba, The Chase* for which she won a Theatre World Award, *Picnic, The Traveling Lady, Bus Stop, A Clearing in the Woods, A Touch of the Poet* (Tony nomination), *Cheri, A Far Country* (Tony nomination), *Natural Affection,* and *The Three Sisters;* as well as the London production of *Cat on a Hot Tin Roof.* Only making appearances in five films, she received Academy Award nominations for two of them. She is survived by a son, two daughters, three grandchildren, and a brother.

Beatrice Straight, 86, Old Westbury, NY–born actress, died Apr. 7, 2001, in North Ridge, CA. She made her Broadway debut in 1934 in *Bitter Oleander,* followed by *The Possessed, Twelfth Night, Land of Fame, The Wanhope Building, Eastward in Eden, Macbeth, The Heiress, The Innocents, The Grand Tour, The Crucible* (Tony Award, Best Featured Actress in a Play), and *Everything in the Garden.* Off-Broadway credits include *All My Sons, Ghosts, The River Line, Sing Me No Lullaby,* and *Everything in the Garden.* Known also for her work on film, she received an Academy Award for Best Supporting Actress in 1976 for her role in *Network.* She is survived by two sons, two stepchildren, seven grandchildren, and three great-grandchildren

Ray Stricklyn, 73, Houston, TX–born actor/publicist, died May 14, 2002, in Los Angeles, CA, of emphysema. A 1953 Theatre World Award winner for his Broadway debut in *The Climate of Eden*, Off-Broadway credits include Truman Capote's *The Grass Harp*, directed by José Quintero, and *Stalag 17*. He relocated to Los Angeles in the mid-1950s and made several appearances on film, one of which earned him a Golden Globe nomination for Most Promising Actor of 1958. Turning to publicity, he joined John Springer and Associates in 1973 and worked there until he developed his one-man show *Confessions of a Nightingale*, in which he portrayed Tennessee Williams, which ran for more than a year. He toured extensively nationally and abroad in the role for over a decade and made numerous appearances in television later in his career. He was awarded the L.A. Ovation Award for Career Achievement during his final stage appearance, at the Ahmanson in L.A. in 2000. His autobiography, *Angels & Demons: One Actor's Hollywood Journey*, was published in 1999. He is survived by his longtime companion, Los Angeles stage director David Galligan, a sister, Mary Ann, and two nieces.

Ron Taylor, 49, Galveston, TX–born writer/director/performer/producer, died Jan. 16, 2001, in Los Angeles, CA, of heart failure. He made his Off-Broadway debut in 1982 as the voice of Audrey II, the carnivorous cactus plant in *Little Shop of Horrors*, which ran for for than 2,000 performances, and garnered Mr. Taylor a Drama Desk Award. He also appeared on Broadway in 1999 in *It Ain't Nothin' but the Blues*, which he co-wrote, appeared in, and helped produce, and for which he received two Tony nominations, for Best Featured Actor in a Musical, as well as for Best Book. He toured extensively with the show, as well as in the first national tour of *The Wiz* early in his career. He also appeared in several television and film roles. He is survived by his wife, DeBorah Sharpe-Taylor, parents, Robert James Taylor and Marian Taylor, two sisters, Roberta Taylor and Frances Taylor-Stovall, and a son, Adamah Taylor.

Robert Weil, 86, New York, NY–born actor, died March 1, 2002. He made his Broadway debut in *New Faces in* 1941, followed by *Burlesque*, *Becket*, *Once upon a Mattress*, *Blood, Sweat, and Stanley Poole*, *Night Life*, *Arturo Ui*, *Beggar on Horseback*, *Lenny*, *Happy End*, and *My Old Friends*. Off-Broadway credits include *Love Your Crooked Neighbor*, *Felix*, *Linda Her and the Fairy Garden*, and *The Golem*.

Victor Wong, 74, San Francisco, CA–born character actor who made his way from journalism to acting with the Asian American Theatre Group, died Sept. 12, 2001, at his home near Locke, CA, of heart failure. Off-Broadway credits include *Sound and Beauty*, *Plenty*, and *Family Devotions*. He is survived by his wife, two daughters, a brother, three sisters, and five grandchildren.

Irene Worth (Harriet Elizabeth Abrams), 85, Omaha, NE–born actress, died March 10, 2002, in New York, NY, of complications from a stroke. She made her Broadway debut in 1943 in *The Two Mrs. Carrolls*, followed by *The Cocktail Party*, *Toys in the Attic* (Tony nomination, Best Actress in a Play), *Tiny Alice* (Tony Award, Best Actress in a Play), *Sweet Bird of Youth* (Tony Award, Best Actress in a Play), *The Cherry Orchard* (Tony nomination, Best Actress in a Play), *The Lady from Dubuque*, *John Gabriel Borkman*, *The Golden Age*, and *Lost in Yonkers* (Tony Award, Best Featured Actress in a Play). Off-Broadway productions include *Corialanus* with Christopher Walken, *The Gypsy and the Yellow Canary*, *The Chalk Garden* (Obie Award), and her solo *Irene Worth's Portrait of Edith Wharton*. Making London her primary residence much of her life, she appeared in many productions in London's West End, as Lady Macbeth, Desdemona in *Othello*, Helena in *A Midsummer Night's Dream*, and Portia in *The Merchant of Venice* at the Old Vic, as Goneril in Peter Brook's acclaimed *King Lear* with the Royal Shakespeare Company, and as Jocasta with the National Theater of Great Britain. Other notable West End productions include *Native Son* and *The Cocktail Hour*. She also made appearances in *All's Well That Ends Well* and *Richard III* at Canada's Stratford Festival. She won the British Academy Award for her role in the film *The Scapegoat*, and made several other notable film appearances. She was renowned for her myriad solo performances later in her career, and was awarded an Obie in 1989 for Sustained Achievement. She is survived by a sister and a brother.

INDEX

JOHN WILLIS (EDITOR) has been editor-in-chief of both *Theatre World* and its companion series *Screen World* for over forty years. *Theatre World* and *Screen World* are the oldest definitive pictorial and statistical records of each American theatrical and foreign and domestic film season and are referenced daily by industry professionals, students, and historians worldwide.

Mr. Willis has also served as editor of *Dance World*, *Opera World*, *A Pictorial History of the American Theatre 1860–1985*, and *A Pictorial History of the Silent Screen*. Previously, he served as assistant to *Theatre World* founder Daniel Blum on *Great Stars of the American Stage*, *Great Stars of Film*, *A Pictorial History of the Talkies*, *A Pictorial History of Television*, and *A Pictorial Treasury of Opera in America*.

For the past forty years he has presided over the presentation of the annual Theatre World Awards. Begun in 1945 and presented by past winners, they are the oldest awards given to actors for a Broadway or Off-Broadway debut role. On behalf of *Theatre World*, Mr. Willis received a Special 2001 Tony Honor for "Excellence in the Theatre" and the 2003 Broadway Theatre Institute Lifetime Achievement Award, in addition to awards from Drama Desk, Lucille Lortel, the Broadway Theater Institute, National Board of Review, Marquis Who's Who Publications Board, and Milligan College. He has served on the nominating committees for the Tony Awards and the New York University Hall of Fame, and is currently on the board of the University of Tennessee Clarence Brown Theatre.

As an actor, BEN HODGES (ASSOCIATE EDITOR) has appeared in New York with the Barrow Group Theatre Company, Monday Morning Productions, Coyote Girls Productions, Jet Productions, New York Actors' Alliance, and Outcast Productions. Additionally, he has appeared in numerous productions presented by theatre companies which he founded, the Tuesday Group and Visionary Works.

In 2001, he became director of development and currently serves as executive director for Fat Chance Productions, Inc., and the Ground Floor Theatre, a New York–based nonprofit theatre and film production company. *Prey for Rock and Roll* was developed by Fat Chance from their stage production into a feature film starring Gina Gershon, Drea de Matteo, and Lori Petty.

In 2003, frustrated with the increasingly daunting economic prospects involved in producing theatre on a small scale in New York, Ben founded NOOBA, the New Off-Off-Broadway Association, an advocacy group dedicated to representing the concerns of expressly Off-Off-Broadway producers in the public forum and in negotiations with other local professional arts organizations.

Ben served as an editorial assistant for many years on the 2001 Special Tony Honor Award–winning *Theatre World*, becoming the associate editor to John Willis in 1999. Also an assistant for many years to Mr. Willis for the prestigious Theatre World Awards, Ben was elected to the Theatre World Awards Board in 2002 and currently serves as the executive producer of the ceremony. He was presented with a Special Theatre World Award in 2003 for his ongoing stewardship of the event.

Forbidden Acts, the first collected anthology of gay and lesbian plays from the span of the twentieth century, edited and with an introduction by Hodges, was published by Applause Theatre and Cinema Books in 2003 and was a finalist for the 2004 LAMBDA Literary Award for Drama.

LUCY NATHANSON (ASSISTANT EDITOR) grew up in Manhattan, during a more heroic and innocent time. She studied fine arts at the High School of Music & Art, ballet at the School of American Ballet, and sculpture and painting at the Arts Students League. The genesis of her love of musical theatre, plays, and cultural performances of all types began at home, nurtured by her theatrical/motion picture press agent father and classical pianist mother. She currently works as a publicist, editor, and assistant to people in the arts. Working for John Willis, Ben Hodges, and *Theatre World* has reinforced her belief that Art, beautifully shaped, can reshape lives.

RACHEL WERBEL (ASSISTANT EDITOR) has assisted on *Theatre World* and the Theatre World Awards for the past two years. She is a graduate of the American Academy of Dramatic Arts and currently a member of the Agency improv group. She has studied performance with the Barrow Group Theatre Company and Holly Mandel's Improvolution.